PENGUIN

JACK OF DIAMONDS

BRYCE COURTENAY is the bestselling author of *The Power of One, Tandia, April Fool's Day, The Potato Factory, Tommo & Hawk, Solomon's Song, Jessica, A Recipe for Dreaming, The Family Frying Pan, The Night Country, Smoky Joe's Cafe, Four Fires, Matthew Flinders' Cat, Brother Fish, Whitethorn, Sylvia, The Persimmon Tree, Fishing for Stars, The Story of Danny Dunn* and *Fortune Cookie. The Power of One* is also available in an edition for younger readers, and *Jessica* has been made into an award-winning television miniseries.

BOOKS BY BRYCE COURTENAY

The Power of One
Tandia
April Fool's Day
A Recipe for Dreaming
The Family Frying Pan
The Night Country
Jessica
Smoky Joe's Cafe
Four Fires
Matthew Flinders' Cat
Brother Fish
Whitethorn
Sylvia
The Persimmon Tree
Fishing for Stars
The Story of Danny Dunn
Fortune Cookie

THE AUSTRALIAN TRILOGY

The Potato Factory
Tommo & Hawk
Solomon's Song

Also available in one volume,
as *The Australian Trilogy*

BRYCE COURTENAY

JACK OF DIAMONDS

PENGUIN
an imprint of Penguin Canada

Published by the Penguin Group
Penguin Group (Canada)
90 Eglinton Avenue East, Suite 700, Toronto, Ontario, Canada M4P 2Y3

Penguin Group (USA) Inc., 375 Hudson Street, New York, New York 10014, U.S.A.
Penguin Books Ltd, 80 Strand, London WC2R 0RL, England
Penguin Ireland, 25 St Stephen's Green, Dublin 2, Ireland (a division of Penguin Books Ltd)
Penguin Group (Australia), 707 Collins Street, Melbourne, Victoria 3008, Australia
(a division of Pearson Australia Group Pty Ltd)
Penguin Books India Pvt Ltd, 11 Community Centre, Panchsheel Park, New Delhi – 110 017, India
Penguin Group (NZ), 67 Apollo Drive, Rosedale, Auckland 0632, New Zealand
(a division of Pearson New Zealand Ltd)
Penguin Books (South Africa) (Pty) Ltd, 24 Sturdee Avenue, Rosebank,
Johannesburg 2196, South Africa

Penguin Books Ltd, Registered Offices: 80 Strand, London WC2R 0RL, England

First published by Penguin Group (Australia), 2012.
Published in this edition, 2013.

1 2 3 4 5 6 7 8 9 10 (WEB)

Copyright © Bryce Courtenay, 2012

Illustrations by Cathy Larsen

'Love Me Or Leave Me' by Walter Donaldson & Gus Kahn © 1928, US Copyright Renewed,
All Rights Reserved, Donaldson Publishing Co. & Gilbert Keyes Music Co.
© 1928 Donaldson Music Co., Estate of Gus Khan. Used by permission of EMI Music Publishing
Australia Pty Limited. International copyright secured. All rights reserved.

The verse that opens the Epilogue is an extract from *Through the Looking Glass* by Lewis Carroll.

Manufactured in Canada.

LIBRARY AND ARCHIVES CANADA CATALOGUING IN PUBLICATION

Courtenay, Bryce, 1933-
Jack of diamonds / Bryce Courtenay.

ISBN 978-0-14-318819-3

I. Title.

PR9619.3.C598J33 2013   823'.914   C2012-908319-4

Visit the Penguin Canada website at **www.penguin.ca**

Special and corporate bulk purchase rates available; please see
www.penguin.ca/corporatesales or call 1-800-810-3104, ext. 2477.

For
Dr Koroush S. Haghighi,
with my gratitude and thanks

PART ONE

CHAPTER ONE

_____

HARRY SPAYD WAS A drunk. He was also my father, but the only thing he contributed to my childhood was a sense of unremitting terror. As fathers go, Harry was by no means unique. In the part of Toronto where I was raised in the 1930s, normal, happy, socially well-adjusted children were non-existent, which meant I was lucky. When every kid is in much the same boat, there is no such thing as a dysfunctional family or even poverty, just life.

We were different in one respect: my mom, Gertrude, had the rare good fortune to have a regular job as an office cleaner across town. It was a small miracle, really. She would get home just after ten at night, always walking the last streetcar stop to save on her fare. She had bad circulation in her feet and in the winter suffered from chilblains.

Treating her chilblains was my first contribution to the welfare of our family, and the nightly ritual gave me a great sense of importance and pride – I was the man of the house, looking after Mom, just as her small salary kept the wolf from the door.

The treatment required careful planning and precise attention to detail. I'd place a big tin pail on the kitchen floor with a chair beside it and another chair beside the stove. Then, anticipating her return from work, I'd fire up the stove with coke and, as soon as it was burning properly, I'd fill the big black cast-iron kettle and lug it over to the chair beside the stove. There was just enough space on either side of the seat for my feet. I'd hop up and heave the kettle onto the stove to boil. I don't suppose the kettle was that big, but to a six-year-old boy it seemed a veritable giant. My mother had inherited it from my grandfather, who had got it from his father, who was a real Iroquois Red Indian. I always imagined it must have been used on an open campfire, it being so black. Such a large heavy kettle filled with boiling water is very dangerous. I'd lift it from the stove using both hands, and place it ever so carefully on the chair between my legs, with the spout pointed to the front. Then I'd jump down, tilt the kettle and pour the boiling water into the pail. Later, when I was eight and had grown a bit, I didn't need the chair any more.

I'd always leave a little water in the bottom of the kettle to return to the stove the moment I heard Mom coming through the front door. It would only take a minute or so to boil, and I'd have the teapot ready with tealeaves in it.

Next I'd fill a white enamel jug with cold water and place it beside the steaming chilblain pail so we could mix it to the right temperature. Then I'd add coarse salt and a tablespoon of cayenne pepper to the pail. This was almost as risky – if you got even the tiniest bit on your hands and later rubbed your eyes, kapow! You were temporarily blinded. Even after you'd washed your eyes at the tap, they stayed red and burning for ages and ages. But the cayenne wasn't all. There was one more special ingredient. I'd unbutton my fly and piss into the pail. My mother explained that it was an old but trusted recipe for fixing chilblains that she got from her mother and also her grandmother; cayenne pepper, urine and coarse salt did the trick every time. I have to say that the pissing part sounds pretty disgusting now, but at the time I accepted her instructions and it simply became a part of my nightly routine.

When I heard her key rattle in the front door, I'd put the kettle on and meet her at the door. 'Hello, Jack,' she'd say, her lips so blue and trembling from the cold she could hardly get the words out.

I'd help her take off her overcoat, and she'd sit down on the kitchen chair with an exhausted sigh. With my precision timing, the kettle would be boiling and I'd make the pot of tea and leave it to steep to the strength she liked, then I'd remove her battered snow boots and her three pairs of socks. Finally, I'd add the water from the jug to cool the pail sufficiently so she could sink her near-frozen feet into it.

She'd start ouching as her feet thawed, until she grew accustomed to the temperature. I was pretty careful and she never ever got scalded. Chilblains affect your fingers as well as your toes, but she wore these big woollen-lined gloves my dad had for his job in winter (he must have got a second pair somewhere) and never got them on her hands.

It was then time to pour her a mug of tea, hot, strong, black and heavily sugared. The mug, one of two royal mugs we possessed, had a picture of King George V on one side and the royal coat of arms on the other, with the legend 'God Save the King' around the base. The second had a picture of Queen Mary and the coat of arms but no legend. Cabbagetown people were almost exclusively of English, Scottish or northern Irish stock. All were obsessively loyal to the Crown and referred to King George as the King of Canada. Mom always preferred the slightly larger King George, as it was about three mouthfuls bigger than the more ladylike Queen Mary and also served to warm her hands more effectively. She always drank two mugs of tea in the time it took for the water to cool in the pail.

It was while she sat and soaked that I performed my next task. She'd undo her bun to allow her hair to tumble almost to her waist. It was thick and black, and I'd brush it and watch the silvered light run across the strands as the brush worked through her hair. 'Jack, what would I do without you?' she'd sigh.

'You could have had a girl and she wouldn't make you go "ouch"! Girls are better at hair than boys. They're always braiding and tying and messing around with each other's hair at school. Hair is definitely a girl thing.'

'I prefer you, Jack. A girl couldn't do the chilblain concoction or even lift Grandpa's kettle.'

I stifled a giggle. Lucky I was standing behind her and she couldn't see my face. As far as I knew, a girl couldn't add the final ingredient like a boy could; she'd have to sit on the cold pail and put the 'you know what' in first. But it was better to add it last thing when the salt and cayenne pepper were mixing with the boiling water.

While I brushed her hair, I had the kettle going again. Our timing for the entire chilblain procedure had to be perfect so we could take turns using the bathroom before my dad came home. She'd go first, taking the hot water in the kettle with her to rinse her feet and legs carefully in a tin tub, before changing into her nightie and cleaning her teeth (we used salt for teeth cleaning). Then I'd clean my teeth and get into my pyjamas, and we'd padlock ourselves in the bedroom I shared with her.

With a bit of luck we'd see very little of my father. He left home at 5.30 a.m., one of the fortunate few men who had a regular job with the Toronto City Council, where he worked as a garbage collector.

I was six when the 1929 Wall Street Crash brought the industrialised world to a juddering halt and the Roaring Twenties to a whimpering close. The factory horns no longer signalled the start and finish of a working day, and the Great Depression that followed was a huge, crushing, grinding machine that demolished society. But we children didn't know any different. We grew up with a set of rules for home, school, street and slum that were simply beyond our control. The strong ruled the weak and children adjusted themselves accordingly. But kids find ways to be happy even in truly miserable circumstances. The real trick was not to be seen to be a loner. Inclusion in any capacity – tyrant or slave, bully or victim – was the first rule of survival, as was knowing your place in the pecking order of a broken-down social structure.

Virtually everybody in the slum area named Cabbagetown where we lived belonged to the bottom of the working-class heap – factory-floor workers and pick-and-shovel labourers. All were ground down by the remorseless tread of economic depression, thereafter to be swept up like a pile of dirt into a hopeless, helpless heap of useless humanity.

The traditional male breadwinner in the family, despairing of ever gaining regular employment and dependent on a labour line already grown long by first light, too often took his misery and shame to the tavern. Drinking away his day's pay, he then brought his anger and guilt home, usually to a small ramshackle two-storey rented workers' cottage, occupied by two or more families crammed into each storey.

Most houses in Cabbagetown were shabby, their broken windows taped up or covered with cardboard. Most were rented, and neither the tenants nor landlords did much to prevent them falling into rack and ruin; you could often smell rotting wood and mould as you passed. Occasionally, you'd come across a house that you knew was owned by a family because it was well maintained, like a good tooth in a mouthful of decay. These few homes usually belonged to people who had government or city council jobs, like policemen, council foremen, clerks or firemen. Most people could never contemplate owning their own home.

Cabbagetown was dirty. The gas plant on Front Street, the silent, dusty factory yards and the railway yards along the Don River added to the grime. In winter, the acrid tang of the coal stoves filled the air, and when the wind blew, the smell from the gasworks would catch at your throat.

There was one good thing about the gasworks and the railway. Kids could sneak down to the railway yards at night with these little carts they'd made and steal coal. There was stuff leftover from making gas that you could burn in the stove and that was stolen too. The unemployed would get a voucher from the government every week for coke for cooking, but it was seldom enough in winter because the stove was what kept people warm. They also gave out a ration of staples and another voucher for milk but, because we were an employed family, we didn't get them. If you were unemployed, you had to report downtown to the House of Industry to sign the unemployment register before they'd give you your weekly rations. Lining up would take the whole day and only the head of the household could go, so this knocked out one day a week on which a man might get a casual job.

The slum landlord and the bailiff from the sheriff's department were both public enemies, feared by all. The bailiff would evict a family, then auction all their possessions until he had sufficient money to pay the landlord the outstanding rent. Finding the weekly rent was every wife and mother's greatest preoccupation. It took precedence even over food and winter heating. While kids went hungry and some were definitely malnourished, no one starved. Food could be obtained from the Yonge Street Mission Soup Kitchen and other local charities. The classrooms were heated and people found ways of not perishing from the winter cold.

The major social problem, aside from a lack of gainful employment, was, as always, alcohol. Once-compliant husbands – essentially happy Saturday-night drunks who had dutifully handed their pay packets to their wives and kept only sufficient for a daily pint with their pals at the tavern after work – now frustrated, helpless and ashamed, became recalcitrant and violent when drunk.

The sound of a drunken man beating the living daylights out of his sobbing wife was not unusual. It didn't pay to interfere – bashed wives and kids were too common to cause much comment, and the maxim at the time was that you didn't intervene in the affairs of husbands and wives. Church and community workers learned to ignore the results of domestic violence and nobody thought to call the police. If they had, the multitude of charges for drunken, violent and disorderly behaviour would have brought all the provincial courts in Toronto to a standstill and put half the men in Cabbagetown in the clink. Teachers simply did the best they could with classrooms of largely feckless, soup-kitchen-fed, snotty-nosed children, often enough with a split lip or a black eye above a swollen cheekbone.

If a teacher – new, young and generally female – was silly enough to ask a battered child what happened to his or her face, she would receive the time-honoured reply: 'I ran into a doorknob, Miss.' Doorknobs had a dreadful reputation in Cabbagetown. In fact, many boys wore their domestic wounds as a badge of honour.

A beating from my father was usually a vicious backhand, the great knobs of hard knucklebone doing the damage and making a mess of my mother's face and sometimes my own. My mom, who must have once had a handsome face, with her dark hair and obsidian eyes, had had her nose broken so often that it might well have belonged on the face of a veteran prize fighter. My father's backhand swipe never extended to a second; if it landed correctly, it had enough power to knock my tiny mom senseless.

As I grew older I'd dream of some day growing big and strong enough to take on the bastard. No warning, just bang, bang, bang! Merely thinking about it would cause me to clench my fists and I could almost smell the blood on my knuckles, his blood, and see him on his knees, whimpering, both hands covering his broken nose, the way I'd so often seen my mom cowering on the kitchen floor.

A battered wife would very seldom leave her brutal husband, even before the Depression. Women's wages were only two-thirds of men's, there was no social security for a woman alone with children, and even should she find work, she couldn't possibly care for her family. In the Depression she had no chance.

The fact that both my mom and dad had jobs was greatly resented by many of the Cabbagetown women, who would snub my mother in public or make snide remarks as she passed by. If we kids understood the pecking order in the playground, this was also true of the wives, who caused most of the problems that weren't the result of liquor. While we were all in the same boat, there were deeply felt differences. A small family such as ours, with two adult wages coming in and only three mouths to feed, caused great resentment, even bitterness, among the women in our neighbourhood.

Most families had a clutch of four or five children, so when neither parent was able to find regular work, feeding and clothing that many kids was a terrible burden. I didn't have any brothers or sisters due to 'complications'. My mom gave birth to me at home, where, like most slum kids, I was delivered by Mrs Spencer, the local midwife. But, shortly after I was born, Mom had to be taken to the general hospital emergency department in Elizabeth Street. 'It was to do with my plumbing,' was how she later explained it to me. The doctor at the hospital said she couldn't have any more children, and that if she did, then she'd most likely die. That's why I was an only child.

While the perception of our financial circumstances was quite wrong, I suppose the envy and anger some wives directed at us was understandable. Had my dad not poured his entire wages down his throat each day, so that we were forced to rely on my mom's tiny income, we would have been decidedly better off than most. In truth, my mom shared all the same fears about the landlord and bailiff as everyone else.

Nonetheless, many of the Cabbagetown wives snubbed Gertrude Spayd completely, never addressing her directly or even acknowledging her presence. Some even spat to the side of their feet as she passed. My mom referred to them as the 'bitch pack' and pretended she didn't give a damn. I was too young to fully understand what was going on, but it must have hurt like hell and she must have been terribly lonely. The only women she could talk to were those she met briefly at work.

The leader of the bitch pack was Dolly McClymont, a very large, big-bosomed woman who lived upstairs with her diminutive, skinny husband, Mac, and twin teenage daughters, Clarissa and Melissa. The entire family had blazing red hair, and none of them was supposed to speak to us, under strict orders from the dreaded Dolly, who would sweep by my mother with a disparaging sniff and her nose in the air in her down-at-the-heel white summer shoes. We got to know 'them upstairs' from what we heard through our ceiling. They, of course, would have learned about us by what passed up through their floorboards.

In 1930, the McClymont twins were thirteen, nearly twice my age, but when they'd pass me in the front passage one of them would bump me aside with her hip or shoulder. 'Oh, didn't see you,' she'd say with mock surprise. Then I'd hear them giggling as they went off down the front steps and into the street. When it was very cold, their pale Anglo-Saxon skin seemed to take on a bluish tinge. My mom would sometimes refer to Melissa and Clarissa as 'them red-and-blue twins'. In summer they would turn red as a ripe tomato, burn, peel and blister.

My mom's colouring was just the opposite of the twins'; she was, in Cabbagetown terms, tainted by a 'touch of the tarbrush'. It was probably her black hair. Not only did she have Iroquois Indian blood but also French Canadian, and in the summer she'd develop a nice, dark, even tan. I was the same. No doubt her olive skin and dark hair were yet another reason why she was ostracised by the Dolly McClymonts of this world.

My mom referred to Dolly as 'a nasty piece of work', not only because of how she treated us, but also because of what happened when Mac was occasionally in his cups. A harmless drunk, he was nothing like my dad, and yet Dolly McClymont would always beat him up. We'd hear him begging her, his voice gone shrill with fright, 'Dolly, Dolly, stop! I'll be good. I promise, I'll never touch a drop!' But Dolly lacked a forgiving nature and would abuse him, cursing him as a 'useless little shit' and far worse. My mother said she had a mouth like a dock worker. Sometimes we'd hear the twins sobbing when Mac was being beaten up. The following day his face would be a mess – both eyes almost closed and a split lip were pretty normal. That woman was capable of doing as much damage to a face as my dad, but I never got to see her knuckles afterwards.

Mac McClymont was an upholsterer by trade but I guess not too many people, even among the city's upper and middle classes, were too fussed about their tatty couches in those hard times, so he only occasionally got work at his trade. No more than five feet tall, he was seldom chosen from the dawn labourer's line he diligently joined most mornings. But I have to say this for Mac McClymont, he was the only one of the family upstairs who would always smile and say, 'Hello, young Jack', if he was on his own. He once gave me a marble he'd found somewhere, a good aggie any boy would be fortunate to own. No one else had one anything like as good as it, and I never put it in danger when we played marbles at school. It became a precious possession.

Mac would have made a much better husband for my tiny mom, and a much better dad for me. Once, in the winter, when Dolly and the twins went to stay with her sister and Mac was on his own, he must have noticed my mom's broken and battered snow boots. 'Mrs Spayd, forgive me for being personal like, but . . . ah, er, me trade is, er . . . I'm an up-upholsterer,' he stammered.

'Oh, that's nice,' my mother said with a smile, not knowing where Mac's announcement about his trade was leading. Seeing she was friendly and wasn't going to bite his head off, he immediately lost his stammer. 'What I meant to say is, will you let me fix yer snow boots? No cost, of course. I'm not a shoemaker but I can darn well repair them boots.' He took them upstairs, returned two hours later and they were as good as gold. He had a cup of tea with us in the kitchen and we talked. It was nice.

See what I mean? He was the same size as my mom and they'd have been good together and I wouldn't have minded. In fact, I'd have been happy to swap my dad for him. But then I suppose Dolly and the twins wouldn't have agreed to take my drunken father at any price. Even by Cabbagetown's standards, Harry Spayd stood out among the drunken bums and bastards. But here's the weird thing: he never came in for much criticism and the men liked him, so their wives left him out of their bitchy gossip, even though he was lucky enough to have a job. It was my mom who had to take it on the chin and silently accept all their abuse, and she'd never harmed a fly.

I'd like to be able to say that I looked up to my dad despite everything, and that we'd shared some kind of father-and-son relationship, even a half-assed one. But that would be a lie. The only role he played was, like I said, to keep my mom and me in a state of constant terror.

I remember four things in particular about my father.

First, of course, was his drinking. In the summer we'd wake to an atmosphere that smelled like a brewery, even long after he had gone to work; in winter, the freezing interior would somewhat deaden the beer fumes.

Second was his size. He was six-foot-four and weighed 290 pounds. He'd brag about one day reaching the 300 pound mark.

Third was his quick temper, usually as a result of drink, but not always. It could flare up out of nowhere; the smallest detail could send him into a fit of rage, often as not resulting in a backhander for my mother and sometimes, if I was foolish enough to try to protect her, for me. His hand was the size of a small dinner plate and his knuckles would make a mess of a face with one blow, like I said.

Finally, there were his loud rasping snores, which came through the wall into our bedroom from the tiny room where he slept alone, and presumably clearly carried through the ceiling to the McClymonts upstairs. Fortunately, in the snoring stakes, the two families pretty well cancelled each other out. Dolly McClymont had a fairly severe snoring problem herself and must have looked like a beached whale in bed. The nights were never silent and I reckon as a kid I could have slept through an earthquake.

My dad beat up my mom so often that my memory blurs just thinking about it, but there were two events of sheer bastardry that stand out from the many violent outbursts that resulted from his drinking. The first occurred on a winter's night during a particularly severe January snowstorm. The streetcar was delayed forty-five minutes and then my mom, as usual, walked the last stop to save on the fare, struggling through the snow. She arrived home over an hour late, so that my pail of salty, pissy, peppery chilblain water was pretty much cold. I had to begin my routine all over, but I managed a small piss while she turned her back.

She was barely seated with her steaming King George mug of tea warming her hands when my father arrived home, drunk and snorting from the cold outside. Kicking snow from his boots, he tossed his heavy council work coat, gloves, cap and scarf on the kitchen floor and demanded a mug of tea. I poured him one from the pot, black and heavily sugared.

'What's this, boy?' he demanded, swaying slightly as he took the cup and raised it to eye level.

'Your tea, Dad.'

'Tea? I don't mean the fucking tea!' He stabbed a finger at the mug. 'The queen? Where's the king? A man drinks out of the king's cup.'

'Mom's got the King George,' I replied.

'"Mom's got the King George",' he mimicked, then added, 'What the fuck's that supposed to mean?'

'She always has it,' I blurted out stupidly.

'That so, is it? Well, now . . .'

'Oh, for heaven's sake, Harry!' my mother interjected. 'Here, I've barely touched it.' Still sitting with her feet in the pail, she reached up and proffered the King George mug to my father, who accepted it but kept hold of the Queen Mary mug.

'Barely touched it, have you? Shouldn't have touched it at all!' His voice rose as he indicated the mug I'd given him. 'This is your mug, woman!' he shouted. 'That is mine!' He nodded at the King George. Then he upturned it over my mother's head and stood swaying as he attempted to pour the tea in the Queen Mary into the empty King George.

My mom leapt up screaming, the almost scalding tea running down her face and neck. Some of the water from the pail spilled onto the kitchen floor as she stepped out of the pail, her dark eyes blazing and her voice a furious snarl I'd never heard before. 'You bastard! You drunken bastard!' she yelled. Then she picked up the pail and hurled the hot, salty, pepper-and-piss-infused water at his face and chest. He let out a howl and dropped both mugs, clutching at his eyes as he sank to his knees. My mother banged the upturned pail over his head and hands. 'Bastard!' she screamed again.

My dad, sobbing and moaning that he was blinded, managed to shake the pail off his head, but he remained on his knees with his hands covering his eyes while we cleaned up around him. Surprisingly, only the Queen Mary mug had smashed. As I picked up the pieces of broken mug, I thought, *I wonder whether the King George mug didn't break because it had 'God Save the King' on it.* The Queen Mary had no such request for God's protection inscribed around her bottom.

My mother's thick flowing hair had carried most of the hot tea away from her face, and apart from a pink scald on her left cheek she didn't seem to be too injured. Finally, Mom was sufficiently calm to attend to my dad, who was weeping uncontrollably. I found out years later that cayenne in the eye causes severe pain, conjunctivitis and something called blepharospasm – contraction of the eyelids – as well as floods of tears. Of course, neither my mom nor I knew that at the time, and it wouldn't have made any difference if we had; she was mad as hell and would still have thrown the pail into his face.

Anyhow, my old man was howling like a baby, still kneeling on the kitchen floor with his hands pressed over his eyelids. My mom told me to fetch a rag and a bowl of cold water, and tried to mop his eyes, but he screamed each time she attempted to touch them. We wrestled him out of his wet clothing, and when he was stripped down to his underpants, we took an elbow each and escorted him into the bathroom, his great hairy beer belly wobbling from his agonised sobbing. My mom got him into the bath and poured fresh water over his head, easing his hands away so she could wash his reddened eyes thoroughly.

At last we helped him into his red flannel nightshirt and led him into his bedroom. I slept okay but my mom said she could hear him howling through the wall and didn't get a wink of sleep all night.

He lay in his bed for three days moaning and groaning, while my mother bathed his eyes in boracic acid eyewash, fed him and took him to the toilet.

I couldn't help wondering what Dolly McClymont and the twins made of my dad's three-day bout of screaming, sobbing and moaning. They couldn't possibly have entertained the notion that my tiny mother had turned the tables on him and had become a fire-breathing dragon.

I'd watch my mom caring for him, gently swabbing his half-closed eyes, which looked like fiery red marbles stuck in flaming eye sockets, and silently hope that my personal contribution – the piss – added to his pain. I'd also ponder why she didn't take the best chance she'd ever had to do some real damage. He was as helpless as Cyclops, who I'd read about in one of my library books. Children don't think much about consequences and I reasoned that if he couldn't see her, he couldn't harm us. Unfortunately, by the fourth day he managed to regain some sight, sufficient to return to his work at the council and, of course, to the tavern. But his eyes were real bad for a long time afterwards and though I don't know if he got blepharospasm, he now had a permanent pop-eyed look that made him even uglier. 'Lucky you don't need good eyes to collect garbage pails,' my mom said with a small smile, 'or good looks.'

Drunken bashings inevitably followed, although it was three months before he backhanded my mom again. We never found another Queen Mary mug, and the pail incident was simply never mentioned again. When he gave me his angry, eye-popping glare and I didn't know what was coming next, I'd remind myself that I'd once virtually pissed in his eye, and take some comfort and courage from that.

Winters always seemed endless, but eventually summer would arrive, with the long summer vacation stretching through July and August. During term, half the class would play truant, girls staying home to mind younger children, boys on the streets learning a different set of lessons from classroom stuff, which was rarely valued. In winter it was the opposite: the classrooms were warmed by hissing hydronic radiators, which were almost too hot to touch. School was packed to the rafters, the girls bringing their preschool brothers and sisters with them to get them away from the bitterly cold cottages. The school principal, Mr Stott, always sent letters home saying babies and little kids were not to be brought to school, but none of the families took any notice. You can't let a toddler freeze, and so the teachers had to give in. Of all the vicissitudes we endured as children, the one we shared with the rest of Toronto was the bitter winter weather. I can't ever recall being totally warm except in a classroom.

The only advantage of winter was that there were fewer fights. Fighting meant partially stripping, and staying warm in the freezing playground was everyone's first priority. My mom would bring newspapers back from the offices she cleaned and mould a thick layer against my skin under my shirt, jersey and overlarge overcoat from Mrs Sopworth at the Presbyterian Clothing Depot. All the kids did the same in winter and some of us looked like the Michelin man. As soon as warmer weather arrived we reverted to looking as scrawny and malnourished as we really were. With babies and small kids squalling and screaming and generally carrying on in class, there was very little effective learning in the winter months.

The children in our part of town were divided into various categories, mean-spirited and tough at the top, weak or compliant at the bottom, with most somewhere in between. If the attitudes and expectations adopted in childhood carry over into adulthood, then, generally speaking, the kids from Cabbagetown were unlikely to live lives filled with much success or happiness.

That I should fall through the cracks of my childhood world was a matter of sheer luck. I was by nature a loner, but at school I mostly managed to conceal my true feelings with the appearance of an easygoing attitude. I was quick with a quip and I used my wit to make the other kids laugh. Strangely enough, I have my father to thank for a piece of good advice that helped me in the playground: 'Son, don't back down from the big guy; fight him and even if yer lose yer'll gain respect. He won't pick on you again and neither will anyone else.'

Fights were how the pecking order was established in the schoolyard, and, in schoolboy terms, they were what decided the future. The toughest guy in my age group was Jack Reading, and he was an inch or two bigger than me. He was virtually obliged to challenge me to a fight, and when he did, I accepted, and though I took a beating, I inflicted a fair bit of damage of my own. He was the one who eventually walked away. 'That's enough,' he growled, unaware that I had just about fought to a standstill. I stood there bleeding from the nose, my lip split and my left eye closing fast, feeling as if Jack Reading had near beaten me to death, but as I looked around at the guys who'd gathered in a circle to watch the fight, I mustered a grin and called out, 'Hey, Jack, come back! You forgot to close the other eye!' This got a big laugh and did a whole lot for my reputation, and I realised then that using humour is generally more effective than using your fists. Although Jack Reading had clearly won, the fight was declared 'evens', an honourable draw. So, I gained the respect I needed to help conceal the fact that I was different and a loner. I knew that isolation or solitude was the single most dangerous situation in which a slum kid could find himself.

Nobody could get away with showing that they really liked learning. Anyone stupid enough to hold up his hand in class in response to a teacher's question would earn the scorn of his peers. It would certainly have blown my disguise to smithereens had I let on how much I loved learning, and I wasn't that foolish. Answering questions in class was left to one or two of the bolder, brighter girls. But I had a secret life in books. Remember, my mom left for work at four o'clock in the afternoon and so I had the whole late afternoon and evening alone at home in which to read.

I'd borrow books from the Boys and Girls House, which I'd joined at age six with the help of a teacher, Miss Mony. Her name was Shanine, and she was very beautiful and always nice to me. One afternoon after school, she took me on the streetcar to where they had a library that, like its name said, was just for boys and girls. We were permitted to take out two books twice a week.

For the next two years, Miss Mony would take me to the library twice a week on her way home, we'd discuss the books I'd read and she'd give me verbal tests that helped me a lot. I'd get off at the Boys and Girls House streetcar stop, and she'd give me my return fare to the east side and continue on to where she lived. I'd get my two books, jump on a returning streetcar and be home by five, an hour after my mom had left for her work. She would leave my dinner for me: sandwiches in the summer and, when she'd managed to get a bone from the butcher, soup in the winter, which she'd keep warm in our old thermos flask.

On days when Miss Mony and I didn't go to the library, she'd give me my hot evening meal soon after I got back from school. So on weekdays I'd only see my mom for half an hour over breakfast and then for half an hour over dinner on non-library days; my only real chance for us to have a proper chat was when she came home at ten o'clock each night.

In the summer in which I would turn eight, Miss Mony left our school to get married and moved to Vancouver. Because the weather was fine, I could walk to the library, but it took a long time and I'd get there in the last half hour before it shut. By the time I got home, my mom was long gone. Nobody knew I'd become an avid reader except the departed Miss Mony and my mom, who could barely read herself and loved it when I read to her. We would share books at night just before we both fell asleep and at weekends, when we had more time. It didn't seem to matter that they were kids' books, although just before Miss Mony left, I was reading books for children aged up to twelve. My mom had never had anyone read to her, not even, she said, at school. It was like she was doing her life backwards. Sometimes she'd clasp one of my library books to her chest, close her eyes and say, 'I wish, I wish.'

But with Miss Mony now gone, I didn't know what I was going to do when winter came and it snowed. I didn't think I'd be able to make it to the library before it shut. Winter loomed even bleaker than usual, and I puzzled over how I could avert this impending disaster. How do you spend the evenings alone at home if you can't read? Especially after you've been accustomed to reading four books a week. I couldn't listen to the radio, like people did later. Radio was just becoming popular, but only very rich people had one in their homes and no kid I knew had ever seen a radio. I doubt there was a single radio in all of Cabbagetown during the whole of the 1930s.

'Them upstairs' had an old wind-up gramophone and the records were all old songs that sounded as if the singer sang them from the bottom of a deep well. Sometimes the needle would get stuck in the worn groove and keep repeating a single line until somebody came and lifted it. But I didn't mind; it was the only nice thing coming through the ceiling. I memorised all the songs, even the places where the voice got stuck. But they didn't play the gramophone a whole lot, so books were usually my only companions at night. While there was a fair bit of summer left, I couldn't help worrying about the winter to come. At night when I said my prayers, I asked God not to let it snow on library days.

But, as it happened, snow was responsible for the second disastrous incident involving my father, my mom and myself. It was to change my life forever.

It happened on the day of my eighth birthday, the 13th of August 1931, but the seeds of the disaster were sown two days earlier, when my dad returned from the tavern in his usual state. For some reason, my mom and I hadn't yet escaped into our bedroom, and she mentioned to him that it was my birthday in two days' time, adding that she would bake a cake and hoped he might come home sober to share it with his son.

'Birthday? What's this? It's the fucking Depression. We don't have money for fancy cakes, woman,' he'd replied.

'And whose fault is that?' my mom couldn't resist muttering, but then she added quickly, 'I've saved a bit, it'll be nothing fancy, just a small cake. Try to come home sober, Harry.'

'Don't! Don't do it, woman!' he'd roared, then stomped off to bed.

But my little mom could be stubborn and knew how excited I'd been when she'd first mentioned the birthday cake. While I now insisted I didn't need a cake, she nevertheless baked what she referred to as a 'plain cake' and iced it with chocolate icing, saving a bit of white icing to write 'Happy 8th Birthday Jack'. Then she decorated it with eight red, white and blue candles. I got to lick the bowl.

I must say, it looked splendid sitting in the centre of the kitchen table, with a small white doily placed under it. I'd never had a cake for my birthday before and was pretty excited. I'd entirely forgotten my father's drunken warning two days previously.

We waited anxiously on the big birthday night. Neither of us said anything as it drew close to closing time at the tavern. But, of course, he arrived in his usual state. He entered the kitchen and glared, his red-rimmed eyes bulging more than ever at the cake resting resplendent on the table with a box of matches beside it.

Lighting the small candles, we'd previously decided, would be his special task. Mom had done the baking, icing and decorating. Dad would perform the candle-lighting ceremony, and I the blowing out and making a wish. (I'd already practised blowing out the unlit candles in a single breath.) Then, wearing her special white lace apron from her grandmother, Mom would cut the cake.

'What's this?' he barked, pointing at the cake. 'I thought I told you, woman!' His anger flared in the familiar way and, if possible, his eyes popped even more. Then he took a step towards the table and drove his fist down hard into the centre of the cake, and kept hammering the broken pieces until the kitchen table was covered in bits of yellow cake, chocolate icing and smashed red, white and blue candles. He even crushed the matchbox, which burst and scattered matches all over the place. 'Jesus Christ, woman! Don't ya ever listen?' he roared, ignoring the birthday boy, who stood in front of his silent mom, frightened enough to piss his pants but attempting to protect her.

I was aware of the backhand that might at any moment drop her to the floor but, even when drunk, he was reluctant to hit me in the face, so if I stood in front of her, I might save her. A wife-beater was one thing; a child-beater was a much lower creature. While, like many other fathers, he qualified on both counts, he'd sometimes be just sufficiently aware to leave me alone. Now, swaying and cussing, he turned towards us, and I stiffened and closed my eyes, expecting his vicious knuckles to crack into my face. But he hesitated, turned again and rinsed his hands under the kitchen tap, then grabbed me by the shoulders. 'Git!' he snarled, hurling me across the tiny kitchen to crash into the wall. Next he dried his big red-knuckled hands on my mom's white lace apron, his ugly, pugnacious face inches from her own. 'Yer don't fuckin' listen, do yer, yah stupid bitch!' he growled, before staggering off to bed, thankfully without his signature goodnight backhander. Never mind the cake, this would turn out to be the best birthday I'd ever had.

Two weeks later, my dad returned from the tavern, reached into his trouser pocket and held out a harmonica, its polished silver shape resting on his huge calloused hand. 'Here, Jack, thought I'd forgotten, eh? Yer birthday present.' Then, seeing my surprise, he added, 'Now, don't get too excited, son. I won it in a card game.' He gave me a sardonic grin. 'Put it to your gob. It'll stop you talking shit. You can blow crap instead.' His great belly heaved as he chortled over his own wit.

I thanked him profusely, though more out of obsequious fear than from delight at the unexpected gift, taking the silver instrument gingerly from his palm. It was obviously not new – one of its silver cover plates bore a small dent and the words 'Johnny's Revenge' was scratched crudely into the chrome – but it still had a metal button that extended from one side that you apparently pressed, though why, I couldn't be sure. But I would later learn it was a genuine German Hohner and a fairly decent one, with an excellent tone.

I guess there are moments in all our lives we later recognise as turning points. This was mine. The moment I brought the harmonica to my mouth and felt the square wooden holes against my lips, I knew something in me had changed forever.

CHAPTER TWO

NIGHTS AT HOME BY myself were lonely, and would have been unbearable without books. I was no longer reading baby books, but had moved on to bigger ones, such as *Robinson Crusoe*, *Treasure Island* and *King Solomon's Mines*. At the library I'd been promoted to a new teenage section, and while it was exciting to have access to all those new titles, you were only allowed to take out one per visit and keep it for no more than a week. I needed at least two books at a time, one to read by myself and another to read in bed at night to my mom.

It always took longer than a week to finish a book with my mom, because we only had twenty minutes or so for reading each night and a bit more time at the weekends. This meant I had to bring the book back even if we hadn't finished it, then re-borrow it, sometimes for three or four weeks. But because of the rule about only taking one book out at a time, you couldn't renew a second book on the same day. I found out that some older kids hadn't been bringing back their books on time and that when they were overdue, they couldn't pay the fine. This was a particular problem in bad weather, and meant that the most popular titles were sometimes missing. So Mrs Hodgson, the librarian, had made this awful new rule that forced me to make two trips to the library each week.

As winter settled over the city, I decided to summon up the courage to ask Mrs Hodgson to let me break the rules and take out and return two books at a time. I'd prepared my argument beforehand, trying it out on my mom and going over and over it in my head during the long walk there, but once I arrived I realised that thinking up a good argument and delivering it to someone as fierce as Mrs Hodgson were entirely different things.

Miss Yolande White, the junior librarian, smiled at me. 'Well, what's your choice this week, Jack?' she asked.

I handed over *The Last of the Mohicans* and tried to gather my courage. 'Please, Miss White, may I see Mrs Hodgson?' I asked.

She looked surprised, then frowned. 'I don't know, Jack. She doesn't like to be disturbed. What's it all about?'

'It's a private matter,' I said, trying to sound as grown-up as I could.

'Oh, I see,' she exclaimed. 'Wait there and I'll ask her.'

So far so good, I thought. She returned a few moments later and said, 'You're in luck, Jack. She must be in a good mood. Go ahead.'

I knocked tentatively on Mrs Hodgson's office door and gazed at the sign:

Mrs Jess Hodgson
Chief Librarian

'Come in, Master Spayd,' she called.

I entered, closed the door behind me, and went to stand in front of her desk with my hands behind my back. I was suddenly very scared.

She hadn't looked up from something she was writing, and I noticed she had a proper fountain pen. 'Yes?' she asked at last. 'What is it?'

'It's about books, Missus . . .'

'Mrs *Hodgson*, if you please. "Missus" means something quite different. It's servile.' She looked up over the top of her glasses.

'Sorry, Mrs Hodgson.'

She removed the cap from the top of the pen and slotted it over the gold nib. 'Do you know what servile means?'

'No, Mrs Hodgson.'

'You will look it up in the dictionary before you leave, young man! Now, what is it you want?' Her spectacles had black rims and made her look even fiercer.

'It's about borrowing.'

'That's what we do in a library.'

I was floundering, my carefully prepared script forgotten. 'Can I take out two on the same day?' I blurted. 'Please,' I added belatedly.

'The answer is probably going to be no you can't, but you have the right to state your case. Go ahead.'

I was panicking. 'Snowdrifts.'

'Snowdrifts? I don't understand.'

At last I had the opportunity to give my prepared speech. 'It's almost winter and soon the snow will come and I have to walk a long way in the biting cold to get here and I could easily fall into a snowdrift and break my leg.'

One eyebrow shot up. 'Oh? Pray tell.'

'Then I have to walk back again in the dark when you can't see the snow and it's even more dangerous.'

'More snowdrifts?'

'Yes. I don't mind the cold because I love to read, but my mom worries about me. You see, she works nights and she's afraid I'll fall into a snowdrift, and nobody would know if something awful happened, like I broke my leg, and then I'd freeze to death.' I really laid it on thick, looking brave, then sad, then pathetic. I admit I got a bit carried away.

I almost told Mrs Hodgson about what a loss I'd be to my mom if I couldn't get home in time to prepare her chilblain treatment but at the last moment thought better of it. People who suffer from chilblains, and maybe she was one of them, are always interested to know someone else's method of treating them and I thought she might ask me what I put in my concoction.

She removed her spectacles, bowed her head, pressed her eyes with her forefinger and thumb and sighed. Then she looked at me again.

'Now, Jack, rules should not be broken. What if I let every child take out two books at a time?'

'It'd be good, Mrs Hodgson. You'd have less work . . . and more time to read,' I said quickly.

Mrs Hodgson looked stern but I could tell she was now smiling on the inside a bit. 'I'll think about it and let you know if we can make an exception in your case, Master Jack Spayd.' Then she gave me a hard look. 'You certainly know how to mount an argument, but the bit about trudging through snowdrifts and breaking your leg was sloppy thinking. Except for an occasional blizzard, it only snows about half-a-dozen times a month in winter, and, as you would well know, a single snowfall is seldom more than four inches deep. The likelihood of any of these factors causing a healthy young boy to break his leg and freeze to death is remote. Do you know what a specious argument is, Jack?'

'No, Mrs Hodgson.'

'Then the word "specious" is the second you will look up before you leave.'

'Yes, Mrs Hodgson, thank you for seeing me.' I knew it was all over; my dramatic account hadn't fooled Mrs Hodgson for one moment. I'd imagined fierce winters and dangerous snowdrifts when I'd read *White Fang*, the book I'd just finished. That's the one problem with books. Facts and fiction get mixed up with your real life.

I turned to leave.

'Wait a minute, Jack Spayd. I haven't finished with your . . . prognostication yet. If I were you, I should be more careful with facts in the future, my boy. Facts remain facts, no matter how you deck them out in fancy dress.' She reached for the fountain pen and tapped its end on the top of her desk three times.

'I shall make an exception in your case, Jack. You're the only child who comes all the way from Cabbagetown, and it's a long walk now that Miss Mony has left and you have no streetcar fare.' She paused and looked at me sternly. 'You are to tell no one that you have been granted this special privilege.'

'Thank you, Miss — Mrs Hodgson.'

'You may take out and return two books to the library on the same day.' She smiled and replaced her glasses and reached for her fountain pen again. 'Go on, hop to it!'

I quietly thanked her again and turned towards the door. I didn't want to overdo it. As I reached the door, she said, 'Don't forget the dictionary! And look up prognostication while you're at it.'

My mom was getting to love books as much as I did, and unknowingly we were educating ourselves – I was educating myself forwards and she was educating herself backwards because, as I said, she didn't have books in her childhood. Not all of what we learned came from books, either. In winter, she'd cut sandwiches and fill the thermos with black tea, and we'd go to the museum for the day. It would take Mom all week to save the streetcar fare, but the museum was free. Sometimes we'd listen to experts lecturing on all kinds of interesting stuff.

We went to the Riverdale Zoo once, for a special treat. I liked the elephant, the lions and the bear, even the hippopotamus, and especially the monkeys. But they looked sad behind bars, cooped up in their tiny cages. I had hoped to see birds but they didn't have any, except for sixteen pheasants and a young crane. When I thought about it later, I was pretty glad they didn't. Wild birds in tiny cages would be horrible. Can you imagine an eagle or a buzzard in a cage?

Toronto has lots of lake birds – too many to mention. We'd been to Lake Ontario once on a school outing and I'd seen lots and lots: ducks, geese, swans, herons, ring-billed gulls, herring gulls and two Caspian terns. There were supposed to be bald eagles and ospreys, but we didn't see any that day.

I liked birds a lot, not that there were many around Cabbagetown: some starlings, sparrows and doves, and occasionally you'd see a chimney swift. Once I saw a screech owl perched on a lamppost after a snowstorm. It just looked at me for ages, all hunched up, the feathers on its back disarranged. I didn't know if it was cold or injured, but then after a while it let out an eerie cry and flew away. I was glad it was okay. Owls eat mice and there were plenty of those around, I can assure you.

On our weekend walks we'd sometimes wander along the banks of the Don River, which wasn't all that far from our cottage, passing all the shut-down factories and industrial sites with their silent cranes and rusting metal. It looked like the world had come to an end. Once we heard this weird sound, like a wooden ratchet, but coming from a maple tree. We stopped and I looked up and saw a belted kingfisher, the only one I ever saw in Toronto. It was so strange; I don't think there could have been many fish in such murky, polluted river water.

My mom talked fondly about how 'the Don' used to be, with all the factory women sharing stories about themselves and their kids and laughing a lot, and how, when the factory knock-off horns sounded along the riverbank, they'd all stream out like schoolgirls and she'd meet girlfriends working in other factories, and they'd find a spot beside the river to sit for a good old chinwag.

Mom and I had lots of good fun times together on the weekends. We'd usually leave the cottage as early as we could. In the summer we'd go to the parks in search of musicians and bands – we both loved music. There were often brass bands in the rotundas, and sometimes musicians playing other instruments. I knew what a fiddle looked like, but the first time I saw a cello I thought it was a violin that was just too big to lift. Massed bands would occasionally play in a park or as part of a veterans parade, and I'd get terribly excited and march on the spot to the beat of the drums. Violins could make me cry, but they were soft tears – not because I felt sad or anything, just because the sounds were so beautiful. For days afterwards I'd hear the music in my head as clear as anything. I'd learned to whistle when I was small, and could easily pick up a tune and whistle it, sometimes weeks later. My mom would say, 'Jack, you have *the gift*.'

'What's the gift?' I'd asked the first time she said this.

'Your ear, you have a musical ear.'

'Which one?'

She'd laughed. 'It's just that you can remember music right off, every bit of it.'

'Can't everyone?'

'It's very rare, I think.'

It was nice having a gift that was very rare, but all I knew was that I loved music and could recall and whistle it weeks or months after I'd first heard it.

My mom once mentioned it to my dad. 'Must come from my side of the family,' he'd grunted. 'My Uncle Joe could play the banjo real great . . . killed in the war, poor bastard.' He showed no further interest in my gift; I guess it was not what he wanted in a boy.

Once, when I'd shown him the aggie Mac had given me, he said it was a good one, then asked, 'You any good at marbles?'

I told him I was seldom beaten.

'That's good,' he replied. His praise was sweeter even than my mom's praise for my whistling. She praised me through thick and thin, but he never did. Funny how when you receive too much approbation you cease to believe in it. My mom saw lots of praiseworthy things in me that I don't suppose were so unusual in a child.

To avoid Dad we'd stay out of the house as much as we could manage at weekends. I confess I never thought that he might be lonely or feel neglected. In winter he'd spend Saturdays at the football or ice hockey and Sundays recovering from his bender. In summer the sport changed to lacrosse or baseball but the bender was the same. Luckily for us, he slept in on Saturday mornings, recovering from a whole week of hangovers and early starts, then again on Sunday mornings as a result of his binge at the game and afterwards at the tavern. I guess the Sunday-morning hangover must have been *really* bad. My mom said she'd often hear him throwing up during the night.

Like most of the men in Cabbagetown he was a sports nut. He'd leave for the game mid-morning, summer or winter, so he and his pals could buy cheap seats in the bleachers. As bottles of beer were too bulky to carry and could easily be spotted by the law, they'd each take a bottle of cheap whisky or bourbon made by Joe Rattlesnake, a local who kept a secret still in the yard of one of the abandoned factories along the banks of the Don River. His liquor was sometimes referred to as Rattlesnake Special, whether it was whisky or bourbon (the only difference was said to be the colour, and no one ever knew what was in the wash). It was even cheaper than the fortified 'bum wine' you could buy, and lord knows the alcohol content of Joe Rattlesnake's distillate, but it could render you pretty motherless at the end of a long afternoon's drinking. Dad and his pals would then retire to the tavern after the game for beer, which, mixed with hard liquor, made for an even nastier drunk than usual. As often as not it ended in the all-too-familiar Saturday-night wife- and child-bashings.

Those fathers who didn't drink at the game would take one of their sons to the football or hockey game as a treat, for a birthday or something like that. My dad took me to a football game once, when I was seven. There was no special reason. Perhaps he wanted to look like a real father. The game at Varsity Stadium was between the Toronto Argonauts and the Ottawa Rough Riders, two teams in the Grey Cup competition. He even made me wear his precious Argonauts scarf, which fell to below my knees, even though I wrapped it around my neck three times. Taking me was a big sacrifice for him as it meant he couldn't go back to the tavern to drink beer with his pals afterwards.

When the Argonauts scored, I yelled and threw my hands in the air, and I think that pleased him, but I knew I was never going to be like him or the other fans at the game. Sport – football, anyhow – just didn't do a whole lot for me. I was not a bad skater, and I was pretty good at shinny, a rough-and-ready type of pond hockey, but that was about it. I played shinny when the pond in the industrial area near the Don River froze, skating in a pair of old skates from Mrs Sopworth at the Presbyterian Clothing Depot.

In truth, my dad seemed more interested in the breaks in the game than in the game itself. 'Stay there. Don't move, son,' he'd say, while he and his pals left to join all the other men behind the bleachers with bottles in brown paper bags. While drinking at a game was against the law, the cops, in an unwritten agreement, turned a blind eye to the area directly behind the bleachers.

After the game, when we were in the middle of the crush leaving the stadium, Dad turned to heckle a group wearing the colours of the Rough Riders. They responded, and he and his pals suddenly lunged towards them through the dense shuffling mass, shoving people aside. The crowd quickly closed behind him, separating us, and moved forward, sweeping me along with it. Outside the stadium I waited for fifteen minutes but couldn't see him. I could clearly imagine Dad and his pals involved in a drunken fight with the Ottawa supporters, and suddenly it seemed like a bad idea to hang around.

I was a pretty observant and independent kid, and on the way in the streetcar I'd taken in all the landmarks. It was a straightforward route down Bloor Street, so I wasn't too worried. But I hadn't anticipated the snowstorm that swept over the city, practically blinding me and changing everything. These severe blizzards were called Panhandle Hooks, and they came up from the Gulf of Mexico, usually in late December and January but seldom in November. Snow in Toronto isn't usually that heavy but when a Panhandle Hook hits the city, watch out.

While Varsity Stadium hadn't seemed a long way from the east side by streetcar, walking home proved quite a different matter. The streets were now deserted and I couldn't identify any of the landmarks I'd seen on the way to the game. I struggled on through the blizzard for what must have been an hour, growing numb with cold. I figured it should have taken me less than that to get all the way home, but soon I couldn't see from one streetlight to the next and somehow, I don't know how, I lost the streetcar tracks in Bloor Street, and after that I quickly lost my way.

The shops were all shut, so I couldn't ask for directions or shelter from the snow. It never occurred to me to knock on someone's front door. I might have done so in Cabbagetown, but I didn't dare knock at houses where there was only one family and a garden. Stupid, I suppose, but in those days everyone knew their place in the social hierarchy and mine certainly wasn't at the front door of a big house. I eventually found a small tobacco kiosk and a fat bald man with an accent redirected me. 'Ven you get lost, come back, I tell you some more za vey.'

Amazingly I was only about twenty minutes from Moss Park, next door to Cabbagetown where we lived. I can tell you now, I was stumbling with exhaustion and cold when I finally arrived home. My frantic mom burst into tears, running to embrace me, but my dad stepped directly in front of her, blocking her way. He was drunk of course, and in a towering rage. When she tried to pass him, he bumped her hard so that she crashed to the floor. She got to her knees, arms reaching for me, sobbing with relief that I'd come home safely. 'Oh, Jack. Oh, my darling, you're home!' she cried.

'Jesus Christ, where yer been ya miserable little bastard?' my dad yelled, standing above me. 'Look what ya done to yer mother!'

'I got lost. It snowed real heavy,' I said through chattering teeth.

'Why the fuck didn't ya wait fer me?'

'I did, then I thought you were in a fight,' I stammered, my teeth still chattering, now even more so from fear at his drunken rage.

'C'mere!' He reached out and grabbed me by the scarf, and yanked me violently so that I near lost my footing and found myself in the centre of the kitchen. 'Git yer fuckin' pants down!' he barked.

My hands were frozen, and I had trouble removing his scarf and my overcoat, then unhitching my braces and dropping my pants. I watched fearfully as he removed his big leather belt. Holding the buckle, he wound it around his fist and snapped, 'Bend!' While I'd received my share of backhands from him, I'd never received a formal thrashing. Most of the guys who'd told me about their experiences said that it wasn't too bad – six across the bum and sometimes you couldn't sit comfortably the next day. But that was when your dad was sober. I was terrified. The leather belt he wielded was at least two inches wide and my knees were knocking, not, I assure you, from the cold.

'Turn round, grab yer ankles!' he commanded. I turned so my ass faced him, then bent, my stiff fingers disappearing into my crumpled pants to grasp my shins. I locked my knees so that they almost stopped shaking.

'Please don't, Harry!' my mom begged him frantically. 'Please don't thrash my boy!'

'Shurrup, woman!' he commanded. 'Teach the little shit a lesson!'

Still bending, I peered around my skinny legs to see him lift the belt above his shoulder. I braced myself, ready for what was coming to me, but suddenly my mom sprang at him, screaming and clawing at his neck and face. The lifted belt came down hard across her back, but I don't think she even felt the blow as her nails raked across his face, opening it in four distinct furrows from just under his right eye, down his cheek and the side of his neck. She was in another chilblain fury but this time she had no pail of cayenne and piss as a weapon, only her nails. My father let fly with a straight left, his fist smashing into her face, and she sank to the floor, bleeding from the nose and mouth.

'Now see what yer gorn and done to yer mother!' my father growled. The scratches on his face had reddened but he seemed oblivious to them. 'Next time you wait for me, if necessary, until the fucking second coming of Christ! Yer hear, boy?' With this, he started lambasting me with the belt, going hell for leather across my ass and the backs of my legs. I started to scream and scream until I fell to the floor, unable to stand any longer. He whacked me one more time across my back, then I could hear him panting. I managed to crawl to my mother, and we huddled together on the kitchen floor, her blood dripping onto my best shirt, which I'd worn especially for the game, both of us howling our hearts out.

Then my father grabbed his coat and gloves and stormed out of the house, presumably heading for the tavern before it closed.

It was the first and last time I accompanied my dad to a game of any sort. I think my mom must have put her foot down. But I don't suppose he needed much persuading. I don't think my dad liked me, and I've got to admit the feeling was pretty mutual. I wasn't the kid he'd wanted, nor was I, like most kids my age, mad about sport and collecting cigarette cards of football and hockey stars. I just wasn't into ball games.

We had never been a proper family. We seldom, if ever, shared anything, not even meals, except occasionally on a Sunday night. Dad must have eaten somewhere, because my mom rarely cooked for him. If she left a plate of food for him to warm up when he got home from the tavern at night, in the morning she'd invariably find it untouched and scraped into the garbage pail. He'd never just leave it on the plate so we could maybe eat it ourselves. Eventually, she simply gave up. You couldn't waste perfectly good food like that.

He can't have been all bad – he seemed to have plenty of friends. One of my school pals said his father had called my dad generous because he'd never let a pal go without a drink. We knew all about that! Perhaps he used up all his generosity in the tavern. At home he was a morose grunter – nothing seemed to please him and I can't remember him ever saying anything nice about my mom or speaking kindly to her.

Maybe he resented her for giving him only one kid, a boy he couldn't really enjoy in the way some other fathers seemed to enjoy their sons. On Sunday mornings he'd come out of his bedroom just as we were leaving. Scratching his crotch, he'd called after me, 'Fuckin' mama's boy! Tit sucker!'

At school we once had to write an essay on the subject 'Why I like my dad'. The girls had to do the same about their moms. I was forced to invent a whole lot of bullshit, saying how lucky we were to have him. Later, Miss Mony handed back the essay and said quietly, 'Jack, imagination in a child is a good thing, but sometimes you have to stick to the facts, to the truth.' She must have guessed the cause of the split lips, bruised cheeks and black eyes I occasionally sported, or maybe she'd heard about my dad somewhere. But she was dead wrong about telling the truth. A boy never talked about having a drunk for a dad, never ever. It was a lousy choice for an essay topic and she should have known better.

A drunken bashing was a source of personal shame, always kept within the family. A thrashing – or a good hiding, as it was sometimes called – was quite different. Six of the best on the bum was the definition of a thrashing, and you could talk about it if you wanted to. Thrashing a child for a misdemeanour was accepted practice in all families and happened when your dad was absolutely sober. The adage 'Spare the rod and spoil the child' was a universal truth at that time and, as far as I can gather, applied in proper middle-class homes as well. You can be sure everyone knew the difference between a thrashing and a beating, and who were the truly violent drunken fathers. There were no secrets in Cabbagetown. But still, you never admitted or talked about a bashing, even when you came to school with a battered face. The doorknob had a lot to answer for.

So my home life was divided into two parts: a father whom I avoided, and a loving mother. Somehow my mother's part outweighed my father's, and all things considered, I was a pretty happy kid. My dad did one good thing that was to change my life: he gave me the harmonica for my eighth birthday.

School was good. With my quick wit and easy manner, I was quite popular, though I never had a *best* friend, preferring my own company. Still, in the summer there were plenty of boys ready to play marbles in the schoolyard, or muck about after school among the deserted factories and along the river, and in winter play shinny on the frozen pond. By the time I'd turned eight, I was well ahead of the other kids my age. I mean, I couldn't help it, with all that reading and with the stuff my mom and I learned on weekends, and especially with Miss Mony pushing me along. Just before she left for Vancouver, she told me I should be at another school, because ours wouldn't let you skip a class, let alone two, which she said was what I needed to do. 'Jack, the principal here doesn't understand children like you who *really* want to learn. He's been at Cabbagetown School too long and simply doesn't know how to handle truly bright children.' But I knew what she'd done for me was much better than being promoted to a class where I'd probably have to endure a worn-out and dispirited teacher, and the snubs and slights of the ten-year-olds, on top of ostracism in the playground by guys of my own age for being too clever for my own good. She'd set me on a course, created within me habits of reading and questioning that would serve me well all my life. One of the last things she'd said to me before leaving for Vancouver was, 'Jack, you don't need me any longer. Keep reading and asking yourself questions, or anyone else you think may have the answers. That's all you'll need until you get a scholarship to a decent high school and then university.'

When I told my mom, she couldn't believe her ears. 'University!' she squeaked. 'Isn't and never was nobody in our family ever could have thought about something like going to university.'

I owe Miss Mony a great deal and mostly because she got me reading, which wouldn't have happened otherwise. 'Curiosity is the greatest habit a human can cultivate and reading is the best way to satisfy it,' she'd say. Reading made me happy for another reason, too. I loved sharing books with my mom. Late at night, when we'd padlocked ourselves in the bedroom, I'd read just for her. Because she'd had very little education, she was anxious that I didn't end up the same as her, just another child following in the pretty miserable footsteps of ignorant parents. She'd constantly ask me about school and Miss Mony's private lessons, and she'd be proud as punch when my report card came in at the end of term with a whole string of straight As. Although you never allowed yourself to appear clever in class, you were allowed to be clever in tests. End of term report cards were regarded with indifference by most kids and never discussed. They were usually bad news, anyhow. The reports probably didn't get too much attention from parents either. Most, recalling their own time at school, didn't harbour great expectations for their kids. In those days people really believed you inherited your stupidity: like father like son; like mother like daughter. Working-class women especially were never expected to have brains and were regarded as breeders and factory fodder.

I remember my mom would give me a hug and a big kiss and shake her head in genuine wonder when she saw my results. 'I don't know where your brains could possibly come from, Jack. In my family nobody was good at schooling, yer father's family neither; hopeless, the lot of us.

Miracles will never cease, dumb marries dumber and, lo and behold, out pops Clever Jack!' Then she'd laugh. 'You don't suppose they swapped babies at the hospital by mistake, eh?' I could see she was surprised that I kept topping my class and it pleased me no end to see her so proud.

My father would just grunt and say, 'Yeah, nice,' in an off-hand manner, barely glancing at my results before adding, 'It's all bullshit, son. Remember yer from Cabbagetown, nothin' here to beat. Only means yer the least stupid of a bunch o' knuckleheads, so don't you go thinking you're God's gift, eh, boy.' Without discussing it, we stopped showing him my report card, and he never asked to see it.

But I had a long time to wait for my mom to come home each night, and sometimes I'd even grow weary of reading. Singing along to the McClymonts' gramophone upstairs would, of course, help pass the hours occasionally. My mom and I had always sung together – mostly Iroquois tribal songs her grandmother had taught her – and often enough she'd say I had a real nice voice, but you couldn't take too much notice of her. With only one child, who she loved to bits, she was a bit biased. Not that it mattered, because the one thing a boy never did at school was sing, except for 'God Save the King'. You were allowed to belt that out because it was an act of loyalty to your king and country. Otherwise, our school was no place for a boy soprano.

I'd long since memorised the lyrics of the songs I heard drifting through the ceiling, and when the gramophone started upstairs I'd sing at the top of my voice, pausing at the parts where the needle stuck in the worn grooves. It never occurred to me that my voice would have travelled up through their floorboards as readily as the music travelled down, but they never complained; perhaps the silent treatment they'd imposed on us prevented them from speaking.

I recall my favourite song was 'Alexander's Ragtime Band', but I loved most of the songs filtering down from the McClymonts': 'It's a Long Way to Tipperary', 'Pack Up Your Troubles', 'Keep the Home Fires Burning', 'A Bicycle Built for Two'. Many of them were popular during the Great War, when, I suppose, someone in the McClymont family had a good enough job to be able to afford the gramophone and seventy-eights. They hadn't added any new records since and all of them were badly worn from being played so often.

But there was worse, much worse, to come for Dolly McClymont, Mac and the twins. The arrival of the harmonica marked the beginning of a whole new musical era. I was desperate to learn to play, and practised for so long that my reading suffered. I knew all the tunes by heart, so I didn't have to wait for the gramophone to start up. Sometimes I'd practise until my lips hurt. When I think back, it must have been sheer hell for 'them upstairs'. The boy soprano might have been annoying but the novice harmonica player would have been far worse. Unknowingly, I had probably paid them back for the emotional hurt they'd so cruelly inflicted on my mother.

I don't know whether it was from kindness or desperation but Mac confronted me one afternoon in the hall when Dolly and the twins must have been out. 'Jack, you're coming along nicely with that mouth organ. I'm surprised how quickly you've learned to play. Well done, and my goodness, all self-taught, eh?'

I was too young or gauche to know how to react, so, instead of thanking him for the compliment, I said, 'Sorry, sir.'

He gave me a knowing grin. 'Can't speak for the missus and the girls, but I reckon you're doing great. I liked it when you used to sing, you've got a real nice voice, Jack. But the harmonica makes a nice change from the records; goddamn gramophone drives me crazy.' He smiled again. 'Jack, I like the way you push the beat, put some *oomph* into the music. I like jazz. "Alexander's Ragtime—"'

'Jazz?' I'd never heard the word.

'Black man's music, from America.'

I'd seen one or two black people on the street, but I'd never met one, and was surprised to learn that different coloured people had different music. 'Do black people have black music?' I asked, curious.

'I'll say!' he replied, obviously enthusiastic.

My mother called the Iroquois songs I sang with her folk songs, but because they were just tunes, they didn't count in my mind as real music. Now Mac was talking about jazz music that belonged to American black people.

'You can hear it at the Jazz Warehouse on Dundas Street, not far from Yonge Street. Take you if you like,' he offered.

I instinctively glanced upstairs.

'No, no, tomorrow.' He glanced up too. 'It's quilting night. They'll leave for St Enoch's just before four o'clock. What say we take off about half past? Plenty of time to catch the jam session.'

'What's a jam session?'

'Oh, it's when the musicians play for themselves. We'll just stand outside and listen. I know just the spot.'

Jazz, black people's music, jam session, and all happening in some warehouse on Dundas Street, not far from the street where the Mission handed out free beef sandwiches, tea and milk. It was close enough for us to walk there, no more than half an hour away, so we wouldn't need money for the streetcar. 'That would be great, thank you, sir,' I said formally.

'Good. Bring your instrument, Jack.'

'My what?'

'Mouth . . . er, harmonica.'

Instrument! Mac was treating me like I was a proper musician. The timing was good – I wouldn't have to tell my mom – and I knew I was safe with Mac, who wouldn't hurt a fly.

The following afternoon when my mother gave me my supper I was having trouble concentrating.

'What's the matter with you today, Jack? Cat got yer tongue?' she asked, after I'd failed to answer yet another question. 'You're jumpy as a jackass!'

I wanted to tell her, but then again I didn't. I knew she liked Mac and was grateful when he fixed her snow boots, but he was still one of 'them upstairs' and she might be worried about Dolly's reaction should she find out Mac was mixing with the enemy. 'We had an exam today,' I said, 'it was hard.' This wasn't the truth – the exam hadn't been difficult at all – but afterwards some of the brighter girls said they'd found it hard, so I was only half fibbing.

'Oh, Jack, you're such a clever boy, I'm sure it will be all right,' she replied, dismissing my concern as she piled my plate with mashed potato and boiled cabbage. 'Eat up. Maybe I'll manage a soup bone from the butcher tomorrow. Never know, eh?'

I felt a bit ashamed because I knew she trusted me completely.

After my mom left for work, I got ready for the grand adventure. It was late November and already pretty chilly. We'd be returning after sunset and so I packed several sheets of newspaper inside my shirt – more than I probably needed, but this way I wouldn't crackle as I walked. Then I put on my big overcoat (the charity lady, Mrs Sopworth, had been right, I had grown into it), my winter cap with padded flaps that covered my ears, and a pair of knitted gloves (same charity lady). I felt a bit overdressed for the time of the year, but walking to the library two days previously a chilly November wind had blown up around six o'clock, and Mac had mentioned that we'd be standing outside. I hated the cold. I decided that when I was grown up I was going to live in the South Seas or somewhere like Robinson Crusoe and Man Friday lived.

I was ready twenty minutes before I heard Mac coming down the stairs into the front hallway. I met him at our door, which led off the foyer directly into our kitchen. 'Thank you, sir, for asking me,' I said.

Mac chuckled. 'Let's get it straight from the beginning, Jack. I'll call you Jack and you call me Mac and we can be buddies, right?'

I nodded, not quite knowing how to reply. Mister or sir was how kids addressed adults. 'I'll try . . . ah, Mac.'

'It's just that all the folk that love jazz think of themselves as the same,' he explained. 'We don't use our names to address each other – kids and grown-ups, we call each other "brother" or "sister". We all . . .' he hesitated a split second then spoke out of the corner of his mouth, stretching his words, 'Jes jazz fans, man! Yeah, you can say that again, Brother Jack!' He grinned. 'That's how we talk.' He patted me on the shoulder and continued. 'I hope you're gonna be one of us, Brother Jack.

The harmonica is a natural jazz instrument.' He grinned again. 'Yeah, man, Brother Jack, I've got a distinct feelin' you are gonna take to jazz music like a duck to water, my good man.'

Mac obviously liked to talk in what I suppose was meant to be black people's language, but my ear told me it was sort of phoney, so I didn't try to copy it.

As we walked along Dundas Street you could hear music coming from this big warehouse, its timber walls practically vibrating with the volume. It sounded like nothing I'd ever heard before.

Outside, there were several groups of young people huddled together against the cold, their feet tapping and their bodies swaying to the music. Some had their eyes closed.

'Come on, Jack, too cold to stand with the brothers and sisters. I know a place where we can be warm.' Mac led me behind the building to a small shed directly alongside a set of eight wooden steps leading to a red door. Three pipes ran from the shed into the building, each of them wrapped in burlap and tied with wire to keep the heat in.

'Boiler room,' Mac said, pointing to the shed as he walked over to the steps and ducked under them, indicating that I should follow. Lucky we were both small; there was just sufficient room for us to sit with our knees practically up to our chins. But here's the thing: the hot-water pipes formed a barrier on one side of the steps, and I noticed the burlap had been neatly removed on the inside of the pipes, and the heat made it cosy as anything.

Mac pointed to the pipes. 'I did that last winter. Makes it nice and warm in here.' He raised his voice above the music. 'Don't touch, hot as hell.'

If this was jazz, I knew almost immediately that I loved it. I liked the rhythm and the wail of the saxophone, and the driving compulsive beat. This music wasn't slow and tired like on the records upstairs, or pronounced and disciplined like a military band, but came at me urgently; it jumped and barked and wailed, hammering into my consciousness. Then it would go smooth all of a sudden and make you smile. It was 'speaking music'. While I hadn't yet learned its language, I knew I must. Black people's music it might be, but it went straight to my white heart and soul. I'd discovered what was to become my first true obsession.

The jam session continued until seven, when, Mac said, the musicians stopped to have their evening meal and a rest before the club opened. On the way home he explained the concept of a nightclub. 'It opens at nine o'clock most evenings and closes at one in the morning, sometimes even later.'

'But who would go to such a place?' I asked, mystified.

'Oh, rich people and people in business entertaining their clients after they've had dinner in a restaurant.' He said it as if he knew all about such things.

My mother cleaned offices, so the term 'business' was vaguely familiar to me, but I'd never imagined the people who dirtied the offices, or realised they ate in restaurants and visited places like the Jazz Warehouse. Rich people, I knew, could do anything they liked and were not like us. I'd never been inside a restaurant. I don't think Mac knew much about businessmen and clients and restaurants either, because all he volunteered when I asked him to explain further was, 'It's called nightlife. They're night people.'

I thought about this for a few moments then asked, 'Are all black people rich?'

Mac laughed. 'No, Jack. The only black people at the Jazz Warehouse are the musicians, and they're definitely not rich. They come from across the border: New York, Chicago, other places in America.'

'Have you been inside?'

'Oh, yes, a year ago, the last decent job I had. Miss Frostbite bought all these old couches and chesterfields – nice, mostly turn of the century, Edwardian and earlier, Victorian maybe – she wanted them upholstered in purple velvet.'

'Miss Frostbite! Is that her *real* name?' I asked, surprised.

He shrugged. 'It's what her staff and the musicians call her.'

'For real or behind her back?'

'No, it's said friendly-like and she doesn't seem to mind as long as it's staff and musicians and workmen like me who call her that. Mind you, Miss Frostbite is not a bad nickname for her.' He turned his head and grinned. 'Believe you me, that lady . . . man, she ain't nobody's pushover, nosirree, def-fin-nitely!' he said in the new jazz accent. Then, speaking normal Canadian again, he added, 'They all say she's hard as nails and I'll admit she didn't give me a cent I didn't earn twice over. She wanted receipts for everything I bought: upholstery studs, lining material, sets of springs, edging tape, tacks . . . every goddamned little thing! She drives a hard bargain, but she always paid me in cash at the end of each week, and in these hard times that was good enough for me. She also told me I done a good job and took my name and address.'

'So, what's her real name? It can't *really* be Miss Frostbite, can it?'

'To tell the truth, Jack, I don't know,' he admitted. 'But her customers call her Fairy Floss. So do those young people you saw standing outside, listening to the jam session. It's a name I believe she got from the soldiers in the Great War when she was a nightclub singer. She was young and very beautiful then. She still plays the piano; she's got an act with an old black guy. I'm told it's very good, but not jazz. I haven't seen or heard it. It's not a part of the afternoon jam session.

'Doing her couches is how I got to know about the jam sessions. She insists her musicians practise every afternoon. It's become a ritual. Late summer afternoons and early evenings, lots of people gather, young ones mostly, but not all, some like me. They come directly from their work. Those we saw today probably don't have jobs. We're all true jazz lovers, the brothers and sisters.'

'Miss Frostbite doesn't mind? You said she was hard as nails.'

'Nah, I think Miss Frostbite does it just for us, the fans standing outside. When I was doing the upholstery, I once heard her telling a visiting musician how much she loves jazz, that it's in her heart and soul. He was an American saxophone player. I reckon she invented these afternoon rehearsals to bring jazz to Toronto. She wants everyone to enjoy jazz. She wouldn't stop them for anything. She knows most of her paying patrons prefer her two-piano act with the old guy, they don't come to hear the jazz. She and the old guy perform twice a night for almost an hour, and the jazz is just in between. But she'd never admit she's being kind and generous to the brothers and sisters outside. I expect it's a tough job running a nightclub and she don't want to be seen to be someone you can take advantage of.'

I didn't quite know how to ask my next question. I had read *Uncle Tom's Cabin* by Harriet Beecher Stowe, and Mom and I had cried and cried, but I was, of course, too young to see it as an indictment of racial prejudice. So although I knew about black slavery in America, I never connected it with Canada because, as far as I knew, we didn't have slaves. Still, even at the age of eight, I knew that most white Canadians didn't have a good word to say about anyone who wasn't white. My dad's opinion of black people was probably very little different from that of most people in Cabbagetown and perhaps the rest of Canada. Asians – 'Japs and Chinks' – as well as Indians from the subcontinent, were all considered to be a lower form of life by most white Canadians. My dad called black people 'Dirty fuckin' niggers'. So how then could Miss Frostbite invite black musicians to play in the Jazz Warehouse? Wouldn't people object? If we were going to be brothers and sisters and talk from the side of our mouths and be make-believe black men, was that maybe against the law or something?

'You said black musicians come from America to play.'

'Yeah, guest artists.'

'Is that allowed?'

'You mean segregation?'

I'd never heard the word segregation before.

'It means keeping coloured people out of restaurants and other places,' he explained, seeing my puzzled expression.

'Yeah. My dad calls them niggers and says they're scum, the lowest.'

'Yeah, well, you see, that's just people. Miss Frostbite don't buy it. Nosirree, she don't! In the entrance to the Jazz Warehouse she has this notice.' He sketched the lines in the air as he spoke.

'Warning!
When you enter
the Jazz Warehouse
you become colour blind!'

That's what I liked about Mac. As he'd promised, he talked to me like we were buddies and I was a grown-up and not some dumb kid. I was grateful for all the reading I'd done because it made me quite a good grown-up talker. Besides, my mom and I always spoke to each other as equals.

We arrived home around half-past seven, a good hour before Mac said Dolly and the twins got back from quilting. When I asked him about quilting, he said he'd saved scraps of material from his upholstery for years before the Depression when he used to have lots of work. Dolly made quilts, which she'd then sell. But now, with the Depression, people seldom, if ever, bought one. Still, she was teaching the twins and other women from St Enoch's Presbyterian Church how to make them. I admit I was surprised she'd do a kind thing like that for other people. I'd have liked to sleep under a nice warm quilt.

'So, what do you think, Jack? Did you enjoy that?' Mac asked, smiling. I think he already knew the answer.

I grinned. 'You can say that again, Brother Mac!' Then we shook hands.

'I did too! It was a real nice night, eh?' He hesitated. 'Like to do it another time?'

'You bet,' I replied.

'Tomorrow?'

'I can't, I have to go to the library.'

'Friday? I can do Friday.'

'Yes, thanks, Mac.'

'Bring your instrument.'

I'd taken it with me that afternoon but there hadn't been any point. 'Why?' I now asked.

'Don't you want to play jazz on that harmonica?'

I stared at him in amazement.

'Jack, I know you have a good ear. I've heard you picking up tunes from the gramophone in no time.'

'Do you think I could? I mean really, really?'

'Well, naturally not at first, not until you work out the chords and what have you. But if you practise on the spot, I do believe you could, Jack.'

'What about you?'

'What about me?'

'Well, I'd be practising and messing things up and it would spoil the jam session for you.'

Mac laughed. 'If it does, I'll go stand with the brothers and sisters. There's a group I stand with in the summer.' He paused. 'Mind, I wouldn't be there always. I get an occasional upholstery job and sometimes a day's work from the labour line, and that always involves overtime. The foreman only picks a handful and you often have to work an extra two hours without pay, sometimes more.'

'That's not fair. My dad says, "a fair day's work for a fair day's pay".'

'Ah, yes, but he has a regular job,' Mac said without malice. Then he added, 'But, hey, you can't complain, it's work, a day's pay.' He glanced up automatically. 'They'll be home soon. Better be going, get the spuds on.'

'Thanks again, Mac.'

'Goodnight, Jack.' We shook hands once more, like proper grown-ups.

Inside I took off my boots and climbed into bed with my coat still on. I had two-and-a-half hours to go before my mom got home. Now I found myself in a real quandary. I got out my harmonica, but I didn't want to play any of the old music, not even 'Alexander's Ragtime Band', and I didn't know how to play this new stuff that had made my heart pound and my feet tap involuntarily. It was music that got into your ear so you couldn't think about anything other than jazz rhythm. I tried to sound some of the notes I'd heard, just a bar or two, and I finally managed a sustained wail from the harmonica, but it was pretty pathetic.

Thinking it might help to stop the sounds reverberating in my head, I grabbed my book, *The Last of the Mohicans*, but I was near the end and half an hour later I'd finished it. Almost immediately, the music returned once more. The jam session had somehow got stuck in my head, and I was trying to pick it apart and bring some sense of order to it without any understanding of the underlying principles. I'd never heard of anyone making up music on the spot. Instruments came in solo, played a few bars and then faded out with only the drummer continuing to beat the time, then the others merged back in and all of it made perfect musical sense.

However, one thing I knew for certain was that now Mac had suggested I take my harmonica, I'd be going back to the Jazz Warehouse as often as I could, even if it was every weekday except my library days. Reading was something I could never give up, but I persuaded myself there would still be plenty of time to read at night. Besides, after three hours my lips were too sore to play. If I could spend two hours playing under the steps at the back of the Jazz Warehouse and then another hour at home, perhaps I might one day learn how to play jazz.

CHAPTER THREE

WITH THE LIBRARY SORTED out, I had four afternoons a week free to
'hit the steps', as Mac had said after our visit to the Jazz Warehouse on
Friday. He'd encouraged me to play my harmonica, but we both realised
that trying to listen to the jam sessions while I worked on a few chord
progressions wasn't going to work. After my initial attempt, he decided
to join his old group out in front so I could mess about trying to follow
the musicians. I'd said to him, 'Mac, I don't mind not playing at the jam
session. I can take stuff home in my head and work on it there.' But he
wouldn't hear of me not playing the harmonica at a session.

'Jack, never mind me. I get to hear the music properly with my
friends and you and me can talk on the way home. Hey, that's what
buddies are all about – leave some space for one another.'

While it was true that I could carry a lot of music in my head, it was
much better trying to work it out on the spot. In this way I could hear a
melody or some piece of musical phrasing, then attempt to play it. Then,
when it was repeated later in the jam session, I could play along and see
how I was doing.

I sensed that Mac was a bit of a loner, too. He never talked about
other guys. I think he'd enjoyed the twins when they were little and
he'd tell me funny stories about them, but now they were teenagers,

going on fifteen, and I don't think it was the same for him. Like I said before, I wished my mom had married Mac and that he was my father. He was always cheerful and didn't seem to have bad moods, even when he'd been in a labour line since early morning or done a hard day's manual labour on a work site. Sometimes he'd come to the jam session looking shabby and dirty after work, but he'd always greet me with 'Hi, Brother Jack,' poking his head under the steps and waving to let me know he'd arrived.

After that first time, when Dolly and the twins had been out quilting, we'd separate when we approached the neighbourhood, just in case someone from Cabbagetown saw us together and told Dolly that the one-time 'enemies' were thick as thieves. I'd go ahead and he'd wait five minutes before following.

Three weeks went by and it was the Christmas school-holiday break, so I had almost nothing to do during the day except practise and read and play marbles with friends or go skating with them on the big pond in the factory area along the banks of the Don. It stank to high heaven in the summer and even frogs wouldn't go in it, but when it iced up and the stench froze it was our winter playground. I was a pretty good skater and shinny player. We'd play in the mornings when the air from the gas depot didn't stink as much and the surface of the pond was freshly frozen. But still, if you fell and got your face near the ice, it smelled real nasty. Pond hockey was the best part of winter.

One night a Panhandle Hook blew in over Lake Ontario, and I knew that next morning the ice on the pond would be perfectly frozen with no slush. I was on my way to play shinny when I met Mac coming down the stairs. 'Hi, Jack,' he said quietly, so his voice wouldn't carry to 'them upstairs'. He pointed to my skates tied by the laces and slung over my shoulder. 'Shinny?'

I nodded. Then he pointed to the front door to indicate that he'd meet me in the street.

Once outside and away from the house, he said, 'Let's have a look at that hockey stick.'

I handed him the worn and battered stick, and after examining it for a moment, he said, 'Bit small for you, isn't it?'

It was true. I seemed to be growing so fast that nothing was the right size for long. But the stick was the least of my concerns. Skates were always the biggest problem. My feet kept on getting bigger each year, and somehow every winter my mom would find the money to get me a second-hand pair.

'Can you hang on a minute, Jack? I might have just the thing.' He turned and hurried back into the house and returned a couple of minutes later holding a nice-looking hockey stick that was definitely bigger than my own. 'Here, Jack, try this,' he said, handing it to me.

Now, Mac was definitely not the ice-hockey type; he'd never even brought the subject up and I'd never mentioned playing pond hockey either. 'Jeez, thanks, Mac, it's a beauty!' I exclaimed. It was, too: almost new and made from maple wood, like a proper professional ice-hockey stick. 'Where'd you get it?'

Mac grinned. 'I've had it for a few years now. It's a strange story. I was re-covering an old chesterfield for someone, and I'd lifted the three big cushions to get to the springs underneath to realign them when I saw that someone had slit the lining and pushed that hockey stick down between two rows of springs.'

'What for?' It was a silly question.

Mac shrugged. 'Damned if I know. It wouldn't have helped stabilise the chesterfield any. Someone must have been hiding it. It's not unusual to find the odd thing hidden in a couch or lounge chair. I once found a gold brooch . . . then, on another job, I found a silver cigarette case. Anyhow, I'm glad I hung onto it. It's yours now, Jack.'

The new maple stick really helped my game. Soon I was among the first to be chosen in a pick-up shinny side. Sometimes, walking back from the pond, I'd make up different stories about why the hockey stick had been hidden in the lining of the couch. Then my mind would drift to the precious gold brooch and silver cigarette case, although the reason why these had been hidden was pretty obvious – probably to stop someone from taking them to the pawnbroker. But a kid-sized used hockey stick wasn't pawnbroker material. Some of the stories I made up went on for ages and got very complicated. In one, a father used it to beat his son and so his mom hid it, but there was much more to the story than that. The imagined boy's name was Tom. I can tell you, life wasn't easy for him. The only fun he ever had was playing shinny.

Anyhow, back to hitting the steps at the Jazz Warehouse. In the three weeks since my first visit with Mac, we'd been eleven times. It should have been twelve but on one of the days there was a blizzard coming through, so I was forced to stay home. Then came Christmas and the Jazz Warehouse closed for a week. The downtown offices closed for four days, so my mom was home and I couldn't practise my jazz. She would have immediately noticed the difference in the music and asked about it.

But the good thing was that I was beginning to get the hang of it. After about three sessions, I'd worked out the button on the end of the harmonica, which up till then had been a bit of a mystery. Playing is only a question of sucking and blowing. On a chromatic harmonica, there are four notes in each individual hole. Two notes are played either by sucking or blowing with the button pressed in; the other two with the button pulled out. This means you can play all the notes in the scale across three or four octaves, depending on the size of the harmonica. This gives you almost unlimited musical possibilities. Not that I could have explained that at the time, of course; I just gradually worked it out for myself.

When I couldn't practise jazz because my mom was home, I'd play other music. Right from the start, I'd played for her while she worked in the kitchen. She had to endure all the 'them upstairs' music, and sometimes, just to break it up, I'd sing Daisy's reply from 'A Bicycle Built for Two' in my piping soprano. But she especially loved the stuff we'd heard together on our walks over the summer. She'd sometimes stop at the sink or stove, close her eyes and say, 'Oh, Jack, that's lovely.' One night she'd said, 'Jack, I'd love it if you played to me while I had my first cup of tea.'

We called them 'First Cuppa Concerts', and it was nice, but now I longed to play the new music I'd learned and see what she thought. Sometimes I'd feel it so strongly that I was glad when it was time for her second cup so I could stop and brush her hair. Every time I played the old stuff and not the jazz I'd learned, not telling my mom weighed heavily on my conscience. It bothered me that I hadn't told her about hitting the steps to learn jazz. Hitherto there had never been a secret between us. I'd tell her everything and she knew all about the gramophone and me teaching myself the harmonica.

Christmas Day came and went, my dad disappearing for the entire day, and soon my mom was back at work. Chilblain time was well and truly upon us, and she always wanted me to play while she soaked. The trouble was that I was totally consumed by jazz. Sometimes I'd practise for hours, and before long I could harmonise a few numbers and play a couple of short solos. I was dying to play them to her but I hadn't even played for Mac. We'd decided I wouldn't show him my progress for two months.

The more I learned and the more involved I became, the more I worried that my mom might not like me going to the Jazz Warehouse with Mac, especially to learn American black people's music. Ragtime I knew she liked, and it was kind of like jazz and kind of like the marches we'd hear at some of the summer parades, only with hiccoughs. In fact, it had helped me grasp some of the elements in the jam sessions. Much later I'd learn that jazz was closely related to ragtime. It also adopted lots of the musical vocabulary of the 'blues', with bent notes, 'growls' and smears. But of course I knew none of this at the time. All I knew was that my mom enjoyed ragtime, so maybe she'd also like jazz.

I knew what my dad's views would be. If he found out I was playing 'nigger music', he'd hit the roof and probably me, and then stop me playing or even listening to jazz again. I wanted to learn enough so that if this happened I could go on playing secretly. But when I thought about it properly, I knew I would need my mom to co-operate. She didn't mind black people one little bit and although there were women in

Cabbagetown who suggested she possessed a touch of the tar brush she was proud of her Iroquois blood, which wasn't white or black but sort of in between. I finally decided that the best way to break the news to her was during our next First Cuppa Concert to play the little I'd learned, watch for her reaction and then come clean.

So, one night, when her feet were in the pail and her hands were warming themselves around her first King George cup of tea, I sat on the second kitchen chair and took up my harmonica, ready to play. 'Mom, I'm going to play you something different tonight,' I announced with my heart thumping.

'You mean something new? That's nice, Jack. Is it from the rotunda or a marching band?'

'No, just wait and see,' I replied, looking suitably mysterious, a kind of half-smile on my face, which I hoped would prevent her seeing how nervous I suddenly was.

'New? What is it? I can't wait,' she replied, then took a sip of tea and looked up over the cup at me. 'Go ahead, Jack, I'm listening.'

I began to play. I'd practised all evening before she came home to make doubly certain I got it right. I'd decided that if she didn't like it, I was going to have to tell her about the Jazz Warehouse anyway, and about Mac and me hitting the steps. It was not something I could keep to myself any longer. Like I said, we never lied or kept things secret from each other and I was feeling increasingly guilty. It was going to be a pretty hairy four minutes and then I'd have to face her questions afterwards.

The music seemed to come out okay, in fact real good, even if I say so myself. I ended it with a long 'bluesy' wail from the harmonica. She'd had this smile on her face while I played, but when I stopped it was replaced by a quizzical look. 'It's jazz?'

'Yes. How did you know?' I asked, surprised.

'I've heard something like it. In 1924, I think it was. I remember it was played at the Canadian National Exhibition by an American orchestra and was called "Dixieland". But where on earth . . . ?'

'Were there black people – Negroes – playing?' I asked quickly, thinking that she could have known about the Jazz Warehouse all this time and it would probably have been all right.

'No, I don't think so, I'd have remembered if there had been. I remember being very excited.'

'Jazz is American black people's music,' I announced.

'I liked it a lot, Jack,' she said, ignoring this last remark.

'Are you *sure*, Mom?'

'Of course I like it! Why shouldn't I? Where on earth did you hear it? Was it during the Christmas break? Why didn't you tell me before?'

'I wanted to surprise you,' I said, not telling the entire truth.

'Well, you certainly have. From the sounds of it, you've been practising a lot. Did you hear it all in one go? And where exactly?' she demanded, perhaps smelling a rat. She gave me another quizzical look. 'Jack, we've never kept anything from each other, have we?'

'Well, it was, you know, Dad finding out and all . . .' Saying it out loud, it sounded pretty lame. 'I was a bit scared, like I said . . . he hates black people, and it's their music . . .'

'So? Black, yellow, piebald – so what? Since when does music have skin colour! And when have we ever shared anything we do together with your father?'

Her questions were raining down on me like hailstones and I felt ashamed, as though I'd betrayed her.

I confessed the whole thing, about Mac and the Jazz Warehouse, and even about the cutaway burlap on the pipes under the stairs, so as to reassure her that I was always nice and warm.

To my surprise, the first thing she asked was, 'Has Mac ever touched you, Jack?'

'Touched me, how?' I asked, puzzled.

'You know, somewhere private . . . on your body.'

'No!' I cried indignantly. 'We shake hands when we meet and say goodbye, just like grown-ups do.' I couldn't understand why she'd ask me such a thing. Mac wasn't a stranger and if he'd been to jail, everyone would have known about it. You couldn't hide your past in Cabbagetown. Someone would have seen him in prison. If he'd gone in for sexually molesting a child, he wouldn't have been coming back to Cabbagetown. And now with the Depression, and homeless men all over the place, kids had been warned to be extra careful.

Of course, looking back, sexual molestation must have been common enough, with drunken fathers sexually abusing their children. But wives and kids were too ashamed or too frightened to talk about such matters. My mom had been right to ask the question. Mac could have been abusing the twins, although I couldn't imagine it. If he had been, Dolly wouldn't be like those other moms who hid the truth. I reckon she'd have simply beaten him to death. Fortunately, as it turned out, Mac was as good as he seemed.

'And Mac takes you when you go to this warehouse and then brings you back?' she asked, still somewhat suspicious.

'Most times we go together or he meets me there and we walk home after. But not always,' I admitted. 'Some days he gets a job and works overtime.' I told her about us parting as we reached the beginning of Cabbagetown, in case someone saw us and told Dolly McClymont.

'Yes, I agree that's sensible. If that nasty piece of work upstairs knew about you and him being together, she'd give him a thrashing he wouldn't forget in a hurry.'

Although she hadn't said so yet, I could see she was dead worried about my being away from home every weekday until early evening, especially in the winter when it was often dark before five o'clock.

'Mom, I promise to be careful. I can see you're worried, but there are kids out much later, stealing coal from the railway yards along the Don. I promise I'll be home by half-past seven every night.' Then I added, 'Even in winter that's not real late.'

'So you like learning jazz, Jack?' she said, ignoring my reassurances.

'I love it, Mom! It's the best thing I've ever done. Better even than books!'

'Oh, Jack, you're not going to neglect your reading because of jazz?'

'No, Mom, I wouldn't do that.' Reading had been the mainstay of my life. It had more or less conquered my loneliness after my mother had landed her job as a night cleaner.

'Good. I can tell you love it by the way you sway and tap your foot. I've never seen you put so much into your music.'

'Mom, I'm sorry I didn't tell you before.'

'Why didn't you, Jack? I thought we shared everything. I'm really disappointed. Working nights, I simply *have* to trust you and I always have done.' I could see she was pretty upset.

'Sorry, Mom,' I repeated.

'Jack, if anything happens with Mac, you are to tell me immediately, you hear? We have to be honest with each other. You know what I mean, don't you?'

'Yes, Mom, I promise.' So she really was worried about Mac perhaps being a pervert. But she didn't know him like I did.

She handed me the King George for her second cup. 'You will be careful, won't you?' She looked at me, her eyes suddenly welling. 'Jack, you're all I've got, my precious boy. You do understand the world can be a dangerous place, especially at night, so you will be on your guard all the time, won't you?'

I wanted to give her a big hug but I was holding the King George.

They say confession is good for the soul, and I have to say I felt a whole lot better for telling my mom what I'd been doing. I resolved that henceforth I would tell her everything. After all, if you didn't count Mac, we only had each other.

Nine months or so after that first time I went with Mac to the Jazz Warehouse, I could actually jam along with the musicians. It was almost the beginning of fall. Fall is one of the best times in Toronto, with the weather perfect and the maple leaves changing colour. Quite often now, Mac would sit with me under the stairs and listen to me playing along. Sometimes when the music stopped indoors, he would shake his head like he was truly impressed. 'Brother Jack, you got what it takes, man! Yessiree! You can jam with the best, Brother Jack! You got the true gift!' he'd say in his phoney black accent.

I didn't take him too seriously. Mac was like my mother, over-generous with his praise. My own ear told me I was still a beginner.

During the summer school break I'd arrive half an hour early and wait across Dundas Street to see the musicians arriving, instead of hitting the steps at the usual time. The first time I saw them, I was amazed to discover that only two of them seemed to be proper Negroes. One was a very tall and stooped old man with grey frizzy hair who walked with a limp, and the other was a guy about the same age as Mac; neither carried an instrument. One of them, I knew, must be the piano player. This wasn't at all what I'd imagined. I'd hardly ever seen a proper black person and all my ideas about them came from *Uncle Tom's Cabin* and other books, like *The Adventures of Huckleberry Finn*. The most surprising thing was that white people could play black people's music. It was pretty exciting, even if the musicians did look like everyone else. It meant I didn't need to be black to be a jazz musician one day.

Of course, the musicians didn't know me from any other kid hanging around the street. They had no idea I was under the steps outside the stage door each day, jamming along with them, so no matter how good I got, I knew I'd never have the opportunity to do an actual solo, and that started to matter to me. Sometimes, at home on my own, I'd have the whole jam session going on in my head and when I came to a part where a solo would fit, I'd pick up my harmonica and invent one just for fun, imagining all the other musicians stopping to listen, smiling and nodding their heads, tapping their feet, then joining in again after my solo ended with a bluesy *'Whap-whap-whap-woo-whaaaa!'* It was an impossible dream but that didn't stop me dreaming it.

During the two months of the summer vacation I practised for hours on end, and my lips became so accustomed to the blow and suck of the harmonica that I could play for longer and longer periods. One day I worked out all the hours I'd ever practised jazz, and it came to almost a thousand.

Once Mac said, 'Jack, I'd love you to perform in front of the brothers and sisters, just to see their faces.'

I hated to disappoint him, but I was scared that someone in the group might know my dad, and if it got back to him, I'd be in real trouble. As soon as I explained, he understood. Mac was good like that.

And then on a Wednesday evening in the last week of the summer vacation, when the jam session was just wrapping up, the music suddenly grew just a fraction louder for a few moments then returned to normal. I did my own 'Whap-whap-whap-woo-whaaaa!' and we ended perfectly in sync. Almost immediately, the steps above me creaked and shook slightly. I glanced up to see someone descending, although I could make out only the soles of their shoes. I sat very still, my heart pounding, hoping whoever it was didn't notice me and would keep on walking once he reached the bottom. But then two long legs came to a halt on my side of the steps and I saw that the shoes were black and white two-tone patent leather, and the pants were shiny and light blue with a black stripe down the side.

Then a deep voice spoke. 'For the past few months I reckoned I bin dreamin'. I heard a harmonica somewhere way back but still comin' through in the jam. "Joe," I says to myself, "You're gettin' old and you is hearin' things. There ain't no harmonica player in the band." Then I'm backstage one day, lookin' for some sheet music, and I hear it clear, this fine jazz harmonica coming through the floorboards. Whoever you are, I'd be much obliged if we could meet, sir. That a real nice sound you got yourself there.'

The legs stepped backwards about four feet, and with my heart still pounding and my face burning with embarrassment and fear at having been found out, I crawled out from under the steps and looked up, then rose to my feet, still holding my harmonica. Standing in front of me was the old Negro musician with the frizzy grey hair and the limp. I'll never forget the look of amazement on his face. 'Oh my!' he said, 'Ain't I just got me a big surprise!'

'Sorry, sir,' I said, looking down at my feet. Above the blue pants he wore a starched white shirt, matching blue suspenders and a blue bow tie.

'Ain't nothin' to be sorry about, nothin' whatsoever, young man. You got a gift from the Lord above and that a matter of joy and jubilation. What's your name, Jazzboy?'

I looked directly up at him like you are supposed to when you talk to adults. 'Jack . . .' I hesitated because kids usually give only their first name, but then added my surname, 'Spayd.'

'Spade?' His eyes widened and his head jerked back. 'Now that ain't a nice word, son.'

I looked at him, puzzled. 'What word, sir?'

'Spade! S-P-A-D-E! It a bad word to call a Negro person.'

'It's my surname, sir.' Then, following his example, I spelled it, 'S-P-A-Y-D.'

'Well, I'll be damned!' He shook his head and chuckled. 'I thought you said Jack was your name and then you called me Spade. I apologise, son. Hey, now a white jazz musician wid a name like that maybe ain't all that bad. Black musicians, they sure going to remember you, Jack Spayd.'

'I didn't know "spade" was a bad word for Negro people. I've never heard that before, sir.'

'Now you learned a derogatory word you didn't need to know. You know what derogatory mean?'

'Yes, sir, it means rude.'

'Hey, smart boy, Jack Spayd. Now it's my turn to introduce myself.' He extended his hand. 'Name is Joe Hockey. I play piano.' We shook hands. His fingers were long and bony, and I decided they must have become that way from playing the piano. 'Now we introduced ourselves, Jack, I'd sure like you to meet someone who'll want to know you. Can you spare a few minutes so we can step inside?'

'Kids can't go into a nightclub, sir. It's against the law.' It was something Mac had told me.

'Well now, that is correct. But only through the front door after it's showtime.' He indicated the red door. 'We can go through the backstage door, though.'

Mac hadn't made it to the jam session so I would have to walk home alone that night. 'Sir . . . I don't think I can,' I apologised. 'I promised my mom I'd be home by half-past seven and it's a half-hour walk if I start right off.'

'Now, Jack, my name is Joe. No need to call me sir.'

'Sorry, s— Joe,' I said, blushing all over again because it still felt strange to call a grown-up by their first name.

'Where do you live, son?'

'Cabbagetown . . . er, Joe.'

'Cabbagetown? Why, that's five, ten minutes the most by streetcar.' He glanced at his watch. 'It's only about five-past seven.'

I didn't want to tell him I didn't have streetcar money, so I said, 'I like to walk, Joe.'

He paused a moment. 'Oh, I see. Most careless of me.' He dug into his blue pants and produced a small leather change purse, removed a quarter and handed it to me. 'Take the streetcar home tonight, Jack.'

I looked at the coin. 'The fare is only ten cents, Joe.'

He smiled. 'Well, now you got two trips, tonight and tomorrow and five cents over to buy candy, Jazzboy Jack.'

I handed him back the quarter. He didn't look like a pervert but I wasn't taking any chances going in alone with him through the red door. I didn't like the sound of backstage, either. 'Joe, I can't go in with you tonight. I promised my mom. But I could do it tomorrow afternoon, anytime before the jam session starts.'

He accepted the coin. 'You got pride, Jack. That's good in a jazz musician. Pride don't let you lose sight of the true black music, so you don't end up playing hokey music to please the patrons in some downtown cocktail lounge, or like Joe Hockey in a two-piano nightclub act. Okay, what say half-past four tomorrow? Come to the front and ask for me. Oh, and bring your harmonica, Jazzboy Jack!'

I agreed and we shook hands again, and I hurried away with my head full of questions going round and round. The biggest one of all was what was going to happen now I'd been discovered under the steps. The next question was easy, but made me feel scared. I was pretty sure Joe wasn't a pervert but I reckoned he was going to haul me up before his boss, Miss Frostbite, and maybe she'd be angry and stop me from hitting the steps. And what if she saw what we'd done to the burlap on the hot-water pipe? I'd have to lie and say I'd done it so as not to get Mac into trouble. The third question was why had Joe told me to bring my harmonica. At school the teachers confiscated things if you were caught playing in class. Could they confiscate my harmonica?

This time I knew I had to tell my mom, so when she got home that night I made her a cup of tea and as I handed it to her, I said, 'Mom, something's happened.'

Her eyes widened. 'Nothing bad, I hope. Don't tell me "her upstairs" has found out about you and Mac.'

'No, nothing like that. I got discovered at the Jazz Warehouse . . . under the steps, by this old man, Joe Hockey.' I then proceeded to tell her the whole story, including my speculation that I was going to meet Miss Frostbite, but I didn't mention the pervert part.

'Half-past four, did you say?'

'Yes, and I'm pretty scared . . .'

'I'm coming with you, Jack,' she announced firmly.

'Could you, Mom?' I asked, relieved. Then, suddenly concerned, I added, 'What about your work?'

'I can go from there. I don't suppose this Miss Frostbite business will take very long, and I can be a bit late. I haven't been late for work in two years.' She laughed. 'Anyhow, I'm the head cleaner now, so there's nobody except me to sack me and if I'm an hour late, the girls know what to do. We'll have a big lunch and I'll make you sandwiches for tomorrow night.'

Boy, oh boy, was I ever relieved! My mom wasn't the fierce Dolly McClymont type, but she could stand her ground if she had to. Mac had said Miss Frostbite was hard as nails, so having my mom with me was good; a kid can't stand up to an adult who's hard as nails. My experience with Mrs Hodgson at the library had taught me that you couldn't always talk your way out of trouble.

I polished Mom's best black shoes, the ones she wore on special occasions that she'd had since before the Depression. They had mildew on them from the damp and I had to wipe it off first. She kept them in a shoebox that was almost worn out and was held shut with a red rubber band. She wore her best dress that smelled of mothballs, and packed her work clothes and shoes in a white cotton bag to take with her. I polished my boots and, even though it was only Wednesday, I wore my good weekend shirt and pants.

We took the streetcar and Joe Hockey was right – it took less than ten minutes to get to the Jazz Warehouse, so we were a bit early. We went around the back, and I showed my mom the steps and pointed to the missing burlap on the pipe, warning her that the topic might come up with Miss Frostbite and that I'd take the blame for doing it.

She nodded. 'Jack, it's wicked to tell lies, but in this instance I'm sure God will forgive you.'

At exactly half-past four we were at the front door. We rang the bell and soon we heard footsteps, and Joe Hockey opened the door himself. 'Ah, Jack, welcome,' he said, then looked at my mom. 'Good afternoon, ma'am.'

I was about to say, 'I brought my mother,' and then introduce her, when she smiled and extended her hand and said, 'Gertrude Spayd, Mr Hockey, I'm Jack's mother.' She didn't sound a bit nervous.

'Nice to meet you, you are most welcome, Mrs Spayd.' They shook hands and Joe stepped aside. 'Would you both kindly come in.' He was wearing a brown business suit and grey-striped white shirt with no collar attached instead of his blue outfit, which must have been for performing.

In the large foyer I noticed three of Mac's purple velvet couches and the famous sign he'd told me about:

Warning!
When you enter
the Jazz Warehouse
you become colour blind!

There were also five signed and framed black-and-white photographs on the walls, which I took to be of musicians who must have come up from the States because most of the people in them were black. Two, the horn and saxophone players, were pretending to play their instruments. Then there was one big hand-tinted photo of a very pretty young woman dressed in a long pearl-coloured satin dress. I took this to be Miss Frostbite when she was young. You could see it hadn't been taken recently because of the fashion she wore, and her short hair and the dark curl sort of pasted down in the centre of her forehead like a kewpie doll's. She had bow lips and dark stuff around her eyes, and she was holding a long cigarette holder with an unlit cigarette in it, like I'd seen in pictures from when women were called 'flappers'.

Joe Hockey indicated a purple couch. 'Please wait here, ma'am. If you'll excuse me, I'll fetch Miss Byatt.'

Miss Byatt? Not Miss Frostbite? Then again, maybe it was. Maybe 'Byatt' was her real surname. Joe Hockey had never used the name Miss Frostbite.

Several minutes later he came back with a lady wearing a posh-looking black lace dress and black high heels, with pearls around her neck. I could smell her perfume and it was nice. She smiled and you could see she was the person in the coloured picture, only older. She was still very pretty but now her hair was longer. I jumped up and clasped my hands behind my back as she came up to us and smilingly held out her hand to my mother. 'Mrs Spayd, how very nice to meet you, I'm Floss . . . Floss Byatt.'

'Gertrude . . . Gertrude Spayd,' my mom answered, taking her hand but not shaking it like a man, just quickly gripping it. I noticed that Miss Byatt had painted nails.

'Welcome to the Jazz Warehouse, Gertrude,' Miss Byatt said, smiling again. 'May I call you Gertrude?'

'Thank you, you may, Floss,' my mom replied, calm as anything and really dignified. I was very impressed and glad she'd come with me.

I'd read about puns and got it right off: Floss Byatt equals Frostbite. I had trouble not laughing out loud. Miss Frostbite turned to me. 'And this is the young man Joe has been talking about! Jack, isn't it?'

'How do you do, Miss Byatt,' I replied, giving a sort of bow, the way Miss Mony said you did when you first met a lady.

'Well now, how long have we got?' Miss Frostbite asked. 'I was hoping you'd play for us, Jack. Did you bring your harmonica?'

'Yes, Miss Byatt.'

'I have to leave by five,' my mother answered.

'Perfect, that gives us just on half an hour,' Miss Frostbite replied.

We were led into a big room with lots of small tables, with an ashtray on each one and comfy chairs around them. Six of Mac's purple couches were at the far end of the room in front of the stage, arranged sort of casually so they didn't look all lined up in a row. There were lots of knee-high tables where I guessed people put their drink glasses, with more ashtrays scattered about on them.

On the stage were what I later learned were baby grand pianos, one on each side. One was the same blue as Joe's pants, and one was white. The space in between them I took to be where the jazz band sat because it had chairs and, at the back of them, a set of drums.

Joe Hockey indicated a couch facing the centre of the stage. 'Gertrude, would you oblige by sitting right here, ma'am?' he said. 'Jack, you go on up, stand in the centre of the stage.'

I hesitated, not sure what he meant.

'Come, Jazzboy Jack, up on the stage, my man,' Joe repeated. My mom laughed at the 'Jazzboy Jack' nickname, but I could see she liked it.

I hoisted myself up onto the stage and went to stand in the middle between the two pianos, suddenly scared. My knees began to knock, like the time my dad gave me the thrashing, only then I knew what was going to happen and now I didn't. I tried to think of something else so they'd stop and I looked about the stage. On the wall to the left was a clock that made no sound but told the time. It was the first electric clock I'd ever seen and must have been there for the musicians.

Then both Joe and Miss Frostbite climbed the steps at the side of the stage and each took their seat at a piano, Joe at the blue one. 'Take it easy, Jazzboy Jack, ain't nothin' to be scared about,' he called. 'Miss Floss and myself, we are goin' to play a few chords and cadences just to see how you follow them. Okay?'

I nodded, still scared as anything, but I reached into my pocket for my harmonica. I didn't dare look at my mom.

'We'll do them one followin' the other right off and we want you to listen, right?' Joe instructed.

'Yes,' I said, my voice all squeaky.

'Then we'll play them separately. After each separate piece, we'll stop, and we want you to try to repeat it on the harmonica.' Joe paused. 'You okay wid that arrangement?'

I nodded. The roof of my mouth had gone dry, so I was glad I didn't have to play right off.

'Good.' He looked over at Miss Frostbite. 'Let's go, Floss,' he called.

They started to play, changing every bit of the music as they went, the beat, the tune . . . I didn't have the words to describe what they were doing, but I could hear it and I knew I could remember it. Then they stopped and before Joe could speak, I played it right through and then ended with my signature 'Whap-whap-whap-woo-whaaaa!' I glanced at my mother, who was trying hard not to laugh, her hand covering her mouth.

'Hey, whoa! Jes you wait a cotton pickin' minute!' Joe exclaimed. 'What you doin', Jazzboy Jack? Why, that was grand, man!' Laughing, he looked over to Miss Frostbite.

'Remarkable. He has a great ear,' Miss Frostbite said, then turning to me she added, 'Jack, that was very good indeed.'

To my surprise, my mom piped in. 'Jack can also sing.' She was leaning forward on her purple couch.

'Oh? Will you sing for us, Jack?' Miss Frostbite asked. But it wasn't like a real ask, more like a command. I nodded, a bit dumbstruck. 'What will you sing? Perhaps I can accompany you?'

'A Bicycle Built for Two' was all I could think of because of the second verse when Daisy replies.

Miss Frostbite laughed then hummed the tune for a few moments. 'I think I can manage that,' she said. 'What key?'

'Pardon, Miss?'

'What note do you want to start on?'

I sang the note I usually started on and she played it on the piano. She and Joe exchanged a look. 'I think this child has perfect pitch,' she said, and then she played the first few bars and nodded for me to come in. I sang it, trying my best, and when it was over she said, 'Let's play it again, Jack. This time I'll only accompany you on the first verse and then I want you to sing the second verse solo . . . that is, on your own.'

I nodded. So we did it again and, like I'd done probably hundreds of times before, I sang Daisy's reply on my own.

There was silence when I finished singing and Miss Frostbite looked over at Joe Hockey. 'Remarkable,' she said.

Joe nodded. 'Atta boy! Not jes the harmonica, hey, Jazzboy?'

Miss Frostbite rose from her piano, walked to the edge of the stage and addressed my mom. 'Has Jack had any formal training, Gertrude?'

My mom shook her head. 'No, his father gave him the harmonica for his eighth birthday and he's taught himself to play. But he started singing before that.' She made it sound like we were a happy family, with my dad being a real nice, caring guy.

'I see, and that's when you discovered he had perfect pitch?'

'Perfect pitch?' my mom asked. Like me, she didn't know what Miss Frostbite was talking about. 'He's always been a good singer,' she said, trying to cover our ignorance.

Miss Frostbite returned to her piano and we played some more, with the music getting more and more complex. I mean, I could hear it in my head but I just couldn't play it quickly enough. I apologised to them both.

'Jack, if you hadn't made those mistakes, me and Miss Floss would be thinking maybe we had George Gershwin Junior on our hands. That ain't kid's stuff, even for good jazz musicians.'

Miss Frostbite left the stage and went to sit beside my mom. They talked quietly for a bit then stood up and left the room together. It was already late and I knew my mom'd be thinking about getting to work. She'd been very patient, just sitting and watching. 'Won't be long,' Miss Frostbite called back. 'Perhaps you can go over the bits Jack didn't understand, Joe.'

Joe and I started working on one of the bits I couldn't play, but I still couldn't quite get it. 'Never mind, Jack, you'll get it next time,' Joe said. Then he laughed. 'It took Joe Hockey a long time to perfect that particular phrasing and those progressions on the piano.'

It was funny how he referred to himself as if he were someone else. He'd also done it the previous night when he told me I had pride and talked about playing twin pianos, like it wasn't a good thing to do for his pride. I'd definitely never heard two pianos playing together in a jam session, so either he or Miss Frostbite didn't play in the jazz band.

The foyer door opened and a head appeared. 'Tony, you gotta wait in the foyer till I holler. Tell everyone!' Joe called to him.

It was a quarter to five, almost time for the jam session to begin, when my mom finally returned from seeing Miss Frostbite. 'I have to hurry, Jack,' she called up to me.

'We can work some other time, Jazzboy Jack. Better go say goodbye to your mama.'

'Wait! I'll come with you to the streetcar,' I called to Mom, running across the stage and down the steps.

When I got to her, she said in a low voice, 'No, Jack, she wants you to stay back a while.'

'Stay? What for?'

'Come outside with me.'

'But the jam session starts in about ten minutes.'

'Shhh, Jack!'

We walked silently towards the door leading into the foyer. All the band members were sitting around talking, and although some glanced up, they went back to talking. It was obvious they didn't think they'd been asked to wait in the foyer because of a boy and a woman carrying a lumpy white cotton bag. We hurried past them, out the door and into the late-afternoon sunshine.

'So, what happened? What did she say to you, Mom? Why must I stay?' I asked, all three questions tumbling over each other.

My mom stopped walking and turned to face me. 'It's all a bit much to take in, Jack. I've got to hurry. Can we talk about it when I get home tonight? As it is, I'm going to be late for work. I don't know why she wants you to stay back; she just asked me if it was all right and said she'd give you your streetcar fare home. I wanted to get away,' she confessed. 'People like her are a bit much for such as us, Jack.'

Just then a streetcar came rumbling down the street towards us. 'Am I in trouble, Mom?'

'No, nothing bad.' She kissed me hurriedly. 'I'm very proud of you, Jack.' Then she turned and broke into a half run in her good shoes, the cotton bag jumping up and down in her hand as she ran. She stopped for a moment, slung the straps over her shoulder and held the bag tight against her body. 'Don't forget to eat your sandwiches!' she yelled as she started to run again towards the rapidly approaching streetcar.

My whole life was changing in front of my eyes and my mom was thinking about my dinner.

I waited to make sure she caught the streetcar and watched as she climbed aboard, then I waited outside for a minute or so to collect my thoughts. My only hope was that Miss Frostbite would allow me to hit the steps again, and that, by doing my best and playing for them on the stage, I had earned the right to continue to jam under the steps. There'd been no mention of the missing burlap on the pipe.

As I turned towards the front door, I thought to myself that so far they'd been very nice and complimentary about my harmonica playing. But I hadn't forgotten Mac's warning that Miss Frostbite was as hard as nails and that this was because a woman had to be tough to run a nightclub. With my mom no longer present, anything could happen. I didn't know what I'd do if I was forbidden to hit the stairs.

It was still summer and lots of brothers and sisters, the jazz fans who hung about outside listening, had turned up and were waiting in their usual groups. The jam session must be just about ready to start. Maybe Miss Frostbite would take me into her office, like Mrs Hodgson at the library, in which case it wouldn't be anything to look forward to.

I finally summoned enough courage to go back inside. The foyer was empty and when I pushed open the door to the main room, I saw that the band was just about ready to begin the jam, with everyone seated between the two pianos.

'Oh, there you are, Jack. Over here,' Joe shouted, summoning me forward with his big bony hand. He was standing at the centre of the stage, right next to a microphone, and his voice, caught by the mike, boomed out in the big room. I cringed at the unexpected sound and the musicians all laughed. There was no sign of Miss Frostbite. 'Jack, come up here on the stage – I want you to come close and see what a real jam session is all about. Come and join us.'

Then the session started with a number I had heard under the stairs a hundred times. I knew the chord progressions off by heart and could join in easily. Three more followed and I was able to play along, but then Joe Hockey pulled up a chair and placed it beside me and said, 'Jazzboy, what you now gonna hear be where you gonna go sometime later when you have learned yourself a lot more jazz and growed up a whole lot. You just sit now and listen, then after, if you want explainin', you come to me, okay?'

It had been easy enough to listen to these guys and then play a few little riffs in the same key, but I now realised, when I was finally among them and not under the stairs, just what they were doing. One guy would get up and start honking on his trumpet and then suddenly tone the whole thing down. He'd do that for a few minutes then begin climbing up the scale. Just when he'd taken it about as high as a note could get, he'd come back down again and give the whole thing a slower and easier blues feel. As soon as it felt comfortable and familiar he'd change everything, as if to say, don't think it's gonna be that easy. And all the while he did this in time with the bass player and the percussionist.

Then another trumpet player picked up from where he'd left off, moving in all directions, going from top to bottom at lightning speed, sometimes making a woofing sound, sometimes honking, sometimes screaming. Then the first guy would come back in. They were duelling! It seemed to be getting faster and faster and yet the beat never changed. The second guy seemed to be coming off the first, as if he was finishing off what the first guy had begun. And then the first would come back again. It was like a conversation where each of them finished off the other's remarks. I had the feeling it was like a kind of boastful argument – one guy says, 'I can do this,' and the next says, 'So what? If that's your best, get a load of this, man!'

Somehow they seemed to know when it was their cue to come back in; there was some unspoken rule I couldn't for the life of me work out. It was pretty friendly, but there was no doubt about it – they were in a contest. I realised jamming was not just about knowing music. They were feeding off each other's music; they needed each other, but they were also trying to surpass each other. Wow!

More solos followed: the piano, drums and clarinet. But nothing compared to those feuding trumpets. I knew it would take me years to be anywhere near as good as these guys, and I guessed they were nowhere near the top players in America. But I knew, I just knew, I would get there some day.

After the jam session was over, I got lots of pats on the back and my hair ruffled, and guys saying I could come back anytime to jam with them and that it was a pity I wasn't eighteen so I could play nights in the band.

Then Joe Hockey took me aside while the musicians went off to have their dinner and handed me a dollar. 'Yeah, I know, Jack, the streetcar fare to Cabbagetown, it only ten cents. You don't have to show no pride tonight, Jazzboy. You played real prideful. I talked to Miss Floss when you were outside wid your mama and she says to give you a dollar, so I am only followin' orders. She says you may call her "Miss Frostbite", like the other musicians, except for yours truly. I call her Floss because we bin together even before the Jazz Warehouse. Miss Frostbite be the name she prefers for musicians and staff, and now, because you been in a jam session, you are like family.'

My head was still full of what had just happened on stage and I accepted the dollar without really taking in what he said. It was too much money for a boy to have, and I was going to walk home and present it to my mom. 'Thank you, Joe, for letting me play in the session. It was the best thing I've ever done! Will you please thank Miss Frostbite for my dollar and everything?'

'Our pleasure, Jack Spayd. You done real good today, earned your respect wid them other cats. Your mama will tell you what she and Miss Floss discussed this afternoon. Now you better get goin', son. You are welcome to jam wid us any afternoon you want.' He grinned. 'Only one rule: no drinkin' rye whisky or bum wine before you come to work. No bottle allowed wid you on stage. Miss Frostbite, she don't tolerate inebriation.' He paused. 'You know what inebriation mean, Jazzboy?'

I nodded. 'Being drunk.' I'd read it in a book and looked it up at the library.

'Hey, that's good!' he said, laughing. 'You is even gettin' yo'self educated. Not too many jazz men had that privilege when they was young.'

Of course, I couldn't wait for my mom to get home that night, and when she arrived it was hard waiting until she'd settled down and I'd handed her the King George. She took a sip of tea and then said, 'I suppose you want to know what happened in Miss Byatt's office, Jack? It's been going round and round in my head ever since, and I couldn't hardly concentrate at work.'

'Same for me!' I exclaimed.

'Did you eat your sandwiches?'

'Yes, they were nice. Now can you *please* tell me what she said,' I begged.

'No, first tell me why she wanted you to stay back.'

'Mom, I asked first!' I protested.

'Yes, but if I know everything that happened it might make more sense, I mean, me and her this afternoon, in her office,' she replied.

So I sighed and told her about jamming with the band and explained that I hadn't seen Miss Frostbite again. Then I fished in my pocket and handed her the dollar.

'What's this, Jack?' she said, surprised.

'Miss Frostbite gave it to Joe to give to me for the streetcar.'

'Oh, so she must want you to go on with the harmonica, too.'

'What does that mean?' I asked fearfully. 'Joe Hockey said I could sit in on the jam session any night I liked.'

'She wants you to learn to play the piano, Jack.'

'The piano!' I was shocked. 'What about my harmonica?'

'She says you've got a huge talent but you need to study classical music as well as jazz. She says you're not too old, but you should have started when you were seven.'

'The piano?'

'And learning to read music.'

'Read? You mean like what's on a song sheet?'

'Yes, I think so. You know, like the music notes the musicians have on those stands in the rotunda.'

I liked this idea a whole lot. I supposed it was like another kind of reading, only music reading. '*Really*, Mom? She said that? But where could I learn? And how would I practise?'

My mother nodded. 'Aha, that was exactly what I was thinking but she said never mind the details – if I gave my permission she'd take care of the rest. In fact, her exact words were, "Leave the details to me – the piano and the tuition, Gertrude. Just let me have your boy."'

'Have me? You mean go and live with her?' I exclaimed, appalled.

My mom laughed. 'No, of course not! How could I ever part with you, Jack? No, she meant give her permission to pay for your training, your lessons.'

'Why can't I have lessons on the harmonica?'

'She said the harmonica wasn't enough for a musician to learn. That if you were going to go far, you needed classical piano training as well.'

'I'm not giving up the harmonica, Mom!' I said, suddenly alarmed.

'I told her I didn't think you would and she said, "That won't be necessary; it's a minor jazz instrument but it's another string to his bow and an excellent skill for a jazz musician to have in his back pocket."'

I was a bit miffed that she'd described the harmonica as a minor jazz instrument, but I had to admit there wasn't a single harmonica player among the Jazz Warehouse group. But the good news was that she'd let me keep my harmonica. 'What will Dad say if I learn piano as well as harmonica?'

'Who knows? She said I should discuss it with my husband.' We both laughed at this. Then she went on, 'Jack, I don't think he'll ever ask, so let's not worry about it. I told her that I would discuss it with you, that we discussed everything and we only did what we both agreed to do. She smiled and said, "Gertrude, I agree your son seems very bright and has a great talent, but sometimes parents have to do what's best for their children even if the child is unhappy at first. You and your husband must surely know this."'

'Mac said she was hard as nails,' I volunteered.

My mom ignored this remark. 'I had to come clean and tell her your father has a drinking problem and a violent nature, and didn't even know about you playing jazz in the first place.'

I was truly amazed. My mom never talked about my dad to anyone. 'What did she say, Mom?'

'She looked a bit puzzled. "But didn't you say he gave Jack the harmonica for his birthday?" So I told her that he'd won it in a card game at the tavern two weeks after your eighth birthday. That it was second-hand and he had never asked about it since. "How extremely fortunate that he's good at cards," she said, and we had a bit of a laugh.'

My mom handed me the King George for her second cup. Even when it wasn't chilblain time, she always had two cups of tea when she got home. That way we could have a good chat right off.

While I poured her tea, I said, 'School starts again next week and there's the library, and now that I can jam with the band I'd be mad to give that up. How are we gonna fit all this in?'

'Jack, she may be hard as nails but she's also smart as a whip. I told her school started again next week and she said: "Mrs Spayd, Cabbagetown is only ten minutes on the streetcar. He could get here by four-thirty, I have my own piano room out back, which he can use, and we'll have a tutor come at five-thirty. He can practise for an hour and then spend the last half hour with his harmonica, jamming with the band, as his reward."' My mom looked directly at me. 'She thinks on her feet. She worked all this out on the spot.'

'What about my dinner?'

'Oops!' My mom covered her mouth with both hands. 'Stupid me, I forgot!' She was clearly upset, like she'd let me down as a mother. 'Oh, Jack, you'll have to tell her! I'm so sorry.'

I nodded, not sure how I was going to manage to change my after-school timetable. Miss Frostbite was clearly nobody's pushover. What's more, I didn't need to be Einstein to see the other catch – no piano lesson, no jam session. Or that was how it seemed to me at the time, anyhow. One of Mac's favourite expressions was, 'I found myself between a rock and a hard place.' Now I knew exactly what he meant.

'What about the library?' I asked.

'Jack, I don't know. After I told her we needed to talk about it and she asked about your school hours, it was time for me to go.'

'What do you think we should do then, Mom? Jamming with the band was one of the best days of my life. I definitely want to be a jazz musician when I grow up.'

My mother was silent for a while. 'Jack, most people, especially now with the Depression, don't get too many chances to improve themselves. Why don't we give it a try, hey? I'm sure she – Miss Byatt – will agree to you having an afternoon off to go to the library. In fact, she doesn't have a choice. I'll put my foot down. She'll soon learn how smart you are, and it's not just that you've got a good ear or perfect pitch or whatever they called it. Besides, just think, even half an hour with your harmonica in the jam session will mean you'll learn a whole lot. It would be worth much more than two hours sitting under the stairs, straining to hear. Then you can always practise your harmonica when you get home.'

'Mom, I can't go to the Jazz Warehouse tomorrow to see her, it's library day.'

'Jack, an opportunity like this one comes along once in a blue moon. We'd be mad not to accept it. I'm sure the library won't fine you for being one day late. Go see her tomorrow and thank her, and I'll give you a note from me to thank her as well.'

I have to confess I was pretty excited, even if I didn't know how it was all going to work out. But Mac had started everything and so I needed to tell him. I needed his reassurance about Miss Frostbite as well. He'd always said she was fair and did the right thing by her staff, and I reminded myself that she'd said I was allowed to call her Miss Frostbite, so that was something good as well.

I managed to waylay Mac real early the following morning as he left for work, and we talked as we walked. He had been given four days' work in a row on a road gang, filling potholes, with unpaid overtime of course, so he'd miss the next four jam sessions, but he was happy. 'Beggars can't be choosers, Jack.' We walked down the pathway along the Don, while I told him everything that had happened and, like he always did, he listened without interrupting. Finally, I asked, pretending that I hadn't made up my mind, 'So, what do you think, Mac?'

'Nothing to think about, Brother Jack, grab it with both hands and hang on tight!'

'Really? But I want to be a jazz musician when I grow up.'

'And so you will be, pal. But jazz *piano*! That's big time, man! Miss Frostbite, she's right, it's better than the harmonica, and you'll learn to read music and play classical as well. Hey, man, now you *really* bustin' outa this rat hole!'

'But what about us, you and me? I won't be hitting the steps any longer.'

Mac stopped on the path, turned to me and spread his arms wide. 'Brother Jack, we're buddies and that's forever. Anyhow, we can sometimes walk home together after the jam session and chew the fat as usual. Be much the same as now,' he reassured me.

That night when she returned home, my mom handed me back the dollar I'd given her. 'I think this is meant to be your first week's streetcar fare. Miss Byatt promised she'd give it to you and I'm very happy you're not walking home alone at night from your *piano* lessons.' She emphasised the word 'piano' and I could see she was really proud.

CHAPTER FOUR

AND SO MY LIFE changed. Being a kid, you just go with the flow, but this was a stream that turned into a river until my whole life seemed to be music. But first I need to tell you about my visit to see Miss Frostbite. I'd have liked my mom to be with me but she couldn't take off any more time. I knew that, even if you were the head cleaner, like my mom, even if you were the best in the whole of Canada, you could still be sacked. You couldn't just take time off to be with your boy because he was a bit nervous.

If my mom lost her job and couldn't get work, I would end up in an orphanage, like two kids who'd been in my class and whose parents both had a 'drinking problem'. When the bailiff threw the family out of their house, their parents couldn't look after them, and they were living on the street and begging, so the Children's Aid Society took them away. If this happened, it would be the end of everything for me. I couldn't imagine my life without my mom, and I sometimes grew real scared just thinking about it. Mac told me it couldn't happen, and that if both parents couldn't work, then the Canadian Government would help with the rent and other stuff.

I couldn't ask Mac to come with me to the meeting because he was with a road gang, filling potholes for another four days, and I knew he was over the moon about it. 'I'm gonna bust my ass to try to stay on even longer. I'll work overtime free until midnight if the foreman wants,' he'd exclaimed.

'If you do, then the job won't last as long,' I'd joked, pleased that he was working.

'It's better than staying home,' he replied. It was one of the few times I ever heard him say anything critical about his home life.

I didn't have an appointment to see Miss Frostbite. All my mom had said was, 'Jack, she wants to talk with you personal.' When I got home from school, my mom was just about ready to leave for work. I gulped down my dinner and we walked to the streetcar stop together. Hers came first and just before it stopped she kissed me. 'You'll be fine, Jack,' she assured me. 'Just tell her you want to do the piano lessons. Be nice and polite and don't forget to say thank you and to give her my note.'

She had written the note to Miss Frostbite the previous night. 'Jack, I *think* I got it right. Can you look at it?' she'd asked. She didn't have much education but she did learn how to write. Mom had once told me that when she was at school they spent hours copying letters and sentences from the blackboard. 'I remember the one we copied the most – *The quick brown fox jumped over the lazy dog.* Did you know it's got every letter in the alphabet in it?' Her writing was called 'copperplate' and it was beautiful. The note had taken her ages to write, using my school pen and inkpot, and she'd made several fresh starts.

Dear Miss Byatt,

Thank you from the bottom of my heart
for what you done for my boy, Jack.
We are most truly grateful to you
and can never pay you back ever.
I work at nite so if you want any cleaning done
in the mornings for free just ask.
God bless you Madam.

Yours faithfully,
Gertrude Spayd (Mrs)

She had worked so hard on it that I felt guilty about correcting it. When I left out the free cleaning bit, she got quite upset. 'Jack, we may be poor as church mice, but we don't take things from people without trying to pay them back. That would be like begging and we don't have to do that yet, thank the good Lord.'

'Mom, I'll just say it in another way,' I promised. 'I can always tell her you'll help if she needs it.'

My mom then did the final copy and it looked beautiful. She wrote it on a page we tore out of my school exercise book.

Dear Miss Byatt,

Thank you for what you are doing for Jack.
We are most grateful to you, and if I can help
you in any way, I would be most happy to do so.
May God bless you.

Yours sincerely,
Gertrude Spayd

Short and sweet, and adding the 'May' to 'God bless you' made it a tiny bit swanky. I'd read it in a book where a church minister said it to a grand lady, and it sounded better than just plain 'God bless you', which is what ordinary folk say all the time.

I got to the Jazz Warehouse at about a quarter to five and decided to wait in the foyer as if I had arrived early, and then if Miss Frostbite decided to see me, that was okay. If she didn't, then I could pretend to be accepting Joe Hockey's offer to jam anytime I wanted to.

I'd also worked out that, if I got off one stop earlier, like my mom did on the way home from work, the fare would only be five cents, which meant I'd have twenty trips to the Jazz Warehouse from Miss Frostbite's dollar. Or even more if Mac came to listen and we walked home together. Maybe, if Mac had been working all day and was dog-tired, I could say, 'Be my guest, let's take the streetcar home, Brother Mac.' It felt real good to be rich.

When I got to the Jazz Warehouse, the front door was open and I went and sat in the foyer alone. Then, a little later, I summoned the courage to try the door to the main clubroom, but it was locked. After a while there was a rattle of keys. The main door opened slightly and Joe Hockey's head appeared. 'Why, if it ain't the Jazzboy!' he exclaimed. 'You come to jam, eh, Jack?'

'Yes, please, Mr Hockey, and my mom said I had to see Miss Byatt, that is, if she has the time and wants to see me.'

'Yessir, she said something about conversatin' wid you if you came today. I'll go tell her you are here now. By the by, she gave you permission to call her Miss Frostbite. That what she expect from now on, you understan', Jazzboy? We family now, so you jes call me Uncle Joe. Okay?'

'Uncle Joe' was much easier and more respectful than calling grown-ups by their first names, which was difficult for me when I'd always used 'sir' or 'mister'. 'I'll try, er . . . Uncle Joe.' Then he repeated more or less what Mac had said. 'Jazz don't know no age. If you can play good, that mean your music is growed up, and so you family, and family don't say sir or mister the one to the other. Wid me, Uncle Joe be jes fine.'

I made a note in my head to look up the word 'conversating' next time I was at the library. It sounded like a real word and you knew immediately what it meant, but I just thought I'd check it to be sure. Mrs Hodgson's insistence that I look up words I didn't know had led to me forming a good habit, and I enjoyed flicking through the dictionary. It wasn't that I'd use words to show off – you couldn't do that at school or you'd be in deep shit – but it was just nice knowing a new word.

Two musicians turned up for the jam, and before they walked into the main room, they both stopped and welcomed me and said they were glad I'd returned to play with them. Then Uncle Joe came back and told me to follow him. We passed through the club and went through the door I'd seen my mom enter. It led to a large kitchen, then a short corridor ended in another door, which, to my surprise, opened onto what looked like somebody's house, only it was built inside the warehouse.

The hallway had a red runner on the floor and on the left was a proper lounge room that looked very grand.

'Jack, will you kindly take a seat? Miss Frostbite, she won't be long now.' When Uncle Joe reached the door, he turned and said, 'When she through conversatin' wid you, you can come join us on stage.' Then he left and closed the door behind him.

I sat on the edge of one of two couches, both covered in yellow silk, I think; anyway, in shiny material that looked too nice for a boy to sit on. The polished wooden floor was covered with a huge yellow and green carpet with complicated patterns, and on the walls there were framed pictures that looked like real paintings. There was also a radiogram big as anything which stood on its own legs. It was made of varnished wood with two half-moon shapes and a circle cut out of the middle of the wooden front and backed with brown cloth where the sound came through. It had a badge on it with a little terrier dog looking into an old gramophone speaker and the letters HMV. I'd seen pictures of a radiogram, but this was the first real one I'd seen. Talk about swanky! There was also a glass cabinet filled with lots of little coloured porcelain figurines, mostly beautiful ladies in old-fashioned gowns. Later I would learn they were Royal Doulton and that the long skirts were called crinolines. Collecting them was Miss Frostbite's hobby and I must say they looked very pretty. It must have been hard to walk around the kitchen in dresses like that, or to get close to someone.

On the top of the cabinet was a framed photograph showing Miss Frostbite when she was younger, together with a fat, bald man with a moustache, who looked much older than her and who held a pipe. She was smiling but he wasn't.

Maybe ten minutes later, just when I was beginning to worry, Miss Frostbite entered. 'Welcome, Jack,' she said as I jumped up and stood at attention with my hands behind my back.

'Good afternoon, Miss Frostbite, thank you!' I said, remembering my mom's last instructions.

She sat on the couch opposite me, and when I stayed standing, she said, 'Please be seated, Jack. I hope that you'll soon come to think of this as your second home.'

My first thought was that if this were to become my second home, then maybe she'd let me listen to the radiogram.

'Well now! What have you decided?' she asked.

I dug into my trouser pocket and handed her the note. 'It's from my mother, Miss.' I forgot to add the 'Frostbite'.

She read it quickly then looked up, smiling. 'So I take it you'd like to learn the piano, Jack?'

'Yes, please, Miss Frostbite,' I said, remembering this time.

'Well, I must say I am delighted. I believe you to have a very impressive talent, young Jack. It would be a shame to neglect your musical education.'

She seemed real friendly, so I plucked up the courage to say, 'I want to play jazz and can I *please* keep my harmonica?'

'But, of course! I will consider it a part of your musical education. That is, sitting in with the band to keep you in touch with the real world of jazz. Joe Hockey will see to that part. He doesn't play much jazz in public these days but he is an excellent teacher. He says you can do a good ten minutes of very competent jazz and several jazz numbers. After only a year that's very promising. Now, do you know what all this is going to mean?'

'No, Miss Frostbite. My mom said she didn't know, only about learning the piano that's classical, and learning to read music and all that.'

'Well, Jack, the key to everything in a musical life is practice. How old are you?'

'Ten, Miss.'

'So, you won't be able to do much more than an hour a day.'

'We don't have a piano, Miss Frostbite.'

'No, of course not, Jack. You will practise here. My own piano room is soundproofed so that my playing doesn't go through to the club. You will have to come here every day. I'm hoping your piano teacher will come here for the two afternoons you have lessons. As you grow older it will be considerably more.'

'Do I have to practise on the weekend, too, Miss?'

'Yes, of course. Why do you ask, Jack?'

My heart started to pound. 'Miss, I can't on the weekend. It's when me and my mom go out together.'

I think she must have heard the panic in my voice and seen the look on my face. 'Let's just get the information down first, Jack. Once we've got a schedule, we can adjust it.' I was to learn that schedules were very important to Miss Frostbite. 'Now, when does school come out?'

'Four o'clock, Miss.'

'So you could get here when? Half-past four?'

'No, Miss Frostbite, that's when I have my dinner.'

'A bit early, isn't it?'

I explained my mother's work hours and how she had to leave at half-past four for her office-cleaning job and didn't get back until ten at night. 'Oh, well, what about half-past five? That should give you lots of time and you can sit in with the band for half an hour.'

'I can't do Thursday, Miss.'

'Oh, dear. Why not, Jack?'

'I have to go to the library, Miss.'

'Oh, I see. Four days, that's only four hours a week. Hmm, that's hardly enough and, besides, you should be practising every day. You couldn't come after you've been to the library?'

I explained about the hour walk each way.

'And if you take the streetcar?'

'Fourteen minutes.' I knew precisely because of Miss Mony.

'Well, then, you shall have money for the streetcar. Could you be here by, say, six?'

'Easy, Miss. Half-past five, if you like. But I can pay for it out of the dollar you gave me, because you gave me too much and I have to give you some back.'

'You shall do no such thing, Jack. Buy yourself a small treat.'

Small treat! Even with the library I'd have money over. My mom and I could spend it on the weekend – tea and buns in the café near the rotunda. 'Thank you *very* much, Miss Frostbite.'

'Now, about the weekends.' I was to learn that Miss Frostbite seldom took 'no' for an answer. 'Could you get here at, say, eight o'clock on Saturday and Sunday mornings? Or do you go to church on Sunday?'

'No, Miss, I think that will be all right.' It was five cents each way for the streetcar fare for two extra days. *There goes another twenty cents of my dollar, just when I thought I was rolling in money.*

'Jack, you shall have a dollar for your travel expenses each week.' She paused. 'Now, if you're going to sit in with the band until seven, why don't you have your dinner with them? You could be home just after eight.'

'I'll have to ask my mom, Miss Frostbite.'

'Now that you are a budding musician and a growing boy, your food is very important. We like to feed the band properly – they're mostly single men and so don't look after themselves. Besides, musicians don't play their best on an empty stomach.' She held up one hand and ticked the meals off on her fingers: 'Let me see, Monday is beef stew; Tuesday, macaroni cheese; Wednesday, shepherd's pie; Thursday, lamb casserole; and Friday, roast beef and roast potatoes. And you tell your mom there's always vegetables.' She smiled. 'Dessert every night, stewed fruit with custard, rice pudding with raisins, bread pudding with dates . . . all you can eat, Jack.'

I now definitely knew my mom would say yes when I told her about the food. I'd never had food that good, not ever. You couldn't turn down an offer like that, could you. 'I think the extra half hour will be okay, Miss Frostbite.'

'I'd like you to start as soon as possible, Jack. I have yet to finalise my agreement with Miss Mona Bates, your teacher. I'm hoping she will take you on. She's very famous but also a friend. Last year I played on two occasions in her ten-piano ensemble for a charity and they turned out to be very successful events. My hope is that by the time you're twelve they'll allow you to sit for the fifth or sixth grade examination at the Toronto Conservatory of Music.'

'What's a conservatory, Miss Frostbite?'

'Oh, it's a place where they teach music to talented students when they've graduated from high school. They also oversee all music examinations – a school for future musicians where every instrument is taught, as well as singing.'

'Do they teach the harmonica?'

'Well, now, that's a good question, Jack. I really don't know the answer to that. But if I can get Mona Bates to take you privately for piano lessons twice a week, and if you make good progress, then her recommendation will help enormously to allow you to take the entrance examinations when you finish school. But she's very fussy about the students she accepts. She will need to hear you play and you'll also have to sing for her. I promise you she won't take my word on it. I expect we'll have to go to her Jarvis Street studio for an initial test. Shall we meet again the same time tomorrow when you've discussed the things we've talked about with your mother?' She looked at her wristwatch. 'Now, go and see Uncle Joe and sit in on the jam for a bit. See you the same time tomorrow. You may eat with the band tonight, if you wish.'

I stayed and had a second dinner in a room leading from the kitchen. We had spaghetti with meatballs and it was hard to eat with all the long strings, until Uncle Joe showed me how to use a spoon to help twirl it around my fork into a neat bundle. It sounds easy but it isn't. I didn't eat as much as I wanted because it was going to take a lot of practice to get right. Real life seems to be all about practising things.

I asked my mom about eating at the Jazz Warehouse and practising for an extra half hour after dinner, then I told her about the spaghetti and recited the other good things I was going to eat, and she laughed. 'That one knows the way to a boy's heart is through his stomach.' But I knew she was glad I was going to eat so well and when I told her about the dollar every week for the streetcar, including the fare to the library, she was very happy, especially when she thought about the winter. But then she said, 'Jack, you must tell her about my cleaning for her. We can't just keep taking like this. I could easily do two hours in the morning three days a week. Tell her I don't mind scrubbing floors and cleaning greasy ovens, doing the dirty kitchen work.' She looked at me sternly. 'You be sure to tell her,' she insisted.

For a boy accustomed to having lots of time on his hands, I was suddenly going to find my life filled to bursting, with only a bit of time left over in the evenings to do my reading before my mom arrived home. My only hope was that piano would be as much fun as the harmonica. I was going from the smallest musical instrument to the biggest in one giant jump.

The following day I returned to see Miss Frostbite, as we'd arranged. She was wearing a brown dress with matching high heels and handbag, brown gloves, and a little chocolate-brown hat with two long feathers sticking out the side, which I immediately recognised from our visit to the zoo as pheasant feathers. It was a lot of brown but she wore her pearls and looked very nice, like a rich person. 'Good boy, Jack, you're right on time. Joe's gone to fetch a taxi. Should be here any moment.'

Taxi! I'd never been in a taxi, although I'd seen plenty, sometimes with only one person riding in the back, who must have been pretty rich. Ours, when it came, was a black Model A Ford with bright orange tyre spokes. The driver jumped out and opened the back door for Miss Frostbite. 'Would the lad like to sit in front, madam?' he asked.

Miss Frostbite looked at me and I said quickly, 'Yes, please.' It was grand driving down Dundas Street, and I hoped somebody would see us, but I couldn't think who that might be; a kid from school, maybe. But I didn't see anyone I knew and we were soon at the address in Jarvis Street. On the way Miss Frostbite said, 'Jack, perhaps it might not be a good idea to tell Miss Bates you live in Cabbagetown. People can be very strange and form wrong impressions about such matters.'

Even before we entered, you could hear someone playing the piano. It didn't stop when we rang the doorbell, but soon enough a lady a bit older than Miss Frostbite answered the door. 'Oh, Mona, it's you. I expected the maid!' Miss Frostbite exclaimed.

'Damnable nuisance. She sprained an ankle falling off a chair while dusting the picture frames. Come in, Floss,' Mona Bates said with a jerk of her head. You'd never know she was a friend of Miss Frostbite; she didn't seem all that welcoming.

We were taken into a small reception room that had lots of framed photos on the wall showing Miss Bates sitting at the piano, or standing up holding a bunch of flowers with musicians seated behind her dressed in suits like Uncle Joe's, only black. 'I shan't be long,' she said, then, turning on her heel, was gone. Miss Frostbite didn't have time to introduce me and Miss Bates didn't even look at me once. Miss Frostbite sat on the leather chesterfield while I examined the photos.

'She's terribly famous, Jack,' she said in a low voice. 'But she gave up her career at forty to teach. Goodness knows why. She was at the height of her powers as a concert pianist. She claims she was tired of living out of a suitcase, the long voyages to Europe . . . If she agrees to accept you as one of her pupils, we should consider ourselves very fortunate indeed.'

We heard Miss Bates's footsteps approaching and Miss Frostbite put a warning finger to her lips. I stood with my hands behind my back, remembering to look up directly into her eyes if she should speak to me. 'It's the one small power a child has,' Miss Mony had once told me.

'Let's get started, Floss,' Miss Bates said crisply, adding, 'I have a very busy day ahead of me.'

'Yes, of course. Thank you, Mona,' Miss Frostbite replied, smiling. But I'm not sure it was a real thank-you smile.

'You do understand that I can't do you any special favours regarding the boy, Floss? Even with the Depression, I have more gifted young musicians applying than I can possibly accommodate.' She glanced at me for the first time. 'Come with me, boy,' she commanded.

'His name is Jack, Mona,' Miss Frostbite said.

'No point in getting personal unless he passes, Floss,' Miss Bates called, not looking back.

I followed her, leaving Miss Frostbite to wait. Miss Bates led me into a large room that contained three pianos and sat at one of them. 'Come and stand here,' she commanded.

I went over and stood at attention beside her. The long row of black and white piano keys intimidated me; the piano wasn't a bit like a harmonica and I wondered how, with my big clumsy hands, I would ever get the hang of it. 'Miss Byatt tells me you play the harmonica,' she sniffed, 'and that you have a very good ear. They all say that, but in my experience very few have. I shall be surprised if, when we give you an aural test, we find Miss Byatt's assessment is correct, and I wonder about your choice of instrument.'

It didn't seem to be a question but I said, 'Yes, Miss,' anyway.

'Miss Bates, if you please,' she replied crisply.

I would have liked to say, 'No point in getting personal unless I pass,' but of course I couldn't.

'Now, I'm going to play some notes on the piano and I want to see if you can replicate them.'

'Does that mean sing them, Miss Bates?'

'Yes, are you ready?'

'Yes, Miss Bates.'

She played four single notes and I sang them for her. Then we did it all again, and again. Then she played a melody and I sang that as well. Of course, at the time I had no idea why she was asking me to sing all these notes, I just did as I was told. 'Now I want you to sing for me unaccompanied. Do you have a song?'

'Yes, Miss Bates, "A Bicycle Built for Two".'

She sighed heavily. 'Oh, dear. Well, I suppose that will have to do.'

'I'll only sing the second verse, if you like,' I offered, knowing this was the best one for my high voice.

She gave me an impatient glance. 'As you wish.' I didn't think my test was going very well.

I sang Daisy's part in the song.

Miss Bates sighed once more. 'Now you will play the harmonica. What have you chosen to play?'

'"Basin Street Blues", Miss Bates.'

'Oh?' she said, but unlike her response to 'Daisy', I didn't know if that was a good 'Oh?' or a bad one. But I played it through and then did my signature *Whap-whap-whap-woo-whaaaa!*

She looked at me and smiled for the first time. 'Well done, Jack. That was all very good. How old are you?'

'Ten, Miss Bates.'

'Oh, dear, you should be well into third or fourth grade by now. But never mind, I think you may be able to catch up by doing two grades a year.' She rose from the piano and I followed her back to the reception room. Miss Frostbite looked up anxiously as we entered but didn't say anything as Miss Bates sat down next to her on the chesterfield.

'Well, Floss, you were right, Jack has an excellent ear. But I want him coming here for his lessons. It's not that far from Dundas Street and I'll give him the extra time, the half hour it would take me to travel there and back to you. He should be well into third grade at his age and so initially he's going to need the extra tuition. Six or seven years to take him to eighth grade is sufficient and I'd be surprised if we couldn't take him a bit further. How many hours have you set aside for him to practise, apart from his lessons?'

'Well, if you have him for an hour and a half twice a week, that leaves him four hours,' Miss Frostbite said.

'Totally inadequate! I know he's young but I want another three. Seven hours' practice and three hours' tuition.'

'Isn't that rather a lot for a young boy, Mona?'

'Less than seven hours' practice and I'd simply be wasting my time with him. Make up your mind, Floss.'

Miss Frostbite glanced over at me. 'Leave it to me. We'll work out something.'

'Good!'

She looked up at Miss Bates. 'The problem is solved. Jack is very keen to be given the opportunity to study piano under your tuition, Mona.'

'Do you have far to come, Jack?' Miss Bates asked.

'No, Miss Bates.' I didn't tell her Jarvis Street wasn't that far from Cabbagetown because of Miss Frostbite saying not to mention where I lived.

'When will he start, Mona?' Miss Frostbite may have been annoyed on the inside but she wasn't going to show it to Miss Bates.

'Let me see now. Today is Friday. Monday week at half-past four will be splendid, Floss.'

Miss Frostbite turned to me and said, 'Jack, put your hands over your ears.'

I did as I was told but not so hard that I couldn't hear. 'Shall I pay you in advance, weekly or monthly, Mona?'

I was too young to realise this was meant as a putdown, it being the Depression and all. But Mona Bates was not to be intimidated. 'You may do as you wish, my dear,' she replied.

'Cash or cheque?' Miss Frostbite asked, smiling, but the smile wasn't in her voice.

'Oh, dear, Floss, you are so good at managing money, running that *jazz club* as you do, and I am so utterly hopeless, perhaps cash every week would be the best thing?' Miss Bates said, smiling like a Cheshire cat. Again, I didn't realise this was a double-whammy putdown.

I was just about coping with Miss Frostbite and now I had Miss Mona Bates to deal with, who seemed to me to be even tougher than nails.

Later, in the taxi going home, Miss Frostbite said, 'It's not going to be easy, Jack. The talented Mona Bates and I went to school together in Burlington, although I was several years below her. She always was a prima donna. She was to become the most famous girl ever to attend our exclusive girls school.' She laughed. 'I was to become the most notorious. But now she is known as an absolute perfectionist.' I made a mental note to look up 'perfectionist' the next time I was at the library. 'But we can truly thank our lucky stars. She only takes the very best, the most promising. You must have done very well indeed. But being accepted is one thing, maintaining the pace is quite another. Children don't have inbuilt discipline, so I'll be keeping a time sheet. Now we simply *must* average seven hours' practice a week. With your lessons, I know that's a lot, and as you get older it will increase. As Miss Bates said, we have some catching up to do.'

We arrived back at the Jazz Warehouse and I thanked Miss Frostbite for everything she'd done for us, and then told her about my mother wanting to help and not minding if she had to do the dirty work in the kitchen. 'That is very kind of her, Jack, and I will certainly call on her in an emergency, as sometimes happens. But you tell her that I shall never marry or have children, and that it's a great privilege to be allowed to share her son on the day shift.'

Because I was only starting with Miss Mona Bates on Monday week, I could go to the jam sessions all week. On Thursday night Mac was there, so I went into the kitchen and told the cook I was walking home with a friend and wouldn't be having my dinner as usual. 'You got grub at home?' he asked.

'No, but it's okay.'

'Hang in there, Jazzboy, I'll make you some sandwiches.' Everyone, except Miss Frostbite, now called me 'Jazzboy'.

He made me two large ham sandwiches, and Mac and I ate one each as I told him about going to Jarvis Street to meet Miss Mona Bates, and how we'd gone in a taxi, a Model A Ford. Then I told him about the new schedule and that in future, because of my musical education, we couldn't meet on school days, though I quickly added, 'But there'll be lots of times during school vacation when you're not working.'

He was real good about it and said, 'It don't change anything, Brother Jack. Friends is friends; jazz buddies are forever. Knowing you're going to make something out of your life, that's the best news, and I want you to know I'm behind you 100 per cent. Education is the only way out of this miserable Depression. Your generation is the future hope of the nation.' He sighed. 'The twins are sixteen already, and they're planning to leave school this year. I think they're fed up with their mother and want to leave home.' He grinned. 'Possibly sick of me, too, although we get on pretty well these days. But I don't know how they'll find jobs, and I get scared just thinking about it. The education they have isn't enough, although their mother says they can cook, clean, knit, sew and mind children and that's all a working-class woman needs to know to get by in life. But that's not true in today's world. It's scary. They're turning out to be very pretty, and that can mean trouble for young girls in these hard times.'

I wasn't sure what he meant by this, but you'd often hear people talking about young girls leaving school and then 'going off the rails', so I suppose that was it. I imagined a streetcar going off the rails: it would be a pretty nasty business for the people inside, all mangled up. It was years since Dolly McClymont put the talking ban on us and the twins still hadn't ever said hello, nor, as they swept past, did they ever smile back at me when I smiled at them. But they'd long since given up bumping into the invisible me in the hallway. Maybe Mac had spoken to them, although I had never mentioned it to him.

I also told Mac about the two shiny yellow couches and he said they would definitely be silk or silk shantung from the Orient. I then told him about the radiogram in Miss Frostbite's home with the picture of the dog. He laughed and said, 'Jack, it stands for "His Master's Voice". Our gramophone upstairs is exactly the same model as the one in the picture. The dog is supposed to be sitting in front of it listening to "his master's voice". Radio is here to stay, and you'll see, one day everyone will have one. Mark my words, with a twist of a knob we'll be able to hear news from all over the world, and what's more, music as well, just as good as a gramophone record. Jazz straight from America, and classical music, like you're going to learn. It's called mass production and it was started way back by Henry Ford. That taxi you rode in to Jarvis Street was an example of it.'

'Yeah, but not everyone can have a motorcar, can they?' I challenged.

'Just you wait and see, Jack. One day . . .'

In my wildest imagination it didn't seem possible to own a car. I couldn't see how the Depression was going to end, but Mac had always been an optimist. I suppose you had to be if you had a wife like Dolly who treated you so badly. But since we'd become friends he hadn't got drunk even once. We'd still sometimes hear her having a go at him, but not anything like so often as before.

Mac was quiet for a while after I told him about my lessons. I hoped he wouldn't be lonely now I was only going to have half an hour to sit in on the daily jazz jam. But when he next spoke he was still thinking about radios. 'Ever thought of making a crystal set, Jack?' he asked.

'No. Only English boys make them, I read about them in a *Boy's Own Annual* I once borrowed from the library. But I don't think we can find crystals in Canada, and you need earphones.'

'I bet we could make one every bit as good as those English boys'.'

'Yeah? What about the earphones? They cost money.'

'Ah, that's just it. You know how I am about collecting stuff. I was working last month on the extension to the Toronto Telephone Exchange. They've got hundreds of girls there who use earphones all the time. I found three broken earphones in an old built-in cupboard when we knocked down a wall. There was nothing else in the cupboard and the room was empty, so I figured they didn't want the earphones. I asked the foreman and he said it was okay to take them, they were obviously trash. I just thought at the time they might come in handy one day.'

I laughed. 'Like the hockey stick?'

'Yeah, sort of. I'm always carting home junk that Dolly throws out unless it's small enough to hide. Well then, when you mentioned your piano practice and not being able to hit the stairs any more, then the HMV radiogram, "*Ding!*", on went the light bulb. "I'll use the earphones and make a crystal set for Jack."'

I could hardly believe my ears. '*Really?*'

Mac shrugged. 'Shouldn't be too difficult.'

'What about the crystals? And you need lots of copper wire.'

'Ah, the crystal is easy,' he said with a grin. 'Dolly's mom left her this quartz necklace that hangs halfway to her waist. She sometimes wears it to church. It's got maybe thirty or forty of these quartz crystal beads.' He gave me a wicked look. 'She's never gonna miss one, is she?

I mean, the pawnbroker says it's worthless. So it's not as though I'm taking something precious.'

I tried to imagine the thrashing Mac would receive if Dolly discovered the bead missing from her mom's necklace. He'd be a hospital case, for sure.

But Mac's enthusiasm for his crystal set was tumbling out as we talked. 'The copper wire I'm gonna need? Now that's real easy, Jack. Lots of abandoned factories along the Don have big electric bells on the outside wall to call the factory workers in to start a shift. If they ever open again, the dome and the hammer will have rusted, but each one has a copper wire coil that will still be good as gold.'

'But wouldn't that be stealing?' I asked.

'Nah, it's all junk now, Jack. Hey, they ain't never gonna bring those bells back to life.'

Carting useful bits of junk from an abandoned factory was so common that most people never regarded it as stealing. If the factory didn't have a guard, then this indicated that the owners didn't consider what was left as worth saving. I felt sure Sergeant Crosby, who was in charge of the Cabbagetown police station, would see it the same way. People in the Depression needed bits and pieces to repair their homes or make something, and there was no place else they could get the raw materials without paying for them. Many of the abandoned factory windowpanes and inside doors had been carefully removed to help fix houses.

'And you'll be able to hear music? I mean, properly, just like from a radio?'

'Yeah, CBS and all the New York radio stations. Maybe even Chicago. But listen to this will'ya, Jack,' he said, grabbing my shoulder. 'The best part is the earphones. No one else hears it except *you* and you can choose your own stuff to listen to, private like. So, you see, it's almost better than a big radio blaring stuff out to everyone and his dog who maybe don't want to listen. You can just sit in bed and jam all you like.'

I imagined myself sitting up in bed late at night hearing jazz played from New York, right under my dad's nose, jazz blaring in my ears and him none the wiser.

Two days before Christmas Mac presented me with the crystal set. 'I couldn't give it to you on Christmas Day because everyone will be home.' Mac wasn't just the best buddy a boy could have, he was like a proper dad. It seemed so unfair: he had Dolly and my mom had my dad and everyone was unhappy and the good guys got beaten up. But, like I said before, I don't suppose Dolly would have done a swap. She was big, but my dad was even bigger, and with his fierce backhand her nose would soon have looked like my mom's, never mind her teeth. Dolly with two black eyes, a broken nose and no front teeth would be a sight to behold, all right. I think my mom had once been pretty but I doubt that this was true of Dolly McClymont. She had these small pale blue eyes, big jowls and a downturned mouth with a large nose that turned up at the end, so she looked a bit like a rhinoceros wearing a red wig. The twins must have got their looks from Mac, who, if he wasn't so little and didn't have a broken nose (it wasn't hard to guess how he got it) would have been quite a nice-looking guy.

My mom had saved up and we had a meat stew for Christmas and I got a new shirt. I'd saved the money left over from my dollar streetcar fare and bought her a washcloth, some perfumed soap and a tiny bottle of scent, all in the same box with a pink ribbon and cellophane.

The new year was the first of my childhood to be thoroughly organised and timetabled. Everything had to be planned around piano lessons; you couldn't just expect to have time when you suddenly wanted to do something. Music and the piano, or, as Miss Bates called it, 'the pianoforte', had become everything from the moment I woke up to the moment I fell asleep at night. I learned to read music in a month and by the end of the first year I was pretty competent at sight-reading. But that was like learning stuff at school; the piano was an altogether different matter. Practice, practice, practice! Scales, scales, scales! Studies and exercises until they seemed to almost spill over the keyboard onto the floor! Then just a bit more practice. It was never enough and seemed as endless as the Depression itself, although more enjoyable.

It wasn't that bad, but because of Saturday and Sunday practice, I had to give up shinny in winter. I still had time to read, and I played harmonica and listened to the brilliant jazz coming from New York and Chicago. Every once in a while you'd get Art Tatum on the piano – oh, man, that was something else! I'd be swaying and bumping up and down in bed with a big grin on my face, and my mom would nudge me and say, 'Jack, I'm trying to get to sleep!'

Mona Bates would say, 'Jack, the pianoforte is judged by degrees of competence. There's never an end point, even if you are Sergei Rachmaninoff.' As I grew older she would sometimes look at my hands. They were going to be like my father's, big as dinner plates, and were already real big for a kid my age. 'With a bit of luck they'll continue to grow, Jack. Rachmaninoff's hands were ridiculously large, which allowed him to stretch huge distances across the keyboard.' Not that I could ever be like Rachmaninoff, but it was nice to think that big hands might one day create something beautiful instead of being used to bash people's faces in. But, big hands or not, my tone was far from even.

I mentioned scales before, but I was to learn that scales are not just scales, they are like musical mountains, each one in a different key. Having a good ear didn't help if your technique let you down every time. Scales were supposed to help me develop strength, control and freedom of movement in all my fingers so that I could produce an even tone, but if I wasn't forgetting a sharp or a flat, I was playing unevenly or varying the volume or speed. 'Jack, stupid boy!' Miss Bates would yell. 'Wrong, wrong, wrong and wrong again!' It was her favourite comment. Even if you made only one small error, you got a 'stupid boy' and four wrongs. I tried and practised and struggled and got yelled at. To use Uncle Joe's un-word, there wasn't much conversating going on, just arpeggios and yelling, and contrary motion and yelling, and staccato exercises and yelling, exercises in thirds, double thirds, trills, octaves and studies, all accompanied by sighs, clucks, and several 'stupid boys' and sets of four 'wrongs'.

In among the yelling I learned to play pieces by Czerny, Scarlatti, Heller and – listen to this! – stuff Mozart wrote when he was only six years old. Can you imagine, what he wrote as a little kid took me ages to learn to play and Miss Bates would listen and, when I got a bit better, sigh, and say, 'For goodness sake, slur those notes, Jack! In these bars I want a nice bell sound!' They got the spelling of her first name wrong; it should have been Miss 'Moaner' Bates.

I must have done okay because after the first year and a half I'd passed the second-grade examination and was halfway into third grade. Miss Bates entered me into my first piano competition – the prizes were not about degrees of difficulty but about how well a piece of music was played on its individual merits.

Before each player performed they announced how long the student had been playing piano. Then the competitor was called onto the stage with their parents and introduced to the audience, so that the parents as well as the performer could be acknowledged. Most parents give up a lot so their talented children can learn piano, and it was like the concert organisers were saying thank you to them. Even though I had no chance of winning, I was dead proud of having my mom standing beside me.

Once or twice during the school vacation she'd come with me in the morning to the Jazz Warehouse, where I'd play for her on Miss Frostbite's piano, but this was the first time I'd played or done anything else in public. I can tell you now it was the big time for both of us.

We got her good shoes out of the box and her mothballed yellow dress and brushed her hair until it shone so that you practically had to squint your eyes. She looked lovely, and she even wore a bit of red lipstick. She'd borrowed a tube from one of the women at work, who offered it when she heard my mom speak about going to the swanky piano concert.

When Miss Bates turned up, lots of people crowded around and made a big fuss of her because she was still very famous from her concert career. We didn't sit with her because of all the people, presumably friends, anxious to be near her. Miss Frostbite couldn't come because it was a Saturday night and she had to work, doing her dual piano act with Joe Hockey.

Well, to cut a long story short, I came third and Miss Bates said she was happy because the other performers had studied at least two years longer than I had. She came over especially, and I introduced her to my mom and she said, 'Mrs Spayd, we both have every reason to be proud of Jack's performance. Considering he's been studying piano for less than two years and he's the youngest in the competition, it is a remarkable achievement. As you will have heard, most of the competitors have had at least five full years at the piano.' It was the first time she'd praised me since she started teaching me.

'That can only be because of his teacher, Miss Bates. Jack and me are very grateful,' my mom replied.

'How very gracious of you, but I cannot accept the credit. Well, not *all* of it, anyway. Jack has achieved a great deal through diligent practice. Both Mozart pieces he played with beautiful tone and expression, showing an understanding of the composer's intentions.'

I could see my mom was very proud, even if she didn't understand all of it. Then, a little while later, just when we were about to leave to take the streetcar home, she excused herself to go to the ladies room. She looked a bit upset when she returned and on the streetcar she was very quiet, when I'd expected her to . . . well, to be honest, now that we were on our own, to tell me how proud she felt of me. But she barely said a word and when I asked her what was wrong, she looked out of the streetcar window and said, 'Nothing, Jack. Just something that happened.' But her voice wasn't normal and I knew it was something bad. Then, when she got home, she burst into tears.

'Mom, what happened?' I asked, alarmed. But she just kept on sobbing. So I sat and held her hand and then made her a cup of tea, and I could see she was shaking when she took the King George.

Eventually she looked up and sniffed and brushed the tears from her eyes, which had gone all red, and told me what had happened.

'Jack, when I went into the ladies room there were two women doing their make-up at the mirror and so they probably didn't see me,' she explained. 'Then, when I closed the toilet door, I heard one of them say, "The young lad who came third is very talented."

'Then the other one said something like, "The early Mozart minuets? Yes, he already has a nice sound."' She mimicked the two voices, making them sound very lah-de-dah. '"But then, he *is* taught by Mona Bates; that does make a tremendous difference."

'I was so proud, Jack,' my mom said, her voice still a bit tearful. But then she started to sob again and choked out, 'Then . . . one of them said – *sob* – "Did you see his frightful mother?" *Sob.* "Most of her teeth missing, broken nose, and that ridiculous chartreuse dress and truly awful shoes. She looked like a down-and-out whore a drunken sailor might pick up on the docks!"'

My mom looked up at me, fresh tears beginning to well. 'Then the first woman said, "If she's seen with him as he gets older and begins to perform in important competitions, it will seriously affect the poor boy's career."' Then my mom started to wail.

That first concert taught me a sad lesson. Classical music isn't meant for poor people, and the parents and audiences were not from places like Cabbagetown.

The following Monday at Jarvis Street I was playing for Miss Bates when she suddenly called out, 'Stop! Stop at once! What on earth has come over you, Jack?'

'Nothing, Miss Bates,' I replied.

'Oh, nothing, is it? Well, your playing is *good for nothing!* Has coming third on Saturday night gone to your head? Stupid, stupid boy!'

I could see this wasn't make-believe and she was truly furious. Sometimes she would give me a meaningful look when I goofed a piece real bad and say something like, 'Jack, I am in the fortunate situation of being able to choose the cream of the crop, *and*, I should remind you, I also have the luxury of weeding out those who don't perform. So far, since I opened the studio, I've never experienced the disappointment of a student failing the conservatory entrance examination. But one or two have been sent packing along the way.' I guess this was meant as a warning to me not to let her down. This time she sounded really angry. So I blurted out, 'I don't care about the concert. Those people hated my mom, Miss Bates.' And then I just couldn't help it, I started to sniff and I could feel the tears running down my cheeks.

'Hated her? On the contrary, I found your mother perfectly charming and I can see the two of you are very close. Now tell me what happened at once, Jack,' she demanded.

I sniffed away my tears and told her the whole story exactly as my mom had told me, my own sniffs replacing her sobs. When I'd finished, Miss Bates was all red in the face and even more furious. 'Jack, I wish I'd been there to give them what-for! What I would have said to them would have made the front page of all the newspapers. No, on second thoughts, it would have been unprintable. How dare they! That's simply too awful for words. They're not just the worst type of snob, they're thoroughly nasty pieces of work!' I could see she was genuinely upset. 'You tell your mother that from now on she always sits with me. Tell her she has nothing whatsoever to be ashamed of, and I'd be proud to have her at my side at every recital and concert we do together.' She looked at me sternly, 'Now, you promise to do that, Jack?'

I guess Miss Bates must have told Miss Frostbite, who didn't say anything to me, but the next Monday as I was practising, she came into the piano room and said, 'Jack, we're short-staffed in the club at the moment with one of the kitchen hands off with pleurisy. The generous promise your mother made about cleaning for us in the club kitchen, do you think I could see her about it tomorrow or the next day?'

My mom was overjoyed! She went on her own to the Jazz Warehouse the following day while I was at school. I only heard the result of it that night and it was 100 per cent Miss Frostbite getting her own way as always. My mom explained what had happened in Miss Frostbite's own words. '"Gertrude, we need a morning cleaner now that Lily is sick – she has a chronically bad chest and may not be returning to work. I must warn you, it's not very nice work. The kitchen is always cleaned at night, but the heavy-duty cleaning is left for the following day, ovens, floors, grease traps . . . "

'"Oh, I don't mind, Miss Byatt, I'm used to hard work," I told her.

'"But we'll have to pay you, of course . . . by the way, please call me Floss, as I said, or Miss Frostbite, if you prefer."

'"Of course, Miss Frostbite," I said.'

Now there was work involved, I don't think she was prepared to call Miss Frostbite by her first name.

'"I can't take any money. I just want to pay you back a bit for Jack."

'"Pay me back for Jack! Why, Gertrude, the boy pays me back every day with his practice and nice manners, and I'm like a mother when I see him eating his dinner with the musicians. I assure you, I'm already emotionally well compensated."'

My mom told me all this because I could see she was proud. 'But, Jack, I wouldn't hear of it and I insisted that I work for free.'

'"Oh, dear, that's difficult, my dear. You see I've always run my business along union lines, and it goes against my principles to have someone work for nothing."'

My mom looked up. 'I felt like laughing. She was just trying to be kind. Everyone knows the unions have lost their power because of the Depression and nobody takes any notice of the rules. But I wouldn't have it, she'd been kind enough, it was time I did something in return. "You can pay me and then Jack can give the money back to you the next day," I suggested. "I honestly couldn't take it, Miss Frostbite," I told her.'

My mother then said Miss Frostbite put her middle finger to her cheek and tilted her head to one side. I laughed because it was a sure sign of danger I'd long since learned to recognise. '"Quit pro something," she said.'

'Quid pro quo,' I said, interrupting. 'It means you scratch my back and I'll scratch yours, like a favour returned.' It was an expression I knew because Miss Bates used it once in 'conversating' with me. This had now become my favourite un-word, borrowed from Uncle Joe, even though it wasn't in the dictionary. But when I looked up *quid pro quo*, it was a real expression and it was Latin.

'Oh, that explains it, Jack. I didn't want to ask her what it meant. Then she removed her finger from her cheek and her head jerked up. "Teeth!" she said suddenly. Just like that, "Teeth!"

'"Eh?" I said. I know it wasn't very ladylike, but I didn't know what she meant by the *quit pro* stuff and all. Now, teeth! I mean, what on earth was she carrying on about?

'Then she said, "You shall have a set of teeth, Gertrude."'

I now need to explain that it was only several years later that my mom told me this next part of their conversation. I'd always thought that the *quid pro quo* part meant Miss Frostbite paid for my mom's teeth in return for an extra two mornings' work, making it four mornings a week altogether, but that's not how it was at all.

When I was old enough my mom explained what had actually happened, prefacing her explanation with these words: 'After paying for your lessons, Jack, I could *never ever* have accepted her paying for my false teeth as well. Miss Frostbite told me, "Gertrude, when you run a nightclub you get to know a lot of people, some good, some not so good, and they sometimes get a little sozzled at the club, or arrive that way from a late dinner and get steadily worse. After Joe and I finish our performance, I mix with the audience while the jazz band plays. You get to hear a fair bit and see a bit, sometimes from the most unexpected quarters – men who are important, politicians, professionals, big wheels in the Toronto business scene. We observe a three-monkeys policy here at the Jazz Warehouse, because men, even married men, are sometimes lonely and arrive with a gal on their arm who probably ought not to be there. I mean, the kind of girl we would normally not permit to come in on her own. But if she accompanies a guest, then that's entirely his business. If someone questions who was with whom on a particular night, we simply say we haven't the faintest idea or if, as sometimes happens, a patron suggests to us that he spent the evening here on his own, we simply do as he asks, unless it is a serious police matter. This is a nightclub after all and not the courthouse." She smiled. "I'm a compulsive note maker. I have a whole filing cabinet full of silly notes. In fact, I'm addicted. I make notes and I have schedules for everything. Jack will have told you about his strict piano schedules.

'"Anyhow, I know a rather wealthy dentist. Dentists in general seem to be an unhappy lot. He is a club regular who is married to a society matron, but invariably has a girl of doubtful reputation on his arm and has often enough asked us to keep mum, which, of course, we do. But there is an unspoken rule in the nightclub business that one good turn deserves another. It's particularly true of politics and the law, but in this instance it also applies to my friend the dentist." Then she stopped and her voice changed. "What say we give that pretty face of yours a little help?"'

My mom looked at me. 'Jack, it was a terrible moment and I think I must have gone purple. I didn't know what to say to her except, "Oh!" But then she just carried on as if she was pointing out that the sky was blue. "You work for us in the club kitchen two mornings a week for a year and in return you get a set of teeth." I didn't even have time to answer before she said, "Now please, don't be fussed, Gertrude. I have exactly the right files to consult and, best of all, no money has changed hands between us."'

My mom laughed as she recalled the incident. 'When I had regained my breath I said, "No, Miss Frostbite, the two mornings' work in your kitchen are for Jack's piano lessons. I will give you an extra two mornings' work for this."

'"Gertrude, that simply won't be necessary. As I mentioned, it isn't going to cost me anything but a nice little chat next time my dentist friend comes into the club," Miss Frostbite protested.

'"Still, I couldn't take it unless I did the two extra days," I insisted.' My mom looked at me. 'Jack, poor doesn't mean taking charity when you have two strong scrubbing arms and capable hands to clean with.'

'So, what did she say?' I asked.

'She laughed and said, "Well, you must do as you wish, Gertrude. I think we are going to be good friends. Perhaps the two mornings can be spent cleaning my office and apartment."'

Then Miss Bates remarked one day, not long after the concert, 'Jack, I have wardrobes filled with evening dresses I wore on various concert tours. They're just hanging there and I can't possibly wear them all. If I'm not mistaken, your mother is the same size as me. I shall bring in four gowns and matching shoes, and you're to ask her to try them on, and if they fit I'd be most obliged if she would do me a favour and take them off my hands.'

And so Mom started to attend performances with me again. I gotta tell you, she looked pretty as anything. After she got her new teeth and in one of Mona Bates's gowns and swanky shoes, my mom never missed a concert or a performance, and people would often comment on her ready smile and quiet and charming ways.

But it didn't stop my dad. Shortly after she got her teeth, we'd got home on a Saturday night from a concert that had gone on quite late and were having a cup of tea in the kitchen. 'My feet are killing me!' she'd exclaimed when we got home. She never said it, but I think Mona Bates's shoes were a bit too small. Anyhow, she'd kicked them off when she sat down, but was still in her fancy concert dress when my dad arrived home.

He was silent, his watery blue eyes taking in everything. 'Shit, what's goin' on here?' he finally asked. 'Where'd you get that dress?' He pointed to the shoes. 'You on the game or somethin', hey woman? That how you payin' for Jack's pee-a-no lessons, is it?' He turned to me. 'Thought I didn't know, eh? Who gave you the harmonica, eh? Me! That's who! Now your mother is paying for yer lessons and her fancy whore-smilin' teeth with her pussy!'

'No, Dad, I can explain,' I yelled, jumping in front of my mother.

'Yeah, sure, you little bastard, think I'm stupid, do yah? The whole of Cabbagetown is talkin' about the boy wonder. Wonder, my fuckin' ass! It was me who give you the harmonica!' he yelled again. Then he brushed me aside and let go with a vicious backhand, knocking my mom's new teeth out of her mouth, and then he did something that had never happened before and let go with a second backhander, this time smashing into her nose so that she fell off the chair onto the floor. He stood over her. 'Dirty fucking whore!' he yelled. I ran at him and punched him as hard as I could in his fat belly. He grunted and grabbed me by the scruff of my neck, sending me hurtling across the kitchen to slam face-first into the far wall. I didn't know at the time that I'd broken my nose, but it bled a lot, and the next day my mom and I each had a pair of black eyes. By some miracle her false teeth didn't break.

When Miss Frostbite saw me and my mom's faces she was terribly angry. 'Right, we'll see about this!' she vowed. Then, quite early on the following Saturday morning, there was a knock on the door and I answered it. It was Sergeant Crosby, the policeman who lived in Cabbagetown. 'Mornin', Jack. Your daddy in?' he asked.

'Yes, Sergeant, but I think he's still in bed,' I replied.

'Better get him up, son,' he ordered. 'Your mother in?'

'Yes, Sergeant.'

'Good. I need to see them both.'

By this time my mom had joined us, drying her hands on her apron. 'Oh, hello, Tony,' she called.

'Mornin', Mrs Spayd.'

My mother had known Tony Crosby for years and years and, before she married, had gone out with him a few times. He was from Cabbagetown, man and boy. He'd been a semi-pro lacrosse player and a champion amateur heavyweight boxer, and was a bit of a legend around the place and owned his own house. He still looked pretty fit. His brother, Father Crosby, was the local Catholic priest, so, as my mom once told me, the two Crosby boys had done well for themselves, because they came from a dirt-poor Irish Catholic family. Also, it was fairly unusual for a Cabbagetown kid to end up with a career on the right side of the law. People sniffed at the so-called 'careers' of the four Crosby girls, who were supposed to be 'dancers' in Montreal.

While Sergeant Crosby was on first-name terms with everyone in the community, especially my mom, he'd chosen to refer to her as Mrs Spayd, so we knew it must be a pretty serious matter, him calling around on a Saturday morning and then addressing her in such a formal manner.

'I need to talk to your husband and I'd be obliged if you'd sit in as well,' he'd said.

'Oh, what's wrong, Sergeant?' my mother asked, suddenly anxious.

'Nothing you've done, Gertrude,' he said, softening his demeanour now that he'd established the official rules. 'But I require your presence.'

My mom repeated that my dad was still asleep and Sergeant Crosby again said to wake him.

My mom turned away to do as he'd asked and Sergeant Crosby said to me, 'Better go outside and play for a bit, Jack.'

Later my mom told me what had happened. My dad came into the kitchen, rubbing his eyes and smacking his lips, and went to the kitchen sink and shamed her by not bothering to get a glass, just cupping his hands and drinking straight from the faucet. Then he looked blearily at the police sergeant. 'Ah, Tony,' he said, 'whatcha want?'

Sergeant Crosby pointed to the third chair, 'Sit, Mr Spayd,' he demanded.

'Mr Spayd? What the heck's that supposed t' mean?' That's what my mom told me he said, but I knew she couldn't say the 'f' word, and that he'd most likely said, 'What the fuck's that supposed t' mean?' Anyhow, he took a seat and rubbed his crotch. 'What?' he asked again.

Sergeant Crosby leaned forward, addressing my dad. 'I could have done this the nice way and had a private chat with you, Mr Spayd.'

'Well then, why didn't't'cha?' my dad demanded, all surly and bad tempered.

'I wanted Gertrude to be present at this interview, Mr Spayd. I emphasise, she didn't call me and has no idea why I am here. I could have taken you to the station and taken down the conversation we are about to have as future evidence, but decided to give you the first and the last warning you'll ever get from me on this matter.'

'Hey, wait on! What'd I do? What's the matter?' my dad objected once again.

'Nothing yet, Mr Spayd.'

My mom said he was *leaning* on the 'Mr Spayd' even though the two of them had known each other all their lives.

'Well, get the fuck on with it then!' my dad shouted. He must have had a very bad hangover to talk to a policeman like that.

'Certainly, Mr Spayd. What I have come to say is that if you ever lay a hand on your wife again – and she won't have to report it because it will be there for all to see – not only will I see to it that you lose your job at the council, but I'll also throw you into a cell and charge you with assault and anything else I can think of that will get you a prison sentence. You're a blowhard good-fer-nothing drunk! Everyone in Cabbagetown knows you drink your wages and not a cent gets home.'

'That's my business!' my dad thundered. He looked over at my mom. 'She been talking?'

'No, not at all. Your pals at the tavern have big mouths and dry throats. Generosity, my friend, begins at home!'

My mom said Sergeant Crosby was getting very angry.

My dad rose from his chair and clenched his fists as he faced the policeman. 'I won't take that from nobody, ya hear?' he spat.

Sergeant Crosby rose to face him. 'Oh my, can't tell ya how much I've looked forward to this moment, Harry Spayd. Just let me remove my jacket and cap so I'm not here officially. I've watched what you've done to Gertrude for years, so now just throw the first punch, will ya?' Then Tony Crosby, never taking his eyes off my dad, removed his cap and jacket and dropped them on the floor. 'Come on, hit me, you bastard!'

It seemed they stood toe-to-toe for nearly a minute, with my dad's unshaven chin jutting out and his bottom teeth showing, and Tony Crosby looking into his eyes and waiting to block the first punch so he could beat the living crap out of him. But then my dad shook his head. 'Just you wait. One dark night, you tyke bastard!' he threatened. Then he pulled back, unknotting his fists.

'I'll be waiting, Harry. Make it soon, won't you?' Sergeant Crosby said, retrieving his coat and then his cap.

'Get outa my house!' my dad yelled.

Believe it or not, my dad never backhanded my mom again. But six months later he didn't come home for a week, and my mom called on Sergeant Crosby to report him missing. Not that we wanted him back, but the lease was in his name. Tony Crosby called in the following night. 'He's taken up with a kitchen hand named Milly Townsend, at the tavern where he drinks. It seems it's been on between the two of them for some time. She feeds him after the tavern closes at night.'

'That accounts for him throwing his supper in the pail when he gets home,' my mom replied. 'Good riddance to bad rubbish.'

'Don't worry about the lease, Gertrude. Give me the name of your landlord and I'll fix it up,' Sergeant Crosby offered.

Miss Frostbite never admitted she'd informed the police, so I still wasn't any the wiser until three years later, when I learned from Sergeant Crosby himself that it was Mac who had gone to see him. When I confronted him – Mac, that is – he blushed. 'Jack, we don't usually talk about things that happen in families, as you know. But your mom looked so pretty, I didn't want that bastard to harm her again. When I told Tony Crosby he seemed very pleased and relieved. "Mac, I'm glad you came and told me. Now we can settle the matter in the Cabbagetown way. I've had a call from the police chief saying I'd better sort it out or he'll be down on me like a ton of bricks. It seems someone very important called him. If you hadn't come in as a local, I would have had to make a formal arrest, court and all the rest, including the slammer."'

I have to backtrack a bit here to the year before I started piano lessons. The principal called me into his office one day and said, 'Jack Spayd, what are we going to do with you? I have a report from your teacher, who says you are well above the standard of your class and should be in grade six, that you're languishing, bored and disruptive and know all the answers so that she can't keep up with you and at the same time be fair to the other children she's attempting to teach.'

He was right, I'd long since given up caring about what the other guys thought. I couldn't just sit in the class and play dumb. Now the principal looked at me over his big horn-rimmed spectacles, even bigger than Mrs Hodgson's at the library, and said, 'So I'm going to take the risk and elevate you to grade six, though you will be young when you enter high school, but I don't suppose that will matter.'

I wrote to Miss Mony, who was now Mrs Pritchard, but would always be Miss Mony to me. She was going to have a baby. I wrote almost every week and saved the letters up until I could buy a stamp. I told her that at long last the principal had done what she'd asked.

She wrote back to say she was researching a bursary into one of Toronto's good schools, and that she didn't want me to languish in the local high school as it was filled with students who'd all leave at fourteen and didn't want to be there in the first place. This was nearly true, but there were *some* kids who would go on to complete twelfth grade at the nearby high school – very few, I admit, but some. You couldn't just write them all off like that, even though girls who were clever were never allowed to continue, partly because of the Depression and partly because of the notion, set in concrete in Cabbagetown, that 'a woman's place was in the home', and that before she was married she was only fit for factory work or to be a domestic servant. Working-class girls were not permitted to have brains. Even I could see, plain as the nose on my face, that the cleverest kids in the class were usually girls.

I know I might be beginning to sound like a bit of a smart alec but I think it was mostly all the reading that I'd done that put me ahead, and Cabbagetown primary was hardly the benchmark for Canadian scholarly excellence. But, anyhow, I was lucky, thanks to Miss Mony and a letter from Miss Frostbite and Miss Bates, that I was asked in March of my final year in primary school to sit the first exam at UTS (that stands for University of Toronto Schools) in Bloor Street, only about two miles from home. I managed to pass in the top quarter, so they asked me to sit a second exam, based on writing an essay. I can tell you now I was grateful for all the years of reading and looking up stuff in the library dictionary and encyclopaedia, because I managed to pass this as well. So I got to the last part, which was an interview with two teachers and an old boy from the school who now taught at the university.

By this time I was doing fourth-grade piano and I think it was this that got me through, especially when I told them my teacher was Mona Bates. It seemed the music school at UTS was excellent. Then later, close to my eleventh birthday, we got a letter accepting me as a bursary student at UTS. We learned that over 600 kids had sat for the entrance exams and only seventy-five of us were accepted. They weren't only bursary students. Most were clever guys who wanted to get one of the very limited UTS places. My mom cried and cried when she heard the news, then started to worry about paying for the school uniform. Fortunately, they had a free clothing pool where parents donated their kids' outgrown uniforms, so I was okay for school clothes. When I told Mac, he clapped me on the back and said, 'Best news ever, Jack. If I could afford fireworks, we'd let them off from every rooftop in Cabbagetown.'

Now here's a lucky thing . . . sort of. The school had lots of extra-curricular activities, where parents paid for their kids to go places and see special things, skiing and camp in the summer, excursions to the theatre or sailing on Lake Ontario, and then, when I got a bit older, there were parties with girls in private homes. But, of course, we didn't have money for equipment or fares or anything else, and my clothes were too shabby for parties – I wore my school uniform for concerts. The reason I say I was sort of lucky was that I could easily have felt just like my mom after that first concert, but because the school accepted that I was a serious music student and had to practise for two hours a day and all through the summer vacation, I had the best excuse not to go on the various excursions, skiing trips, camps and so on, which saved me from being completely humiliated.

My mom proved she could be as stubborn as Miss Frostbite, and when she discovered that there was no union involvement at the Jazz Warehouse, she insisted on continuing to work an extra morning a week for Miss Frostbite after her teeth were fixed. Now she no longer worked in the kitchen doing the dirty work, but had become Miss Frostbite's house cleaner four mornings a week. Like I said before, I know she felt proud that we weren't taking Miss Frostbite's charity without giving something back.

And so time passed and I grew into my teenage years, and the worst part was that I hardly ever had time to play the harmonica, except during the summer school vacation. I took to playing it on the streetcar going home from my piano lessons at night. The passengers became my very first jazz audience and seemed to love it, invariably clapping as I got off at my stop. More often than not the conductor wouldn't accept my fare, so it was almost like being paid to play.

I was doing an awful lot of piano practice, but Mona Bates was a pretty formidable teacher in more ways than one. She demanded technical perfection as well as beautifully expressive playing. I worked my way through the grades and learned to play with absolute precision, as well as great feeling. 'Emotion, Jack! It's what makes the difference. It's a great part of your musical signature,' she would often say. Music is addictive and I loved the piano and all the classical music I learned, but I still hungered for jazz. I told myself all this technique I was learning would translate to jazz when I had more time. I learned theory, harmony and counterpoint and began to study Bach's fugues, after a lot of work with Miss Bates 'stupid boy-ing' me and 'wrong, wrong, wrong, wrong-ing' me. I also worked at being able to modulate from any key intuitively, knowing it would be a great asset when I turned to serious jazz piano.

Of course, I said nothing to Mona Bates. I could see she had this big career in mind for me but it wasn't where my heart was. By this time I knew a fair bit about the life of a concert pianist, and even if I made the big time, it wasn't where I wanted to end up. If I'd told Miss Bates I had decided to turn to jazz when I left school she'd have had a major heart seizure. She was obsessed with my large hands and made me learn challenging pieces of music just to test me. When I succeeded, she was very pleased. 'See, Jack, you can do it. It's the hands, the Rachmaninoff hands!'

I told my mom about my feelings on one of our Sunday walks in the park. We'd just heard massed military bands playing in Queen's Park, then a politician had spoken to the crowd about how war in Europe in the coming months was almost a certainty. His final words were 'If you're a man over eighteen and under forty, Canada will expect you to do your bit on behalf of the British Empire!' Everywhere you went people were talking about the coming war and that Canada must be involved. Lots of the older final-year guys at school said they'd be joining up for sure, but I'd be too young if it came in the next few months. I was still in year eleven, and you had to be eighteen to enlist. But if war was declared and continued into late 1941, I'd certainly join up. It wasn't the reason I didn't want to go to the conservatory and study classical music, but it was certainly a good reason for not going. I pointed to a park bench. 'Mom, I have something to tell you. Why don't we sit down for a moment.'

'Oh, Jack, it's not about joining up and going to the war when you leave school, is it?' she asked, clearly worried.

'Mom, I'd be too young. It will probably be over by the time I turn eighteen.' I then proceeded to tell her that I'd decided I didn't want to go to the conservatory and that I wanted to become a professional jazz pianist.

'Oh, dear. Jack, what will Miss Frostbite and Miss Bates say?'

'I don't know. I don't suppose they're going to be happy. But I wanted to talk to you first.'

'Oh, deary me, however shall we pay her back the money she's spent on you?' she said, clearly distressed.

'Mom, I'll find a way, I promise.'

'I'll work as her housekeeper forever,' she said firmly. 'That way we can eventually pay the money back.'

'Mom, I told you I'd find a way and I will, I promise. But how do you feel about it? I mean, are you angry?'

'No, Jack, just very shocked and sad. Everyone had such high hopes for you.'

'You mean I've failed you?'

My mom looked at me tearfully. 'Jack, you've never failed me for one minute of your life. It's . . . it's just that it comes as a tremendous shock.' She brushed her eyes with the back of her hand. 'One thing I know for sure, you'll become a very good jazz pianist and that's all that matters.'

'Mom, I haven't wasted my time. Almost everything I've learned from Miss Bates can be adapted to the jazz piano. Miss Frostbite once said an education in classical music was the very best training a jazz musician could have. Mom, jazz is the coming music, it's not as though I'll be going backwards. Bands like Count Basie's, Louis Armstrong's, Cab Calloway's and Duke Ellington's are leading the way. I can spend the next five years at the conservatory or learn my trade as a jazz musician. I'll be scuffing – I mean, earning very little – but it will be better than the nothing I'm earning now.'

'Oh, Jack, you won't be leaving your school as well, will you?'

'No, of course not. I think I can get an A-grade pass that would allow me to get into university.'

She looked relieved. 'Maybe you could study something else as well, Jack?'

With only a year to go at school, I knew I also needed to tell Miss Frostbite about how I felt. I was scared stiff. After all, she'd been the one who'd paid for my lessons all these years and she'd never once mentioned that she hoped I'd turn back to jazz one day. Though jazz was gaining in popularity, it still wasn't what talented young white musicians were expected to choose. Even though I knew Miss Frostbite loved jazz, it would probably still come as a big and unpleasant surprise. I plucked up sufficient courage after four days of rehearsing what I was going to say, then one afternoon after school, instead of going directly to her piano room to practise, I knocked on her office door.

'Come in!' she called.

'It's me, Jack, Miss Frostbite. May I see you, please?'

She had her back to the door. 'In the lounge, two minutes, be right there. Just completing a schedule for the club,' she answered.

We sat opposite each other on the yellow couches, just like the first time.

'What is it, Jack?' she asked.

'Ah, hmm, er . . . I wanted to ask your advice, Miss Frostbite.'

'Oh, that's nice, Jack. Nothing bad, I hope?'

'I don't know, I hope not,' I replied.

'Well, go ahead. In my experience most things can be worked out.'

This was when I was supposed to launch into my prepared speech, but all that came out was, 'Miss Frostbite, I don't want to be a classical musician.'

'Oh, Jack, you're not thinking of giving up music?' she exclaimed, plainly shocked.

'No, of course not,' I hastened to assure her, 'I could never do that! Just classical music. I want to play jazz piano when I leave school.'

She put her hand up to her breast and sighed deeply and then took a deep breath. 'My goodness, for a moment there I thought I was about to have a heart attack.' Then she laughed. 'Jack, I can't say I'm not surprised. You're doing so well and we are all so very proud of you. Next year you complete high school, and then, of course, we all took it for granted you'd attend the conservatory. But you're old enough to know your own mind. However, you should be aware that making a living as a jazz musician, unless you're at the very top, isn't going to be easy. Most of the band here are scuffing and would be out of work if we didn't have the club, and goodness knows how long this Depression will continue. But I respect your decision and, as you know, I'm a jazz fanatic.' She laughed. 'I ask you, why else would a well-bred gal from Burlington run a place like this?'

'I can't say, Miss Frostbite, but Miss Bates said you always did exactly as you wanted and were stubborn as a mule, even as a young girl.'

'Oh, did she now! I must say, that's a clear case of the pot calling the kettle black. She expects to get her own way as much as I do.' Her lips puckered and then she said crisply, 'Although, she usually goes about it less pleasantly. By the way, have you told her about your decision?'

'No, I wanted to tell you first, to see how you felt. Then, if you weren't very angry, I wanted to ask for your advice.'

'Thank you, Jack, that's nice and I appreciate it. No, I'm not angry, but I am surprised. As for telling Mona Bates, I suggest you don't . . . well, not for the time being, anyhow. She's likely to have a conniption!' (Another word I had to look up.)

'I thought you'd be very angry with me, Miss Frostbite. What I mean is, you giving me such a wonderful chance in life and then me not wanting to go on to the conservatory. I thought I should tell you now because if you kicked me out, then I could concentrate on schoolwork and getting into university.'

Miss Frostbite leaned back and smiled. 'If you're going to be a jazz musician, it's always as well to have a contingency plan, Jack. I know your music takes up all your available time but do try to do well at school.'

'Even if I did go to university, or if there is a war and it's still on in 1941, I'd still want to play jazz piano.'

'We probably have a great deal more in common than you may think, Jack. I suspect I know just how you feel. While we are from different backgrounds, I felt the same about being a popular singer when I was eighteen and had just left school. I'd studied piano and voice at school and privately, like every well-bred Burlington gal. I was even considered quite promising, though I admit I was no Mona Bates, who everyone knew even then was going places. My parents wanted me to study for the opera because I had a pleasant contralto voice. But I wanted to sing ragtime and the blues and be an entertainer. In those days singing in men's clubs, taverns or music halls was considered wicked and probably regarded in much the same way as becoming a prostitute. Besides, you did what you were told, and so I dutifully studied classical singing, as my teacher called it. It was excellent voice training, just as classical music is wonderful music training for you, Jack.

'But when I was twenty-one and free to leave home, the war broke out and I flew the coop and came to Toronto. My father never spoke to me again. He wrote to me to say that, as far as he was concerned, I was dead and he had instructed my mother to accept this notion. He was a dreadful old curmudgeon and I was glad to be free of him. But I missed my mother desperately. In those times a man's wife was expected to obey his wishes.' She paused and smiled. 'So you see, Jack, we are not all that different.'

I was becoming increasingly amazed at Miss Frostbite's story. It seemed that bad things could also happen to the rich and not just to poor people.

Miss Frostbite continued. 'I had been singing blues and ragtime in my spare time, as well as playing the piano, for four years without my parents' permission, so I wasn't wholly unprepared for what awaited me in Toronto. But I got lucky: I did an audition for a nightclub and I got the job. By the end of the war I guess I was pretty famous among the troops. It was the soldiers who gave me the sobriquet Miss Fairy Floss.'

She smiled. 'The club owner, Wayne McCarthy, would hand out photographs of me in a slinky evening gown to all the soldiers. I thought the way he'd made me pose was a bit risqué.' She laughed. 'But compared to the evening gowns I now wear, the photograph was the very soul of modesty.'

'I bet you looked really pretty, Miss Frostbite,' I said.

'Why, thank you, Jack. Wayne McCarthy would often say, "Floss, you weren't much good when I hired you, but you turned out to be the best investment I ever made."

'The Mail and Empire newspaper wrote an article about Miss Fairy Floss, the "It" girl, in which they said that a lonely serviceman needed a dream, and that my picture could be found in the wallets of Canadian soldiers and sailors wherever they were posted in Canada or overseas.'

'I didn't know you sing as well as play the piano with Uncle Joe,' I said.

'Alas, Jack, I don't. On a club tour to Alaska in 1924 we got caught in a blizzard when our motorcar got stuck. I contracted pleurisy and then a severe dose of pneumonia that wasn't treated properly and I lost my singing voice.' She laughed brightly. 'I sound worse than Joe these days, my dear. My career was effectively over, for while my piano wasn't bad, it was only an accompaniment for my voice, and so I was down and broke when I met a gentleman and we fell in love. He was a local politician and before that a real-estate developer, but a Catholic and married, so that was that.' She hesitated, then continued a moment later. 'I became his mistress.' She paused again. 'You're old enough to know what that means, are you not, Jack?'

I nodded. 'Yes, of course, it's very hard when people are in love,' I said, trying to sound sophisticated. I'd read words somewhat like that in a book and was paraphrasing, because I knew very little about loving a girl. I'd only just begun to have problems 'down there' when I woke up, which was a pretty late puberty, I guess. I no longer shared a bedroom with my mom, thank goodness, but had a bed under the outside stairs. Someone had built in the space under the stairs to make a real big cupboard, and there was a door to it from inside our house. You could fit a narrow bed into that cupboard, but we took the door off to let air in, otherwise I'd have suffocated. The only trouble was that lying directly under the stairs I could hear everyone coming and going.

Miss Frostbite continued. 'Well, I lived in an apartment he owned, and he encouraged me to take up piano and forget about singing. It wasn't a great success, but then in 1928 I met Joe, who was American and trying hard to get a basement jazz group going but without much success. At the time two-piano acts were just beginning to become popular and so we teamed up with some small success.

'My father died in 1926 and I was reconnected with my mother, which was wonderful. It turned out she was rather proud of me breaking away from "the old curmudgeon" – her name for him, not mine. Then the crash came. My gentleman had a lot of money invested, and when the stock exchange collapsed in New York, he had a heart attack and tragically died. As it wasn't polite in my family to ever talk about money I assumed that my father's considerable fortune had also suffered in the crash. My mother had previously sold the big house in Burlington to move to Toronto, where she bought an apartment so that she could be closer to me. After the crash she seemed to manage quite well and so I never asked about her assets. My gentleman had left me my small apartment and an old warehouse on Dundas Street. I sold the apartment and Joe and I, perhaps very stupidly, decided to open the Jazz Warehouse on the smell of an oily rag. We both slept in two tiny offices at opposite ends of the original warehouse for a year while we built the club and got it going. My mother was unaware of this or she would have insisted I stay with her. But I guess I'd been independent for too long.' She looked up at me. 'Jack, don't ever think I don't admire your mother's self-respect and her stubborn belief in paying her way.'

I grinned at her.

'You have a very precious mom, Jack,' she said, then went on with her story. 'Well, we soon discovered that Toronto wasn't quite ready for us, that is to say, for a nightclub that played only jazz. Still isn't. So we went back to the dual piano act, but developed it into the showbiz affair it has become, using mirrored illusions, costume changes and elaborate popular music arrangements. Thank God I have kept a reasonable figure, and Joe in his blue satin tails and top hat looks the part and is a real character, so our act can hold the attention of an audience that's usually "well oiled" for an hour-and-a-half twice nightly.

'However, Joe and I still wanted our jazz dream, hence the band. We may not feature Scott Joplin, Duke Ellington or Louis Armstrong, but it's jazz, and with the money I inherited when my mother passed away last year, we can now afford a visiting American instrumentalist every once in a while. It turned out that my father's estate didn't go down in the crash. He was a rotten old grump but evidently had been a very canny one. It's very good for the boys to work with a top-notch jazz and blues musician. They do their best, and that's pretty good, and this is their reward. It's very good for Toronto, too. It gives Joe and me great encouragement when the young people stand outside for the afternoon jam sessions and they have the privilege of hearing someone very special playing.'

'I'm glad you're not angry with me for giving up classical music,' I said, relieved.

'Miss Bates believes you could have a concert career ahead of you, but I would be a hypocrite if I tried to persuade you against turning back to jazz. But, if you'll take my advice, sit for the conservatory entrance examination and that way she will know she's done her job. Then I shall inform her that I am no longer willing to pay for your tuition, that now it's up to the conservatory to grant you a bursary. That will be the time to tell her you want a career in jazz. She'll be absolutely furious, of course, but as she herself gave up her concert career when she was at the height of her powers, she may understand. It won't be easy, Jack, but it's your life.'

'And you? I mean you've been paying for my tuition.'

'Jack, let's hope you turn out to be an exceptional jazz musician and I will have been more than compensated. Besides, your mother has paid your tuition fees by cleaning my house all these years.'

It wasn't true, of course. Four mornings a week as a cleaner wouldn't have come near covering my tuition with Mona Bates, but my mom and Miss Frostbite seemed to have become good friends and she was very proud of making a contribution to my career.

War broke out that September, a fortnight after I turned sixteen. The whole eligible male population of Cabbagetown rushed to join up. Toronto was full of men in uniform. If nothing else, war heralded the end of the Depression for the working class. There was talk of factories reopening, and going to war meant a weekly salary coming in for men as well as women; it was the promise of regular work. War was a tragedy for people in Europe and Russia, but in Canada it was seen as a return to the good times.

A year later, in June, I took my grade twelve exams at UTS, two months before my seventeenth birthday, and while I got an A grade, which meant that I could go on to university if I wanted to, it wasn't the most brilliant result and I only just scraped in. But when you play piano three hours every school day, something has to give. I had all but completed eighth grade when I sat for the entrance exam for the conservatory. I played Beethoven's *Pastoral Sonata* in D major and the

G major Prelude from Bach's *Well-tempered Clavier, Book Two*. It was stretching it a fair bit, but I worked my ass off and Mona Bates was fairly certain I could manage both pieces.

She had miscalculated: I failed to impress with the Beethoven. I will never know what happened but I just fell apart on the day. I was devastated, and Mona Bates was furious with me. 'Jack, what on earth happened?' she cried. 'I was confident that you knew the sonata and we'd done the work. Stupid boy! You got it wrong, wrong, wrong and wrong again!'

We were both bitterly disappointed, but mostly my disappointment was for her. I hadn't yet told her I wasn't going to go to the conservatory. Mona Bates's students didn't fail; I'd been the first to do so and I believed I had thoroughly disgraced her.

But then a week later we got a letter from the chief examiner, and in it he said that attempting to play that movement of the *Pastoral* was more than they required for eighth grade, and as I was only being examined to enter at that level, they had decided to give me another opportunity because I had played the G major Prelude with assurance. Miss Bates was still angry with me and felt that I'd let her down, but this time around I played a study from Clementi's *Gradus ad Parnassum* that I had worked on for ages and *The Tempest*, Beethoven's sonata in D minor. After it was over, the chief examiner, Mr Hogan, told Mona Bates that not only had I passed but I had done so with flying colours, and that they greatly looked forward to welcoming me into the 1940 conservatory year, beginning in August.

Mona Bates was clearly relieved she had an unblemished record for her students but on the way back to her studio in the streetcar she said, 'Jack, I can't help feeling you've lost some of your enthusiasm. I know you had to work hard on your final school exams and perhaps that's it. I hope to continue being your teacher after you enter the conservatory, but you'll have to buck up, my boy. From now on, if you want a concert career, then you're going to have to learn what real application and dedication mean.'

Normally I would have continued on in the streetcar after she got off at Jarvis Street, but I asked if I could come back with her to the studio.

She looked surprised. 'Isn't this a rare day off for you, Jack? You've passed your entrance exam. I don't expect to see you back until your Monday lesson.'

'It shouldn't take long, Miss Bates,' I replied. I wasn't a timid small boy any more, but I can tell you I wasn't looking forward to the next half hour. Mona Bates wasn't an easy person to confront and I knew she regarded me as one of her star students.

Fortunately the studio wasn't far from the streetcar stop, and for three weeks there had been guys with jackhammers digging up the road, much to the annoyance of Miss Bates, who complained, 'While the government invents needless work for the shiftless and the lazy, they're driving those of us who work for a living to utter distraction.' She'd called to complain twice and was unimpressed with the response she received, telling them in no uncertain terms that she was Miss Mona Bates and that they hadn't heard the last of the matter. As she knew everyone of importance in Canada, including the prime minister, Mr Mackenzie King, it wouldn't have surprised me if she'd called him personally to complain. Now I was glad of the jackhammering, because the noise meant we didn't have to talk until we were in the privacy of her studio.

'Well, Jack, what is it?' She pointed to the lobby couch. 'Shall we sit?' It was more a command than a suggestion. She walked ahead of me and sat down. 'Out with it.'

'Miss Bates, I don't want to go to the conservatory,' I blurted out.

'Oh?' I waited for her to say something more but she remained silent.

'I want to be a jazz musician.' Then I added, 'I don't want to be a classical pianist.'

To my surprise she didn't explode but remained silent. Finally, she said, 'That's why you deliberately messed up the Beethoven, wasn't it?'

'No! Not at all, I promise!' I protested, appalled at her accusation.

'Well then, you know what you've done, don't you, Jack?'

I'd expected her to be furious and yell at me, so this quiet, even voice she was affecting was disconcerting. 'No, Miss Bates.'

'You've elected to be a *nobody* when you might have been a *somebody*.'

'I . . . I don't see it like that, Miss Bates.'

'Oh, of course you don't, you're still wet behind the ears.'

'But, Miss Bates —'

'Don't be impertinent, Jack! You're giving up years of study, and for what? To play in some smoke-filled basement with third-rate musicians when perhaps you could have played in the great concert halls of the world – Vienna, Milan, Paris, London, New York . . .'

'You gave up *your* concert career, Miss Bates.' I knew I was being provocative, in fact, clearly overstepping the mark.

Then the explosion came. 'How dare you! You think it was easy . . . a woman alone, lonely, often exhausted, in a hotel room by myself or with some jumped-up impresario trying to get me into bed? I always put my art first. I was dedicated, diligent and I didn't complain about the pokey changing rooms, bad organisation, arrogant European concert organisers, pedantic and stupid conductors, ignorant audiences!'

I could have said touché, but instead I said, 'But then you wisely decided to quit. Miss Bates, I don't want all that. I don't want to be a concert pianist,' I pleaded. 'I want to play jazz piano and what I've learned from you will be the best possible training anyone could have.'

'Balderdash! Don't patronise me, Jack!'

'I'll be eighteen next year and I'll have to join up. I'd have to leave the conservatory after only one year anyhow.' It was a futile attempt at amelioration.

'Oh? That's your excuse for not continuing, is it?'

'No, that would be a lie. It's just that I want to play jazz. I want to make it my future. I'm truly sorry, Miss Bates. I just can't . . . I just *can't* do it.'

'What about your poor mother?'

'She's disappointed, I admit. But she understands that I've made up my mind.'

'Well, I don't suppose someone from her background would know any better,' Miss Bates said, her tone acerbic, lips pursed. She'd been so kind to my mom and this is what she truly thought of her?

'My mother thinks very highly of you, Miss Bates. She is enormously grateful for what you did for her, letting her sit with you at concerts and the dresses and shoes. She thinks it's one of the most generous and kind things that has ever happened to her.' It wasn't very often anyone got the better of Miss Bates. 'She just wants the best for me,' I added, immediately feeling guilty and trying to soften the smart-ass comeback somewhat.

'Doesn't everyone! All those years I've put in so you'd have the best chance possible to dig yourself out of poverty! I am appalled and humiliated! You've let me down, and as far as I'm concerned you are a disgrace and I have wasted my time and my gifts trying to teach you!'

'I'm truly sorry. I hope some day to make you proud of me, Miss Bates.'

'Proud? I've given you the benefit of the best teaching in Canada and you turn on me like a rabid, snarling wolf. I had high hopes for you, Jack. Playing jazz is like spitting at my feet! Proud? Of what? Your return to the gutter? I don't think so, boy!'

'You've taught me wonderfully, Miss Bates. I will always be grateful to you.'

'Well, I must say, you have a very strange way of demonstrating your gratitude, Jack Spayd. We, Floss Byatt and I, pulled you out of a stinking social sewer and now you're diving straight back into it! How dare you insult us both like this!'

'I have already spoken to Miss Byatt. She has accepted my decision.' I didn't tell Mona Bates this had taken place almost a year previously.

'Spoken to her? You've spoken to *her* before you spoke to *me*?' Her cheeks had blown out and her eyes were so furious they were practically spitting sparks. She was nearly apoplectic. It was the worst possible thing I could have said and now she completely lost control. She jumped to her feet and leaned over me, her lips spit-flecked. 'I am your teacher and you . . . Oh! I knew I should never have trusted Floss Byatt! She disgraced her family and became a soldiers' slut! Everyone in Toronto knows that place she calls a jazz club is just a brothel in disguise! And as for that disgusting old black man in his pale blue satin suit and their gauche and sickly sentimental piano duo, it's horrible, cheap and thoroughly nasty!' She pointed to the front door. 'Go to Jezebel's arms, boy!'

I hesitated, wanting to defend Miss Frostbite, but at that moment she screamed, 'Go! I never wish to see your face again! Damn you, Jack Spayd. I hope you have a truly rotten life!'

As I closed the front door to leave Jarvis Street forever, I was glad I didn't say what I had in mind because that would have made me as nasty to her as she'd been to me, and I had no cause to do that. Leaving Jarvis Street forever was terribly sad. I'd seen it in summer heat and when the maple leaves changed colour to the rose red and pure gold of fall. Mona Bates had taught me everything I knew about music. She'd taken a small boy and turned him into a good musician. The rest was now up to me.

Could I make it to the top in jazz? It was a momentous and perhaps a foolish decision for a boy to make and her curse, *'Damn you, Jack Spayd. I hope you have a truly rotten life!'*, was to haunt me for the rest of my days.

CHAPTER FIVE

————

SO THERE I WAS, tossing away the best opportunity I'd ever had, or was ever likely to have. Brilliant decision! But I just couldn't see myself under the bright lights playing classical piano.

Over the years Miss Bates had mentioned the life she'd led as a concert pianist and why she'd finally given it up. The stories came in dribs and drabs, often as casual asides, and I knew she wasn't saying all this to discourage me, but simply to toughen me up – a grown-up reminding a kid that life is never easy and success is a long, hard road.

From memory, it went something like this: 'Now, Jack, if you're going to be among the one per cent who get to the very top in this profession, you're going to have to give it everything you've got, every waking minute of your life. You're going to have to do your apprenticeship in the larger towns and smaller cities, in halls with bad acoustics and in front of audiences who are less interested in the quality of your playing than they are in being *seen* by others.

'You'll have to become accustomed to fat sanguineous old men in evening suits whose wives have dragged them, bellowing, to your concert and who, after half an hour, are fast asleep and snoring. At the conclusion of your performance they'll be wakened with a sharp dig in the ribs and then, taking their cue from their wives, they'll jump to their feet clapping and yelling "Bravo!"

'You'll live in cheap hotels, eat bad food and be invited after the performance to endlessly boring dinners with the local mayor, his wife, and those members of the community he's hoping to impress with his sophistication.

'The local newspaper critic, who probably failed grade three, will comment on the inaccurate way you played a Beethoven sonata – too soft, too loud, at the wrong tempo and most certainly not the way Beethoven intended it to be played.

'It's all a part of your training and there's no guarantee you'll move further up the ranks. You may never become a member of the elite, play at Carnegie Hall, travel the world and receive the applause from the *cognoscenti*, people who come to hear you because they love the way you play. But I believe you have the talent; the rest is persistence and dedication and a ruthless will to succeed. You *must* show me you have these qualities as well,' she would say.

Of course, she had no idea that I still loved jazz and assumed that classical music had taken possession of my soul and was all I lived for. But I craved participation, rather than the solitary glory of the soloist; I loved improvising and the spontaneous response of people who hear the beat and the bump and the grind in their heart and soul.

That's not to say for one moment that I didn't enjoy, even at times love, playing classical music, because I did and knew I always would. Music is its own reward but I would carry in my heart forever my mom's pride as she clutched to her chest the blooms I'd won and smiled her shiny new smile.

But in the end I was the son of a garbage collector and a cleaning woman, an Anglo-Celtic gentile Canadian boy from the slums of Cabbagetown, and I wasn't heir to generations of European culture and musical tradition. I needed different rhythms to make my blood race and my heart beat faster.

Boys of seventeen can be difficult and stubborn and convinced they know everything, and I guess I was no different. There would be times when I would regret the impetuosity of my youth, but now ambivalence had no part in my life, and every decision needed to be unequivocal. I saw the dream clear and clean as if in a polished crystal ball – Jack Spayd, earning respect at the jazz piano.

The boy who thought all his Christmases had come at once when his mother managed to buy a soup bone from the cut-price butcher, who dipped his spoon into the delicious broth and sipped it slowly to make it last, was one day going to show the world how to play jazz piano so that everyone sat up and took notice. What I could imagine myself achieving in jazz piano I never imagined with classical piano. I knew myself capable of tremendous concentration, perhaps to the point of addiction, but I couldn't reach the pinnacle in both classical and jazz at the same time, so one of them had to take precedence over the other.

But what could I have possibly known? I was barely seventeen, and young for my age, that is, if you compared my experience of life with that of your average slum kid, who by seventeen belonged to a street gang trained in petty crime and had already received his first tongue-lashing from an exasperated magistrate. While I was practising endless scales, the local kids were becoming experts at stripping factories of copper wire, lead piping, faucets and other brass fittings – any stuff you could take apart quickly and quietly while the guard slept in his hut. They sold it to a junk dealer on the Don, who paid them cash and whose yard seemed shut and padlocked during the day but remained open all night to take deliveries.

If piano lessons and hours of practice weren't sufficiently isolating from the normal routine of other young guys in Cabbagetown, I was also a scholarship kid at a private school, where I was clearly a misfit. Clever, bookish, isolated by serious music and unfamiliar with the life and privileges of a well-to-do family, I was caught between the devil and the deep blue sea. If I'd attended tech or a local high school, I might have at least stayed in touch with the world of my childhood. All I had was my mom and my music. Not surprisingly, I was as confused as any boy might be living in a slum while learning to reach for the stars.

I hadn't neglected the harmonica and played jazz as often as possible. I also played jazz piano whenever Joe could fit me in for a lesson. 'You're good, Jazzboy. Just gonna take time and practice. Ain't nothing gonna happen 'less you practise,' he'd say, and I'd long since realised that nothing happens in life without practice. I'd often spend an extra half hour in Miss Frostbite's piano room fooling around with the jazz numbers the band played, but there had been no real opportunity to practise jazz while I was studying classical piano with Miss Bates.

Had I possessed a crystal ball to see the full disaster we euphemistically term life, I could well have changed my mind and returned to the safe and secure world of classical music where, even if you don't hit the big time, you can always find a role as teacher, academic, repetiteur, accompanist or, as a last resort, a regular musical hack.

But life doesn't work that way and we don't have the ability to see the future. When you squander opportunities you inevitably pay for your lack of judgment. But then, in my experience, some (certainly not all) of your more costly mistakes turn out to be the parts of your life where you were the most alive and where the human capital you spent turned out to be a worthwhile investment.

Mistakes seem to me to be the force that changes the status quo and that's not necessarily a bad thing. Most humans hate change. We love to sit clutching our knees within a well-worn, familiar and comfortable groove. We are trained young in the hope of acquiring a set of skills that will grow steadily until we grow old and the final bell tolls. Here lies Jack, who played piano.

The thousands of hours of practice for frenetic travel, polite applause and a bunch of flowers wrapped in cellophane didn't add up to the exciting life my febrile imagination had conjured up. I'd read too many books about here, there and everywhere and firmly believed there were adventures to be had. The harmonica and not the piano seemed the perfect metaphor for where I saw myself going. It was light, bright, versatile and instant and could earn a man a welcome, a meal and a bed wherever he went.

It was not that I wanted to return to the harmonica – my ardent desire was to be a truly good jazz piano player – it was just that, as a Canadian boy who'd emerged bruised from the Depression, my head was full of visions of a vast new land of snow, endless prairie and space, where men were rough and women stoic, where a Mountie always got his man and where cattlemen and lumberjacks rubbed shoulders with adventurers and rogues. Childish, I know, but we are the sum of our own myths and the sons and daughters of our larger environment. I was Canadian and not Russian or Polish or Austrian, and this, I told myself, accounted for my different mindset.

Of course, these imaginings assume I could have made it as a concert pianist in the first place. There was no such certainty. Five or even ten more years at a conservatory were no guarantee that I'd make it onto the hallowed concert stages of Europe and North America. Had I failed, the choices left to me did not fill me with wild excitement. Every kid hopes to grow up and be famous for something; with me it was jazz, not classical piano.

Although, just for the hell of it, I'd sometimes reflect on what might have been. For instance, whenever I see a soloist receiving a sheaf of flowers at the conclusion of a recital, I imagine that I am him. Then moments later I will be going backstage, my black tie ripped free and my sweat-stained collar unbuttoned the moment I'm alone. On the way I'll meet the cleaning woman (ugly term) waiting for me to leave so she can tidy up the mess I've made and then sweep the corridor and the stage before going home. In my mind's eye she's the same age as my mom at around the time she got her new teeth and, like her, she gets home late and exhausted. I'd smile and hand her the flowers and say, 'Here, my dear, brighten up the parlour a bit.'

But the glorious, heart-stopping moment I'd experienced the first time I heard jazz had never left me. Even today, when I hear the grand masters of my idiom, men such as Duke Ellington, Erroll Garner, Ray Charles, Thelonious Monk and, topmost, foremost and every possible most, the incomparable Art Tatum, I want to urgently repent my sins and die a good man simply because I've had a taste of heaven and want more of the same in the afterlife. Great jazz makes my heart race like a furiously beaten set of bongo drums.

Alas, the Cabbagetown boy in me never felt the same way about playing the *Piano Concerto Number 2 in C Minor* by 'Big Hands' Sergei Rachmaninoff, who, by the way, having once heard Art Tatum play at the Onyx Club later told a reporter, 'If this man ever decides to play serious music, we're all in trouble.'

Some of the great classical musicians had started to take jazz seriously around the late 1920s, even incorporating elements of the jazz idiom into their compositions. Three among many notables in the twenties and thirties were George Gershwin with *Rhapsody in Blue, An American in Paris* and *Porgy and Bess*; Maurice Ravel with *Violin Sonata Number 2, Piano Concerto for the Left Hand in D Major* and *Piano Concerto in G Major*; and, even earlier, Igor Stravinsky in 1918 with *Ragtime for Eleven Instruments*. But despite this homage, concert audiences had not yet welcomed black jazz musicians to the great classical music venues in North America and Europe.

Arthur Rubinstein, for instance, would visit the jazz clubs when he was in New York to hear Art Tatum play. On one such occasion at the Onyx Club a noted professor of music walked up to him and said, 'Maestro, this is not your usual habitat.' Rubinstein placed a finger to his lips. '*Shush!* I am listening to the world's greatest piano player.'

Like I said, it wasn't that I didn't enjoy learning classical piano, I did, very much. I am also eternally grateful to Mona Bates, who, by the way, kept her word and never spoke to me again, but who was nevertheless a good person, always generous to my mom and a simply wonderful teacher to the boy she so often castigated. Whenever I do something foolish, which happens frequently enough, her immortal words echo through my mind: 'Stupid boy! Wrong, wrong, wrong and wrong again!'

However, self-analysis and speculation about the future were pointless. War had been declared; the army was where I was headed as soon as I turned eighteen; that is, if it wasn't over by the end of 1941, as some people were speculating in the news.

Anyhow, I had one year to kill before anything much could happen in my life. In the meantime, with my school days over, Miss Frostbite had given me a job as general factotum and kitchen hand in the club. I started at two o'clock in the afternoon doing anything and everything, scrubbing down the kitchen walls and the floor, cleaning ovens and stoves, and washing and polishing the previous night's glasses and ashtrays until the club opened at nine o'clock. Then I became the general dishwasher, running three sinks, one for dishes, one for drink glasses and the third for pots and pans. I knocked off at eleven o'clock, three hours before the club usually closed. Miss Frostbite had decided a boy of seventeen should be in bed before midnight.

I earned six dollars a week, and now that I had to make my way in life Miss Frostbite gave me a choice: I could jam for an hour every night with the band, with twenty minutes of this time allocated to the piano, but it would mean a deduction of two dollars from my salary. Naturally I grabbed the opportunity with both hands. My hope was that, with this experience every night, plus Joe's lessons, I'd be good enough to do a solo improvisation by the end of the year. I'd worked up a piece on the piano based on a theme the band always included in its repertoire.

I had planned to spend the whole year before joining the army on a return to jazz. I hoped Miss Frostbite would let me continue to practise in her piano room, so that I could adapt what I'd learned in classical study to jazz piano. I'd also be taking formal lessons from Uncle Joe, who, while very competent, would never be a great jazz pianist. Nevertheless, he was a great teacher. I wanted to maintain more or less the same schedule as I'd had with Miss Bates, realising that in some ways I was starting all over again, with work hours replacing school hours and jazz lessons replacing classical lessons, and practice replacing any leisure hours I might have had. While my day was now turned upside down, the amount of effort I'd have to put in would be much the same. This was the well-worn, familiar and comfortable groove I was speaking of earlier, and I was as addicted to routine as everyone else.

When I'd approached Uncle Joe about formal lessons shortly after I'd started as a kitchen hand at the club, he'd thrown back his grey peppercorn head and laughed. 'Jazzboy, welcome. Personally I am dee-lighted! You're already good, but you ain't great. That don't happen until you gone out and gotten yo'self some life and done yo'self some dirty livin'. So now we gonna teach you the fine art o' scuffin', so you learn to take care yo'self in dis big bad world that Mr Bad-ass Adolf Hitler want to make even worse, if that possible. In the next three months I is gonna learn you ragtime, swing and big band jazz.' He paused to explain what he meant. 'Dat when you can't improvise none and gotta read the music strict and play accordin'. After you learn all this you gonna go out play yourself some bars, clubs, taverns, hotels, any venue you can find for a musician that eager to learn himself in.'

'Couldn't I just play here at the club? I know the routine and the musicians and you'd be watching and teaching me . . .' Then I added, 'I've been working on a solo piece for piano.'

'Jazzboy, you ain't hearin' me correk!' Uncle Joe said. 'Playin' here at the Jazz Warehouse, what you gonna learn, hey, boy? You gonna learn same old same old. You gonna eat good, wash a few dishes and have yo'self a jolly time. No, sir, I gonna teach you the ways of scuffin' for three month, then you gonna go out, get yo'self gainful employed any how you can wid the piano.' He paused then stabbed me in the chest with a big, bony forefinger. 'And don't you forget your harmonica. Some crazy joints dey don't have no piano, but if you can play good ragtime on your harmonica, they gonna give you some grub and a bed when you hungry and weary. I don't want you should stay here in the big smoke neither.' He chuckled, then appeared to be thinking. 'Now let me see. Maybe Cowtown, Calgary, Alberta? Go mix wid the cowboys, smell yourself some cow shit, eh? What say?'

'But, Uncle Joe, all the good musicians are across the border in New York, Chicago, Memphis, New Orleans – I mean, surely that's where —'

I didn't get to complete the sentence. 'Hey, whoa, Jazzboy! Uncle Joe gonna tell you why you ain't crossin' no border. Now you listen to me good. Firstly and foremost you ain't good enough to mix it wid them cats. What you gonna need is seasonin'. You gotta harden up. Need some space to grow some. What I sayin', you gotta get yo'self some life to put into your music. Dump some ex-peery-ence in them chords. You got talent, sure, but that don't mean nothin', sonny boy. You got yourself a musical education, that gonna be useful later when you growed up a bit. Now, this exact moment we is speakin' . . . why, you just a dumb kid wid a bit o' fancy technique you learned from that piano woman.'

'Jesus, Uncle Joe, go west? It's just cow shit and prairie!'

'That pree-cisely what you gonna need, boy! Log cabining, snowshoes and bad liquor. Now there is also other places you gotta acquaint yourself wid. Edmonton, the Rockies . . . you never seen them mountains? They like you looking in the veri-table face o' God! It put wonder in your soul that gonna go straight back into your music! Then Vancouver, that by the Pacific Ocean that stretch way out to Australia.'

'You want me to go to Australia?' I exclaimed.

'No no, that the end o' the fuckin' world, man!' It was the first time I'd ever heard Uncle Joe use such language. 'I want you should do yo'self a whole parcel o' good. Do some hard things, hungry things, tough-goin' things . . . but good things all the while.'

'But, Uncle Joe, I'm going to join the army in less than a year.' I was implying that this would surely be tough enough. 'I mean, I could get myself killed.'

'Ho! That pree-cisely my whole point. You learn scuffin', you learn a whole lot more than scuffin'. You gonna learn yo'self survival.'

'What does that mean, Uncle Joe? I mean, I understand what you said about playing piano and going west, but in the war if you survive it's not really up to you, is it?'

'My goodness, son, you sure is one big greenhorn! Ever-thing is up to you, boy. Scuffin' – that about learning to figure the odds, you know what I mean?'

'Yes, I think so. You're saying it's about knowing a bit of everything – ragtime, jazz, swing, big band – then sort of instinctively getting to know the joints that might give you work. Is that it?'

'Hey, hey, not so fast, Jazzboy. That only a part; the other part is maybe you learn somethin' about stayin' alive. You ever heard an army band? Soldiers got to have music, not jes for marching but also for their rec-ree-a-tion. They gotta have dance bands for the officers, also dinner music and entertainment for the big brass. That what I gonna learn you and you gonna practise out west. That the scuffin' music that gonna save your butt. Ain't no music playin' in them fox holes they gonna make you dig wid your fingernails. You do that kinda work, your hands ain't gonna be worth a dime next time you meet a piano. You got good hands, big hands, you gotta protect them and also yo'self. You gotta be out the way when the Germ-man come runnin' wid their bay-on-net fixed so you crap your pants and you shiverin' and shakin' so much you can't pull the trigger point blank.' He said it all in a rush of words put together in Joe style with no pauses so that I must have looked blank as I was cobbling it all together in my mind. 'Hey, Jazzboy! You hearin' me good? You understan' what I sayin' to you?'

'Yes, but that would be shirking, Uncle Joe!' I protested, shocked at his suggestion. 'It would be cowardly looking for a cosy, safe job in the army when other guys are out on the battlefield.'

'Shirkin'? Cowardly?' Joe's face took on a look of disdain. 'You got too much Boy Scout in you, Jazzboy! O' course savin' your butt well in advance o' the moment when you got to do it for real ain't cowardly! It in-telly-gent and just plain sensible, you hear? A man don't want to die just because he can't make up his mind, and so he gonna leave it to somebody else, some high-rank dude who gonna do the decidin' for him. When you go out west you ain't gonna practise no dyin'. You gonna practise stayin' alive, man! That the battlefield you gotta learn. This lousy world full o' bad asses like Adolf Hitler. Once you learned them by character you knowed them by action. Only battlefield you gotta learn to know is the battlefield o' life. Ain't no war wid them Germans gonna teach you that.' Joe Hockey paused and jabbed his finger at me once again. 'You got one bad problem . . . you wanna know what it is, Jack the Knife?'

It was a name he'd not previously used for me. 'Only one?' I grinned sheepishly, trying to recover my equilibrium. Joe was stamping down hard on my increasingly battered ego.

'You got too many women bin runnin' your life too long. Time you got yourself a ticket on the Canadian Pacific Rail train. Time to vamoose.' He grinned. '"Go west, young man." It time to tell Miss Frostbite and your mama goodbye, like you already told Miss Bates.'

Joe was never short of a word or an opinion, but he seldom handed out direct advice unless it concerned teaching music. He'd sometimes say, 'White man advice you can take or leave; black man advice you ain't most times gonna bother your head at listenin'.' Then he'd add, 'So, I ain't botherin' my head none wid givin' out that kinda wise-ass stuff.' So, this was a world record for advice. I also knew he wasn't kidding and joking around like he sometimes did and that he meant every word.

Moreover he wasn't wrong. Except for Mac and Joe himself there was an absence of influential men in my life. Both had played important roles, and but for them, I might have grown up thinking most men were bastards like my dad. Mac had introduced me to the Jazz Warehouse and Joe Hockey had found me under the steps and dragged me inside, where my life miraculously began to change. But, like he'd said, it had basically been three women – my mom, Miss Frostbite and Miss Bates – who'd more or less dictated my every move since I was a small boy. No, not three, five women, because you'd have to include Miss Mony and even Mrs Hodgson from the library, who'd taken over from Miss Mony when my reading habits grew more sophisticated.

'Yeah, okay, I hear what you say, Uncle Joe,' I said, perhaps a tad annoyed.

'Okay, Jazzboy, now you heared me and you thinkin' about takin' a black man's advice and you mad at me some. But now I said it, I ain't never gonna say it again. By the way, Floss want to see you pronto.' He said this last bit in the same tone as the general flow of his other words so that I almost missed it.

My heart skipped a beat. 'Is it about my job in the kitchen?' I asked, at once anxious. Disastrously, on my third night as a kitchen hand, I'd dropped a tray and broken twenty cocktail glasses, though fortunately not in front of the club patrons. Just as I was coming into the kitchen I'd slipped on a cocktail snack – we were supposed to call them *hors d'oeuvres* – that a waiter had dropped. I went ass over tea kettle, broken glass was scattered across the kitchen floor, and the chef was near ready to decapitate me with a meat cleaver. Just picking up the glass screwed up the kitchen routine completely and the rest of the night had been a major disaster. Miss Frostbite had entered the kitchen and read the riot act to the furious chef while not saying a word to me. The whole scene hadn't been pretty and I thought she might have been saving her pique for a later time to avoid risking her dignity by shouting at the dishwasher.

'I ain't sayin', 'cept it ain't about them Manhattan glasses you broke,' Joe chuckled.

Miss Frostbite wasn't in her apartment when I called around, so I decided I'd catch up with her later when I came on shift that afternoon. I could arrive fifteen minutes early. It wasn't one of my mom's cleaning days so I'd stay and have lunch with her.

When I got home Mom kissed me then pointed to the kitchen sideboard. 'Note there for you, Jack.'

'From?'

She shrugged. 'How should I know?'

'Mom!' I said somewhat pointedly. 'You're talking to me, your beloved son Jack, who's been with you seventeen years, remember?' It was nice being able to answer back after the verbal hiding I'd taken from Joe Hockey.

'It's from Mac.'

'And?'

'He wants to meet you after you get out from work tonight. He'll be waiting outside the Jazz Warehouse.'

'Did he say why?'

'No, just that. Read it for yourself.'

'Thanks, Mom. Can you make a cuppa? I need to talk with you about something that happened this morning.'

'Oh, Jack! They've fired you over breaking them cocktail glasses, haven't they!'

'No, Mom. It's about a long talk I had with Uncle Joe this morning. Make the tea and I'll tell you.'

She made a jam sandwich and a cup of tea for each of us, and we ate lunch and I told her about going west and scuffing.

'Scuffing? It don't sound very nice, Jack. What is it exactly?' my mom asked, looking anxious.

'Gaining experience, moving around, learning how to stay alive. You know, feeling the pressure of making a living, getting exposed to the world outside, learning about life by playing music,' I explained.

'Don't them things happen here in Cabbagetown every day?' She was now beginning to look decidedly upset.

I explained how, in Joe's opinion, it was essential if I wanted to become a jazz piano player. But, long before I'd finished speaking, the tears began to roll silently down her cheeks. I didn't tell her about Joe's lecture on survival and finding a job playing music in the army because, despite what Joe said, I still wasn't sure I wouldn't be dodging my duty.

Finally, when I fell silent, she sniffed and used the backs of her hands, like a little girl might do, to brush away the tears. 'Oh, Jack, you're going to go west then return and join the army, and you might die,' she sniffed.

There it was again, the war and dying. 'Mom, who knows? The war might be over by then, for all we know. Lots of people are saying it might.' I'd been so busy telling her about scuffing that I hadn't given a thought to her. I was all she had in the world. Once I left she'd be on her own and terribly lonely. Sometimes the plans we make for ourselves have consequences for others we can't do a lot about, but I felt sure that in her mind she'd calculated on my being with her until I turned eighteen, when I'd be off to the war. The news of my departure would have come as a nasty shock.

'I hope so, Jack. I do hope so, but the prime minister says we need to prepare for a long conflict, and he's right about most things,' she said softly.

I'd always planned that some day I'd hit the trail and kick the dust, or plough through the slush and snow of the Canadian prairies, but I'd seen this happening later in my life, maybe after I'd returned from the war. It was one of those *sometime whenever and possibly never* ambitions we all carry in our heads, often into our dotage, like sailing singlehanded around the world in a 30-foot yacht or climbing in the Himalayas, or dog-sledding across Alaska, or some other wild dream of the ultimate adventure. I'd often enough 'gone west' in my imagination and I'd read half a zillion books set in the Canadian prairies, Alaska and the Yukon. Canada was a vast country – I owed it to myself to explore it.

However, once his 'do it now' advice had sunk in I realised Joe Hockey was right about leaving the primary influences in my life and heading westwards. I had only left my mom's side for two nights in my entire seventeen years, when Miss Bates and I had travelled overnight by train to Montreal to a piano competition. Travelling overnight on a train in effect meant I hadn't really seen anything more than railway stations on the way, and a bit of Montreal going from the station to the concert hall, and returning in the early evening to the station.

While my excitement mounted at the prospect of heading west, it was nonetheless a somewhat scary notion to drop everything and head out of town with nothing in my back pocket but a battered harmonica. But the more I thought about it the more I began to embrace the idea. I'd been on a strict schedule since the age of seven and I'd largely lost the sense of careless, casual and intrepid adventure a boy of my age might possess. Even the girls often kicked over the traces. For instance, the twins had fulfilled Mac's worst fears by leaving school at sixteen despite, according to their teachers, being exceptionally bright. They'd left Toronto for Montreal to work for Dolly's sister in her fish-and-chip shop. Seven years later they'd returned from their various adventures in an altogether different feminine guise from the lowly one their mother had envisaged for them as well-trained working-class women, at the lower end of the social pecking order: equipped to mind children, change nappies, cook and scrub other people's kitchen floors in return for a daily pittance and the breakfast, lunch and dinner leftovers.

The Depression had left the rich both greedy and mean. With so many near-destitute women to choose from, for the most part they treated their domestics like slaves. But the twins had envisaged their working lives differently and, judging from their looks and the way they behaved, they had rarely scrubbed floors when they'd been down on their knees.

I'd learned of their return to Toronto in the final months of my senior matriculation. Occasionally a kitchen hand would fail to turn up and I'd work the last half of a shift washing dishes and clearing glasses from the tables. The head waiter who'd instructed me had emphasised, 'You lift the empty glass from the table when the patron's attention is some other place, on the stage or talking to someone; now it's there and then it isn't. You're the glass ghost, Jack.' Like my mom, I didn't want any payment, but at the end of the week if I'd done an extra half shift, Miss Frostbite would add a couple of dollars to my streetcar fare. It was usual for someone doing my job to put on a waiter's long apron for ten minutes every hour to enter the club and retrieve the dirty glasses. Washing and polishing cocktail glasses was my main job. It was on one such occasional shift that I saw the twins for the first time since they'd left. Surprise wasn't the right word for how I felt. I almost dropped the tray of glasses I was carrying. Both were with men much older than themselves, and I knew immediately that it wasn't simply because the twins preferred the company of older men.

If I seem to have pre-judged them, I assure you, one didn't need to be Einstein to know what was going on. The heavy make-up, revealing dresses and high heels, the highly suggestive dancing, told you all you needed to know about the profession they'd decided to pursue.

We'd ignored each other like always, but this time it was a management instruction. They were patrons and the rule was that the hired help only responded if first spoken to – collecting glasses was a silent and hopefully unobtrusive operation. The twins either hadn't recognised me or they didn't let on.

Now, with the last of my pimples finally gone, I was big, somewhat clumsy and, when it came to young women, more than a little naïve. Their presence intimidated me more than it ever had in the stairwell at home. I prayed that they'd maintain their aloofness or that my glass ghosting was so good they wouldn't see me. Then on one occasion – I remember it was on the second-last night before the regular dishwasher returned – Melissa or Clarissa had winked at me and the following night had blown me a silent kiss. I have to admit that on both occasions I could feel my face burning and the cocktail glasses on the tray I carried set off a clinking tintinnabulation as my hands started to shake.

Even just looking at them filled me with lust and longing. The nasty teenage brats who had once shouldered me aside in the passageway with the words, 'Oops, sorry! Didn't see you,' had undergone a metamorphosis and turned into two identical but astonishingly sexy creatures. Alas, I confess, I lay in bed at night in what had once been my dad's bedroom, aching with the mental image I'd carried home of a pair of scarlet lips blowing me a kiss, my overheated imagination finally no longer able to resist the dark impulses that had my heart thumping and set my hand to doing its urgent relief work.

Two spectacular and identical new young creatures appearing on the Toronto nightclub scene didn't pass without comment and I learned that they'd bought a nice apartment downtown and paid cash for it. Rumour had it that you didn't bother to call them unless you were filthy rich. The fact that the men on whose arms they appeared were never young and handsome seemed to confirm this, and despite the Depression, they would invariably summon the cocktail waiter who'd served them, then make a point of being seen to tip him a five-dollar bill, in those hard times a very big gratuity. I was more interested in watching each of the girls leave, sashaying along with the delicious bounce of firm buttocks under a tight silk dress, the sight of which drained most of the blood in my body to a central location.

On one occasion, when I'd been fairly close and was watching Melissa or Clarissa leave unobserved, she'd suddenly stopped within earshot of where I was standing, tugged at the sleeve of her partner's suit jacket, and said, 'You forgot to tip the cocktail waiter!' Her voice carried easily to the surrounding tables, and I noticed something else – they'd left behind the argot of Cabbagetown and assumed awfully swanky accents.

'Oh, ah . . . next time,' the guy grunted, clearly embarrassed. You could see he wasn't accustomed to being pulled into line.

'No! Now!' Clarissa or Melissa demanded. 'He's probably got a wife and kids at home.'

The man had called the cocktail waiter over and, grunting, slipped him a five. So, I had to hand it to whichever twin she was, she had guts and hadn't entirely forgotten her humble beginnings.

A week or so later Mac was waiting outside the club when I came out of Miss Frostbite's piano room after the last bit of early-evening practice. 'We knocked off early 'cause the foreman had to go to a funeral, so I dropped around for the jam and thought we might walk home together,' he suggested. Even though I had the money to pay the streetcar fare for both of us, it seemed like a nice idea. Any time spent with Mac was time well spent. He was more a buddy than a mentor these days, and while I'd ask for advice, I had no qualms giving it as well. This was perhaps partly because of his size – by now he could have fitted neatly under my outstretched arm.

Shortly after we'd set out for home he announced, 'The twins are back in town.'

'Hey, that's nice for you,' I replied, not telling him that I already knew.

'Hmm, not sure about that,' he mumbled, but explained no further. Mac was a proud man in his own way and as we both had lots to talk about, we went on to other topics. He hoped to join up, and said with one of his rare laughs, 'Jack, fighting the Germans won't be nothing after all my years living with Dolly.'

I would have loved to know what Dolly thought about her recently returned daughters, who, as it were, now worked under the flip side of the quilts she'd taught them to make. Naturally I never mentioned their regular appearance in the club to Mac. I wondered why he'd come to see me after my shift. It must have been fairly urgent or he'd have waited until the next time we met, which we made a point of doing at least once a week, even if sometimes only briefly.

It was late September and while there was a definite nip in the air, it was nice being out of the steaming kitchen, where I'd spent most of the night up to my elbows in soapsuds. We'd barely got underway when Mac said, 'Jack, I want to ask your advice. The twins have come up with something.'

Apart from the disconcerted mumble when he'd first told me they'd arrived back in town, Mac had never mentioned them to me again, correctly assuming, I expect, that there was little to tell me I didn't already know.

'What is it, Mac?'

'They want Dolly and me to move into a garden apartment they've bought in High Park North. But I don't know that it's such a good idea. It's a pretty snooty neighbourhood, as you know, and I'm not at all sure it's for such as Dolly and me. It seems they made a bit of money in Montreal and with houses and apartments now cheap as chips they wanted us to own our own place.'

'That's nice, Mac, that's real nice,' I replied.

'Yes, but you see they've given us a choice. They've also bought the house in Cabbagetown. We can stay there if we want.'

My heart sank. Whatever happened, Dolly would give us the instant shove and my mom would have nowhere to go. 'Dolly know all this?'

'Yeah, but for once she can't make up her mind. She's got all her friends in Cabbagetown.'

'No, what I meant was about the twins owning our house?'

Mac looked taken aback. 'Jack, buddy, what do you take me for? I've made them promise that whatever happens you can stay until the end of the war. You see, we either stay put or it's an investment for later, that's why they bought it in the first place.' Then he added as an afterthought,

'They know they can't sell it now, and you're actually doing them a favour by paying rent.'

'Thanks, Mac, I'm grateful. Mind if I don't tell my mom for now?'

'Of course.'

'So you want my opinion – move or stay – is that it?'

'Yeah. I'd like to know what you think.'

'That's simple, Mac, you move to High Park North. The other day you called Cabbagetown a shit hole and you're dead right, I can't think of a better word to describe it.' I laughed. 'Mind you, perhaps we've got something to be proud of. I read in the paper the other day that Cabbagetown is the largest Anglo-Saxon slum or, if you like, shit hole in North America.'

'You think we should then?' he asked. After a moment or two he said, 'I don't know, buddy. Have you seen them big houses and gardens in High Park? There's garages for cars!'

'C'mon, Mac, how long is it since you walked down one of our streets? The buildings are shit houses, bug- and rat-infested and in need of repair. Everywhere smells of rot, old wallpaper and mould. In the winter it's dirty snow and coal smoke. It's a bit better now the chemical factories have closed – at least your eyes don't water – but all of Cabbagetown still smells of shit. I mean, do you really have to think about staying or vamoosing?' (Like conversating, vamoosing was a 'Joe word' I'd decided to adopt.) 'Cabbagetown is a broken-down old whore and High Park is a sassy lady.' I'd read that somewhere and enjoyed being able to use it.

'Yeah, but still and all, it's what we know, where we come from,' he mumbled.

High Park was pretty swanky – one of the better suburbs in Toronto, with this big park right at the centre with fancy houses and low-rise expensive-looking apartments surrounding it. My mom and I used to occasionally go there on our weekend walks. Just by visiting the High Park neighbourhood you definitely got the impression you were a long way from the scruff and general deterioration of Cabbagetown. But still, vehement as I'd been about his moving away, I knew exactly what Mac was worried about. It was about fitting in; he was scared of sticking out like a sore thumb.

'Well, it's a nice thing the twins have done for you both and for my mom and me, but you say Dolly's not sure?' I replied.

'Yeah. Devil you know, sort of.' He looked at me. 'Know what I mean, Jack?'

'Mac, why bother asking me for my opinion? Whatever Dolly decides will happen. A house is a woman's decision; men don't come into it.'

'Yeah, I know, but the twins are no longer under their mother's thumb and they take none of her bullshit no more. They want it to be *my* decision. As a matter of fact, they're insisting it's what I want to do that matters.'

I threw back my head and laughed. 'And if you make the wrong decision, guess who lands in the shit.'

Mac grinned. 'So what's new?'

There would never be a better opportunity to ask him, so I said, 'Mac, what does Dolly think about the twins returning and . . . you know what I mean . . . the rest of it?'

Mac grinned again. 'You *really* want to know?'

I nodded and smiled a little sheepishly. 'It's a bit personal I know, so don't say if you don't want, but I've often wondered how she felt when they returned from Montreal.'

'Okay, the whole of Toronto seems to know about the twins, so what the hell. It doesn't matter now anyhow. Well, after a while Dolly couldn't ignore the rumours no more, you know, what was staring her in the face, so she sat me down one night and handed me a bottle of Molson's. She'd actually opened it for me. "Siddown, Mac, I've got something to say to you," she says. Well now, handing me a Molson's wasn't her usual way of going about things, except maybe on Christmas or my birthday, but when she went and fetched a glass as well I started to *really* worry. So, hoping for the best, I poured the beer and sat down, not sure what to expect. Then she drew up a chair and sat right up close to me, I mean real close. She sort of clamped my knees between hers. I couldn't move an inch. You know how big she is. I reckon if she'd clamped them any tighter I'd'a lost me circulation and never took another step again!'

I'd never heard Mac talk in such a personal way about his wife before. He must have really wanted to get this off his chest, but maybe he hadn't the courage, or felt too ashamed or something. Now he continued.

'She seemed to fill the room, you couldn't see nothing either side of her.' He laughed, recalling the moment. 'If I'd wanted to take a sip of my beer I'd have needed to lift the glass over her boobs. I tell you, buddy, I could barely breathe.

'"What is it, Dolly?" I ask.

'"Now don't you go judging the twins, you hear, Mac?" she says right off, leaning forward so I can smell her breath.

'"Judging? How do you mean?" I ask her.

'"Just judging!" she shouts. "Every woman has to do her duty when there's a war on. If they can't fight, they can send our boys away happy. Some of them kids ain't comin' back and God understands this!"

'"You mean when there's a war on, God grants women special permission to . . . yer know, be extra kind to soldiers?"

'"Only the good ones, not the Germans. It's our special women's way of thanking them for protecting our families. The twins have decided to help the war effort. They're doing their bit for their king and country!" She stabbed me in the chest with her finger. "Yer hear me now, Mac, I don't want no judging!"

'"Dolly, you're not serious!" I say, flabbergasted.

'"Don't you *dare* look at me like that! Mr Mackenzie King says what our women do is just as important for Canada as the men going overseas: working in the factories making war supplies, farming, driving ambulances, doing hospital work and all that."

'"But he didn't say they should, you know . . ."

'"Oh yes he did! He said we should *entertain* the boys, give them a good time, that it's all a part o' the war effort."

'"Dolly, that's bullshit. Everyone knows Mackenzie King used to find prostitutes and persuade them to give in their trade and turn to God."

'"Mac, you callin' me a liar, are ya? I just told you that's peacetime. War's different. They're not only doing it for Canada but also for our nice new King George and not his shameless brother that's took up with that American woman Mrs Simpson! Gawd only knows where that one's been! Our boys deserve a good country, a nice king and a beautiful memory to take with them when they go overseas to fight."

'"You mean they'll take a memory of the twins with them? Not all of them, I hope?"

'"Don't be smart, Mac!" she yells, not seeing I'm joking.

'"Have the twins said all this to you?" I ask.

'"Don't have to, I know personal from the last war," she says, calm as anything. "We knew our duty them days."

'Holy smoke!' Mac looked at me, his eyes grown wide. 'She says it right off, like she's not ashamed and she'd only done what's right and now the twins will be doing the same.' He stopped and squinted up at me. 'You know something, Jack, I think she's proud of them following in her footsteps. Now the war's come they've got a true purpose that both the prime minister and the king would say was okay. What were a sin yesterday is now being a loyal Canadian that's helping win the war.'

I couldn't help thinking that even as a young woman Dolly would have been a very big girl and she probably would have been capable of making an entire platoon happy prior to their day of departure overseas – Dolly's last hurrah for king and country.

Mac stopped in his tracks and turned to face me. 'Jeez, Jack, life has a strange way of turning out, don'tcha think? I took them in the streetcar to the railway station to send them off to Montreal to work with Dolly's sister in her fish-and-chip shop. Who'd have thought, eh? I remember we had to sell and pawn some stuff to buy their tickets, but I didn't have any money over so they could eat on the train. They had a bread and dripping sandwich each and two apples I bought at the station kiosk with my streetcar fare home.'

'I remember you were dead concerned they'd go off the rails.'

Mac sighed, shrugged and spread his arms. 'Well, it turned out different. Between them they now own their own apartment downtown, and the one at High Park and the house we both live in.'

'That's not just because they're pretty, that takes brains,' I replied.

'Yeah, damn right. Dunno where they came from, though. Dolly and me don't have a decent brain between us.'

'You're selling yourself short, Mac.'

He propped and turned again. 'Jack, when Dolly told me about, yer know, her war effort, sending them soldiers away happy, it all fell into place.'

'What did?'

'The twins; you'd agree they don't – thank gawd – look like me, nor Dolly neither. More like, you know, refined, better class.' He looked at me steadily. 'Well now, that ain't entirely impossible, Jack. We were both just kids when we sort of started going together, not all that regular neither. I was doing my apprenticeship with an upholsterer out the lakes way, staying at a boarding house during the week and comin' back to Cabbagetown weekends to see my folks and also to squire Dolly.'

'How'd you meet?' I asked as we continued to walk.

'Meet? We didn't, we're the same age and we'd been at school together since we were little kids. It just sort of happened. My parents and hers were friends. They lived just three doors away from us. It was always, you know, expected; her and me were an item.' Mac shrugged. 'That's mostly how it happened them days.'

'You didn't love her or anything?'

Mac laughed at the thought. 'Nah, nothing like that. Dolly was getting taller and I wasn't growing none too fast. I suppose we were both kinda misfits. She was already six foot in her teens and I'm five foot one inch. I have to say it, she was big but not fat back then, and not too bad on the eye neither.

'I had to work until midday each Saturday and Dolly was working as a waitress downtown all week and Saturday until 7 o'clock at night. In them days unless there was a dance or a party at someone's place you didn't go out Saturday night. So I'd only see her mostly Sundays, when we went to church and then we'd have lunch with my folk or hers, alternate like. Then I'd have to start back to the lakes. We were sort of engaged but goin' to wait until my apprenticeship was over and we'd both be eighteen. But the war broke out, of course, although I was too young to join up.

'Anyhow, Dolly started to volunteer at night as a waitress, doing her duty for king and country at an officers' canteen. She'd get home real late and sleep in Sunday mornings, so I was lucky if I saw her for an hour before lunch. We'd go for a walk along the Don or to Queens Park.

'I completed my apprenticeship just before my eighteenth birthday. The war had been going for two years, and Dolly had changed a lot. She was much more worldly in her ways and used different words, like more lah-de-dah ones, and even swore sometimes. She was always goin' on about the officers at the canteen, but somehow we were still together.

'As soon as I turned eighteen I wanted to join up, but my birthday was on a Sunday. I remember we went for a walk along the banks of the Don, and we were walking along chatting – well, she's chatting and I'm listenin' – when suddenly we came to this group of bushes a bit away from the path. "Come on, soldier boy, it's your birthday!" She laughs and takes me by the arm and drags me into the bushes. "Get your pants down!" she says.' Mac laughed. 'I'm still a virgin. I didn't know a thing except how to jerk off.'

I laughed nervously. I wasn't used to adults talking like that, and also because Mac might as well have been talking about me. 'Jesus, Mac, what did you do?' I was trying to imagine how I would have acted but all I could see in my mind's eye was the Dolly I'd always known – a giant – in the bushes and it wasn't a beautiful or seductive vision, I can tell you.

'Jack, you're about the same age as I was . . . I don't know how much I should tell you,' Mac said a little sheepishly. He'd gotten carried away telling me the story and forgotten my age, and I suppose he was now remembering my innocence as well.

'Mac, I'm going scuffing. I'm a virgin like you were, so maybe you can tell me something useful, you know, in case I find myself in a similar situation.'

'Okay, but understand, Jack, I'm no expert. I knew damn all then, and I still don't know that much. You'd be better asking Joe Hockey or one of the musicians at the Jazz Warehouse.'

'But what happened in the bushes? You can't just leave it like that,' I said.

'Well, I'm too surprised to, you know, get a hard-on. "I ain't got no rubbers," I say.

'Dolly just reaches into her bag and hands me one. "Your second birthday present," she says. Then she unbuttons my fly and gets to work on me, and we fit the rubber and I'm up for it. She lifts her dress and pulls down her bloomers and . . .' Mac pauses. 'I'm not sure how she managed it, but next thing I know I'm in. Holy shit! But I ain't no Casanova, it's biff-bam-thank-you-ma'am. I'm ashamed of meself because I should've lasted longer or something.'

I couldn't help laughing but I was curious too. 'How come Dolly knew all that stuff?'

'At the time it don't occur to me, only much, much later. I apologised and Dolly said it don't matter, at least I ain't going to the war a virgin and she'd done her duty for king and country and happy birthday.'

'How did it feel?' I asked. 'I mean, did you feel any different afterwards?' It was a serious question.

'Nah, just a bit of a failure because it'd been so quick. But by next morning, on my way to the recruitment centre, I was quite pleased. I imagined myself in the barracks and being able to say honestly that I'm not a virgin. I've got, like, bragging rights. But of course I got knocked back: flat feet and too short.'

'Then you must have known this time they were going to reject you?'

'Yeah. I sort of hoped maybe the rules had changed, but obviously they hadn't.'

'Go on, so what happened next?'

'Well, when she heard I'd been rejected Dolly gave me the cold shoulder. She wouldn't have nothin' to do with me no more.' Mac glanced at me. 'She even gave me an envelope with a white feather in it, calling me a coward. A fucking coward!'

'Holy smoke! She did that?' I exclaimed. 'A white feather, but, but . . . she knew you'd tried to enlist. I mean, it wasn't your fault you were rejected!'

'You know Dolly, she ain't the forgiving type, even then.'

'So how come you got together again?'

Mac stopped and turned to me. 'That's the whole point of everything I've bin sayin'. It all made sense when she told me about doing her duty for king and country and the twins doing the same.' He turned and threw his fists in the air and looked up like he was appealing to the Almighty. 'Jack, I am some dumb fucker!' he yelled.

'Mac, you're not dumb, I assure you,' I said, putting a hand on his shoulder in an attempt to comfort him.

'Yeah, thanks, Jack, but let's be honest. Anyhow, a month after it's all off and she'd given me the white feather I got home from looking for a job, and her parents and mine were at my place and Dolly was with them. Then Dolly starts sniffing and acting kinda tearful. Well, it turns out she's pregnant and she's told them about my birthday present. It ain't no big deal, like now. Most of the girls were knocked up by sixteen, and she's eighteen so practically an old maid. "We'll arrange the weddin' pronto," Tom Butcher says, that's her father. Everyone nods, that is, 'cept me.

'"No, I ain't doing it!" I shake my head and say. "She handed me a white feather when they wouldn't take me in the army!" They can all see I'm mad as hell, like all the disgrace and stuff is coming out.

'"She what?!" her father shouts. "A white feather? She did that to you, young Mac?"

'"Yeah," I say. I don't even call him Mr Butcher, like usual.

'He's a real big guy, bigger even than your dad, Jack. He gets up from his chair and whacks Dolly across the head so hard she falls off the chair. Nobody says nothin', not even my mother. What she's done can't be forgiven. Dolly gets up and she ain't even blubbin'. Sniffin' a bit, but that's all. But she's got a black eye coming, sure as mustard.'

'So, I mean, what happened then?' I asked.

'Well, her old man takes mine to the tavern and they get legless and come home supportin' each other and singing "Daisy" and the wedding's on. They don't even wait until her black eye is gorn.'

'Oh,' is all I can think to say, and then, 'Tough luck.'

'Six months later the twins are born.'

'Six months!' I exclaim. Even I know it takes nine months.

'Yeah, well, they said they was three months premature. They looked okay to me, but what would I know? I'm no expert on what's premature and what's not.'

'But surely folk would have remarked. I mean, when they saw the twins?'

'What, in Cabbagetown? You should know. "Premature" was a word used as often as "pregnant". Nobody took no notice. Besides, all the girls, even from school, were dead scared of Dolly Butcher. They knew not to mess with her.'

'Jesus, Mac. What are you saying?'

'Well, it took me a long time to figure it out. I mean, it stands to reason, don't it? I'm wearing a rubber. It ain't broke or anything, I remember that much.'

'So you think . . . ?'

'It ain't too hard to figure out, is it? The twins don't look like me or Dolly or anyone in our families.'

'But they've got red hair like Dolly and you.'

'Yeah, perhaps that's why I never questioned it until now. But Toronto's full of redheads, Irish and Scottish, that's not such a coincidence.'

'So, you reckon . . . ?'

'Well, you've seen the twins, Jack. See any resemblance, 'cept the hair?' Mac shrugged. 'Bit late now. Probably wouldn't have made any difference anyhow. I guess you have to take the rough with the smooth in life; whatever will be will be. Poor folk are not usually given a choice, but the twins made one for themselves. That's another reason I think I'm not their father. They went and got themselves out of the shit hole they was born in and I never done that until now and then only with their help.'

'Yeah, they made their own luck. Some people may not like it, but the girls haven't forgotten their parents and that, for a start, says a lot for them.'

'Yeah, I guess. Even if I wasn't their dad, that don't happen every day, do it, Jack?'

'You can say that again, buddy.'

Mac may have been diminutive, but as far as I was concerned he was a giant. He'd stuck by Dolly and the twins through thick and thin, though God knows why. I suppose it was like my mom would have stuck with my dad and continued to take his drunken backhands if he hadn't gone with that Milly woman at the tavern. Poor stupid thing, it wasn't hard to imagine what her nose must look like by now.

So it seemed, despite all her nastiness, Dolly McClymont possessed a strong streak of pragmatism as well as a sense of duty towards king and country. The sad thing was that moving to a swanky apartment in High Park wasn't going to change a thing for Mac. He would still be sleeping with the enemy. I don't mean, of course, in the literal sense, although if nocturnal dalliance still occurred between them this conjured an instant picture in my mind of tiny Mac disappearing between Dolly's gargantuan thighs, never to be seen again. I could see that despite my recommendation they make the move to High Park, he hadn't yet entirely made up his mind. Mac, in his own way, was an independent man, and while he was dead proud of the twins for what they'd done, he couldn't change a lifetime's habit.

'Mac, didn't you say it was a garden apartment?'

'Yeah, but I wouldn't know a rose from a daisy, Jack. It's even got a bit of grass out front.'

'So maybe you could build a shed – your own workshop. You've always wanted one. You know, put in electric light so you can spend evenings there in the summer?'

Mac stopped in his tracks. 'Jack, you're a goddamn *genius*!' he cried, suddenly very excited. 'There's plenty of room out the back. I could have me a turning lathe and build me a proper workbench, eh?' Then, as an immediate afterthought, he said, 'Hey, I could put in heating for the winter as well!'

'Great! Give you a bit of time on your own, buddy.'

He gave me a knowing smile, but then suddenly he stopped, the grin leaving his face. 'But what about us, you and me? Our being buddies? We don't see much of each other now – once a week at the most these days.'

'Mac, something happened this morning with Joe Hockey I need to tell you.' I then began to tell him about Uncle Joe's scuffing tour to far-flung places starting with Cowtown, Calgary. As usual he listened quietly. I then explained why this hardening up was necessary for my future as a jazz pianist and, of course, he already knew I'd be joining the army when I returned.

'Be great to go with yer, Jack. I've always hankered to see the rest of Canada. Be nice to be together a stretch before yer go off to the war.'

I had an instant vision of Mac informing Dolly that, to use Joe's word, he was vamoosing to all points west for nine months with the goddamned little guttersnipe downstairs, informing her just as they were moving into the new apartment in High Park. I didn't like the picture in my imagination of his poor little battered face. I'd seen enough smashed noses to last a lifetime, and now that my dad was no longer around I had decided that as soon as I made a decent salary in a regular job I would pay to have my mom's nose straightened. But with poor little Mac, that would have been a terrible waste of money.

'Yeah, both of us together going west . . . would have been good, Mac,' I said, not wanting to start any more senseless speculation.

'Yeah,' he answered, 'yeah, it sure would have been, buddy.' He sounded resigned, the idea already in the past tense. We both knew Daunting Dolly would be an impossible obstacle to overcome. I reckon if Dolly was standing at the front door with her great big pink hams folded across her enormous bosom, not even Joe Louis, the heavyweight boxing champion of the world, would get past her.

'I'll keep in touch,' I promised, then in an attempt to cheer him up I said, 'Just think, you'll have your workshop truly up and going by the time I return.'

'Then, lucky bastard, you'll be off to the war.'

'Yeah, as soon as I turn eighteen next August.'

Poor Mac, how desperately hard he'd tried to join up, almost going down on his knees and pleading with the recruitment officer. But, alas, he'd been rejected on three major counts: he was one year over the age limit, he was too small, and he had flat feet. Every eligible male in Cabbagetown had practically wrestled each other out of the way to be the first in the voluntary recruitment line. For them it meant the Depression was finally over.

Due to the burgeoning war economy, Mac had all the work he could manage, but people still weren't re-upholstering their couches, which would be a low priority after the Depression. But the point was he had a regular wage coming in. With practically the whole male population strutting around in uniform, it wasn't the same thing, and he found it hard to conceal his disappointment. On one occasion he'd lamented, 'Jack, I'm helping to build a soldiers' canteen at the camp, and I'll never get the chance to relax and share a beer with an army buddy after a day of firing a rifle on the practice range.'

Mac, more than anything, wanted to fly the coop, to leave Canada and fight for his country. But instead, he was stuck with the odious Dolly for the entire duration of the war. Still, a new workshop in High Park would at least be better than remaining in Cabbagetown.

We walked home like old times and when we got to the point where Mac traditionally went on ahead alone he turned to me. 'Jack, you've been real good never mentioning the subject of the twins after they come back from Montreal and don't think I don't appreciate it.'

It was late when we shook hands and Mac disappeared into a Cabbagetown where most of the men were away in a military camp and only women, children and old men slumbered. Dolly must have known for ages about our friendship, but she still hadn't spoken to my mom or me, so Mac and I continued to go through the dumb masquerade of appearing not to be on speaking terms. All I could think was that I hoped Dolly also wanted to move to High Park.

My mom was in bed but still awake when I came in. 'What happened with Miss Frostbite, Jack?' she called. 'I haven't slept a wink from worrying.'

'She said to see her tomorrow afternoon, but she didn't seem angry. I don't think it's about the broken glasses,' I called from the kitchen.

'What did Mac want?' she called out.

'Shhh, Mom!' I called, then hurried from the kitchen to her bedroom. I pointed towards the ceiling. 'They'll hear you if you shout.' I sat on the edge of her bed. 'He wanted to tell me about the twins, you know, tell me himself so I got it from the horse's mouth.' I bent and kissed her on the forehead. 'Go to sleep, Mom. I'll tell you all about it tomorrow.' My mom already knew about the twins from working at the club, so I wouldn't have cause to tell her about the apartment in High Park. She'd love the story of Dolly's contribution in the First World War and I went to bed chuckling to myself. The thought of Dolly servicing a platoon or all the officers in a battalion on her own would be a sweet revenge for my mother to carry around with her.

The following afternoon I checked in early to see Miss Frostbite.

'Well, Jack, how's it all going?' she asked.

'You mean the . . . ah, cocktail glasses? Miss Frostbite, you must take it out of my pay.'

'Don't be silly, Jack. These things happen. I should dock the careless waiter who didn't clean up the mess you slipped in.' She laughed. 'Cook grumbles he's still finding bits of glass in the kitchen.' She paused, took a breath and smiled. 'I have a proposition, one that I hope you'll like, Jack. Four of the band members are joining the army and we've been managing with only one trumpet player for a while, so that's five missing. But Joe thinks, and I agree, we could reduce the band numbers to seven if we can find the right musicians. Not easy, though, with the war on. We've got clarinet, drums, double bass and trumpet, not a great sound. We need an alto saxophone, and possibly a tenor sax as well, and, most essential, a piano player who can sing. Joe says he could sit in for piano, but the twin-piano act is what keeps the club doors open and it seems unfair to have him double up.'

Oh my God! My heart started to beat faster. *She's going to let me play jazz piano in the band!* Although my voice had long since broken, I'd been left with a half-decent baritone. But then, what about everything Joe had talked about yesterday? Maybe they hadn't compared notes. But then again, he seemed to know what she was going to say to me.

'Oh, that's a shame they're going, Miss Frostbite.' It was all I could think to say.

'Well, I can't complain. After all, they're doing their duty to their country. But here's what we've decided to do. The war promises to be a busy time for all of us – soldiers need entertainment – so we're going to shut the club for two weeks and paint and generally spruce the place up. The kitchen needs updating and the couches will all need to be re-upholstered.'

'I know just the man for the job – the upholstery, I mean,' I said quickly.

She laughed. 'You mean your friend Mac McClymont?'

Why hadn't I guessed she'd know Mac and I were friends? Miss Frostbite missed nothing. 'Of course, tell him to come and see me tomorrow. His work was excellent, as I recall.'

'He can only come at night. He's working at the new military camp at the Exhibition Grounds,' I explained.

'Have him announce himself to the doorman, say about ten-thirty, when our first performance concludes.'

'Thank you, he'll be very pleased, he liked working for you before.'

'That's nice, Jack, but I'll need a firm quote. He knows what's involved. Now, we're going to have to find three or four new musicians, and as America doesn't look like joining the war in Europe, Joe and I have decided to go to New York to find them. Joe has friends in Harlem with whom he can stay and we'll stay at the Waldorf-Astoria.'

'We?'

Miss Frostbite smiled. 'Yes, Jack, I thought you might like to accompany us.'

She must have seen my astonished expression. 'You're kidding?' was all I could think to say. I could hardly believe my ears. 'New York? Art Tatum? Billie Holiday? Count Basie?'

'And the rest of them, Jack . . . all the greats of jazz. Well, almost, they're not all in New York, of course. We'll be gone for a week, then I must get back to make sure the painters and carpenters are following my instructions.'

As I previously mentioned, I'd left Toronto only once in my life, on that trip to Montreal with Miss Bates. Now I was struggling to keep calm in front of Miss Frostbite, but then I decided there was no point. I was trembling with excitement and simply couldn't conceal my feelings a moment longer. 'Oh, thank you, *thank you*, Miss Frostbite!' I exclaimed.

'Oh, and Jack, the World's Fair is still on. Shall we visit that as well? What do you say?' She laughed and clasped her hands. 'Why, I think I'm almost as excited as you are, Jack.'

A little more composed, I now said, 'I doubt that, Miss Frostbite, but that will be grand.' I'd come across the word 'grand' in a book, of course. Now that I'd said it out loud I realised how pretentious it must sound. As someone who was about to have the shit kicked out of him in the process of scuffing in rough joints, I'd have to mind my vocabulary. I loved words, but the trouble with using the swanky expression of a character in a book is that when you say it out loud yourself, words don't land quietly into a sentence like leaves falling from a tree; they hit the ground like an overripe apple with a noticeable thump.

But if Miss Frostbite noticed she didn't show it. 'It's nice that you want to come, Jack,' she said graciously.

What a panic, what a scramble to get ready. I could no longer wear my school uniform as I had at concerts, and my everyday clothes, while okay for kitchen work, were not exactly appropriate for visiting New York. But my mom discovered one good thing. With most of the men under forty in uniform, the second-hand clothing shops were bulging with civilian clothes, and for next to nothing we bought a brown suit and whatever else I needed, including a blue striped shirt like Joe's that I particularly liked. It was the first time I could remember not wearing darned socks. We even bought a white shirt with two detachable starched collars, and a red tie for when we went to see Art Tatum and Count Basie's Big Band. I also took plenty of boot blacking and my mom packed a new bar of soap. 'Be sure you keep yourself nice and clean, Jack,' she'd cautioned. 'Don't forget to clean the basin afterwards.' Miss Frostbite suggested I bring my birth certificate along, for I was big for my age and she said the Canadian border guards were on the lookout for draft dodgers trying to get into America. The government was already conscripting men for wartime production work.

CHAPTER SIX

WE LEFT UNION STATION at eight-thirty in the morning and arrived at Penn Station, New York, at 10.30 p.m., so I spent most of the day looking out of the train window. We didn't see Niagara Falls because they were two-and-a-half miles upstream, but it was pretty sensational crossing the Niagara River gorge on a high – I mean, *very* high – steel bridge and seeing the water still churning from the falls way down underneath, with a small boat about to sail under the bridge looking about the size of a large leaf. The track ran for the most part due east, before turning towards the south and running down to a big city I at first thought must be New York but was Albany, where we crossed the Hudson River. We travelled through small and big mill towns and past farms, and threaded through pretty wooded valleys, but mainly we clung to the banks of the river. Everything, it seemed, depended on the river.

We had lunch in the diner, and Joe and I had steak, because I hadn't had that too often in my life, with mashed potatoes and green peas and gravy. Miss Frostbite had grilled fish and she squeezed lemon juice on it. I've eaten less fish than steak in my life, but I reckon that as far as fish is concerned I'm ahead of the game. Even cooked it smells horrible. She said it was sole and tasted delicious.

In the lounge car after lunch Joe and I played poker. The musicians at the club played it all the time, and I'd picked it up from watching them. It was always penny-ante stuff, like now with Joe, so you couldn't lose much. But I really took to it. Memorising was easy for me and I was getting quite good, so I'd go home with an extra half a dollar more often than a loss.

For dinner we had roast chicken with roast potatoes and beans. Miss Frostbite had fish again – Canadian salmon that smelled even worse than the sole at lunch, and she put lemon juice on it again. For dessert we had apple pie and Miss Frostbite had smelly cheese and crackers, then I had a milkshake while she and Joe had coffee. I reckon if they did scuffing on trains – I mean, like musicians working their way across the country entertaining the passengers in the dining car – I'd be in on that in a flash, with all the good food going around. As we approached New York that night I'd never seen so many lights in one place. You couldn't see the skyscrapers because there didn't seem to be a moon, just the lights in square patterns; some rose as high as the stars would have been in the sky above Toronto. What I want to know is how a train can travel for fourteen hours from one place to the next, winding and twisting, and arrive exactly on time, not a minute too early or late. How can that be? But that was how it was; we arrived at Penn Station exactly at 10.30 p.m. and the porter took our luggage to a taxi stand where the taxis were all yellow and lined up.

Joe said goodbye and that he'd catch the L line then take a bus for the last bit to Harlem and see us in the morning. Like me he only had one small suitcase but Miss Frostbite had three big ones and they wouldn't all fit, so we had to take two taxis to the hotel. At that time of night the streets were busier than downtown Toronto during the rush hour. You've never seen anything like it, horns honking and people everywhere with nobody in military uniform and in Times Square neon lights blinking on and off, that many in all the colours of the rainbow that you could have stood and counted them all night and not got to the end.

Now, how can I tell you about the Waldorf-Astoria? Put it this way, I started to panic the moment we arrived. They had an awning, and carpet running from the front door across the actual sidewalk, with a big black guy in a charcoal-grey uniform with a whistle in his mouth calling taxis for people coming out of the hotel, all of them dressed to the nines; you could see they were rich. The women tittered and touched each other, and you could see the diamond rings on their fingers, and the men were wearing dinner suits with white scarves hanging round their necks and smoking big cigars. I noticed the light shone on their plastered-down hair.

I'd also had my first real haircut – for once my mom didn't do it in the kitchen – and the barber called it 'The Sheik'. It was parted at the side and oiled then brushed flat. When I asked him why it was called that name, he said it was because of Rudolph Valentino.

I said, 'But he's dead, isn't he?'

And he said, 'Yes, but it's in memory of him, because he'll live forever.'

He then wanted to sell me a jar of Brilliantine, but I told him no. I reckon he was bullshitting anyway and just wanted to sell me the hair grease. Instead I just used water on my hair, which was okay until it dried. Then it looked as if I had two black lopsided wings that flapped if I ran. I think my mom's way of cutting my hair was better, you didn't have to worry about it and it was how I'd always looked.

But now I saw that the barber had been right and most of the men, unless they were bald, used Brilliantine, because their hair was stuck down and shone and this was obviously the fashion. So Toronto can't have been the hick town I'd begun to imagine it was, coming into New York on the train and then from Penn Station, and now walking across the sidewalk on a green carpet with two bellboys pushing our luggage ahead on a trolley with two big polished brass hoops, one at either end.

Holy smoke! If you thought the outside was good you shoulda seen the inside! Miss Frostbite had earlier explained that she'd chosen 'The Waldorf' in Manhattan because it was the only top-notch hotel in New York that allowed women without an escort to register. The lobby looked like a royal palace, which was how I suppose it was meant to look. My battered cardboard suitcase tied with twine was conspicuous on the very top of Miss Frostbite's suitcases on the trolley, but my head was turning this way and that so fast with the sights and sounds around me that I guess my new Sheik hairstyle made my head look as if it was about to fly off on its own.

I'd been in a few quite nice concert halls before, but nothing like this. You couldn't help but feel a bit out of place, like you didn't belong. Miss Frostbite later explained the decor was called Art Deco. If I felt a bit intimidated by everything, she fitted into the grand hotel like a hand into a silk glove, people calling her madam and kowtowing and 'this way please-ing' and generally carrying on.

Our rooms turned out to be what the desk clerk termed 'a two-bedroom suite': two bedrooms, two bathrooms, a hallway and a parlour Miss Frostbite referred to as our living room. I'd read about living rooms being rich people's parlours and concluded from the name that, unlike parlours, which you only opened for important visitors, rich people must actually use living rooms like poor people used kitchens. They were places where you could sing around the piano, listen to Amos 'n' Andy on the radio and have a cup of tea or even a drink before you had your dinner. We didn't even have one – a parlour, I mean. To have one you were usually middle class or owned your own home.

Now I've got to come clean – the other room most Cabbagetown houses didn't have was a bathroom. For instance, we had a small room at the back of the house with nothing in it but the privy. If you lived downstairs, as we did, it had a cement floor that was freezing in the winter. Some people used it not only as a toilet but also for storing coal in winter so they didn't have to go out in the freezing wind to the coal shed. They then used the kitchen or a bedroom for bathing on Saturday nights. During the week people simply washed their faces and hands at the kitchen sink, using a damp square of sugar bag to wipe away any dirt not concealed by their clothes.

When it was time for your weekly bath, you filled two large tin jugs with water, or, if you were like us, you used kerosene tins with the tops cut off and the edges beaten flat, fitted with a wire handle and a wooden grip. These were then heated on a coal stove. When they were hot enough you carried them into the bedroom or stayed in the kitchen if you were still a small kid. You then poured the first container of hot water into a large enamel basin or small tin tub and then, stepping into the basin or tin tub, you soaped yourself. Then you emptied the basin down the privy or the kitchen sink and filled it with the second jug, rinsing yourself using a sugarbag flannel. But you didn't use all the water in the second jug. At the very end, and best of all, you tipped it slowly and ever so carefully over your head and shoulders so it didn't splash on the floor. This last bit was sheer heaven: hot water running from your hair down your face and the back of your neck and over your stomach, back and legs and into the dish or tub. When you were still very young and your mom did it for you it was even better.

So, you can imagine my surprise when I entered my own bathroom at the Waldorf-Astoria hotel and there was this gigantic, gleaming white bathtub, and a washbasin and toilet with two toilet rolls fitted on the wall in a cavity specially made for them. The walls were tiled white and the floor was black marble with a fluffy mat next to the huge tub for when you stepped out.

Now, I don't expect you to believe me, because I couldn't believe my eyes, but the tub had two faucets, hot and cold, which you just turned on to fill the bath with as much hot water as you wanted. But of course everyone knew about hot and cold water faucets even if you didn't have both in your own house. What was unbelievable was that these faucets were made of gold with the spouts shaped like a dragon's head, so the water ran out of the dragon's mouth! The faucets on the washbasin were smaller but the same shape. I don't suppose they were solid gold, maybe just gold coated, but still – I mean, talk about sheer luxury.

There was also a towel rack with two white fluffy towels and two more on a shelf above it. The towels were embroidered in dark green with 'Waldorf-Astoria' in fancy writing. I'd never been in a bathroom with a bath in it and hot and cold faucets, much less ones made of gold and shaped into dragons' heads.

There was also a double bed in the bedroom with a cushioned backrest and two lights with little shades on the wall behind for reading, a chest of drawers for my clothes, as well as a wardrobe for stuff I didn't have, except my suit jacket. There was a little notice on the bedside table that said to put your shoes outside the door to be cleaned by the boot boy. No way I was going to do that. What if, by mistake, he mixed up the boots? I'd wake up with no boots. I'd brought boot blacking anyway. This boot business was the only thing in the whole place that wasn't perfect.

What a day! You couldn't want for a better one even if you wished your hardest! What I also liked about a day like this one was that I'd learned a zillion things I didn't know when I woke up that morning.

I was dog-tired and I'd already said goodnight to Miss Frostbite, so I took off my pants and put them under the mattress to bring the centre creases back, then cleaned my teeth, but there was no salt so I had to do it with just water. Then I washed my face and hands and dried them on a smaller fluffy white towel folded and placed beside the basin. Now, I suppose you're wondering why I didn't take a bath after such a long journey. Well, two reasons. I'd done nothing that would make me dirty and the other reason was that you only had an all-over wash if you were going somewhere, like on a weekend with my mom or to a piano competition. You never bathed just to go to bed, because that would have been a big waste of effort and hot water. I changed into the pyjamas we'd bought at the second-hand clothes shop and crawled into bed, where I reckon I fell asleep in about one minute flat.

How do I start describing the six days we spent in New York? Next morning Miss Frostbite and I had breakfast at the Waldorf (you didn't use the second part of the name if you were staying there). I had cornflakes then ham and eggs that were really bacon and eggs, but in America they said 'ham', and she had an omelette with mixed herbs, whatever they were. I looked at her plate when she opened up the omelette but couldn't see anything.

Joe was waiting outside for me at ten o'clock. Even though I'd been up since early, ten o'clock was real early for Miss Frostbite, because of the late hours she kept at the club, and she wasn't coming with us. Joe had explained to me that the top hotels in Manhattan were for white folk only, so I didn't have to wonder why he hadn't come in to have breakfast with us.

Miss Frostbite had also explained that she and Joe would be spending their days conducting interviews, and suggested I might like to spend my days at the World's Fair, and then at night we'd hit the jazz joints and dives together. With this in mind, she'd handed me ten dollars, more than a week's pay. The idea was that Joe would take me to the fair on the first day to explain how to catch the subway to Flushing Meadows and how to return to Manhattan in the late afternoon.

Joe accompanied me to the gates where there was no entrance fee. 'You be okay, Jazzboy?' he'd said. 'If you get lost, everyone know where Manhattan is and what subway, so you just ask polite.' We shook hands and he left to do his interviews with Miss Frostbite.

So I just walked in with thousands of other people and started looking around. There were 1216 acres and the whole thing was called 'The World of Tomorrow'. With hundreds of countries and companies showing their vision of the future, you'd have to practically run from one exhibit to another for more than a week to see it all.

I loved being on my own. It meant I could see whatever I wanted and didn't have to be tentative or polite.

The first thing I did was to look for the Canadian pavilion. I don't know what I expected but whatever it was, it wasn't there. There was lots of stuff about the Royal Canadian Mounted Police, with Mounties in their scarlet jackets crawling all over the place. But for all that, it was dull as dishwater. There were lots of American pavilions (the General Motors Exhibition was the best), and when you visited them, they made Canada look even duller by comparison.

Later on in the week I decided to find the Australian pavilion, because Joe had called it the 'end of the fuckin' world', and I thought it might somehow be different from all the other places, being so far away. But it was worse than Canada, with only one main theme – 'The

Story of Wool'. I mean, seriously, they had a couple of stuffed sheep, one with all its wool on and one that had been shorn, and lots of big photos about shearing, with the sheep on its back and a guy called a shearer clipping off the wool in a long shed. There was nobody in their pavilion and I didn't blame them. I couldn't figure out what wool had to do with the world of the future, but then Canada wasn't much better with its Mounties.

There was truly lots and lots to see and you couldn't take it all in, even going every day for a week. For me the two individual highlights were The Arctic Girl in Her Tomb of Ice, and Elektro the Motorman, a seven-foot-high robot that talked and sang, could see and smell things and count on his fingers. I don't know how they did it, but people would hold up something, an apple or a leather purse or a dollar note, and he'd say it right off.

But the weirdest was the Dream of Venus at the Dali pavilion. Now, okay, I was only a young kid, fascinated by robots and a girl buried in ice and something called television and the General Motors Exhibition that showed a huge diorama of New York where the whole city was connected with bridges that sometimes spanned tall buildings. These showed the future, or a possible future, although nobody mentioned the war in Europe and how that might change things, and the Germans weren't there to give their opinion about what was going to happen if they won.

However, this Salvador Dali exhibition was something else and I would always remember it, which is strange for a boy like me who knew very little about art, except what my mom and I had seen occasionally at the Art Gallery of Toronto on weekends when it was raining and you couldn't go anywhere else. I remember my mom once said, 'Modern art is like the Depression; it shows a world falling to bits that don't make no sense.' Once, before my dad left us, we saw a Picasso painting of a woman's face all squiffy, with her eyes and mouth and nose in the wrong places, and Mom said sadly, 'That's exactly how it feels after one of your father's drunken backhands.'

I went back three times to the Dali pavilion, and each time people were coming out and shaking their heads and saying things to each other like 'Disgusting!', 'Simply awful!', 'Too crude for words!' One short, fat old guy with a droopy tobacco-stained moustache came out and stood under the huge girl's legs at the entrance, shook his fist and yelled, 'You filthy Dago son of a bitch! This is the United States of America! Go back home!'

I admit it was pretty darn weird but I couldn't figure out what all the fuss was about. Dali's Dream of Venus was the creation of the famous surrealist painter, Salvador Dali. I confess, at the time I'd never heard of him. But his pavilion was surreal, all right! A strangely shaped building with no corners, it contained a wet tank and a dry tank. In the wet tank real girls swam under water, where two of them milked a bandaged-up cow that must have been dead because it couldn't stay down there and breathe, or maybe it was just a model. Other girls tapped on typewriters like they were busy in an office. Then I noticed a piano keyboard painted on the body of a girl lying down that looked very real until you realised she was made of rubber. Then, in the dry tank was what was called the Sleeping Venus: another rubber lady reclining in a 36-foot bed covered with white and red satin, live flowers and leaves. Oh, I forgot to say the girls in the wet tank had uncovered breasts, which was what all the fuss was about, I think. Then, on various parts of the ceiling were upside down umbrellas and telephone receivers hanging down, and above the big bed were lobsters grilling on live coals and bottles of champagne.

I must say, although it was meant to be highly erotic, it didn't affect me anything like seeing from the back one of the twins walking out of the club in a tight silk dress and high heels.

But it was what was outside the pavilion that was really funny and got people's backs up so that some just refused point-blank to enter. I remember one woman shouting, 'I am a born-again Pentecostal Christian and this is the Antichrist!' If she was born again, then it was a while back because she was no spring chicken and reminded me of Dolly McClymont. What Pentecostalists and the Antichrist were all about I hadn't any idea, but she was sure steamed up and practically foaming at the mouth. Then she started shouting, 'Jesus saves!'

First, you bought your ticket for the Dali exhibition at an office shaped like a large fish's head and then, to go into the pavilion, you had to walk through these giant parted female legs wearing stockings and high heels, where the man with the moustache had been standing. I mean giant legs so you couldn't touch either side with your arms spread out wide and with the tops of the stockings way above your head and the high-heeled shoes the size of a baby's pram.

I loved it. Every other pavilion was sensible and about the future and showing stuff off, but this one took no notice and just went mad all by itself with fish's heads and ladies' legs and umbrellas upside down and telephone receivers, and they must have done it all without asking permission.

Each day at the Waldorf started with the same breakfast: ham and eggs. I'd say to the waiter, 'Over easy, please,' and he'd reply, 'Yes, sir, with your ham crisp as usual?' I told Miss Frostbite I needed to tell him not to call me sir, but she said he had to because it was his job, and this was the Waldorf, after all, and if *they* didn't maintain standards, then who would?

Then there was the travelling back and forth to the World's Fair every day in the subway. Lots of black and brown and white people, with everyone laughing and joking, kids pushing each other and their moms and dads carrying baskets with food and thermos flasks and having a good time even before they got there.

I really, *really* wished my mom could've been with me. I don't think she'd have minded the Dali pavilion one bit. We'd seen nude ladies in the art gallery – I mean, in pictures, of course – and she'd said they were a bit fat, but beautiful, and the artists were very clever; you'd think looking at it from a distance that it was real skin that hadn't ever been out in the sun. That was when I was much younger, because now, of course, I know all about nineteenth-century figure and portrait paintings from school, as well as the French Impressionists – Degas, Cézanne,

Renoir, Monet – and lots of others. It was part of all the stuff I knew that wasn't about life here and now, or living in Toronto and waiting to be old enough to go to war.

The real big thrill was hearing some great musicians. First came what Miss Frostbite called 'housekeeping', that is, the interviews to find three new jazz musicians. The piano player was the most important because if you got him right the rest would follow. The reason the piano was so important was that the left hand could supplement the rhythm of the double bass and the right hand could play the melody; also, the pianist was free to sing. I was secretly a bit disappointed. As you will recall, I'd hoped they'd invite me to be the pianist, but Miss Frostbite, as usual, read my mind and said that, while she'd love to have given me a chance, she didn't dare break the law – I'd have to be eighteen to play in a nightclub legally.

They found a piano player from Memphis who could also sing the blues, which was good. His name was Noah Payne and he was fifty years old and was willing to move to Toronto. He'd only just moved to New York and hadn't settled down there yet. His wife had died of breast cancer the previous year, and his two boys were both in the American army and stationed in Hawaii. He said that in jazz circles he was known as No Pain and that was what he preferred to be called. Miss Frostbite explained that she and Joe had heard him play and he was pretty good and had a good blues voice, but it was between him and another pianist from New York, and he was also very good so they couldn't decide. But then Noah Payne chuckled and said, 'Ma'am, I got me that name because when I play piano, your patrons, they don't feel No Pain no more.' She'd liked that and he was hired on the spot.

The next musician was much younger – in his mid-thirties – and played the tenor and baritone sax. He hailed originally from Chicago and his name was Jim Shantyman, and Joe said he had a sound that was sweet and big and pure. 'That good to find in the one and only player. Usually they got one sound better than the other.' Both he and No Pain were Negro guys. But it was the third musician who was causing Miss

Frostbite to bite her nails and for once making Joe unsure of what they needed at the Jazz Warehouse.

He was a white guy from Tennessee named Elmer Perkins, who played the electric guitar. He was thin as a beanpole, with straw-coloured hair you couldn't comb because it grew in five different tufts on his head and stuck out every which way. He had pale blue, red-rimmed eyes, and eyelashes that were almost white, lighter even than his hair, and his skin was practically transparent. Joe said to me the night after the first interview, 'You gotta believe, this cat, he ain't no pretty sight. He play the 'lectric guitar with his tongue hanging out the side his mouth and a look he got on his face like he 'bout to cry.' Miss Frostbite and Joe both admitted Elmer Perkins was good, very good, but the problem was that the band had never contained such an instrument and it meant a new sound in the Jazz Warehouse combo. Joe explained that the electric guitar, made by companies such as Gibson and Rickenbacker, had been introduced into jazz in the early 1930s, so it hadn't worked itself into the blood and sinew of jazz yet.

'Old man like me don't hear that 'lectric sound too good. For me it got a twang like there's cats caterwauling on a tin rooftop. But that don't mean it ain't good. I ain't saying that. I got to keep my heart from decidin' and my min' open. It a good jazz sound, and it young and got good rhythm and can go solo. All that gonna be mighty handy in a jazz combo. Floss, she like it, but she ain't sure 'bout the boys back home. They ain't worked with no 'lectric guitar before and we don't want no dis-cor-dant note in the band music. Mr No Pain says no problems, ain't no 'lectric guitar gonna concern him wid the piano.' Joe paused. 'That worth considering seriously; when the piano man don't concern himself, then no trumpet or sax or rhythm section got nothing to complain themselves about. Mr Shantyman says he worked wid one such before in Chicago and he say it was just great. He says that 'lectric sound is where jazz music heading in the future, and we gotta in-cor-por-ate it because Mr Gibson and Mr Fender, they made a whole new 'lectric sound that gonna stay wid us a long, long time.'

All this discussion would take place in Harlem or Greenwich Village, where we'd go someplace Joe knew for our dinner, because you had to be careful you were welcome, him being Negro. We went to a different place every night and then afterwards we'd hit the clubs.

Now, I'm going to begin with Billie Holiday, nicknamed 'Lady Day' by her great friend and musical partner Lester Young because of something she sang that I will never forget. Now that I'm older and can understand even better, it makes me want to cry for the human race every time I hear it sung. But when she sang it that first time at the Café Society in Greenwich Village you wanted to cry anyhow. It was so sad, but also so beautiful.

But first about the name, 'Café Society'. Miss Frostbite explained that it was a send-up because a lady named Clare Boothe Luce, who was the wife of the man who started *Time* magazine, had coined the phrase 'Café Society' to describe the rich New York socialites who were still plentiful even during the Depression. I think they must have been the same people coming out of the Waldorf the night we arrived, the men with cigars and white silk scarfs and the women waving their long red-painted nails and wearing gold high-heeled shoes.

Miss Holiday had her shiny black hair pulled back tight over her scalp and tied at the back, like my mom sometimes wore hers after I'd brushed it to a shine every bit as good as hers. As a matter of fact I think my mom's hair was even better. On one side of Miss Billie Holiday's head were these white flowers Miss Frostbite said were gardenias. She had a beautiful voice but when she sang this song I could see there were tears rolling down Joe's cheeks and he didn't speak for quite a while afterwards. Miss Billie Holiday was dressed in a red evening gown, and she had a nice figure and was also quite pretty.

The song was 'Strange Fruit', and the description of southern trees hanging with the bodies of lynched Negroes almost made me cry, too. After listening to a song like that, I was really scared Elmer Perkins might be like those southerners who hanged Negroes, being from Tennessee as he was. I couldn't help it, although as it turned out I was proved quite wrong. I thought perhaps that was why Joe was a bit concerned about the electric guitar player, and that the 'discordant note' wasn't about the music at all but about having a white man and a southerner in the band.

But Elmer Perkins loved jazz, black music, and even sang the blues real well, but when he did, those people would have this look on their faces as if they couldn't tell where the sound was coming from. Surely it wasn't coming from the white beanpole with the blue red-rimmed eyes and hair going every which way? Because hearing blues from somebody who looked like Elmer was truly weird and unnatural. Joe would sometimes chuckle and shake his head. 'Elmer, when you singing them blues, it like Mrs Roosevelt using bad cuss words when she givin' out her famous quotes to American women. Ain't never suppose to happen.'

Elmer would laugh and pick up his electric guitar and sing a verse from Dixie. Joe would later say, 'Inside Elmer, his soul, it black as the ace o' spades, only that the good Lord, He spilled too much Clorox in the mixture when he was stirring up to make him.'

At The Famous Door on Fifty-Second Street we heard Count Basie. How do you describe the greatest big band that ever was? They were in full-tilt boogie and it was like trying to keep ahead of a runaway express train. Then he followed this with his belting Memphis- and Kansas City-flavoured piano solos and my head was spinning. It was receiving more than it could take in in one go and still stay sitting on my shoulders. I'd lie in bed at night at the Waldorf and the sounds would come rushing, one smashing into the others, swirling and gyrating and booming and soothing and I couldn't stop them; they were so real that I used the cushion to cover my ears.

Then, the next night at the same place we heard Lester Young play saxophone and clarinet, and it was so marvellous that for a moment there I wished I'd taken up those instruments instead of piano. Miss Frostbite said he was breathtaking and if only . . . I think she meant if only she could afford someone like him as a guest at the Jazz Warehouse.

Then, on the last day in New York Joe said, 'This afternoon, Jazzboy, we gonna go down to Harlem and we gonna pay us a visit to my good friend.' That morning Miss Frostbite took me up to the top of the Empire State Building, the tallest building in the world! Did you know it has 2500 toilets? If you used a different one every day, it would take you six years and 310 days!

Joe was waiting for me outside the Waldorf at two o'clock. 'Where we going, Uncle Joe?' I asked.

'Oh, we gonna see an old friend o' mine I think maybe you gonna like some,' he replied, but didn't explain any further. Miss Frostbite said she had to arrange a few things and pack for the following morning so she wouldn't be coming. Later Joe would explain that where we were going was sort of for men only. Not official but understood.

We got to Harlem and made our way to a restaurant called Jerry's Chicken Place. It wasn't ritzy or anything, not like the other places we'd been, just some restaurant with a tin cut-out of a rooster that was rusting a bit hanging above the door. I thought maybe Joe's friend was just someone who sold fried chicken who he knew way back when and we were paying him a polite visit. Inside there were tables and chairs and a piano. A chicken shop with a piano was different, but this was in Harlem, so who knows what's different? There was a Negro man sitting at the piano when we walked in and I followed Joe, who walked up to him and placed his hand on the piano player's shoulder. I saw that the man sitting at the piano was nearly blind. 'Who this?' he asked.

Joe chuckled. 'It your old buddy, Joe Hockey, Mr Piano Man.'

'Hey, Joe! Welcome, back! Where you bin, man? You still that damn place in the boondocks other side them Great Lakes? They cain't play good jazz there because you gone and stayed and they never found out you no good.' With this he threw back his head and laughed uproariously. 'Welcome home, brother Joe.'

'Art, I want you should meet my good friend Jack Spayd.' Joe turned to me. 'Jazzboy, say hello to Mr Art Tatum.'

You could have knocked me down with a feather. I completely lost my voice and when it finally came back I squeaked, 'Good afternoon, sir.'

Art Tatum grinned. 'We don't do no "sir" at Jerry's Chicken. Here we all brothers and buddies.' He looked up at Joe. 'And even old chil-hood friends who once every ten years maybe they bother themselves to come by to pay their respect is still welcome.' He turned to me and extended his hand. 'Welcome, Jack. You play piano, white boy?'

'Only classical piano, sir . . . but I hope to play jazz piano some day,' I stammered. There was no way I could ever call the greatest piano player on earth by his first name.

'That where I got myself started. It the best training if you gonna play jazz piano. It jes a matter of practice, practice and more practice. Now you remember that good, son!' He held his hand out palm upward. 'Let me see your hands, first the left then the right.' I did as he asked and he gripped each hand in turn, his fingers feeling, kneading, pulling mine, then he released them. 'Big hands, that real good, Jack. Now you got to learn yourself speed, big hands and speed, that the beginning.' He reached out again and touched me on the arm. 'Good luck and play good, always from the heart, you hear? Jazz ain't about reading music, it about reading the life and the pain that's in plain folk.'

Art Tatum then began to play for an hour and a half with only one or two pauses to drink black coffee. Joe explained that he played nights on 'The Strip' on West Fifty-Second Street not far from where we'd heard Count Basie, and was getting his hands limbered up. Only his personal friends were ever allowed to come to Jerry's Chicken Place in Harlem, where he hung out during the afternoon.

When we were about to leave Joe and me went up and said goodbye and I shook Art Tatum's hand a second time. 'Next time you come to New York you come see me, Jack. You come play jazz piano. I wanna see them big hands working and the speed you meantime learned yourself. You come back here to Jerry's Chicken, you hear now, white boy?'

I nodded, too dumbfounded to reply, knowing that I'd never, even if I lived a thousand years, be good enough to dare play jazz piano in front of Art Tatum. 'Yes, sir . . . thank you,' I managed to squeak.

Going home I thanked Joe over and over, and then said, 'Uncle Joe, I don't think I've got it in me. I'm wasting my time with the piano.'

Joe put his hand on my shoulder. 'Never you mind, Jazzboy. Ain't nobody ever heard Art Tatum play piano who don't say that. He the best there ever was and the best there ever could be. Maybe you can be number two. That the only place left for anybody else to play piano.'

For an hour and a half almost non-stop I'd listened to the finest piano playing I had ever heard, jazz or classical. I also knew with certainty it was the best jazz piano sound I ever would hear.

We left Penn Station at eight-thirty the following morning, and as we crossed the Hudson and I saw the New York skyline for the last time, I knew I had just had the most remarkable week of my life. I also knew that my life could never be the same again and that I'd be going scuffing knowing that Art Tatum had held my hands and that this was like sitting at the feet of God himself. You can't do better than that, can you?

CHAPTER SEVEN

DOLLY'S CLAIM THAT SHE'D given her all during the First World War as her contribution to king and country certainly contrasted with the twins' attitude. The time they spent on their backs had precious little to do with altruism. In fact, they planned their war extremely well, based on a healthy respect for profit. They were frequently seen, separately or together, at the Jazz Warehouse on the arms of captains, lieutenant colonels and full colonels, and occasionally the arms had even more impressive insignia.

Joe Hockey, seeing one of them squired by a top-brass military or air force officer, remarked with genuine admiration, 'Them twins, they got foresight and behind sight and to the side sight. They got the soldier-pleasing business down perfect.' He'd then turned to me. 'Jazzboy, that pree-cise-ly the way you got to look at scuffin'. You don't do no charity, you hear? Iffen you got to sing for yo supper, you make damn sure it gonna be worth yo while. Free piano playin' soon enough make you taken for granted.' Over the first few months of the war, Joe had gotten to know the twins well, in an entirely platonic way, I hasten to say. My fondness and respect for their father may have had something to do with it. Because Joe was a natural listener and a wise counsellor, folk seemed to tell him just about everything you could safely tell a man.

Between Mac and Joe I was kept fairly well in touch with the details of the twins' wartime lives. While the twins didn't entirely neglect their former customers, they near doubled their rates. The implication (never stated) was that, with so many needy military men away from home, civilian clients would need to pay a premium. According to Mac, far from discouraging their pre-war customers, this seemed to elevate the twins' status. War is an opportunity for everyone to make money and this was the view of many former civilian clients who now saw the pair as even more desirable and well worth the higher rate.

I guess there's nothing quite like a world war to perk up a languishing economy, and Ottawa found the resources, or simply printed paper money, until the economic wheels were spinning once again. The Depression was effectively over. Sending its sons off to die in defence of a motherland the vast majority had never seen, whether it be Britain or France, put Canada back on its feet. Meanwhile, our daughters were stoking the home fires and the wartime boom. A million young men marched off to war and were replaced by their sisters, mothers, wives and daughters, working in shifts around the clock, running the factories, utilities, transport, offices and farms, to become a workforce that not only rivalled the menfolk's but more often than not surpassed it. It was perhaps the first time in the history of humanity that women were no longer simply taken for granted, or not entirely.

Meanwhile, I set out to find my way as a man and a musician. I was off, free of the strictures of the women who so far seemed to have largely controlled my life. I was anxious for my seventeenth year, the year of my waiting, to pass as quickly as possible, but I also wanted to test myself in an unknown environment, so that I would be worthy of wearing a uniform and doing whatever my country thought was necessary to help to win the war.

Like any guy my age I considered myself bullet-proof, and while the idea of being killed in action was something I'd considered in an abstract kind of a way, it wasn't that I thought of it as *death* – the snuffing out of life's candle – it was simply something that happened, a peculiar and occasional outcome of military action.

In all the countless war stories that I had read as a kid of eight or nine in *Boy's Own Annual* – from the North-west Frontier in India, the Zulu Wars or Boer Wars in Africa to the Boxer Rebellion in China and, of course, the Great War – the hero went through a series of harrowing experiences but survived and triumphed in the end. Such early formative notions endure until experience or maturity finally erases them.

I didn't see myself as a hero, even secretly. Playing piano and reading books had taken up so much of my childhood and teenage years that I'd never acquired the derring-do of the street kid – that first taste of dangerous excitement in a hostile environment that most of my schoolmates underwent as a rite of passage. Nevertheless, I accepted my invincibility without thinking.

Old men, the politicians and generals who start wars, exploit this impulse in the young to happily volunteer as cannon fodder. If the compulsory minimum age for joining up to fight was fifty, I doubt there would be too many long-lasting wars. But in any nation there is a plentiful supply of young men anxious to die without questioning the motives of those who wage war.

Joe, hoping to knock some sense into me, had suggested scuffing, a musical baptism of fire that would 'grow me up some' so that I'd see the world as a sufficiently dangerous place without needing to go to war. Joe's wisdom and advice usually proved valuable, but I still felt pretty strongly that I must do my bit for my country.

As the day of my departure approached, my increasingly tearful mother became convinced she'd never see her precious son again. Furthermore, given Dolly's and the twins' longstanding attitude to both mother and son downstairs and the fact that they now owned our house, my greatest fear was that my mom would find herself out on the street.

I decided to wait for the right opportunity to talk to Mac, who, along with Dolly, had moved into the apartment in High Park. Despite his earlier concerns, the move had turned out happily for him and he had since built himself a splendid workshop as a private retreat from Dolly.

Furthermore, Mac had gradually found sufficient work as an upholsterer to resume his old craft, starting with the couches at the Jazz Warehouse.

Dolly, also somewhat surprisingly, settled into the nice middle-class neighbourhood, where she was accepted with very few raised eyebrows. This she achieved by joining the quilting society, a group of women recognised as the local powerbrokers who saw her as the truly exceptional quilter she was and a good churchwoman who, despite her gargantuan size, brusque manner and coarse accent, was a true artist or, as one of the women was heard to explain, a rough diamond waiting to be polished.

Dolly's acceptance wasn't all of her own making; the twins clinched it. Most of the ladies in the quilting group marvelled that a woman with such an obviously working-class background and the voice and manner of a sergeant major could have brought up two such pretty, well-spoken, refined, beautifully mannered and clearly successful daughters who spoke French in addition to English. The girls' true vocation was never revealed in High Park – Dolly always said they were in the real-estate business, which was not entirely a lie.

While they were away in Montreal, the twins had been tutored in the French language, as well as the manners, style and fashions of the most socially acceptable, privately educated, modern young French Canadian women. Back in Toronto they'd quickly adopted the accents, manners and speech of the upper middle-class English-speaking Canadian women of their age. Their intelligence, astute memories (a prerequisite for their profession), and uncanny gift for mimicry no doubt helped.

Although they acted the part of well-bred young women, the twins never attempted to conceal their past and never denied their humble background. This had little or nothing to do with humility. They'd long since discovered that it was good for business to admit to their initial lack of breeding. A wealthy client will happily condone a girl being on the game if she is attempting to better herself, but will quickly condemn one who, accustomed to wealth and privilege, takes up the oldest profession, no matter how compelling her reasons might be. Climbing the next rung on the ladder of success was seen as highly commendable; descending to one several rungs below was totally reprehensible.

The twins were, of course, now our landladies. They rented their old place upstairs to a rather nice woman, Mrs Debra Calderbank, and her two young boys, Zachery and Ethan. Her husband, Adam, a drill instructor, was absent during the week at a local military training camp. She'd explained that his job moved him from place to place, depending on where young recruits were being trained. He lived in the camp during the week, but enjoyed regular weekend leave and so, for the sake of their two boys, the family followed him to wherever he was posted in Canada.

With Dolly elevated to High Park matron, she was now unable to speak to my mom because we were from Cabbagetown, but here's a strange thing: she officially lifted the 'no speak' ban for Mac, who had laughed when he told me. 'At least it's nice to know our friendship is out in the open at last, buddy.'

As for the twins, whether or not Dolly reasoned that it wasn't practical to be on non-speaking terms with your tenants, I don't know. We simply received a notification in the mail concerning the new owners, together with a post office box number where we were to send the rent. My plan to speak to Mac about my mom's continued tenancy was proving unusually difficult. Shortly after Dolly had lifted the ban, Mac had been contracted to do the upholstery for a country golf club way out of town and I hadn't seen him for nearly three weeks, including the weekends when, understandably, he hadn't bothered to come home. Knowing Mac, he'd probably worked seven days a week.

Then one day, after my usual afternoon band practice, Joe approached me with some unexpected news. 'Hey, Jazzboy, how ya going? Them twins, they want to have a meeting wid you.'

'With me, why?'

Joe shrugged. 'They sayed it was somethin' to do wid yo mama and the Cabbagetown house.'

My heart sank. This was it: I'd be off scuffing and my mom would be out on the street sitting on a cardboard suitcase. While it wouldn't be impossible to find a new place for her to live, rents had gone through the roof since the war and we had still been paying Depression rent – in other words next to nothing – which was about what she could afford.

I was already seated when the twins entered the downtown café in Queen Street West where we'd arranged to meet. I confess I was nervous as hell, but relaxed a little when they arrived wearing woollen skirts, sweaters and scarves. They wore almost no make-up apart from a dab of lipstick, although even stripped down they were awfully pretty. God knows, in the loneliness of my bed I'd often enough taken their interchangeable names in vain.

I rose as they entered. They smiled and each extended a hand. 'Hello, Jack,' one said, then the other smiled this gorgeous smile. 'Long time no speak.' It was obviously intended to break the ice, but I was too nervous to respond with a laugh. Instead I smiled weakly, trying not to show my nerves.

'Ah, please join me,' I said stupidly, immediately wanting to backhand myself. After all, why else were they here?

The owner, an Italian-looking guy with a permanent five o'clock shadow, introduced himself as the ubiquitous Tony and took our orders. We talked briefly about the Jazz Warehouse and Joe Hockey until our coffees came – the twins drank theirs black, no sugar; I had cream and sugar.

'I guess you're wondering why we want to talk to you,' one of them said.

'The house, Mac told me you'd bought it . . .'

The second twin frowned slightly. 'The house? Oh, yes, I suppose that too . . . but no, not really.'

The first twin turned her coffee cup around on the table and said, 'We wanted to apologise to you, and then to your mom, for our rudeness since we were kids.'

'We were simply horrid brats! I'm sorry . . . we're so sorry, Jack,' the other exclaimed.

There wasn't anything I could say because this was the honest to God truth. Since as far back as I could remember they'd been perfect little bitches. Seizing the initiative, I said, 'How do I tell you apart?'

They both laughed, accustomed to the question, though I later learned they seldom told anyone, least of all their clients. Swap-ability, I expect. Now one of them placed a manicured forefinger on the left side of her neck. 'When I remove my finger you'll see a tiny mole. I'm Melissa.'

Sufficiently composed, I now tried my urbane act. Leaning back in the chair, I said expansively, 'It's all water under the bridge. Now that you're our landlords – ah, landladies – would you like to meet your other tenant?'

To cut a long story short, they came the next day at three o'clock for afternoon tea. We all, especially my mom and Melissa, seemed to get on like a house on fire. I'd never imagined we'd ever be friends, but later I learned that it wasn't only Joe who'd said nice things about my mom and me, but also Mac, who'd asked them to apologise to us once the ban had been lifted.

Anyhow, at the conclusion of our first meeting and just before my mom had to leave for work, Melissa said Mrs Calderbank and the two boys, who we'd grown to know and like a lot, were moving on to follow her husband to Vancouver. We already knew this, but neither of us expected what came next. Melissa went on, 'Mrs Spayd, with new people moving in, would you consider keeping an eye on the place?'

Clarissa added, 'Of course, we'd reduce your rent in return.'

'By half,' concluded Melissa.

So much for my gloomy predictions – the three of them were soon as thick as thieves. The tale of the twins' success, largely gleaned from stories my mom told me, as well as information from Mac and Joe, was amazing, and well worth recounting. Rather than being shocked by the twins' activities, my mom admired their initiative. I think they loved having her as a confidante. When you think about it, they had no one to talk to other than each other; no female friend, I mean. Maybe Dolly, but

I doubt it. She wasn't that sort of mother. They talked to Joe and Mac and occasionally to me, but we were men and that's always different. My mom was down to earth and practical, quietly spoken and a good listener who wasn't in the least judgmental. Some of their stories were hysterically funny and, had she cared to repeat them, would have ruined the reputations of many of Toronto's most respected and conservative citizens, as well as several of the bristly moustached top brass among the Canadian army and air force. Mom, like the twins, had a natural talent as a mimic and had the girls' accents, mannerisms, syntax and grammar down pat. Sometimes it was almost like being in the room with them. Apart from confiding in me, as she'd always done, my mom possessed the tightest lips in Canada. The twins knew they were safe and had a shoulder to lean on, an ear to listen to them and a mouth to laugh with them. As my mom noted, 'Jack, every woman needs someone to share her thoughts and her secrets with, and to laugh with her over the strange ways of menfolk.'

Conventional wisdom has it that earning a living on your back is easy, whereas it is, in fact, very hard work and seldom fun. The twins accepted this with equanimity; they knew the name of the game and did their utmost to play it expertly. They planned to work hard while they were still sufficiently young, save all they could, then leave the profession and find something they'd enjoy doing. I learned later that both of them wanted to go to university, but would not have dared to express the hope for fear of being mocked. Whores taking university degrees was going just a teensy-weensy bit too far in the prevailing moral climate of the late 1940s.

By the standards of Cabbagetown, the twins had already acquired an impressive property portfolio and would have been considered by local slum standards to be filthy rich already. But it hadn't come easy. From slum kid to landlady was too great a leap for any of the locals even to comprehend, especially in a woman, so instead of quietly applauding, the locals mocked their efforts with the usual remarks about how opening your legs was an easy ride to fortune. It was no such thing, of course. The twins had skimped and scraped together the funds to buy the three properties while working in Montreal and later in Toronto. But there was one upside – when you sleep with the very rich, you get the soundest advice, and the twins hadn't missed a trick.

Now that money was flowing freely, and men were prepared to pay generously for a good time before they went off to fight and perhaps die, the girls were earning a lot. They had an arrangement with various bell captains at two or three discreet hotels, which proved very profitable for all parties. However, Melissa, the more thoughtful of the twins, could see that hotel rooms and bribes were a large part of their overheads, along with expensive underwear, shoes and evening dresses, cosmetics, and much, much more.

Then they got really lucky.

They were introduced to Lodge G. Calgary, whom they dubbed Mr Logical, a member of one of Toronto's famous banking families. He was in his mid-fifties, carrying a little too much weight and possessed of peculiar sexual needs that had originated in early childhood with the harsh ministrations of a redheaded nanny and her sister, a maid in the household. He had become addicted to being humiliated and punished with severe whippings, accompanied by role-playing necessary to his humiliation, though not all of it was sexually perverse.

The twins possessed the correct shade of titian hair, and had the slum accent they'd once shared with the perfidious nanny and her sister, which they were required to use for the duration of the dalliances. They took the procedures seriously, performed the role-playing expertly and afterwards showed complete discretion, thereby earning his absolute trust. In return, Lodge G. Calgary gave them invaluable advice about making their money work for them, and pointed out that, while it was admirable that they'd paid cash for the properties they already owned, there was a better way.

'You'll have to register a property trust right away, using the three properties you already own, so you can channel your illegal earnings through a legitimate front and eventually use the trust, with its assets and cash flow, to borrow funds. After the initial ten title deeds we can't have you paying cash or using your own money every time you purchase property.'

'The bank will lend us money? I mean *us*, Melissa and me?'

'No, of course not, but they'll lend it to a trust with sufficient equity. That way there will be no awkward questions. Greed is always tight-lipped. The trust will pay taxes, so the government won't come snooping.'

The twins took his advice, and at the conclusion of my year away scuffing, they had increased their property portfolio considerably, having bought several downtown workers' houses. They were becoming increasingly bold and Melissa had spotted a penthouse flat to let, the largest in the block, with its own private lift and entrance at one side of the building. She'd been thinking hard about how to improve their business income and asked Mr Logical for his opinion. It centred on difficulties they had working independently of a brothel.

'Well, my dears, it must be obvious to you from working in both Montreal and Toronto that both are pretty conservative cities, where a brothel by any other name is still a bordello to a city council driven by religious dogma. Both cities are controlled by those invisible religious strictures that decide how everyone will think and behave. In Montreal it's the rosary-rattling Catholics; here, it's my lot, the sanctimonious Presbyterians, the evangelical Methodists, the Bible-thumping Baptists and, bringing up the rear, the moribund Anglicans, none of them having yet come to terms with the Industrial Revolution, let alone anything that came after it.'

Clarissa smiled. 'You can say that again! Melissa and I entered a beauty pageant in Montreal before we went on the game. Our bathing suit parade and judging was done behind closed doors at a very swanky hotel. At the semi-finals we wore evening dresses and were told there were to be no plunging necklines or slits down the side of the skirt to show a glimpse of stocking.'

'That would have been interesting,' Mr Logical remarked. 'However do you judge identical twins in a beauty contest?'

'Oh, they didn't,' Melissa replied. 'They eliminated us in the semi-finals. Later we were told they'd thought we were the prettiest, but the judges felt that two identical winners would insult the other girls because it would mean second place would really be third.'

'It's how we first got into the profession,' Clarissa explained. 'One of the judges ran a young ladies' deportment school and modelling agency and approached us afterwards. We thought we were going to be fashion models, that is, once she'd taught us fancy manners, how to dress, sit, walk and talk in the French manner. Her name was Madame Chastel, and our first client was a millionaire magazine owner and businessman. After we'd done the fashion shoot for his magazine, he invited us to his country estate for the weekend. Madame Chastel said it was an opportunity not to be missed. He sent a chauffeur-driven limousine, a black Cadillac, to fetch us and I guess we were knocked off our feet. His country chateau was a long way up the scale from our aunt's fish shop. Anyhow, after supper on the first night, and after our first taste of red wine —'

'Which we thought was horrible,' Melissa interjected.

'But which must have had the desired effect,' Clarissa continued, 'he offered us a rather large sum of money to sleep with him in a huge bed he claimed was once owned by Marie Antoinette.' She laughed. 'The queen of France must have owned a lot of beds. We've supposedly slept in three of them!'

Melissa shrugged. 'He must have liked what he saw in us. Goodness knows what – we hadn't a clue then – but we must have made it seem like fun. Anyhow, he suggested we meet some of his friends, and Madame Chastel said they were useful contacts for young models and would help us earn more. She said fashion parades in department stores, with an occasional magazine shoot, wouldn't make us a lot of money, and that it was the Depression, after all . . .'

'We simply had to get out of that fish shop,' Clarissa laughed.

'Little did we know that we, a couple of Cabbagetown kids, had discovered a pot of gold!' she went on. 'We were a true double act and the millionaire businessman had, on that first occasion, set the price, so all his rich friends knew the rate. Madame Chastel must have known but she never brought it up; we stayed on her books – even got the occasional modelling job – and she continued to tutor us in how to be perfect ladies.'

'Oh, she knew, all right,' Clarissa jumped in, 'because she'd book us for weekends at country chalets or châteaux at the lakes or in the mountains, saying that the male owners were throwing a party and wanted two pretty hostesses to serve drinks and canapés —'

'That's what she called all the naughty stuff. It was all unspoken but it seems we were by no means the first to pass through her hands. She had a great many rich friends to whom twin "hostesses" in a double act were irresistible.'

Clarissa took over again. 'Well, one thing led to another and . . .' she paused and raised her right eyebrow, 'here we are at your service, sir.'

Mr Logical laughed. 'Well, my dear, you're quick learners and Madame Chastel obviously taught you well. But what you have yet to learn is how to properly utilise money to purchase or lease real estate.'

'So you think we should rent this penthouse or not?' Melissa asked.

'Well, that's hard to say. As I said, you're in a hostile environment here in Toronto. Hotels and taverns are deliberately unwelcoming places to consume alcohol, gambling is forbidden and the sex trade is forced to operate in a clandestine and underground manner. Supper clubs like the Jazz Warehouse, where I know you often go, are a prime example. They cannot allow women in without a male escort. Furthermore, if a dalliance is to follow, you are forced to bring your clients to a hotel, where I imagine the overheads add greatly to your expenses. I agree. You should think about acquiring your own premises, girls.'

'Buy? But this penthouse is in a very nice neighbourhood. Wouldn't it be rather expensive?' Melissa asked. 'So far we've only bought cheap workers' houses as speculation.'

'Sooner or later someone in the building – there's always someone – will name it a bordello and the neighbourhood will be up in arms. So why not consider buying the whole building? That way, if there's any brouhaha with any of your leaseholders, you can account for yourselves as perfectly respectable tax-paying, property-owning citizens. Your clients can then simply be presented as your friends. In my experience, people on a lease tend not to antagonise their landlords if their apartments are well maintained. Incidentally, a building in that area is bound to become a sound investment after the war.'

With advice and help and the equity they possessed already, the trust fund they'd established was able to buy the entire block, their biggest financial move yet, or, as my mom put it, 'a pretty big gamble'. They then renovated the penthouse to replicate the premier suite in the Royal York Hotel, Toronto's swankiest.

To her delight and surprise, the twins asked my mom to act as caretaker and cleaner, and offered her one of the small flats downstairs rent-free, plus double the salary she earned as an office cleaner, if she'd become the caretaker and cleaner of the penthouse and the girls' downtown apartment. She was to clean, change the linen, take it to the Chinese laundry and prepare the various rooms each morning, and then repeat the process after the afternoon sessions. In the winter she was to keep the fires going in the two bedrooms and sitting rooms, designed so that when each twin was busy a client could come and go unseen.

My mom took considerable pride in her new job. As far as she was concerned, working for the twins in such salubrious surroundings was, frankly speaking, money for old rope. She was no prude, and didn't feel in the least compromised. She'd also been careful not to write and ask my opinion. When I returned from my year's scuffing, she sat me down at once and, to my considerable surprise, explained exactly what was happening. 'Mom, how long . . . how long have you been doing this job?'

'Long enough to know that for the first time in years I have a day job and the pleasure of listening to the radio beside a gas fire, which the twins put in for me, plus all this.' She swept her hand to indicate the neat little apartment with its freshly painted interior and new gas stove. 'Jack, don't be a prig, please.'

What could a man say? Besides, she'd become very fond of the twins, who, as I said, often confided in her and trusted her completely. They also proved to be very generous to her in lots of other small ways and one big one. It so happened that one of Clarissa's civilian clients was an eminent plastic surgeon. Most of his work was skin grafts and reconstructive work on soldiers sent back to Canada with bad facial injuries sustained in combat, but he agreed to work on my mom's nose as a special favour to Clarissa, who no doubt granted him some special favours of her own. It wasn't sufficient to fix her nose entirely, but when I got back to Toronto from my travels, I was able to pay for the rest of the work to be done. A year later, when I returned on a week's leave from the army, I couldn't believe how pretty she'd become. She was still a woman of only forty. Hard work as an office cleaner had kept her figure trim, her hair was still raven black, and as far as I was concerned, with Miss Frostbite's teeth and Clarissa's nose job, she'd turned into a stunner. Joe Hockey later remarked, 'She be too old to be cheesecake, Jazzboy, but I do declare your mama, she the sweetest dee-sert ice cream wid a cherry on top served in one o' them parfait glasses!' Even Miss Frostbite now referred to her as 'your pretty mother'.

But, to return to the story of the twins, now that they no longer had to pay for hotel rooms or bribes, they were well and truly on their way, and took advice not only from Mr Logical but also from some of their other powerful business clients.

Amazingly, they'd managed to repay enough of the apartment block loan for the bank to offer them even more investment finance. Mr Logical and others among their clients advised them against buying properties in Cabbagetown, or anywhere in the centre of Toronto, and suggested that they should be looking to the land surrounding the city. 'After this war ends, Toronto is going to boom, my dears,' Mr Logical advised. 'You have equity in the houses and the apartment block, bricks and mortar you already own; now you should move into cheap land outside the city. The slums are beyond repair, and automobiles will mean that people can live further and further out. You mark my words, after the war Toronto is going to expand. There'll be mass migration from Europe at least.'

Accordingly, they purchased great tracts of farmland around Toronto, especially in Scarborough, which they rented back to the farmers on short-term leases or used for agisting stock. What the banks liked was that the twins were surprisingly conservative by nature, and always put down half cash and borrowed the remainder, so the value of their assets amounted to roughly twice their debt. After the war, this ratio often became five times what they owed, and no bank could wish for better or safer clients.

In later years the twins were often referred to as financial geniuses, but their particular genius lay in their ability to make good use of some of the best business brains in Canada. Under the direction of Mr Logical, they used what they laughingly referred to as their human resources very well. Now, what they had given in pleasure was returned in knowledge, influence and credit guarantees by establishment and entrepreneurial figures, all of whom depended on their utmost discretion. When they left the profession in 1948 at the age of thirty-one as rich and successful property developers, their old clients, with one or two exceptions, took real pleasure in (and even personal credit for) their success in the world of commerce.

For two slum kids who had left school early, they'd done remarkably well, but they didn't stop there. As if they weren't busy enough, each twin studied and passed her remaining high-school grades and entered Toronto University, studying for Bachelor of Commerce degrees, taking turns year and year about: Melissa graduating first in business management and Clarissa a year later in accounting. They were the first members of the McClymont family who had ever attended a university.

I wasn't around to witness most of what happened with the twins after the war, but my mom stayed with them and continued to act as their senior housekeeper and confidante. They'd given up their original profession as planned, and their dubious past was disguised by money, as well as the greater social mobility of a new, larger and more diverse population. The two fiery redheads were well on their way to the utmost social respectability.

However, they had both remained unmarried. When the second wave of the women's rights movement was a mere ripple, Clarissa was asked to deliver a speech at a women's college. A student asked her whether she had ever contemplated marriage, and her answer had been unequivocal: 'There is little about the human male that my twin sister and I don't understand. Why then would either of us be foolish enough to tie ourselves to one simply for the sake of having children? There *are* good men, but you should all choose very carefully. Make sure that, as the dependant mother of your children, you don't become a servant to their father.' Perhaps the twins had learned more from their mother than they let on.

Now wealthy and respected as successful businesswomen, the twins never brought up their past, but they also never denied it. Among female academics there was almost a level of admiration for what they'd achieved, a perverse pride in it, so that the context in which Clarissa spoke was not lost on her audience.

But to return to 1940, I was able to prepare for my trip with a clear conscience now, knowing that my mom could manage in my absence. Apart from the twins, there was Mac, Miss Frostbite and Joe, all of whom she could turn to in an emergency. At seventeen, I was six foot one inch tall and, although I was still growing, my warm clothes would just about last me through the winter. All I needed was a good heavy-duty anorak. So a week before leaving, I'd stopped by the Presbyterian Church Charity Clothing Depot and got one for a song.

Old Mrs Sopworth, known as 'The Camel', ran the depot and was responsible for almost everything I'd ever worn up to that moment. I told her what I was hoping to buy and explained that I was going west to the prairies for a year before I joined the army. 'It gets pretty cold up that way – down to minus twenty degrees,' I explained, a touch melodramatically.

She clapped a hand over her mouth. 'Oh my goodness, Jack, I have just the thing. It came in several days ago and you won't believe this, but I actually thought of you.' She beamed up at me. 'And here, dear boy, you are!' She showed me a splendid, almost new anorak, explaining it had come from a church family who had recently lost their grandfather, a man over six foot, which was why she'd thought of me. 'It's yours for two dollars, Jack.' It was an absolute bargain and with a decent warm coat I was finally ready to depart. 'You'll be requiring a good grey suit, my dear, for when you play at swanky places. I have one of his that's practically new, also six white shirts with detachable collars, and his neckties.'

While I doubted that the sort of scuffing jobs I'd get would require such formal attire, she was so enthusiastic I couldn't say no. I figured a suit would always come in handy, so I selected three shirts and the box of collars, as well as three neckties, and thanked her sincerely.

Armed with a battered harmonica, an ability to read music and play piano – jazz and classical – and, as I foolishly saw it at the time, whatever musical corruption fell between these two pure forms, I prepared to head west on my getting-to-know-myself expedition.

My mom, Miss Frostbite, Joe Hockey and Mac had all promised to see me off at Union Station. I was headed for the prairies, my first stop the town of Moose Jaw in South Saskatchewan.

Why Moose Jaw? Well, no special reason. *Moose Jaw in Southern Saskatchewan* read like the opening line of a Rudyard Kipling poem. I was by nature a romantic, and with the choice to go anywhere I desired, I couldn't pass up a conjunction of names like that. In my mind it evoked wide-open spaces, sun-dried bones, hard men and women who were not afraid to use a gun, the Canada of the tough-minded north-west frontier. Which proves you should never be beguiled by a name and that it might be just as well to do some research before you settle on a destination.

For a start, Moose Jaw was no small town nestled on the never-ending prairies. It was in the prairies, all right: the rich agricultural part – wheat and meat. It also turned out to be a railway junction for the transcontinental Canadian Pacific Railway with branch lines heading down into the US and up into northern Canada. If Toronto was the city of the Temperance movement, with evangelical Protestant watchdogs barking Christian dogma, then Moose Jaw was the red-light district of the prairies, actively doing the devil's own work. I was to discover that Moose Jaw was the Canadian capital of vice, booze, gambling and wayward women.

If Joe had personally selected my baptism of fire he couldn't have chosen better. I later realised that when I'd mentioned Moose Jaw to him, he must have quickly decided it was probably a good thing that I be thrown in at the deep end. It was Joe's intention that I arrive with very little money and then support myself by playing the piano. In truth, I didn't expect to have much over after I'd paid my second-class rail fare. I'd given my weekly wages from the club kitchen to my mom, so that for once in her life she'd have some money over to spend on herself – a new dress or a pair of shoes or a good winter coat from Eaton's Department Store – and not have to depend, as she'd done for most of her married life, on second-hand stuff from Mrs Sopworth.

I had sufficient to live on anyhow, plus all the food I could eat at the club. Miss Frostbite had always insisted that the customers' tips (she called them gratuities) were shared with the kitchen staff. Now, with the war on and with more money around and servicemen anxious to spend it, these tips were often substantial. I could depend on at least five dollars a week and with a further two dollars or so won at poker, I could live quite nicely and save my rail fare with a little left over.

Then, the night before I was due to leave Toronto, Joe sprang a big surprise. Miss Frostbite had decided that, despite the law preventing me from playing in a nightclub because I was under-age, I was to play for the first band session after their double piano act. 'You got your solo part chance jes one time, Jazzboy. Play good. It be yo farewell present from the cats in the band. Mr No Pain gonna step aside, but if'n you no damn good and cain't hack it, he gonna kick yo sweet ass an' shift you off that pee-ano seat pronto. Don't let me down now, you hear? This yo first scuffin' job and it pay two dollar. Yo mama, she gonna be here also. This the last time she gonna hear you for a long, long time, so play good, Jazzboy.'

There had been times when I was younger that Miss Bates had remonstrated with me, yelling, 'Stupid, stupid boy! Wrong, wrong, wrong and wrong again!' until she'd left me emotionally tattered. But Joe's injunction not to let him down gave me perhaps the most anxious moment in my musical career.

I'd practised my solo part a hundred, maybe five hundred times, maybe even more, but when the moment came I could feel my knees begin to tremble beneath the keyboard. Having my mother seated at a table directly next to the stage, along with Miss Frostbite and Joe, didn't help calm my nerves either. Though my mom was no jazz expert, she'd heard me on the harmonica so often that there was no doubt she knew a good musical passage when she heard one.

Noah Payne, alias No Pain, handed the piano over to me and introduced the band: 'Ladies an' gennelmen, welcome once again to the Jazz Warehouse, where the band gonna play you some real nice jazz. Tonight for the first session we have us a special privilege to introduce the one and only Jazzboy!' He paused, then, raising his voice like they do at a boxing match, went on, 'From Toronto, I give you Mr Jack Spayd at the piano!' A bit of sporadic clapping followed and No Pain brought us to life with a sweep of his hand.

I knew the opening routine like the back of my hand and played it almost effortlessly. It was smooth, easy and relaxed – 'smooth as whipped cream on a satin bedspread', as Mickey Spillane had said, describing the skin on the thighs of one of his fictional molls. With the extra musicians from the US, this was now a truly good jazz band, perhaps even the best in Canada at the time.

Then the awesome moment arrived when No Pain signalled the start of the solos, pointing at me to begin. I took a deep breath and began to play, all the while looking at my mom. The band had already played through the basic melody and progressions, so first of all I repeated the chords. Then I started embellishing a little with my left hand and doing a few showy bits like trills and fast scale runs with my right hand. The grins from the other musicians boosted my confidence and I turned back to the keyboard to concentrate as I threw in some passing chords to make things more interesting. Then, halfway through my solo, I grabbed my harmonica and stepped over to the microphone and jammed with it, keeping the musical thread and pumping out the beat. This was a complete surprise for the band, and glancing down at Joe I could see his eyes were near popping out of his head. But equally surprising was the burst of applause from the audience as I moved back to the piano to complete my solo.

Joe would have handed me my two dollars scuffing money anyhow, but he seemed genuinely pleased, and at the break No Pain and the other musicians came over and congratulated me, as did Miss Frostbite. Turning to my mom, who was standing shyly off to one side, she said, 'Gertrude, I truly think the boy has made the correct decision. That solo piano with the harmonica interlude just summed up everything for me – from that first day Joe brought Jack in out of the cold until now. It was splendid, truly splendid. You can be justifiably proud, as indeed am I.'

My mom smiled her best new flashing smile, but I could see she was close to tears. 'Thank you, Floss, for giving us a chance,' she said quietly.

Joe gave me ten dollars and Miss Frostbite gave me fifteen. It was generous of them both and meant that if I didn't immediately find a job, I'd be financially secure for a month at least. But that wasn't all. What had actually happened was that my mom had saved every cent of my wages, a sum that amounted to $150, and she wouldn't take 'no' for an answer when she gave it to me. 'At least I'll know you're going to eat properly and sleep warm, Jack.'

So when I took off for Moose Jaw I was stinking rich with $175 in my wallet. I determined that, come what may, I wouldn't touch my mom's money, and when I returned it would go towards her nose job. At that time, the twins' contribution to her plastic surgery was still in the future.

The kitchen at the Jazz Warehouse set me up with three days' worth of sandwiches, mostly meat and pickles, a dozen hardboiled eggs, six apples, a packet of peanut biscuits and finally, as a special treat, a large Hershey's chocolate bar. Even the cook shook my hand in the end and said he'd half forgiven me for breaking the glasses and making the kitchen floor lethal for days, and concluded that I had been a top dishwasher.

Mac, Joe Hockey, Miss Frostbite and, to my surprise and delight, Mrs Hodgson from the library were all at the station to farewell me. Remarkably, the twins appeared, having given up an evening's work to support my mom, who was trying hard not to cry. These were some of the people who had made me what I had become at seventeen. Miss Bates and Miss Mony, who had also profoundly influenced my life, were absent, but all of them would remain forever in my mind.

Now I was to leave them all behind to find myself. It seemed paradoxical that I had to leave the people who'd influenced me most to find out who I truly was. This was the first time I'd be on my own, I mean with nobody, absolutely nobody, I knew at my side. While the prospect was exciting it was also sad – for all of us. Even hard cases like Mrs Hodgson and Miss Frostbite shed a quiet tear. It was nice being loved but I knew in my heart of hearts that Joe was right: it was time to go it alone. But whatever was to come, these people would always be a part of me.

With a shrill blast of his whistle, the conductor shouted, 'All aboard!' Then the train, metal wheels screeching on steel rails, let off a blast of steam and started to pull away to much shouting from passengers and those who had come to farewell them. My last glimpse of my mom was of her back as she wept in the arms of the twins. As the train gathered speed and the wheels clicked over the rails, the rhythm seemed to be announcing *Wrong-wrong-wrong-and-wrong again! Chuff-a-chuff-a chuff-a chuff – stupid-stupid-stupid boy!*

I had all I could possibly eat for the journey, with plenty left over to share with a young guy in my compartment named Pat Malone. He was small in stature, like Mac, maybe an inch or so taller, but undernourished, thin and weak in appearance with a body that seemed reluctant to coordinate itself with his mind. He looked as if he lacked the strength or energy for physical work.

He'd been rejected for military service because he suffered from asthma and was going on to Moose Jaw as a volunteer agricultural worker on a combined wheat and cattle ranch. The army doctor had sent him to work on the land saying it would be good for his asthma to be out of the city. All they'd given him was a warrant for his train fare and he was almost stony broke with only two dollars in his pocket.

As it turned out, Pat Malone was a bit of a chucklehead. He'd shared my grub for breakfast and lunch on the first day out of Toronto, and seemed to relish the beef and pickle sandwiches, wolfing them down like he hadn't eaten for days. Around midafternoon it occurred to me to ask him if I could take a look at his rail warrant. He handed it over and I saw that he was entitled to eat in the second-class dining car. 'Hey, buddy, it says here you can eat in the dining car,' I explained.

'Yeah?' he said, astonished. 'Here . . . right here on the train?'

'Where else?' I laughed. 'Compliments of the government.'

'I can't do reading that well,' he admitted, adding, 'I never was no good at school.'

He trotted off to dinner that first night and returned with a roughly tied napkin which he handed to me.

'Open it, Jack,' he said, giving me a goofy smile.

I untied the napkin and saw that it contained a broiled chop and two roast potatoes. 'I didn't bring them green beans – anythin' green's no good for ya, Jack,' he'd explained, his expression serious, as if it was a universal truth.

'You shared your dinner with me, Pat? That's real nice of you, buddy.'

'You did the same for me, Jack. They gimme two o' them chops and four o' them roast potatoes and a heap o' beans I couldn' eat.'

'Pat, I *really* appreciate it, but I've already eaten.' I pointed to the chop and two potatoes. 'You've only had half your dinner.'

He looked guilty. 'I ate all the puddin' . . . rice custard.'

'Better finish it, eh? Can't let it go to waste, can we? I hate rice pudding,' I fibbed.

He looked uncertain. 'You sure, Jack?'

'Absolutely!' I patted my stomach. 'Chock-a-block. You're going to need all your strength as a farmhand and cowboy, buddy. Eat up. Never know where your next chop's coming from.' I handed the napkin back to him.

Pat Malone began to wolf down the chop and roast potatoes and it was surprising to see how someone so puny could have such an enormous appetite. He ate voraciously, as if he were catching up on all the meals he'd missed in his life.

When Pat had first mentioned the ranch near Moose Jaw where he'd be working, it had suddenly occurred to me that this was no dry-boned prairie I was heading into. You've got to wonder which of us was the chucklehead. Geography had never been my strongest subject at school, and most of my ideas had come out of books, such as *The Great Lone Land* by the Irish-born army officer William Francis Butler, in which he evoked tenantless solitudes in prose that Mrs Hodgson at the library claimed was almost poetic. Hence there was little room in my head for any modification of my imagined landscape of the north-west prairies and Canada's west.

Whenever the train pulled into a station along the way, I would buy coffee or a soda for Pat and me, and the whole journey cost me the grand sum of three bucks, which left me $172 in my wallet, but most of that was my mom's nose money. I knew I'd have to find a job quite quickly, but I could probably stretch Joe's and Miss Frostbite's money and the little I had over from my rail fare to last me a month. After that, I told myself that if I failed to find a job in Moose Jaw, I'd be riding the rattler.

Arriving late in the afternoon, the steam train let off a loud hiss before coming to a halt beside a very long platform teeming with people waiting for the passengers to alight in what proved to be an enormous railway station.

'Jesus, Jack, how'm I gonna find the man supposed to meet me?' Pat said in a near-panicked voice, looking every which way out of the compartment window.

'Keep looking, they'll probably be holding up your name,' I suggested. Then, as luck would have it, I saw a big guy two carriages down from us holding up a large piece of cardboard above his head on which was painted in crude black letters: PAT TORONTO. The paint had dripped down to the edge of the board so that it looked as if each letter was held up by a haphazard arrangement of black sticks. Pat Malone didn't make the connection until I pointed out the guy, a thickset man who looked to be in his late forties or early fifties. 'Buddy, I think that's for you.'

'Nah, me name's not Toronto.' Pat glanced at me reproachfully. 'I ain't *that* bad at readin,' Jack.'

'Still, I think you should try him,' I suggested.

'He don't look happy,' Pat said, hesitating.

I heaved my large rucksack onto my back (another example of Mrs Sopworth's kindness), Pat grabbed his battered suitcase, and we stepped down into the milling, shouting, gesticulating crowd on the platform. 'Hang onto me, Pat,' I instructed, making my way to where I thought the guy stood. I pushed my way further through the crowd, saying, 'Excuse me! Excuse me!' with Pat hanging on to my rucksack until we reached the guy. 'Are you looking for a Pat Malone from Toronto?' I asked.

'You him?' he demanded with a scowl.

'No, he is,' I said, jerking my thumb back at Pat.

'Frank Farmhand,' he said, addressing Pat and ignoring me. I wasn't sure if 'Farmhand' was his surname or job description. 'You got here,' he barked at Pat, then, ignoring his proffered hand, he glanced upwards as if at the sky, even though the platform was under cover. 'More snow comin'. Got to hurry. Chevy don't like travelling through mush without snow chains. Fuckin' idjit ranch mechanic don't put them back'a the truck.' He punched a fat forefinger in the direction of Pat. 'Follow me, Toronto.'

'Pat! Pat's me name, sir!' he called out, but Frank Farmhand had dropped the cardboard sign at his feet and was already pushing his way through the crowd.

'Go, buddy!' I yelled, giving him a shove.

Pat set out after the big man. 'Thanks, Jack,' he called back and then disappeared into the crowd.

'Good luck!' I shouted in his general direction. Poor bastard, it hadn't been the most propitious start to his new life as an asthmatic cowboy.

I decided to wait until the crowd thinned and dug into my rucksack for my Mrs Sopworth anorak. I put it on, zipping it to the neck and fitting the hood over my head, then moved over to a station wall clear of the pigeons overhead and sat on my rucksack with my back against it. Jesus, it was freezing! I silently blessed Mrs Sopworth for her two-dollar anorak.

The crowd eventually began to thin and I was about to leave when a train pulled in on a parallel track and the platform was soon crowded again. I began to realise that I hadn't arrived at a terminus, a town at the end of the line, the *Nowheresville* I'd always imagined Moose Jaw to be, but at a city that acted as a junction to just about everywhere. All passenger trains on the CPR stopped here to take on coal and water, while transit passengers left the train to grab a meal in one of several dining rooms. I was to learn that, for the most part, these stayed open and busy twenty-four hours a day.

I suddenly felt very alone. It wouldn't be the last time, but the first time is always the worst. Miss Mony, then Mrs Hodgson, then Mac followed by Joe, Miss Frostbite, the boys in the band, the kitchen staff, even Miss Bates and latterly the twins, they had all been my anchors and understood the why and how and what of me. Was it the same in the country? I was in a strange place with people milling around like a cattle roundup, everyone seeming to know someone or have some sort of purpose, even if it was only to have a nice dinner and then hop back on the train and head for some familiar destination, where they would be met by family and friends and taken to a home with a fire in the hearth, food in the oven and a warm bed. A city is full of disparate people so you can always find someone who shares your peculiarities and understands your background, where you are coming from the moment you open your mouth or behave in a particular way. But I suddenly found myself a dot, a nothing, a cipher, nobody. Shit, I was lonely.

On the train Pat Malone had protected me from feeling the full force of my isolation. Despite his slowness, Pat had been enthusiastic about his new life, peering out of the compartment window like a small child, exclaiming about the smallest things he saw in the passing landscape, gleefully counting the grain elevators whenever we approached a small town or country siding. Would little Pat be happy and find his feet? Could he discover new skills, get to know and love animals? Dogs, for instance. Dogs don't judge you, just love you for who you are. I'd always wanted a dog. But dogs live off scraps and there was never enough left over. Could Pat make himself useful and needed? All these questions racing through my mind sounded like the end of a weekly radio serial I'd listen to on Mac's crystal set, with the announcer building anticipation for the episode to follow.

But I couldn't help worrying. Here out on the prairies there would be no crowd where Pat could lose himself. Would country folk look upon him as a simple-minded no-hoper who everyone could yell at and kick around with impunity, laughing and humiliating the clumsy city kid? Was Frank Farmhand the first of many? Pat's smallness would count against him. Huge and slow-witted lads could always be put to work doing the heavy lifting, the grunt and heave that was part of farm and ranch life, but Pat's puny frame would be a disadvantage even without his chronic asthma.

My worries about Pat were probably distracting me from worries about myself. It was getting dark and I had to find a place to stay the night. My sandwiches were gone and so were the peanut biscuits. Despite eating breakfast and lunch in the dining car, Pat had polished off most of what remained of the food the kitchen had prepared for my journey. His eyes had almost popped out of his head when he saw the Hershey's bar and he'd eaten most of it, not letting it melt slowly in his mouth, but gobbling it down like there was no tomorrow or as if someone was going to snatch it away from him.

My own life hadn't contained too many Hershey's bars either, but now I urged myself to buck up, pull myself together. My own childhood and teenage years had been filled with opportunity and the kindness of people I had no claim on, not to mention private school, piano concerts, the eye-opening trip to New York and meeting the jazz greats. I'd even been lucky enough to be born with a decent brain. Pat Malone had been given so much less than me, and it was high time I put my brain into gear to solve my immediate problem – food and shelter.

I wasn't really hungry but I reasoned that the staff in a railway restaurant would be accustomed to strangers asking them for information, and so I decided to blow a buck or two on a steak. It was an indulgence, but if I picked one of the better restaurants at Moose Jaw station, the waiters or waitresses would have been chosen for their initiative, serving as they did a passenger prepared to pay a bit more for their food. Sloppy joint, sloppy waitress: they invariably go hand in glove.

I finally selected one called The Watering Hole, which had white tablecloths and three fancy chandeliers. Miss Frostbite had long since instructed me on table manners, so I didn't feel out of my depth as I was shown to a table by a head waiter. I also told myself that this was my first and last indulgence, and that I could only justify it because of the situation in which I found myself.

As luck would have it, I was served by a woman who appeared to be in her forties. She was very obliging when I asked if she could recommend somewhere in town for me to stay the night. I explained why I had chosen her dining room and that I wanted somewhere cheap. She nodded. 'I thought you looked a bit young for this restaurant, sir, but I completely understand.'

'Please call me Jack, ma'am,' I hastened to say.

'I'm Marge and this is our busy time with a train just come in. If you can order now and eat slowly, I'll come talk to you later, Jack.' She smiled.

I ordered my steak. It wasn't cheap – $1.75 – more than I could ever remember paying for a meal. In fact the prices were pretty extortionate and I didn't dare order anything else, like an 'appetiser', whatever that meant. I think it was what the menu at the Waldorf-Astoria had called an entrée. Although why someone would need something to tempt their appetite when they were already in a restaurant was beyond me. I glanced around. At the next table a couple were tucking into these appetisers. I checked the menu and identified Cream of Tomato Soup (fifteen cents) and Fresh Shrimp Cocktail (forty-five cents)! No way I'd be having an appetiser at that price, or even bread and butter, ten cents, and no jam on the table. Miss Frostbite would have been happy, though: there was Fried Fillet of Sole for seventy-five cents. I couldn't look too long as that would have been rude, so my eyes flicked all over the place. On the other side of me a family were already on to their main courses, all of which seemed to cost $1.25: the mother had chosen Half Chicken Broiled, and the father was tucking into Calves Liver Sauté with Bacon. The two rather plain children had chosen fish. I'd never seen a kid who liked fish, and wondered where they came from. But whether they were eating Broiled Halibut Steak Maitre d'Hotel or Baked Fillet of Flounder Veronique I had no way of knowing and as far as I was concerned fish is fish and best avoided.

Marge brought my steak and a side plate of beans and French fries. 'Enjoy,' she said. 'See you later, Jack.'

I tried to eat the steak slowly but it wasn't possible; it was thick and juicy and absolutely delicious. The fries and beans in butter were also pretty good and I scoffed the lot. At these prices, leaving something on the plate, as Miss Frostbite said nice people always did, just wasn't on. It would be like ignoring a nickel you came across on the pavement.

I didn't have dessert, although the Waffles and Pecan Maple Syrup (thirty-five cents) sounded good, but I lingered long over two cups of coffee until the train finally departed. With the restaurant empty but for myself, Marge finally approached me. I asked her if she'd care to sit down and she gave a grateful sigh. 'Thank you, be nice to be off my feet. That's me for the night – not my turn to set up for the next train, but the others will want to get going. Why don't we go sit in the foyer?'

I paid the cashier as we left the main dining room, and Marge led me into the entrance, where we sat in two comfortable chairs. She sighed again. 'Always a rush when a train comes in,' she said, then handed me a slip of paper. 'The head waiter let me make a call, Jack. I've booked you a shared room at Mrs Henderson's boarding house. It's six doors down from where I live with my husband, just clear of the main part of River Street. It ain't the best part o' town, but it's near everything, almost in the centre of the city.'

'That's terrific, thank you, Marge. May I pay you for the phone call?'

'*Tush!*' she said with a dismissive sweep of her hand. 'The railways can pay, they make enough.'

'It's just until I can find my way around, see what's what around the place.'

'It's Friday today. Will you stay the weekend?'

'What? At Mrs Henderson's? Yeah, I guess.'

'Oh, then I'd better warn you about Sunday. By the way, Mrs H. doesn't take boarders who drink.'

'Is she Temperance?'

'No, no, Apostolic.'

'Huh? Can't say I've heard of them. Anyhow, I don't drink.'

'Wish I could say the same for Mervyn.'

'Mervyn?'

'My husband. It's why I need to warn you about Sunday.'

'The Apostolics? If they're not Temperance, what are they . . . like, a kind of church?'

Marge sniffed. 'Well, if you want to call them that. They're in an old theatre across the road. It's a religious denomination – the Apostolic Church of the Pentecost. It's a breakaway from one of them holy-roller churches I think started in the deep south . . . Tennessee, some place like that in the States. They call themselves Apostolics for short.'

'So why warn me about Sunday?'

'The church is right opposite Mrs Henderson's boarding house and they make a fearful racket.'

Racket seemed a strange way to describe a church service. 'You mean singing hymns?'

Marge sniffed again. 'Songs, more like. They have a loudspeaker right out onto the street, so what happens inside comes right on out. They start singing at seven Sunday morning, then at nine there's the main meeting – fiery sermon, yellin' out *hallelujahs* and *praise the Lords* – then jabbering holy ghost gibberish – they call it speaking in tongues – gospel singing, raising the roof. In the summer, baptising grown people in the Moose River and Thunder Creek. Lordy, it goes until noon, almost non-stop.' Marge laughed. 'I can recite some'a their songs off by heart. Their hymns of praise sound to me like black people's music – jumpin' and thumpin', harmonising, horns, piano, you name it, they got it; they got the lot 'cept no church organ like a proper church.' She shook her head. 'I can tell you one thing for sure, Jack. If God's trying to sleep in of a Sunday mornin', He's got no hope.'

I secretly liked the idea of gospel music, if that's what it was, the real raw thing from the south. I had my doubts, though. Joe said it was particular: 'White folk don't know this music. This black folks' only.' I'd definitely check this out, come Sunday. But then I asked the obvious question. 'Don't people, you know . . . complain?'

Marge laughed again. 'Well, yes, my husband, Mervyn, for all the good that does. He works at the railway workshops and has a regular card game Saturday nights that goes well past midnight. He and his buddies drink a fair bit and he always has a hangover come Sunday mornin'. But what can you do?' She sighed. 'Men will be men.'

'Well, he's part of the majority. They, these Apostolic whatevers, I imagine they're in the minority. Surely he and the people in your neighbourhood can complain to the police or the mayor, someone in authority . . .'

'Jack, this is Moose Jaw, the city where anything goes. It's also right up on River Street, where we don't have regular authority; it's only grubby hands held out, greedy palms to be crossed. If the nightclubs and honky-tonks, dance halls and red-light district in the River Street area can go all Saturday night doing the devil's work, the Apostolic Mission say they have the Lord's permission to do His work in the same area, so they spread the gospel loud and clear for three hours on God's own Sunday mornin'. That's how the *Times Herald* said the Apostolic Church of the Pentecost put it to the mayor and the councillors when they applied for a street broadcast licence, and they couldn't hardly refuse, could they? "It's God fighting back in a godless city," the newspaper said.'

'Yes, but every church is supposed to do that, I mean, fight the devil. But not with loudspeakers blaring out onto the street.'

'Ah, that's not how it works here. The Apostolics say the devil's out there in the streets, not in their church.'

I was beginning to wonder what kind of place I'd landed in. 'Good thing I don't have hangovers but I admit I don't mind a bit of a sleep-in on a Sunday. What do you suggest, I move on before Sunday?'

'Just warning you, Jack. Suit yourself. Mrs Henderson keeps a nice clean place. Mary Spragg, her cook, makes a good breakfast and dinner, I'm told, and at least your room-mate won't be a drunk; in this town that's rare enough. But like half the top end of River Street, Mrs H. has become a born-again Christian, so no cussing's allowed neither and no drink at the table or in your room.'

Marge had drawn me a map, and it looked as if Mrs Henderson's wasn't far from the station. 'I told her you wouldn't need dinner, Jack.' Marge smiled. 'Must go. Mervyn always forgets to put the dog out for a wee. Glad you enjoyed your steak.'

'Best ever,' I replied. Mind you, my life hadn't been filled with juicy steaks any more than it had been with Hershey's bars.

'That's good, Jack. You don't wanna go paying fancy prices for a steak and find it don't meet your expectations.'

I'd left her a tip under my side plate and was now worried she might not get it and think me mean, but I couldn't bring myself to mention it, so I thanked her profusely for her help. While she hadn't asked me a single question about myself, I figured that must be the way at a railway restaurant – come and go, never to be seen again, no point in knowing any further details. Anyhow, she didn't strike me as someone who could advise me about the music opportunities available in the city. Still, she'd been very kind.

As Frank Farmhand had predicted, it was snowing quite heavily as I set out to walk to Mrs Henderson's boarding house. I couldn't help laughing to myself, wondering if playing gospel hymns – black people's music – on the Apostolic piano qualified as scuffing. Joe Hockey had taught me several Negro spirituals, saying at the time, 'that the Lordy Jesus side o' jazz'.

Talking to Marge had been one of the drollest and most unexpected conversations I could ever have imagined. I was in Moose Jaw, Saskatchewan, at the confluence of Moose Jaw River and Thunder Creek, where it seemed I was immediately caught up in a struggle between God and the devil.

If only I'd known at the time what a perfect analogy this would be for my life to come.

PART TWO

CHAPTER EIGHT

WHAT MARGE NEGLECTED TO tell me was that her home and Mrs Henderson's boarding house were plumb in the middle of the red light and entertainment district in downtown Moose Jaw. Both were a short walk from the railway station, and as I turned into River Street just around the corner from the address I'd been given, my eyes were soon popping out of my head. There were girls waving and calling from the windows and balconies of cheap hotels and boarding houses on both sides of the street. It didn't seem to matter that it was snowing steadily; both sidewalks were crammed with people, mainly men, shoving in and out of the brightly lit bars, honky-tonks, gambling joints, saloons and taverns. Even on our famous trip to New York I had never seen anything like this. River Street was the devil's playground and I had come here to play piano.

In the first ten minutes I witnessed two street fights. Three policemen were endeavouring to halt one of them and the crowd was giving them a really hard time, booing and catcalling. I stopped to watch and asked another onlooker what had caused the fight. 'Say, you must be new here, buddy. Just the usual – them American and Canadian railwaymen are always at each other's throats. CPR and the Soo. It's a regular part o' Friday and Saturday nights. Don't do no harm.' He pointed to the police. 'It's them bastards cause most of the trouble.'

In this part of town anyhow, the city police were obviously resented and I would later learn that they were widely regarded as corrupt, in the pay of the big gambling, drinking and prostitution interests in town.

I was to discover that the fabled Mounties, whom I'd always thought of as synonymous with all that was good, honourable and incorruptible, were loathed by the workers and small farmers in the Western Provinces. The Depression was accompanied by a severe and long-lasting drought, which hit farm produce first. Wheat prices crashed and thousands of farmers were forced off their land. As the drought and Depression ravaged the country, the Canadian prairies had their own version of the Oklahoma dustbowl made famous by John Steinbeck in *The Grapes of Wrath*. Like the Oklahoma families, prairie people were forced to seek work elsewhere, many of them being close to starving and penniless. The mounted police suppressed labour unrest, almost as brutally as the thugs hired by business, a practice that was rampant in the US at the time. They beat and arrested men for riding the rails – hitching rides in empty railroad wagons. They joined the goons from the CPR to attack workers in the marshalling yards, beating men senseless with baseball bats as they tried to scramble onto trains going almost anywhere, attempting to find work away from the prairies.

The government in Ottawa labelled these desperate men communists and brutally crushed all protest. The biggest protest ever held in Canada was termed the 'On-to-Ottawa Trek'. Over 1500 unemployed men travelled from work camps in the west towards Ottawa to have their grievances heard. In 1935, in nearby Regina, Mounties and police wielding baseball bats beat the living daylights out of the protestors and sympathetic locals. These people's only solace was that six months later the hated conservative government was unceremoniously thrown out.

The Canadian Mounted Police had to work for years to regain the respect of the common people in the west, and when I arrived in Moose Jaw in 1941 this certainly had not yet happened. Police of any description were suspect, and more than once I was to witness some old guy turn aside and spit at his feet at the mention of the local or federal force.

The guy I'd queried about the fight seemed to know quite a bit about the place, so I asked him why there seemed to be a lot of men about but very few women, apart from those yelling down from the windows and balconies. 'Itinerants,' he said. 'Harvest's long over but they're having a last fling before goin' home.' He then explained that special trains were run to bring labour in from the big cities in the late summer and fall. Saskatchewan alone needed 20 000 extra men to help with the harvest. 'They got a pocketful o' cash and soon they'll be home again with their wives and children. This is their last chance to get drunk and get laid with nobody giving a damn,' he concluded.

My conversation with Marge in the railway restaurant concerning the proselytising Apostolics seemed increasingly bizarre. God and the devil, it would seem, had found a place where they could coexist. Downtown Moose Jaw was positively jumping. Several 'girls' had called out to me, and one had made me laugh, yelling down from an upper-storey window, 'Hey, big boy! Come on up and lay down that heavy pack. I'll lay you down real nice, honey!' If only she'd known I was the original virgin.

Every weekend during the harvest the prairie city filled with itinerant labourers; then all year round there were railway workers, grain elevator and meatworks men and, of course, young people, many over from Regina to enjoy the wicked ways denied them in the prudish provincial capital. The city was the junction for three railway networks, so there was a constant stream of commercial travellers passing through. Despite having cut my teeth on the Jazz Warehouse, I knew nothing about an urban scene like this, but at first sight, it seemed as if Moose Jaw was the ideal place to begin scuffing.

I rang the bell at Mrs Henderson's boarding house and presently heard footsteps approaching and saw a light go on in what I presumed was the hallway.

'You him come from Marge?' a gruff woman's voice demanded from behind the front door. It sounded like, 'You him come from Mars?', which seemed apt; after River Street, staid old Toronto did feel like another planet.

'Yes, ma'am,' I called back, thinking it must be Mrs Henderson.

The door opened a fraction. 'Mrs Henderson?' I enquired.

The door opened further and a large woman sniffed then stuck her head out. Ignoring my presence she checked the street in both directions and said, 'This time of a Friday night, you never know what's outside – soldiers from the camp up to no good, still some of them itinerants around; scum o' the earth, them harvesting lot – drunks. Rubbish people everywhere!' Having thus demolished the neighbourhood, she finally turned to face me and demanded, 'It's mister who?'

'Spayd. Jack Spayd.' I smiled. 'Please call me Jack, Mrs Henderson.'

She made no move to allow me to enter but instead looked at me sharply. 'I'll call you "Jack" after you've paid,' she replied, lips pursed. 'How long do you want to stay?'

With the hall light behind her I couldn't quite make out the colour of her eyes – green, maybe hazel – but their expression was far from friendly. Perhaps she'd once been a proper redhead, but what I was looking at was, to use my mom's words, 'hair that came straight out of a bottle'.

'Well, I guess a week at least, so I can look around and find a job. If that's okay, ma'am?'

She sniffed and I took this for acquiescence. It wasn't the warmest welcome I could remember.

I judged Mrs Henderson to be in her mid-sixties. Stout, big breasted and heavy limbed, she was a tough-looking old buzzard, who gave the impression there wasn't much she hadn't seen or experienced of the human race. Almost certainly life hadn't been kind to her, and she seemed largely unimpressed with it and her fellow humans. Her thinning hennaed hair was a particularly bright shade of ginger and was somewhat disarrayed. Beneath it, her features were almost lost in matt white powder, which stopped abruptly at her pink jowls. Otherwise, her face was devoid of any make-up, even lipstick (the devil's paint, I was to learn). The powder had clogged the myriad creases and deep lines around her mouth, making them even more pronounced, and marking her for the heavy smoker she was, or must have been in the past. I took it that the Lord condemned lipstick but found face powder acceptable.

Most of the rest of my landlady was concealed behind a heavy woollen knit-one purl-one no-nonsense brown cardigan, a baggy skirt and faded floral apron, below which heavy grey woollen stockings, and black felt slippers the size of small canoe paddles protruded. Taken together with her ginger hair and ghoulish face, she was an altogether formidable-looking woman and I confess I was immediately intimidated. Mrs Henderson could well have passed for Dolly's older sister.

'That will be three dollars for bed and breakfast, four dollars fifty with dinner. We don't do lunch, but you will let me know if you'll be out for dinner – can't go throwing out good food – and there's no reduction, unless you say so the night before; cook needs lots of notice so she don't waste money marketing.'

Still standing on the doorstep I reached into my wallet and handed her five single dollars, whereupon she drew fifty cents from her apron pocket in change, then stepped aside and smiled for the first time . . . well, sort of twitch-grimaced. 'C'mon in,' she instructed, as if I'd only just knocked and she'd opened the door to welcome a not particularly good friend or a tradesman. Then, reaching for a key on a rack beside the door, she beckoned me to follow her.

As we walked down the hallway towards the rear of the house, she kept up a flow of instructions. 'I always need the rent a week in advance. We don't want you sneaking off in the dead o' night, do we now, Mr Spayd? You wouldn't be the first. I'll show you to your room. You'll be sharing with Mr Greer; he's long term, clean, tidy, don't snore week nights 'cause he works nightshift at the grain depot, don't come home till eight in the morning and don't drink.' We'd turned into a dark passageway in what seemed to be the rear of the two-storey house. She stopped to click on a light. 'Always switch off the light if you're going out at night; can't waste electricity.' We proceeded a little further down the passage and came to a halt outside a door marked 7, a lucky number for me when playing cards and the first good omen. Mrs Henderson made no move to open the door but turned instead to face me. 'Mr Greer is a born-again Christian and so am I, *praise His precious name.*' The last four words were said as an attachment to the sentence, almost as a throwaway, and I would come to learn that they were always attached whenever she mentioned matters of salvation, witnessing for the Lord, the church, its pastor or congregation, known collectively as *the Lord's work.* 'We don't allow strong drink on the premises. Come home drunk, you'll get your marching orders quick smart and no rent returned, can't say it more plain than that, can I?' She paused fractionally, her green eyes pinning me down. 'You a drinker, Jack?'

It was the first time she'd used my name in this one-way conversation. I smiled in what I hoped was a reassuring way. 'No, ma'am. Marge at the railway explained about drink. But it's okay, I never touch a drop.' She looked at me doubtfully so that I felt the need to explain further. 'You see, my father was, ah . . . is an alcoholic.'

'You mean a drunkard?'

'Well, yes, I suppose that's another word for it.'

'Ain't no other word for it. No point in using fancy names. Strong drink is the devil's way of leading the world into temptation. You smoke?'

'No, ma'am.'

'Dirty, filthy habit, wicked, wicked. This is an iniquitous city, Jack.' She fixed me with another warning look. 'You'll want to be careful, *fall thou not into temptation, saith the Lord, praise His precious name.* A young man like you can easily get into trouble. There's plenty of that around here, all of it the devil's work and he's lurking, Jack. Satan is everywhere you turn.'

How was I ever going to tell her I was in the entertainment business, a jazz piano player and potentially a part of the wicked and iniquitous city? Hoping to change the subject, I asked, 'May I have a shower every morning, ma'am?' Miss Frostbite had advised me about the importance of personal hygiene after discovering that a daily shower wasn't customary among the populace of Cabbagetown. As a schoolboy,

I'd become accustomed to having a shower after I completed my piano practice at Miss Frostbite's place. She had installed three showers at the Jazz Warehouse and so there were no excuses, everyone on her staff was expected to be clean. She could smell what she called 'BO' from ten feet away. If she passed a kitchen worker who hadn't attended to his or her personal hygiene for two or three days, she'd say in a reproving voice, 'There is absolutely no excuse for body odour.' Once said, it wasn't lightly forgotten.

Mrs Henderson's head snapped back at my request. 'Certainly not! You're not a labourer, are you?'

'No, ma'am.'

'Well then, two hot showers a week ought to be quite enough and they come with the rent. Anything extra is ten cents a shower, fifteen cents a bath. Money don't grow on trees, but someone's got to chop them down to heat the water. All that lumber and lugging and bath cleaning costs.' She made it sound as if she was the lumberjack responsible for the entire process involved in feeding the furnace.

Perhaps it was her first attempt at levity. I wasn't sure. I handed back the fifty cents change she'd given me, wondering how much more she would extract before she finally let me into the bedroom. But that, for the time being anyhow, seemed to be that. She unlocked the door and handed me the key, but not without further admonishment. 'You must *always* lock it when you're going out. I can't be responsible for your bits and pieces, so don't come crying to me if anything gets stolen. Take your keys with you. I don't need no careless and inconsiderate person waking me up in the middle of the night and asking me to walk down them stairs with my lumbago to let them in. And be quiet when you come in. Have some consideration for others.'

'Thank you, Mrs Henderson, I will be very careful. Just where is the bathroom, ma'am?'

'Down the end of the passage, the door without no number, and don't leave your things lying around in your half of the room, and kindly clean up the bathroom and wipe the floor after you've been. I don't want no ath-a-letes feet. Only men on this bottom floor, no men allowed upstairs. Brush next to the privy, don't want no dirty splashboard neither. Breakfast seven to eight-thirty, till nine o'clock on Sunday, though you won't want to sleep in with the Lord's work going on outside, *praise His precious name.*'

With this last remark Mrs Henderson's demeanour suddenly changed and she smiled a more or less proper smile, the cracks in her face powder shifting and her voice assuming a slightly softer tone. I was to learn that there were two Mrs Hendersons: the first was *God's precious child*, who was working towards what she referred to as her sanctification; the second was tough as old boot leather and worked at keeping her boarding house shipshape.

'We are having a revival meeting, starting at noon after the regular prayer meeting this Sunday, *praise His precious name.* Perhaps you'd like to come, Jack? The church is just across the road. It's the old theatre, you'll see it in the morning.' She indicated a window above what was to be my bed and my half of the room. 'Snowing too heavy now, but you'll see it when you go out in the morning. Don't do the neon Friday night.'

I didn't ask what she meant by this last remark. Mrs Henderson in her guise as boarding-house keeper had given me a fair old verbal bludgeoning. Surprised by the sudden change in her persona, I agreed to attend a revival meeting, whatever that was supposed to be.

Later, having been to the bathroom and cleaned my teeth and changed into my pyjamas, I lay in bed in my half of the room trying to justify my pathetic spinelessness in acquiescing so quickly to my landlady's suggestion. I told myself I was only going for the music, though I doubted there'd be Negro spirituals. Joe had once told me, 'Negro spirituals, that like white folk tryin' to have themselves their own jazz. Ain't pretty but sometime it got itself some nice Lordy Jesus rhythm.' I was going to hear the Lordy Jesus rhythm. After all, I was a musician, it was my professional duty to check out every type of local music. Comforting myself with the thought of this act of musical piety I felt considerably better about my moral cowardice. I assumed my room-mate would be home on Saturday and Sunday nights, and asked myself if it meant that these were his big snoring nights. I'd simply have to wait and see, but for now I was dog-tired, and soon drifted off to sleep.

Mr Greer, my room-mate, turned up for breakfast, and after Mrs Henderson introduced us – 'Mr Spayd, Mr Greer' – he said quietly, 'Call me Jim.' He seemed a nice enough gent and informed me he worked permanent night shift as a grain blender at the grain terminal, explaining, 'I like to do the Lord's work at the railway station.'

When I looked blank he explained that he handed out tracts and testified to passengers passing through Moose Jaw. 'Otherwise I sleep until it's time for my dinner, then I have my quiet time with the Lord, then it's time to go to work.'

After breakfast – oatmeal, toast and tea (two fried eggs on Sundays) – I left to explore Moose Jaw. The theatre church across the road was easy enough to spot and I asked myself why it was that an abandoned theatre, despite being occupied for a different purpose, still looked forlorn, like an old dancer who had sustained a permanent hip injury. The large and lonely-looking building explained Mrs Henderson's cryptic reference to 'the neon'; on the front of the theatre-cum-church was a large white neon cross with APOSTOLIC CHURCH OF THE PENTECOST spelled out in pink neon tubing. The sign was turned off during the day, but it was sufficiently large to dominate the building.

I must have kept my head down in the heavy snowfall of the previous night, because somehow I hadn't noticed this proclamation in lights of God's residence. I was to learn that the neon sign was turned on every night as soon as it grew dark. There was a church service every night of the week, each with a particular purpose for members of the congregation, the point being that the Apostolic Church of the Pentecost was active seven days a week, and not just on the Lord's day. They were busy 'grabbing the devil by his tail daily'.

The Sunday revival meeting I was to attend with Mrs Henderson was after the regular church service from nine o'clock to eleven o'clock, where the Holy Spirit seemed to be especially present. That in turn followed the Sunday quiet time meeting that came after the gospel record broadcast at 7 a.m. to rouse the neighbourhood. The revival meeting began shortly after 11 a.m. and had the singular purpose of saving souls, with singing and hellfire preaching to encourage us sinners to be born again, *washed in the blood of the Lamb*. The revival reinforcement meetings on Tuesday and Friday evening were to strengthen the faith of those who were born again at the Sunday revival.

My visit with Mrs Henderson, who had previously attended the earlier service, therefore had as its primary purpose the saving of my soul, along with the souls of other sinners dragged in by members of the congregation. We were to *look into the glorious face of the Lord*, confess our sins and be born again.

I was too young at the time to understand the mechanisms of conversion, although later I came to understand that any fundamentalist cult requires at least two indoctrinating events per week to reinforce the message and further isolate the convert from the society outside the cult to which they had belonged in the past.

It must have snowed all or most of the night, for River Street and the surrounding streets were blanketed in snow and looked pristine despite the previous night's mayhem. Nothing looks more shut than a nightclub or tavern or other place of entertainment with the neons and the lights switched off and a chill morning-after wind battering at the barred and padlocked doors. Bright artificial light has the advantage of concealing the creaking and aching bones of tired buildings that are all too apparent in the harsh light of day. On this Saturday morning, much of River Street above its blanket of snow looked a little like Mrs Henderson's face, beaten but not entirely bowed, the whiteness from the newly fallen snow covering all but the creases and disrepair on the older buildings that had remained unmaintained during the previous decade of the Depression.

Reading the billboards and posters outside the clubs, saloons and gambling joints, I made a note of several likely places I might apply to for a job. Nothing appeared to be open except for the slightly better hotels, where the whirr of hoovering and the smell of floor polish indicated the major activities of the morning.

I soon discovered that it was pointless enquiring after the entertainment manager. Nevertheless, I did the rounds, asking anyone I could find for the name of the manager or person I should ask to see, and writing this down for later. Finally I approached a uniformed bell captain at the entrance to the Brunswick Hotel, a three-storey building that was seemingly one of the best of several hotels in River Street. He was an older man and I introduced myself and asked him if I could see the entertainment manager.

'What's your business, Jack?' He was obviously accustomed to authority.

'I play piano,' I replied.

'What sort?'

'Jazz . . . ah, just about everything else as well,' I added quickly.

'Bit young, ain't you?'

'Well, the keyboard doesn't know my age.' It wasn't an original line and could probably have been attributed to Mozart in his day.

'Hey, I like that!' he exclaimed. 'You're going to need all the cheek you got in River Street, Jack. There are more ways to fleece a greenhorn in this street than I've found to swear at a bellboy.'

'Yeah, I must say it's a bit different to Toronto.'

He laughed. 'Well, yeah, chalk 'n' cheese. Moose Jaw is the New Orleans of Canada, and River Street is where a man can find the most joy and trouble in the one place.' He stuck out his hand. 'Peter Cornhill.'

'Pleased to make your acquaintance, Peter.'

'When'd you get into town?' he wanted to know.

'Last night,' I said. 'If you hear about anything going on the street, I'd be most obliged.'

Peter Cornhill laughed again. 'Jack, that's my job, son. But in my profession the only way to open my ears is to unzip your wallet.' I reached into my pocket. 'No, no, not now.' He grinned. 'Most musicians are on the bones of their ass. It's the one trade where money don't stick. You pay if I deliver the goods, the information you need.'

'Thanks, Peter, much obliged.'

'May as well take it easy for the rest of the day, son. Ain't nothing happens in this street until the girls have risen from their beauty sleep, painted their faces on and are back leaning on the windowsills and showing off their titties. That's the signal, that's the time when the joints start jumping and the saloons and the gambling dens get to thinking about the action for the night to come. Come by maybe five-thirty, six o'clock, be someone you can talk to in most places. I'll have a word to Mr Kerr, the assistant manager, when he comes in. Reggie Blunt, who plays piano here, is getting a mite grumpy, been one or two complaints from the ladies at the Thursday tea party. Do you do, you know . . . light classical? They like that.'

'You mean Johann Strauss, Franz Lehar, Fritz Kreisler? Yeah, sure, I can do them.'

'Huh? No, never heard o' them. Don't suppose they have neither. You know, English classical . . . "Keep the Home Fires Burning", "If You Were the Only Girl in the World", "Roses of Picardy" . . . them?'

I'd come full circle from Dolly and Mac's ancient HMV gramophone squawking through the ceiling boards and my battered, belated birthday harmonica. 'Sure, practically play them in my sleep,' I assured him.

'I'll see what I can do, Jack. Come back round about six. Mr Cameron Kerr will be in to get ready for the dinner crowd. He's a nice guy, bit sharp sometimes but don't take no notice. Drives a hard bargain but he'll give you a hearing.' Peter Cornhill grinned. 'Old Reggie says he's getting too old to play ladies' afternoon-tea-party crap. Says he's gonna toss it in if he has to play to a bunch of cackling old hens much longer. Long as I can remember he's bin saying he's going to live with his son and daughter-in-law in Winnipeg and only play nursery rhymes to his grandchildren. "A definite step up the rungs of the musical ladder, Peter, old chap," Peter Cornhill mimicked. 'Only by now his grandchildren must be teenagers.'

'Thanks, Peter, I'll be here on the dot.' I knew just how Reggie Blunt, the resident piano player at the Brunswick, must have felt. I'd never played any of the First World War songs on the piano and it had been a good while since I'd done so on the harmonica, but as I said, I could have played all the sentimental favourites on a comb wrapped in tissue paper and not missed a note.

I spent the remainder of the day looking around the centre of the city and walking along both rivers, but it was too cold to go far. Around five in the afternoon I returned to River Street and began knocking on doors. Six premises of various sorts more or less fitted the bill. Three of them featured bands, two were setting up for the night to come, and one place featured a solo piano. For each of the two bands that were setting up, the piano player was the bandleader and both gave me the heave-ho, my feet barely touching the ground. The third band hadn't yet arrived but the manager asked me to play a medley, and after I'd done so he told me I was too good and would show up the rest of his band, so thanks but no thanks. The solo piano player turned out to be a part owner of the club and asked me to play. I did and he said he'd hire me for the nights he had off and asked me to leave my phone number. Like an idiot I hadn't asked Mrs H. for the phone number of the boarding house. Some professional I turned out to be. I'd been so intimidated by my landlady that I'd left without thinking of her at all, except to be hugely relieved that she hadn't turned up in the dining room at breakfast. I could of course have asked the cook or Jim Greer, all the other guests having left or eaten earlier. I told the piano-playing club owner I was new in town and would drop in a contact number as soon as I had one.

I was beginning to realise that most of the musicians were older men, the younger ones having gone off to war. Because I was over six foot and shaved every other day I probably looked a little older than seventeen. In fact, I was pointedly asked by two of the four bandleaders, both short, paunchy and somewhat recalcitrant, why I wasn't in uniform.

At six o'clock sharp I reported to Peter Cornhill at the Brunswick Hotel who put one of his bellboys in charge of the front door and took me in to see Mr Kerr, whose office adjoined the main foyer. The interior of the hotel smelled of beeswax and floor polish. The assistant manager was busy writing at a small desk when Peter knocked on the half-open door, and before the doorman could open his mouth to introduce me, without looking up he said, 'Thank you, Peter, that will be all. Please sit down, Mr . . . ?'

'Spayd, sir, Jack Spayd.'

'Won't be a moment, Mr Spayd,' he said, still not glancing up from his writing. Peter Cornhill touched me lightly on the shoulder, smiled reassuringly and left while I lowered myself into the only chair.

'Now, what can I do for you?' The assistant manager looked up at last. 'Oh,' he said, obviously surprised, 'You're young.' Then, recovering quickly, added, 'Mr Spayd, you said? What is it?'

'Well, I play the piano and I was hoping . . .'

'What? What do you play?' he interrupted.

I smiled, attempting to ignore his sharp manner. He obviously saw me as some over-ambitious jumped-up kid. 'Rachmaninoff to ragtime and most everything in between.' It was a line I'd rehearsed in bed that morning and I rather liked the sound of it – neat, concise, competent but not overly boastful. But now it sounded pretentious.

The assistant manager of the Brunswick Hotel frowned. 'I see, a piano hack.'

I smiled, trying to conceal my surprise. 'No, sir, I've had a classical training but I prefer jazz, the blues in particular.' It wasn't what I'd intended to say. Jazz still wasn't all the go in Canada, and way out here on the prairies it may have been even less popular.

'Jazz? It so happens I know a bit about jazz.' It was said in a smug, slightly amused manner as if I had trapped myself and he was about to find me out. He gave me a supercilious smile. 'Care to play for me, Jack?'

'Be delighted, sir.'

He rose. 'Follow me. We have a piano in the ballroom. It's not new but it's a Steinway and recently tuned.' He was warning me not to blame the piano. 'Dinner doesn't begin until 6.30 p.m., plenty of time to hear you out before Mr Blunt, our regular pianist, arrives for work.'

The clipped manner in which he pronounced the word 'out' left me in no further doubt that he wasn't expecting much and that the word was intended to convey more than the obvious meaning. We reached the ballroom, a big echoing room with pale blue walls, a high white ceiling, and polished wooden floors for dancing, now covered with tables set for a big dinner with white damask tablecloths and napkins, silver and good china. There were wine glasses on the tables too, something you didn't see very often. The Steinway sat on a bandstand some distance from the tables, as if the music was not meant to intrude on the conversation of the two hundred or so diners the room seemed set up to accommodate.

'Just jazz?' I asked.

'No, give me . . . what did you say? Rachmaninoff to ragtime and everything in between,' he said, amused, and with his arms clasped about his chest, he chuckled. 'I want your full repertoire, Mr Spayd.'

'Range or repertoire, sir?' I queried, hoping to gain a little respect.

'Range,' he snapped, clearly annoyed at me for picking him up on his misuse of a word.

He still hadn't called me Jack, which wasn't a good sign. I sat down and started with the main theme from the second movement of Rachmaninoff's *Second Piano Concerto in C Minor*. So as to continue the mood I did a couple of Chopin *Preludes*, then moved effortlessly into the first movement of Beethoven's *Moonlight Sonata*. I looked up and smiled to indicate my confidence (ha ha) before moving into 'Tenderly', a slow jazz piece in the Art Tatum manner, though, of course, with nothing remotely like the master's effortless finesse, switching from style to style. Part of Art Tatum's genius was his marriage of classical and jazz and it was this I was now trying to emulate. From here I eased into 'St James Infirmary Blues' and then bridged this with Gershwin's 'Summertime' from *Porgy and Bess*, his recent musical. After this soft, tender and beautiful melody, I opened up and thumped my way merrily through 'Alexander's Ragtime Band', grinning and stomping. Finally, so as not to exclude the Thursday ladies' tea party, I ended with 'Roses of Picardy', actually singing the lyrics, my voice having long since turned from boy soprano to baritone.

Closing the piano I waited for the assistant manager's reaction. To my mind I'd played reasonably well but wasn't sure what he expected or wanted, if anything at all. Maybe he was simply humouring me.

'Jesus! What are you doing applying for a hotel job, Jack?' Cameron Kerr cried. 'You're concert material!' His expression indicated that he was more than mildly impressed.

I breathed a huge sigh of relief. 'Not quite, sir,' I grinned. 'Jazz is a difficult medium and I'm still too young to fully grasp its nuances,' I said pretentiously.

'Well, I can tell you you're the best we've heard around these parts for a while. What brings you to Moose Jaw?'

'Learning to grow up some before joining the army, sir.'

He grinned and came towards me with his hand extended. 'What can I say? You've got the job.'

'Thank you, sir . . . thank you very much,' I said, stretching out my hand to shake his. Then, stupidly, in spite of Joe's warnings, I said, 'But what about Mr Blunt?' I could hear Joe Hockey's words clearly in my head. 'Jazzboy, you on yo own in the wide wide worl'. Don't do no soft-hearted non-sense, you hear? No free, no one-week trial wid no pay. Do that you soon gonna starve yo'self to death. Scuffin' means every man fo' hisself, tramping over and stomping on ever-body to get yo sweet ass on that there pee-ano stool.'

'What about Reggie Blunt?' Cam Kerr asked.

'Well, ah, the doorman, Peter, told me he, Mr Blunt, was the resident pianist and an elderly man. Be hard for him to get another job . . .'

Cam Kerr laughed. 'Jack, he's been threatening to quit for years. Wants to go live with his son, daughter-in-law and grandchildren in Winnipeg. He's not broke and he only plays piano for his stake so he can play and lose at poker every week. He keeps the local gamblers in pocket money. Don't worry, he'll be secretly pleased. He can never make up his mind, not about cards, not about anything. Now it's done for him, he can go and see his grandchildren.

'Can you play here tonight? This Saturday's a big night for us, it's the annual Rotary shindig. The police chief will be attending, as well as some of the big wigs from Regina. We have a band coming – couldn't get the one we wanted, this one's second-rate – but I'll put them in the fine dining room. I want you to play as you've just done for me, Rachmaninoff to ragtime, and everything in between. You'll knock their socks off, Jack.' Cam Kerr had transformed from cynic to enthusiast.

'Sure, be a pleasure, sir.'

'It's Cam. Call me Cam. Musicians aren't formal. Always wanted to be a musician,' he chuckled. 'Never got past "Tea for two"!'

'Pretty sophisticated if you're Art Tatum; it's practically his signature tune,' I replied.

'Not with two fingers,' he laughed again.

I swallowed. 'Cam, ah . . . what about . . . you know?'

'Oh, yes, almost forgot. Your salary? How does eleven dollars a week sound, dinner thrown in?'

This time I took Joe's advice. 'Fifteen. I'll bring in new customers. Younger crowd. Give me a few weeks and I'll be on your billboard.'

'Fourteen! With lunch thrown in as well as dinner? Days off, Sunday, Monday.'

'It's a deal, but with a salary review in three months?' (Joe Hockey once again.)

'Done!' he said, reaching out and clasping my hand in both his own. 'Welcome to the Brunswick, Jack.'

Effectively I was a dollar fifty a week better off not having my dinner at Mrs H.'s and I'd be saving on lunch money, too. I had my first scuffing job and it was a damn good one – I couldn't have asked for better. I ended up playing the foyer and the cocktail lounge of the Brunswick Hotel from 4 p.m. to 6 p.m. with half an hour for dinner, then the main fine dining room or ballroom if they had a gala event. Tuesdays to Saturday, 6.45 p.m. until 9 p.m. (10.30 p.m. for ballroom events) or back to the cocktail lounge until 10.30 p.m. for a normal night. Of course, I did the Thursday ladies' tea party, 3 p.m. to 5.30 p.m.

After paying my board I had more than ten dollars left over a week. I wouldn't have to touch the money for my mother's nose job and felt I was positively rolling in cash. I handed Peter Cornhill two bucks for the introduction. 'Thanks, young Jack; more than generous. Welcome to the Brunswick.'

I'd pressed a white shirt and my only pair of dark blue flannels for any interviews I might have obtained, but I certainly wasn't dressed for playing piano to a celebrity audience in a ballroom. My Mrs Sopworth suit was back at the boarding house but it was still squashed into the bottom of my rucksack along with the starched collars and shirts.

'What time would you want me here, Cam?' I asked.

He glanced at his watch. 'Now, in ten minutes,' he replied.

'What about Mr Blunt?' I asked, Joe's advice once again ignored.

'Oh, I'll tell Peter to explain and I'll pay him off tomorrow.' I was beginning to understand the cutthroat world of the entertainment business. Poor old bastard, I hoped he really did want to get to Winnipeg and wasn't broke.

I glanced down at my clothes. 'But I won't have time to get home and change.'

'Oh, I see what you mean. Wait on, we'll find you a bow tie. The manager's a big guy and always has a spare suit in his office. We'll borrow his jacket. Nobody will notice your pants, just remember not to get up to take a bow.' I could see he saw me as a feather in his cap.

That was my first Saturday night, in fact, my first night scuffing. When I finished playing just after 11 p.m., half an hour beyond my official time, the maitre d' congratulated me and added that a number of his Rotary diners had commented favourably on the music. After most of the guests had left, I earned two dollars in tips playing for the stragglers, old friends chatting on and enjoying a last drink. Finally, at 11.45 p.m., my first night's scuffing came to an end. Altogether it had been a good night's work and I felt rather pleased with myself. I could now truly call myself a professional musician and it felt good. The big wide world wasn't as frightening as Joe had said. All that remained was the prospect of attending the Sunday revival meeting the following day with Mrs Henderson, and coming clean about earning my living doing the devil's work.

I spent the next hour canvassing River Street to check out the other sinners before finally heading to my half of the bedroom. It had stopped snowing and the white neon cross was pumping out the true light, testifying for Jesus to the heathen horde still Saturday-nighting along River Street. The bright candy-pink lettering below it flicked on and off – APOSTOLIC CHURCH OF THE PENTECOST – and under it in blood-red neon ran the words I hadn't noticed when the neon had been switched off: *The wages of sin is death!*

I'd mentally backhanded myself several times for being so weak and now I did so once again. I should have told the white-faced old dragon to go jump in the lake, or in this particular case, Thunder Creek. I'd only just obtained a paid job in the devil's playground and now, in a few hours, I was going to attend a revival meeting where I would be asked to give my life to Jesus.

I unlocked the door to my bedroom close to midnight. My room-mate Jim Greer's snoring practically battered down the door before I'd even opened it. Should I switch on the bedroom light or leave the light on in the hall and hope I could see enough? I decided to risk waking him up by turning on the bedroom light; it was half my room after all.

Jim Greer lay on his back with his mouth open, his false teeth, fixed in a Machiavellian grin, in a large glass of water on the small bedside table beside his gilt-edged Bible. His big belly and chest were covered with three heavy blankets and a brown quilted eiderdown with the words *Asleep in the arms of Jesus* appliquéd in white down the middle. At breakfast he'd made it sound as if he led a neat, ordered and fulfilled life; he'd certainly earned his sleep.

His snoring didn't bode well for future weekend sleep, but I told myself I'd cut my teeth on my dad's drunken snoring and then Dolly's far from dulcet tones fret-sawing their way through the ceiling, but Jim Greer's nocturnal snorts and barks were really something. Inhaling grain dust must have permanently affected his sinuses.

I grabbed my wash bag and repaired to the bathroom, then returned to the bedroom, changed and switched off the light and lay in bed listening to the cadences of his breathing, broken occasionally by a long pause and then an alarming snort. It had been a good day and I was on my way to making a living as a musician. The last thought I remember was that if I averaged two dollars a day in tips, this added an extra ten bucks per week to my income. I was already earning more than Mac had made on any week I'd known him over the past ten years.

Gospel hymns blaring into the street over powerful speakers at seven o'clock on a Sunday morning could be described as a rude awakening. A blast of music and singing practically lifted the covers off my bed. I was to learn that they played gospel gramophone records for an hour on Sunday mornings, followed by silence for an hour until the church meeting began at nine, whereupon the sermon, the witnessing and the attendant vocal pyrotechnics took over, all of it broadcast live onto River Street.

Jim Greer was already up when I awoke with a decided shock and parted the curtains to look out. The neon blazed in the December dark, with the blood-red threat to sinners punching out a warning to stragglers and the last of Saturday night's lost souls that they were being closely watched.

It was difficult to comprehend how this dawn chorus or the fervent religious carry-on that followed would ever switch the Saturday-night and Sunday-morning ne'er-do-wells to God's way of thinking. With all the noise and a sore head to boot, you'd have to have been a pretty desperate sinner to come running in from outside to be born again. The Apostolic Church of the Pentecost owned River Street on a Sunday morning and the whores and their hungover clients were most certainly getting their comeuppances.

It was just after eight o'clock when I arrived in the dining room.

Thankfully, neither Jim Greer nor Mrs Henderson was present. The singing had ceased and the street outside was now blessedly silent. No doubt my room-mate and hostess had departed early for the church service, even though it was only a hop, skip and a jump across the street. Jim Greer would later tell me they always attended a Sunday morning pre-service Bible reading and prayer meeting when they all '*drew unto themselves*' and prayed silently for their personal sanctification.

'It's completely silent? No speaking in tongues or shouting out?' I'd asked.

'The Holy Spirit isn't required for the eight o'clock meeting, Jack.'

'Isn't required or isn't invited?' I asked somewhat cheekily.

He looked at me as if I were a child in need of a patient explanation. 'The Holy Spirit descends as a dove, a white dove among us. Sometimes it turns into a flame. It is always welcome and sometimes arrives quite unexpectedly when a blessed brother or sister bursts spontaneously into tongues. But the Lord Jesus also allows us silence to contemplate His word. *Ask, and it shall be given you; seek, and ye shall find; knock, and it shall be opened unto you.*'

'This dove descending, can you actually see it? I mean with your own eyes?' I asked, more than a little sceptical.

'Of course! That is once you've been *washed in the blood of the Lamb* and have accepted Jesus into your heart as a born-again Christian.'

There was no point arguing. I was to learn that born-again Christians witnessed and experienced phenomena not seen by or given to those who are not embraced within the arms of Jesus.

The cook, Mrs Mary Spragg, handed me a note from Mrs Henderson saying she'd hop over the road to fetch me at 8.45 and to wear a clean shirt and necktie if I possessed one – if not, Mr Greer had left one of his own on his bed for me – and not to forget to polish my boots. Mrs Spragg seemed to be everything Mrs Henderson wasn't, thin as a rake and a chirpy, cheerful soul who took one look at me and declared, 'Ah, a four-egg young man, I do declare! How do you like them, Jack, over easy or sunny side up? Call me Mary.'

After breakfast, I spent ages trying to press my crumpled suit, using a sheet of brown paper to avoid making the material shiny, as my mom had taught me to do with my school blazer and grey flannels. I then ironed a shirt, pressed a blue tie from the back and polished my boots.

Mrs Henderson, arriving to escort me over the road, appeared somewhat taken aback by my appearance. 'My goodness, Jack, you do look splendid!' she exclaimed. I told myself once again that I was only going to church for the sake of the music, although the 7 a.m. blast of sound, presumably from a recognised and recorded gospel choir, undermined my argument.

Though everyone seemed to be having a good time at the revival meeting, to me it felt and sounded chaotic. My mom and I hadn't been to church all that often in my childhood, but when we had it had been the Presbyterian church, mainly out of gratitude for their help in clothing us throughout the Depression. They were a pretty staid lot, almost as far removed from this lot across the street as the dreaded Catholics themselves. Joe might have said of the Apostolics, 'Them cats they really jumpin'! They got the devil by his tail and they be swingin', man!' What ensued in the next two hours of the revival meeting was, to my mind at least, complete chaos, but joyous chaos, people letting their hair down in a manner I'd never before witnessed.

Pastor Mullens, wearing a lounge suit instead of robes, welcomed us and announced that, unfortunately, Sister Hammond, the pianist, wasn't well and asked us to include her in our prayers. Fortunately, Brother Bright on the clarinet and Brother Simmons on his new electric guitar would accompany us whenever the spirit took them.

He then prayed, which turned out to be a series of injunctions to the Lord to send down the Holy Spirit to bring light into the lives of the heathen and to strengthen our resolve to fight the devil on every front. There were frequent interjections from the congregation, with 'Hallelujah!', 'Yes, Jesus!' and 'Praise his name!' being the most popular.

Then the singing started, with Brother Bright's clarinet sounding anything but bright. The audience didn't seem to mind, belting out the words of praise. Then followed more fire and brimstone from the pastor, and invitations to come to the front and declare for Jesus, *the one and only precious redeemer.*

After more singing, the dove or the flame or both must have arrived because one woman jumped from her seat and, throwing her hands in the air, started speaking in tongues, a surprising gabble of words that made no sense but was nonetheless impressive – not the sort of sounds you could make from a standing start. Two others followed her, one having to be restrained by a companion as she attempted to throw herself to the floor.

More imprecations were directed at the devil, and those sinners in the congregation were urged to accept Jesus as our saviour. We were warned not to delay but to come forward and give our lives to Christ Jesus and be saved *from the everlasting flames of hell.* Several people, or rather sinners, came forward to kneel and be embraced by the pastor. Kneeling at his feet with his hands on their heads, they were declared saved, *washed in the blood of the Lamb.* More singing followed, with neither musician doing anything to improve the sound, and there was more crying out in praise.

I could feel Mrs H. beside me almost willing me to go to the front and accept Jesus as my saviour and precious redeemer, but the appalling clarinettist and excruciating guitarist were getting to me so much that I wanted to run for my life. Bad instrumentalists are painful to anyone and these two were agony personified. The piano stood empty, with what I took to be gospel sheet music resting on the stand above the keyboard. I could sight-read just about anything, and judging from the tunes we'd sung so far there was nothing difficult about the music, so I rose to a tremendous shout of *'Hallelujah! Praise His precious name!'* from Mrs Henderson, who, thinking she'd brought me to her redeemer, clasped her hands in joy.

Instead I made my way to the piano, glanced at the music and began to play 'Nothing but the Blood of Jesus', which was taken up happily by the congregation. 'On Christ the Solid Rock I Stand' followed, with Pastor Mullens beaming at me. I played several others over the next hour, interspersed with messages, speaking in tongues, and urgings to accept Jesus into our lives. Two songs I remember were 'I Have Decided to Follow Jesus' and 'There's Room at the Cross'. Fortunately my playing was too accomplished for the other musicians to follow me, and they laid down their instruments and quietly resumed their seats. Finally, and to my surprise, I found 'When the Saints Go Marching In', a piece Joe had long since taught me to play with a very black feel. To my surprise the congregation took it up with alacrity, clapping their hands, and even dancing on the spot in a couple of cases. This seemed to signal the end of the revival meeting and the pastor concluded with a prayer of thanks for the six precious souls who had given their lives to the Lord, then a general blessing – Go forth in the light of the Lord. We all left the church then and spilled out onto the sidewalk, filled with the glory.

Taking me to be a visiting born-again Christian, several of the congregation including Pastor Mullens came over to thank me. Mrs Henderson stood by introducing me, pigeon-breasted with pleasure, basking in the light of her new find.

When at last we crossed the street to the boarding house, she said, 'Jack, why didn't you tell me you'd already found the Lord?'

'Mrs Henderson, I'm afraid I haven't. I've been meaning to tell you, I'm a professional musician.'

A stunned silence followed. 'You mean it was the devil's child at the piano?'

'Was the music not just as sweet?' I replied. It was a quote from somewhere, though I couldn't remember where. Maybe Shakespeare . . . no, that's wrong, of course; that's 'a rose by any other name would smell as sweet'.

As we reached the front door she announced in a clipped and angry voice, 'I shall pray to the Lord for your salvation, Mr Spayd.'

'Thank you for your invitation today, Mrs Henderson. I found work last night at the Brunswick Hotel and I'll be home rather late on Saturday nights in future, which will mean I'll need to sleep in some, come Sundays.'

'Hmmph!' she grunted, proceeding to climb the stairway, her broad back and hips rigid with indignation. Halfway up she turned. '"I am not mocked," saith the Lord,' she shouted down at me.

Reaching my half-room, I decided Joe Hockey had been over-generous. Lordy Jesus music was a long way from jazz and was not in any sense rhythmic, the exception being 'When the Saints Go Marching In', which is almost impossible to play badly. Even Brother Bright on clarinet and Brother Simmons on his recently acquired electric guitar wouldn't have been able to screw it up entirely.

Thankfully, Jim Greer was out on the Moose Jaw railway platform, sending the gospel down the line by passing out tracts and witnessing for the Lord, and so I had the room to myself for the afternoon. Although the revival meeting had been both bizarre and unsettling, it had also been an intense experience, so much so that there were moments when I felt frightened to be a sinner, and had consciously to resist the offer of salvation and of taking Jesus into my heart and life. I didn't know if I even qualified as a sinner to be saved. Apart from thinking lascivious thoughts about the twins when I was in bed at night, and the self-pleasuring that invariably followed, I couldn't think of any particularly wicked thing I'd done. Did any of that require me to be washed in the blood of the Lamb? I played cards, penny-ante poker, but was that a sin? I wasn't sure. I tried always to tell the truth, unless doing so was pointless and would result in someone being hurt.

The piano had been my true salvation and had kept me from being swept off my feet during the revival meeting. Now I needed an hour or two on my own to regain my balance and exercise some control over my emotions.

I have no idea how many lost souls in the ensuing months were brought begging for salvation into the converted theatre on a Sunday morning by the blazing white cross and its attendant warning in red neon, but I felt fairly certain that tackling the devil head-on with a 7 a.m. Sunday broadcast was counterproductive, an act of poor judgment by the Apostolic Church of the Pentecost. I remained fairly certain

Marge's Mervyn wasn't the only bleary-eyed sinner, suffering a hangover and desperately in need of a sleep-in, who cursed God's children singing His amplified early-morning praises. For my part, I continued to wake up with a start at the first strains of the Sunday morning choral alarm and then, covering my head with the blankets, I slept a further hour before going down to Mrs Spragg's breakfast of four eggs over easy.

What did I know about scuffing? Not a lot. I'd landed myself just about the best job in town and after two months young people started to appear on Sunday afternoons to listen to me practising on the Steinway in the ballroom. Somehow word got around, and every Sunday the crowd grew bigger until Cam Kerr asked me to make it an event and increased my weekly pay cheque. It seemed I'd attracted a new younger crowd. The hotel began to advertise me actively with the banner 'Jack Spayd Digs the Sunday Blues', and I soon played for two hours to a packed ballroom on a Sunday afternoon from three till five.

Like the audience outside the Jazz Warehouse, the younger adults in Moose Jaw were jazz hungry, and when you play to an appreciative audience, you always play better than you imagine you can. I enjoyed these sessions immensely, and while they earned me another eight dollars, playing the devil's music on a Sunday was to prove the final straw for Mrs Henderson. She may have passed the Brunswick and seen my name 'in lights', so to speak, because she now never spoke directly to me and accepted her weekly rent with a grunt and a curt 'Thank you, Mr Spayd'.

I expected her to send me packing and I guess I could have moved out, but the boarding house was convenient for work. Besides, I spent very little time there and when I was in, Mrs H.'s silence proved a blessing. She was a woman who could only think in negatives and saw everyone as a potential cheat, liar or threat.

Jim Greer's presence on weekends was bearable because on Saturdays he slept the sleep of the dead until the afternoon while I played a regular poker game at the Caribou Café just off River Street. This regular card game came about through a nice happenstance. After my first night playing at the Rotary dinner I reported for work only to be called over by Peter Cornhill. He introduced me to Reggie Blunt, who greeted me in a most friendly manner despite my having stolen his gig. 'Glad to meet you, Jack,' he said, immediately extending his hand and putting me at ease.

'Mr Blunt, I —'

'No, no, say no more, dear boy, you have relieved old Reginald of a great burden.'

I judged him to be in his early sixties, a short, almost square man, bald on top, although the remainder of his grey hair curled over his coat collar. He had blue eyes and what my mom would call a whisky nose, purple and veined. 'Peter tells me you wowed the Rotary crowd on Saturday night, Jack.'

I laughed. 'Not really an overly demonstrative lot, but thankfully I got through unscathed. I don't think they cared for the blues much, but they liked the ragtime and the old sentimental songs . . . ah, classics,' I added quickly for Peter Cornhill's benefit.

'Good for you, Jack. The mayor is a pain in the backside and the police chief only knows two movements.' He demonstrated, his arm outstretched with the palm up, followed by a quick retreat into his trouser pocket. We chatted for a while and he assured me I had one of the better music jobs on River Street. 'I suppose you might make a case for Grant Hall on Main, with all that black marble in the foyer, the rotunda, grand staircase and musicians' gallery, but is it the top of the Christmas tree? I think it lacks the cantankerous and brash atmosphere of River Street.' Cackling, he observed, 'Ragtime and whores go together like prairies and bad weather, no, blues and whores, even better,' he added, then asked, 'Do you play cards, old chap?'

'Yes, but penny-ante,' I replied cautiously.

'Poker?'

I nodded. 'Five-card stud or five-card draw mostly.'

'Excellent! We have a group, three other River Street musicians and my good self. We play Monday mornings from eleven until two in the afternoon. Like you, musicians have a day off on Mondays. Would you care to join us?' He nodded towards Peter Cornhill. 'Peter's also a part of our group.'

Peter laughed. 'I'm the flat note. My poker isn't much better than my music, I'm afraid. I have to be back on duty at two-thirty in the afternoon because Monday is the hotel chauffeur's day off so I take his place. Sunday evening is always busy with commercial travellers and company men arriving in town for the week.'

'Hah! Beware this man!' Reggie Blunt warned. 'Always remember, he's a hotel bell captain and doesn't miss a trick. Sharp as a shark's tooth, old chap!'

'I'd like that very much,' I said.

'We play at the Caribou Café, Jack, though I should inform you it is always referred to as the John Robert Johnson Caribou Café, don't ask me why, it just is and always has been. Excellent chap, by the way, most accommodating fellow.'

If Cam Kerr had been right about Reggie Blunt's poker game, I wouldn't be out of my depth. There is a saying in poker that if you can't find out who's the bunny in the game, then it's you. I hoped this wouldn't prove to be the case. It would be nice meeting a few of the local musicians. Maybe there'd be a chance to form a bit of a group later on. I already missed playing sessions with a band.

The poker game took care of Monday mornings and I used the afternoon as well as Sunday mornings for serious piano practice. Cam Kerr had kindly agreed that I could use the Steinway in the ballroom on both days. It was sufficiently isolated from the general business of the hotel for the sound not to intrude and I practised three hours on Sunday and another two on Monday after the poker game.

During the week I'd read in the mornings, or visit the first-rate city library. To get out of my bedroom I'd go to the parlour. Mrs H. had earlier agreed to a request I'd made via Mary Spragg, the cook, for permission to chop wood and light a fire, provided I cleaned the grate after it had cooled and paid twenty-five cents extra on my rent.

Saturday I'd usually do a long walk of about three hours' bird-spotting along the Moose River or Thunder Creek. I'd never lost my love of birds, first developed on walks with my mom along the Don and still very much a part of me.

I didn't see much of the remaining boarding-house guests, apart from at breakfast time; all of them, it seemed, were permanent. There were two elderly ladies: Mrs Throsby, who suffered from Parkinson's disease, and Miss Darlington, a frail birdlike woman with a heavy walking stick, which she clunked alarmingly on the floor when she walked. Both complained constantly of their aches and pains and competed over the number and severity of their 'ops' (surgical operations). Having to negotiate the stairs was a double daily nightmare. Fortunately Mary Spragg took their breakfast to their bedrooms so that the mornings were free of surgical references. The two remaining boarders, Mr Hardacre and Mr Fobbs, were in their fifties, silent men who wouldn't say boo to a mouse, although they ate so noisily one could almost imagine it was their means of conversing. Both were clerks at different meatworks: one was stout and rubicund, the other painfully pale and thin. According to Mary, they hadn't spoken to each other for eight years. She referred to them as Pork and Beef.

For the next six months I really enjoyed the weekly poker game. The group consisted of Chuck Bullmore, tenor sax; Charlie Condotti, drums; Mort Smith, clarinet; and Reggie Blunt, piano like myself; and of course Peter Cornhill, who referred to himself as 'playing the fool'.

I usually came away from a game with five or six bucks in my pocket, but most importantly, I enjoyed both the company and the game. Poker seemed to suit my personality. I had what Miss Bates called an eidetic memory, that is to say, I could fairly easily visualise a sheet of music I'd seen once or, as I discovered when learning to play poker, remember the cards my opponents were dealt and have a fair idea of the hand they might hold. There is, of course, a lot more to the game of poker than a good memory, but it's a helpful skill to bring to a game and, as I said, I usually left with a little more change in my pocket than I'd had when

I sat down to play. The poker school rather predictably dubbed me Jack of Spayds.

I confess, while the five-card stud we played involved only pennies and was not to be taken too seriously, alas, my approach to poker differed somewhat from that of most social players.

Most young guys learn how to be competitive at a very young age, but I had somehow missed out on that aspect of growing up. I learned music instead, where you compete against your previous best effort rather than against an opponent. If I'd missed this important survival skill, I'd gained another, perhaps doubtful, one in its place. I was possessed of a highly obsessive nature. This was one of the reasons I felt compelled to run to the piano during the revival meeting. It was the only way I could protect myself from being overwhelmed. Any person who claims that the charismatic religions don't have the power to pull at some deep atavistic emotion is quite wrong. There is a need in many people for blind belief or, as it's usually more politely put, faith. Like all fundamentalist beliefs, it provides a safe haven and can easily become an obsession.

I had been watching the guys in the band at Miss Frostbite's playing poker for ages. The thing about musicians – well, musicians who play in a band anyway – is that they mostly practise together and have a fair bit of time to kill – time between rehearsals, time waiting for gigs to begin and time after a gig, when they're often too high simply to pack up and go home. Musicians entertain others, but are often left with no entertainment themselves. So they reach for a pack of cards and most often the choice is five-card stud poker, a simple game anyone can learn to play but that few play with expertise.

I'd begun to play poker with the band after I'd completed my schooling and before I left for the prairies; *begun to learn* is a better way of putting it. I'd often stay back after dishwashing and get home at two in the morning. Joe, observing me, called me aside one night and issued one of his more pertinent warnings. 'Jazzboy, now you gonna be careful with that there card playin', yo hear?'

'But it's only for pennies, Joe. Nobody gets hurt,' I protested. 'It's harmless fun and I can sleep in late now school's over.'

'Ha, that ain't no harmless fun, boy, that the beginning o' big, big trouble. You wanna know why it only penny-ante allowed? That because Miss Frostbite hear dey playin' for big money she gonna cut off their balls, make dem sing soprano, that's why.'

'But surely it's just a good way to unwind after a heavy night's playing?'

'Yeah, for some folk, sure, but poker ain't no unwind for some them cats. While you may be unwindin', they windin' up. Ain't nothing breaks up no band like poker gamblin'.'

I scratched my head, not understanding. 'But why? It's better than booze, isn't it?'

'Ha, now that prob-lo-mat-tic, Jazzboy. Booze don't make no hate in a band.' I looked at him, still not understanding. 'Now, you lissen up real good, son. The first rule o' poker, any kind poker, straight poker, draw poker, five-card poker, five-card-stud poker, seven-card-stud poker, don't matter what, always somebody gonna take all the cash and ever-body gonna set to hatin' that par-tic-u-lar dude. You know why? Be-cause he gonna do it again and again and one more time, and them other cats they gonna try to chase their stake. What they lost before and what they bring'd for chancin' money. Next thing you know you ain't got no band no more. No, sir, there ain't nothin' worse than money hatin', and poker the place where you gonna fin' it most likely gonna happen.'

Joe never gave advice he hadn't earned the hard way but it hadn't stopped me growing to love the game. I wasn't unduly troubled that I hadn't taken his advice. I'd never played cards for a decent stake, nor ever thought I would. In the first place I lacked the resources, and in the second, I told myself money wasn't the object. I was a Cabbagetown kid, after all, and knew that nothing is for nothing. You earn money or you steal it. The first comes from the sweat of your brow, and the second inevitably brings nasty consequences. The idea that you could simply gain a fortune by betting on a horse, a number, a card or a sporting result was patently stupid; any mug could work out the odds and they were never, or very seldom anyway, in your favour. It wasn't why I was growing more and more to love five-card stud or any other form of the game I was eventually to learn.

I've mentioned my memory for music but now I could use cards to exercise my brain. It was as if I was receiving brain nourishment, feeding my hungry mind. This was one of the reasons I read so voraciously and certainly what attracted me to jazz, to the endless possibilities it contained. Art Tatum never played a piece in the same manner twice. His musical genius always saw another possibility and his musical memory always told him where he'd been before and, perhaps more importantly, where others had been before him. Nobody before or since has brought, or probably ever will bring, what the greatest piano player of all time brought to his medium, but his prodigious memory was a part of it. In some small way I shared that with him; I could visualise what I'd previously seen almost as clearly as if it were in front of me.

I liked five-card stud because I knew so much more about the hands I was facing. I could recall the face cards players had received for the entire session. This meant patterns in their play started to emerge before very long. It never occurred to me that everyone in the poker school didn't have this same facility until Reggie Blunt and I discussed the subject one afternoon several months after I'd joined the game.

Yet again, he'd lost the two dollars he'd held as his stake and I'd been fortunate enough to end the game some six dollars richer, somewhat more than any of the other players had made and with everyone remarking that Jack of Spayds had scooped the pot again. Reggie wanted a final whisky. We'd strolled over to the Brunswick from the John Robert Johnson Caribou Café and were sitting at the bar, where I'd ordered a sarsaparilla to nurse through the half hour it would take for Reggie Blunt to consume his fifth Canadian Club for the afternoon. For want of anything better to say, I'd remarked, 'Wasn't it funny you having the same face cards in two hands, Reggie?'

His head jerked back and he looked genuinely surprised. 'I beg your pardon, old chap,' he said in his affected Anglicised manner.

'You know, early on you held the ace of diamonds, nine of diamonds, queen of spades, jack of clubs, and then, in your second-last hand this afternoon you had exactly the same face cards.'

'I know no such thing, my boy. Nor can I for one moment see how you could know this.'

It was my turn to be surprised. 'But surely you remember . . . I mean . . .'

'Indeed no! Are you telling me you can remember the cards I held in my hand all afternoon? How, pray tell? What's the trick, old son?'

'It's not a trick. It just seems to stick in my head . . . in my memory. I think it's because I've had to learn so many piano scores. Surely you'd be the same. The brain starts looking for patterns.'

'Well, perhaps yours does, old boy. I can't say the same for mine, which seems increasingly to be falling to bits.'

'But you know you need a good memory in music, just like you need a good memory for cards.'

'No doubt it helps, old chap, but my memory's like a sieve.'

I admit I was surprised. I'd thought up to this point that this was what I had to learn, this was the essence of the game and that, for the most part, people who had played a lot were experts at just this sort of information gathering and processing. 'I enjoy playing cards and I try to remember the face cards everyone gets and my mind starts to see patterns in how they play their hands,' I explained.

Reggie seemed to be getting a trifle edgy. It was as if what I was telling him was bullshit or, alternatively, dangerous. 'Bully for you, Jack. So you think you know what their hole card is?'

'No, that's too simple. It's more a matter of knowing what cards have been face up during the hand already, so you know they're out of play, combined with how someone has played similar card combinations all through the game. That way you can eliminate a lot of possibilities and calculate the odds of them having the hole card they need to beat you. You sort of accumulate information . . .'

Reggie appeared to be thinking. 'Hmm, that doesn't work as well when you don't have face cards, does it?'

I laughed. 'Dead right! That's why I like five-card stud. You have more information to work with. You see most of the cards. It's much easier to work out what players are likely to do and what their hole card may be.'

Reggie Blunt shook his head slowly then sighed and lifted his whisky glass to his lips. 'Christ almighty, and this is what I'm up against.'

'C'mon, Reggie, you're a lot more experienced than me,' I protested, though I was secretly pleased to have impressed him a little.

'Jack, you've obviously read Jacoby's new book. It already looks like becoming the holy grail of poker players.'

'No. Sounds interesting.'

'Oswald Jacoby on Poker, it came out earlier this year or late last year. It's already become the poker player's Bible, the Gospel According to the Prophet Jacoby.' I admitted again that I'd never heard of it. 'Allow me to lend you my copy, although with your luck . . .'

He left the sentence hanging, so I added quickly, 'No, thanks, Reggie, that's very kind of you, but I tend to be a bit rough on books. It sounds like I may have to read this one several times; I'll buy one first thing.' I'd have to stash it in my rucksack. If Mrs Henderson saw it beside my bed – my version of Jim Greer's Bible – it would be the final straw, I'd be out in the street before my feet could touch the ground.

I've already mentioned that Reggie Blunt was generally considered the school bunny but it wasn't because he was stupid, far from it. He had a quick mind and was famous for his one-liners, the opposite end of the spectrum from his convoluted sentences. Here are just a couple I recall. *Don't take life too seriously – you're not going to come out of it alive. God must love stupid people, he made so many of them.* I recall discussing John Steinbeck's new book, *The Grapes of Wrath*, with him. Lifting his whisky glass, he commented, 'But then again, a hangover is *The Wrath of Grapes.*'

The fall of the cards was obviously important, but it seemed in my limited experience that Joe was right, the same players almost always ended up with a pile of pennies in front of them while others constantly complained about their bad luck. Perhaps Jacoby, could explain why this was so, among other things, or why Reggie always seemed to draw the short straw.

'Good for you, old son,' Reggie said now. 'I've only had my copy three months and it's almost in tatters. Wouldn't want it falling into further disrepair. I guess my brain doesn't function quite like yours, otherwise, having chewed and digested Mr Jacoby's wisdom, I really ought to have won a couple of pots in the past month. I guess I'm just plain unlucky. I do, however, recommend you read this book, Jack. If you are going to play the game properly, you might as well assemble the mental tools you're going to need.' He smiled at me in an avuncular way. 'My boy, while I think you've probably got a natural gift, there's still a lot you can learn . . . we can all learn,' he added, I guess so as not to sound patronising.

I'd come to regard Reggie Blunt as a decent, generous-minded guy, especially considering I had pinched his job and, in a manner of speaking, snatched the bread from his mouth. Though Cam Kerr and Peter Cornhill had assured me he had other means of support, just what they were was never explained; they merely insisted he could afford to lose a few bucks every week at the poker game he so loved.

Well, the book was everything and more that Reggie Blunt had promised it would be. *Oswald Jacoby on Poker* was a treatise on how to play poker to win, written by one of the world's leading bridge players. It was mainly about five-card stud and five-card draw poker. He also dealt with seven-card stud, high, low and wild-card games and other variations, but these mainly cropped up in dealer's choice games, which he didn't think were worthy of serious players.

I read the book twice over during the following week, my brain snatching at the contents, hungry for more as the possibilities of the game became increasingly apparent. To use an apt comparison, it was as if I was back at my first lesson with Miss Bates at the piano. Or later, standing bewitched by Art Tatum. I realised, as I had when first confronted by both classical music and jazz, that I knew next to nothing and that the mountain to climb was exceedingly steep.

Years later I would admit to myself that it was at that very moment in my life in Moose Jaw that I took the first step on my way to becoming obsessed with poker. Jazz and then poker – honey mixed with arsenic. Stupid, stupid Jack Spayd! Why oh why hadn't I remembered that Joe's advice was always sound?

CHAPTER NINE

SOMEWHAT TO MY SURPRISE, my performances quickly grew in popularity and the Sunday jazz lovers now crowded into the ballroom at the Brunswick, much to the delight of Cam Kerr and the hotel management. Young guys in uniform, on weekend leave from the camps, drew an appreciative following of young women who, I hoped, also enjoyed the music. It all did wonders for the general ambience of what had formerly been a dull and unprofitable hotel Sunday.

My salary had been raised to $30 a week and, taken together with my poker winnings and odds and ends, I was clearing a good $45 with lunch and breakfast thrown in. I'd hit the jackpot in terms of my scuffing experience, a fact that left me feeling vaguely guilty because Joe Hockey had sent me into the wilderness to grow up and get some life experience and here I was living off the fat of the grasslands and actually adding to the money I had brought with me. My mom's nose job was looking ever more affordable.

Jack Spayd had once again fallen on his feet and I guess was still pretty much the same kid they'd all tearfully seen off at union station almost eight months previously. No doubt they'd imagined I'd have to endure many hardships before we all met again, especially Joe, who'd been damp-eyed at the station.

I couldn't help feeling rather smug. Sometimes I'd imagine myself arriving home and sitting at the kitchen table in my mom's flat. I'd casually reach into my jacket and place a bulging envelope on the table. 'Here, Mom,' I'd say, sliding the envelope towards her.

'What is it, Jack?' she'd say, picking it up and opening it. 'Oh my goodness! Jack, what on earth . . .'

'The money to do the rest of your nose,' I'd say with a little smile.

Of course I'd written to them all often enough saying I was okay but I could read between the lines of my mom's weekly replies and knew that she believed I was merely putting on a brave face. Stoic young Jack out there in the wilds among the savages. Joe would be wondering about the musical compromises I was being forced to make as a price for my hard-won maturity. Miss Frostbite had urged me to remember I was a gentleman and not to fall into coarse ways. She'd taken a lot of trouble to turn the gauche Cabbagetown kid into 'a charming young gentleman'.

I felt reasonably sure I'd become a better jazz piano player despite having to play the popular music my audience demanded. Swing was now sweeping the county and I didn't mind because in Joe's words, 'You gotta go where the hep cats goin'. You don't want to get yo'self stuck in no jazz lullaby land.'

Furthermore, with the aid of Mr Jacoby and his wondrous book, I was slowly becoming a better poker player, beginning to realise that while you win and lose over time, the better player usually comes out in front. I felt I was improving and the others were standing still. If Reggie Blunt had dog-eared Jacoby's book, the information didn't seem to have sunk in – he was still the bunny. I was becoming the winner of the game rather more often than not, so I'd throw in the odd good start to a hand, just to keep things interesting for the others. Ours was a small-stakes Saturday social game and I didn't need Joe's warning to know I'd soon mess things up in the group if I won too often; nobody needs some show-off punk kid repeatedly snapping up the stake they've had to save to bring to the game. As it was I was doing nicely, even if I was being careful not to rock the boat. They were my buddies after all and in a strange place far from home friends are not easily made and should not be taken lightly.

Like many an only child, I'd spent most of my life with adults, and although most of them had been women, there had been Mac and Joe and the members of the band as well, so I didn't feel out of place among these men. While it would have been nice to have friends of my own age, I'd never quite managed to have a buddy at school. I'd always had my days mapped out for me with music and the library and weekends spent accompanying my mom to museums and parks.

As I passed through puberty I longed for a girlfriend, but girls had always been scarce in my life and when I did meet one she usually thought I was a bit weird and we had nothing to say to each other. What does a classical pianist say to a Cabbagetown girl when he's either got his head in a book or he's practising scales and she believes she's hit the jackpot if, at sixteen, she can leave school and get a job as a kitchen hand in a downtown café and eventually become a waitress?

I'd been a kitchen hand at the Jazz Warehouse, but you soon exhaust the conversational possibilities of dishwashing. The most fun I could ever remember with my peers was during winter when we'd play shinny on the frozen pond, but even that had ended when Miss Bates noticed a bad bruise on my left hand where some kid's hockey stick had connected with it. 'Your hands are your future, Jack!' she'd scolded. 'Broken fingers could put an end to everything. I simply won't have it!'

It seems crazy, but as a kid I understood women better than men and men better than boys my own age; girls I understood not at all. The twins were the closest I ever got to girls, and they were six years older than me, and light years removed because of their experience. At seventeen I was going on forty but I'd missed out on the experience of getting there. My childhood adventures had all come through the characters I read about in books and most of them were either English or American.

I guess this was why Joe wanted me to get the hell out of Cabbagetown and live a bit, fall flat on my face a few times and harden up. Life wasn't meant to be as easy as it had been for me, and if the Depression had taught kids anything it was that few avoided an apprenticeship in hardship before they launched themselves into the world. I'm sure he was right. But while most young guys my age were going through the tedious and difficult process of growing up, I needed to grow down, or backwards, if such an experience is possible. The only thing I had in common with a normal teenage boy was puberty, that strange time when nothing makes sense and your hormones are going berserk and you are happy for no reason, and angry at most of the people you know at some stage, or at life in general and most particularly yourself. Of course by the time I got to Moose Jaw this onerous time was pretty much over for me. Still, I needed to grow down to seventeen or eighteen and my best hope of doing so was, of course, the army – lots of young guys together seemed an ideal way for me to grow backwards into becoming a normal kid, young man and soldier.

I missed jamming at the Jazz Warehouse and longed to play with other musicians. Finally, after a lot of discussion over many hands of poker, I persuaded my older buddies in the poker school to form a small group. The owner of the Caribou Café, John Robert Johnson, had agreed we could have a gig for an hour and a half before our poker games. He was a truly great guy and trucked in a piano from home which he claimed his mother had once played and then his daughter. It had stood idle in the parlour for five years because, to his disappointment, his daughter had lost interest as a teenager, married early and become a young mother almost immediately.

It was a Grinnell, an old upright from before the Great War, but he'd had it tuned and the key pads replaced and it wasn't all that bad. We played to the Saturday-morning coffee crowd which soon grew in size and we were able to repay John Robert Johnson in a small way for his generosity as his takings increased.

I offered to play the harmonica and leave the piano for Reggie Blunt but he insisted that he'd been fascinated by the electric guitar ever since it had appeared on the musical scene as a new instrument and had purchased one three years back. He had been taking lessons by correspondence, he claimed. I'd never really appreciated the skill Elmer Perkins had brought to the Jazz Warehouse from Tennessee until I heard Reggie play; there's a lot more to the electric guitar than meets the unfamiliar ear, though of course Reggie's guitar, despite being the butt of many a joke among the other musicians, was welcomed.

As for me, I was attracted to the free forms adopted in the twenties by Louis Armstrong and his Hot Five. Those dazzling extended solos were where I wanted to go on the piano. I was groping towards my own style, and it was this, I believed, that was attracting a more involved audience to the Sunday solo concerts where I had possibly cornered the market for jazz purists in Moose Jaw and Regina.

While the group muddled along and played well enough without a bass player, we all felt the lack. A group without a bass instrument is like chewing without back teeth. Then several weeks after we'd started, a guy from the audience introduced himself as Robert Yuen and asked us if we had room for a double bass. Whoopee! There must be a god in heaven!

Robert Yuen was twenty-five and the son of the wealthy owner of more than a dozen small hotels in towns along the rail line and the Trans-Canada Highway. He must have known we'd grab him with both hands. We now had the final instrument to allow us to achieve a characteristic jazz sound, and his addition made all the difference to the group. Although all of us were professionals who played in other bands on River Street, our group began to have its own sound and pretty soon people were begging us to play at private parties. We all had night jobs elsewhere, so we had to decline most of the invitations.

In honour of our generous patron we called the group the John Robert Johnson Caribou Café Band. A bit of a mouthful I admit, but such was his generosity that we never shortened it to the Caribou Café Band, and I think he liked the tribute. He was a great guy, 'salt of the earth' as Reggie would say.

My hope was that we'd progress sufficiently to do a Sunday afternoon gig at the Brunswick, but, as I said before, the kids who came were essentially purists, cool and demanding, insisting on a standard of jazz

I could only barely reach. While I'm not suggesting I was all that much better, the others were set in their ways and had always been functional middle-of-the-road musicians making a living. We were pretty good by Moose Jaw standards, but that wasn't quite enough for my diehard Sunday fans.

However, Robert Yuen, the ring-in who'd approached us, turned out to be good, I mean *really* good. He'd studied at the Juilliard, and was back in Moose Jaw because his dad had cancer. As the oldest son he was expected to take over. Although he didn't say much, I think he was pretty disappointed at having to give up a musical career. He'd once said to me, 'Jack, man, you saved my life. I always wanted to play jazz and now at least I've got something going aside from fucking buildings and leases.' He and I soon worked up a gig that was pleasing enough for the Sunday aficionados. Cam Kerr could hardly refuse a $10 Sunday salary for Robert when we were so popular, but he wasn't all that keen to begin with. Piano and bass are an unlikely combination, but it worked.

I'd bought a state-of-the-art harmonica, the magnificent Hohner Echo Elite, from a Main Street music shop, the last one of its kind in stock. I felt guilty just owning it, not because it was German, but the word 'new' to me had always been preceded by 'almost' and meant *second-hand in good condition*. We'd get an item of clothing from Mrs Sopworth and my mom would exclaim excitedly, 'Why, it's almost new!'

I also bought a lot of sheet music, then once I knew it by heart I'd start extemporising. Even Joe had once remarked, 'Yo real good, Jazzboy. Yo bin the fastest ever I seen to get a melody in yo head.' Miss Bates, pretty stingy with her compliments, had said much the same on more than one occasion, commenting that she believed my big hands and musical memory were going to be my greatest assets in classical music.

I must have been improving because the Sunday afternoon ballroom crowd continued to grow, despite the five-cent surcharge on drinks and despite swing being all the rage. When Robert Yuen came along with his bass I think we both took a big leap forward.

My most ardent desire was to return to the Jazz Warehouse, casually sit down at the piano knowing they'd be expecting a bit of backsliding, and then positively knock their socks off. I wanted Joe to say, 'Hey, Jazzboy, you three notch up the Tatum totem pole.' He'd told me when I'd left (as a huge compliment) that I was past the first notch and 'jes toe-touchin' the secon'. When I asked him how many notches there were on the totem pole, he'd laughed. 'Maybe twenny-five, maybe fifty, maybe dat totem pole be the stairway to heaven. Ain't nobody ever gonna get all the way up. Mr Fats Waller? No! Mr Earl Hines? No! Mr Teddy Wilson? No, no, no!'

Joe never explained his antipathy for Teddy Wilson, whom I greatly admired. He was simply up there with the very best and it wasn't like Joe, who, by his own admission, was never a great jazz piano player. I knew he was better than he made out, but he was nowhere near Teddy Wilson's class. Few jazz musicians were. But he knew a great jazz player when he heard one and I was yet to meet a musician, including Art Tatum, who didn't respect his judgment.

Jazz wasn't my only obsession. I mean, here I was, in the epicentre of sin, with girls leaning from windows and balconies everywhere I looked. They called me Honky-Tonk Jack, and had come to know me as a regular and not as a mark, a professional who worked on River Street as they themselves did, but this hadn't stopped me imagining dozens of scenarios with different girls. Once, a very pretty, dark-eyed girl with skin the colour of milk coffee and a smile that would have lit up a moonless night, had opened her coat and flashed me the entire bodyworks, leaving nothing to speculation. What I witnessed had sent my imagination into a fever for two weeks. Jim Greer's nightly absence during the week permitted some blessed release, but not before I'd turned my back on his *Asleep in the arms of Jesus* quilt.

Which goes to show how mixed up I was about sex. I knew I was hungry for love, *starving* in fact, yet I lacked the courage to confront Miss Flash, as I termed her, or for that matter any of the other girls. As for meeting what might be termed a 'nice' girl, I was even less certain about how to go about it. There were lots of them at my Sunday concerts, but there was nowhere to go afterwards and besides, as I'd learned at the Jazz Warehouse, Miss Frostbite's first immutable rule was no fraternising with the patrons.

Reggie Blunt seemed to know most of the balcony sisterhood, as he called the girls, I suppose because he had been a widower and had hung around River Street for so long. He and I used to walk over to the Brunswick and he'd have a whisky after our poker game. One day he said, 'My dear boy, the balcony sisterhood are putting a dollar each week in the proverbial hat towards a party. They're selling raffle tickets at 25 cents each to be drawn at the shindig to see who'll be the first to put Honky-Tonk Jack on his back.'

I laughed, though I could feel my face burning as I tried to conceal my embarrassment. 'Reggie, do they know how old I am?'

'Ah, exactly, that's half the challenge, old boy. A good-looking, tall, broad-shouldered, seventeen-year-old virgin who is clean as the driven snow and yet still a legitimate part of the River Street scene is close to a miracle. A mark who is untainted and talented – you're the dream of every member of the sisterhood.' He laughed. 'You're big time, you draw a hundred and fifty or more young people to the ballroom on Sunday. I know for a fact that six of the River Street girls attend religiously. They see you as the big prize, my boy, the scalp they all want, the status symbol, the notch on the rifle butt, or in this case, on their own butt.'

He paused and gave me a bloodshot, weepy-eyed, whisky-nosed look. 'You *are* a virgin, are you not, Jack?'

All I could think to say in reply was, 'Not in my head, Reggie.'

I immediately recalled Mac's story of being seduced by Dolly and how he'd returned to his apprenticeship having only gained one thing from the altogether frightening experience in the bushes beside the Don River: the right to nod sagely when the loss of virginity was discussed and, if asked, admit casually and modestly to being a veritable stallion.

While I was certainly ignorant, there wasn't a skerrick of innocence in my head. I imagined doing sexual things to a woman that I could never talk about to anyone. While they were neither vicious nor violent they didn't allow her any choice in the matter. In my head she'd be completely compliant and go along with whatever it was I wanted and if I wasn't absolutely sure what I required, nevertheless it was all one way, all about me and my pleasure. I am ashamed to say that if my imagined partner had any needs of her own in my torrid fantasies, they had never occurred to me.

Despite this, Reggie Blunt's words filled me with terror. It was not what I wanted, it was what *they* wanted, and they were professionals. They'd actually know the what, the where and the how. If they'd won me in a raffle they could do whatever they desired and I was terrified that I might prove entirely inadequate.

Apart from the glimpse of the neat triangle of dark hair on the milk-coffee-coloured Miss Flash, I had absolutely no idea of the precise appearance or use of the intimate parts of the female anatomy when it was naked. I had even less idea of whether women enjoyed sex, and if so, how they went about it. It wasn't a subject discussed in any of the hundreds of books I'd read, other than in the most unspecific phraseology. Couples 'made love' or 'consummated their relationship' and were therefore happy, satisfied and mutually fulfilled afterwards. It was the words 'made' and 'satisfied' that preoccupied me. 'Made' suggested at least one specific task that led to a highly satisfying conclusion known as 'mutually fulfilled', but there were no books that told you the details. I was a man. How the hell could I be expected to know how to satisfy a woman?

It was not until twenty years later when Penguin published D.H. Lawrence's *Lady Chatterley's Lover* in 1960 that kids like me had access to any descriptions of sex. If only I'd had some of his words in my head at the time, many of which I found so beautiful that I never forgot them.

Of course I knew about male climaxes but hadn't any idea how it happened for a female. The twins could have explained, but I was too terrified to go near them. Just observing one of them from the back filled me with lust and guaranteed a nocturnal assignation with my hand.

Miss Flash had the same effect on me as the twins, and although she never exposed herself a second time, I had great trouble walking past her when she was consorting, flashing her brilliant smile down at me from her balcony. I usually carried a paperback in case I had a spare moment to read, or had to cover my tent pole, as if the usual way to walk around carrying a book that could just as easily have slipped into the side pocket of a lumber jacket or the back pocket of one's trousers was to clutch it to one's groin.

However, if Reggie Blunt was right and I was to be a raffle prize, what was it that I was expected to do to fulfil my role and satisfy the winner? If they thought I knew anything about how to please a woman they were in for a big, big disappointment. I wasn't just a novice, I'd missed out on most of the salacious gossip boys shared with their peers. None of us had been told about the birds and the bees, we were simply expected to follow the chirping made by someone's sister when we reached nineteen or twenty. If she proved too willing she was called the town bike, if too cold, the ice maiden. Mac and Dolly's experience (well, Mac's anyway) was typical of teenage sexual experiments, most of which ended in a confab between both sets of parents with a bit of chest stabbing and shouting before a hasty marriage in a hand-me-down wedding dress or, if the bride's waist was expanding too rapidly, in her best dress let out round the middle. Cabbagetown had an astonishing number of premature births.

'Well, what do you think, old chap?' Reggie said in his Canadian version of Colonel Blimp.

'Think? I'm not sure I know what to think, Reggie.'

'Well, if it's any reassurance, Jack, I can honestly say in the thirty-five years I've been in Moose Jaw, I've never known this to happen before. I think you ought to take it as a huge compliment. I'd say Honky-Tonk Jack is the man of the moment, the ant's pants, the star on the top of the Christmas tree.'

'Reggie, I don't have any idea what . . . you know . . . what to expect. I mean, it is just ah, one girl who wins the raffle, isn't it?'

'Good lord, yes, just one. They want to have a party on a Monday. That's what the hat money is for – booze and canapés. Even the madams have made a contribution. Everyone is surprised at how much money they've collected with the raffle. It's a real tribute to your popularity, old chap. You don't work Mondays and it's almost as quiet for them with River Street virtually closed down. The party would be at the Caribou Café – John Robert to supply both booze and eats. A nice little earner for him I daresay. The band would play and then you'd be, ah . . .' he paused and cleared his throat, 'the raffle prize! Splendid, what?'

'And if I refuse? What then?'

'Well, that would be extremely awkward, old son. Not the done thing at all. The sisterhood are paying you the ultimate compliment.' He shook his head as if he couldn't quite believe what I'd just said. 'Very churlish, very churlish indeed.'

I thought immediately of Miss Flash. 'But . . . but I don't even get to choose the girl I want.'

'Well, no Jack, that wouldn't be fair. They've all put in their money and bought tickets. No jealousy that way, see? No resentment among the various houses.'

'Houses? What's that mean? Whorehouses?'

'Bordellos, Jack, much nicer word,' Reggie corrected, looking quite hurt. 'The girls are not freelance. That would never work. Like everything in this town they need the protection you can buy with a little zigzag or they'd be in front of a magistrate every other week.' He demonstrated 'zigzag' with the gesture he'd used initially for the chief of police – the hand outstretched to accept a bribe and then the quick retreat to the trouser pocket.

'But what if I end up with, you know, some old crone?' I protested. I guessed my chances of scoring the coffee-coloured flasher were pretty remote, one chance in who knows how many. 'You said even the madams made a contribution!' In my mind's eye I saw a Mrs Henderson lookalike. Holy smoke! Imagine that. Lumbago Lil!

Reggie looked me in the eye. 'There's no likelihood of that happening, dear boy. Possibly a girl in her mid-twenties, and you should pray that this is the case. There is simply no substitute for experience. There's plenty of time for young and pretty later. The kind of instruction you'd get isn't that easy to come by. An experienced professional can teach you how to please a woman, which will, I assure you, pay off handsomely in the years to come. You should be very happy if she isn't a comparative novice.'

Here we go again, Jack Spayd being managed by an older woman – Miss Mony, Miss Frostbite, Mrs Hodgson, Miss Bates and now, with my luck, Miss Wrinkles.

'And I'd wear a rubber, of course,' I said, trying to sound as if I knew more than I did.

'But, of course old chap, a contraceptive is mandatory. Would you like me to make the purchase for you? You'll need five or six, I should think.'

'Five! I'd feel a bit foolish . . . like I was bragging!'

'You don't have to use them all.' He drew his head back. 'Strapping young chap like you – better to have too many than to find yourself short.'

'Thank you for your advice, Reggie. If I agree to the raffle I'll buy my own.' I thought for a moment. What the hell, I'd be joining up soon. Who knows, I could die in a muddy trench in Europe, still a virgin. I grinned sheepishly, not looking directly at Reggie Blunt. 'Okay,' I said quietly, adding in musician's jargon, 'that's cool.'

Reggie hugged himself, plainly pleased. 'Oh, that's excellent, Jack!' He then reached out and took my hand in both of his. 'It may well be an experience you'll cherish for the remainder of your life, old son. What a grand party we'll have, one you'll never forget, that much I can guarantee!'

I recall hoping that the party wasn't the main thing I remembered from the day, but having agreed to go along with the plan I felt sufficiently emboldened to ask, 'Did ah, did you lose your . . . um . . . you know, in the same way?' I couldn't bring myself to say the word *virginity*. It seemed somehow a word that marked my immaturity and which, once removed, would allow me to mysteriously grow up; by losing it in a single sexual act I would gain my manhood and thus my maturity. In a sense it felt like a barrier I must leap so that I could get on with my life as a man. The sooner the word was tossed away the sooner the metamorphosis could take place.

'What? My virginity? Did I lose it in such a grand manner?' Reggie shook his head. 'No such luck, old boy. Olga – God rest her soul – and I were complete neophytes. Married, dumped on the doorstep of a friend's lakeside cottage, uninstructed, ignorant and simply left to our own devices. We had no idea! Hadn't a clue! Made a ghastly hash of everything. She ended up sobbing all night with her back turned to me in bed. We didn't attempt it again for a week and the second attempt wasn't much better. As I recall, it took several months and always in the dark before she could or would allow me . . .' he grinned, 'free passage.'

'But when it happened, did you . . . I mean, were you, you know . . . able to . . . ?'

'Get it up? Good God, yes! Horny as a charging rhinoceros! Walking around bow-legged with lover's balls for days. I just didn't know how to . . . well, of course, I knew the anatomical part concerned, but it didn't seem to want to cooperate.' He paused momentarily, recalling. 'I guess it was made even more difficult probing – so to speak – in the dark.' He laughed uproariously, then reached for his whisky and took a slow sip. Licking his lips, he observed, 'But that won't happen to you, old son. You'll be in expert hands and the doorway to heaven will be opened wide and welcoming. Chorus of angels, fanfare of trumpets, all sorts of glorious things.'

'Shit, Reggie, I hope you're right.' The thought arose again that my unknown partner might not be all that discreet and if my performance ended up a disaster I'd be the laughing stock of River Street.

'Never been more certain, old son. Strapping young lad like you, Jack. She'll think all her Christmases have come at once.'

I thought this unlikely, given the way these girls earned their living, but I didn't want to say so. The less I thought about the number of comparisons she could make, the better.

'Do the other cats in the band know about this, um, raffle being the reason for the gig?'

'Well, no, I thought best not to tell them the purpose of the party. They might tell their wives.' He took another sip from his glass. 'Womenfolk don't see these things quite as we do. Sanctity of marriage, that kind of thing . . . Charlie Condotti is Italian, strict Catholic, his brother is a monsignor; Chuck and Mort, I'm not sure, Presbyterian I think; Robert would probably just laugh, after all, he's a bachelor and he'd probably wish it were him. All they know is that the River Street girls want to have a party, no males present except for the band. It's a chance to help John Robert Johnson. He gets to buy the booze wholesale and make a few bucks on the food as well. Monday evenings are a pretty slack period at the Caribou, he informs me.'

'And he didn't object?'

'On the contrary, the girls use the Caribou a lot, he knows most of them, strictly legitimate of course, no hanky-panky . . . no fraternising. But they like him because he treats them just the same as any other customer, which is with due deference and kindness. He's a good man.'

I'd once read somewhere that there's no such thing as a good man, not through and through. The misanthropic author believed men are imperfect creatures, their minds a roiling mass of primitive, violent urges, and that controlling those violent forces gives men a sense of goodness. If my own father was a typical example, he was a bastard, drunk or sober, but drunk, all that bastardry towards women emerged from the dark recesses of his mind.

If most women's minds are motivated by the same instincts then I haven't personally observed this to be the case. I've witnessed frustration, bitterness, anger, despair, jealousy, bitchiness and sometimes racial bigotry in women, but most of it seems to me to have been directly or indirectly caused by men. Dolly McClymont may have been an exception, given the way she treated poor little Mac.

I thought of all the women who had been important in my life. Miss Mony was married but I had no idea how she was faring; Mrs Hodgson was divorced; Miss Frostbite and Miss Bates were determinedly single; the twins were showing no signs of marrying; and my mother was rid of my bastard father at last. Most of these women made a deliberate decision to remain on their own. My mother was plainly a victim. I couldn't imagine any of the others tolerating a permanently flattened nose and broken teeth while still remaining loyal, nor being afraid to walk out on the bastard who beat her to alleviate his guilt, anger and pathetic weakness. The tragedy was that Gertrude Spayd was not the exception but rather the Cabbagetown stereotype, while my dad wasn't a rarity either.

I have often wondered if men who were born into a higher social class were any better. Certainly they seemed to be outwardly, but what about deep down inside? I'd read enough to know that women in good homes were also beaten up by their husbands, men who took out their frustrations on their women, whatever those frustrations might be.

'When is the gig?' I asked Reggie.

For some curious reason he removed his fob watch, his fingers flicking along the gold chain to the pocket that housed it in his vest, then he clicked open the gold cover and looked into the watch face as if the date might be registered upon it. 'Let's see, today's Saturday,' he glanced up. 'Next Monday week, Jack.' Then clicking back the cover he replaced the watch.

'And how should I dress?'

'Mustn't insult the girls, must we, old boy? Your grey suit, of course. Trust it's virgin wool, eh?' He placed both his hands on his paunch and began to heave with laughter, very pleased with his own wit.

I didn't think at the time it was very funny but there was no doubt Reggie thought it extremely clever, one of his better *bons mots*. His affected English manner could at times be extremely tedious, as if Canadian English was somehow lesser or indicated an inferior people. All the other musicians used music slang as a matter of course, words such as hep (with it), cats (other musicians), wicked (very good), cool (good), chick (girl) and gig (job or performance), but Reggie Blunt never did, specialising in pomposity. His mind seemed stuck somewhere in the English prose spoken by British officers who'd attended Sandhurst prior to the First World War. For instance, he would order a 'double whisky and splash', as if he were a Canadian version of Bertie Wooster, P.G. Wodehouse's famous character.

Still, he was very kind and helpful and lord knows I needed all the advice I could get. He'd been honest about his own experience and in doing so helped to encourage me to agree to my initiation via the ministrations of a professional.

I told myself that it was all in line with Joe's advice to get myself some experience of real life. Once, when feeling particularly poetical, as he termed it, he'd sat down at the piano and begun to play and sing. 'Jazzboy scuffin' and roughin', huffin' and puffin' when you ain't got no women and yo drownin' from swimmin' 'gainst the waves and you ain't gettin' no raves and yo just about beat and there's holes in yo feet from the soles that wore out and you're askin' and prayin' and nobody's sayin' it's time to get playin' and your belly it groanin' and yo angry and moanin', and yo cain't take a trick and nobody give a fig you ain't got a gig, that life, man, that learnin' to be grow'd up widout no mama to call yo her baby and cook yo no grits that flavoured wid gravy.'

Of course, the party and raffle would never have happened in Toronto – I'd have been too afraid of the formidable women who had hitherto controlled my life. I'd often fantasised that one or both of the twins would offer to initiate me into manhood (wearing diaphanous nightgowns and leading me into a carpeted bedroom with a gigantic bed). But I'm not sure whether, had they made such an offer, I would have had the courage to accept.

Monday week came much too soon. I arrived at six o'clock sharp at the Caribou Café, shaved, showered and dressed in my Mrs Sopworth suit, white shirt and starched collar, navy blue necktie with a small anchor motif on the front, shoes polished so you could see your face in the toecaps, ostensibly ready to play in the John Robert Johnson Caribou Café Band to entertain a multitude of River Street 'balcony babes'. There must have been fifty or more girls in the room – I had no idea there were so many. They gave a squeal as I entered and quickly surrounded me, some clutching at my arms. *Jesus, what now?* I thought to myself. Sometimes some of the chicks at my Sunday jazz concert would gather around and shout a bit, but nothing like this. These were girls who were accustomed to men and had few inhibitions. I, on the other hand, was filled with them, a stuttering, mumbling, stammering, blushing fool with a confused and no doubt inane smile on my silly mug.

Fortuitously Reggie Blunt arrived only a minute or so later. 'Now, now, girls, hands off the prize!' he shouted, then mounting the bandstand he flicked his fingers across a drum and *rat-ta-tat-tatted* to bring the room to silence. 'You've now all bought your tickets in the raffle and until the winner is announced at the end of the evening,' he turned to me, 'Honky-Tonk Jack is just another member of the band.'

'I've bought five!' a pretty blonde shouted.

'Ten!' It was Miss Flash. God, wouldn't that be something. Plainly she liked me as much as I liked her.

'We've formed a syndicate, me and the eight girls in the house!' a redheaded lady a lot older than the others shouted. 'Forty tickets in all we've bought . . . it's a certainty, Mr Blunt.'

This brought gales of laughter and even I had to join in.

'I hope then that the winning ticket doesn't include you, Madam Rose,' Reggie grinned to further laughter. 'Shhh, now! No more, please, ladies. The remainder of the band is due at any moment and they know nothing about the raffle. When it's announced it will simply be referred to as a night on the town with the partner of your own choosing. Now enjoy the party, there can only be one winner, and in the meantime it's eyes only, no touching. We don't want Honky-Tonk Jack too exhausted by the time the raffle is drawn. Have a good time, all of you.'

'Speech, Honky-Tonk, speech!' someone called out and the room broke into spontaneous applause. I was certain that the worst moment in my whole life had arrived. I thought briefly of Rudyard Kipling's poem 'If', where he talks about what it is to be a man. He hadn't mentioned women, but according to him you needed to be able to cope in just about any situation to be a real man. The room had grown deathly quiet with a sea of carefully made-up eyes fixed on me.

I cleared my throat, locked my knees to keep them from shaking and began. 'I can honestly say that I've never been in a room that contained only pretty women. Whoever among you has the misfortune to win the raffle, I can only say I shall be extremely honoured and will try to do my . . . ah, um . . . very best.' I could feel myself blushing furiously. 'Thank you.' The room broke into thunderous applause, fortunately, because I couldn't have added another sensible word if my life had depended on it.

Chuck Bullmore and Charlie Condotti arrived at that moment. Reggie banged the drums to bring the room to silence and rather cleverly said, 'Ladies, *another* big clap for Chuck Bullmore and Charlie Condotti!' The ladies immediately cottoned on and gave them a big welcoming yell and loud applause and did the same when a couple of minutes later Mort Smith and Robert Yuen entered the Caribou Café. Peter Cornhill was absent, having to work at the Brunswick.

It was all rather well done and a minute or so later I led off on the piano with the song 'Tenderly'. The River Street girls didn't seem to miss the presence of men, and certainly knew how to throw a party and have an outrageously good time. I found myself trying to think up a good collective noun for a gathering of working girls such as this. It was hardly a fellowship and certainly not a congregation, both terms having been stolen by one church or another. Perhaps, a prancing of pros? They were having an absolute ball and while several had consumed a glass or two too many, others took good care of them. Hopefully one of the girls in her cups didn't turn out to be the eventual winner.

John Robert Johnson later said his greatest fear was that there might be a cat fight, because according to him, prostitutes were notoriously competitive and combative. Reggie Blunt, I was to learn, had paid the necessary zigzag, in this case to a police captain named Charles Coville, responsible for what was laughingly known as law and order in River Street. Coville claimed he'd have extra men on standby to deal with any fights that broke out, the implication being that a generous bribe would prevent him from doing his duty and banning the event before the streets ran with blood. He also pointed out that the Apostolic Church of the Pentecost would be having a stern word to him the following morning.

Had Coville been so inclined, he might have labelled the anticipated catfight a war of whores or a protest of prostitutes. However, no such ruckus occurred. The girls were out to enjoy themselves, and while some got pretty drunk, they didn't turn ugly or even vulgar. Much to my disappointment, I didn't glimpse a single garter belt or peek-a-boo nipple all evening, both mainstays employed by the girls on the balconies to attract passing men. In this respect their behaviour was as chaste as girls at a high school prom. But the dancing was wild and the laughter infectious, the girls partnered each other and there were no wallflowers; even the madams flounced their skirts and giggled like schoolgirls. As Joe might say, 'Ever-body included in, ain't nobody included out.'

The music seemed to please everyone and as the evening drew on there were calls from several of the girls, perhaps those who regularly attended the Sunday concerts, for me to play a couple of jazz solos. I didn't want to be too much of a purist, so I played a short blues number then one of the free-form pieces by Louis Armstrong and his Hot Five I mentioned previously. I then led the band back into easygoing swing so as to avoid appearing to be the focus of the night in case the other band members suspected anything. Even so, both pieces got rather more applause than they deserved, and Chuck Bullmore laughingly remarked, 'Oh to be seventeen again and tender meat. The chicks are eating you up, Jack.'

When ten o'clock arrived it was time for the band to pack up and leave and for all but one of the girls to go home or back to the balconies after a certain 'dreaded event'.

The four other guys in the band finally left, armed with a great story to tell their wives that night in bed. After all, you don't play too many all-girl gigs where the partygoers are all hookers or madams and you, the band and the owner of the venue are the only males present.

Reggie Blunt and I stayed back under some pretext or other he invented on the spot. Then, with my heart pounding like a Charlie Condotti drum solo, I realised that the moment for the raffle to be drawn had finally arrived.

Reggie Blunt stood on the bandstand and brought the room to silence with his now familiar drum technique. 'Ladies, I pray your indulgence for just a moment longer before we reach the grand finale of the evening. I trust you all enjoyed yourselves?' (Much clapping, some whistles and lots of cheering made it clear they all had.) Then he sat down at the old Grinnell and began to play the Fred Astaire and Ginger Rogers number 'Top Hat', ending with an unnecessary glissando to show off. John Robert Johnson walked up and handed him a silk top hat. 'Ah the repository of joy to come!' he announced to a sudden outburst of excited clapping from the girls, some of whom were jumping up and down or crossing their fingers and yelling, 'Me, me, me!'

'I now call on Honky-Tonk Jack to come up to the bandstand and draw out the winning number . . . or should that be the winning slumber?' (Much laugher for a witticism he'd most certainly rehearsed.)

Reggie stretched his short arms straight up, holding the top hat high and still not reaching that far above my head, as I stepped up, nervous as hell. He gazed around at the girls, crying, 'Who's going to be the lucky damsel to win the *Jack*pot!' They laughed generously, but I was shitting my britches and his uncalled-for levity didn't help. My hand trembled as I dipped into the hat and withdrew a single ticket and handed it to John Robert Johnson without looking at it.

'Number 61! Jucilla Fruitino!' he shouted.

There was a moment's pause then a squeal from a clutch of girls in the centre of the room as one of them pranced up, waving her ticket to a mixture of groans, cheers and clapping as some of the girls good-naturedly hugged and kissed the winner.

I was forced to grin despite my nervousness. The winner broke away and the first thing I noticed about her was her wide, generous smile. Reggie Blunt's wish for me had come true: she looked to be in her mid-twenties, fair skinned with dark brown hair done in a style that had just come into fashion, referred to as the victory roll. The hair was swept up off the face into big rolls, like tubes of hair, and the rest curled softly around the neck and shoulders. She was good-looking – not pretty or beautiful but by no means plain – the girl-next-door type with nice brown eyes. She was also a willowy five foot seven, and the nice curves of her body showed through a silky dark green dress. Her nails were painted bright red to match her lipstick.

She handed John Robert Johnson her half of the ticket so he could confirm that they matched and then she turned to me with a smile. 'Hello, Jack, how lucky am I,' she said, and stretched out her hand.

'I . . . um . . . ah . . . hope so,' I managed to mumble.

'Kiss! Kiss! Kiss!' the girls began to chant from the floor, and I think that was the moment my knees started to shake and my mind went into a blind panic. Except at the movies, with, say, Rita Hayworth and Cary Grant in *Only Angels Have Wings*, I had never witnessed a passionate kiss and I'd certainly never experienced one, not even at the Jazz Warehouse where couples sometimes left a bit the worse for wear.

Jucilla Fruitino immediately understood, smiled then said softly, 'Jack, take a step forward and open your arms wide.'

'I . . . I . . . can't . . . m-my knees are sh-shaking . . . too much,' I stammered, my teeth rattling. The moment was much too big for me.

'Then drop to your knees, honey.' I did as she instructed, my legs almost giving way in the process. I looked up into her eyes as she bent down and whispered, 'Put your arms around me and just relax. I'm in charge.' I felt her soft lips press against mine and at that precise moment I suddenly went deaf. It was only later that I learned that our kiss was met with thunderous applause. When I came to, I wondered how the hell I was going to stand up again, my legs having gone to water.

As for the sensation of the kiss, I'd love to say everything changed and all of a sudden I was transformed, different forever, the chrysalis broken, the butterfly emerged. Alas, it was not the case. I was as nervous as ever, and confused, shaken and embarrassed as well, as if I'd suddenly awoken in a room full of strangers.

I had recently read a great new book by an American writer named Ernest Hemingway called *For Whom the Bell Tolls* in which there is a love scene between a Spanish girl named Maria and an American named Robert Jordan. After they've made love Jordan asks her, 'Did thee feel the earth move?' It was to me at the time simply dynamite and wondrously beautiful. But now the closest I came to the earth moving was that I regained my hearing and a floorboard squeaked as I drew back from the kiss.

I was so completely stunned at what had just happened that I felt not even the faintest stirring of desire. Thankfully Reggie Blunt sat down at the Grinnell and started to thump out 'For they are jolly good fellows . . .', his fat little arms and legs bouncing up and down in an exaggerated manner as he sang. Thank god I managed to rise to my feet unassisted as all the girls sang along with Reggie, their arms around each other's shoulders, their heads rocking from side to side.

Jucilla Fruitino, who now stood with her arm around my waist, was obviously a popular winner. When the serenade ended to much clapping and cheering, John Robert Johnson touched me on the arm and said, 'Come on, Jack. Bring your girl, the car will be waiting.'

Car? Nobody had mentioned a car. When I'd asked Reggie where we'd be spending the night he'd replied, 'Secret, old chap. Nice surprise, though.'

'Not a . . . ?'

'No, no, not a bordello. Trust me, nothing as disconcerting as that, old chap.'

Now a car was somehow involved? The girls had all rushed to the café door, lining up as if we were the bride and groom leaving our wedding reception. Jucilla Fruitino clasped my arm tightly above my elbow lest I make a dash for freedom and led me through our guard of dishonour as Reggie might say, smiling like the cat that got the cream. I could feel my face burning up.

However, there were no rude calls or suggestions, only smiles and applause. One or two of the girls touched me lightly on my sleeve and said, 'Be happy, honey,' and 'Good luck, Honky-Tonk Jack.' One near the end, the older woman Reggie Blunt had referred to earlier in the evening as Madam Rose, shook her finger and shouted out to Jucilla Fruitino, 'Now you be *real* nice to that good-looking boy, you hear, girl?'

Then – holy smoke! – there, standing under the streetlight directly in front of the Caribou Café, was the big black Brunswick Buick with the rear door held open by Peter Cornhill. 'Welcome, Jack,' he said. 'You're a lucky man.' Then with a broad smile he exclaimed, 'Hello, Juicy Fruit!'

Jucilla Fruitino, now that she was free of the mob, smiled a somewhat enigmatic smile. 'Thank you, Peter,' she said, stepping into the back of the Buick. So far she was acting like a proper lady. Of course it was a part of Peter's job to know all the girls on River Street – stupid of me to be surprised – but he seemed genuinely pleased that I'd scored Jucilla Fruitino, evidently known as Juicy Fruit. But as I stepped into the back of the car it left me in an immediate quandary, what the hell did I call her?

I was settling into the back seat when she leaned over and kissed me lightly on the cheek. 'If you promise never to call me Juicy or Fruit I'll promise not to call you Honky-Tonk,' she laughed.

Alone for a moment in the car as Peter walked around the back to get into the driver's seat I was feeling a little more composed. Maybe it would become awkward again when we reached our destination and prepared for the dreaded you-know-what, but I reminded myself firmly that I knew how to handle women when they were dressed. After all, I'd been doing it for most of my life. 'What shall I call you? Jucilla?' I asked.

'Lordy, no!' She giggled. 'What everyone else calls me, just plain Juicy Fruit.' Then she cautioned me, 'But mind, always together like that . . . like the chewing gum.'

I could almost hear Reggie Blunt remarking, 'By gum! I wonder if she'll stick around, old chap.'

'I promise,' I laughed, and at that moment Peter Cornhill slipped into the driver's seat, slammed the door and gunned the engine, saving me from having to reply.

'Right then, let's be off. Just time to catch the late train to Regina.'

'Regina!' we both chorused.

'Ha ha! Big surprise, hey? All arranged – personal suite. Night clerk knows you'll be coming in late.' He glanced quickly over his shoulder then back at the road. 'No questions asked, you're already registered as Mr and Mrs Kupple.' He spelled it out, 'K-U-P-P-L-E,' then added, 'it was Reggie Blunt's idea.'

I nodded. 'Yeah, that figures.'

'Hotel Saskatchewan, it's just a short ride from the station. All very grand – vaulted ceilings, marble, all that jazz – looks over Victoria Park. There'll be a hotel car to pick you up at the station. The driver's name is Alf . . . Alf Fields. You'll be catching the midday train and arriving back here shortly after 1.00 p.m. tomorrow. Alf will take you back to the station and we'll meet you here. Everything's been paid for, no gratuities, that's all been done. You can order breakfast from room service or you can have it in the grand dining room, whichever you decide.'

With Peter in the car chatting away as if everything was perfectly normal I was gaining in confidence by the minute. 'Peter, how come? Is this all your work?' I asked.

He laughed. 'Only a small part. It seems you were a very popular prize, Jack. The amount for the raffle tickets and the dollars in the hat were much more than anyone expected. Madam Rose handed the logistics over to Reggie and I did my part.'

Juicy Fruit laughed. 'I bought several myself.'

'Well, my bit was easy. My brother Noel is the concierge at the Saskatchewan – special rates, all in the family if you know what I mean?'

Juicy Fruit leaned forward and touched Peter on the shoulder. 'Thanks, Pete, I owe you,' she said. 'What a lovely way to come back to Regina!'

'Oh, you've been there before?' I asked.

She squeezed my arm. 'Might as well know, Jack. The last time I was in Regina I spent the night in the Queen's Hotel.' When I looked blank she said, 'Jail, honey. I was caught soliciting in the cocktail bar of the Hotel Saskatchewan quite late, it's the best time for us when customers have had a bit to drink and are feeling lonely. I was only eighteen, a country girl, and very new to the game. I didn't know my way around the city and I hadn't negotiated a cut with the barman. Just to teach me a lesson the bastard called the cops. At the police station they locked me in a cell and soon after the fat police sergeant gave me an either or.'

'You didn't refuse?' Peter interrupted.

'Yep. I did so. I told you I was a greenhorn.'

'Oh, dear. And then?' Peter asked.

'The fat bastard kept me overnight in a cell.' She laughed. 'It wasn't just that, he removed the blanket and it was late fall, almost winter. "Teach you a good lesson, girlie," he said.'

She had a truly infectious laugh that suggested nothing in life should be taken too seriously. Nevertheless it was the first suggestion that Juicy Fruit wasn't entirely the nice-looking, friendly, girl-next-door type she'd appeared to be at first glance. I reminded myself she was a professional who, from the story she'd just related, now knew her way around. I guess you grow up quickly out on the street. As far as I knew, the twins had never done street work, or been forced to solicit in a cocktail bar, but then what would I know about their time in Montreal? Juicy Fruit wasn't as pretty and glamorous as they were, but she had the face, dress and demeanour of a well-turned-out young woman you might see walking with her equally well-dressed partner downtown and you'd think immediately how lucky he was to have someone like her at his side. She'd earlier confessed to being a Saskatchewan country girl but you'd never have known it from her appearance.

Miss Frostbite would have called her handsome, with a certain charm. I could hear her in my head saying it.

My mom would have said, 'That's a sassy young lady.'

On the other hand Joe had once taught me not to trust appearances. I remember he was watching one of the twins leaving the Jazz Warehouse on the arm of a top-brass officer and had no doubt seen the lust and longing in my eyes. 'Jazzboy, what on the outside of a wo-man, that be cam-o-flage. What on the inside, now that sheer mys-tery. That ain't known to no hep cat. Cain't nevah tell. No wo-man she the same to no two cats! She change colour anytime she want, like a cam-e-leon. She got a long, sticky tongue and even if yo other side the room she got you, zzzzzzip! One mo-ment you got yo Wee Willy livin' quiet in your pants and then before you knows you got yoself Long Dong Silver who's a pushin' and strainin' so you cain't walk no ways normal.' He shook a long bony finger in my face. 'Now that hard earned what I jus tol' you, Jazzboy. So don't you do no forgettin'. A wo-man ain't nevah what she seem. Even what she bin tonight ain't what she gonna wake up an' be tomorrow mornin'.'

Joe would have made some woman a great husband, and while his advice to me may have seemed cynical, I never heard him be anything but polite and gracious in the company of a woman, and this included the kitchen staff. My mom adored him and I don't think Miss Frostbite could have done without him constantly by her side. She could be stubborn as a mule, and beware any male who crossed her, but she'd usually come around to his way of seeing things. He was also a much, much better jazz piano player than he ever let on. Sometimes he'd see me attempting a difficult new piece and sit down and do it effortlessly, instructing me as he went. He stuck with their two-piano act and his powder blue tails because it gave the unsophisticated nightclub customers a plausible reason to come to the Jazz Warehouse and drink in a civilised way and gave Miss Frostbite a musical as well as a proprietorial presence. *Fairy Floss & Hockey*, as they were billed, was a lot more than a musical act. I sometimes wondered if, when they'd been younger, Joe and Miss Frostbite . . . you know . . . may have been somewhat more than a musical item. One thing you could be sure of, he would never tell you and, come to think of it, I don't suppose she would either.

We'd reached the Moose Jaw station and Peter Cornhill jumped from the car and opened the door for Juicy Fruit before I could get to it. Then he opened the boot and produced two small suitcases and handed one to Juicy Fruit, explaining, 'Reggie Blunt asked Madam Rose to see to all this. It's got all you'll need I'm told.' He handed me the second, saying, 'Same for you, Jack, packed it myself – clean shirt, the rest.' He then turned towards the conductor who was walking down the platform getting ready to blow his whistle. They moved away out of our hearing and I saw them talk a moment and then Peter put his hand in his trouser pocket and they shook hands. I felt reasonably certain some paper money changed hands, because the conductor nodded and looked towards us. 'All aboard!' he shouted and blew a long blast on his whistle.

Peter shook hands formally with both of us. 'Good luck to you both,' he said, as if there was more than one novice embarking on an unknown journey.

We found our second-class compartment and discovered it contained a couple, both of whom had already folded down the bunks and were in bed. I looked at Juicy Fruit. No words were necessary – the trip to Regina was going to be in silence and more than a little awkward, to say the least.

However, moments later the conductor appeared and instructed us to follow him. The train had started to gather speed and he eventually unlocked a vacant first-class compartment. 'Be more comfortable in here,' he said. I went to my pocket but he waved me aside. 'You'll be able to talk in here. We get into Regina in an hour.'

The time has come. We are alone. What now? These were my immediate thoughts. There was no point in being scared or even nervous, the train was going too fast for me to jump out of the window, we had an hour and I guess we could talk and get to know each other a bit better. That way . . .

'Well, Jack, we'd better get to know each other,' Juicy Fruit said, stealing the words right out of my mind.

'You mentioned you were from the country?' I said casually, hoping I sounded urbane and that this was simply easy talk between two people who, despite the evening just past and the trip to the station, were still strangers.

Juicy Fruit giggled. 'Yes, I'm a flatlander born and bred but that's not what I meant, honey.' We were seated opposite each other and she now stood and pointed to the bunk where I sat. 'On your back, young man,' she ordered.

'Oh no! Not now! Not here on a train!' I panicked. 'Are we, I mean now, right *now* . . . going to . . . make love?'

'Jack, perhaps you forgot. This is my gig.' She said it quite sternly but her eyes were filled with amusement.

'You mean —?'

'I make the decisions.'

I nodded, then gained sufficient courage to say, 'Juicy Fruit, I have to . . . I mean, I haven't any idea what to do. The kiss, the one on the bandstand, that was the first romantic kiss I've ever had.'

'Romantic, that's a lovely word, Jack. I don't get to hear it too often.' She rested her forefinger on her chin. 'You know, I think that's the first time I've ever heard it said to me and I think you should be rewarded.'

I suddenly wondered if the same was true of my mom, that no one had ever said anything romantic to her. I grinned sheepishly. 'I really don't know a thing. I'm sure you're going to find me a big disappointment.' I tried desperately to tell the truth but at the same time not seem like the naïve young fool I was.

'That makes it even nicer for me, Jack.' She paused and grinned. 'Now, do as you're told and lie down, please. Perhaps, now that we're alone, we can try a second kiss and make it a little more passionate than the first, eh?'

I started to raise my legs and then stopped. 'Do I take off my shoes?'

'Always a good start,' she giggled.

I fumbled with the laces and pulled them off.

'Jacket, tie and collar might be a good idea as well,' she instructed playfully, putting me at my ease.

Grinning like a chimpanzee I did as I was told, removed my jacket, tie and the stud from my heavily starched collar so that it sprang open, held only by the stud at the back of my neck. 'Allow me,' Juicy Fruit said, removing the back collar stud and placing the collar with my jacket and tie on the opposite bunk. I must say it was nice being in only my shirtsleeves – the starched detachable collar had been chafing my neck all night. 'Now, what were your instructions, Jack?'

'To lie down.' I swung my legs up onto the bunk and stretched out, only just fitting. Almost before I'd adjusted myself Juicy Fruit had climbed aboard and placed her body on top of mine with a little wriggle of her hips. My very shy friend Wee Willy had been hiding all night, but now, seemingly in seconds, he rose to the occasion, demanding that I introduce Long Dong Silver, as Joe would say. There wasn't much I could do about it. With Juicy Fruit directly on top of me there was no chance of escape.

Moments later, her mouth rested on mine and I thought I felt her tongue between my lips. Then she drew back and whispered, 'Open your mouth, Jack.'

Now I know this is hard to believe, but as I noted before, my only experience of a passionate kiss had happened at the movies between Cary Grant and Rita Hayworth and hadn't involved (or I hadn't noticed) open mouths. So I opened my mouth as if I was at the doctor's about to say 'Ah'.

Juicy Fruit burst out laughing, but it was kind, not cruel, and I couldn't help laughing with her. 'I don't believe it! I just *don't* believe it,' she cried. 'It's like you've been thrown in the deep end and you can't swim a single stroke!'

'What?' I asked, chuckling. 'What have I done?'

'Open your mouth just a little, Jack, so I can get my tongue into your mouth. It's . . .' she seemed to be searching for a word, 'deep kissing, like passionate. I think I'm going to enjoy tonight. How lucky can a girl get, eh? A lover I can train to please me.'

I had no idea what was expected of me but I decided humility was the best option. In fact there was no alternative, so I attempted to say in what I hoped was a more or less gallant manner, 'Of course, whatever you want, Miss Juicy Fruit. But you'll have to show me.'

She lowered herself onto her elbows. 'Oh boy, I'd never have thought this would happen in my whole life!' She was plainly delighted. 'So, let's begin then, Jack. Now open your mouth only slightly when I kiss you, just enough for my tongue to enter,' she said, bringing her slightly parted lips down softly onto my own.

The effect was magical, it was . . . well, just wonderful, and I slid my own tongue into her mouth and it was even better, our two tongues making love. Eventually Juicy Fruit drew back.

'Wow!' I announced, lost for words.

Juicy Fruit moved off me and came to kneel beside the bunk. It was a relief down below, but now I faced yet another embarrassment: I was unmistakably tent-poling. Juicy Fruit leaned over and kissed the tent. 'Time I made you comfortable, Jack. Then we can sit down and chat and when we get to the hotel we'll continue, eh?' She grinned. 'I'll be teacher and you can be teacher's pet.' She had a nice turn of phrase and was obviously smart. She undid my top button, then glancing up at me, she went to work on the rest. 'Oh my, and what have we got in here?' she exclaimed, easing my penis from my Jockeys.

My imprisoned member shot up and out like a ramrod. 'Wow! What a lucky girl am I!' Juicy Fruit exclaimed again, leaning over and holding the base gently between her forefinger and thumb, then, to my astonishment, kissing it. My first thought was that she was going to . . . well, you know, start to rub me using those pretty hands with the long red nails. But then, to my astounded delight, she brought her mouth over the top and a good half of my rampant juddering manhood disappeared into it.

Perhaps if I'd known what was coming it might have been different, but it was simply the happiest surprise of my life as she began to stroke me with her tender beautiful lips.

I'd like to report that this went on for ages and ages but I was much too excited and after a few minutes I started to moan and, though I tried to hang on, Juicy Fruit gripped me more firmly and also increased her speed and with a huge, wonderful surge I came. It was as if I had reached some new pinnacle of pleasure that was so unsustainable it simply had to end. Of course, the act of ejaculation wasn't new to me, but this was infinitely more pleasurable. It was the first time I'd experienced oral sex – any sort of sex! – and there could be no possible comparison to the simple bodily function that leads to relief for every teenage boy. To have a woman willing to give freely with no thought of immediate return was, in itself, an exquisite act of unselfish lovemaking. I instinctively knew that, although it could have been performed dutifully, somehow that wasn't what Juicy Fruit was doing for me.

Although I was still by definition a virgin, I had now, with her tender ministrations, learned that the first joy in making love was sharing – I was dying to give back what I had received. I had fallen in love with womankind, not just the person with whom I had experienced this first act of love, but all of womankind, the gender itself. Alas, I didn't know how I was ever to please Juicy Fruit as she had so wonderfully and selflessly pleased me.

I know people reading this may think, 'Oh well, she was a prostitute and probably gave oral sex routinely when men demanded it, so what's the big deal?' But that's not what it was for me. Juicy Fruit had won me in a raffle, she didn't have to prove her credentials, she had a young guy who knew nothing and it could well have amused her to make fun of me or make demands on me I couldn't or didn't know how to meet – the hooker's ultimate revenge for all the men who had abused, insulted and taken her for granted. The fat cop when she'd been eighteen was just one of what I imagined had been dozens, possibly hundreds of such men. But she'd done no such thing. She'd made me unselfconscious and eager to learn as much as I possibly could. She had prepared me for what was to come.

The first-class sleeper cabin had its own bathroom, or at least a nice washbasin with hot water and other facilities. By the time we'd washed and brushed our teeth we had no more than half an hour to go before arriving in Regina, when it was going to be my turn to perform. Moreover, I knew, metaphorically speaking, this was no Rachmaninoff

Prelude in C Sharp Minor party piece. I would be expected to give a major performance using a sexual musical score I'd never seen before in my life and which, after the oral sex experience, might contain unimaginable feats. Mostly I feared I was now running on empty, and that Wee Willy would be incapable of raising his weary head from the twin oval cushions on which he rested.

I thought about confessing there and then, but remembered that Juicy Fruit had previously warned me that she was the one in charge; she was making all the decisions. After all, she knew all about men and we might just sleep and then start whatever lessons were to come in the morning. What can a girl do when a boy can't . . .?

'Well now, what shall we talk about, Jack? We're about to be lovers and know nothing about each other, so let me guess . . . you speak nicely and use big words and you're seventeen and haven't yet been with a woman; you play jazz piano and Peter Cornhill says you also play classical and come from Toronto. That tells me heaps.'

'Well, what for instance?'

'Oh, you know, decent family, good education, safe and secure, I'd say born with a bit of a silver spoon in your mouth, but then what I can't figure out is what on earth you're doing in Moose Jaw on River Street playing the piano.'

I laughed. 'On my eighth birthday my dad, who was a council garbage collector, came home drunk as usual, smashed the little birthday cake my mom had baked with his fist and threw me against a wall. Usually he beat up my mom, but he didn't that time. Two weeks later he won a battered harmonica in a craps game and gave it to me as a belated birthday gift. He told me I could blow crap instead of talking shit.'

I then gave Juicy Fruit a brief summary of my life in Cabbagetown and the luck that reading books and a talent for music and the careless gift of a battered second-hand harmonica had brought me. I fished into my jacket pocket and produced my shiny new Hohner Echo Elite. 'I don't feel secure without a harmonica,' I confessed. 'My dad's thoughtless gift started everything. The rest I owe to four older women, if you don't count my mom.' I stupidly enumerated them, 'Miss Mony, Mrs Hodgson, Miss Frostbite and Miss Bates,' as if Juicy Fruit would have been any the wiser for knowing their names.

She smiled wickedly. 'And now it's five older women . . . Miss Juicy Fruit!' she cried happily.

'Oh my god, you're right!' I exclaimed.

She laughed. 'We'll soon see about that, Jack. You'll have to tell me how you feel in the morning, eh?'

My heart sank. I knew I was going to fail her for sure.

'Now you have to guess about me. I got you all wrong. See how you do,' Juicy Fruit challenged.

I pretended to be thinking hard. 'Well, let me see, Fruitino, that sounds Italian. You've already told me you're a born and bred flatlander. Italian? That's food, eating it or growing it. I'll take a guess and say you come off the land from a big Italian family battling on a small farm, the long drought and the Depression, dust and debt. Your family was forced to leave the land and do the best they could.' I shrugged. 'At eighteen, with maybe younger brothers and sisters, you had to help support your family, so you did the best you could to survive.' I was cheating of course. Almost all of this was sheer speculation that came from reading John Steinbeck's *The Grapes of Wrath*, where he talked about the Oklahoma dustbowl. But, of course, I knew Saskatchewan had been through the same experience and with much the same suffering for people on the land. It was just a guess but it paid off. Miss Frostbite would often say, 'Jack, if you listen carefully, people will tell you everything about themselves.'

I had always been a good listener. Mostly, I suppose, because my entire life had been controlled by instructions, other people's plans and aspirations for me. Listening is what got me out of poverty and gave me a life, unlike most Cabbagetown kids who were destined for a job that involved little more than brute strength. My own father, a garbage collector, was a good example of what I could have expected. And while there was no shame in what he did, he was somebody who never listened to anyone. He knew everything he thought he needed to know but he had no say in his own destiny other than to become a vicious and bitter drunk.

Juicy Fruit now looked at me open-mouthed in what I took to be a mixture of admiration and incomprehension. 'Why, Jack, how could you possibly know all that? We only met tonight. You couldn't have known I'd win you in the raffle.' She laughed. 'I'm still putting my baby sister Maria through her last year in high school; she wants to be a hairdresser.' She pointed a long painted fingernail at me. 'I got you dead wrong and you got me dead right and I'm the one supposed to be doing the teaching!' She shook her head. 'Oh my, oh my! Ain't that something now? When I was seventeen I was just a dumb kid with nice tits and a starving family and look at you, eh. Same age and reading books and playing the piano so folk come from everywhere to hear you.'

'Yeah, look at me, real bright *I don't think*! I didn't even know how to perform a passionate kiss. All theory and no practice, books and piano but nothing else.' I grinned. 'Believe me, if what you can teach me could have been found in books I'd have been a Lothario by now.'

'A what?'

'No, not a what, a *who*; he was a character in a book written a long, long time ago. A Lothario has his wicked way with women and doesn't always treat them very well.'

'Sounds like most men I know,' Juicy Fruit said, then collecting herself she leaned forward and touched me on the knee, excited as a schoolgirl. 'Oh, Jack, baby, we're going to have us some fun tonight. Just you wait and see. It's been a long time since I got excited over a man.' She gave my thigh a squeeze. 'Ain't no puppy fat there. All good muscle!'

Leaning forward with her dress falling open a bit at the top she gave me a glimpse of her truly beautiful breasts, and as the train approached Regina with a rhythmic *chuffer, chuffer, chuffer, chuff, chuff, chuff*, I could feel a vague stirring. Wee Willy was either waking up or stretching in his sleep.

CHAPTER TEN

WE ARRIVED IN REGINA to be met at the station by Alf Fields, the hotel chauffeur, in a chocolate-brown 1939 Pontiac. Judging from his expression and curt response to my ebullient 'Good evening, you must be Alf', he was clearly not thrilled at having to make such a late pick-up. 'We're sorry to bring you out so late, Alf,' I said.

'Taxis,' he said, pointing to a cab rank. He was as tall as me but impossibly thin. I carried no fat but I must have been twice as broad across the shoulders. It was as if his long string-bean body only had the capacity to produce one word at a time and each word had to be curt or mean. The way he slammed the rear door of the Pontiac after we'd ensconced ourselves, then the deliberate omission of 'sir' left us in very little doubt about his attitude. Juicy Fruit glanced at me, her right eyebrow slightly arched in silent comment.

Even though the train trip had gone so well and we'd got on like a house on fire, I was anxious that nothing should dampen our spirits before we arrived at the hotel, and Alf the driver wasn't being helpful. God knows this was going to be difficult enough without us having to put up with a bunch of sour-faced staff looking down their noses and making silent though undoubtedly snide judgments about the late-night advent of Mr and Mrs Kupple (thanks very much for the moniker, Reggie, about as subtle as a slap in the mouth).

As if the name wasn't a giveaway, we were carrying identical suitcases, small Woolworths overnight bags, which were highly indicative of a one-night stand and certainly not of an extravagant and carefully planned twenty-four-hour honeymoon.

I almost envied Reggie his abortive wedding night. At least it was his wife who couldn't cope. It was different when the woman was the virgin. Innocence and ignorance, purity, faithfulness and love lay folded in the pleats of the pure white surplice she wore figuratively as her nightdress on her wedding night. She was allowed, almost expected, to weep in lamentation for her lost virginity, while I was expected to rise like a stallion on his hind legs, whinnying in exultation that I'd been given the opportunity to get rid of a tiresome and unfortunate boyhood affliction.

'Nice guy!' I said now, turning to Juicy Fruit.

'Take no notice of that long streak of dry shit, Jack,' she advised, her River Street language reminding me abruptly of who and what she was.

'No, he's not going to get away with this!' I exclaimed, though I wasn't quite sure what to do and was feigning courage I didn't think I had. Politeness had always been my main defence, but I was damned if he was going to spoil things. I may only have been seventeen but I'd been to the Waldorf in New York with Miss Frostbite and they'd treated her and me with the utmost courtesy. We'd often arrived back very late at night from a jazz show or concert and the polite welcome we received had never varied. I may have been an ignorant teenager in some respects but I wasn't a punk kid and if he was taking it out on Juicy Fruit, having guessed or been told her profession, I wasn't prepared to allow him to humiliate her.

When Dolly McClymont had snubbed my mother and refused to speak to her, my poor little mom had simply accepted this gross indignity for years. I only understood later how much this must have hurt and humiliated her, and how much it had affected me. The Dolly McClymonts, Mrs Hendersons and Alf Fields of this world can inflict a great deal of harm because they rely on their victims being too timid to retaliate. Yelling or pulling rank might not be the answer but I had seen not only my mom but Mac permanently damaged by bullying and I knew that being a victim could easily become a habit. Something always needs to be done, and early. It was just like when I was at school: you might end up with a bloody nose, but it will be the last one you have to endure. Bullies do not come back for more if you show them there is always going to be a price to pay. It was the only useful thing my father, a perfect example of a brutal bully, taught me.

I knew confrontation wasn't going to help me with Fields, it would simply make the atmosphere even frostier, and I could hardly complain to the management after we arrived. I guessed that if this scrawny bully in jumped-up chauffeur's livery knew our true identity he probably thought he had us on the ropes. Something was required from me if I were to prove myself anything more than a cowed boy.

I didn't usually confront people directly; it just wasn't my style. As Joe would say in one of his semi-biblical maxims, 'Bad mouth begets bad mouth. Yo talk shit yo gonna end up eatin' it.' I remembered how Joe handled things once or twice when there'd been a sudden altercation in the Jazz Warehouse – two drunken businessmen at war with each other or two local Mobsters huffing and puffing and muscling up, sometimes even a couple of women shrieking at each other. Joe would simply turn to the band and say, 'Drum solo! Loud. Real loud!' The drums usually did the trick. 'No use hollerin' at each other when they cain't hear nothin'.'

I reached into my jacket pocket and drew out the Hohner Echo Elite and started to play, leading off with 'I'll Never Smile Again', sung by Frank Sinatra, then into Jimmie Davis's 'You Are My Sunshine', and Bing Crosby's 'Only Forever'. As we turned into a park I moved on to 'In the Mood' by Glenn Miller. They were some of the popular songs I'd play at the Brunswick most afternoons, then mix a bit of jazz for the cocktail lounge in the evenings.

Juicy Fruit loved every minute and joined in singing the lyrics to 'Sunshine', which everyone in the world seemed to know. She had a nice clear contralto voice and followed the music well. Alf sat there stiff-necked and straight-backed, radiating disapproval as far as I could tell. It came as a big surprise therefore when he opened the back door for Juicy Fruit wearing a smile as big as a slice of melon.

'Welcome to the Hotel Saskatchewan, Mr and Mrs Kupple,' he beamed as I slid over to emerge through the same rear door. 'That's the best station pick-up I've ever done and I thank you most kindly. Why, you sure known how to handle a harmonica, sir! I play a bit myself, but sure as damn I've never heard it played like that. You're a master, sir.'

Two 'sirs' in a row! We were suddenly experiencing an entirely different Alf Fields who insisted on taking our luggage, such as it was, and escorting us into the hotel, shouting out to a sleeping desk clerk, 'Randy, git movin' boy! We've got important guests. Mr and Mrs Kupple have arrived. You see they get everything they need now.' He placed our suitcases down and shook us both by the hand. 'Damn, that was good!' he exclaimed, shaking his head before departing.

Randy, startled out of a peaceful sleep, jumped to his feet and hastily straightened his necktie and put on his jacket. 'Welcome, sir, madam,' he announced in a flustered voice. 'Musta dozed off.'

'That's okay, buddy, it's pretty late. Lousy time to arrive anywhere,' I said. He didn't seem any older than me but somehow I'd grown since we left Moose Jaw and he seemed more like the Jack of yesterday than the Jack of today. The harmonica had given me back some of the initiative. Juicy Fruit clung to my arm like a new bride and I felt her squeeze it gleefully.

Randy, seemingly the only person on duty, was a model of obsequious attention as he escorted us in the lift to our eighth-floor room, which turned out to be a whole suite, not as swanky as Miss Frostbite's suite at the Waldorf, but terrific just the same. There were silky curtains and fancy upholstered French chairs with those bent legs that bulge at the top, and carpets your toes sank into. 'The honeymoon suite, sir,' Randy announced proudly, handing me the key. Bringing his feet together and bowing slightly, he touched his head in a salute. 'Just call the desk if you need anything, sir.'

'Have a good sleep, Randy,' I said, still a little high on the success of my harmonica ploy and feeling much more in control.

The moment the door shut, Juicy Fruit burst into laughter, threw up her hands, danced over to me and flung her arms around my neck. 'Oh, Jack, you were terrific. The harmonica sure turned that bastard around!' She released me and twirled across the room, her outflung arm taking in everything around us. 'Jesus, Mary and Joseph, Jack! Look at all this! I think I just died and went direct to heaven!' She ran through to the bedroom where she let out a cry of delight. 'Jack, come quick!' I walked across to the bedroom to join her. 'Look, Jack, the bed's got curtains, like a love nest!' She slipped between the lace hangings surrounding the four-poster bed and flung herself full length, like an excited eight-year-old. 'Oooh-ah, feel the springs!' she said, bouncing up and down. I noticed the cover had been removed and the bed turned down for the night.

I grinned to see her so obviously happy, but I must say I was surprised. I'd imagined she'd have been pretty accustomed to . . . you know . . . assignations, lonely commercial travellers sneaking girls into their hotel rooms at night. But then again, I don't suppose many commercial travellers booked the honeymoon suite, and I'd learned along the way that most of them stayed in cheap accommodation, boarding houses and the like, and entertained at the cocktail lounges of the big hotels to give their clients the impression they were staying there. They'd be the guys who'd drop me a quarter during the afternoon while I was playing in the foyer and say, 'Hey buddy, when I come into the cocktail lounge with a client, will you just nod or smile and say, 'Welcome back, Mr Brown.' It helped to have a good memory – some nights I'd make a couple of dollars.

'Jack, I've never seen anything like this!' Juicy Fruit was excited almost to the point of tears. 'Oh, we are going to have us such a good time, baby!'

She brushed the curtains aside and headed for the bathroom. Moments later she was at it again. 'Oh, quick, come and look! Jack, what luck!'

I wasn't much of an expert on hotel bathrooms – bathtub, tiles, towels, taps, soap holder . . . I mean what else could you expect? Gold dragon's head taps at the Waldorf, maybe, but not here. 'What?' I asked, seeing nothing unusual.

She pointed. 'The shower, it's on its own. Look, behind those curtains. Oh Jack, let's have a shower! Get lovely and clean for bed.'

'Righto, you go first,' I said, not thinking.

'Jack Spayd! Now you listen to me, boy!' Juicy Fruit announced in a voice that made me jump. 'We're alone and I'm in charge, remember?'

'What . . . what is it?' I asked, perplexed.

'Get your clothes off.'

'Huh? Right now? At this moment?' I asked stupidly.

'Ain't any other moment I had in mind, honey,' she said, undoing a zip in the side of her dress. She bent over and promptly pulled her green silk dress over her head and moments later stood in her panties, brassiere, garter belt, stockings and black court shoes. 'Well, go on! Off with it,' she said, flicking a scarlet-tipped forefinger in the direction of my suit. 'We haven't got all night!'

Unfortunately that was exactly what we did have.

She picked up the dress, shook it out and draped it over her arm then turned to me. 'When I get back you be in your birthday suit, you hear me now Jack Spayd?' she scolded.

'Yes, ma'am,' I replied, touching my brow in an informal salute. The confidence I'd so recently gained was slipping away like quicksand. I watched as she click-clacked across the tiles and out of the bathroom in her heels and undies. She had a perfectly splendid bottom and nice long legs and what her bra contained was simply too marvellous for words.

Alone in the hotel bathroom as I wrestled my necktie loose, I could think of few more awkward moments in my life up till then. The anchor motif on the tie was a perfect symbol of my predicament: I was sunk in deep water. I removed my jacket, shirt collar and shirt, draping them across the edge of the bath, then I sat on the edge and pulled off my shoes and socks and stood to undo my belt, so that the trousers, always slightly too big around the waist, concertinaed around my ankles. Stepping free, I folded them and smoothed them over the edge of the bath. I'd have to hang them up somewhere later on if I was going to wear the suit in the morning.

Standing in my Jockeys I gazed down, but nothing stirred, nothing stretched, nothing woke from deep slumber. At that very moment Juicy Fruit entered the room entirely naked and without a glance at me she stepped behind the shower curtain and turned on the shower. I stood where I was, growing increasingly anxious, unsure what to do next. I could see her blurred silhouette through the curtains and she seemed to stand there motionless for ages. When she finally emerged her hand and arm glistened with water. 'Perfect,' she announced. I realised then that she had been adjusting the temperature.

Now she faced me full frontal and pointed silently at my Jockeys. Keeping my eyes fixed on hers I slowly slid my underpants down to my ankles and stepped out of them. She'd removed the hairpins that held the victory rolls and brushed out her hair. It now fell softly from the crown of her head to her shoulders. Juicy Fruit was Mary Magdalene; in every possible way she was every woman that ever was, not beautiful but much, much more than that. She wasn't young or old, innocent or experienced in the ways of men; the only way I could think to describe her was that she was of the earth and perfectly, delectably ripe. The word fecund sprang into my mind, beloved of D.H. Lawrence, who seemed to like his women rich, lush and flourishing. It seemed to apply to the glorious woman who now fixed me with large brown eyes that glinted with gold flecks.

I would come to know a lot of women and make love to a great many of them, but there is always one moment when you know that you are about to make love to every woman at once. In barely a few seconds it seemed to me I stood rampant. 'Come, Jack,' Juicy Fruit invited, then, not even glancing at my erection, she took my hand and we stepped into the shower together. 'Hold me tight, Jack,' she said.

'How?' I asked, glancing down.

'Oh,' she said, laughing. She reached down and held my cock then shook it like a recalcitrant child.

'Don't!' I cried. 'One more like that and I'm a goner!'

'Oh, this is such fun,' Juicy Fruit cried, stepping into the shower. As the water streamed over her head and shoulders she lifted her face into it, allowing it to cascade over her tightly closed eyes and down her cheeks. She stepped back and wiped the water from her face, sweeping her palms down her neck to her wonderful breasts, her nipples bouncing as she swished the water from her skin, her lovely body glistening. Finally she opened her eyes. 'Now it's your turn, Jack,' she said, laughing.

I wet myself down, rubbing the water over my skin and being careful to avoid the unsheathed but overeager erection that couldn't be trusted to behave for a moment. I told myself I had to concentrate on something else until we got into bed so that I could lose my virginity properly. I greatly feared what was to come, and worried that I would not last a minute before I disgraced myself.

I turned Juicy Fruit back into the warm cascading water. She searched blindly for the soap and handed it to me with her eyes tightly shut, her face directly under the shower rose. Speaking in a bubbly sort of underwater voice she said, 'Jack, soap me everywhere, with your hands, with your fingers, every part. You got to know every part of a woman when you go to bed with her, so I want you to wash every single woman's part of me.'

Instructing me like this under the shower made it seem a bit more natural. I'd never touched a woman's breasts before, much less the neatly clipped pubic bit I'd observed only once before, when Miss Flash had opened her coat and shocked me to my core. It was central to all of this and the grand entrance to manhood. I'd spent hundreds of hours imagining the naked female body, this part in particular, but I still knew nothing about it. Sure, I knew you could slide in and move up and down and soon grand things would happen, or they were supposed to. In Reggie Blunt's case, he'd discovered that even though he possessed a marriage licence, free entry was barred. But I knew this wasn't going to happen to me, just the opposite in fact. Juicy Fruit's suggestion that I soap her was a stroke of genius. Armed with a bar of soap I could guard against any lascivious thoughts. I had a task to perform, almost a duty, which allowed me to curb my prurient fantasies. After all, I'd been obeying instructions from women all my life.

I set about with gusto, soaping my large hands before I began at her feet and ankles, deciding I'd do the parts we had in common first. After all, while a woman's back might be more shapely, it didn't differ all that much from a man's. Legs, bottom, back. In this manner I could delay, or work up to, soaping the major differences, all of which seemed to be situated at the front. Or so I'd hitherto imagined.

It was lovely to soap and lather her as the shower splashed over her front, and soon enough I arrived at her delicious bottom, the walking wiggle, the part of the female anatomy that had turned me on a hundred times, mostly when it belonged to one of the twins as they left the club. I knew the twins used it as a weapon, showboating, strutting their stuff, but I guessed that while it had a powerful effect on a male, it probably didn't have the capacity to make a woman feel horny. I soaped her rump carefully, my big hands moving in circles over both cheeks, then suddenly she bent over, her hands grasping her ankles. 'Holy smoke!' I stumbled back into the shower curtain and what hove into view very nearly caused me to fall on my ass. 'Jack, soap me, sweetheart, right inside,' Juicy Fruit said. Of course I knew what I was looking at, but never in my wildest imaginings had I expected to see it from such a viewpoint, two lovely mounds with paradise valley enfolded between them. 'Soap me, Jack,' Juicy Fruit instructed. I did as she requested, gently soaping this astonishing female part, which I had long imagined. She ran her hands up her calves from her ankles, resting on her knees but still bent over in full display. 'Now rub your finger along inside, just a little at first, at the very top. Not hard, gentle, with the pad of your finger.'

Again I did as she asked and my finger slid in so effortlessly I had to draw it back to meet her requirements. 'Yes, yes, just like that, at the top, that's nice . . .' then a little later, 'a little harder, baby, but don't dig . . . slide. Oh god, that's lovely,' she gasped. 'Now just a little deeper, slide the whole finger up and down, Jack. Oh, Jesus! You're giving little mama pleasure, darling,' she said breathlessly. I could see her bottom starting to grind. 'Gimme the whole finger, Jack! There,' she guided my hand. 'Deep!' she said as I hesitated, afraid I might hurt her. 'Go, Jack, faster!' Then suddenly her bottom went berserk, moving so quickly that my finger had almost no work to do. Then, several gasps and whimpers later, she suddenly grasped both taps and cried, 'Oh, oh, oh my god! Oh my god!' The strength of her muscles was awesome. When at last she quietened, the sound of the water masked her panting as it splashed and trickled over her body.

Juicy Fruit straightened and kissed me. 'You passed your first exam, Jack. I'm giving you an A-plus, honey,' she said, her beautiful breasts rising and falling from her previous exertions. 'You've still got my back and then the front,' she said, giggling.

I continued to soap her, bemused by the way the night was unfolding. Already I'd been taken way beyond my imagination, which hitherto I'd always thought of as dangerously extreme.

I lathered her lovely back and neck and then her breasts, which felt soft and firm at the same time. Her nipples were taut and lovely, little pink rosebuds that pointed upwards. 'Kiss them, Jack,' she instructed. On a sudden impulse I dropped the bar of soap and cupped each breast in my hands, allowing the water to sluice the soap from her breasts before I took each nipple into my mouth in turn. It was a bold move, the first deliberate sexual act I'd ever initiated. I played with each one for a short while, rolling it around my tongue as if it were a delicious sweet. Miraculously, Juicy Fruit said breathlessly, 'Oh, Jack, that's lovely. I want more of that later.'

Suddenly I felt good about myself. I was still a virgin, but now I possessed a sort of rough road map, some experience at least. Not much, but some. I retrieved the soap and continued to lather her stomach, moving my hand down onto the soft pad of dark wet hair. I felt as if this was not entirely unfamiliar territory, although I was approaching it from a different perspective. Nonetheless it was one I treated with great circumspection, careful not to attempt any further innovation.

Breast kissing was one thing, I had imagined that before, but I had to be careful because I had a sudden urge to kiss every part of her, to use my tongue again. It seemed only natural, especially after what Juicy Fruit had done to me on the train. She grabbed my hand and grasped my forefinger, saying, 'Lovely big fingers,' as she guided it into her body, then, removing her hand she wriggled her thighs until my forefinger had been completely accommodated in what I can only describe as a firm but altogether surprising grip. 'See, Jack, it works from the front as well,' she said wickedly.

The soaping ploy had worked like a dream. I had been so preoccupied, applying myself with my usual obsessive concentration to learning all this new information and trying my best to please Juicy Fruit, that by the time it was my turn to be soaped I found that I had regained a measure of control over my body. If I could just maintain that control, then at the very least, I might be able to learn something about making love.

Just watching Juicy Fruit was a joy, as we finally rinsed ourselves under the shower and turned off the taps. She grasped her hair and wrung it out, squeezing the last of the water from the thick, glistening rope down over her breasts. She looked simply glorious as she smiled mischievously and said, 'I think the boy could go places.' She looked happy.

Clean and stark naked seemed so natural and easy as Juicy Fruit and I towelled each other dry and hopped into the four-poster, pulling the curtains around us. 'Jack, you have a nice young body so we're going to make love with the light on, and if you'll let me tell you what I want, I think you'll find it more fun, eh?'

Inwardly I jumped for joy. 'Suits me,' I replied, attempting for a moment to sound nonchalant. I knew nothing about naked women, but I knew a fair bit about the dressed variety, and soon realised that acting suave and assured, especially at my age, was doomed to failure. I decided to come clean. 'Juicy Fruit, I've loved learning what you've shown me so far. I'd really like it if you were in charge. I want to remember tonight forever, but I'm afraid I'm going to mess it up for you . . . you know, wham, bam, thank you ma'am and that will be that.'

She looked at me with amusement. 'Jack, sweetheart, you have no idea what that body of yours is capable of doing. You think I'm gonna let you get away with givin' me woe? Honey, no way. You wait and see, it'll be just fine. If it ain't . . .' she paused and chuckled, 'I brought me a real sharp bowie knife and you don't need to know what I'm gonna use it for,' she laughed. 'You cost me five raffle tickets and I ain't gonna let myself have a bad time, so you might just like to come along for the ride, eh?'

Quite how she managed it I shall never know, but Juicy Fruit made my passage into manhood a sustained and wonderful experience and was kind enough to have an orgasm, although at the time I was too ignorant to understand exactly what was happening or why, let alone to know what it was called.

I was so elated and grateful that I leapt out of bed and ran to the bathroom to retrieve my Hohner Elite. Jumping back into bed I serenaded Juicy Fruit with 'Night and Day' by Cole Porter. She knew the lyrics and the song suited her distinctive deep voice.

Miraculously we managed to make love three more times that night and each time, as we lay side by side, she'd request a song. She knew all the lyrics and seemed to enjoy herself immensely. Even today when I hear certain old songs I can recall the ways she wanted to be gratified. 'Night and Day' was the first song I played her, and I guess a fairly predictable choice, but it never failed to conjure up in my imagination the four-poster with its curtains and the sense of being totally enclosed and private the first time I'd actually made love to a woman.

Each time we made love that night my loving partner taught me something new and after each time she chose a song for me to play: 'Cheek to Cheek' by Irving Berlin, 'My Funny Valentine' by Rodgers and Hart and after that came Gershwin's 'Summertime'. Finally, when we were both dead tired and lying in each other's arms, Juicy Fruit paid me a simply lovely compliment by singing, 'Thanks for the Memory'. Hearing her unaccompanied I realised that she had a damn good voice. Dawn was just showing through the lace curtains as we both fell into an utterly exhausted sleep, marking the end of the night that had made Jack a man.

But it wasn't quite over. I woke to find Juicy Fruit kissing me. 'It's ten o'clock, baby,' she said, smiling down at me. 'Time for you to have a shower.'

I sat up in bed and stretched, yawning. 'God, it feels like I've been asleep for ten minutes. Okay, you go ahead, I'll be there in a tick.'

'No, I've already showered, Jack. There's something I have to ask you . . . a favour.'

I grinned. 'Sweetheart, after last night, you can have whatever you want.' She'd brushed her hair and look glorious. 'You look beautiful, Juicy Fruit,' I said, reaching out for her.

'Jack, remember last night, the first thing we did in the shower when you were soaping me and I bent down?'

I nodded. 'Lesson number one. How could I ever forget?'

'Well, this is the last lesson and this is a fresh day, so you are no longer mine to command. It's a special treat for me and you can say no if you want.'

I shrugged. 'Anything . . . anything for you, Juicy Fruit.' I grinned. 'I need all the knowhow you can give me.'

'No, this is just for me, Jack.' She kissed me gently. 'Will you do what you did with your finger, but this time use your tongue?'

I couldn't believe my ears. It was what I'd wanted to do in the shower. It had seemed completely natural and the equivalent of what Juicy Fruit had done for me on the train. But of course I hadn't had the courage to suggest it at the time.

I pretended to think for a moment, to add a little comic tension. Then I growled softly at her. 'Grrrrrr! Come here gorgeous, delicious Juicy Fruit. I'm going to eat you up!'

Juicy Fruit had taken my virginity, and in return she had given me the most important lesson a man can learn in sexual good manners: that sex isn't merely for your own gratification. With lovemaking, as with almost everything else between men and women, it is as well to remember that there is a time to give and a time to receive. I would spend most of the years to come in the presence of women and learn that, unlike Juicy Fruit, who had the courage to ask for what she wanted, most needed to be given the confidence to demand from a man the same satisfaction as he demanded from them.

On the journey back to Moose Jaw we had a compartment to ourselves where Juicy Fruit and I talked like old friends rather than recent lovers. At one stage she looked me in the eye and said, 'Jack, I'm a working girl and that's not goin' to change for a while, honey. So I guess it's friends, eh?'

I nodded. 'Yeah, I'd like that, I'd like that a whole lot.'

Juicy Fruit reached out and touched my hand and chuckled, keeping things light. 'Jack, that was lovely and on my terms for a change. Let's not spoil it. One day, perhaps, when I'm free again, who knows?' She laughed suddenly. 'I truly loved last night but it's cost me dearly!' She lifted her skirt to show a ladder starting at the top of the nylon stocking on her left leg. 'It's my only pair of nylons. I got these from a Yank commercial traveller and his offer was the nylons for the trick, or he'd pay me. The nylons won hands down. They're precious.' Pointing to the ladder, she said, 'It's saying a heap, Jack, but you were worth it *and* the five raffle tickets. Such a pity you can't be a virgin twice. Next time I'd buy ten.'

'Thanks, Juicy Fruit. Everything was great for me, thanks to you. If this ever became a River Street tradition, raffling a virgin, I mean, I can't imagine anyone ever getting a better deal than I got. You were simply fantastic!'

'Jack, about being a working girl – I don't mix business with pleasure. But loving ain't just that . . . if you know what I mean. Any time you need a bit of loving, you let me know. You need me, just holler and I'll come,' she repeated.

I nodded. It was generous of her to say the least. I guess she meant like a big sister. 'Sorry about the nylons. Rare as hen's teeth, I know.'

I knew the twins were drowning in nylons, given to them by their top-brass clients. Senior officers could get as many as they needed from the Americans who had cornered the entire market for their own troops. A soldier, sailor or air-force guy armed with a couple of pairs of nylons when he went on rest and recreation was practically guaranteed a girl for the night. A pair of nylons was pure gold. Juicy Fruit had been forced to trade sex with some dumb commercial traveller for the pair that was now lamentably laddered. I'd write my mother to get a couple of pairs from the twins for her.

'I've been thinking,' I said.

'What, Jack?'

'You've got a nice voice, sweet and low, good accurate pitch – you're obviously musical.'

'My papa used to play the piano accordion. As kids we'd sing every night – 'O Sole Mio', 'Santa Lucia', 'La Danza', 'Carmela', and heaps and heaps more. One of the last things he sold before we were forced to leave our little farm was his accordion. He died in Winnipeg last year without ever playing a note of music again.'

'Oh, I'm sorry,' I mumbled, the way people always do. 'You seem to know most of the lyrics of the popular songs. If you like, I'm sure I can arrange it with Peter and Cam Kerr for you to sing in the cocktail lounge for an hour or so some nights when it's, you know, quiet on River Street. I can accompany you on the piano, you can put on your green dress, maybe make a couple'a extra bucks doing requests?'

Juicy Fruit looked at me in astonishment. 'Jack, you could *do* that?'

'No, I can't *absolutely* promise, but I can try. Of course you couldn't, you know, solicit.'

She nodded. 'Of course! I don't anyhow,' she replied, then went on, 'but . . . but will I be good enough?' She looked me in the eye. 'Jack, I don't want no favours, eh? I can or I can't. I want you to be honest, no —'

'Patronising?' I interrupted.

She scowled, not sure what the word meant. 'Yeah, if that means no favours.'

I laughed. 'You sing well already. I suspect you'll do just fine. No one can be sure about these things but let me put it this way, I can't afford to have a second-rate singer beside me at the Brunswick. We'll do a little practising at the Caribou Café for a few mornings, get our phrasing right, work up a bit of a routine and repertoire.' I grinned. 'Maybe even throw "Santa Lucia" into the mix in memory of your papa. What do you say? A bit of practice . . . instruction . . . never know your luck, eh?'

'Oh, Jack!' Juicy Fruit jumped up and sat on my lap, put her arms around me and kissed me passionately. When she finally drew back she said, 'I would've bought twenty raffle tickets!'

Juicy Fruit's gratitude made me feel slightly uncomfortable, because I had plans that I was not prepared to admit to her or anyone else just yet. I guess after my single night's education at the hands of Juicy Fruit I was like a kid in a candy store confronted with all the choices in the world. Anything seemed possible now, and I wanted to taste every piece of candy in the shop. Given the generosity of women towards me all my life, my aspirations seemed thoroughly unworthy and ungrateful, and considering my tender age and lack of experience, possibly foolish and arrogant as well. I knew I could never be the sort of man my father was, treating women brutally and cruelly, nor even a man like Mac who accepted whatever marriage and family life handed him. I wanted to be a man who truly loved women but I was uncertain that I could love or be possessed by only one of them. All this was entirely hypothetical, since I had never had even one romantic relationship with a woman. But, I told myself, I wanted these potential dalliances to be more or less on my own terms; I didn't ever want to be tied to one woman in the usual death-do-us-part manner. Most of the men I knew thought of marriage as a trap and children as a burden. Some, like Mac, endured, others were violent and some appeared to be reasonably happy family men. Nonetheless most men saw women as objects, necessary objects perhaps, but still a kind of general factotum to have at their side, almost as an unpaid servant. The worst of them saw women as simply a way to 'get the dirty water off their chest' as the saying goes.

I told myself I didn't want to endure any of this; I wanted something quite different. I wanted women to want me, not as a good little boy who did what he was told and played the piano nicely and worked hard, thereby giving them a certain amount of personal satisfaction. I wanted them to be falling over themselves to get their hands on me, but I never wanted any of them to own me. Nor did I want to be the kind of cruel, ruthless and violent man who seemed to attract women. At the Jazz Warehouse you would often see beautiful women, perhaps driven by some misguided primordial instinct, who seemed deeply attracted to absolute unmitigated bastards. Joe would shake his head and say, 'Ain't it strange, Jazzboy? Sometime the most beautiful wo-man, she fine herself a cruel asshole, then she happy.' I had grown up in Cabbagetown during the Depression and had witnessed every kind of male behaviour – desperate, mean, violent, ashamed, mean-faced, sour, miserable, beaten. Usually men took out their misery on hapless and generally blameless women and kept what joy they experienced for their drinking buddies.

I didn't want to be that kind of man, but I wanted independence. It was, I thought, my only way of getting to know who the hell I really was. I never again wanted to be beholden, not to women or anyone else. My last experience of doing what I was told would be the army. After that I wanted to be free.

When we arrived in Moose Jaw I was surprised to see the Brunswick Buick waiting for us. The train usually carried people for the hotel but John, the regular hotel chauffeur, had received strict instructions from Peter Cornhill to give us priority. 'What the bell captain wants, I do, Jack,' he'd laughed. 'No arguments, that's how any good hotel is made to run smoothly. Get on the wrong side of the man at the front door and you may as well pack it in, find another hotel.'

He dropped Juicy Fruit off first and then drove me to Mrs Henderson's, just in time to change, after which I barely had time to walk to the Brunswick to start my shift. I'd no sooner finished playing in the cocktail lounge, when Reggie Blunt appeared. 'Evening, old chap, I take it this is a brand new Spayd I'm digging? Care for whisky now you're a man?'

'Mr and Mrs Kupple! That was pathetic, Reggie. Thanks for nothing. Sheer bastardry,' I said with a grin.

'Sorry old chap, spur of the moment.' He didn't appear the least upset by my rebuke. 'Well, we couldn't get much out of Miss Juicy Fruit on her return. Very circumspect, I must say. The girls did their best, gathered around like crows at a road kill, but she simply smiled. Must have been good or it would be all over River Street by now. Harlots don't hide these things as a general rule. A man's performance with his pants down is passed around, part of the sisterhood conspiracy. Not a peep from Mrs Kupple, though. You haven't answered my question. Whisky?'

'Reggie, what is it with you? How come you were even around to ask?'

'Ah, even harlots have to have a confessor, a man they can rely on for guidance, and after three decades or more playing piano on River Street, they've chosen me as their confidant.'

'Sure, but the raffle, you organised that; you and Madam Rose were thick as thieves.'

'Intermediary, old chap, like I said, father confessor. Besides, I've come to think of you as my protégé, Jack.' He smiled a smug, whisky-nosed, weepy-eyed, grey-stubble smile. 'Couldn't have you carrying your virginity around like a sad sack, could we now, old boy? I've known Rose O'Shannessy since she was a young gal. She started working on River Street at the start of the Great War. Likes a wee dram herself.'

'Reggie, thanks for the offer of a scotch, but I *still* don't drink.'

'Jack, there's a saying among men, "Never trust a man who doesn't drink".'

'Sounds like an excuse rather than an aphorism, Reggie.' The conversation was developing into the usual flurry of competitive ripostes and I wasn't in the mood. 'I haven't had breakfast or lunch and —' I glanced at my watch, 'I've got half an hour to have my dinner. Afraid I'll have to pass on the offer of a drink, even a soda pop, but thanks anyhow, Reggie.'

Reggie Blunt ignored my refusal. It was as if he hadn't even bothered to listen, too busy constructing his next remark, making sure it came out in the usual pontifical manner. 'Damned lucky you got one of Rose's girls, Jack. A most fortunate choice, fortunate indeed! Lady Luck smiled on you, dear boy. But then you're a lucky young sod, noticed that in poker on several occasions. Lucky with cards, unlucky in love, eh? I daresay

Miss Juicy Fruit will eventually tell Rose and I'll pass on her take on the weekend for your elucidation, dear boy. Whore's worthy words, eh? Still, couldn't have done worse than me and the dearly departed Olga, the vestal virgin, ha ha.'

I rose from my piano stool. 'Reggie, I have to get something to eat or I won't get through tonight. You really *must* excuse me.'

Reggie grabbed at my jacket. 'Jack, never mind the drink, I wanted to talk to you about a poker game – Monday night, three weeks' time, out-of-towners, farmers, railroad men, couple of older "commercials" from the east, harmless types. They're looking for one or two locals to sit in on the game.'

'Bunnies, you mean?' I said, half joking.

'No, nothing like that, old boy . . . just between the two of us, nod and a wink if you know what I mean, they're in town to use Madam Rose's establishment, the poker game is incidental, a bit of a tradition, post-coital recovery, ha ha. Something I do . . . arrange every year. Thought you may like to sit in?'

'And you? You'll be playing?'

'No, I'm usually the dealer. Thought you might like to try your luck, old son. Nothing you can't handle I assure you, but a bit too rich for me. Think about it? Could be fun. I'll wait for your answer in the cocktail lounge after you've played the dining room.'

Reggie Blunt of course knew the routine and when I would return to the cocktail lounge after helping Cam Kerr create the right atmosphere in the fine dining restaurant. 'Starched damask, polished crystal, monogrammed silverware, flowers, rosy-cheeked country girls waiting on tables in frilly aprons and caps and some of your light classics, Jack, then Hilda's nice tits at the cashier's desk.' (Cam was a tit man.) His face would split into a satisfied grin. 'Irresistible combination. The food is incidental, except of course for the quality of the beef and pork. Every peasant on the prairies is a goddamned meat expert when we get that wrong.'

I'd had more than enough Reggie Blunt on an empty stomach, and with no more than three or four hours of sleep. To get rid of the fat little punning machine so I could get some grub into me before I faced the diners, I said hastily, 'Yeah, okay, count me in. Unless the entry stake is too big.' For a moment he seemed surprised and, I thought, relieved at my speedy acceptance. I put this down to imagination brought about by hunger. The poker game sounded harmless, and I'd been playing more serious poker for months now.

Playing Mondays with the boys was pleasant enough, but after studying Jacoby, I'd felt I needed some real competition. I had to make myself lose in the penny-ante game almost every Monday. Peter Cornhill solved the problem nicely. He soon had me fixed up in several late-night games that started after ten-thirty and usually went on until around one in the morning. I could sleep in until nine so the hours didn't matter and Mrs Spragg, who ruled the kitchen so fiercely that even Mrs Henderson didn't dare venture there, would cook me up a mess of eggs which I'd eat at the kitchen table around nine-thirty.

These games involved more serious money, but Peter had made sure there were no crooks or con men involved. I was using a much bigger stake, often taking three or four hundred bucks along with me, some of it, I confess, money I'd put aside for my mom's operation. But I was holding my own and after three months I was ahead, not by much, but not behind anyhow. My mom's money was still intact and I'd added a little more.

I'd long since realised that Reggie seemed to know almost everything going on at night on River Street. Now he gave me the facial grimace that passed for his smile. 'Capital! Nothing you can't handle these days, dear boy,' Reggie exclaimed. 'The two railroad men I believe you know, Grover and Fred, from previous late-night games when they're in town. The others, as I've just explained, are all of them old friends.'

I nodded. 'Nobody else from the Monday game?'

'Lordy, no!' He chuckled. 'Jack, don't think we haven't noticed you throwing in your hands far more often than you customarily did. You've moved on, we've stayed put. We don't belong in this game, although it's by no means beyond you, old chap,' he said in a clumsy attempt at flattery.

'Okay,' I repeated, glad to get away at last. I told myself I could always throw in my hand, call it quits if the game got too hot for me.

Now I don't want this to sound like fairy-tale stuff, but Juicy Fruit proved, with a little coaching, to be a very capable singer. Her voice was deep with a husky edge to it, and she was naturally musical, thanks no doubt to her parents. Of course she had one or two bad habits but nothing disastrous. Moreover, this wasn't New York or even Toronto but Moose Jaw, and I felt sure she could pass muster in the cocktail lounge and we'd use her as well in the John Robert Johnson Caribou Café Band where she'd gain further experience.

The main problem was her 'other' night job. I decided to bring it up before her first performance, just in case. 'Juicy Fruit, how well are you known on River Street? I only ask because, if we're going to do this, the Brunswick won't have a bar of you if you're well known for your, ah . . . other job. How come I've never seen you soliciting?'

'On the street . . . River Street?'

'Yeah.'

'I work for Madam Rose, Jack. She keeps five of us for the wealthy out-of-town clients and the local big nobs. We don't do the street, if you mean getting out on the balconies or standing in doorways. No migrant harvest workers for me. I've long since graduated.'

'What's that mean?'

Juicy Fruit laughed. 'The street is for the beginners and the old beat-ups, it's obvious you're unfamiliar with how a house works, Jack. A good house like Madam Rose's has street girls to attract the passing trade, and the in-house girls. Just like a restaurant – walk-in diner or fine dining, bookings only. It's all very discreet, separate side entry from a lane, our own rooms and by appointment only. Clients arrange a time by telephone. Some of the important local citizens have their own key to the side door – we're down a separate lane half a block from the main brothel. Oh, that reminds me.' She dug into her purse and produced a Yale key. 'You never know when you might need it, Jack. Five doors down from Madam Rose towards the city centre on the left is a small lane called Riverside Lane, it's door number seven. This can be a rough town and I know you've been playing poker late at night.'

Juicy Fruit's arrangement wasn't all that different from the twins' in Toronto, only she didn't go out in public with her clients and neither did she manage her own enterprise. 'Your clients?' I asked. 'They wouldn't give you away? You know, if they suddenly saw you on a bandstand at the Brunswick?'

She gave a snort. 'Be very damned stupid if they did. But first they'd need to recognise me.'

'Eh?'

'Wigs.'

'Wigs? What's that mean?'

'Well, Jack, even a whore wants a private life. Well . . . an in-house hooker, anyhow. We all wear wigs: I'm a blonde in-house, and I wear quite different make-up.' She threw back her head and laughed. 'Men are so stupid. I've been passed in the street and I've even met one or two important public figures, officials and the like, in public and they've never once cottoned on.'

'You sure they weren't . . . you know, just playing dumb, being discreet?'

'Jack, men don't have to play dumb when it comes to women – they *are* dumb, otherwise they'd mention it the next time they were in bed with me. Men simply can't resist being smart-asses and know-alls. No way.'

I pointed to her hair. 'But your hair was brown when we went to Regina.'

'Of course, there were only girls present at the raffle dance, so I was in street dress.' She looked at me and gave me what I had come to learn was her reproving look. 'Jack, I'll have to trust you or someone, perhaps Peter Cornhill, to tell the boys in the band not to mention the raffle.'

'Yeah, okay, I'm pretty sure the band will keep quiet. Anyhow, they don't know the details. But I'll mention it to Peter; he'll have a quiet word to them.'

The next task was getting Cam Kerr to agree. 'Mr Cameron Kerr isn't one of your regular clients, is he?' I asked, just to be sure. The assistant manager of the Brunswick, as I'd previously mentioned, was a breast man and they didn't come any better in that department than Juicy Fruit's.

'Lordy no! He's number-one watchdog when it comes to keeping girls out of the cocktail bar. But I don't use the hotels in town anyhow, Jack.'

I was beginning to realise how lucky I'd been to win Juicy Fruit in the raffle. She was obviously at the top of her profession in Moose Jaw and only had clients of the more discreet kind.

Cam Kerr proved easy, especially as Juicy Fruit agreed to three nights' free trial during the cocktail hour. The free part wasn't her idea. 'Jack, I'm a working girl, I don't do free, eh?' she'd protested when I'd suggested it. We'd compromised when I said she could have all the tips as well as the salesmen who wanted to be 'recognised' to impress their clients. This was more than she could have expected as an hourly rate for an untried singer.

If I'd expected her to be grateful and a bit humble, she wasn't in the least. Juicy Fruit was a tough customer, willing to put in the hard yards, but she wasn't going to be a Little Dorrit. She may not have been a professional singer but she was a professional nevertheless and didn't do grateful. Miss Frostbite had once explained to me that to a clever woman 'grateful' is a weapon, not a sentiment. But Juicy Fruit didn't even seem to need to use it in this way.

I was soon faced with another problem: she needed at least two evening gowns for the gig. 'Jack, I can probably afford to buy one, but can you help me with the other?' she asked, then added, 'I know a good dressmaker who won't charge the earth.' She looked directly at me. 'I'll pay you back if I get taken on permanently. But if I don't,' she shrugged, 'I can't.'

I agreed, stressing that they should both be low cut. 'Should be cheaper, uses less material,' I joked, then added more seriously, 'we're going to need all the help we can get to persuade Cam Kerr to take you on after the trial. He's pretty mean with a buck and won't be easy to win over. But he's a notorious breast man. There isn't a single woman front of house at the Brunswick who doesn't have good boobs.'

'What are you saying, Jack, that I have to show my tits?'

'Yes, I guess I am,' I said, feeling myself blushing, but determined nevertheless to be professional. 'I'm afraid you must make sure the dresses you choose have a plunging neckline.'

Juicy Fruit nodded. I'd taken instructions from her about sex, now she did the same with me about performing. I advised and she accepted without protest, knowing that she had to get past Cam Kerr and her voice alone might not be sufficient. She had one chance, and either she made it onto the bandstand or she didn't.

Juicy Fruit took the stage name Miss Prairie Gold, after Golden Prairie, the town nearest to the small family farm where she'd been raised. She behaved like a professional from the moment she leaned her sexy body against my piano during the cocktail hour a week later. Somewhat to my surprise, the entire cocktail lounge fell silent the moment she started to sing, her deep voice easy and embracing with a warm personal quality that seemed to love the microphone. Afterwards Cam Kerr, who'd come in to make sure she wasn't going to be a disaster, approached us. 'Very good, very good!' He couldn't take his eyes off her décolletage, but that had also been true of most of the men. 'What do I call you? Miss Prairie Gold?'

Juicy Fruit laughed. 'No, Mr Kerr, sir, just Prairie will do. After all, it's the name I was given at birth. My parents were Italian immigrants and came here directly from Naples and thought it had a nice sound and was a . . . you know, loyal thing to do in their new country.'

'Why, that's real nice,' Cam said, addressing her cleavage. 'A prairie girl through and through then, eh?'

'That's me, sir!' Juicy Fruit said with her best smile, pushing her breasts forward and sketching a little salute. Her lie about her name was faultlessly delivered with a twinkle in her gold-flecked eyes as if she was poking mild fun at the innocent naivety of her newly arrived parents' earnest endeavour to do everything they could to assimilate.

'Well, Prairie, why don't we go to my office for a talk while Jack has his dinner?'

Juicy Fruit glanced down at me. 'Jack's my partner in this, sir. I'd prefer it if he sits in.' She turned to me. 'Okay, Jack?'

I nodded. 'I'll grab a sandwich after the dinner session.'

Seated a minute or two later behind his desk, and very much in control, Cam Kerr said briskly, 'Can you play, I mean with Jack here of course, the fine dining room tonight, then return to the cocktail lounge afterwards for the final session?'

Juicy Fruit gave me a questioning look. 'Jack said only the cocktail hour, Mr Kerr.'

I'd previously requested she take no clients for the night, even offering to pay her if she was out of pocket. I'd reasoned it was her first professional night beside the piano and I thought she should enjoy it without having to rush back to Number 7 Riverside Lane to resume work as if nothing significant had occurred in her life. She'd declined my offer of payment for any clients she'd have to refuse and said she'd come and sit in the cocktail lounge after the dinner session and listen to me play and if I wanted her to sing again that would be okay.

'That's correct, Cam,' I replied. 'It was only for the cocktail hour. An opportunity for you to hear Prairie for yourself at no expense to the hotel.'

'Well I liked what I heard. Tell you what, I'll give you three dollars for the night. That's all three sessions.'

Juicy Fruit sighed, her expression suggesting regret. 'I'd love to if Jack's happy, but not tonight, Mr Kerr. I have a previous engagement.'

Cam Kerr was a pro. 'Pity, great pity.' He looked at her steadily. 'You couldn't postpone your appointment?' It was said with just a tinge of 'you better-or-else'.

Juicy Fruit smiled charmingly, head to one side. 'No, I'm afraid not. I don't break appointments and I always arrive on time. But I could return for the last session in the cocktail bar tonight.'

'Bravo, yes, let's do that then,' Cam said, though I could see he was still a bit annoyed. There was no doubt it was a win for bosoms or he wouldn't have agreed so readily. He was a man accustomed to getting his own way. Juicy Fruit was not responding in the usual obsequious manner. He would have found this pretty galling. Female hotel staff, almost inevitably, were expected to have style and smile, but not under any circumstances to show any guile. 'A dollar then for the late session.'

'I take it that would be two dollars for tonight, Mr Kerr.'

'Yes, that's right.'

'And if I work all three sessions on future nights, that's three dollars, right?'

'Well, yes, and we'll throw in your dinner. You and Jack can eat together.'

'No. I'll accept two tonight but then it's five for a night's work, three sessions,' Juicy Fruit said firmly.

'Five? No way, Prairie. I'd only pay that for a professional. I'm taking a chance on you.'

Juicy Fruit's eyebrows shot up. 'Hey! I've been singing in public since I was five years old. That's fifteen years. Jack's been playing the piano since he was eight – that's ten years. You ain't taking no chances, sir, I'm a professional just like him! You saw the crowd in the cocktail bar; they liked what they saw.'

'They did, Cam. People kept coming in from the foyer,' I said.

Cam remained silent for a good while, thinking he was adding to the pressure or something.

Juicy Fruit shrugged, then glanced at her wristwatch. 'If I don't cut the mustard, then you can fire me, Mr Kerr. But it's still five and I've got to go or I'll be late for my appointment.'

Cam Kerr sighed, clearly frustrated. Tits or no tits, he had to assert himself. 'No, my dear.' He looked at me. 'Jack here only started at, what was it? Yes, fourteen dollars a week, and that was for five days.'

I think he was expecting me to nod or something, as though I agreed with him – two men putting a pesky woman in her right and proper place.

'I feel sure a good singer like Miss Prairie Gold is going to greatly add to the attraction of the cocktail bar and fine dining, Cam. It's certainly worth a try. As Prairie says, if it doesn't work out . . .' I spread my hands. 'Well?'

Juicy Fruit was on her feet. She reached across the desk to shake hands. 'I enjoyed tonight, Mr Kerr, and thank you.' She gave him a genuinely nice smile. Miss Frostbite would have clapped. I knew how badly she wanted the job. It was a pretty cool performance.

Cam Kerr sighed. 'Okay, but understand I'm taking a big chance on you. We'll try it for a month.'

Juicy Fruit smiled. 'If you don't fire me, then what?'

'Well, we carry on.' Cam said, puzzled.

I held my breath. *No, don't screw it up now, Juicy Fruit*, I prayed silently.

'Six.' Just the word, like a single note sounding from a gong.

Cam Kerr threw back his head and laughed. 'Six dollars! You're not serious?' he exclaimed.

I flinched; that was pretty near a living wage. She'd already explained the four nights only, Friday and Saturday were her busy nights elsewhere. I was sure, in fact certain, Cam wouldn't agree, if only as a matter of pride.

On the other hand things had changed since he and I had negotiated. Cam had gained something of a reputation by securing me to replace Reggie Blunt, an old piano hack. The Brunswick takings were up considerably in the cocktail lounge and fine dining room and we were doing more special events in the ballroom. The Sunday concert, now with Robert Yuen, was now advertised as *Jack Spayd Digs the Sunday Blues with Robert Yuen*. It attracted a sell-out crowd and people had started turning up early. The cocktail lounge, with its five-cent premium on each drink, was doing a roaring trade. Peter Cornhill would often remark that I had brought the assistant manager great credit and with the manager due to retire in a year, Cam Kerr was a sure thing for promotion. Now, if he added a singer with a body as well as a voice he would have an even greater mid-week attraction. Cam had clearly seen the advantage of a partnership, but six dollars a night? Holy smoke!

Juicy Fruit turned and made for the door of his office. 'I don't like being late.' Her voice, though resolved, showed no trace of emotion. Nevertheless I was pretty sure she'd blown it. Why hadn't she left it until she'd done a month and proved herself? It would have forced Cam's hand.

'Wait a minute!' Cam Kerr said. 'We haven't finished, Miss Gold.'

'Oh?'

'Sit, please sit.'

Juicy Fruit sat down slowly, clutching her handbag. It was sitting but sitting ready to go.

'Six after a month?' he asked needlessly.

'Or you fire me, Mr Kerr.'

'I thought I'd asked you to call me Cam.'

'Only after we have a deal,' Juicy Fruit shot back. It was said with a brilliant smile.

To his credit, Cam Kerr laughed. 'Righto,' he leaned over extending his hand.

I had just received a lesson in negotiation. Juicy Fruit was no country bumpkin. Joe would have said, 'Now don't go use the last slice o' bread to wipe all the gravy from the plate, Jazzboy,' meaning that there should always be something in every negotiation for both parties. Juicy Fruit had proved him wrong; she'd make a good poker player, I thought.

'Thank you, Cam,' Juicy Fruit smiled prettily. Then, without a hint of triumph in her voice, said, 'I really must hop it or I'm going to be very late. I'll be back in time for the last session.'

I must confess, while hugely pleased for her, I was also a bit disappointed at her taking a trick when I'd already offered to pay so she could have a night off. Later that evening, after we'd done the final gig and just before I was due to join a late-night poker game, I asked, 'How did your appointment go?'

'What appointment?' she replied, laughing. 'Jack, I sat in my room on the bed hugging my knees!'

It was at that moment that I knew Juicy Fruit could make it all the way as an entertainer. Although we never discussed it, my hope was that she'd eventually decide to change careers. I had no idea how much a high-class hooker earned, and all she ever said was, 'Jack, my singing means a lot of re-scheduling and not all of my clients are happy.' I took this to mean she was sacrificing some of her income for her singing career, but at least it was a start – twenty-four bucks a week was just about a living wage.

It really was surprising how quickly and how well we came together. By the time Reggie Blunt's big poker game rolled around three weeks later it was almost as if we were an established gig. Reggie, the walking punster, came into the late-night session at the cocktail lounge to escort me to the game. The last number we performed for the night was 'Thanks for the Memory', the song Juicy Fruit had sung in bed in the hotel in Regina. Predictably, Reggie had remarked, right eyebrow slightly raised for effect, 'Shouldn't that be, "Thanks for the Mammary", old chap?' Thankfully Juicy Fruit had already excused herself to go the powder room. But I nevertheless felt it was in poor taste.

'A bit tired as puns go, don't you think, Reggie? Besides, it's not an appropriate thing to say. She sang the lyrics beautifully.'

'Ah, dear boy, good puns never wear out. As for Juicy Fruit, she wouldn't want me to tell certain people around here what she does as a second profession, now would she?'

'Reggie, you don't mean that!'

'No, of course not. You know me.'

'I hope so,' I said sharply. 'I'll see you at the main door in a couple of minutes.'

'We ought to be going,' he said.

'I won't be long.'

'Jack, I know you won her in a raffle, but take my advice, whores don't change. You can't make a silk purse out of a sow's ear.'

'True. A pig is always a pig!' I shot back, still upset.

Reggie laughed. 'Only a warning, old chap. 'Don't want you to get hurt.'

I sighed. 'Maybe I'll give the game a miss tonight . . .'

A momentary look of shock crossed Reggie Blunt's face but then he assumed an expression of extreme disappointment. 'Jack, don't be foolish. This is a big game, with good players. It's time to test your mettle. You've been playing inferior opponents up until now. Even the late-night games have been easy pickings. Now's your chance to see what you can do against some good players for real money.' He paused. 'It wasn't easy to set up this game, they're all from out of town, but I think you can win.' He grinned his fat-nosed, piggy-eyed grin. 'Feather in your cap if you do, Jack . . .'

I have to say this for Reggie Blunt, it was exactly the right psychology to use. I needed to know if I was good enough to tackle experienced players. I had two hundred bucks in my wallet to say I was. Some of it was the money for my mother's nose operation. 'Give me a couple of minutes,' I said.

'Do hurry, dear boy,' Reggie said.

Juicy Fruit returned from the powder room. 'What's wrong? You look mad, Jack. Something happen while I was gone?'

'Nah, just Reggie.'

'Jack, be careful tonight, won't you? Reggie Blunt isn't what he seems to be. If it gets rough, cut your losses.'

I laughed. 'You know me, always careful.' There wasn't time to ask her what she meant. I'd long suspected there was more to Reggie than he admitted. He and Madam Rose, for example. She kept cropping up in his conversation. The raffle. One or two other things he'd said, though all of it seemingly pretty harmless. No time for that now, though; I had to get going. 'You were very good tonight, Miss Prairie Gold. I can't see Cam not coming to the party. Hey, six bucks a night, that's not to be sneezed at.' I kissed her lightly on the cheek. 'If I win tonight I'll buy you the best dinner in town. No, better still, a new dress to wear when you get your raise.'

'And if I don't?'

'We're packing them in, Miss Gold. There was barely enough elbow room to lift a drink in the cocktail lounge tonight. I'm told fine dining's takings are up as well. See you tomorrow evening. Got to go. Reggie's waiting!'

The poker game took place down the wrong end of River Street, as it was called, although there wasn't really a right end, it was a matter of sleazy and sleazier. The name of the joint was, predictably enough, Girls Etcetera, the second half of the name indicating that it was a place where just about anything goes. The general racket, not to mention the bad music blaring out onto the street, should have been enough to warn me to keep away.

Reggie led me through a throng of late-night drinkers to a small back room where the poker game was to take place. There was nothing in it apart from a table and six chairs, and a side table that held two bottles of Canadian rye and six glasses. The wooden floor hadn't been waxed in twenty years, and a small high window was open in one of the yellowing mottled walls.

We were the first to arrive, and I asked Reggie if he could arrange for a jug of water. 'Could be a problem, old man. Service isn't great around here.'

'You mean everyone drinks their whisky neat?'

He seemed to realise that it was more than a question about drinks and that we were alone in the small back room and that I might walk out there and then. 'I'll see what I can do,' he mumbled, leaving me alone. I selected the chair farthest from the window, realising it was the only way cigar and cigarette smoke could drift upwards away from me. Fuggy, smoke-filled rooms are one of the more unpleasant aspects of poker games.

Reggie returned five minutes later clutching a chipped white enamel jug. He was followed by four men, one of them a big, burly, dark-haired man I knew was Grover Smith, a long-haul engine driver on the Canadian Pacific and therefore one of the local aristocrats. I'd met him on a previous late-night game and knew he was a very competent poker player. 'Hi there, Grover, where's Fred tonight?' I asked. Fred O'Reilly was Grover's chief fireman, a bit over five feet tall and almost as wide with not an ounce of fat on him. His neck, what there was of it, was thicker than my thigh, his legs were tree stumps and his arms carried more muscle than my calves. Stoking the coal-fired steam engines, shovelling several tons of coal on what was one of the more difficult routes in North America, required men such as Fred. Both were prairie legends, tough, hard men who were seldom apart. Apparently they'd been an inseparable team since they joined the CPR on the same day twenty years previously. I immediately felt better. They were tough, but straight.

Grover grinned. 'Delayed. Be along later.' He poured himself a whisky and sat down before the others. 'Know any of these guys, young Jack?' he asked.

'Nah, Reggie's friends.'

'Yeah, Grover and me saw them at the cat house.' There was nothing in his voice that offered an opinion.

The other three guys, whisky glasses in hand, seated themselves. In a poker game, players come and go, so that introductions are not obligatory, and yet I was surprised when Reggie made no move to introduce me. This was meant to be a friendly game. Oh well, I knew Grover was straight and wouldn't put up with any crap; pity Fred wasn't around, though.

In friendly games, you usually shared the news of the day, or a joke or two before you got started. But in a serious game you didn't come to make friends. Once people started to lose money, things could get a bit edgy, especially if the players had been drinking, and the manner in which this lot had made directly for the whisky table was a little disconcerting. I told myself if they'd been 'in the saddle' for the earlier part of the evening they probably needed a drink, but two of the three strangers had knocked back half a tumbler of neat whisky standing at the side table then immediately refilled. Curiously, Reggie Blunt abstained. Still, as Juicy Fruit had suggested, I could always leave if the game got out of hand.

One of them, in sports jacket and open-necked shirt, hadn't touched his whisky and placed it on the table to my left. Without bothering to introduce himself he sat down beside me and was immediately all over me like a bad rash, asking me questions, commenting on the fact that I played piano, saying he'd heard I was a bit of a local poker star (all of which must have come from Reggie) so that I was so busy answering or brushing off his compliments that it took ages until there was a gap in the conversation so I could say, 'You obviously know who I am, but you haven't introduced yourself.'

'Jim . . . Jim Negas.'

I extended my hand, 'Jack Spayd.'

He made no move to take it. 'Nah, poker game, better leave it at that.'

But this didn't stop him asking me questions. He knew nothing about jazz and was being far too curious. In fact, he was insulting my intelligence, thinking me just a kid. But when you're brought up to be polite and respect guys older than you it's difficult to be rude. Even with Reggie I'd felt a bit guilty making that crack about pigs.

The guy sitting directly opposite me was a big lummox in farmer's overalls and a red tartan shirt. He had a strange unblinking stare, snake's eyes, which he directed at me as if he were trying to establish his dominance over a younger player. Apart from his fixed stare there was something else disconcerting about him: his nails were clean and his fingertips weren't split and stained with ingrained dirt. As a Cabbagetown kid, I knew about labourers' hands.

Negas, the big mouth next to me, was proving a nuisance. Being a polite kid was one thing, but poker has certain unspoken but universal rules, and unless it's a social game among friends, you keep the chat to a minimum. I realised he was trying to disrupt my concentration. No chance; I'd been trained by Miss Bates to concentrate; he could jabber on all night and it wouldn't make any difference. I'd simply ignore him.

The guy sitting next to the so-called farmer was perhaps in his mid-forties, brown hair parted in the centre and slicked down against his skull, the hair oil turning his hair a shade darker. He was in a grey suit typical of a commercial type, necktie, white shirt, a small dark cigarillo stuck unmoving in the corner of his mouth. He hadn't said a word since entering the room.

All of them smoked, so that soon the fug was rising towards the high window. I had picked my seat well and most of the smoke drifted away from me.

It was five-card draw poker, with a fifty dollar buy-in, and no limit on raises, so I needed my wits about me. The first three hands didn't even render me a pair to start with, so I was watching rather than playing, picking up body movements, anything I could see, which wasn't much. It was still too early.

Grover won a small pot, so did Cigarillo and Negas on my left, who made a big fuss over winning a few bucks, again addressing most of his enthusiasm at me. ('See how it's done, kid? Whacko!')

The next hand I was given a pair of kings, a reasonable start.

The first bet was from Jabber on my left. 'Check,' he called, meaning he wanted to see if any of us would bet before he came in.

The starter, the farmer type who I'd decided to dub 'Mr Manicure', bet two dollars and Cigarillo raised it to four. Grover put in his two bucks to make it six. This meant it would cost me eight bucks to stay in the hand and draw three more cards in an attempt to improve it. I added my chips to the pot in the centre, but apart from the eight dollars I didn't raise it further. My hand simply wasn't strong enough, although it could still, with the right three cards, lead to a good one.

Jabber decided to come in and added ten dollars and took three cards, probably like me trying to improve a pair.

Mr Manicure, the starter, discarded two cards and Reggie dealt him a further two, dealing each of us in turn the number of cards we'd discarded.

Doing a quick calculation (not necessarily correct), this possibly meant that before they got their new cards, Mr Manicure had three of a kind; Cigarillo two of a kind; Jabber, like me, two of a kind; Grover maybe two pair and looking for a straight or a flush.

Everyone arranged their cards and the serious betting began. The three strangers, Jabber, Mr Manicure and Cigarillo, all raised each other's bets so

I had to put in an extra ten just to stay in the game. My cards had fallen the way I needed, with another king and two aces – a full hand – and the two aces meant no one could have a better full hand than the one I held. It was good but not unbeatable if someone had four of a kind.

I matched the bet. This implied I had something and probably wasn't bluffing but wasn't overconfident either.

Grover threw in his hand; he obviously hadn't received the cards he needed and there was no point trying to bluff with four of us still in the game. Jabber matched the previous bets and raised it another ten, all the while jabbering in my ear. Mr Manicure only matched Jabber's bet, saying 'See ya'. But then Cigarillo raised it another twenty dollars. This meant thirty dollars if I wanted to stay in and at least forty dollars to bet again. I took a hundred from my wallet and bought chips. 'Your thirty and another thirty,' I said quietly. Grover gave a soft whistle and at long last Jabber shut up and to my surprise folded. The remaining two players matched my bet and paid to see my hand.

I wasn't surprised when both folded their hands without showing them. These guys were giving nothing away. For a moment I toyed with the idea of turning to Jabber and saying, 'See how it's done, kid? Whacko!' But, of course, I didn't. Poker, well played, means you button your lip and show nothing when you fold. My full house had won, though frankly I would have been unlucky to lose; four of a kind doesn't happen along too often and straight flushes are even rarer. At least thus far the Spayd luck was holding.

The stakes were not higher than some of the games I'd played in over the past few months, but the early aggressive start indicated that these guys were serious players. The game was hotting up. This was no friendly game arranged by Reggie Blunt. One wrong move could quite easily cost a hundred bucks. I was already up nearly two hundred but knew it could disappear in a single hand if these guys continued the way they'd started. I didn't have to be Albert Einstein to know that Jabber, Cigarillo and Mr Manicure were playing to a plan and that Grover and I were on our own.

The way it went was that if the two of us were still in the game, or if Grover was in on his own, putting in chips to draw the extra cards we needed to attempt to play a winning hand, then they played normally, dropping out or bidding up. But if Grover was out and I was left to play against the three strangers, then they went to town, raising aggressively and forcing me to match or better their bets if I wanted to stay in the game.

The very beauty of the game of poker is that it is one man against another, individuals daring their particular genius against each other. But when there is collusion, say two or more opponents working together against you, then they can just keep on raising the ante until you drop out and lose the money you've put on the table. Unless you have a good stake to start with, possibly more than their combined stake, you lose all your money and walk home with the linings of your pockets on the outside of your trousers.

If I'd been sensible when I began to suspect what was happening I would have told myself I'd had enough. But it was early, I was ahead, and it's a kind of unspoken rule that you don't leave a game early when you're ahead. It's . . . well, it's not done if you want to be invited back.

Not that I wanted any more of these guys now or in the future. It was becoming increasingly apparent that Reggie Blunt was stitching me up, but why? One of his favourite sayings was, 'Revenge is a dish best eaten cold,' but as far as I knew, I hadn't done anything to upset him. He'd even thanked me for taking his job. But he hadn't left Moose Jaw to catch up with his possibly mythical grandchildren in Winnipeg. Nevertheless, he'd organised the raffle night. Admittedly he could be a crushing bore, but I'd never been anything but polite, sitting through endless sessions over his 'whisky with a splash' and enduring a thousand bad puns. On one occasion Juicy Fruit had remarked casually, 'Our Reggie isn't all he seems.' It was a throwaway line, delivered with a laugh, as if she didn't want or need to explain further. Then again, her warning tonight had seemed a lot more serious. As the game continued I was beginning to realise that Reggie's favourite saying about revenge had been intended for me all along. He was going to clean me out. My heart skipped a beat when I remembered that I'd once told him about my mom's nose money. Holy smoke, I was in deep shit. *Cut and run while you can, Jack Spayd. Get the hell outa here, son.*

The only thing keeping me in the game was the extraordinarily good cards I kept getting. Every poker player hears stories of nights when every hand you play turns out perfectly – opponents drop out, the right card turns up to complete your hand and you keep getting better hands than the other players when it comes to a showdown and they call you. Even Jacoby had mentioned this phenomenon in his book. Now it was happening to me.

Every time they came after me in a combination of two or three I had the hand I needed. I lost a few hands, smaller ones when Grover played and the game normalised, but the big hands where Grover couldn't afford to be involved kept on falling my way. Three kings would beat their three nines, my straight would beat their three of a kind and the biggest hand of the night to that point was when I held four tens and I beat Cigarillo's full house of three aces and a pair of eights. It was the first time the cigarillo, which had been unlit throughout the game, jumped in the corner of his mouth. There was an angel sitting on my shoulder; the cards just kept falling my way.

After two hours or so Fred, Grover's fireman, appeared. Oh, how I pitied the poor girl he'd been visiting. Reggie invited him to sit in and he glanced at Grover, who shook his head. 'Thanks, but nah, I'll just sit in an' watch for a while,' Fred said, then jerked a thumb as big as a medium-sized cucumber at the whisky table. 'Mind if I help meself?'

Grover's wordless sign to stay out of the game was unusual. In the previous games we'd played together, Fred was a pretty competent poker player and Grover, playing within his original fifty-dollar stake, was up at least a hundred and fifty, whereas I was up nearly two grand.

Two thousand dollars! Holy mackerel! Jabber had shut the hell up, but was drinking heavily, and the second bottle of rye was all but gone. Mr Manicure continued to give me the evil eye, not that I cared, and except for the jumping cigarillo, Cigarillo kept his cool.

After a few more hands where nothing much happened and Grover increased his takings another eighty bucks, Reggie Blunt called a break. 'I need to get more whisky, gentlemen. Time to stretch your legs.' But it wasn't said with the usual Reggie ebullience. Looking into his weepy eyes I could see he was mad as hell or panicking; something was definitely different. The usually urbane pontifical Reggie Blunt was falling to pieces.

Grover stood up, nodded to Fred and then turned to me. 'Let's take a break, kid,' he said, indicating the door. As we made our way out onto River Street, Girls Etcetera had almost ground to a halt, with no sign of any girls, nor as far as I could make out, any Etcetera, beyond half-a-dozen drunks in a circle with their arms around each other's shoulders singing 'Rosemary'. Out on the street it was a beautiful clear mid-summer night with a near full moon, perfect prairie weather.

Grover touched me lightly on the shoulder. 'Say, kid, have you seen these guys before?'

'No, first time; Reggie Blunt set things up. Old friends in town looking for a game, he said.'

'Yeah, thought as much. You've had an amazin' run, Jack. Never seen the likes, but you've played your hands damn well.'

Grover looked over at Fred standing silent, big as a tree stump. 'Tell him, buddy.'

'Nah, no good them dudes . . . them lot. We played them a while back over in Calgary. Reggie was with them.'

'It was a set-up, kid,' Grover said, taking over from Fred again. 'Some poor small-time sodbuster just sold his wheat crop, took him for near four thousand.'

'But . . . but I don't understand. Why? I've done nothing to Reggie.'

'Hey! Whoa, kid, you took his job. He worked half his brothel clients from his piano seat at the Brunswick.'

'Eh?'

'You mean you didn't know? He owns a share in Madam Rose.'

'You for real?' I asked, flabbergasted. Like I mentioned before, I thought they might have something going between them, but I never suspected the brothel, that Reggie, for all his bluff and bluster and stories of innocent Olga, was a shareholder in a bordello!

'Had to let four girls go when you nabbed his job,' Grover said. 'You've cost him a lot of bread, kid.'

'Hates your guts, Jack,' Fred said, cackling. 'Tonight's supposed to teach you a lesson. Only the goddamned furnace fired up and the Jack engine is comin' full speed down the tracks and they're in a truck stalled at a crossing.'

It was a nice compliment but I was smart enough to know I'd been dead lucky and that luck doesn't hold forever, in fact it can turn on a single card. I was still trying to make sense of the Madam Rose connection. Why hadn't Juicy Fruit mentioned it? Now I thought about it, it made sense. But this was no time to speculate, I had to turn my attention to the problem at hand. 'So what next, Grover?' I asked, genuinely confused and in need of some advice. Then a nasty thought struck me. Why were the two of them in the game? Maybe he and Fred were a part of the scam!

Grover looked at me steadily. 'Jack, Reggie isn't your problem right at this moment. He's set this up but he was simply relying on the three of them being good enough to take you to the cleaners, suck you dry. The guy with the slicked down hair, the quiet one, he's the real pro. He pretends to be a commercial traveller, sells lubricants and fancy condoms in whorehouses, probably does it for a cover, but he's really a professional player. So is the guy with the big mouth.'

'And the big brute, the farmer?' I asked.

'Ah, the farmer . . . ha ha. Only thing he'd ever do with a pitchfork is stick it up your ass. He's the muscle, although he's not a bad player. He's little league hockey compared to the other two.'

'But how . . . I mean you and Fred . . . ?'

'How do we happen to be in the game?'

'Yeah.'

'Well, it has its advantages. When we get into town it's an evening spent free with one of Reggie's girls.' He glanced over at Fred and chuckled. 'Though tonight Fred made a deal with a special girl he's been after for three years, that's why he come in late. She had another client or something till ten o'clock. Couldn't see him until after ten-thirty.'

'Great tits,' Fred added by way of explanation. 'I've wanted her real bad. Got her tonight.'

'First a poke, then a game of poker,' Grover continued, smiling at his play on words. 'It's a good way to spend the evening before we stoke up and pull out for other parts. We're the first train out in the mornin'.'

'But you just said this game is rigged.'

'Not for us, Jack. The game is straight for Fred and me. We carry our own muscle and we give the game a wholesome look, so people like you can be . . . enticed . . . is that the word? Yeah, brought in so the game doesn't look like a set-up. You would have seen for yourself, there's no screwing around when I'm in the game and generally I can get out without losing my pot. Tonight's been good, I'm well up.' He glanced at Fred. 'Kid's brought me luck.'

'So why are you taking the trouble to warn me?'

'Madam Rose. She usually doesn't interfere. But she told us to look after you. She must have a soft spot somewhere after all, though you could have fooled me. Said to never mind Reggie, she didn't want you harmed or cheated.'

'Thanks, Grover, Fred. I'm obliged. But what now? Head on home?'

Grover shook his head. 'No, cain't do that, Jack. Not smart. If you hadn't been gettin' them great hands we'd have taken you aside before you got cleaned out and told you to get the hell outa the game. But with what you've won you cain't cut and run now. They'll sure as hell come and get you. Mess you up some and take your winnings. The tall lummox playing Farmer Joe is a bad case. Don't got no conscience like other folk. There's a fancy name for it.'

'Psychopath?'

'Yeah, maybe. Tough *hombre*, got no conscience,' he repeated, 'kill yer and then eat a big breakfast. Fred here could handle him, but I don't know anyone else who could.'

'So I stay in the game?' I said fearfully.

'Got no choice. Reggie's got his ass in a crack. He's got them over here specially. Give them the full free whorehouse treatment and a chance to clean up. But between us we've taken them for the better part of three grand. They don't mind me getting a small share. Matter of fact, it makes it look like a straight game. Which, like I said, it is, when Fred and me are sitting in. But tonight you've took the birthday cake and all the candles so there's no party.' He grinned. 'By the way, you play real smart poker, Jack. But all I can say is you must be fucking Lady Luck or something. Never seen anything like it. You're the problem, kid.'

'But if my luck holds, then it gets even worse?'

'Dead right, deep shit,' Fred allowed.

Grover then asked, 'Do you know what a cold deck is, Jack?'

'Yeah, sure, the dealer swaps the deck for a stacked one, dealing the players the hands he wants them to get.' I'd read about it in Jacoby's book.

'That's correct, he'll give you something crazy, a routine or a running flush, something you think can't miss, then he'll give one of them a higher routine that will beat yours.'

'So I'll just keep on betting until it's all in the centre?'

'Yeah, down to your last cent. They'll suggest we make it a no-limit game.'

Fred nodded. 'That's when you know the fix is in. That Reggie's gonna top-swap the deck.'

'Too right, that and the crazy good hand he deals for you. They'll believe that with the great hands you've been getting all night, you'll think it's your luck holding.'

'What if I throw in my hand?' I asked.

Fred looked at Grover. 'The kid ain't no idjit.'

'That's it. They won't know what to do. Nobody in his right mind would throw in a hand like the one you'll've just been dealt.'

Fred chuckled. 'They'll think Reggie Blunt stuffed up and you didn't get the hand they'd planned.'

'I'll throw in as well. Be nice to see the bastards squirm,' Grover added.

'Okay, thanks. I owe you both. Thanks for keeping me out of trouble.'

Grover smiled. 'We've been in three games together, kid. We've been watching you. You're not some punk kid acting like some young smart-ass. You play it straight down the line. We respect that.'

Fred grinned. 'Besides, Madam Rose runs the best whorehouse in town.'

'But why would you agree to help me? You just said you get a free run at Madam Rose?'

Grover looked at Fred. 'Well, now you ask, we got a favour in return. Tell him, Fred.'

Fred chuckled. 'There's this girl, she doesn't do free. I've had me eyes on her for three years, like I said. Great tits, great everything, but she won't be in it and Reggie can't make her.' He shrugged his huge shoulders. 'So we made a deal, I get her and Madam Rose gets her wish.'

I knew at once he was talking about Juicy Fruit.

'Wicked world, Jack,' Grover said as a throwaway line. 'Okay, time we went back in?'

Reggie Blunt and the other three were seated, waiting, replenished whisky tumblers on the table in front of them. 'Where you bin?' Jabber yelled as we entered. He was clearly somewhat the worse for wear or otherwise was putting on a damn good act.

'Takin' a *real* long piss,' Grover answered, settling down in the chair beside the whisky table then reaching over and pouring himself a stiff drink.

Reggie didn't look at all happy. He was shuffling the cards and looking down, ignoring our entrance.

Jabber then said, 'Hey, man, what say we make it a no-limit game? Give us dudes a chance to get our money back, eh?'

Cigarillo simply gazed into his whisky glass and Mr Manicure stared venomously at me. Expecting this, I simply shrugged my shoulders and turned to Grover beside me, who nodded. 'Okay,' I said quietly, taking my seat.

'Attaboy!' Jabber exclaimed. Cigarillo looked up at me quickly, making sure Jabber hadn't overplayed his hand. But then, almost instantly, his eyes returned to his whisky glass. I watched as their cigarette smoke rose towards the high window. Cigarillo had a fresh unlit cigarillo in the left-hand corner of his mouth. Funny that. The last one had been stuck in the right-hand corner. No point in reading anything into it, though, this guy was 'Mr Cool' and the fix was in anyhow.

Reggie turned and plucked a large red silk bandana from the top pocket of his jacket which was hanging from the back of his chair. Dapper Reggie always sported one of these spotted bandanas spilling from his top pocket. 'Touch of Oscar Wilde', he called it. It went with his 'whisky and a splash' affectation. Now he used it to dab his lips, a curious use to say the least, except that the large square of silk fell to the table and just happened to cover the deck he'd placed there prior to reaching for it. Quite how he made this one-handed swap, I can't say. Grover said he wasn't a mechanic, a dishonest dealer, but it was nevertheless well done, so that when he turned to stuff the bandana carelessly back into his top pocket, a deck of cards, presumably the doctored pack, rested on the table in front of him slightly to the left of where the original one had been placed. If I hadn't been alerted I'd have had no cause to notice. 'Right then, gentlemen, let's play,' he said in a serious voice with none of his customary bluff manner.

I turned my first five cards. Holy smoke! I had a straight flush, eight, nine, ten, jack, queen of spades. Virtually unbeatable! I'd never seen one before. Normally I would have happily bet all my night's winnings on it. The only thing that could top a straight flush is a higher routine, with a king or an ace instead of the queen I now held. The probability of someone holding such a hand was unthinkable, in fact, you could say, impossible. Even Jacoby would have turned in his grave in astonishment.

Cigarillo was the first to bet and pushed ten dollars into the centre, a mere gesture to get things rolling as if everything was normal. The silence was palpable as they waited for me to react, go to town, or so I imagined. The table was suddenly very quiet. 'I fold,' I said, throwing in the best hand I'd probably ever have in my entire life.

There was a collective gasp, Cigarillo's brown cigarillo bounced several times but remained in his mouth. Reggie Blunt cleared his throat . . . *aahrrh, aahrrh!* Not like clearing a blockage but more like I imagined a pig or a sheep might gurgle when its throat was cut. Jabber Negas's mouth fell open – he may have been a pro, but he was also drunk. Mr Manicure turned his snakelike eyes from me and fixed them on Reggie.

Grover sighed and threw in his hand. 'Nothing there for me, either.' He brought his great engine driver's fist to his mouth and yawned. 'Reggie, settle me up, it's late. Fred and me, we've got a long haul in the mornin'.'

'Me too, time to go. Been a long day.'

Reggie was sweating. 'Jesus, no, you guys can't quit now!' The urbane Reggie Blunt was gone and a short, fat, weepy-eyed, whisky-nosed very frightened brothel keeper had taken his place.

Fred rose from where he'd been sitting next to the whisky table and took a step forward. God, he was big! 'Best time to quit, Reggie,' he growled, barely raising his voice. Mr Manicure made as if to move and Cigarillo tapped the table with his forefinger and the great hulk remained in his chair.

Reggie Blunt started counting out chips, his hands shaking like a morning-after drunk. Then he counted out the money. Grover got back eight hundred dollars and my pile came to two thousand six hundred dollars, less the two hundred dollars I'd brought to the game. I'd netted two thousand four hundred, enough to buy two houses in Cabbagetown or half-a-dozen new noses for my mom.

'We'll see you out, kid,' Grover said. 'Walk you back home. That's a lot of money to carry without a little muscle on either side of you.' It was said quietly, but well within the hearing of the group.

'Thank you for inviting me, Reggie,' I said politely, 'goodnight, guys.' How I managed to keep my voice from trembling I'll never know.

Once outside, Grover asked, 'Where do you live, Jack?'

'Oh, ten minutes' walk, a boarding house, down the far end of River Street.'

'Well, that's where you ain't goin', son. Got anywhere else?'

I thought of the key in my wallet that Juicy Fruit had given me, together with her door number in the alley. 'Yeah. I guess.' I pointed towards the lower end of the street. 'Opposite end.' It was 1.30 a.m. Fred had turned up at the game around midnight. She'd be asleep, but she'd insisted anytime, so I guessed it was okay.

'We'll wait here. Let you get in some distance while we watch yer back, they'll be expecting you to go home,' he pointed towards the boarding-house end of the street. 'If they ask, we'll tell them you headed that-a-way.'

'Thanks, Grover, thanks, Fred.'

Grover grabbed me by the shoulder and looked me directly in the eye. 'Good luck, kid. Take my advice, *don't* tell no one where yer holing up, you hear me, Jack? Don't even go back and collect your stuff at the boarding house. Get yer sweet ass out of town or we'll be indentifying you in the city morgue.'

'Lying next to Reggie,' Fred said, laughing.

Grover gave me a push. 'Go now, Jack, scram.'

'So long, buddy, good luck!' Fred called as I started to run.

Ten minutes later I knocked on Juicy Fruit's door. I didn't want to use the key if she was in. I didn't know if the room was where she lived or where she carried on her business. Barging in when she was with someone wouldn't be a good idea. Juicy Fruit and I had become very close in one sense, but she didn't talk about the other side of her life. We hadn't slept together since Regina. I remembered her exact words, 'Jack, that was lovely, and on my terms for a change. Let's not spoil it. One day, perhaps, when I'm free again, who knows?' This was the closest she'd come to suggesting she might give up the game. I confess I longed to have her again, but I didn't want to force the issue, and couldn't have even if I'd wanted to. But she hadn't discussed it, or asked my advice, and once or twice when I'd said she was doing real swell as a singer and I could see her with a future, she'd given me the Juicy Fruit look of disapproval. 'You're hassling me, Jack. Leave it be.' This had been enough to make me shut up and mind my own business. Juicy Fruit was in her own way just as strong minded as Miss Frostbite, and as Joe would say, 'She done know her shit from Shine-ola.' She didn't talk about her family, except the one time she mentioned her little sister's education, and once when she'd explained she'd gone on the game to take care of them all. Whether she was still responsible for them I had no idea. As I mentioned previously, she was a professional and didn't do gratitude or even feel the need to explain herself.

Suddenly I heard her say, 'Who is it?' from the other side of the door.

'Jack!' I called back. 'Are you alone?' If she wasn't I didn't know what I was going to do. Spend the night beside the river, hiding in the brush?

I could see a light go on from a small window set above the door. Moments later there was a rattle that sounded like a chain latch, then the door opened. She was in a pair of striped pyjamas, two curlers stuck into her brown hair, so she was done for the night. 'Jack, what's wrong?' she asked, her expression surprised and concerned. 'Come in.'

I entered, still a little out of breath from running. She quickly closed the door and replaced the chain latch. 'What's happened? The game?'

'Yeah. It was a set-up, but I won. The bastards are coming after me.'

'Jesus, Mary and Joseph! Reggie's friends?'

'Some friends! They were meant to clean me out – Reggie's revenge for taking his piano job.'

'Yes, I suspected as much.'

'Eh? You know? You *knew* it was a set-up?'

Juicy Fruit sighed. 'Jack, I tried to tell you to watch out. I didn't know it was a set-up, but that lot are pretty suspect. And I thought it would be okay with Grover and Fred in the game. They're not thugs.'

'Then do you also know Reggie owns half of Madam Rose?'

'Yes, of course. I work here!'

'And you didn't tell me?' I was beginning to lose it. 'You didn't think to tell me?'

'Jack, I work here,' Juicy Fruit said plainly.

'So?'

'So, how would that have helped? If the game was a set-up, he was only going to take your money. Big deal, it's a wicked world, it can't have been that much anyhow.'

'Well, it didn't work! If it hadn't been for Madam Rose I'd be lying in the gutter bleeding to death,' I said somewhat melodramatically. I was angry and didn't care if she chucked me out and I'd have to spend the night out in the elements.

Juicy Fruit started to laugh. 'Madam Rose! You mean Grover and Fred?'

'Yeah, and it didn't take too much figuring out that you fucked Fred!' I snapped, irrelevantly.

'So what? Anything for a friend.'

'What's that supposed to mean?'

Juicy Fruit folded her arms. 'And who do you suppose went to Madam Rose? Me, that's who, you stupid boy! Fred was the price I had to pay! Fred's free fuck!' Now she was angry. 'It was like mating with a grizzly bear only the bear would have had better bed manners. Jack, they promised to pull you out of the game in time so you didn't lose your shirt.'

'Well, I won two-and-a-half grand.'

'Uh?' Juicy Fruit's anger dissolved instantly and she looked worried. 'Jesus, that true, Jack?'

'Yeah. I thought you'd be happy?'

'Happy? You're in serious trouble.'

'Yeah, I know. You said if ever . . .' I held up the key.

'Jack, Reggie Blunt is a bastard, but he's not stupid, he'll work out where you've come. Those three guys are hoods, bad news. One of them's got a mental problem.'

'The guy with the stare?'

'Yes, that's him, Snake Eyes. The girl who services him says he can barely get it up. Just sits and giggles and drools, than gets her to give him a blowjob. But he's capable of killing you with his bare hands. We've got to get you away . . . away from here now, *immediately*, before Reggie works it out.'

'Grover said to leave town, not even to go back and get my things from Mrs Henderson's.'

'Good advice.'

After all my petulance I felt like a real asshole. 'Juicy Fruit, I'm truly sorry I went off at you like that. I'd better get the hell out of your room or you won't be safe yourself.'

Juicy Fruit sat on the edge of her bed. 'Jack, let me think a moment.' I glanced around the room, which I saw was just a single room serving as both bedroom and sitting room, quite nicely furnished with a bathroom somewhere, or maybe not even that. 'Give me the money,' Juicy Fruit said. 'If they catch you and you don't have the money on you, they're not going to kill you until they've got it. It's safe with me.'

'I could go hide by the river, in the brush. It's not cold out this time of year.'

'No, go to the Brunswick. You know all the night staff, have them give you a room, tell them to say nothing if Reggie or anyone else comes by. They never liked him anyway, treated everyone except Peter Cornhill like servants with his hoity-toity ways. He's nothing but an old whore!' she spat contemptuously. It was a curious description.

'More fool me. I thought of him as a friend.'

'C'mon, no time to talk about that now, they'll probably go to the boarding house first. It's two o'clock in the morning. If we're lucky they'll just let Snake Eyes wait outside until the morning, till you come out. Get over to the Brunswick now, get a room, lock yourself in and call me.' She pointed to the telephone. 'They all love you at the hotel. Nobody's goin' to give you away, not even for money.'

'Juicy Fruit, I've got to get out of town! Out of Moose Jaw!'

'Leave that part to me. Can I use some of the money? I may need a favour or two.'

'Yes, of course.'

'Jack, call me, give me your room number, then whatever you do, don't move. I'll come and get you when it's time.'

I was beginning to feel like a wimp. Rescued by women, always women. I was almost eighteen, almost six foot two inches tall and broad as my father without the gut, without the guts either. I was hiding as I'd always done, behind the skirts of a woman. I was a matter of four weeks away from going into the army to fight for my country and here I was being locked away in a hotel room while Juicy Fruit sorted out a way to get me out of town. It had been like that all my life, except that one time when I was a kid and I took my dad's advice and tackled a bully in the schoolyard. Apart from that I'd never been in a fight. I was a piano player and my big Rachmaninoff hands were designed to make beautiful sounds, not to smash into another man's face and beat it to a pulp. I wasn't afraid; I'd never been afraid. As I grew older, my size had always kept the other kids at bay. But I knew a man like Snake Eyes, who was almost my size, would make mincemeat of me if we fought. Juicy Fruit could probably defend herself better than I could – defend me, it seemed, better than I could. If I left the money with her and went looking for him, after he'd beaten the living Christ out of me, would I feel vindicated? Is that what a real man would do? Get beaten up, half killed, on a point of principle?

Juicy Fruit seemed to read my thoughts. 'No, Jack, if you're thinking of going after them, don't. Take Grover's advice. You don't stand a chance. Live to fight another day. Get going, we've got no time to lose. Give me the money. If they find you and you haven't got it on you, you'll be safe – they're not going to leave without it. If they threaten you and you are in real danger, tell them where it is. I'll handle it.'

I removed my wallet and quickly counted out two-and-a-half grand and handed it to her. This left me a hundred bucks – plenty – a month's salary for a working man.

Juicy Fruit took the money, waving it in front of her face. 'Jack, I could buy our farm back and then some. I've never held so much money, it's . . . well, frightening. People would kill for this.'

'That seems to be the nub of it,' I said, attempting a sardonic smile. 'I feel like a real wimp.'

'Don't be childish, Jack. Now get going. If I don't hear from you in an hour I'm calling the police.' She held up the wad of notes. 'Some of this will see to it that they go looking for Reggie's friends. I have a client I can call who's high enough in the ranks to create a fuss if I really have to. Use the staff door at the hotel. Now go!'

I made for the door, then realised how buttoned up I was being. 'Juicy Fruit, I want you to take five hundred bucks for yourself, okay?'

She nodded, not making a big deal of it. 'Thanks, Jack.'

'No, thank *you*, Juicy Fruit,' I replied softly. 'Also, when things have cooled down a bit, could you give Mrs Spragg, she's the cook at the boarding house, fifty dollars from me and tell her thanks for all the over easies?'

Juicy Fruit nodded again. 'Good night, Jack. Oh, and make sure there's a phone in your room,' she repeated. She sounded just like Miss Frostbite or maybe Mrs Hodgson at the library. So much for the new grown-up Jack who'd decided he'd given up accepting generosity from the opposite sex. If I skipped town, Juicy Fruit's singing career was over. Cam Kerr wasn't going to hire her as a solo performer. Besides, she wasn't really ready yet. She needed more time with me at the piano; I could cover for her when she made mistakes. No other piano player was going to do that for her, and her breasts, lovely as they were, weren't sufficient on their own. She was pretty well finished. I'd effectively pushed her back into the brothel for the Freds of this world to salivate over.

The night clerk at the hotel didn't even ask for an explanation when I told him I needed a secure room with a telephone that not even the management would know about. 'I'm in a spot of trouble,' was all I said, adding hurriedly, 'but not with the police.'

'Jack, say no more, buddy. Mind if I tell the switchboard? Otherwise your calls won't get through. It's Marion and June, you know them both. We'll call you what?'

'Rachmaninoff.'

'Eh? Too hard.'

'Rachman then?'

'Okay, Mr Rachman it is. No disturbances, not even the cleaning maid, okay? Hey, you'll need a bathroom, I'll put you in a room with one right next door.'

Within twenty minutes of leaving Juicy Fruit I'd called her and given her the details.

'Jack, I'll need to talk with someone. What about Peter Cornhill? We trust him and he's never really been a friend of Reggie and he likes you a lot; thinks you're the best thing to come to the Brunswick in years.'

'Yeah, okay.'

'I'll call you in the morning about ten o'clock. I'll bring you some breakfast. Good night, Jack. Don't worry, the giant ain't gonna chop down the magic beanstalk as long as I can help it.'

I think I was asleep in ten minutes.

I awoke at nine, the usual time, ready for a quick shower then Mrs Spragg's breakfast before my mind clicked into place. I needed to go to the bathroom, so I grabbed my towel, opened the door in my Jockeys and scanned the corridor. Nobody appeared to be around so I gathered up my clothes and slipped next door unseen. There was no sign that anyone had used the shower before me. I had a lightning shower and dressed in clothes that smelled of stale cigarette smoke. There was a rind of collar dirt where I'd sweated the previous night. I considered asking Juicy Fruit to buy me a shirt on her way in but then thought better of it. Maybe Peter Cornhill would, later.

The phone rang around ten o'clock.

'Hello?'

'Mr Rachman, this is Peter Cornhill, the bell captain,' Peter's familiar voice announced.

'Good morning, this is Jack Rachman.'

'Listen, buddy, Juicy Fruit has been round. Don't worry, everything's under control, she's told me what happened.' There was a moment's pause. 'I'm not surprised. Reggie Blunt can be a nasty piece of work.'

'Peter, I'm sorry if this is, you know, splitting your loyalties.'

'Hey, buddy, I'm a bell captain, I need guys like him, but it don't mean I have to like him.' He chuckled. 'Don't give it another thought, Jack, Reggie Blunt needs me more than I need him. This town is full of whorehouses.'

'Thanks, buddy, I owe you.'

'Nonsense, we're long past that stuff, Jack. Sit tight, I'm sending up a maid with your breakfast. How do you like your eggs?'

Despite myself I had to laugh. 'Over easy.'

'She'll tap on the door and leave the tray outside for you. Call you later, son.'

'Oh, Peter, if this isn't stretching things too far, can you organise a shirt, extra large?'

'Yeah sure, I'll get one from the hotel laundry. People leave them behind. Must be fifty there. What colour do you prefer?' He was trying to put me at ease and doing a damn good job.

'Anything, long as it fits.'

'Good, I'll choose a nice loud Hawaiian, something people will notice,' he shot back, laughing.

Breakfast arrived with a plain white shirt on a wire hanger, a brown paper packet pinned onto the back of the shirt, containing a clean pair of Jockey shorts. I guess bell captains have to be good at detail.

Juicy Fruit called shortly after I was dressed. 'Hey, Jack, lucky you went when you did. Reggie called round about half an hour after you'd left. He was in a real state and wanted to know if I'd seen you. "What, after we left the Brunswick?" I said. "No, of course not. He was going to your poker game, that's what he told me anyhow. Why? What's happened? It's two-thirty, Reggie, he'd be at his boarding house, Mrs Henderson's." "No, we've checked, he's not there," he said. "Why do you want him?" I asked again. "Money, he stole our money," he said. "At the card game? C'mon, Reggie, Jack wouldn't do that!" I said. "Never mind. None of your business, girl! You haven't seen him then?" "I told you, Reggie, no!" I said. He left without even apologising for getting me up. Jack, he was in a real funk, kept licking his top lip. They must have knocked up Mrs Henderson, too.'

'They'd have got a right mouthful at that time of the morning,' I replied, thinking she'd have shown them very little Christian charity at that hour.

'Now, down to business, Jack. We're more or less organised. John the chauffeur has gone off, pretending to be sick. Peter's taking the hotel car and driving you on to Indian Head. That's in case Reggie's friends are waiting at Moose Head station. You'll catch the Winnipeg train at Indian Head – I used some of your money for the ticket and Peter needed money for the booking clerk at the station; the rest I'll give you when you're safely on the train. Never know, they may be waiting at Indian Head. Peter has your money in a sealed and taped envelope in case I get stopped and searched. They wouldn't search him. I took out some money for the night clerk and kitchen and laundry staff too. I don't know how Peter's done it, but you've got a compartment on your own. Best I'm not seen in the hotel. I'll turn up as usual dressed for the cocktail-hour gig and play it dumb. But I'll be in the car with Peter . . . plenty of time to get back for tonight. Staff entrance at eleven o'clock, don't be late.'

'Wait on! Don't ring off,' I yelled down the phone, than in a calmer voice I said, 'Juicy Fruit, I've really screwed things up for you, haven't I? I mean your singing career . . .'

There was a slight pause. 'Jack, it was fun. Think no more about it, I'm a big girl.'

'Sorry,' I said. Which is sometimes the most inadequate word in the English language.

'Forget it, Jack, it never happened. A bit of fun, chance to show off a bit, that's all.' She hung up before I could frame another pathetic apology.

The trip to Indian Head was mostly spent giving Peter and Juicy Fruit a blow-by-blow account of the game. Peter had timed it so that we arrived ten minutes before the train from Moose Jaw. Juicy Fruit kissed me thoroughly and said, 'For old times' sake, Jack,' finally drawing away from me. God, I was going to miss her.

Peter Cornhill shook my hand. 'It's been a pleasure, Jack, a truly great pleasure. Breath of fresh air.'

I thanked him for everything, asked him to explain to everyone what had happened, and climbed aboard. He handed me a large sealed brown envelope, not just sealed but thick with Scotch tape. I pushed it into the inside of my jacket and shouted my final goodbyes as the train started to pull out of the Indian Head station. It was a lousy way to end my scuffing experience, but at least I wasn't returning to Toronto on the bones of my ass. And I still had my mouth organ. Come hell or high water, it always remained on my person.

As we headed east through Pilot Butte it occurred to me to check the money in the envelope to see if Juicy Fruit had taken the five hundred dollars and whatever else she may have had to spend to get me out of Moose Jaw. I'd always been a bit careful with money, because of my Cabbagetown background and the Depression, I guess. But I had plenty left for my mom's nose job and money to spare. By Joe's standards I'd get an A-plus for scuffing. I briefly wondered if Jim Greer would get my Mrs Sopworth suit for his Sunday best and the shirts and collars. I hoped so – his were looking a bit the worse for wear, although mine would be a bit big. I'd miss my anorak come winter. Hell no, I'd be in the army.

I plucked away at the Scotch tape – she'd made a damned good job of it, even taping the edges of the envelope so it couldn't be ripped open willy-nilly. Finally I opened it. Inside was a wad of neatly cut strips of newspaper, two hundred dollars in tens and a written note in a careful schoolgirl's script.

Dear Jack,

A girl has to do what a girl has to do. Your generosity will get my little sister through her hairdressing school and help me also. I'm off to New York to take me a bunch of singing lessons. Hey-hey!

You want to know something, Jack Spayd? This girl loves you and not just for the money! You are simply the best! I hope we meet again some day.

Juicy Fruit

P.S. One day if you see the name Prairie Gold, give me a call.

CHAPTER ELEVEN

I USUALLY ENJOY TRAIN journeys, but I spent a lot of this one staring blankly out of the window, probably due to my preoccupation with the events of the past twenty-four hours. I was returning home broke. Well, not really, I had two hundred dollars and some loose change which, when you think about it, was almost two months' salary for a waitress or road construction worker. Nevertheless, it fell short of the money I needed for my mom's nose. I'd effectively lost the opportunity to properly repair the damage my father had inflicted on her, at least until after I got out of the army. But with the Canadian forces due to go overseas and into battle, who knew when that might be, if ever.

This upset me more than anything else. She was not yet forty and still very attractive, in spite of her nose. Perhaps I should use the money, the two hundred bucks I still had, to find a poker game somewhere – I might get lucky. But every poker player believes that if you go into a game chasing a buck it always runs away faster than you can hunt it down.

Banking on winning enough to pay for her nose only showed that I was becoming addicted to chance, or was an addict already. I was young and foolish and thought myself more or less bullet-proof. That big win, despite the danger I'd only just escaped and the loss of the money, convinced me I had the touch, the ability to get to the top.

Naturally I wouldn't have admitted this to anyone, but I knew, I just knew I was lucky with cards. To prove how stupid this conviction was, I truly believed that I would be dealt a royal flush at the very next game I played – the odds are a mere 2,598,960 to 1, no problem at all. If I could win almost two-and-a-half grand with all the cards coming out right for me, why not? As they say, that first big win is the worst thing that can happen to a young player. It sets him on the wrong path, which often, if not inevitably, leads to his destruction.

At first I was furious with Juicy Fruit for stealing my winnings, especially after I'd given her a very generous five hundred dollars. It was, I told myself, a lowdown dirty trick only a slut and a whore would do to a man. But I realised that using such words to describe her saddened me, and did little to relieve my feelings. I was sort of half in love with her and fully in lust. She was a lovely woman who had been forced into the life of a prostitute in order to keep her family safe from harm. I had even used the term courtesan when I thought about her, which sounded a lot more honourable. But I had been wrong, dead wrong.

However, there's nothing quite like a train journey for a little self-analysis. Long before we got to Winnipeg I'd more or less sorted myself out. Sometimes just owning up to the truth isn't such a bad idea. In my case a couple of hundred thousand or so clickety-clacks of the train wheels straightened out my thinking.

For a start, all my pathetic stammering remorse on the hotel phone about ruining her chances of a singing career was utter bullshit. Irrespective of what had happened at the poker game, I would have left in three weeks to join the army. Three more weeks beside the piano with me wasn't going to turn Juicy Fruit into a smoking-hot chanteuse. The five hundred I'd offered her wasn't money I'd reserved before the game to give her specifically for singing lessons; it wasn't even money I'd previously possessed. Okay, perhaps you could say it was generous, but even this wouldn't be true. Of course I liked to imagine myself looking into her eyes and handing her an envelope: 'Sorry, Juicy Fruit, but my country needs me, so please accept this small token of my love and gratitude. My hope is that you'll use it for singing lessons.' But nothing of the kind had ever occurred to me. Convincing myself that I was Mr Nice Guy and had planned for Juicy Fruit to have singing lessons was arrant nonsense. The gift, given on the spur of a panic-stricken moment, had no such strings attached and I was certainly no generous-minded hero.

I've learned that self-deception usually follows something reprehensible or unwise and I'd been attempting to justify my actions to myself. But it's a psychological slippery slope and when I make these self-deluding excuses, that is, forgive myself for my actions, it inevitably turns out badly in the long run. Looking at things clearly might be painful, but in my experience it removes the roadblocks in your mind and leaves a clear pathway that's uncluttered with excuses and procrastinations. It allows you to learn from your mistakes. I'd sorted out that much before we'd reached Maryfield, a town almost halfway down the line to Winnipeg, where I bought myself a hamburger and sent a telegram to my mom to tell her when I'd be arriving in Toronto.

It didn't mean Juicy Fruit was off the hook. No way! Dealing with the theft of most of my winnings – a veritable king's ransom and sufficient to pay for several nose operations – took a few hundred thousand more clickety-clacks and a good deal of silent invective tossed in for good measure. Owning up to a bit of self-deception over the gift of five hundred dollars was one thing, but coping with outright stealing was quite another. Thief, con artist, swindler, morally depraved low-life, these were just some of the words and descriptions I hurled at Juicy Fruit in my mind.

However, I was wrong again. Nobody had expected me to win. In fact, quite the opposite was meant to happen. Reggie's idea was to leave me destitute, to completely humiliate me and send me back to Toronto with my tail between my legs, his revenge a satisfying, stone-cold dish.

Juicy Fruit must have known there could be trouble the moment Reggie's dubious friends had appeared at Madam Rose's for their free evening's dalliance. She'd have realised Grover and Fred had been included to make the game appear to be honest. Reggie's pals would have arrived around the time she was getting ready to come over to the Brunswick for our cocktail-hour gig. She'd done the only thing she could do for me and at some real personal sacrifice. It was clear that she had refused to sleep with Fred on previous occasions even though he'd lusted after her, but had agreed to do so when she'd gone to Madam Rose to ask if the two railroad men could take care of me if something went wrong. She knew they were straight even though they were fairly rough characters. Fred, grasping the opportunity, had made screwing him the condition for their protection. Sleeping with Gorilla Fred for free when I was certain she wouldn't have agreed to do so even if he'd offered to pay, was more than a gesture of friendship.

She'd tried to warn me. 'Our Reggie isn't what you think he is . . . be very careful.' And she'd returned two hundred bucks, which meant I had *exactly* the amount I'd had when I went into the game. In theory, anyhow, I hadn't lost a dime. She'd taken money that wasn't really mine, and I no longer thought of it as stolen. I couldn't begin to repay her for her generosity of spirit, nor for what she'd done for me, which was something I would never forget.

On top of this she'd got me out of Moose Jaw unscathed. You couldn't put a price on that, could you? I wasn't under any illusions about what my fate would have been without Grover and Fred standing by: Snake Eyes would have beaten the living daylights out of me and taken my winnings. If I'd been found battered and bleeding in the gutter outside Girls Etcetera at two in the morning it would not have given the police any cause for alarm. Losing the money was by no means the worst thing that could have happened to me.

Here I was sitting in a compartment heading home with my body and mind intact. What, I asked myself, was that worth? What had I lost? The money won in a single night's gambling, my Mrs Sopworth suit and anorak and a few bits and pieces – books, a framed picture of my mom, a pile of sheet music.

And then it hit me. Of course I had the money for my mom's nose! I'd been feeling so goddamned sorry for myself, so preoccupied with losing my winnings, that my memory had done a blank. See what I mean about self-deception?

I'd only taken two hundred dollars to the game, leaving one hundred and fifty dollars back at the boarding house. That was only twenty-five bucks short of the hundred and seventy-five dollars my mom had returned to me from what she'd saved out of my wages as a kitchen hand at the Jazz Warehouse. The rest of my stake had come from my personal savings and small poker winnings while in Moose Jaw. Now when you added the two hundred I had from Juicy Fruit and deducted the three dollars in rent I owed Mrs Henderson, I had a total of three hundred and forty-seven dollars. I only needed three hundred for the nose operations. I hadn't broken my promise to myself that my mom would be pretty again.

Jim Greer and Mrs Henderson were born-again Christians; I guessed they could be trusted. I'd write to ask them to send back my stash, which I'd buried in a tin box in a corner of the woodshed where I went to fetch wood for the fire in the parlour so I could read there on winter mornings. Mrs Henderson would get her money and be able to pay for the postage, Jim Greer could have the clothes and there'd be enough money for my mom. So there you go, clickety-clack, clickety-clack, all's well that ends well, as Shakespeare said.

I don't know how it happened – probably the thrill of winning big money – but I'd well and truly caught the gambler's disease. I'd never before seen such a huge amount of money, let alone won it, but I told myself it wasn't the money, it was the game. The bug had bitten deep. Poker made me feel independent, totally reliant on my own wits and nerve; Jack Spayd pitting his skill against all comers. I liked that, I liked that a lot, mind against mind, mine against my opponents', winner takes all.

It was nonsense of course, but I believed it at the time, believed it was something only I could do and that, like jazz, it gave me an opportunity to be myself. The reason I'd given up classical music was because I didn't want to be always playing in the past tense, demonstrating someone else's genius, someone who was long dead. While I was never going to be Art Tatum, jazz let me be an individual – it was music that began in the heart, satisfied the head and gave me the opportunity to extemporise and add something of my own.

But with poker I was *really* on my own. Win or lose, every game started afresh, every game was my own doing or undoing. (Ha ha, and who was it who rescued me when I was about to be undone playing poker? Well, a woman, of course.) But this didn't change my idea that, come what may, I would henceforth make my own decisions. Up to this moment I had always done as I was directed. Even scuffing, though it was meant to teach me independence, had been Joe's idea. I was determined right or wrong to be solely responsible for the man I was to become.

I foolishly believed that if I played fair and didn't cheat or lie or steal that everything would be okay and I'd come out on top. In other words, that life was just and fair and that whatever you sowed you would ultimately reap.

Even though the poker game had been a set-up, I'd been unaware of Reggie's bitterness over my taking his job at the Brunswick, so how could I have possibly been aware that he'd want to take his revenge by fleecing me in a crooked game? Juicy Fruit had told me Reggie wasn't what he seemed to be, a remark I'd conveniently forgotten, and when Grover informed me the game was rigged, I'd still played it straight. As a result of playing good poker, in other words, sticking to my principles, I had beaten a bunch of crooks. Didn't that show that good always triumphs over evil? Which goes to show that being almost eighteen isn't exactly a wise age. For a guy with a dad like mine I should have known better. But then again I was also the kid who believed that a royal flush was only as far away as the next hand. Talk about being naïve! Looking back I now realise that I was far from qualified to be my own man, independent of the opinions of others.

The irony was, of course, that I was determined to be at the recruitment centre as soon as I turned eighteen, where my newfound manliness and independence would count for nothing. My life for the foreseeable future would be totally controlled by other men, but I comforted myself with the thought that where there are men there's bound to be a poker game. Clickety-clack, clickety-clack . . .

I arrived in Toronto two days after I'd left Moose Jaw, and choked up when I saw that everyone was there to meet me: Miss Frostbite, Joe, Mrs Hodgson, Mac and of course my lovely mom, who burst into tears the moment she saw me sticking my head out of the carriage doorway waiting for the train to slow sufficiently for me to jump down onto the platform. This could only have been Miss Frostbite's doing. I'd given my mom very little notice and here they all were at the station to greet me. Or perhaps working for the twins had taught my mom a whole lot about organising things. I knew from her weekly letters how happy she was with her new job, but despite my constant assurances that I was doing well, eating well, enjoying my life and, of course, that I missed her greatly, she always ended with the same sentence: *Jack, I pray to God every night that He'll keep you safe in those dreadful endless prairies.*

I hopped off the train before it had fully stopped and while the brakes were still squeaking. There were hugs, kisses, handshakes, back slapping and laughter all round. Everyone seemed to be talking at the same time as I gathered my sobbing mom to my chest, her arms clasped tightly around me.

'Where are your bags?' Mac asked, about to enter the carriage to retrieve them.

I shrugged and said, 'Nothing worth keeping except memories.' Yes, I admit I'd rehearsed it, and it didn't sound anything like as good as I'd imagined.

Joe laughed, slapping me on the back. 'Jazzboy, that skuffin', my man. You done gone and survived. That good! You ain't got nuthin' lef' 'cept your own skin and a whole heap a' ex-peer-ee-ence. That ex-cee-lent!'

Miss Frostbite held me close. 'Jack, becoming a man is a difficult process, especially with so many women in your life. I guess that's why you want to join up.' She laughed. 'But do be careful, won't you? We don't want to waste all the effort that's gone into making you the splendid young man you are.'

My mom couldn't stop weeping and eventually I asked Mac to get us a taxi. Still sniffing, she protested, 'Jack, we can't afford a taxi!'

'No, it's okay,' I reassured her.

To my astonishment, Mac had hailed another black Model A Ford with bright orange wheel spokes just like the one that had taken Miss Frostbite and me to visit Miss Bates that first time to see if she'd accept me as a music pupil. While there were still lots of Model A's around, bright orange spokes were rare and so I remarked on the coincidence to my mom, explaining that the first taxi I'd ever been in had orange wheel spokes and here we were, all these years later, in yet another taxi with orange wheels. The driver overheard me. 'Sir, this is the only taxi in Toronto that's got orange wheels. I painted them myself when she were brand new because I thought folks goin' to see me better with them coloured wheels.'

'Then this is the same taxi and I guess you must have been the driver?'

'Ain't nobody but me ever drove this old gal, sir.'

My mom, who'd stopped crying at last and was clutching my hand, said, 'Fancy it being the same taxi, and fancy remembering it had orange wheels! That has to be a good omen,' she said excitedly.

I laughed. 'Mom, it was the first time I'd been in a taxi! I don't know about an omen but it seems as if I've kind of come full circle, beginning my music education with a ride in an orange-wheeled taxi and returning home from scuffing in the same taxi ten years later.'

'It's an omen, all right. God is telling you your musical education is over and now you're a professional musician. Oh, Jack, you've worked so hard – I wish you didn't have to go off to war.'

Miss Frostbite had suggested at the station that we all meet the following night at her apartment for a welcome-home celebratory dinner at eight o'clock. 'Jack,' she said, 'Joe and I have cancelled our performance for the night – the band will jolly well have to manage on its own.' It was a lovely gesture. I can't remember an evening at the Jazz Warehouse without their double piano act, Joe in his pale blue tails, flipping them free of the piano stool as he sat down, Miss Frostbite in one of a dozen elegant evening gowns, a gardenia in her hair in spring and summer, looking pretty as anything.

It turned out to be a lovely evening, and after dinner Joe suggested we go through to Miss Frostbite's practice room and 'See what scuffin' done do to you, Jazzboy.'

I sat down at the Steinway and played a medley, a sort of updated Rachmaninoff to ragtime but with a bit of fancy finger work he wouldn't have seen or heard before – some of the stuff I'd used for the Sunday concerts. It was satisfying to see the look of surprise on his face as he turned to Miss Frostbite. 'Maybe Mr No Pain can take that holiday he been hankering for. He got hisself jes two weeks to visit his old folks in New York.'

Joe explained that No Pain's parents were getting on, his dad wasn't well, and he'd wanted to visit them for some time. Would I take my seat at the Jazz Warehouse piano for the two weeks until I turned eighteen and went off to 'take care of that Hitler bastard'?

Would I ever! Even Miss Frostbite, who was a stickler for the law, said she could hardly see the police making a fuss if I was going off to fight for king and country in a fortnight, the day after my eighteenth birthday.

I was still at the Jazz Warehouse when Mrs Henderson sent the money and my mom's picture minus the rent I owed her and the postage. She included a note:

Dear Jack,

Praise the Lord you are safe. We were all very worried and Mrs Spragg and Mr Greer thank you for the money and the clothes and I thank you for the rent money.

I will continue to pray that Jesus, Praise His Precious Name, will save your soul and that you will be Born Again. You are a good young man and one day will see the Truth and the Light and be snatched from the clutches of Beelzebub, the prince of demons and the devil!

Yours, in His Precious Name,

Mona Henderson (Mrs.)

So Juicy Fruit had even handed over the fifty dollars to Mrs Spragg, as I'd asked her to do.

My eighteenth birthday was to be celebrated alone with my mom. It was something she'd asked for especially. The previous night – well no, it was after 2 a.m. so it was actually my birthday – when we'd finished at the Jazz Warehouse, the band, Joe and Miss Frostbite gave me a small presentation, popped three bottles of champagne and gave me a solid gold signet ring, the face inscribed with the single word: *Jazzboy*. I had half a glass of champagne, which tasted awful, the first and last drink I'd have in my life. I was terrified that I might go the same way as my father, sensing from my obsessions with both music and poker that I had an addictive personality.

On the afternoon of my birthday my mom had to go out to take care of a chore for the twins. She hadn't been gone ten minutes when the front doorbell rang and I opened it to find both twins standing there. 'Happy birthday!' they chorused, then Melissa (I remembered she was the one with the mole on her neck) said, 'Have you got a moment, Jack?'

'Yes, of course, come in.'

'No,' Clarissa said, 'we have something we'd like to give you, upstairs.' They both smiled mysteriously.

My heart skipped a beat. Upstairs . . . did that mean what I thought it meant? I'd lusted after both of them and now they were inviting me upstairs! All I could think was, thank god for Juicy Fruit and her careful instructions. We took the clanking old lift to their penthouse apartment and on the way up I was trying desperately to appear relaxed and cool.

At the door of their apartment Clarissa produced a silk scarf. 'We have to blindfold you, Jack,' she said, standing on tiptoe to tie the soft fabric over my eyes. I heard the keys rattle and the lock on the front door click open and then both of them took me by the hand and drew me into the apartment. As the blindfold was removed they cried, 'Tah-dah! Happy birthday, Jack!'

Standing in the centre of a dark green carpet was Dolly and Mac's ancient Victor gramophone with the giant lily-shaped speaker and the emblem showing the loyal little dog.

'We've had it reconditioned and polished and there's all the records to go with it,' Melissa cried excitedly.

'Jack, it seemed so very appropriate. This old darling is where it all started for you, isn't it?'

It wasn't just my hopes that deflated like a punctured bicycle tyre. Thank god they mistook my expression for stunned surprise, which of course it was. It was a lovely thought and, once I'd recovered, a truly wonderful gift.

That night my mom and I sat at the kitchen table. On it was a cake with chocolate icing identical to the one she'd baked for my eighth birthday which my drunken father had smashed to pulp and crumbs with his huge fist. The little cake was now positively overloaded with eighteen red, white and blue candles with the inscription *Happy 18th Birthday Jack*. Beside it was a small bottle of soda pop. My mom wore the same little white lace apron as she lit the candles and I blew them out in one breath, the way I'd practised but never had the chance to do all those years ago. I cut the cake and then we both had a good cry.

I put on one of Mac's records, now mine – 'For Me and My Girl' – and my mom started to cry all over again.

I took her in my arms. 'C'mon, Mom, stop your crying. Jack's back and he loves you.'

'Oh, Jack, I've missed you so much!' she sobbed.

'Mom, it was good I went away, I've learned a lot.'

'I can see that,' she sniffed. 'You've come back a man. I can see it in your eyes and the way you walk. Oh, Jack, I'm so proud of you!' Her eyes were filling up again.

'No more crying, Mom, or I'll remember my eighteenth birthday for the sobs and not the laughs.' I pointed to the cake. 'What happened the first time you baked that cake is long over and he's out of our lives forever.'

'I don't bear him any ill will,' she sniffed.

'Why not? He was a drunk and a bastard who beat you up.' I was trying not to get angry.

'Jack, he gave me you. He could have smashed my face to a pulp, just like he did the cake, and I'd have forgiven him because he gave me a son who's turned out beyond my dreams.'

I was suddenly embarrassed. Trying not to show it I said hastily, 'I'm glad, Mom, but I have something to say too.'

'Oh, please, not about your father, Jack.'

'No, Mom, this is about you.'

'Oh, what?' she asked, her expression suddenly alarmed.

'It's what I want you to do,' I said, smiling.

'Oh, goodness, what is it, Jack?'

'Mom, you're still young and a very pretty woman and you've had a raw deal. What would happen if you started all over again?'

'Started all over doing what?'

'Well, you don't need to be alone for the rest of your life.'

Both my mom's hands involuntarily crept up to her face to cover her nose. 'Jack, no one would want me,' she said quietly.

'What, because of your nose?'

'Well . . . yes, that and . . .'

'Mom, stop!' I interjected. 'I want you to go into hospital.'

'What on earth for?' she asked, genuinely amazed.

'Mom, I contacted the surgeon and the hospital – you know, Dr Freeman, who did the first operation to your nose. I've paid him for the two operations you're going to need. The first one will be as soon as you can make it, and the second one in about three months.'

'Jack, how could you do that? You came back from those awful prairies with nothing.' Then almost as quickly she said, 'I can't accept. My nose doesn't matter, nobody is going to want me.'

'Mom, will you do it for me? The money has been paid.'

'Jack, you shouldn't have. My life's over, my nose doesn't matter. Who cares what I look like?'

I knew that bastard who I no longer recognised as my father had damaged her self-esteem, but now I saw just how much harm he'd done. She had only hung in for me; everything she'd done had been for me. 'Mom, everything we've achieved was because of you – not Miss Mony, Mrs Hodgson, Miss Frostbite, Miss Bates – it was all *you*! They all played a part but you were always there, always fighting to keep us going. If you hadn't been with me every inch of the way I'd just be another slum kid on the bones of my ass. If you hadn't believed in me, worked your guts out cleaning offices at night, getting chilblains, getting off one section short to save a few cents on the fare, I wouldn't have had any of the breaks. Now it's your turn, and there's one tiny thing I can do for you. *Please*, Mom, let me do this for you!' I begged, close to tears.

'What about the twins? They need me here,' she said, still stalling, putting herself last once again.

'I've spoken to them and they're delighted for you. Mac's coming over to fill in while you're in hospital.'

'Oh, Jack, I love you so much,' she gulped.

Then I held her in my arms and she wept and wept and wept for all the years of struggle and hardship and pain and humiliation. Finally she stopped and I got up from the chair and found the record I wanted and wound up the ancient gramophone and put it on. It was the very first thing I ever learned to play on my father's belated birthday gift, imitating the music coming through the ceiling. The first time I ever played it was to her, waiting up for her to return from work and preparing her chilblain water: 'Daisy Bell', or 'A Bicycle Built for Two'. She'd sat in the kitchen soaking her feet in the hot pail and I'd played it. When I'd reached the end of what was probably an excruciatingly bad effort, she clapped her hands and said, 'Oh, Jack, didn't I say you have a real talent for music?'

CHAPTER TWELVE

I GUESS EVERYONE HAS a different war. My combat experience was ten minutes of abject terror. I received a medal for being there and another, thoroughly undeserved, for bravery, which entitled me to call myself a veteran.

At the time I had no idea that my combat experience was entirely the result of incompetence, although the events leading up to it should have given me sufficient warning that the guys in gold braid with red stripes down the sides of their pants were, generally speaking, by no means as smart as the uniforms they wore.

If the men recruited to fight were over the age of fifty-five rather than the men in charge, wars would last no more than a few days. Instead we let these old men, resplendent in braid and brass, send the next generation off to die while they study battlefield maps I'm reasonably sure some of them couldn't even orient so they were the right side up.

Canada only sent volunteers overseas to fight, boys like me who couldn't wait to shoulder a rifle, but the old men in charge were well aware that in times of war young guys virtually line up to die. They also know that war is an opportunity for them to gain more braid and glory for themselves. As far as Canada's top brass went, I feel sure I could count those generals who died in combat on the fingers of one hand and still be guilty of overestimating.

I had been one of those misty-eyed kids, my appetite for war boosted by a boyhood diet of adventure storybooks, but it took just ten minutes of actual combat to disabuse me of the notion that war was glorious, or an adventure that would prove an exciting interlude in an otherwise predictable and almost certainly dull life to follow.

Mind you, the eagerness of young Canadians to be slaughtered in the name of king and country may well have been the result of the decade or so of poverty preceding the war. The Depression had been well named, not only for the collapse of the New York stock exchange in 1929 but for its effects on communities worldwide. By the time war broke out in Europe, many young Canadian lives had been blighted by poverty and shame. Joining up meant three square meals a day, free clothes and accommodation, equality in the barracks where you were given a purpose and were no longer ashamed of being useless and unwanted in a crippled society. What's more, a dollar or so a day was thrown in for good measure.

Anyhow, there I was three days after my eighteenth birthday, lining up with thirty or so other guys at the Fort York Armoury on Fleet Street for a medical examination. Passed fit we were given a train ticket to London, Ontario, for two months of basic training. I was young, didn't smoke or drink, and fortunately wasn't carrying any excess weight on my big frame, but piano playing isn't the best fitness training and I struggled for the first few weeks until I got fit. This, of course, delighted the NCOs responsible for training, who seemed to take particular pleasure in their assigned task of breaking us down and forming us into a cohesive unit.

I learned much later that this is done using essentially the same techniques as brainwashing: fear, tension, physical exhaustion and a total lack of privacy. I found this last aspect the most difficult. I'd always been a loner and now I lived in a barrack room with twenty other guys farting, snoring and yelling out in their sleep on their unscreened beds. Showering en masse was hard to endure, but easily the most difficult was being forced to defecate in a line of toilets in full view of all the other recruits. This was intended to desensitise us, working on the premise perhaps that those who shit together kill together. I don't know about you, but crapping in public seemed to me a strange way to bond.

Basic training is designed to make you a part of a unit and at the same time set you apart from those outside this peculiar experience. Put crudely, it is supposed to teach you how to kill 'the enemy' with impunity, and the enemy are those you are taught to regard as different from you.

Not that I resisted – there wasn't any point – it was just that I was incompetent at most army tasks apart from drill. 'Square bashing' came easily because I had a better sense of rhythm than many of the other guys, but in most other tasks I was pretty pathetic.

I missed being able to play the piano every day, and felt almost as if I was missing a limb. I began, for the first time, to realise how one-dimensional my life had become: without a keyboard I amounted to very little. Being a loner didn't help, and being intelligent made matters even worse so that I soon learned to conceal this aspect as I had done at school in Cabbagetown. If I knew the answer I kept my big trap shut. Besides, it's not much use knowing all the theory if you can't put it into practice.

Most young guys my age had practical experience and could do mechanical stuff – like taking a machine-gun apart and putting it together again – that left me completely mystified. I was good at the spit 'n' polish aspect of army life because I'd had to take good care of the stuff we got from Mrs Sopworth, but that was nothing special, because most of the guys came from similar backgrounds.

I confess, while I hadn't been conscious of it at the time, I had become accustomed to being respected for my playing. Now I was a nonentity, or even worse, an incompetent. Life in the barrack room was like being a kid of seven back in the Cabbagetown schoolyard where you were required to show you couldn't be pushed around. Pecking orders needed to be established, and while I was big I wasn't aggressive; in fact, I was pure marshmallow. In the army there's nothing more pathetic than a big guy who doesn't know how to defend himself. As a consequence

I took three or four good lickings before I started to get the hang of things. The fifth guy who decided to take me apart to cement his place in the pecking order faced a Jack who was now both fit and strong. A lucky right to the jaw dropped him to the floor unconscious, and when he took several minutes to come around it caused a degree of panic in the barrack room, not least in me.

The tale of the five-minute knockout became vastly exaggerated in the retelling, finally reaching the ears of Sergeant Major Mark O'Brien, who called me out on parade. A huge man, standing stiffly to attention with his drill stick jammed under his arm and his nose almost touching my own, he shouted at me loudly enough for the entire company to hear. 'Private Spayd, now you'll be listening to me! While I'm not a man to stop a certain amount of horseplay, I'll not be having you throwing yer weight around! So, I'm warning you, Private Spayd, if I hear of another incident I'll put you on a charge that will keep you so busy you won't have the fuckin' energy to pick yer nose for a week! Do you understand me?'

'Yes, Sergeant Major!' I shouted in the required fashion, knowing there was no point in trying to explain the truth. This public dressing down only served to validate the story of my phenomenal physical prowess. It seemed that nothing had changed since I faced the bully in the schoolyard, and after this I was left pretty much alone.

If my vastly overrated fists earned me a certain reputation, it was once again the harmonica that gave me a lucky break. I could play just about anything and this gained me not only a certain amount of respect but a lance corporal's stripe. During basic training we had not been granted town leave and so on Saturday nights in the mess hall they'd set up a microphone and a makeshift stage and we'd mount an impromptu concert. My harmonica playing stood out against most of the pretty amateur performances, which traditionally were howled down, so I guess the audience could tell the difference. In addition to playing solo, three of the guys in the barrack room had reasonable voices and with a little instruction the four of us soon had a reasonable barbershop quartet going. This pretty well made me immune from any further barrack-room bullying. That barbershop quartet did a whole lot more to bond the men than latrines without walls or doors.

Predictably enough, the favourite Saturday-night piece was 'When the Saints Go Marching In'. Everyone knew the lyrics and it always resulted in a grand singalong. Surprisingly, 'Amazing Grace' was the second most popular, and responded well to being jazzed up a bit. 'The Saints' was a rowdy, joyous all-in-together affair, but you could have heard a pin drop when I played 'Amazing Grace'. Of course I played a lot of other crowd-pleasers and the quartet sang all the popular songs.

One evening a month after I arrived I asked for permission to play piano in the officers' mess. I offered to give them a bit of an impromptu concert, even though my real purpose was to get my hands on a piano after weeks without one. Apart from a single short session at the Jazz Warehouse when we'd been allowed our first weekend leave after basic training, I hadn't been near a piano and I was starved for a bit of jazz. I had to do my Rachmaninoff to ragtime routine before they'd believe me, but once I'd played for a couple of minutes, I was in. Music had once again saved my ass. Not just the big black piano but also the simple little metal music box you can put in your pocket, just about the best travelling companion a guy can have. You can stand up and face the world and still hide behind it.

Not long after, I found a poker game, made up of a mixture of players from other units. On a soldier's pay of a dollar fifty a day it was penny ante but the players were of a high standard, and as I was often successful, poker gave me added status among my peers. Funny that if you show too many brains during theoretical military tactics in the company classroom men soon set you apart and taunt you for being a smart-ass, but if you use the same intelligence to win a game of cards they marvel at how clever you are.

Once we were through with basic training we headed back to Toronto. I couldn't wait to board ship and sail off to war. I'd read far too many *Boy's Own Annual* stories in my childhood and they had clearly influenced my views about soldiering. In my imagination I was manning a machine-gun against advancing hordes of Afghans crazed on hashish, or launching a hand-grenade attack to wipe out an entrenched German machine-gun post. Like most guys of eighteen I preferred the image of dying heroically rather than having to spend the war somewhere safe and secure.

But back in Toronto I joined my unit, the Royal Regiment of Canada, one of the oldest and proudest in the army with all the attendant traditions, and from there was thankfully seconded to the Royal Canadian Army Medical Corps to be trained initially as a stretcher bearer and then as a medical orderly. The fact that I didn't carry a weapon was disappointing to say the least, but the medic training immediately appealed to me. It didn't rely on mindless obedience but required a fair amount of initiative. Soon after I started training I began to change my mind about being a machine-gunner. Here was something I could get serious about; I was doing something useful and after all that basic killing practice I'd undergone in London, Ontario, I was slowly beginning to realise that rather than at best becoming a mediocre killer I could be the opposite, a soldier who saved lives. The brainwashing and bonding that had taken place in basic training obviously hadn't entirely taken me over and was beginning to wear off. I was becoming obsessed (here we go again) with medical and first-aid duties. The years of piano playing meant that my big hands were nimble and efficient and I threw myself into the task with huge enthusiasm. In fact, all the abilities and aptitude I'd sorely lacked in basic training as a soldier and potential fighting man I now seemed to possess as a medical orderly.

My concerts in the officers' mess went down very well and I was approached afterwards by one of the officers who introduced himself as Captain Nick Reed, an army surgeon. He was, he said, an ardent jazz fan and knew a good jazz pianist when he heard one.

'A bit rusty, sir. It's been hard to find time for piano in the last three months.'

'You're completing your training as a medical orderly with us are you, Corporal?'

'Yes, sir.'

'It's obvious you're a professional musician, Lance Corporal . . .?'

'Spayd . . . Jack Spayd, yes, sir.'

'Nice to know you, Jack. Damned shame military bands don't include portable pianos, eh?' He smiled. 'How are you liking your training as a medic?'

I grinned. 'Loving it, sir. I only wish it was more than twelve weeks.'

'Oh? You'd like that?'

'Yes, sir.'

'Would you like to become one of my assistants? When we are posted overseas I'm taking over as the medical officer in the First Battalion, the Royals, in the UK. I can arrange for you to be posted with me as an orderly if you'd like?'

I decided to take a risk. 'Does it mean further training?'

'Corporal, we're going overseas, possibly into combat. The more a medical orderly knows the better for all of us.' He laughed. 'We'll take you as far as you're allowed to go without a licence to practise medicine.'

'I'd sure appreciate that, sir.'

'It'll mean less blues and more bandages.'

I grinned. 'I don't imagine there are many pianos on the battlefield anyway, sir.'

'But you'll play piano regularly for us in the officers' mess?'

'With pleasure, sir.'

On my return to Toronto we were allowed our first weekend leave prior to my being seconded for medical training. It was a couple of months since my mom's nose operation, and I knew from her letters that it had gone well, but she was due for the final one in a couple of weeks and I was dying to see how she looked. Joe had invited me to play a bracket with the band on the Saturday night and to bring my mom. I told him I was a bit out of practice and he'd given one of his Joe cackles. 'Hey, Jazzboy, we gonna play the old time easy blues so you don't go get yo'self hu-mil-ee-ated.'

My mom's nose looked great and she was all for not having the final op, which was to give her a clearly defined and straight bridge. 'Jack, it's so much better but you can't make a silk purse out of a sow's ear, you know.'

Her self-esteem was still very low, not surprising I guess after all those years of being pummelled by my dad's fists. It was going to take longer to fix than her battered nose. 'Mom, I told you before, you're a very pretty woman and you're going to be even prettier when the bridge is back where it belongs. Men are going to be falling over themselves to get to you.'

She'd blushed furiously. All she could manage was, 'Oh Jack, you are such a silly boy!'

By the time I'd finished my training with the Medical Corps and moved over to the Royals with Captain Reed, the last operation had been successfully completed. I tell you what, it wasn't just me – Joe, the twins and Miss Frostbite all agreed Gertrude Spayd was a damn pretty woman. The twins took her to have her dark hair cut and styled (still no sign of grey) and gave her lessons in applying make-up, and she'd have looked a treat on the arm of any man over the age of thirty-five. Her skin was still smooth and blemish-free and soft as silk. Moreover the Depression and all her hard work had kept her figure trim. The only parts of her that showed the hard life she'd led were her hands. Being a cleaner had taken a toll. Quite frankly, I was dead proud to be seen with her.

Captain Reed was a true jazz aficionado. Because we worked together and I played often in the officers' mess, we'd become friends off duty. He was in his early forties and quite old to join the army, but his wife had died two years previously of cancer and as they didn't have any children he decided to join up when there was a national call for more surgeons. He was also willing to serve overseas.

He'd taken me under his wing and I was learning a lot, and not just from being with him; he'd send me to all the courses he could. I learned how to do emergency transfusions of plasma under battlefield conditions, safe injecting practices, anti-tetanus injections, the use of sulpha drugs for infections, dressing battlefield wounds using the soldiers' first-aid kits, shell dressings, splinting of compound and simple fractures and the special care required for head injuries.

It may not sound like much, but it was miles ahead of simply lugging a stretcher around the battlefield. I was trained to give first-aid treatment in the first hour after a soldier sustained a wound, this often making the difference between life and death. I felt I was being trained to be useful and necessary, not just cannon fodder. If only I'd known how accurate that last seemingly exaggerated reference to cannon fodder would prove to be.

Anyhow, I'd told Captain Reed about the Jazz Warehouse and suggested that he might like to visit it one weekend, but there was one problem – an officer and a lance corporal were not usually companions. But when I'd mentioned that my mom's final nose operation had recently taken place and that I was taking her to the Jazz Warehouse to celebrate, to my surprise he'd said in a very tentative voice, 'Jack, I'm also a reconstructive surgeon. I'd like to see the work on your mother's nose. Perhaps you'll allow me to buy you both dinner at this Jazz Warehouse.' He'd laughed in a slightly embarrassed manner. 'Kill two birds with one stone, eh? Hear some jazz and have a look at her nose.'

Of course I agreed right off.

To everyone's surprise, there was an instant connection between the two of them. Physical attraction led to infatuation, so that by the end of the first evening Captain Reed asked if he could call on my mom. What I hadn't realised was that Captain Reed's childhood had been very similar to my own. He'd grown up on the wrong side of the tracks with a single mother who suffered from an intermittent nervous complaint. 'We managed somehow,' he said. 'Lucky that it wasn't the Depression; part-time jobs were easy to get, even for a kid, and I'd work at two jobs over the long summer vacation. So when my mom couldn't work I would somehow manage to pay the rent, usually late, as well as put a bit of food on the table.' He'd won scholarships at every level of his education. Far from being born with a silver spoon in his mouth, he'd come up from humble beginnings the hard way.

Without my knowledge, Mom and Captain Reed started to see each other whenever they could. When Captain Reed realised that

I thoroughly approved he laughed and said, 'It's been two years since my wife died, Jack, and they've been just about the loneliest of my life. It's lovely to meet someone like your mother. It feels as if we've known each other all our lives.' My only concern was that my mother might not be able to match his intellectual acuity; he was a doctor and she'd left school early. But she had a hunger for knowledge, and had always been smart. She also had a lot of love to give to a good man and when it came to good men Nick Reed was one of the best. I don't suppose the disparity in their education mattered, since it was still relatively rare for women to have professions, and it was nice to know she'd be going out with a guy, something she hadn't done since I'd been born. I can't ever remember her and my dad going out together. Pity Captain Reed would be shipping out with us. It would have been nice if they'd got to know each other better; it was high time she had some fun.

In late May we learned that the battalion was going to England, though no more than that, no date, no port, no name of ship, it was all top secret in case of German U-boats. Captain Reed called me into his office.

I knocked on the open door to his surgery, waited for permission to enter, then stood to attention. 'You called, sir!'

'Close the door, Corporal,' he said quietly.

I closed the door and he indicated a chair on the other side of his desk. 'Please sit down, Jack,' he invited. He'd never previously used my name while in barracks or invited me to sit down. I did as I was told and waited, a bit nervous at the sudden informality while we were both in uniform. He too seemed a little nervous, not looking directly at me for a few moments then clearing his throat before he glanced up. 'As you know we're moving out, overseas, probably to England. Quite when I don't know, but I feel it will be soon.' He paused and cleared his throat again. 'I've asked your mother to marry me.'

I did a double take. 'What? You . . . you're going to . . . marry . . . my mom?' I gulped, only just remembering to add, 'sir'.

'Well, yes, is that so strange?' he asked with a half grin.

Then it sank in and I couldn't contain my delight. 'No, not strange, just . . . that's great, sir!' I said, almost leaping from the chair.

He grinned, holding up a restraining hand. 'No, no, not so fast, Jack.'

'What, sir?' I asked anxiously.

'She'll only agree if you give your permission.'

'Done, sir!' I said, grinning like an ape, then I stretched over the desk and shook his hand, perhaps more vigorously than I should.

'Not *sir*. In private you must call me Nick. After all, I'm soon to become your stepfather!' He laughed.

'When, sir? Er, Nick.'

'As soon as we can arrange it. Of course I'll need the CO's permission and I'll have to arrange for the Anglican chaplain to marry us here at the barracks. But there's no time to waste. Never know when we're going to embark for overseas now we've been informed. I don't want to give some other guy a chance, do I! You'll be required to give her away, of course. Just a quiet affair, no fuss.'

But of course when Miss Frostbite heard about it that was the end of the quiet affair with no fuss. Nick's mom, Jean, a widow, came down from Vancouver and proved to be as nice as her son. We had a Saturday afternoon wedding reception with the whole band in attendance at the Jazz Warehouse. There was a proper wedding cake and everything else thrown in by Joe and Miss Frostbite. Mom and Nick invited only good friends: the twins, Mac of course (without Dolly), and the rest of the gang, Joe, Miss Frostbite, Mrs Hodgson and Mrs Sopworth, with the boys in the band and some of the kitchen staff who'd worked with my mom when she was trying to compensate Miss Frostbite for paying for my piano lessons, also five of her team who'd worked as office cleaners with her. All seemed to love her and I could see how truly happy she was. Captain Reed, now to become not only sir but Nick and stepfather, was an only child like me, so apart from his mom he had only a couple of buddies from the army and medical school. He made a speech at the reception saying he couldn't believe his luck finding someone like Gertrude. I agreed with him, although I knew they were both lucky to have found each other.

Later, when they were about to depart for a three-day honeymoon at Windermere House, a grand hotel on the lake at Muskoka (wedding gift from the twins), my mom hugged me. 'Oh, Jack, I'm so happy, I do love him so,' she whispered, close to tears.

'Don't cry!' I laughed. 'You'll spoil your nice make-up and make that beautiful new nose all sniffy and red!'

They were leaving in a military staff car with a driver (a gift from the CO), and as it drove off my mom and Nick turned and waved to us from the back window. They were both beaming.

In early June 1942, the Royals Regiment boarded a troop train to Halifax, Nova Scotia, and arrived two days later, a train journey that normally takes half that time, but our train seemed to be shunted into every siding on the way to let everything else pass. Tired and fed up we embarked on the pre-war Cunard liner *Queen Mary*, now turned troopship and destined for Southampton in England. All we wanted to do was stow our kitbags and find a spot below decks before the grand old lady sailed down the harbour. Less than an hour out to sea the war proper started for me.

With fifteen thousand officers and men on board from various Canadian regiments, the medics were busy almost from the moment we left port. The men were weary and dehydrated from the long train journey and while the sea was no more than choppy, some of the men started almost immediately to feel seasick.

Seasickness is no joke in such crowded conditions. The men and their equipment were crammed below decks, each man allocated a bunk eighteen inches wide as his only personal space, each bunk stacked four high. The officers, of course, were given the use of the decks and billeted in the first-class and second-class cabins with the dining rooms now turned into messes. To add to our misery the ship had all its woodwork covered in leather to protect it. Perhaps it hadn't been properly cured because a strange, nauseating smell pervaded below decks even before the first guy threw up. By the time we were two days out to sea, it had become a stinking miasma.

The medics and orderlies, together with the doctors, worked twelve-hour shifts as a matter of course, but when we hit truly bad seas four days out, I think we worked sixteen hours straight from then on. During this worst period of turbulence I received a message to report to the bandmaster, Sergeant Major Leo Leader, an NCO of the bristling moustache type who demanded perfection. Earlier, I had managed to rehydrate him sufficiently so that he was able to stand on his own two feet, but only just. When I arrived I was surprised when he apologised for keeping me from my work, apologies being contrary to his nature. He then handed me a note. 'Read it, Lance Corporal Spayd,' he ordered. 'It came to me because they assume all musicians are in the band.'

> Dear Sergeant Major Leader,
>
> As you may imagine in these rough seas things are pretty miserable in the officers' quarters. It may help to cheer them up if you'd direct Jack Spayd to report to the main mess at 1700 hrs to play the piano while we have our dinner.
>
> He will return below decks no later than 1900 hrs. Have him report directly to me.
>
> Thank you,
>
> Capt. John 'Bull' Fuller
> Officer Entertainment

I was barely able to contain my surprise when Sergeant Major Leader grinned. 'They don't call that miserable *sonofabitch* "Fuller Bull" for nothing. Don't worry, lad, I've sent the captain a message to say that you are seasick and too weak to rise from your bunk. Never put your trust in an officer until you've fought at his side in battle. You're doing good work, lad, we're all proud of you.'

The *Queen Mary* had a distinctive slow roll in the heavy Atlantic seas that added greatly to the general sense of misery. Underlying all this was the pervading fear of German U-boats. We knew the North Atlantic was infested with them and we were following a zigzag course supposedly designed to frustrate these scavengers of the sea. Fear of being torpedoed pervaded every moment of that seemingly endless voyage as we lay there like sardines in a can.

Added to all this was the fact that because the *Queen Mary* travelled at high speed to avoid U-boats, she left the slower warships, a cruiser and a destroyer, too far behind to have any hope of defending us against attack, so we were sitting ducks.

When I think back on the horrible threat of being torpedoed during that single voyage across the Atlantic my admiration for the navy and the merchant marine, who were almost constantly at sea during the war years, knows no bounds. In fact one of the few times I've grabbed a man by his shirtfront and threatened to punch him was several years later when he called the merchant navy a bunch of combat dodgers. I later learned that, although he'd been in the Canadian armed forces, he'd never left Canada's shores.

Bruised, battered and almost broken in spirit we eventually reached safe harbour in Southampton. I know I was on the verge of collapse even though I hadn't suffered from seasickness. It was probably the best practice I could have had before going into combat. One thing was certain, if I ever became as accustomed to the sight and smell of blood as I had become to vomit I knew I would have earned my stripes, both of them, as I was made a full corporal shortly after arriving in England.

We were accommodated with the other Canadian troops in temporary barracks and billets near the town of Crawley in West Sussex, just twenty-eight miles out of London. We now had five divisions in the United Kingdom. We were there to fill the gaps in the First Battalion as men were rotated into other units and special tasks.

Upon our arrival the battalion was abuzz with rumours of an imminent raid on some part of the French coast. The battalion had been training for some weeks culminating in a disastrous mock exercise that had our battalion and other Canadian forces assaulting beaches on West Bay on the English south coast near the town of Bridport. We were to learn that the practice landing had been a total shambles with the landing craft dumping troops late and miles from their true objectives.

This, we were told, was not an isolated incident. The First Battalion, along with other Canadian troops, had been landed at the French port of Brest after the mass evacuation of British troops from Dunkirk, to prop up the French army in the surrounding area. Upon arrival they discovered what the British War Office *must* have known, that the French army was on the verge of collapse and well beyond propping up. Three days later the Canadian landing force was evacuated only just before the French surrender.

While no men were killed, they lost all their equipment, their transport and most of their artillery. This was not because of undue German harassment but because of mismanagement in the panic to get them onto ships and away from France.

As a consequence the men felt humiliated being forced to scuttle back to England with their tails between their legs, knowing the entire operation had been pointless and that they were the victims of bad planning and administrative stupidity.

Now, the botched landing exercise at West Bay did little to boost our confidence in those responsible for planning the upcoming raid on France. I had accepted I might die in battle, but I didn't want to think that my demise might be due to incompetence, my life thrown away because of someone's crass stupidity. But that's war, I guess; you have no say in how they decide to dispose of you.

We had barely found our land legs when our first and the battalion's second practice at West Bay took place. While pretty iffy in parts, generally speaking it wasn't too bad and so we waited anxiously, hoping that the top brass would get it right when the call came to embark on the real thing. We told ourselves that maybe things had changed and that in the ensuing two years since Brest those responsible for our lives may have learned a bit. I've talked about self-deception on a personal scale but this was self-deception on a grand scale.

Finally, after further weeks of training on the Isle of Wight, on 19th of August 1942, six days after my nineteenth birthday, the order came for what would become known as Operation Jubilee, the infamous raid on the French port of Dieppe. The operation was to be a practice run for the future invasion of Europe. We were to seize the port and surroundings for twenty-four hours, destroy the enemy defences and then be evacuated back to England pretty well intact with German prisoners in tow and lots of useful intelligence.

We left Southampton after dark on the transport *Queen Emma* and arrived ten miles off the French coast still in darkness, the plan being to hit the beaches before dawn to catch the enemy napping. But we should have known the best laid plans of mice and men seldom come together and the business of getting the men into the landing craft meant that it was close to dawn before most of us set out.

To make matters worse for the hundred or so men in our landing craft we developed engine trouble soon after leaving the mother ship. We bobbed around for an hour while the cursing sailors attempted to repair the engine.

The rest of the battalion was headed for a narrow shingle beach fronting a headland named Puys to the east of the main landing point with daylight approaching rapidly. Capturing this headland was considered critical, as German artillery and anti-aircraft guns sited there commanded the main landing beaches in front of the town.

By the time they reached the narrow beach fronting the headland it was already broad daylight. The enemy were ready and waiting for us, well protected in their pillboxes and block houses perched on a ten-foot high seawall and further protected by barbed wire. By 8.30 a.m. it was all over. Not a single man of the 554 who reached the beach got back, most were killed while some few were taken prisoner.

As it turned out those who commanded the operation offshore were oblivious to the total destruction of the first landing on the beach at

Puys and sent in a second wave of troops, presumably to consolidate the victory. They too were all but destroyed. The failure to eliminate the German gun batteries was disastrous; they were able to fire on our troops on the main landing beaches, mowing down men until a partial evacuation was hurriedly organised. Once again we had been thoroughly beaten in combat.

That's the problem with military operations – they always look so plausible in theory. 'Gentlemen, when we reach our objective, the men will come ashore in landing craft and take the beach before moving on to . . . blah, blah, blah.'

Allow me for a moment to describe a landing craft. Officially termed a 'Landing Craft Mechanised', or LCM for short, it is a steel box fifty feet long with a ramp at the bow. They are large enough to carry vehicles and are equipped with machine-guns. The sides are sufficiently high to protect the men inside from everything except a direct artillery hit and each is meant to carry a hundred men together with the required officers jammed in with their equipment like a can of sardines. The theory (always the theory!) is that the steel box pushes up onto the beach and the ramp opens onto a gentle wash over sand or beach pebbles. In practice it is more often a case of jumping from the landing craft into waist-high or even deeper water. If it is deep enough, a man laden with heavy equipment sinks like a stone, drowning being just one of the hazards of any beach landing.

Bobbing around offshore we were unaware of the slaughter on the beach at Puys and when an hour later we set off in our repaired landing craft, the coastline was veiled by clouds of artillery smoke and the general fog of battle. Real life sometimes is stranger than fiction and, unbeknownst to me, Captain John 'Bull' Fuller, the guy who had sent the note to Sergeant Major Leader demanding I play piano on board, was in command of our LCM. I'd never seen him before, and had I known, I probably would have panicked even more than I did.

Long before we got close enough to land, the German batteries must have sighted us through the smoke and fog and their artillery shells began to rain down around us, sending plumes of water often twenty feet high. I was close to shitting myself and have seldom since been as terrified.

We must have gone offcourse because we hit the shelving beach well to the west of our intended landing and slap-bang in front of a heavily armed German position. We dropped our landing ramp in waist-deep water and were immediately exposed to a storm of deadly accurate small-arms fire. Anyhow, when the ramp was dropped, Captain John 'Bull' Fuller was one of the first to jump into the water and presumably one of the first to be killed. At least he'd personally led his troops into battle.

With nothing else to distract them the German machine-gunners and snipers found our range and were firing directly into the landing craft. The wounded still in the water were trying to clamber back while others, attempting to disembark, were taking direct hits or stumbling over men crawling on all fours across the ramp in an attempt to reach the main deck. It was absolute mayhem around me, with terrified and wounded men screaming and the lapping water turning scarlet over the ramp. I stood on the edge, pulling the wounded back on board, yelling out in sheer panic. At one stage I leapt into the water to lift a wounded man up and flop him on the ramp, but he was dead with a bullet through his mouth. I pulled myself back onto the ramp and continued to haul wounded men up and in; I decided I'd go back and fetch the dead later.

All this occurred over a period of no more than two minutes before the naval officer on board realised we were on a suicidal mission and ordered the ramp to be raised. I vaguely recall screaming at him to delay it another minute so we could pull the remaining wounded back on board. This extra minute seemed like an eternity, and it felt awful leaving the dead behind.

Then, just as the ramp started to crank up, I felt as if someone had hit my tin hat with a baseball bat and I went straight down on my ass. There was a loud ringing in my ears, then I felt warm blood trickling down my neck, although no pain. With the engines screaming we began to reverse off the beach and by the time we were in deeper water my head had cleared somewhat. One of the other two medics ran up to where I was sitting, examined me then yelled that I had a shrapnel dent in my tin hat and a bullet had taken the lobe off my right ear. 'Slap a bandage on it!' I yelled as he helped me to my feet. It was only a superficial wound and the steel LCM deck, slippery with blood, was littered with around forty wounded men who were badly in need of attention.

We began to retreat in a choppy sea and to add to our misery men started throwing up, but we three medics were far too busy attending to the wounded. Vomit soon mixed with the blood and gore covering the deck. The extra courses I'd taken under Captain Reed's supervision were paying off and the other two medics allowed me to call the shots, sorting the urgent cases out for immediate attention. We all knew that badly wounded men attended to in the first hour are more likely to survive. Assessing the nature and consequences of a wound is critical and this was an area of instruction Nick Reed was very particular about. 'Jack, that's where you save lives and avoid future complications,' he'd stress over and over while I was training.

In all, including the forty-two wounded, only sixty-seven of us remained, including two officers and yours truly with a very sore head from the shrapnel blow to my tin hat. I never set foot on dry land in France and my entire combat experience lasted mere minutes.

Later we learned that the sixty-seven survivors on our LCM and a handful of others were the only ones from our battalion of close to a thousand men to return to England from the landing on the beaches of Dieppe.

The biggest joke (the only joke) in all this was that I was awarded the Military Medal for courage under fire as I attended the wounded, *while himself wounded in action* according to the citation. I freely admit there wasn't a scintilla of courage involved. With the artillery shells landing all around us and sending plumes of water into the LCM I was shitting myself long before the ramp opened and until three minutes later when it closed and we finally pulled out of range of enemy artillery.

In fact, if the truth were to be known, the only thing that prevented me from collapsing in a hopeless gibbering heap during the withdrawal was that I was too busy attending to the wounded. But once the medics on the mother ship took over and I was free to find a small dark corner below decks, I collapsed with the shakes and it was an hour or more before I stopped shivering and whimpering and started to pull myself together.

My one consolation was that my stepfather and medical mentor Captain Nick Reed didn't take part in the raid on Dieppe. Instead, he was away on a course in reconstructive plastic surgery at the Burns Unit established at Queen Victoria Hospital in West Sussex to care for pilots and crew shot down, many of whom had been injured in the Battle of Britain. His training was under the supervision of the famous surgeon, New Zealander Archibald McIndoe, who pioneered many treatments for serious burns. God knows he had plenty of poor devils to work on.

When Nick returned to the virtually non-existent battalion he admitted to me he felt guilty that he hadn't gone to Dieppe, saying his conscience was further pricked by what he'd witnessed at Queen Victoria Hospital. 'Jack, they only tell us about the courage shown in the Battle of Britain. You don't see the missing faces and twisted limbs that result from being trapped in a burning aircraft.'

Although our battalion was a shattered wreck, new recruits were beginning to arrive from Canada to provide the required numbers. I continued as a medic under Captain Nick Reed, spending most of my time either at the Casualty Clearing Station or on training courses. Six months later, to my great delight, Nick was sent back to Canada to work on repatriated Canadians requiring plastic surgery. It meant that my mom had her new husband back and safe from harm. By that time, I was just about the best-trained medic in the Canadian army and my stepfather was urging me to study medicine after the war. 'Jack, those big piano hands of yours have the healing touch. You have a real feel for medicine.' I confess it was a nice compliment from a man who, while polite, fair and honest, set pretty high standards for his medical staff and wasn't overly lavish with his praise.

In the meantime we'd pulled together an excellent pick-up group from the few remaining members of the band and were playing at concerts and dances for the Canadian forces and at village dances all over West Sussex. We were also invited to do several gigs for the American air force stationed at nearby Gatwick airfield. With the Americans in the war, jazz, hitherto thought of as Negro or black music, was becoming popular and I guess I earned a bit of reputation for playing piano.

But everything was about to change for me. While many of the Canadian troops in England were sent to the Mediterranean, our battalion, with all its raw replacement recruits, was considered in need of further training and remained in England. Then in December 1942, barely four months after Dieppe, the CBC back in Canada started broadcasting the Canadian Army Radio Show, starring comedians Johnny Wayne and Frank Shuster. Unbeknownst to those of us in the UK, this proved an enormous success and some smart-ass general decided that it should be expanded to include a touring show to entertain troops both in Canada and overseas. He picked a guy named Rai Purdy as commanding officer.

What followed was a classic case of not what you know, but who you know. In this instance it was Miss Frostbite who knew Rai Purdy and saw this as a way to get me out of what she considered the danger zone. She asked Lieutenant Purdy to recruit me to the newly formed Canadian Auxiliary Services Entertainment Unit on his arrival in England. Rai Purdy, his full name being Horatio, tracked me down and invited me to join him.

He was all smiles and clearly pleased with himself. 'Jack, I can get you out of this crappy medic's job and you'll spend the rest of the war safely tickling the ivories.'

'Thank you, sir,' I reply politely, 'but I would prefer to remain a medic.'

His tone immediately changed. 'Corporal Spayd, you disappoint me!' he said, giving me a prize-winning performance of hurt and regret.

'Nevertheless, sir, I feel I will be more useful serving my country as a medic than as a musician.'

My answer clearly annoyed him. 'There's a war on, soldier! You will do what you're told,' he barked.

Alas, he was perfectly right and despite an appeal from the new MO who had replaced Nick Reed, in December 1943 possibly the best-trained medic in the Canadian army was forced to switch from bandages to band.

Although he was a mere lieutenant, Rai Purdy seemed to me to be rather full of himself and gloried in his new responsibility, which, to be fair, was not inconsiderable. With his radio background he was big on melodramatic introductions and was inordinately proud of the one he'd composed for me and insisted it be used whenever I was introduced.

Introducing Corporal Jack Spayd, the only professional musician in the entire Canadian army who is a recognised war hero, having won the Military Medal for bravery attending to the wounded while in combat, when he was himself severely wounded. I give you the finest jazz pianist in the Canadian army!

I had gone to him and asked for this stupid introduction to be abandoned. Even though there was no formality among the various musicians and entertainers, he'd stood me to attention and, wagging his finger in my face as if I were a recalcitrant schoolboy, yelled, 'Corporal, my introduction is good for the Entertainment Unit and good for army morale. Do you understand?'

'No, sir,' I replied. 'It is inappropriate and untrue, sir.'

'Corporal, I will make a note that you continue to be difficult. I will decide what is appropriate and what is not! So put that in your pipe and smoke it!'

The only way I could find to counteract this stupid introduction was to point to my right ear and comment, 'If you look *very* carefully, you'll see the extent of my terrible wounds – my right earlobe is nicked, so naturally I'll lead off tonight with "St James Infirmary Blues".' This implied the band master's introduction was a deliberate set-up for my explanation. It always got a big laugh as I launched into the famous blues number.

Until Joe corrected me, I'd always thought that 'St James Infirmary Blues' was one of the greatest of all American blues songs, originating in the eighteenth century as a Negro folksong called 'The Gambler's Lament'. In fact, according to Joe, it went way, way back to sixteenth-century England. 'The Unfortunate Rake' was the most common of its various titles over the past four hundred years or so. It tells of a young soldier who laments the death of his fine lady in St James Hospital for lepers. Having spent all his money on whores, he then sings about his own inevitable death from venereal disease. When the folksong reached America in the eighteenth century, the wayward youth's premature death was put down to gambling and alcohol, and since then the lyrics have been adapted repeatedly, but the unforgettable tune remains unchanged. I was intrigued by the song's long history, so as soon as I could get to a library, I looked up St James Hospital and discovered it was demolished in 1532, thirty-two years before Shakespeare was born. In its place Henry VIII built St James Palace, still on the same site in the heart of central London today. I visited the palace once, and standing beside the guard I took out my harmonica and played the 'St James Infirmary Blues'. Soon enough an old guy stopped and listened. He had sharp blue eyes and spiky grey hair swept back like a hedgehog. When I'd finished playing he pointed a gnarled forefinger at me and said, 'Thank you for remembering, son.'

The Entertainment Unit was based in London and we spent the remainder of the war touring the UK performing for troops and civilians. The group we'd formed before I was forcibly drafted to the Entertainment Unit had played mostly on Saturday nights for our troops and on one or two occasions for the Americans at the local Gatwick airfield. It was here that I was invited to join one of their local poker games and soon after became a regular, playing whenever I had the chance. It was a pretty decent standard and another reason why I didn't want to leave my battalion or West Sussex.

One of the Yanks, an air force sergeant named Sam Schischka, one of the regular players, suggested I look up his cousin, US Marines Master Sergeant Lenny Giancana, who was part of the marine guard at the US

Embassy in Grosvenor Square. He assured me he ran a pretty good poker game and was also a jazz fanatic and so I would be welcome. 'I'll give him a call in London,' he promised. 'He'll take good care of you, Jack, buddy. He's a member of the family.' I was not to know until some time after the war that 'the family' wasn't meant in the domestic sense.

Lenny Giancana proved to be everything his cousin promised. He loved jazz and invited me to play in his sergeants' mess and, when off duty, attended every concert where I was playing in and around London. When it came to poker he really knew his onions and ran a serious game where I struggled to stay ahead and in the process learned a whole lot. In poker luck is one thing but experience is everything.

He would often urge me to come to Las Vegas after the war. 'Hey, buddy, you cain't go back to Canada. No way, man. It's fuckin' cold up there. Freeze ya balls! You gotta come Stateside – Vegas, that's where the sun shines all year round and the girls are happy to oblige a good-lookin' jazz musician like you. Jack, the family they gonna take good care of you, buddy. You got the hair and skin to make you a honorary I-talian.' He laughed. 'You'd pass for a wop any day the week, buddy. You come see us, we gonna treat you real special.'

I recall asking him how come his cousin was called Sam Schischka. 'That's Polish, isn't it?'

He sighed. 'My old man's sister married a fuckin' Polack. Never did work out any good. Useless fuck! We got only Sicilian blood in our family since fuckin' Noah. Then he come and contaminate. But she brought Sam up I-talian, he got the dark eyes and hair, so that's okay. Now he included in the family.'

At first I thought he was simply being nice about my coming to Nevada, but he persisted until I was forced to say, 'Lenny, when we're demobbed I'm thinking of taking a scholarship from the Department of Veteran Affairs to study medicine.'

I recall his look of alarm. 'Shit, man, you goin' back to school? Whaffor? Medicine? Hey, Jack, what you saying to me? You kiddin' me or somethin'? What kinda bullshit is this? Goddamned doctor can mend a broken body. Jazz pianist good as you can mend a broken heart!' He pointed to my big hands. 'God, don't go put no surgeon's knife in your hands. Nosirree, no way! Them fingers meant for one thing, for playin' fuckin' piano like a fuckin' angel, man!' He'd laughed. 'Also,' he pointed upwards, 'the Big Man gives you good poker hands real regular and that ain't just luck, buddy.' He tapped the side of his head. 'You got it, man. In Vegas you gonna be a big hit, Jack. You can play two ways, piano and poker. Where I hail from, that combination's just about the most perfect a man can get himself.'

And so I eventually played my final piano note in London some time after the war in Europe came to an end in May 1945. The Japs were still fighting in the Far East but this too came to an abrupt halt in August when the US dropped the atomic bomb on Hiroshima and then on Nagasaki. If these so-called atomic bombs brought hostilities to a sudden end they didn't affect the Entertainment Unit. There were still tens of thousands of our guys milling around England waiting for a ship to take them home and they needed entertaining. So it was business as usual for us. Finally most of the Entertainment Unit was repatriated, but Horatio John Purdy hadn't forgiven my intransigence and set up a series of solo concerts for me, so that I was among the very last of the musicians to be demobbed, arriving back in Toronto in March 1946, ten months after VE Day.

Lenny Giancana was right. It was freezing in Toronto.

PART THREE

CHAPTER THIRTEEN

THE GOOD PART OF returning to Toronto was finding the now Mrs Gertrude Reed settled in and a very happy woman. There was no doubt Nick Reed was being loved to bits, and he seemed calmly content – in his world of burn victims I guess normalcy was a blessing. My mother looked splendid and seemed to have gained in confidence. Under the guidance of Miss Frostbite, she had learned how to behave in company, and, in her stylish new clothes, she looked the part of a top surgeon's wife. In fact, she confessed to me that, after all the years of hand-me-downs, the most difficult part of becoming Nick's wife hadn't been the novel sensation of conjugal bliss or sharing a double bed again but the seemingly simply act of going into a dress shop to purchase something off the rack for herself.

'Miss Frostbite took me into Eaton's to buy a dress to wear to a fundraising do at Nick's hospital,' she recalled not long after I had returned to Toronto. 'I didn't sleep a wink the night before, and that's not an exaggeration. When we got off the trolley car outside the shop I froze, absolutely terrified. Miss Frostbite took me by the arm and urged me on but I couldn't, for the life of me, budge. It was like I'd been cemented in, Jack.'

I laughed. 'When was the last time you'd been to Eaton's?'

'Oh my, let me think . . . 1929 . . . just before the Wall Street Crash. Miss Frostbite wanted to buy new shoes as well, but that was going too far; I had the shoes Miss Bates gave me, which were still good, the ones I wore to all your concerts, and the fashions haven't really changed all that much. The lovely new dress she made me buy was all that was needed and I felt very smart.'

I grinned. 'She finally got you into the shop then?'

'Yes, but the worst part was that I felt so guilty.'

'Guilty? What for, spending money or for creating a scene on the pavement?'

'Yes, both, but mainly for not going to Mrs Sopworth at the Presbyterian Clothing Depot! All those years she'd keep an eye out for me, dropping me notes: *Gertrude, I have a little something I think you're going to like.* Or she'd say, "My dear, I have some good practical delicates", meaning of course, undies.' She smiled. 'She was generally right, too, about me liking it.'

Miss Frostbite had also made her change her hairstyle. '"Gertrude, you have lovely hair but that long, straight look just has to go, it's much too plain. Nice, but rather too predictable," that's what she said to me. I nearly died at the very thought. All those bitter nights when you soaked my chilblains and then brushed my hair – they're among my most treasured memories, Jack.' She smiled rather sadly. '"No, it *mustn't* be cut, I *can't* have it cut," I'd insisted. "Cut?" she said. "Who mentioned anything about cutting? It's beautiful, my dear. I thought just a bit of a wave, *a la* Veronica Lake." Can you imagine, Jack? At my age, with hair like a film star . . .'

I looked more closely at her hair. She still wore it down to her shoulders but sort of softly curled, falling across her right eyebrow. It looked very glam and its blue-black gloss was still as deep as ever. Gosh, she was pretty, and with her straight nose and her new-found happiness, the new, improved Gertrude Reed was even more of a pleasure to be around.

While she and Nick were both keen for me to share their house, I knew my stay would be a short one. In fact, if I hadn't thought she'd be terribly upset if I didn't, I probably wouldn't have stayed with my mother in the first instance. She and Nick needed time alone together, not a great lump of a returning soldier landing on their doorstep and messing up her neat-as-a-pin home. If I was going to stay in Toronto, which in my mind seemed increasingly unlikely, I'd get a place of my own.

The little house was everything she could have wished for, small and cosy and not all that different on the outside from our original Cabbagetown home. The big difference was that it was in a nice downtown neighbourhood and she and Nick owned it outright. Despite the post-war shortages it was nicely appointed, with a parlour (now referred to as the lounge room) featuring Mac's wedding present, a second-hand chaise longue he'd found somewhere, and repaired and freshly varnished and upholstered in Miss Frostbite purple. With his penchant for hoarding I have no doubt the purple velvet was left over from a past Jazz Warehouse foyer job.

The post-war Mac was happy as a pig in a wallow, with plenty of work to keep him out and about. When he was home he spent all his time in his workshop in the backyard. He'd had heating and electric lighting installed so he could spend his evenings there safe from Dolly's acerbic tongue, her presence restricted to the evening meal and a goodnight grunt. He'd taken to making guitars as a hobby. 'Just you wait, Jack, jazz soloists – just a singer on guitar – are gonna be the next big thing and they'll all want custom-made guitars.'

'Sing while playing the guitar? Yeah, blues maybe, but jazz? I've heard Django Reinhardt, but he doesn't sing and he often plays with a jazz violinist – Stéphane Grappelli. They set up the Quintet of the Hot Club of France,' I said, showing off a little. 'Even then, I don't think you're going to get too many imitators. Solo guitarists? I can't see it, Mac.'

'Mark my words, Jack, the jazz singer guitarist – solo – will be the next big thing.'

'Cost a bit to set up, won't it?' I asked.

'Jack, that's the nice part, the twins are backing me, anything I want.'

Mac loved jazz and as a craftsman he never cut corners, so a handmade Mac guitar would be a nice thing to possess. He seemed pretty certain about what he was saying, but I wasn't going to hold my breath waiting for his prediction to come true. In the meantime, Mac was enjoying himself, and it was long overdue. I was happy for him.

The twins were well on their way to making their mark in respectable financial and property circles, backed, as I mentioned, by the advice and financial help of Mr Logical and the services of his bank. Whether they continued to provide their unique services to him as part of the deal I shall never know, but it looked as though they were destined to become very wealthy, their past as high-class whores soon forgotten. It was as if the trauma of war and the euphoria of a lasting peace had expunged any dubious aspects of their pre-war past. There would always be a few old families whose doors would remain firmly shut to post-war upstarts such as the twins, but new money had a way of overcoming most obstacles, providing one behaved oneself, and if Mommy and Daddy were not up to the mark, you kept them out of sight, used your knife and fork correctly, voted for the right party and donated to the right charities.

For her part, Dolly was now established as the 'Queen of Quilt', having won a blue ribbon at 'The Ex' (Canadian National Exhibition) in the last show before Canada got serious about the war. She had set up the Dolly McClymont School of Quilting, also financed by the twins, in a new shopping centre they partly owned together with Mr Logical and his bank. According to Mac, she was becoming very popular. It seemed her forthright, no-nonsense style was proving to be an asset. 'She gets results. People say she's the best in the biz,' Mac claimed, not entirely without a sense of pride in his churlish spouse, who, though I found it hard to believe, may well have softened now that she was financially independent and free of Cabbagetown and the constant grind of poverty.

As for my own post-war life, I found myself in somewhat of a dilemma, with a contest between the head and the heart. Dr Reed, now my stepfather, was convinced I'd make an excellent doctor after my work with him as a medic during the war, and was anxious that I apply for a veteran's scholarship to study medicine. My mom was quite overcome by the notion that her precious son might someday be a doctor. In her eyes there could be no more worthy vocation – this was the top of the Christmas tree. A jazz musician was something, but an MD was something else; in one generation the family would have leapt from poverty and obscurity to the pinnacle of social success.

I'd sent in my application and subsequently attended the first two interviews with the War Veterans Department, armed with all the correct references from the relevant top army medical brass, organised by Nick. My medal as a medic in the battlefield didn't do any harm either. I felt I'd gone well in both interviews, and was yet to undergo a third and final one in front of army and civilian medical men and a solitary woman, a professor of something at McGill University in Montreal, before being accepted. Nick assured me that it was pretty much a rubber-stamp process.

I tried to convince myself that I could continue with jazz as an amateur and that being an MD would somehow compensate me for staying in my homeland. I'd had my fun in the Army Entertainment Corps, sowing my wild oats with some generous English girls who had allowed me to put Juicy Fruit's lessons to excellent use, so maybe it was time to settle down. But in my heart I knew these attempts to convince myself weren't succeeding.

During the war I'd developed into a reasonable poker player, skilled enough to take my place confidently at almost any card table, provided I had the appropriate stake. You grow up fast at a poker table, but now I found myself in Toronto, a town of Scots Presbyterians, which, despite a burst of post-war activity, continued to progress slowly and cautiously. Like a lot of veterans I felt unsettled and out of place among those who had stayed at home during the war, so the prospect of settling down again to study to become an MD, so I could write prescriptions for cough mixture and play the odd bracket at the Jazz Warehouse on weekends, seemed a little too much like crawling backwards into the future. War and travel change a young guy more than he realises, until he returns to his old environment. Or, as Joe put it, 'Jazzboy, I guess you jes forced to grow up some in a hurry, son. You gone put new footprints in da old ones ain't gunna help none.'

To add to my discomfort, I learned that a highly exaggerated version of my war experiences was circulating, recounted in hushed tones when I wasn't around to set the record straight. If you left out the details it reeled off the teller's tongue very neatly – I was a young lad whose manhood had been forged in the heat of fierce combat. As I gathered from Mac, my battle experience now featured men dropping like ninepins around me while I tended the wounded, despite being severely wounded myself. The most colourful version was that a German sniper's bullet had removed my ear and gouged a ditch in my skull. The most heroic was that I'd personally rescued several men who were wounded and unable to reach the landing craft, throwing myself into the sea and heaving them out before they drowned. If I protested that the sea was sufficiently shallow to stand in and that I'd merely yanked a few wounded men aboard, my listeners glanced at each other in a knowing way.

In truth, there had been so much blood around and my own adrenalin had so distorted my perceptions that I hadn't felt the bullet nick my ear until later, when we were underway and someone pointed to the blood dripping onto my shoulder. Somehow, I emerged covered in unearned glory, with a medal and a citation for bravery while tending the wounded under so-called relentless enemy fire.

Jack Spayd was hardly made of the white-hot metal that, once beaten into shape, makes a hard man. I felt like a phoney. I had learned to play the man game perfectly. I was confident around other men, a big guy who was well liked. I'd attended to men who were wounded and who trusted me to save their lives. I had gained their respect and, while my efforts on the landing craft had been no more than my training and duty required, they seemed to look at me differently after those three frightening minutes.

I was afraid that if I became a doctor or stayed in Canada I'd never live down my hero status, phoney as it was. People want heroes in their lives and I had been branded one whether I liked it or not: poor Cabbagetown boy, with a drunken and violent father, and a mother who worked nights and couldn't give him the love and attention every child needs, goes off to war, wins a medal for bravery, is wounded in battle, returns and becomes a doctor. Wow!

In reality, I had led an absolutely charmed life, with the right teachers and librarians to form my early years: Miss Frostbite, Miss Bates and, of course, Joe, and the enduring love of a wonderful mother to set me on my way. I'd always been a loner as a child, but somehow I never missed the company of friends.

There was just one aspect of my childhood that didn't fit the picture – the sight of my bleeding and broken little mother cowering and sobbing over my vile bastard father's dirty garbage collector's hobnailed boots. It was a vision that was never to leave me. The reconstruction of my mother's nose wasn't merely my attempt to bring back her looks and to help her to regain her self-confidence, it was also a vain attempt to rub out the past. But now, with my mother pretty again, I discovered that I still couldn't forgive my father. If I ever came across the motherfucker I'd break his neck. But then, here again was a paradox. It was my father who gave me a second-hand harmonica for my eighth birthday and, in so doing, effectively changed everything. The only person I hated and continue to hate had inadvertently given me the thing I treasured most – music – as well as a possible future.

Good fathering had been in short supply in my childhood. Mac had always been my good buddy, but I don't believe he led me along the path to manhood. His relationship with women had been almost the opposite to my own: while I had been shaped and nurtured by women, he'd been battered and broken by them, or by one woman at least. While I cherished him as a friend he was no substitute father. Joe, wonderful Joe, was a jazz man who regarded me first of all as a young musician. I guess he came close to being the mentor every boy needs, but he concentrated on turning me into a jazz musician, teaching me about the meaning and privilege of playing jazz and giving me a musical understanding that was probably beyond my years.

What I needed was a challenge, something that wasn't handed

to me on a plate, by a woman in particular. Women had almost singularly made my life a good one and I was grateful, but it was high time I discovered what kind of man I *really* was. I had taught myself to be comfortable in the company of men, whereas I had always loved women. As Joe would say, 'Jazzboy, jes remember, the wo-man yo kiss goodnight ain't the same you gonna kiss good mornin'. Ever'day she gonna be a bran-new in-ven-tion o' herself.' It may sound simple but becoming your own man is a very difficult process to execute alone, while, it seemed to me, women were born with an innate ability to be themselves, in all their glorious variety. One thing was certain, the idea of a career as a Toronto MD and part-time jazz pianist was no longer enough for me.

There was another aspect of my own country that I found stifling. Before I'd gone overseas and mixed with people who came from America, Britain and the Commonwealth, I hadn't thought much about language; that is, the vernacular used by various English speakers. I began to realise that my own mother tongue was more concerned with damping down emotions than portraying them. Canadian English was too polite. Even our street argot lacked the bite of the well-chosen and accurately directed invective of the British or the Yanks or, in particular, my fellow colonials, the Australians and New Zealanders. Words and phrases shot off the tongue like mortar bombs, creating a verbal explosion that couldn't be ignored. The best way to illustrate this, if you'll excuse me, is to take the word 'fuck'. The Australians seemed to have mastered its robust use better than most, not simply adjectivally, loosely scattered through a sentence, but also to express a range of meanings. For example, fuck off! (leave, you're dismissed); to fuck over (to treat badly); to fuck up (to bungle something); you're fucked (you're in serious trouble); don't fuck with me (don't mess with me); no, fuck that (no, I disagree); you little fuck (you contemptible person); he really fucked me over (he took advantage of me); well, fuck me (I'm surprised).

There are, of course, many more uses for this word, most of which have no sexual connotations. Australian men use it frequently and colourfully, the Americans and the British have their own particular uses, while Canadians seem to be able to use it without adding much colour or intensity or inventiveness to their speech. Or so it seemed to me. Such free and creative use of street argot was much less pronounced in Canada, where language lacked the flashes of electric blue such a word could add. Canadians, myself included, seemed reluctant to express their emotions. It was almost as though we had decided to become the world's most conservative English-speaking people. When you damp down emotion, you restrict the expression of anger and other strong feelings, and, as a result, people tend to simmer inwardly. Australians refer to a quarrel as a 'flaming row' or 'having a blue'; they don't hold back. I was beginning to realise that language wasn't simply a mark of class, it expressed the national character.

When you're looking for faults, I guess you can always find them, but when I met other veterans returning to Canada, they often expressed the same restlessness and inability to settle down. Perhaps it was simply the aftermath of war, but it appeared that nothing had really moved forward. We were greeted with the same mild and rather smug surprise: 'Oh, so you're back? How was the war?' The wealthy were as superior as ever and the post-Depression poor still carried the same haunted look in their eyes. The whole city seemed to be running on a slow and endless treadmill.

Let me attempt to explain. Canada had helped to win a war that had taken place elsewhere, so back home there was nothing to mend, or build, or change, no need to begin again, no reason to gird your loins and roll up your sleeves. There was nobody to shout at or blame, as there was in Europe. There was no anger, no invective, no taking of chances in a new environment, no repairing of old mistakes. Buildings stood solid, intact and dull, schoolchildren chanted their lessons and neighbourhoods remained much the same, the same ducks quacked on the same ponds. Canada seemed fixed in a pre-war time warp. The women who had taken over the men's jobs in factories, farms and institutions were now required to put their aprons back on and return to the kitchen, as if nothing had happened. Everything was the same, yet everything was different. Of course, I had to assume that, in time, post-war, post-Depression Canada would eventually change, but I felt I couldn't wait around until it did.

After a couple of months in Toronto I was going stir crazy but, in defence of my homeland, perhaps I didn't want to admit the degree to which I had become addicted to gambling. I had my winnings from London – not a lot, but sufficient to sit down at a reasonable card game – and yet I couldn't find a half-decent poker game that didn't involve a criminal element of some kind. In all, I had around two thousand Canadian dollars – my accumulated back pay, my demobilisation bonus, and a couple of hundred bucks I'd won at Lenny Giancana's poker games in London. I hoarded this like a miser, a poker miser waiting for the chance to get into a game where the stakes weren't penny-ante, which tells you something about my aspirations. I seemed to be, more than ever, addicted to having five cards in my hand, certain that a rare royal flush would be mine some day. In Toronto, the chances of satisfying this need were looking smaller and smaller. Medicine as a career wasn't going to satisfy this craving but playing poker and leading the free and easy life of a jazz musician would. Running a general practice or slicing people open in surgery just didn't compete.

Even if I had taken up a medical scholarship and tried to satisfy my craving for jazz by playing a few nights at the Jazz Warehouse, I would be going backwards, I felt. Miss Frostbite and Joe were still doing their dual piano act, and the musicians in the band were growing older and more set in their ways. Joe, for the first time, was looking his age, his thick mop of wiry hair now sporting a fist-sized patch of pure white above his brow and grey streaks at the temples. He looked like some fierce ageing prophet from the Old Testament.

The jazz scene in post-war Toronto was going nowhere. And then a letter arrived from Lenny Giancana at the Jazz Warehouse address I'd given him. His letter was as direct as the man himself:

Dear Jack,

How you going, buddy. Still freezing your butt? I still remember the cold in Chicago, and Toronto ain't any warmer.

Here the sun shines and the gals at the hotel pool are wearing these new bikinis, turning themselves a nice shade of tan.

Now comes a proposition, the same as before, but this is a definite offer.

I don't think I mentioned to you the Family have this casino, the El Marinero in Las Vegas.

To you ignorant Canadians, that's in the State of Nevada where gambling is legal.

Now they're building a new casino, state of the art, The Firebird, on 'The Strip'. Think – casino, resort, gals – there ain't never been anything like this before. The Family also has a share in this new one. Catering contracts, cocktail bars, we doing the guest luxury accommodation side.

So, here's the deal, buddy. This is what I'm proposing:

Come play at the El Marinero, then we'll give you your own piano bar at The Firebird when it's all done.

Jack, buddy, Las Vegas is going to be real big time pretty damn soon.

We'll fix you up with a Musicians Union Card so you're legit.

Think about it carefully – sunshine, girls, poker, good pay.

You'll make yourself $50 tax-free a fortnight. We'll guarantee this and it don't include your tips and what you can win at poker!

Poker and black jack is why this town exists, buddy.

I promise you the suckers will be coming to the desert with a truckload of cash from all over the States!

C'mon Jack, don't freeze your balls no more!!

What say you little buddy?

Your good friend,

Lenny Giancana

PS Give me a call, LV 2397.

Lenny was both right and wrong. I'd read a bit about Nevada and the town of Las Vegas and knew that it was largely a Mormon state and that the town had been known in the early days for the silver mines in the desert. It was near where they'd built the Boulder Dam in the Depression. Some of the air force guys I'd played poker with at Gatwick had been trained at the US air force base just out of Las Vegas, and they usually referred to the town as Hicksville. Of course I had no idea about its re-emergence as a gambling town, but thought it curious that Mormons would make gambling legal in Nevada.

Despite these doubts, it didn't take me long to decide. In my heart I knew I was a musician. I'd asked Joe what he thought, and he said, 'Jazzboy, a man gotta do what a man gotta do. You ain't been happy since you come back from the war. Maybe you got to keep kickin' the dust some. Moose Jaw and the war ain't enough. Yo not ready for no settlin' down in one place. Maybe you got to be a bit more troubadour? You good now, make no mistake, you a real good jazz man and you kin work anywhere yo want. If somebody hear yo but they cain't see yo, they gonna think yo a black man. Hey, son, whaffor yo want to become a doctor 'n' cut folk up or feed 'em pills? The good Lord, he put jazz music in yo heart and in yo fingers. He jes done forgot to change the colour yo skin.'

Miss Frostbite put it more simply. 'Jack, dear, your mother has a perfectly good doctor in the family and is extremely happy with him.'

While I probably didn't need their encouragement to leave, it was nevertheless nice to have their blessing.

My mom, thinking she'd got me home at last, was pretty upset when I handed her the letter. 'Oh, Jack, please, you can't possibly,' she cried, turning to Nick and thrusting the letter at him. 'Your stepfather says you'll make a wonderful doctor. I know you will, Jack. You were such a kind boy, treating my chilblains. You've always cared about people, always,' she repeated, very close to tears. 'You've *been* a musician, in Moose Jaw and the army, isn't that enough?' Now she was crying openly.

'Mom, it's difficult to explain. Becoming a doctor is about learning stuff; being a musician is about feeling stuff, in your heart, your soul.'

How could I possibly explain my physical and emotional need for jazz, let alone my compulsion to hold five cards in my hand as a means to test my intuition, judgment and mental stamina against my opponents'?

Then she suddenly cried, 'Oh, how I wish your father had never given you that stupid mouth organ when you were a child!'

I was shocked. My mom had sat through endless concerts, encouraged and praised me; could she possibly mean what she'd just said? 'Mom, I just need a little time to find myself. I was too young when I went scuffing. The army was all about obeying orders without question. I need to find out who I am.' I looked across at Nick. 'If it doesn't work out for me in, say, a year or two, can I still take up the offer to study medicine?' I asked.

'Yes, I think so. I'll need to confirm, but I think you'll have at least that long to decide. I'll have to check to make certain and get back to you,' he said quietly.

'Jack, *please* reconsider!' my mother begged. 'A doctor . . . a doctor is a *somebody*! We've always been nobodies . . . the dregs!'

'Mom, you've never been the dregs,' I protested.

Nick, who wasn't a man to show his emotions, took a step towards her and folded her into his arms. 'My darling, you *are* somebody, the best somebody I've ever known,' he said quietly, kissing her on the top of her head as she sobbed against his chest. I'd never before heard him use that endearment. He turned to me and went on. 'Jack, whatever happens, your mother is proud of you. However, I need to add that, while I know very little about music, I am certain you would make a splendid doctor.' He waved the letter in his hand. 'Would you mind if I read this?'

'No, of course.' I realised he was playing for time, allowing my mom to recover.

He gently lowered her into a chair and reached for his reading glasses, while I lowered myself onto my haunches beside my mother's chair and put my arm around her.

Finally, Nick looked up from the single page and then down at me. 'Jack, this fellow Lenny – what's his background? Giancana is Italian, isn't it?'

'Sicilian; he was a master sergeant in the marines at the American Embassy in London. I met his cousin, Sammy Schischka, at a card game, and he suggested I contact Lenny when the Entertainment Unit arrived in London.'

'This Lenny, you say he's Sicilian? But his cousin, that doesn't sound like a Sicilian name.'

'No, Polish, it's a relationship by marriage. Lenny's mother's sister, I believe. '

Nick paused, then said, 'He mentions Chicago . . .'

I nodded. 'But, before the war, Lenny lived with his parents in LA, where his dad had something to do with the entertainment business; in Hollywood, I think.' I pointed to the letter he was holding. 'The Las Vegas thing comes as a bit of a surprise, though. I thought he'd go back to Los Angeles.'

'Jack, this is probably a coincidence, but in 1929 I attended a conference in Chicago on reconstructive surgery. One of the case histories presented to us was that of a mobster, Mafiosi, who had severe facial burns from having been attacked with acid by a rival gang. It was shortly after Al Capone and the St Valentine's Day massacre, so we all thought it was pretty sensational. It was a nasty facial injury, bad scars; sulphuric acid isn't nice. I'm almost certain the victim's name was Giancana, or something very similar.'

Nick looked down at the letter he was holding. 'He mentions "the family" twice in this.'

'Well, I guess that's because he's Italian – Sicilian – family is important.'

'No, that's not what I mean. He doesn't say *my* family, the way you and I might do. In both instances it's *the* family.'

My mom, alarmed at his tone, looked up at him. 'Oh, Nick, whatever does that mean? Is it bad? You sound as if you have suspicions. The Mafia, why that's terrible!'

Before Nick could speak I said, 'I'd be very surprised, Nick. The US marines wouldn't have let him in with a criminal record. They're pretty firm about that sort of thing.'

'Criminal!' my mom gasped. 'A criminal family?'

Nick reached out and touched me lightly on the shoulder. 'I'm sure you're right, Jack. But it may be worth asking him once you get to Las Vegas. Just to make sure everything's as it should be . . . you know . . . legitimate.' He paused. 'If you know what I mean, son?'

'Sure, I'll do that,' I said, more to reassure my mom, who looked on the point of tears, than to take my stepfather too seriously.

Nick, aware of his wife, added, 'You can always turn them down if you're not comfortable and come back here.'

'Yup, of course.' I didn't tell them that, whatever happened, I wasn't going to spend the rest of my life in a jazz backwater like Toronto, wondering if I could have made it as a musician out in the big wide world. Unless I proved to be a complete musical disaster, I was going to try my luck in New York, if Las Vegas wasn't for me.

'Oh, but what if it's true?' my mom asked.

I gave her a quick hug. 'Mom, Lenny Giancana is about as decent a human being as you'll ever find.' Then, wanting to change the subject, I said, 'You have the best husband any woman could possibly have. And, Nick, you do know that you're greatly loved, don't you?' I guess I was trying to say that they had each other and that my leaving wasn't the end of the world.

'Ah, *hrrrumph* . . . yes,' he admitted, clearing his throat, lest he be caught sounding sentimental. 'And, Jack,' he said, 'it feels very good to be loved by your mother.'

'Tell you what,' I said brightly, 'I'll sleep on the Las Vegas thing and we'll talk again in the morning. What say, eh?'

My mother was silent for a moment; then she said, haltingly, 'No, Jack, you've already made up your mind.' She looked up at me, brushed the tears from her eyes and sniffed. 'Whatever happens, remember that I love you, dear.'

I felt a sudden childish impulse to cry. When I was growing up she had given me every ounce of everything she had to give, everything! Now, in the end, I had disappointed her. I could feel a tear running down my cheek. But, as always, she was correct. I'd made up my mind.

I booked a person-to-person phone call to Lenny in Las Vegas. When he answered, I simply said, 'Got any sunshine to spare?'

'Hey, Jack, how ya bin, buddy? Here the goddamn moon shines hotter than the sun in Toronto!'

I wasted no time on pleasantries. 'Thanks for the invitation to join you, Lenny – I accept.'

'Hey, that's great, man!'

'Only one condition.'

'What, buddy . . . anything.'

I swallowed hard. 'A baby grand . . . a Steinway.'

'You got it, kid. What colour you want?'

I laughed. 'It doesn't matter; black, I suppose.' Then, thinking of Joe's powder-blue piano, I said, 'Blue; pale blue, maybe? But I'll leave it to you.'

'Blue? That the colour of fucking ice! Cold! Freeze yer balls off!'

'It doesn't really matter, Lenny. I'll leave it to you, buddy,' I repeated. It was good to hear Lenny's familiar voice down the telephone line.

'Lissen, Jack, I'm gonna send ya the tickets for the train, first class all the way, nothin' too good for my pal . . .'

'Whoa there, Lenny; no, no, buddy, I can pay my own way.'

'Save it for yer stake, Jack, we ain't broke.'

'No, *really*, I'd prefer it that way.'

'Hey, I like that! Ya always was ya own man, Jack. Real cool. Can't never tell what yer thinkin' . . . What ya next move gonna be.'

It was a nice compliment coming from a very good poker player, but I wanted an out if Las Vegas didn't suit me. I could afford the fare even if it meant dipping into my stake money. And it meant I wasn't beholden. As Joe would say, 'Jazzboy, when you owe nobody nothing, losing be only a small hes-i-tation on the path to winning; a mistake, just a hiccup to success.'

CHAPTER FOURTEEN

THE TRIP TOOK FOUR days and three separate railway companies, but at last I arrived in Las Vegas on the last day of May 1946, a Friday, just before lunch.

The train station was slap-bang in the centre of Las Vegas. Lugging my old army kitbag, I'd stepped from my carriage and worked my way across the crowded platform and through the station hall packed with people; some, like myself, intent on leaving, attempting to avoid others hurrying to get onto the train, and seemingly very little love lost between the opposing forces. I finally stepped out into the blinding sunshine and momentarily glimpsed what seemed to be a parking lot across from the station entrance before being forced to close my eyes against the fierce metallic glare of the sun bouncing off the parked automobiles.

My very first impression of Las Vegas had been the streamlined modern station, but once my eyes adjusted to the glare, I realised I'd arrived in a brassy town of transients and people out to try their luck. Somewhere unseen a band played 'The Yellow Rose of Texas', perhaps because some Texan dignitary or millionaire gambler was arriving.

I'd sent Lenny a telegram with my arrival details but he hadn't responded and I figured I'd need to take a cab to the El Marinero. But, squinting around for a cab stand, I saw a green limousine parked directly to my right under a sign that clearly announced: No Parking. It was the biggest automobile I had ever seen, gleaming in the bright sunshine and obviously brand-new. It seemed to announce to the world that the good old USA was back in business. Standing, with one hand holding the trunk open, was Lenny. He saw me at the same moment and yelled, 'Hiya, Jack! How ya doin', buddy?' I grinned and gave him a wave. 'Come throw ya kit in the back and get the fuck in,' he said as I approached. 'Too goddamned hot and anyhow I ain't supposed to be parked here!'

Nothing had changed. It wasn't possible for Lenny Giancana to construct a sentence in male company without a liberal scattering of expletives. I hefted my kitbag into the trunk of the four-door sedan and noticed the soft purr of the engine. The car was polished to within an inch of its life and designed to make a statement about its owner, who was grinning back at me. He still had a marines-style haircut and was wearing cream slacks and a hibiscus-patterned Hawaiian shirt, a tuft of black hair showing at the open neck. His shoes were black and white patent leather. We were both big men; I was now six foot two and Lenny was perhaps an inch or so shorter but broader across the shoulders. It had been less than a year since I'd seen him and he was already beginning to thicken around the waist. He gave me a bear hug and, when we'd pulled apart, he must have been conscious of his softer gut against my own because he patted it and laughed. 'Too much pasta.'

I had broken into a sweat just crossing the road and the first thing I noticed upon entering that light green monster of a car was the blast of cold air that smacked into me. 'Christ, Lenny, you got a fridge in here!' I called out.

Lenny walked around the front of the Caddie and opened the door. 'Air-con, new invention; only Cadillac and Packard got it for now,' he said, hopping behind the wheel. 'Jack, I thought maybe I'd take you down Highway 91 first. I wanna show you two new construction sites, the Flamingo and the Firebird. The Firebird's where we gonna build you the best piano bar in America, buddy.'

We pulled away from the station precinct and I indicated the air-conditioning. It was not only blasting us with cold air but making conversation at a normal level plainly impossible. 'Thanks, Lenny, but if you don't turn that thing down I'm going to die of pneumonia,' I shouted.

Lenny pulled over, climbed into the back seat and fiddled with something until the roar of the air-conditioning faded. 'Essential as pussy, buddy. Can't go nowheres widout air-con. Summers are hunnerd degrees most days here. This is the middle of the fucking desert.' He pointed through the windscreen to the shiny green bonnet. 'Leave her outside . . . fry an egg on that by nine o'clock in the morning.'

'Nice car.'

'Yeah, chartreuse – good thing I didn't buy a black one, eh? Heat suppose to bounce off chartreuse; that the idea, anyhow. Cadillac, they bringing out a new range next year and I got me a convertible on order. They got a waiting list long as Highway 91.' He laughed. 'I told the car dealer I wanted him to jump me up the list or maybe I'd have to organise a visit from one or two of my Chicago friends. He looks at me and salutes two fingers and says, 'Right away, sir. I'll call the head of General Motors tomorrow and tell him to watch out for suspicious characters.'

I laughed, not quite sure what he was telling me. Was it his way of saying he was Mafia? I decided to let it go for the meantime and asked instead, 'Why a convertible? You just said it's a hundred degrees out there.'

'Fall, the nights cool down some.'

'You mean you're ordering a convertible to use at night?'

'Jack, this Las Vegas, man! Daytime ain't nuttin'. That's when decent folk sleep. Nights are the day here, everything lit up.' He grinned. 'It's show time for the Family business when the casino gets busy; it also pussy pick-up time, so that's Cadillac convertible time!'

'Lenny, sorry to interrupt, but can we stop right there. "The Family" – you've mentioned it a few times, on the phone to Canada and in your original letter. I stopped off in New York on the way and went to the public library and looked up the newspaper files for the *Chicago*

Tribune. Your family, who are they exactly? Because various Giancanas and a guy named Tony Accardo seemed to feature in the news a fair bit.' I was putting it mildly; the Giancana 'Family', according to the newspapers, were big-time Mafiosi.

Lenny pushed himself back in his seat, driving with his arms fully extended. He seemed to be thinking, then finally said, 'You mean, am I a gangster?'

'Well, yes. Anything I should know about? I only ask because I don't want to settle in Las Vegas and get a nasty surprise.'

'Fair enough, buddy. Glad you asked. Lemme set it out for you.' He gripped the wheel and straightened in his seat. 'We'll have this conversation and I tell you everything you wanna know; then, if you ain't happy, no hard feelings, you can be on the next train tonight, okay?'

I nodded. 'Sure.'

'Just one thing before I start. It's a conversation we *never* had. If you're asked, you know nuttin'. You're just the guy who plays piano. Understand?'

'Sure, Lenny,' I replied, somewhat hurt that he felt he needed to explain that.

We'd turned onto the highway. 'Now, first I'm gonna show you the Flamingo, or what's gonna be the Flamingo some day; then we'll go see the construction site of the Firebird; then I'll take you home to the El Marinero, where I hope you gonna play piano till we got the Firebird finished in six months, tops.' He glanced at me and grinned. 'That's of course if you decide to stay after this talk. Jack, buddy, I'd trust you wid my life. But not staying *schtum* on this thing is more than your life is worth, mine too.'

'I got the idea in one, Lenny,' I said.

He nodded and continued. 'I don't deny some of them – my cousins, uncles – they did some bad things, still do – Chicago, New York, LA – but not here in Las Vegas. Sure, my name is Giancana, an' I ain't ashamed a that. I'm a US marine, you know that, one year college, then the war. Interfered wid my education. I coulda took a degree maybe.

Yessir, master sergeant, US Embassy, London, England – I'm a cleanskin just like you, Jack. The US marines, they don't accept criminals. Also, the state of Nevada is controlled by Mormons. Nevada gaming laws don't permit illegitimate business or operators wid a criminal record.'

'So, the casinos are legit?'

Lenny hesitated then said, 'Yeah, one hunnerd per cent . . . on the surface. That's all that counts wid the Mormons. Jesus, Jack, the business we got here, the business we *gonna* have wid the Firebird, you won't believe how good it's gonna be. Lemme put it this way, it's so good we can afford to be legit but not to be stoopid, like the kike wid his head up his ass who's building the Flamingo.'

'The kike?'

'Benjamin "Bugsy" Siegel! He's a big-time gangster, works outa LA for the New York syndicate. Meyer Lansky give him the job of looking after their New York interests when they bought into the project with Billy Wilkerson. Problem is the stupid kike got himself some big ideas of his own. But when it come to construction he couldn't organise himself outa a shithouse wid no door.' He pointed up ahead. 'It's coming up soon. We'll stop and have a look, see for yourself the future of Las Vegas. Ha, ha, if Benny Siegel ever gonna get it finished. Supposed to be by Christmas, that's the big joke around this town. He already way behind schedule and way over budget. This may be the biggest building fuck-up in Las Vegas history.'

'Lenny, you're losing me. Meyer Lansky, Billy Wilkerson . . . ?'

'Meyer Lansky, the accountant of the New York syndicate. They don't have no godfather like us. He the guy calls the shots,' Lenny explained. 'Now, Billy Wilkerson also from LA, owns the *Hollywood Reporter*, nightclubs, some other things. The Flamingo his personal project, but he gone and got himself into financial trouble and Meyer Lansky bought a controlling share for one mill. That's what it's supposed to cost in the first place, but now it's already way, way, more wid Mr Big Ideas Bugsy Siegel in control.'

We'd pulled off the road in front of a huge building site.

'See, no fence.' Lenny pointed out.

'Should there be one?'

'Jesus, Jack, c'mon! This a fucking building site! Wid building material so short it's a licence to take whatever ya want. Should be a fence, guards at the gate, dogs patrolling the perimeter, the whole fuckin' shebang! The joke around town is that the builders Bugsy Siegel hires during the day come back at night and steal the material, then sell it back to him the next morning. Dumb fuck don't realise it's happening. Also, like I say, he got some very grand ideas and keeps changing his mind, tearing down, adding stuff, going bigger. We using the same tiling company for the Firebird and the foreman tell us the kike has changed the colours of the tiles four times. You know how many hunnerd bathrooms they got? That's just one example.'

'So, is he going to run the Flamingo?'

'No, worse luck. He's a gangster. You have to have a cleanskin up front. That's all the Mormons worry about.'

'So, who is going to run it?'

'You mean day to day? Christ knows, they haven't said.'

'I take it you'll be running the Firebird?'

'Yeah . . .' He paused. 'Well, Mrs Fuller, really. I'm front of house.' Lenny gave a self-deprecating laugh. '*Mr Meet 'n' Greet Lemme Show You Your Suite*. That's me. I'm doing the same now at the El Marinero, where she's showing me the ropes. Then we both move over to the Firebird when it opens.'

'I take it this Mrs Fuller is a good operator?'

'Jesus, Jack, she's the best. When we bought the El Marinero, beginning of the war, it was a heap of shit, nothing but a few old-fashioned slots and faded baize tables. They say the roulette wheel squeaked. It was just another sawdust casino goin' nowhere fast. Rooms like any hotel, bathrooms down the hall. Now it's rated with the El Cortez the most profitable small casino in Las Vegas. She gotta get the credit for that when she invented the GAWP Bar.'

'The what?'

'G-A-W-P.' Lenny spelled it out. 'It stands for the Girlfriends And Wives Piano Bar, but that's our name for it. Official name is The Princess. Baby grand, snazzy decor. It's where you'll be until we move to the Firebird.'

I shrugged, still not understanding. 'So, what's so special about this piano bar?'

'Well, the GAWP Bar isn't just any old piano bar, buddy; it's why the El Marinero is the best sawdust casino in town and why we finally decided to build the Firebird.'

I must have looked as confused as I felt.

'It was Mrs Fuller started it, had the idea. Lemme explain. When the Family bought the El Marinero just after the Japs bombed Pearl Harbor we had ourselves a vision. America at war and military and air force bases planned for Nevada. It's only natural we gonna attract airmen and soldiers from the bases and camps coming into Las Vegas for R&R. A brand-new population of single guys. So, what they gonna do when they come into town?'

I shrugged.

'They gonna go looking for some pussy, right?'

I nod. 'Sure.'

'Wrong! Fucking Mormons. No girls, no whores in the entire state, according to them; no entertainment 'cept gambling, and the real gamblers among them are few and far between, and those who blow a few bucks on the slots are spread among all the Glitter Gulch casinos. We got nothing special goin' for us. We just one outa lotsa sawdust casinos. Airmen, soldiers, they moving, comin' and goin' . . . there's a word for it . . .'

'Itinerant?'

'Yeah. So, they don't stick around for long. On top of that we paid too much for the El Marinero and we'd hired this fancy dame from the East Coast at great expense.'

'Mrs Fuller?'

'Yeah, she's working at the Waldorf-Astoria in New York at that time, one of them assistant managers, and we're hoping she'll give us a touch of class. But the casino's falling apart. We're losing dough hand over fist. So, Bridgett goes to Chicago wid a business proposition. Tony Accardo, he the godfather, he ain't accustomed to no dame comin' up wid a plan, even a dame with nice manners and a fancy East Coast accent. She says to him, "Mr Accardo, forget the servicemen, go for the high rollers." She says she's made a list, while she's at the Waldorf-Astoria.' Lenny glanced at me. 'Understand, this a lady who likes making lists. So, this list is of all the rich people who stayed in the Waldorf-Astoria when she was working there. She's got their home addresses, every goddamned one. She says she wants to write, invite them to a complimentary holiday in Nevada, all expenses paid 'cept their airfares. Wives or girlfriends to come along and get a poolside tan in the middle of winter. She says, wid a war on, the rich can't go no more to Europe – Monte Carlo, French Riviera, Paris – so they lookin' for a holiday nearer to home. Some of the men she reckon got potential as high rollers if they got the opportunity here in America.'

Lenny was away, his face lighting up as he told me the story of this Mrs Fuller. I began to wonder if he felt more for her than he was letting on.

'But that's not all. She says he gotta upgrade the El Marinero's rooms – all with their own bathrooms, then put in a swimmin' pool and restaurants, and a cocktail bar with a piano and different pianists from Hollywood every month!

'Accardo don't believe his fucking ears. In his whole goddamned life he never heard a plan so stoopid. Ferfucksakes, the US at war wid the Japs, this ain't no time for complimentary holidays, luxury suites in a two-bit gambling town middle of the fuckin' desert that suppose to attract the rich just in case some of them want to – perhaps, who the fuck knows? – gamble!

'So, naturally he thinks this fancy dame gotta be off her fuckin' rocker. So, he tells her to go screw herself, or words to that effect, and when her contract comes up in six months some other casino gonna have to employ her because it ain't gonna be the El Marinero.'

'So what happened?' I asked, intrigued. I was becoming slightly concerned that Mrs Fuller, who was likely to be my boss, might be a bit unreliable.

Lenny continued. 'Well, she don't sulk none, she ain't that type. It so happens that Benjamin 'Bugsy' Siegel is visiting the El Cortez, where the New York syndicate got an investment. This is long before they decide to build the Flamingo. They, the El Cortez, they doin' okay, they been in the biz a long time and they got a local client base and they also gettin' their share of the servicemen as well. Compared to us they doin' great. So, Mrs Fuller goes to see him. I guess she's got nuttin' to lose. She knows he's a gangster and she thinks maybe his New York Mob could be interested in her ideas.'

Lenny paused. 'Now, what you gotta understand about Bugsy Siegel, he looks like a Hollywood movie star, and he loves women. His regular girlfriend is an actress, Virginia Hill. She likes to gamble, so that's why they come to Las Vegas. But this time she ain't wid him, an' Bugsy Siegel ain't exactly the faithful type. He takes one look and then it's, "What can I do for you, Mrs Fuller?"'

'Oh, so Mrs Fuller's young and good looking?' I asked, surprised.

Lenny, impatient to continue, replied, 'You better believe it, Jack, she's a knockout. Then what happened I cain't say wid my hand on the Bible, buddy, but she's pretty smart and a girl's gotta do what a girl's gotta do. I mean, you don't gotta be Albert Einstein. Anyhow, she's got nothing to lose, has she?' Lenny paused for a moment. 'Okay, so she uses her natural advantage, and he, well, he's gonna tell her it's a great idea, ain't he? That he definitely wants it for the El Cortez. Maybe he even promises he gonna phone Meyer Lansky.' Lenny laughed uproariously. 'In the meantime, will she be so kind as to remove her pants, lift her skirt, then bend over and touch her toes.'

I laughed at the picture Lenny had painted. 'It's as good a guess as any. I wonder if she followed through?'

'Frankly, buddy, I don't think so. She's too smart to go wid Bugsy Siegel, 'specially knowing Virginia Hill is his girlfriend. Virginia, she's a tough broad. She's also a *bona fide* member of the Mob. Virginia Hill is white trash from Alabama and Mrs Fuller is a classy lady from New York. It ain't gonna happen wid a gangster like Bugsy Siegel.'

'So, do you know what *really* happened?' I asked.

'Now, Mrs Fuller goes back and tells Accardo the Jews are definitely interested in the idea for the El Cortez and she wants to resign pronto. Accardo don't know if it's all bluff, but if her idea works wid the Jews, he's gonna look like a fuckin' idjit! So, he agrees to let Bridgett go ahead. Later he claims he's got some spare cash he gotta use in a hurry because the IRS been sniffin' round asking questions.'

Lenny went on about the renovation of the casino, and my concentration lapsed as I gazed around me, until he mentioned a Mrs Anna-Lucia Hermes, the mayor's wife.

'So, will I be answering to Mrs Hermes, too?' I said. It sounded as if I'd come to the wrong place if I wanted to avoid women controlling my life.

'You ain't listnin', Jack. Bridgett – Mrs Fuller – discovers the mayor's wife is an interior decorator. Worked in Hollywood, so she engages her to do the work.'

I nodded, relieved that the number of females I'd have to answer to wasn't increasing.

'Like I said, Jack, Mrs Fuller ain't stoopid and having city hall on side is very useful, especially when we do the inside of the Firebird. And there's other stuff . . . it's a connection we don't wanna lose.'

He looked uncomfortable, so I changed the subject. 'You haven't mentioned the GAWP Bar yet.'

'Oh yeah, of course. Well, she uses her list and the rich start to come. First just a few husbands with their wives or rich guys with their girlfriends, and Bridgett's right. Some – in fact, most – like to gamble. What you gotta unnerstan' about the respectable rich and even the not so respectable, the men all know each other. Word gets around. Nothing the rich like better than a classy holiday in the sun, "wid compliments".'

Lenny paused. 'But that ain't the secret of Bridgett's success. Most of the wives and girlfriends don't gamble and they don't know each other. Texas don't know Alabama, don't know New York State, don't know Nebraska, don't know Washington State, if you get what I mean. That's how come the GAWP Bar's such a great idea. Every night the rich dames get together for cocktails and to listen to the piano player. But that ain't the real attraction. The dames like to get to know each other, to gossip, exchange addresses, make friends, just like their menfolk. The GAWP Bar is like this exclusive club where the rich dames come to dish the dirt. Ain't nothing like it in America ever. Mrs Fuller's got the class to go wid it and she knows how to mix 'n' fix. The dames love her – she's one of them. They tell her everything. She keeps her lists and soon she knows more about the rich 'n' famous than anybody in America. But she's discreet, they know she won't blab – see no evil, hear no evil and keep your trap shut, that's her.

'Every year she invites them back to the El Marinero. Not the husbands – the wives and girlfriends.' Lenny paused and raised his eyebrows. 'Ain't no guy gonna gamble at any other casino in Las Vegas. His wife, girlfriend, she ain't gonna let him go no place else now she's a faithful member of the GAWP Bar. Bridgett runs the best club, the classiest venue in town. Soon it ain't just winter, the El Marinero is full most all year round. Take it from me, Mrs Fuller is the real deal.'

'So, with such a success on your hands, why the Firebird?'

Lenny gave me a foolish half grin. 'Well, yeah, it's Mrs Fuller again. Come, lemme show you the future of gambling in Las Vegas.'

'You mean it's not the Flamingo?'

He swung the car around and we moved away smoothly. 'Yeah, of course, whenever it's finished, but she believe there's room for more. She point out we cain't accommodate all the high rollers and dames who wanna come to the El Marinero. She says sawdust casinos, they a thing of the past. The war is over; now we should build a casino with a hunnerd rooms, all *en suite*, with three, maybe four luxury penthouses as well. Her idea is we make a luxury resort for the rich *only*. Everything "comped": wives, girlfriends get to use all the amenities so long as their guys spend big at the tables. She says it's possible to attract three times the number of patrons we got already. Post-war America gonna boom.'

'So, this time they listen, right?'

Lenny grinned and shook his head. 'Mafiosi don't listen to dames, Jack. What does a dumb broad know, anyhow? They long since forgot it was her idea about the rich high rollers and the GAWP Bar. Besides, Accardo took the credit for the idea of investing money so it don't go to the taxation. He says the El Marinero suits us just fine; he don't agree Las Vegas and gambling gonna be the future, an opportunity for the Mobsters to turn legitimate. We already got what we want, a small casino the feds don't even notice. He can skim a bit off the top and launder money. Far as he concerned, it the perfect arrangement. Why change?'

'Skim? Launder? You're losing me, Lenny.'

'Yeah, I forgot, you don't know the business. "Skim" means we take maybe ten per cent of the winnings in cash before we declare the profit to the state. Launder is when you bring in dirty money from outa town and you put it through the casino as your cash float, so it come out the other side washed clean. For any godfather, that's the main benefit of a casino. Now Mrs Fuller wants to build something bigger, a luxury resort.'

I was gazing out at the brilliant blue desert sky, as Lenny continued. He'd always been a good talker, and clearly this town was his passion.

'Like I said, Chicago ain't convinced. Accardo is certain the Jews gonna fuck up big time wid building the Flamingo, and he could be right. The building, the site, it ain't goin' good, they over deadline, over budget. Rumour says Bugsy Siegel's stealing from his own Mob, that he's got two-and-a-half million bucks of New York's money in a Swiss bank account in the name of Virginia Hill.'

'Lenny, why are you telling me all this? You've hired me to play the piano!'

'Jack, I know you've come a long way – Canada, then near across America. You must be beat, man, but if you gonna stay in Las Vegas, you should unnerstan' who you working for. Things ain't never what they seem to be here. Everything is fine, so long as everybody mind their own business. Everything on the surface legit, but unnerneath? Unnerstan' we still gangsters. Every casino got a cleanskin like me runnin' the joint. Some investors ain't even Mobsters, they just businesspeople got themselves a good investment. Mafiosi don't always own the majority shares neither. They like to hide behind legitimate business investors. But the Mobs own the skim and they got the money-laundering facility, also some nice legitimate profits. They run the gambling and the strong-arm bad-debt collecting.' Lenny glanced at me. 'Jack, step on the wrong toes in this town and suddenly you gonna disappear.'

'Well, thanks for the warning, Lenny.' Had I known all this when he offered me a job, if I'd have accepted. But now, under this brilliant sky, I felt like a new man, and Lenny had trusted me enough to be honest. I decided to trust him in return. 'I guess I'll be working for gangsters, right?'

Lenny didn't answer directly. 'People are the same everywhere. They just want to have a good time, relax a little. For ten years during prohibition the Sicilians and the Jews were where the action was. Everyone had a personal bootlegger – judges, doctors, big businessmen – they all buying their liquor from us. Do ya think those cocksucker senators and congressmen in Washington stopped drinkin' for ten years? Or whoring? Course they fuckin' didn't. Ferchrissakes, life, liberty and the pursuit of happiness, ain't that what America is all about? Check the goddamn Declaration of Independence! We give them what they want and that's why they tolerate us. That's what we do, except here it's all legal.'

'What about prostitution?' I asked, thinking of the twins. 'Is that legal here?'

'Not right here in Las Vegas, but near enough. It's just a hop, skip 'n' jump to the county line.' He laughed. 'On the other hand, one of your patrons picks himself up a nice-looking gal in your piano bar, she ain't gonna tell him it ain't legal and to keep his money in his wallet to buy his wife roses. Besides, the local cops know the drill. The Mormon pricks that run everything here depend on us for the majority of their state taxes. They ain't stoopid, they don't do in-depth investigation. This is American apple-pie land. Everything's legit and we ain't gonna spoil that none, no sirree, this is a crime-free city and everyone gonna see it stay that way – the I-talians, the New York Jews, the Irish, all of us.'

'What about drugs? I've read it's the new street crime in America.'

'Not so new, Jack. But that's nigger stuff. The Mafiosi don't run drugs; no way, man! That stuff is poison. The niggers can sell it to each other, who fucking cares?'

I thought of Joe and the others in the band. The term 'nigger' was so unjust. My old man was a vicious drunk and Joe was the best man I had ever known. But this didn't seem to be the time to take Lenny to task about such a common, cruel, unthinking and stupid American term.

'I don't tolerate staff using here at the casino, not even the kitchen and general staff.' He paused and glanced at me. 'Marijuana, weed; you not one of them musicians who uses that shit are ya, Jack?'

'Lenny, I don't even drink!'

'The last thing we want around the hotels and casinos is police looking for drugs. It's the one thing the Mormons won't tolerate. If I find any staff using here, they're out on their sweet ass.'

'Yeah, well, thanks, you've kind of answered all my questions and much more, but I'm curious to know if I'll be working for you or Mrs Fuller.'

'Bridgett Fuller runs GAWP, so you'll be working for her, Jack.'

'So, I guess she'll teach me the ways of the casino?'

Lenny laughed. 'Sure, but I'll be there also.'

'And I'll take my instructions from her?'

'Yeah.'

'Okay, then let's go meet her. Lenny, I'm grateful for the advice.'

'Jack, we buddies, I want you to come and work wid us. I think you gonna enjoy it. But you right, you gotta see Mrs Fuller and she gotta see you.' Lenny paused. 'Sometimes these things, they don't work out.'

'Oh, is there something I should know? Something you haven't told me?'

'Jack, you were never easy to bullshit. GAWP, that's her bag, that's her strength wid Chicago, she got complete control of that aspect and it the main reason why we building the Firebird, so . . .' he hesitated, a sheepish grin on his face, 'it only natural she want to decide who works for her, who gonna play in the new piano bar.'

'Oh . . . I see. So, it's not a done deal?' I'd come a long way on the strength of Lenny's letter and a single phone call. Now it seemed that the job was only mine if Mrs Fuller agreed. 'Couldn't you have told me this on the phone, buddy?'

Lenny shrugged expressively. 'Jack, I know you two gonna hit it off. But she got six piano players from LA and they take turns, two weeks each, to play in the GAWP Bar. They all old guys, left over from the silent movies. In my opinion the Firebird gonna need new blood, young guy like you.' Lenny smiled. 'You the best, Jack. I told her she ain't heard nothing yet.'

'But, naturally, she's not prepared to take your word for it?' Before Lenny could react, I added, 'Well, that's hardly surprising. I'm a Canadian, she's never heard of me. Why didn't you arrange for a record?'

'Hey, I never thought of that!' Then, almost as quickly, he added, 'But understand, Jack, the GAWP Bar ain't just good music, it's also personality. The rich broads, they gotta like you. There's an I-talian word, *simpatico* . . .'

'Yeah, I know what it means.'

'Well then, you cain't send no personality rating on no gramophone record.'

I was beginning to see why Lenny had spent all this time building up Mrs Fuller. 'So, it's really not up to you at all?'

Lenny frowned. 'Jack, gimme a break, will ya? I'm front of house. What do I know about running a casino, eh? When the Firebird comes on stream, if the authorities come askin' questions I supposed to own the joint. I got some influence, sure.' He tapped the rim of the steering wheel. 'Mrs Fuller wants to rehearse the new piano player at the El Marinero for the next six months, before we open on The Strip. She wants a young guy wid all-round musical talent who'll be popular with the high-roller broads.' He grinned. 'So, I told her I knew just the man.'

'Thanks, Lenny.'

'Hey, man, no harm done. If it don't work out, you have yourself a nice vacation while you here, compliments of us; free room, chow, give you a chance to look around, check out the scene. If you not happy, we send you back to freeze your butt off in Toronto. Or you stay in America, get yourself another piano job in some jazz joint. I got you a Musicians Union card and, believe me, that ain't easy. We don't control that union, that's another Mob. Somebody hadda lean on somebody.'

I was silent for a while. Despite being somewhat piqued, I knew Lenny was right. I'd always wanted to work in America and I was more than happy to have a reason to leave Toronto. After all, Las Vegas was just another form of scuffing, another Moose Jaw with legal gambling, poker on tap and a chance to see if I was good enough to make it as a jazz piano player in America. That was pretty much all I'd ever wished for.

'Lenny, thanks for levelling with me. I'll audition for Mrs Fuller and if she doesn't like my playing, no hard feelings. If she does, then I'll play a week for her GAWP Bar patrons, to see if they take to me. If they don't, then I'll move right along. Maybe chance my hand in LA or New York. No, you don't need to pay my way. I've got enough money.' I grinned. 'Or maybe I'll stick around and see if I can sit in on a few poker games and do some scuffing someplace else in town.'

Lenny smiled. 'Hey hey, Jack, you was always your own man. I appreciate what you just said. If Bridgett likes you, then you spend the next six months working up a great routine for her new and improved GAWP Bar at the Firebird. Mrs Fuller, she smart, she on the ball, but you right, buddy, she don't know you. She's only got my word. She want to be sure you the right person for the Firebird.'

'Lenny, I understand. Only one thing . . .'

'Yeah, what is it, Jack?'

'If it doesn't work out, may I keep the Musicians Union card?'

Lenny laughed, clearly relieved that I hadn't made a fuss. 'It the least

I can do, Jack. I apologise for bringin' you all this way for an audition; it ain't dignified, but I know Mrs Fuller, she gonna like you. We gonna build the best new piano bar in America, just for you, man. We already got you your baby grand Steinway. Nobody else played it yet 'cept the Latino guy who tuned it.'

Lenny slowed down, and pulled off the road and stopped the Cadillac in front of a high fence topped with barbed wire, surrounding a block of flat land that seemed to stretch away into the desert. There were workmen everywhere and a buzz and rumble of machines – what you'd call a busy site. It was by no means as large as the Flamingo site, but Lenny gazed at it proudly and announced, 'Well, buddy, here it is, the Firebird!'

Over the noise of the cement mixers and jackhammers, I could hear dogs barking. Lenny pointed to a large fenced-off area some way within the complex, piled high with building materials. 'See the dogs, Jack?'

Six German shepherd dogs were pacing restlessly around the perimeter and I could see a security man on duty at the gate.

'You reckon it will be finished by December, Lenny?' I asked doubtfully.

'Yeah, the builders seem confident. These guys were building army bases during the war and they know their shit from Shinola. Our guys know all about how to run a site. We reckon by the time they get the Flamingo finished, we'll be open.'

'Well, if you run short of anything, you'll know where to get it. The Benjamin Siegel Building Supply Company.'

Lenny grinned. 'Ya know, Jack, I call him a kike, a yid, a fucking Jew incompetent, whatever, but Mrs Fuller still calls him a true visionary. I hope she's right.'

'You don't think, you know, with Bugsy Siegel's mess down the road, that you're taking a chance building out here on the highway?'

'Good question, buddy. The godfather agree wid you, Jack. He wanna keep it small, he don't wanna move from Glitter Gulch. The most he wanna do is, say, buy the property next door, add a few more suites, timber construction, cheap, easy.'

'So?'

Lenny laughed, then switched on the ignition and reversed onto the highway. 'Mrs Fuller don't like that idea. She tells Tony Accardo the Jew got vision, The Strip is where it all gonna happen in the future.'

'So, you – I mean, the boss in Chicago – went along with her?' I said, somewhat surprised.

Lenny gave a snort. 'Went along? No way, buddy!'

'So, what happened?'

Lenny thought for a moment. 'I cain't say I rightly know, buddy. Maybe she got somethin' on the boss, or maybe the Family, or maybe she sweet-talked him.'

'I'm intrigued. What do *you* think?'

'Intrigued, what that mean?'

'Well, curious.'

'It musta bin somethin' big because Tony Accardo rang me from Chicago. "Don't you let nuttin' happen to Mrs Fuller," he says. *Mrs Fuller!* That ain't like him. Usually he says, "That fuckin' bitch" or just "the bitch", and I suppose to know who he mean.' Lenny glanced quickly at me. 'So, I says to him, "Hey, Godfather, I thought you ain't happy wid the idea the Firebird in the first place and out on The Strip the second." Then he say, "Lenny, she got the goods on us. Time being we gotta go along wid her . . . but unnerstan', I ain't happy."'

'And that's all he said?'

'Yeah, Jack, just about. He say one more time I gotta keep her happy, an' the rest none my business. *Capisce?* That mean "unnerstan'" in I-talian.'

We'd arrived in downtown Las Vegas and Lenny turned the Cadillac into Fremont Street East. Moments later we slowed and turned into a gravelled driveway. I confess my first impressions were disappointing. The El Marinero casino was built in what is generally referred to as ranch-style: white stucco plaster over a timber frame with terracotta roof trim, its architectural antecedents almost certainly Spanish Mission. It was anything but imposing; small, even, by Canadian hotel standards, and from the outside it didn't appear to have any of the pizzazz I'd anticipated.

My heart sank, and I feared that, despite the talk about future luxury casinos on The Strip, Las Vegas might be the American version of Moose Jaw. I resolved on the spot that if I was rejected by Mrs Fuller or her GAWP ladies, I'd move out of Las Vegas and try my luck in LA or New York. Maybe at night, with the neon blazing in Glitter Gulch, it might improve, but by day this area looked like a dump. One Moose Jaw is more than enough for any musical career.

Lenny eased the big car to a halt and the doorman rushed to open the Cadillac's door. Lenny stayed him with his hand and turned to me. 'Jack, buddy, I'm glad you had the balls to front up to me about the Mob here in Las Vegas. Most people, they hear mention of the Mafia or the Family and they act real careful.' He slapped me on the shoulder. 'We're buddies, real buddies, brothers in arms. That's something special and don't never forget it. Las Vegas is something else and it's gonna work out just fine if we stick together. You have a problem, you come direct to me, you hear? Buddy, I ain't gonna let you down.'

'That is if Mrs Fuller and her ladies like me,' I said with a laugh.

Lenny didn't reply but said instead, 'Lemme take you to meet Mrs Fuller.' He glanced at his watch. 'Jesus, I'm late for a meeting wid Manny "Asshole" de Costa – my lawyer – and the Nevada Gaming Commission.'

I grinned. 'How did he get his middle name?'

Lenny laughed. 'He's a mean bastard, does the dirty work for the godfather. Regular asshole, that's all.'

He beckoned to the now-hovering flunkeys and they came over to unload the car. For the few steps across the hotel driveway the heat felt like a slap in the face; then, as we entered the hotel, the cold blast of air-conditioning almost knocked me over. Lenny stopped, as if he'd suddenly remembered something. 'Jack, do you remember Sammy Schischka, my cousin?'

'Sure, nice guy, played cards with him at the American air-force base at Gatwick airfield in England. You could say he introduced us. Remember he gave me your name when I left for London?' I had developed the poker player's instinct of never forgetting the technique and habits of someone with whom I had played three or four times, no matter how long it had been since the last game. Sammy Schischka was ticketed in my mind as a born loser, at least at poker.

'That's right, of course. Well, he's here, Jack. But he's changed a lot. The air force gave him a really hard time.'

'What? Wounded?' I asked as we crossed the lobby.

Before he could answer, a tall, attractive brunette appeared. Not really beautiful or even pretty, she was still a knockout, with a strong, intelligent face, wide, generous mouth and astonishing eyes. She also had long legs and a figure that I knew was going to feature in my dreams for a very long time. This was obviously Mrs Fuller. I judged her to be in her late twenties, already too old for me, and married into the bargain, yet my heart was pounding.

'Tell ya about Sammy later,' Lenny muttered as an aside, then smiled. 'Lemme introduce you to Bridgett, Jack.'

To my surprise, Bridgett Fuller extended her hand without smiling, her striking green eyes seeming to take me in at a single glance. Perhaps the stern expression indicated she didn't like what she saw. I'd last changed my clothes in New York and I guess I was pretty scruffy, if not somewhat on the nose. Or, as I had learned to say while in England, I guess I ponged a bit. 'Welcome to the El Marinero, Mr Spayd.'

I took her hand and smiled. 'Thank you, ma'am. Please, call me Jack.'

I've always been sceptical about love at first sight, perhaps because of my parents' awful marriage, and Lenny had told me enough about Mrs Fuller to make me cautious. Even so, I'd felt a charge go through me at her touch. It wasn't just lust, or sex, it was a reaction to the whole of her. Yet, I knew almost nothing about her. Patently, my reaction was ridiculous, and I hoped she hadn't noticed it. I forced my voice to sound cordial and friendly, but nothing more.

Bridgett Fuller pressed her lips together, then said, 'Thank you, that is most kind but, if you don't mind, I would prefer to call you Mr Spayd.'

'Oh! Yes, of course,' I replied, my face burning. *Shit! Over-eager. Bad start.*

'It makes things so much easier,' she said.

Lenny stood by, looking somewhat foolish. 'Bridgett even calls me Mr Giancana in company,' he said a little sheepishly. I now understood why he often referred to her as Mrs Fuller.

'You'll want to see your room, take a shower and change, Mr Spayd. I presumed you have no clothes for the desert climate, so I've left out a pair of slacks and a shirt belonging to Mr Giancana.' She gave me a second swift assessment. 'The trousers will be a bit big around the waist and perhaps an inch or so short in the leg, and the shirt will be too big, but I can arrange for someone to take you shopping or call a tailor, should you need your own clothes.' This was all said in a calm, even tone, but I'd picked up the hint that I might be moving on before I needed a new set of clothes.

'Thank you, that's very considerate, ma'am,' I said. I was damned if I was going to be forced into calling her Mrs Fuller, just because she insisted on calling me Mr Spayd. Her access to Lenny's wardrobe suggested that their relationship might be more than simply a professional one.

However, almost as if she'd read my mind, she turned to Lenny and said, 'I hope you don't mind, Mr Giancana, but I made the selection from the ironing maid's basket in the laundry.'

'No, sure; thanks, Bridgett, good idea,' Lenny said hastily.

She glanced at her wristwatch. 'The tax people are waiting for you in the boardroom, Mr Giancana. You're twenty minutes late. As you know, they don't care to be kept waiting.' She had an east-coast accent, one my mom would have described as a bit hoity-toity. If she'd been a stranger and we'd met under different circumstances, I could hear Lenny describing her as 'a beautiful ball-breaker'.

'Jack, gotta go! I'll see you later,' Lenny announced and touched me lightly on the shoulder as if to reassure me. He glanced at Mrs Fuller. 'Has that shyster of a lawyer of ours arrived from Chicago?'

'Yes, Mr de Costa is waiting in your office.'

'His usual happy self, I take it?'

This last remark almost brought a smile, and certainly the beginnings of one, to Mrs Fuller's pretty lips. 'Cheery as frostbite,' she replied.

Lenny grinned at her riposte. 'Jack, Bridgett's right, take your time, have a shower and then perhaps a nap. These meetings usually last a coupla hours, pain in the butt. Ask for Gina at the desk when you come down. She'll know where I am and she'll bring you over. I've got you a nice surprise wid the piano,' he said as he left.

I confess I was in two minds about being welcomed again downstairs by the redoubtable Mrs Fuller. Part of me couldn't wait to see her again, but the other part quailed at her cool self-possession. Being from Cabbagetown, I was naturally class-conscious and found Mrs Fuller's manner, combined with her stunning good looks, more than a little intimidating. It didn't augur well for my audition. If it didn't work out, I'd either take a train to San Diego or find a boarding house. One thing was sure, I wasn't going to take Lenny up on his offer of a free vacation, not with those intelligent green eyes judging me a failure.

With two hours or so to spare, I showered thoroughly, then unpacked and took a somewhat fitful nap before changing into Lenny's gear. I splashed my face in the basin and ran a comb through my hair, which I'd allowed to grow out into a dark mop. Now that the war was over, most musicians no longer sported their army crew cuts.

I walked out of the lift into the lobby, approached the reception desk and asked for Gina. One of three attractive young women, a brunette, looked up and smiled. Before I could introduce myself, she announced, 'You must be Mr Spayd.' With a gorgeous smile, she continued, 'Welcome to the El Marinero. Mr Giancana is in the Longhorn Room with Mr de Costa. If you'll kindly follow me, I'll take you to him.'

I returned her smile and in what I hoped was a disarming manner, said, 'Please, would you consider calling me Jack?'

Gina laughed prettily. 'But, of course. Hi, Jack. We're all looking forward to hearing you play.' She emerged from behind the reception desk and I noted the tight-fitting grey pencil skirt, high-heeled black pumps and seamed stockings. Following her neat derriere was going to be a pleasure.

It seemed the Longhorn Room was a casual luncheon room and cocktail bar, with several lounge settings as well as dining tables. Lenny was seated with a tall, thin, dark-haired man with a pockmarked face. Obviously the lawyer from Chicago, Manny 'Asshole' de Costa was wearing a slick brown double-breasted suit. They were seated in the far corner of the large room, having a cocktail. Gina crossed the room with me in tow and announced, 'Mr Giancana, Mr Spayd is here.'

'Hiya, Jack,' Lenny said, then, raising his hand, he indicated the tall Italian-looking guy. 'This is Manny de Costa, our lawyer from Chicago.'

'Good afternoon, sir,' I said, extending my hand. Manny de Costa remained seated and gave my hand a limp squeeze. As the saying goes, it was like shaking hands with a squid. 'How ya doin'?' he mumbled without bothering even to glance at me.

'Jack, siddown, siddown. You look rested – that's good, ' Lenny said in an ebullient manner, then, turning to de Costa, was all business again. In a brusque voice, he said, 'I guess that's about it, Manny. Hotel driver be waiting to take you to the airport. See you next month, same time, same place. Don't forget to bring them papers, licences, the new slot machines for the Firebird.'

De Costa mumbled something, rose from his chair and glanced briefly, and without interest, at me. 'See ya 'round. If ya get the fuckin' job, we'll fix ya a tight contract. I don't like no loose ends.' He departed without shaking hands and before I could reply.

'Nice guy to have at a funeral,' I remarked, taking the chair Manny 'Asshole' de Costa had vacated.

'Not even at a funeral, buddy,' Lenny murmured, glancing up at Gina, who was hovering tactfully. 'Thanks, Gina. Get Jack a drink before you leave,' he instructed, then, turning to me, said, 'what's your poison, Jack?'

'Just a sarsaparilla, thanks, Gina.'

'Right away, Mr Spayd.' We both watched as her trim backside undulated across the room.

'Nice ass, but she's out of bounds, Jack.'

I turned to him and grinned. 'Gimme a break, Lenny. I just got here and may not be staying long enough to disobey the rules.'

Lenny laughed. 'Jesus, Jack, you ain't changed from London. Still a bunny banger, huh?'

I laughed. 'Look who's talking!'

'Yeah, that's the downside of Mrs Fuller's rules, but this one is a damn good one. Don't get your meat where you get your bread. Stops a lotta drama and keeps things runnin' smooth.'

'Bridgett sounds like she could use a little meat herself.'

'Eh?'

'I mean, she herself possibly needs, you know, a guy in her life . . . what's the matter with that husband of hers?'

Lenny looked over my shoulder and grinned like an ape. 'Say, why don't you suggest that to her yourself, Jack?'

I turned to see Mrs Fuller standing directly behind me. Plainly, she had heard my remark, but her face remained impassive. 'Good afternoon, Mr Spayd,' she said, *sotto voce*, 'I hope you are feeling refreshed?'

I could feel my face burning but managed to mumble, 'Ah, yes, thank you, ma'am!'

Jesus, there goes my audition! Gina returned with my drink and, before I could thank her, Mrs Fuller smiled at her and said, 'Thank you for taking care of Mr Spayd, Gina.' Her tone was pleasant enough and didn't change when she turned to me and said, 'We'd like you kindly to audition in half an hour, Mr Spayd. I'll come over to take you to the piano bar. I'm greatly looking forward to hearing you play. Enjoy your drink.'

'Thank you, ma'am, I'll do my best.' I felt like a schoolboy in front of the headmistress, though no headmistress had ever had the style and charisma of Mrs Bridgett Fuller.

Seated again, Lenny raised his glass. 'To your successful audition,

Jack. I know you gonna be fine, buddy. It's only natural she's a little anxious. My word is all she got. Cain't entirely blame her, eh?'

'Lenny, you mentioned the piano?'

His face lit up. 'Steinway, baby grand – only the best for you, buddy.'

'Thank you. Hope I get to play it more than once.'

Lenny ignored my remark. 'Sorry, Jack, couldn't do it in blue. Bridgett decided she cain't do nothin' wid a pale blue Steinway. The one we got is black as a nigger's ass.'

First the Jews, now that word nigger again. Was this simply white gentile America or was it something worse? I decided to ignore it, for now. 'Piano sounds great, Lenny, but with all the shortages, how the hell did you get hold of a Steinway baby grand?'

Lenny looked slightly apologetic. 'Jack, buddy, it ain't new, but almost. We couldn't get no new one, but we've ordered a bran' new one for the Firebird. The fucking krauts in New York are having trouble getting their act together – same thing as us, post-war shortages.'

'Have you had it tuned?'

'Of course, poifect, best tuner on the West Coast, come originally from San Diego. Mexican. Blind guy – Manuel Picconas – he's got ears can hear a pin drop a thousand yards away! He's done piano tuning for Erroll Garner, Duke Ellington. Also Count Basie, W. C. Handy, you name it.' If Lenny was being truthful, this was impressive. 'You ain't never gonna believe this, Jack. You know that movie – Humphrey Bogart and what's her name, that actress, Swiss, Swedish, somethin' like that, speaks foreign.'

'Ingrid Bergman, *Casablanca*?'

'Yeah, that's the one.' He laughed. 'Maybe I'm the only guy in America ain't seen the movie.'

I laughed too. 'I've seen it four times.'

'Yeah? Well then, you'll remember the bar.'

'Rick's Café.'

'Yeah, right . . . Well, we got the Steinway baby grand they used in the film. It's bin in storage at the props department; never been used since the movie.' He grinned. 'Nice, eh?'

I agreed it was. 'I'll be honoured to play it,' I replied. The only problem was that the piano Dooley Wilson played in Rick's Café was a small decorated upright. The Hollywood props department was probably correct. I knew Lenny liked a bit of a story. Why present a naked fact if you can dress it up and give it a bit of style, a pair of tap shoes and a red bow tie?

On the dot of half an hour later, Mrs Fuller appeared at the door of the Longhorn. I watched as she came towards us. She was sheer class, every inch. I was back in the library, a small boy fronting Mrs Hodgson.

Lenny rose in anticipation. 'Jack, I'd love to listen to you play, but I gotta meeting wid Sammy. He reckons one of the kitchen hands is pilfering from the meat freezer. Perhaps we can have a drink later, after you finish. How long you reckon you gonna be?'

'I really don't know,' I said. 'I plan to play a composite of jazz, blues, classical and popular . . . maybe three-quarters of an hour?' Mrs Fuller had almost reached us. 'It depends on . . .' I completed the sentence by raising my eyebrows.

'Right on time, as always, Bridgett,' Lenny said.

She gave Lenny a brief smile, then turned to me. 'Mr Spayd, if you'd like to follow me, we're ready for you,' she said crisply. Or perhaps that's just how I imagined it.

'Is there to be an audience? Lenny told me about the GAWP Bar, ma'am,' I explained.

'No, not this time.' Mrs Fuller smiled, a bit like the Cheshire cat, I thought. 'I shall have the pleasure of having you all to myself.'

She turned on her heel and marched off without a backward glance, leaving me to scramble after her. *Jesus, what am I letting myself in for?* It was pretty obvious I'd got off to a poor start. Then Joe's words surfaced once more. 'Jazzboy, when you get to mess up big time, it a great chance to know yo'self. Pro-ceed upwards and onwards wid that knowing.' I played piano and thought of myself as a professional; it was time to grow up.

I caught up with her as we crossed the foyer and headed down a thickly carpeted passageway towards a large, dimly lit room with *The Princess* in gold metal script against rose-pink velvet directly above the words *Members Only*.

The décor consisted of old-rose velvet drapes, cream walls, subdued lighting and leather booths in the same old rose as the drapes. The bar occupied half of the wall at the far end and was upholstered in the same leather as the booths, studded in gold and topped with marble. Gold pseudo-antique tables and chairs clustered around it. Beside the bar, an archway draped in old-rose velvet with gold tassels led into another room. At a pinch, the room could hold fifty people.

Miss Frostbite, had she observed The Princess, might have declared, 'Too much, much too much, my dear,' but I know my mom would have clapped her hands in glee, then almost immediately felt the room was too grand for her.

However, the décor was less important than the acoustics, and the tone and tuning of the beautiful black Steinway baby grand standing on a small stage. My fingers suddenly itched to try it, even if I was destined to play it only once. What the heck, this was one sweet shining black baby.

Attempting to conceal my excitement over the piano, I clapped my hands several times, turning in a different direction with each clap.

Mrs Fuller raised an eyebrow. 'Mr Spayd, I think you'll find the acoustics are adequate.'

It was another putdown but I no longer cared; I was too anxious to lay my hands on that beautiful keyboard. 'Do you have any requests?' I said, stepping up onto the small stage and adjusting the lid so that every note would carry. Any performer would have to be careful not to push the stool too far backwards after a set or they'd tumble off the stage. There was barely sufficient room for the piano and stool. It was an obvious design fault, but one that, happily, focused my attention and calmed my nerves.

'Just play one or two examples from your usual repertoire, please, Mr Spayd. Mr Giancana informs me you have considerable musical range.'

The tone of this last remark was, I thought, just a touch acerbic – Mrs Fuller was preparing herself for the worst. Clearly, she'd made up her mind about me: I was merely one of Lenny's wartime buddies and she wasn't about to trust his judgment on anything.

I sat down and adjusted the stool. *What the heck, here goes nothing . . . I can always go scuffing*, I thought. Settling myself, I began to play, softly at first, just warming up my fingers and testing the piano's touch and tone, easing myself into the music. It had been nearly a week since I'd played and being back at the keyboard felt like coming home. Jack Spayd became whole again. Nothing mattered, the world around me simply disappeared, I was in my own shining universe.

I began with an almost languid version of 'Sentimental Journey', the Les Brown hit from 1944. As my fingers warmed up, I segued into the more upbeat 'Chattanooga Choo Choo', just giving the keys a bit of a workout. I ran through several popular songs, then added a little ragtime followed by some blues – 'St James Infirmary' to begin with – then I launched into the aria of Bach's *Goldberg Variations*, moving on through the first variation until I was completely immersed in the intricate short pieces that had always been among my favourite pieces. After indulging myself with several of them, I moved onto the first movement of Beethoven's *Sonata Pathétique*.

When I came to the end of the movement, I paused for a moment and suddenly realised my audience was no longer only Mrs Fuller. To my immense surprise, the room was filled with people standing in utter silence. Suddenly, they were clapping, yelling and whistling. The piano bar was filled to capacity – standing room only – and I could see the restaurant and kitchen staff in their uniforms, crowding three deep through the archway at the side of the bar. One of the chefs, in a tall white toque, was beating on a saucepan with a wooden spoon, adding to the din. I was completely taken aback. 'More! More!' they began to shout.

There seemed no graceful way to refuse, so I launched into a selection from George Gershwin's *Porgy and Bess*, an all-American finale.

More clapping and yelling followed, and one of the kitchen staff called out, 'Brother, we got ourself a jazz man, the best there could be! I gone heard myself in heaven!'

To their delight, I turned towards the kitchen and dining-room staff and performed a stiff little bow. 'Oh, man, brother, you da best!' The chef's opinion was generally supported, and there was much nodding of heads and more clapping. It felt good to be back at a keyboard and, while I appreciated the obvious delight of the ladies, whom I presumed were the girlfriends and wives of the high rollers, the response of the black folk working in the dining room and kitchen seemed to me to be the best affirmation of all.

I stepped carefully to the edge of the tiny stage in an attempt to see Mrs Fuller in the happy murmuring crowd. A manicured female hand appeared, and reached up and pulled me into the mayhem. Overcome with emotion, she embraced me and kissed me hard on the cheek, her eyes swimming with tears. 'Jack, that was . . . well, what can I possibly say? That was *wonderful*!' She kissed me again, this time a little more decorously. 'You had the crowd in the palm of your hand; they loved you, I loved you! Jack, your repertoire is so divinely eclectic and all of it's excellent. The music was beautiful, simply marvellous,' she went on, then added, 'for once, Lenny got it right. Please, please stay!'

'What about your GAWP members, shouldn't I play for them?'

'You just did. Word got around ten minutes after you began and they all came in from the pool.' She grinned. 'I think they'd lynch me if you didn't agree to stay.'

Of course I loved her reaction, and if at heart I was a jazz musician, I'd at least established my credentials here as a solo entertainer. Nobody had been forced to listen and obviously they thought I was providing them with more than reasonably competent background music for a busy cocktail bar. 'Thank you, Mrs Fuller,' I said, in an attempt to recover from her surprising reaction to my playing.

'It's Bridgett from now on, Jack; plain Bridgett,' she said. *Lady, there is nothing plain about you*, I thought as she dropped a small curtsy and added, 'At your service, maestro.'

Wow! What a turnaround! I thought it was as good a time as there was likely to be to apologise for my crude comments about her to Lenny, which I was certain she'd overheard.

'Bridgett, I want to apologise for the remark I made to Lenny.' The crowd was drifting away and we followed it through into the foyer.

'What remark, Jack?' She looked directly up at me, her big green eyes wide and innocent. It was a gracious gesture and I realised Bridgett Fuller was a very charming liar. Then she added, 'I think I'm the one who needs to apologise, for doubting your ability and for not taking Lenny's recommendation seriously.'

She had cleverly turned the conversation away from any awkwardness. 'No, of course not. I understand. I'm Canadian, a complete unknown – you had every right. I'm glad I exceeded your expectations.'

'And then some, Jack. Your looks were . . . well, you seemed too good to be true. I guess I just didn't expect to find everything in the one package.'

I could feel my face burning. Juicy Fruit was the only other woman, apart from my mom, who had ever remarked on my appearance, and while I liked Juicy Fruit a lot, she belonged to a profession practised in the ways of making a guy feel good. And, of course, nobody can trust their mom's views!

I'd never given my looks much thought, always assuming that my luck with women was due to my skill at the keyboard. I guess the Iroquois blood from my mom's side added an exotic touch – dark hair, dark eyes, skin 'like an early summer tan', as my mom would say when I was a child. I'd been a big kid, not much interested in games, and I'd grown into a big man. That was about it. The harmonica, then the piano, had always seemed to me the only thing that separated me from every other guy.

Now I could feel my heartbeat increasing by the second. *Christ, what is it with you and this lady, Jack Spayd?* I realised that, after just two demure kisses and one hug, she'd burned herself into my nerve endings so that I was acutely aware of her standing by my side, as if there were an electric charge between us.

'I'd like to stay,' I heard myself murmur. 'Thank you, Bridgett.'

Just then I observed a bulky figure hurrying across the dining room. It was Lenny, and clearly something was wrong. A deep frown was fixed on his normally genial face and, as he reached us, he hissed, 'Ferchrissake, Bridgett, call an ambulance. Fuckin' Sammy's damn near killed a kitchen hand wid a meat cleaver!'

CHAPTER FIFTEEN

NEITHER LENNY NOR BRIDGETT discussed the details of the attack on the kitchen hand and I could hardly ask. I was too recent an employee to be able to discuss it with the kitchen or front-of-house staff, and when I asked Gina at reception what had happened, she'd said only, 'It was horrible, Jack. We're not allowed to discuss it.'

I later learned that Lenny had covered the hospital bills and paid the rail fare for the unfortunate man and his family out of Nevada, as well as a modest amount to help them settle in another state. Two days later I saw Manny 'Asshole' de Costa in the foyer, coming directly towards me. I said 'Hi' but he seemed oblivious and brushed straight past me. I saw him fairly often over the next two weeks and had to conclude he was staying at the casino to help out in some way with the meat-cleaver incident, but plainly it was none of my business. As far as I could gather, Sammy Schischka had been sent back to Chicago by plane the morning following the incident and I presumed – incorrectly, as it turned out – that he might not be coming back to Las Vegas.

The atmosphere among the staff was tense, with only perfunctory smiles for the guests, and I couldn't help wondering if I was getting into something I'd later regret and that I ought to get the hell out of Las Vegas while I could. But there was the lovely Bridgett. Although she must have been preoccupied with the attack, she nevertheless made a special effort to see that I was happy in my new job, giving me the use of one of the suites while I looked for accommodation in town. When I told her I'd be happy with a room in the staff quarters, she said warmly, 'You're welcome to stay here at the El Marinero as long as it takes, Jack.'

I decided to find an apartment of my own as soon as possible and create some space between the El Marinero and my private life, although I was in no hurry to create space between myself and Bridgett. However, Lenny had warned me against becoming involved with any of the staff, so I decided I'd find a poker game to distract myself. The gaming floor of the El Marinero was off limits to staff for recreational purposes and Lenny had also suggested I stay away from the other sawdust casinos. 'Get a debt you cain't settle pronto ain't a good look, Jack. This town, everyone knows your business.'

It seemed unlikely I'd have money worries. With tips, discreetly handed to me in hotel envelopes, I'd made a little over two hundred bucks in my first week, more than I'd ever earned playing piano. Two hundred dollars a week was three or four times the income of a normal family and I felt I was at last entitled to call myself a professional musician and entertainer.

My evening gig in The Princess – or the GAWP Bar, as we all called it – started at six-thirty and around five-thirty Bridgett, Lenny and I usually met for a drink in the Longhorn Room to discuss the business of the day (kitchen-hand incident excepted). Bridgett could then brief me on any special requests her ladies might have – something for a birthday, wedding anniversary, a sentimental piece of music to please a friend, that sort of thing. On one particular evening a couple of weeks after I arrived, Bridgett couldn't be there, so I took the opportunity to bring up the subject of Sammy's personality change.

'Lenny, the day I arrived you mentioned Sammy, and what happened to him in the air force . . .'

Lenny emptied his glass, raised two fingers and waited until a waitress nodded. I had no idea how long he'd been drinking before I arrived, but in the weeks I'd been at the El Marinero I'd realised he'd become a heavy drinker, always with bourbon and usually doubles; at least three in the time it took Bridgett and me to finish one drink. He'd usually have them lined up in front of him so we wouldn't be interrupted. Bridgett drank a single Manhattan and I, of course, stuck to sarsaparilla or an occasional Coke. But, on this occasion, two of the bourbon glasses were already empty. There was no doubt he could hold his liquor, but I'd never seen him drink this much at a sitting. 'Wait on, Jack, I'll tell you after Sue brings my regular poison, buddy.'

Sue was a real good-looking young lady: chestnut hair, brown eyes, light summer tan, lovely legs. In fact, it was obvious that all the waitresses had been selected for their looks, wearing their uniform of tight grey skirts, fresh white blouses and black high heels with style. It was the same with the waitresses in the GAWP Bar, only their skirts were more fashionably wide but not as sexy looking. Bridgett explained that the tight skirts were also worn on the gaming floor, so that if a high roller felt frisky he couldn't get his hands too far past the hem.

While we waited for Sue to return with Lenny's bourbon and my Coke, we chatted about my house hunting. I'd found an apartment on the edge of town in a block originally built in the early thirties for the engineers building the huge dam in the Boulder Canyon. It was a way from the El Marinero but only a couple of miles from the Firebird, sufficient to give me a good walk into work when we finally moved up the highway. Lenny kindly volunteered the casino odd-job man for if I decided to work on the interior.

Sue returned with our drinks, smiled sweetly and left. Lenny must have sensed something, perhaps due to the way I inadvertently glanced at the two double bourbons. 'Bin a tough coupla weeks, Jack,' he said. Then, remembering my original request, he went on, 'Thanks for not asking about the incident in the kitchen.' He paused. 'It was ugly. Sammy's changed a lot. He got into trouble and ended up in a military prison, then later, 'cause he did something else real stupid, they sent him to Fort Leavenworth.'

'Leavenworth . . . isn't that a pretty serious place?'

'You gotta believe it! Those son-of-a-bitch MPs at Leavenworth, they treated him like some animal. Beat him up so bad he ended up in hospital for four months. The army patched him up and gave him a dishonourable discharge. His body is more or less okay – face a bit rearranged and he got himself a nasty limp where they busted his kneecap – but what can I say?' He shrugged. 'They've fucked his head. It not somethin' we talk about, but you oughta know he can snap at the slightest provocation. Frankly, I had my way, he wouldn't be here, but Chicago trust him, he's got a criminal record, and that makes him legit, so now he's a senior soldier in the Family. Not just a soldier, the godfather takes a personal interest in him.'

'A senior soldier?'

'That's Mafiosi for a member of the Family called on to do whatever the godfather wants. Ain't nothin' he kin refuse.'

'Not even murder?'

'Nuh, whatever dirty work; he a strongarm, a soldier, no questions asked, do what he told.'

'And you?'

Lenny thought for a moment. 'No, wid me it's different. The Family don't trust nobody who ain't got a criminal record but, like I told you before, I'm the necessary cleanskin.' He laughed. 'Strictly front of house. *Mr Meet 'n' Greet Lemme Show You Your Suite*,' he added. I was to learn that it was an expression he used when he'd had a bit to drink. I guess being not much more than the front-of-house man for a casino was pretty hard to take after he'd been a marine master sergeant at the American embassy in London, where, I daresay, his every command would have been instantly obeyed. He continued, 'If I decide I wanna walk away, I can, so long as I keep my mouth shut.' He paused and his head jerked back as he gave a short dismissive snort. 'Mind, that strictly theory and I ain't about to test it. You don't never leave the Family. Anyhow, I ain't a working member, know what I mean? But Sammy's been inducted, that's different; he's a senior soldier and he gotta follow instructions unquestioned, like in the army, whatever the godfather want. In return he's got their absolute loyalty until death.' He grinned, then added, 'Which, in the bad old days, wasn't usually from old age.'

'So, what did he do to get into Fort Leavenworth?'

'Jack, you need to understand, he was never air force as a pilot or crew. He was senior sergeant in change of the kitchens at Gatwick, bringing in supplies and stuff like that. Wid the shortages in England, most of the food – meat, cheese, lotsa tinned stuff, even some vegetables – was coming in from the States. He was caught running a black-market operation. I guess everyone in military food supplies, they had some sorta racket goin', but Sammy, he got too greedy and they zapped him and sent him back to the States, where he got four months in the clink. But then the stupid fuck had himself an argument with a prison officer, and he called the Family and got three Chicago soldiers to come up and beat the livin' Christ outa the prison officer as a warning Sammy cain't be touched no more.' Lenny paused and shook his head. 'Not a real smart move, Jack. Mafia, maybe they can beat up a member of some other gangster organisation wid no consequences, but a prison officer with the US military . . . shit, man, that a definite no-go zone. They sent him on to Fort Leavenworth wid "suitable instructions". When he was finally released, his mind was completely fucked.'

'So, why is he here? I mean, this is a casino for high rollers and their wives; surely he wouldn't be called upon for, you know, strongarm purposes here, would he?'

Lenny sighed. 'Brain damage ain't necessarily a bad thing where Chicago concerned. He has expertise in food supply and he bin sent to set up the food contracts for the Firebird; at least, that's what everyone says. Meantime, he's here at the El Marinero to learn the catering needs for a hotel that got high-roller guests and fine dining. That's why he can go into the kitchen wid the staff, the niggers, any time he wants.'

'You mean after what happened in the kitchen, he'll come back to Las Vegas?' I asked, surprised.

'Yeah, far as Chicago concerned, that a minor incident, some nigger hurt, who gonna care?'

'And you, do you feel the same way?'

Lenny took a long slug of bourbon. 'Jesus, no! Widout niggers, we ain't got kitchen staff. Widout Sammy, we got peace and happiness.'

I cleared my throat. 'Lenny, I've got a problem – might as well get it out. It's . . . it's the term "nigger".'

Lenny looked surprised. 'Hell, it ain't meant bad, Jack. Kike, wop, mick, chink, canuck, wetback, nigger, it all part'a the American language, it don't do no harm.' He smiled, suddenly recalling, ''Cept I was always a big kid, someone call me a wop, I busted his head good and he don't do it again, I guarantee.'

'But coloured folk can't do that, buddy,' I said. 'As I understand it, if they touch a white man, they're in serious trouble.'

Lenny, for all his intelligence, looked bemused. 'You know, Jack, I never thought about it like that. Kikes, micks, wops like me, they kin hit back, retaliate, bust someone in the mouth if they insulted.' He paused fractionally. 'Yeah, you right, niggers . . . er, coloured folk, hey, yeah, I suppose they cain't do nothin'. The consequences ain't gonna be good if they hit a white guy.'

'So, Sammy takes a cleaver to a coloured man and nothing happens. Do you think that's fair?'

Lenny shrugged. 'Jack, you gotta understand, you cain't change the world and nobody else round here gonna abuse the kitchen staff. Bridgett, me, we not gonna tolerate that. Manny 'Asshole' de Costa come up and fixed things wid the police. Also, I made some compensation to the nig . . . er, man's family.'

I realised this was about as close as Lenny was ever going to get to understanding the issues. 'But can't you say something to Chicago?'

He shrugged. 'Sure, but it won't help. Like I said, to them, it a minor incident, I'm simply told to butt out, keep my nose clean and do as I'm told. They send Manny Asshole to tidy things up wid the cops. I try to reason wid Tony Accardo, the godfather; to tell him if some'a the high rollers get to hear about what Sammy done, they won't be too happy, that maybe he should stay away . . .' He gave a short laugh, which was more of another snort, 'but he don't take kindly to criticism. He hates Bridgett even though she's made us a success. He still ain't happy about the Firebird on The Strip and he think I'm in cahoots wid her.' He looked at me steadily. 'Jack, Sammy ain't only here for the catering contracts.'

'Oh?'

'He's here to keep an eye on Bridgett, and me also. Cleanskins like us, Chicago needs us but it don't mean they trust us. Sammy is Chicago's eyes and ears. Manny Asshole and he, they the same, they the spies. Manny Asshole, he do the heavy liftin' wid the local administration – police, others, stuff that maybe ain't strictly legit. He checks the hotel receipts to see that Bridgett and me, we not stealin' from the casino.'

'Stealing? You're kidding?'

Lenny nodded, then continued. 'On the other hand, Sammy's the resident spy. Every night and mornin', the gamblin' takings are counted, then locked up in the basement safe. Sammy supervises the count and he also got the combination to the safe. Now, Manny Asshole, he didn't only come up after the kitchen business to fix things wid the police; he's stayin' to count the gaming money and he got the safe combination till Sammy gets back. See, Jack, the Family need to wash a lotta money.'

Lenny went on to explain that the Mobsters were rolling in cash made during Prohibition, money they couldn't legitimately spend or deposit in an American bank without some very nasty questions being asked by the tax man. The extra bourbons were lowering his guard, and I wondered if I should stop the conversation before I learned something I shouldn't.

'See, Jack, things are different now. No easy money from booze, illegal gambling . . . The money's dried up. What they gonna do?'

Lenny explained that gambling had been legal in Nevada since 1931, and that the Mafia had moved in with none of their usual swagger or obvious strongarm tactics, being careful to hide their investments and their involvement in various casinos. The Mormon state didn't believe in looking too closely, provided the surface was squeaky clean. The Mobsters made sure they had ultimate control, and each month skimmed ten per cent off the takings before the profits were distributed and tax paid. Furthermore, they could quietly launder the cash they'd made during Prohibition and from their other rackets.

Casino security was fanatically close. Every dealer, every player, knew they were probably being watched. There were walkways above the casino ceiling that had spy holes, so security could observe individual tables if they suspected a dealer might be cheating. All the money received was counted onto the table under the supervision of the pit bosses and chips were treated in the same way. Slot machines were unlocked and emptied under strict supervision. This produced a veritable river of cash, way too much to count. The take had to be weighed, then every few days the money would be delivered to the bank by armoured car. That was the official routine. But, unofficially, there was the skim.

Duplicity was the name of the game. At regular intervals, a Mobster – in our case, Sammy – would be let into the room where the takings were weighed by one of the three staff responsible for the count. There, he would pack a briefcase full of large-denomination notes, the case would lock automatically, and Sammy would quietly leave, shadowed by two goons with bulging suit jackets. He would fly to Chicago and hand the case over to the Family money man, who held the key. It was the best possible money: untraceable used US currency.

The bosses back in Chicago and the other Mobs knew when they were on a good thing. They resisted the temptation to loot the operation. They were sufficiently smart to leave enough to keep the taxman and the casino's other shareholders happy and to grow the business in a more or less legitimate way. Shareholders in a Las Vegas casino, even the straight ones, never complained about their generous dividends. The Mobs, like any good businessmen, had learned to take the long view.

As I sat there listening to Lenny telling me things he shouldn't, I realised Bridgett must have known about all this. I would have been surprised if there was anything Bridgett didn't know. Another Joe lesson came to mind. 'Jazzboy, ever-thing you hear be useful, information got power, but only provide you don't tell nobody till it gonna be useful to you personal.' Perhaps Bridgett's power came from what she knew.

As if Lenny had read my thoughts, he returned to the subject of Bridgett and her mysterious power over the godfather. 'Don't know what it is, but the godfather don't like it. He punish her every chance he gets, tryin' to suggest she's cheating him, that he got his eye on her. Sammy hates her, but Mrs Fuller too smart to show him she feels the same way about him. Sammy understand being hated; in fact, he depend on it. What he cain't stand is to be ignored. But, like Manny Asshole, he cain't do nothin' . . . they think she laughin' behind their back. Jesus!'

I could see Lenny was getting seriously drunk. He shouldn't have been telling me any of this stuff. I decided to steer him onto safer ground. 'So, Sammy will definitely be coming back?'

'You got it in one, buddy. Ain't nothin' we can do.'

'How do I handle him, Lenny? I mean, is there anything else I should know?'

'Don't ask him about Leavenworth. He bitter as all hell, totally unpredictable. Otherwise, don't worry, Jack buddy, just act normal, pretend you're old pals.'

'Sure, Lenny. I'll stay clear of him as much as I can.'

'That's a good idea. He's pretty excitable since he came back . . . hair-trigger. But don't worry, anything happen you tell me, eh, buddy?'

'Sure,' I said again.

Lenny nodded approvingly. 'I sent him to Chicago the morning after . . .' he cleared his throat, 'the meat-cleaver . . . thing. They say they sending him back next month. Manny Asshole already fixed it all up wid the authorities and it ain't no longer on police records.' He snapped his fingers and stared at them a little too long. 'Gone, kaput, it ain't never happened.'

I decided that Lenny's revelations should meet the same fate, for the sake of all of us.

Sammy returned to the El Marinero two weeks later, and a couple of days after that I ran into him quite unexpectedly. He was standing in the driveway of the El Marinero as I was returning from my lunchtime walk, getting to know the town. He looked at least twenty pounds heavier and recognised me at once. As he walked towards me, I noticed he seemed to be dragging his left leg. His face was the biggest shock. Although he was smiling at me, the whole left side of it seemed to be sagging a little, like someone who has suffered a stroke or severe facial nerve damage. His left eye was at least a quarter of an inch below the right and the bottom lid sagged, wet and red. He stopped just short of the distance it took to shake hands. 'Jack Spayd. Hey, how ya doin', buddy! Welcome to Las Vegas!' His voice was an unfamiliar growl. 'Lenny told me ya was here. Piano player. Hey that's good.' His gravelly voice was difficult to understand. I stepped up to him so I could hear him more clearly, but he looked up at me and immediately stepped back. 'Whaddaya think'a the joint, eh?'

'Great!' I replied and extended my hand. 'Good to see you, Sammy.' He ignored my hand and stood, suddenly silent, his face expressionless, looking directly at me with unblinking eyes. I began to feel a little foolish and, in an attempt to cover my discomfort, I lowered my eyes and patted my stomach. 'Lenny tells me you're responsible for the catering contracts. I've got to compliment you, the grub's first rate.'

He remained silent sufficiently long to force me to raise my head and look directly at him again; then, after what seemed like an eternity, he said, 'Yeah, that's right. I put on some poundage.' His tone seemed to challenge me to take it further.

There was nowhere for me to go. 'No . . . no, that's not what I meant,' I stuttered. 'The restaurant food . . . I mean here, in the casino, it's excellent.'

'I know what ya fuckin' meant, Jack Spayd, ya always bin a fuckin' smart-ass poker player cheat,' he growled.

I felt my temper rising and, remembering Lenny's warning, said simply, 'Sammy, excuse me, I'm running late for a meeting.'

'Widda greedy bitch?'

'I beg your pardon?'

He spat at his feet. 'Her! The fuckin' Noo Yoik whore!' he hissed.

'I don't know who you mean, Sammy,' I said, tight-lipped, then turned towards the entrance to the casino.

His voice, raised an octave, was still a growl but with an hysterical edge to it. 'Hey, I mean the stoopid bitch suppose to run this fuckin' joint! That who! Stay away from her, ya hear? Ya cosy up wid her, ya gonna have to answer to me, Jack Spayd. Keep ya prick clean!'

It was too much. I turned and covered the few paces to where he stood with his arms folded across his chest. Seeing me coming, his crazy lopsided face took on a frightened look. 'What did you just say?' I demanded. The fat little bastard barely came to my chin and I grabbed him by the front of his Hawaiian shirt, my right arm drawn back to bust him on the mouth. His hands came up to protect his face and I saw a look of terror in the moment before he averted his head, his eyes now tightly shut as he anticipated the punch. At the last moment, I managed to restrain myself. Instead, I jerked him momentarily off his feet, then set him down again. 'Sammy, I don't know what you're on about but, whatever it is, keep me out of it, you hear?'

Suddenly, there was the sound of running feet, and Sammy opened his eyes and glanced over his shoulder, then quickly turned back to me. I released my grip on his shirtfront and felt him sag, then relax, wiping his chest to straighten his shirt. I looked over his balding head and saw two guys approaching fast. Then, pathetically, he raised his fists like a boxer. 'Or fuckin' what, Jack? Tell me, or fuckin' what?'

I ignored his taunt and waited as two tall men dressed in identical brown suits and hats, the brims drawn low over their eyes, came to a halt on either side of Sammy, both of them breathing hard.

'Move away, Mister. Ya don't want more trouble than ya can handle!' one of them gasped, gesturing with a flick of his hand towards the casino entrance.

'These guys belong to you?' I asked. They were both big but I was too angry to care about the threat.

'Piss off!' the second guy added, his right hand sliding inside his jacket. It was as if all this were taking place in a low-budget movie and he was the villain reaching for the pistol in his shoulder holster.

I was breathing hard. I'm not the kind of guy who loses his temper often – in fact, I do it almost never – but now I realised I was mad as hell. Sammy dropped his pathetic fighting stance and again brushed at the front of his Hawaiian shirt. 'You'll keep, Jack Spayd,' he growled. 'You'll keep.' The fearful look had gone and the unblinking stare was back.

'Christ!' I exclaimed and turned away.

'Oh, Jack,' Sammy said, his voice suddenly calm.

I spun around angrily. 'What?'

'I hear you a big success at The Princess.' He spoke in a mincing feminine voice. 'I reckon the bitch thought you'd be a loser, but Lenny's got a lotta faith in you. Wouldn't pay to let him down.' He stabbed his fat forefinger at my chest as he continued, 'If you ever got a mind to leave, take another offer, maybe the Flamingo, somewhere like that . . . don't be tempted. Take my advice, it wouldn't be a good idea to accept.' All this was said in an even tone.

Despite my anger, I attempted to cool down and said merely, 'Lenny's my buddy, Sammy!'

The doorman drew up in a new Chevy sedan and hopped out, holding the door open for Sammy. Then, in the same friendly voice he'd used to greet me, Sammy said, 'I've got to get going, Jack. So long, nice ta welcome ya to the El Marinero. See ya round.' He shifted behind the wheel with some effort while his two thugs climbed into the back. The doorman closed the car door and, without thanking him, Sammy slammed the car into gear and dropped his foot down hard on the gas, to send the Chevrolet on its way, waltzing its rear tyres. It was as if he were using the car to compensate for his broken body.

I reported the incident in the driveway to Lenny, going into detail with what had been said. 'Yeah, Jack, that's Sammy. You got the bastard to a T. Gravel voice, lotsa different tones, that's him. Quiet, that's normal . . . he raise his voice, you gotta watch out 'cause he's about to snap. Then comes the yellin' and the threats. Just as sudden, back comes the calm. He all over the place like a mad dog's breakfast! Glad ya didn't bust him a good one in the mouth. The two hoods, they Chicago soldiers, they dangerous.'

'Christ, Lenny, he's bad enough to have around, but those two in their gangster suits . . .'

'Contracts for food for the Firebird about to be signed, so Chicago thought Sammy might need a little help, maybe leaning on the wholesale suppliers. That's how they explain it, anyhow. You kin bet that ain't all of it. I'll speak to Sammy. In some things, he gotta listen to me. I'll tell him to lay off you, no exceptions. Messing wid you, he's gettin' into high-roller territory, GAWP Bar. Chicago ain't gonna tolerate that.'

In the weeks and months that followed until the completion of the Firebird, it wasn't too difficult to avoid Sammy most of the time. The food business seemed to take him away from the casino a fair bit and I was also to learn that he was involved in the Chicago Mob's slot-machine business. Now, after the war, they were supplying new machines, made in a plant they owned in Detroit, to most of the casinos in town. This business was more than just a sideline but it could be tricky, one Mobster organisation dealing with another, hence the need for Sammy's 'protection': his two brown suits with the permanent scowls. When they were around, it was easy to see him coming, and avoid him and his two hulks. A weak gesture maybe, but Sammy Schischka was avoided by most members of staff. I'm certain he noticed their reaction and liked being regarded as a nasty piece of work. Imparting fear was, after all, his new profession.

The two hoods had developed a special walk to keep pace with him, a kind of rolling wobble. Had I not been warned that they were dangerous, I'd have considered them laughable. The left side of their suit jackets always seemed to bulge a little, as if to remind everyone that they were the real McCoy. As Lenny said, 'Not nice guys, those two.'

Occasionally we did meet; usually unexpectedly, in the Longhorn Room. Sammy would ensure he was impossible to ignore, and would make a point of coming over, offering to buy me a drink, always 'forgetting' I didn't drink alcohol. 'Yeah,' he'd growl, 'yeah . . . maybe ya oughta try booze sometime.' It was as if his words arrived ready-mixed into the gravel of his growl. The kitchen staff learned to interpret the different tones of his growl, usually standing close and often to attention, some plainly deferential, some few simply straining to hear. He seemed to create a permanent sense of unease around himself.

Sam never enunciated his surname clearly, and if he introduced himself, the name came out in a gargling hiss. While it was fairly straightforward – 'Shish-ka' – people who dealt with him in business, often gangsters themselves, were reluctant to use it, in case they got it wrong. Behind his back, they referred to him as Sam the Snake, a title he knew of and evidently relished. He was addressed by the hotel staff as Mr Sam, and only Bridgett called him Mr Schischka. It was clear Sammy interpreted her formal tone and careful pronunciation of his name as yet another example of her disdain and, having experienced her coldly polite manner myself when I first arrived, I could almost sympathise with him.

Only Lenny and I called him Sammy, and I expect I was only permitted to do so because we'd known each other during the war. He seemed to have entirely forgotten our first meeting in the driveway; it was as though it had never occurred.

Bridgett was initially much too professional in her manner to offer an opinion on Sammy. Her attitude towards him was cool and efficient, and she never seemed fearful or anxious in his presence. I think it was probably this that riled Sammy the most. 'Dames,' he was fond of growling, 'gotta learn to keep their legs open and their mouths shut.'

Not too long after the incident with the kitchen hand, Sammy attacked another staff member with a cleaver, taking exception to the way one of the Negro men was trimming fat from steak to prepare it for barbecuing. Being from Chicago, the meat capital of America and, furthermore, trained in the catering business, Sammy regarded himself as a meat expert. He hadn't liked the fact that the man was using a cleaver rather than a butcher's knife. In a sudden rage, he'd snatched the cleaver from the man's hand and brought it down hard across the fingers of his left hand, removing the middle three.

Sammy, it seemed, showed no respect for anyone he didn't regard as a hotel patron, but was particularly disrespectful to the coloured staff: the Mexicans, who mostly served as maids, and the black folk, who mostly worked in the kitchens, where Sammy felt he reigned supreme.

I soon got to know the staff and, in particular, the kitchen workers. When the four o'clock kitchen shift came on duty to prepare for dinner, I'd sit down and play several brackets of jazz, and rehearse any new numbers that had recently become popular on the hit parade. This was a quiet period in the piano bar, when the cleaners were preparing the room for the evening. It was outside my official hours but, after the marvellous reception they'd given me at my audition, I wanted to repay them in some way. I let it be known that the staff were free to give me requests for any special occasions, such as someone's birthday. It also gave me the chance to play some straight jazz, which was always popular. As a result, I was on the best of terms with the kitchen folk, especially the head chef, known always as Chef Napoleon Nelson, an excellent combination of names that no white family would have had the courage to choose. I was to learn that he was invariably addressed by his full title, even in the most casual circumstances and even outside his kitchen. He always spoke to me freely, knowing it would go no further, unless we agreed it was a problem that could be fixed by Miss Bridgett or Mr Lenny without Sammy's knowledge. He saw me as a friend and fellow jazz man, and not as a white guy on the casino staff.

Our friendship began when I met Chef Napoleon Nelson by chance away from the El Marinero. As a child, I'd always enjoyed walking with my mom. We'd spent most weekends and the school holidays getting to know places on foot, which also gave me an opportunity to observe birds, an early interest that had never really left me. I'd walked the streets and parks of London, and increased my knowledge of water birds and much else besides, and from the second day at the El Marinero, I had begun to explore Las Vegas. My shift at the GAWP Bar ended around two in the morning, so I usually rose at ten-thirty and was out and about shortly before noon.

I'd taken the apartment I'd mentioned to Lenny. It was quiet and cheap and, instead of renting it, I'd put down a deposit, intending to buy it. It was in a fairly rundown part of town, quiet during the day, with scruffy apartment buildings, auto repair shops and the like, and a few bars frequented by working men, but it was reasonably close to the partially constructed Flamingo and Firebird casinos. I guess the local realtors and developers were not yet entirely convinced by the two new casinos emerging on Highway 91. Though quite large and solidly built, my new home was no luxury apartment, and Lenny had been true to his word and sent the casino odd-job guy to paint it and install one of those newfangled dishwashing machines as a personal gift. As I seldom, if ever, ate at home, it was a kind but pointless gesture, and the gleaming white-enamelled machine gave the freshly painted old-fashioned kitchen a somewhat professional look.

On one of my morning walks a week after I'd moved into the apartment, I'd ventured into the Westside, the part of town largely inhabited by Negro people. I slowly realised that there were no white people there, but, to my surprise, there seemed to be no resentment at my intrusion; people smiled as I passed and some even greeted me. I'd been walking long enough to build up a thirst, and a little food would have been welcome, too. I'd usually grab something to eat at a bakery or some such, as a late breakfast or early lunch. Soon enough, I came across a bar from which I could hear good blues music being played on a piano. I decided I'd have a hamburger and fries, something you could get at any neighbourhood bar in Las Vegas, and I guessed the Westside would be no exception.

I entered to discover a lone musician playing and singing the blues
at an ancient upright piano; singing very well indeed. Several men sat
around drinking beer and nodded as I entered. I ordered a sarsaparilla,
with a hamburger and fries.

'We got hamburger, the best on the Westside; fries also, but we don't
do no soft 'cept Coke 'n' Pepsi. Beer we got, pale ale, India pale, red
ale, brown ale, stout, barley wine, Bud, Coors, Busch and Kentucky
bourbon . . .' the barman shook his head, 'but, nossir, we ain't got no
sars-a-pa-rilla.'

Several of the men sitting around grinned and one of them said,
'Now ain't that the truth, brother.'

This brought some laughter, and caused the piano player to stop and
glance over at me. 'My, my, if it ain't Mr Jack,' he beamed, obviously
surprised to see me in his part of town. 'How ya doin', sir?' he asked.
Puzzled, I turned to look at him and he gave a deep laugh and said,
'I work in the kitchen at the El Marinero, Mr Jack. I'm Chef Napoleon
Nelson.'

'Hi,' I said, surprised, not recognising him without his chef's toque,
then added, 'you play good blues, sir.'

I saw one or two heads jerk back at the 'sir'. Chef Napoleon Nelson
chuckled. 'Why, thank you, Mr Jack, that a fine complee-ment coming
from such as you.'

I grinned. 'Thank you.'

He turned to the others. 'You cats ain't heard nothing till you gone
heard mah friend here, Mr Jack Spayd, play "St James Infirmary", maybe
also "St Louis".' He turned back to me and nodded at the piano. 'She's
old but she's in tune,' he said, half rising. 'Maybe while they fixin' your
fries, you like to play some for us, Mr Jack?'

'Please, call me Jack,' I said, laughing. 'You play pretty good blues
yourself, Chef Napoleon Nelson. That's what pulled me in.'

He laughed too. 'I cain't play it like what you done play, Jack. These
cats don't believe no white man can play black folks' music. They gonna
have themselves a big surprise.'

This caused a general laugh, but still I hesitated. 'I wouldn't want to intrude . . .'

'White man got hisself nice manners,' one of the men remarked.

'Now, you just wait and see, Booker T.,' Chef Napoleon Nelson called to the guy who'd paid me the compliment. He rose from the piano. 'Now, you cats listen good, we got ourselves somethin' special comin' up.'

The ancient upright was a little tinny but, as Chef Napoleon Nelson said, in tune. When I'd played the two blues numbers, they all stood up and clapped; then the barman called me over to eat at the bar and Chef Napoleon Nelson took over at the piano. I finally got up to leave, and pulled out my wallet to pay. 'The burger and fries were excellent, thank you.'

'Ain't no charge, Mr Sars-a-parilla,' the barman laughed. 'You already paid your dues good as can ever be! My, my, dat 'firmary somethin' else.'

'Hey, you ain't gonna go widout playin' some more?' Booker T. called in a pleading voice, and the other men murmured approvingly.

I glanced at Chef Napoleon Nelson, who looked over at the little guy who'd called out. 'Booker T., he a railway man an' he ain't 'fraid to open his big mouth. "All aboard what's going aboard!"' he mimicked.

This brought a big laugh. 'Ain't that the truth,' someone said again, grinning at Booker T., a small, scrawny man with a disarming grin that seemed rather too wide for his face. Chef Napoleon Nelson turned back to me and said quietly, 'If it ain't imposin' too much, Jack?'

'Sure,' I grinned, happy he'd paid me the compliment of using my first name. 'If you'd like me to, but that blues number you just played, "Gamblin Man" by Mr Washboard Sam, why, it doesn't get any better than that.'

'Hey, white man knows his stuff!' someone else called.

Chef Napoleon Nelson made to rise from the piano. 'No, no, please stay,' I said, removing my harmonica from my pocket. 'We'll do this together.'

'Hey, hey, my goodness!' Chef Napoleon Nelson grinned. 'What I believe we got ourselves here, gennelmen, is a nice music-making surprise!'

We began to jam and I played for maybe an hour, while he sang the blues and played piano. When he eventually had to leave for work at the El Marinero, two hours had passed and the bar was standing-room only. The pavement outside was packed with people, leaning through the windows or propped in the doorway. The applause was deafening. As we left, the bartender, Mr James Jefferson Baker, called out, 'Hey, Mr Sars-a-parilla, nex' time you come see us, we got ourselves sars-a-parilla for sure, you hear!'

Chef Napoleon Nelson subsequently invited me to come back to join a group that played in a local church hall late afternoon each Sunday. 'We call it "The Resurrection Brothers", because folk eat der Sunday dinner after church, then have themselves a nice nap, then they resurrect theyselves to come back and play or lissen. Jack, you like to come visit Sunday four o'clock, maybe you decide you like to jam wid the brothers, you mos' welcome.'

Sunday was my day off and I jumped at the chance, deciding not to mention it to Lenny. I didn't feel it was necessary to explain to anyone what I did on my day off.

Chef Napoleon Nelson assured me the black kitchen staff could be relied on to keep their mouths shut about my Sunday foray into the Westside to play with The Resurrection Brothers' jazz band. I suppose neither of us wanted to acknowledge just how unusual the arrangement was. Also, we never discussed work on those Sundays, either before or after a jamming session, even when, as occurred often enough, things were really bad in the kitchen with Sammy Schischka.

Sammy's violent eruptions at the kitchen staff were, of course, not infrequent and one particularly memorable one occurred four months after I'd joined the El Marinero. I'd been practising that afternoon, taking requests from the staff as I always did when Sammy was absent or out of town. I'd developed the habit of dropping into the kitchen to share a cup of Java with Chef Napoleon Nelson or his assistant, who the rest of the kitchen staff referred to as Mr Joel, the title of Chef belonging exclusively to Chef Napoleon Nelson. Incidentally, the kitchen staff all referred to me as Mr Sars-a-parilla after my jam session on the Westside, and although I'd asked them to call me Jack, I was to learn that once you got a nickname, it was for keeps. What's more, the name proved convenient because if any of the staff happened to mention me for whatever reason, Sammy would have no way of knowing to whom they referred. Only Chef Napoleon Nelson called me Jack.

Sammy and his two minders had left for San Diego on this particular day, and I was having my afternoon cup of Java with Chef Napoleon Nelson in his tiny cubicle at the far end of the kitchen. Sammy's absences were always happy occasions, with the staff smiling or laughing as they went about their work. But on this afternoon, Chef Napoleon Nelson wasn't his usual ebullient self, and the atmosphere was muted and oppressive.

After several minutes, I asked him if something was wrong, or if there was anything I could do to help.

The head chef shook his head slowly. 'This ain't for you, Jack.'

Normally I would have accepted this with a nod, but he looked so concerned and confused I decided to persist. Chef Napoleon Nelson wasn't the confused type. No head chef worth his salt is. 'Sure,' I replied, 'but sometimes it helps just to talk.'

After a long pause, he said quietly, 'You know that Mr Sam has to make all the decision, even about the smallest thing. He got to be informed. It got so ever-body they scared to do der job. Nobody kin do nothing right, Jack. Mr Sam, he always shoutin' at somebody all the livelong day. He convinced we all stealin' from the kitchen. Two days back, he count all the forks! Nobody know how many forks we got, not even the scullery maid. "You fuckin' niggers stealing mah forks. There's fifty-six missin'! Everyone gonna have his pay cheque docked fifty cents!" he shout at us.'

'So, that's it? The forks?' I asked. I made a mental note to mention the incident to Bridgett, so that the staff didn't have their pay docked. Fifty cents isn't peanuts to a poor family.

'No, that ain't it, Jack.'

'Oh?'

'Mr Sam, he come stormin' in the kitchen 'bout eight o'clock holding a plate that got a porterhouse steak with jes a bite out of it. '"Where the fuckin' meat cook?" he shout so ever-body can hear him. Ever-thing in the kitchen stop, silence ever-where. Me, I, the head chef, I sees it porterhouse he holding, so I know it's barbecue. So I says, "That Hector, Mr Sam, he the barbecue chef."

'"Meat chef, my fuckin' ass! Get him!" he yell. He gone red in the face and he plenty mad.

'Hector cain't stop. He got steak on the grill. I call for somebody take over then he come over to us.

'"What you call this, nigger?" Mr Sam, he ask him.

'"That porterhouse, Mr Sam," Hector, he says, pointin' at that plate.

'"It's fuckin' raw!" Mr Sam yell out. He so mad he got white spit both corners of his mouth.

'"That table nine, Mr Sam. Order slip, it say that diner want medium rare." Hector point to the porterhouse. "That medium rare perfek, sir, Mr Sam."

'"Bring me a fuckin' knife!" I go get Mr Sam a carving knife and he cut that porterhouse steak in four pieces. It a big steak and I can see it through all the way medium rare. Hector, he a good meat chef, he done a fine job like always. Then Mr Sam he tip the plate o' meat on the floor and he stamp it, each piece meat wid his heel, hard down on every one them four pieces steak.'

'Christ!' was all I could think to say.

'He hand Hector the plate. "Pick it up, nigger!" Hector bend down and he put the four pieces of steak back on that plate and stand up again.

'"Open yo fuckin' mouth! Eat it!"

'"Nossir, Mr Sam, I ain't," Hector say.

'Mr Sam, he call out and soon he got his two . . .' Napoleon paused to find a word that wouldn't offend.

'Gangsters,' I suggested.

He nodded. 'They come up and they got pistols, automatic. They put a gun each side Hector's head,' Napoleon demonstrated, holding both forefingers, one to each brow. "Eat that fucking steak, you crock o' nigger shit!" Sammy yell out one more time.' Chef Napoleon Nelson looked up at me and his eyes welled with tears. 'I know they cain't shoot Hector – too many witness. Hurtin', that one thing, but shootin' black folk wid so many witness, even in the south they cain't do that. But I don't say nothing, you hear . . . it my kitchen and I a coward, I don't say nothin'. Hector take one piece stepped-on steak and put it in his mouth, but it too big so he cain't chew, one side stickin' out. Mr Sam grab a kitchen towel and he ram dat piece meat into Hector's mouth while dem two gangsters hold his head.' Chef Napoleon Nelson made a twisting motion. 'Hector, he begin to choke hisself. "I hope you die, you fuckin' piece a shit!" Mr Sam says. Then he turn and he hand me that cloth. "Clean my fuckin' shoes, chef!"' Chef Napoleon Nelson hung his head in shame, shaking it from side to side, and said softly, 'Then I done that.' He looked up. 'Mr Sam, he stab Hector in his chest wid his finger. "You cook one more steak like that, you fired!" he say. Then he says to me, "You also, nigger!" Then they gone leave, the two gangsters laughing and slapping Mr Sam on the back, imitatin' his limpin', that way they do it.'

I was silent a moment, shocked by the story. 'Please let me tell Mr Lenny or, if you prefer, Miss Bridgett.'

'No, Mr Sarsaparilla, please don't you say nothin', you hear now. Hector got nine kids and his wife, she pregnant one more time, also his daughter, she work here.' He paused. 'Only one thing . . .'

'Yes, anything, just tell me and I'll do it.'

Napoleon shook his head. 'No, no, ain't nothing you can do. Only trouble we got . . . what happen now when some diner he gone order a porterhouse, medium rare?' He was still thinking like a chef and the need for perfection for his diners.

I realised that I had been accorded a special privilege as a white man. The story of the porterhouse steak would never leave the kitchen. The staff would have understood Chef Napoleon Nelson was protecting

Hector's and his daughter's jobs, as well as his wife and kids, and he would be respected for his restraint. They would have shared his humiliation at having to wipe Sammy's shoes. As a coloured man he, and they, were so accustomed to being pushed around and bullied, this latest humiliation had simply to be endured. Life was hard. A roof over your family's heads and food on the table, hungry mouths and shelter took precedence.

I felt ashamed that there was nothing Chef Napoleon Nelson would permit me to do, lest I jeopardise the positions of his staff. I guess he'd seen more than one 'porterhouse incident' and no doubt there would be many more.

Sammy and his two cohorts made quite an impact on the El Marinero; Sammy, in particular, with the kitchen staff, but around town they were a bit of a laugh. Sammy was an inveterate gambler but well known as a regular loser, which meant he was welcomed at any of the other casinos. If he had one of his mind snaps, his two soldiers would guide him off the premises. Sammy was short, fat, physically and mentally damaged, and without his two offsiders, decidedly unintimidating, with his inflated idea of his own abilities, at the gaming table and beyond. Adding necessary muscle was one of their jobs, keeping him out of trouble was the other. As long as he kept losing his gambling stake, which he did regularly, he was tolerated in Glitter Gulch, although he was forbidden to sit in on any of the high-roller games at the El Marinero.

Lenny supervised the gaming staff, with a foreman by the name of Johnny Diamond, a simply terrific guy with whom I often shared private poker games on a Sunday night. Like me, we didn't play the casinos but we were always up for a private game, sometimes held in a private room at one of the casinos but mostly in a downtown apartment. The stakes were high enough to interest the truly good players, many of them professional gamblers. You could win or drop around a grand but not much more. It was big money, certainly – for me, over a month's salary – and way, way out of the league of most Las Vegas working guys, so that your fellow players were invariably from out of town: Texas oil men off a rig, guys in the entertainment business, nightclub owners, professional sportsmen and the like, even an occasional banker who'd flown into town looking for a game but didn't want to be seen at a casino. One of these guys would set up a game, and Johnny and I, and one or two others, would be invited to play. We rarely declined because we were playing with guys we respected for their skill.

Sammy would regularly attempt to play in one of these Sunday-night games. He'd hear of an out-of-town gambler setting up a game and arrive early before the locals, such as Johnny and myself, turned up. On these occasions, we'd make our apologies and leave immediately. It seemed Johnny and I were popular among the local players and the out-of-town guys who visited regularly, and they soon got the message and gave Sammy the brush-off. Curiously, playing with someone who isn't up to your standard isn't much fun, even if, as usually happens, you take all his money. It was like taking candy from a kid, and somehow the game lost status when it lowered its standards. Luck played a part, but skill was respected.

The fact that Johnny and I refused to sit in a poker school with Sammy was yet another reason for him to dislike me, and his main reason for disliking Johnny, whom he constantly tried to force Lenny to dismiss. Sammy complained to Chicago that Johnny was stealing money from the take then passing it, after first deducting his percentage, to Lenny to share with Bridgett.

Lenny, in turn, pointed out that Johnny Diamond was one of the most respected pit bosses in Las Vegas and greatly liked by the high rollers, who would be most upset if he were forced to leave the El Marinero. In Mobster terms, greed always wins out over revenge, and Sammy had not a shred of evidence to support his accusations. The El Marinero was very profitable and suited Chicago's needs ideally, and Tony Accardo didn't want to rock the boat. He was also well aware of Sammy's ability as a poker player.

Lenny was nothing if not loyal, and he clearly admired Bridgett Fuller as much as I did. When I questioned him one day about the wisdom of building the Firebird, he grinned. 'The kikes ain't stoopid, Jack. The highway, it's gonna woik. And I reckon the deal Mrs Fuller got wid Chicago includes a cut from the Firebird profits, know what I mean? It stands to reason. She ain't stoopid.'

I grinned too. 'No, she's a very impressive gal.'

Lenny leaned towards me. 'Rumour is, she's already got three points in the El Marinero. They say that was one of her conditions when she proposed the GAWP Bar, payment for her list of high rollers from the Waldorf in New Yoik. Makes sense, don't it, buddy?'

I nodded gloomily. This new knowledge, if true, put an end to my romantic fantasies. The intensity of my reaction to Lenny's guesswork forced me to acknowledge that I had become infatuated – no, besotted was a better word – with Mrs Bridgett Fuller from the moment she had planted that kiss on my cheek after my audition. Despite her stern warning about fraternising with staff, my overheated imagination had often placed her at the door of my apartment in the early hours of the morning, eager to fall into my arms and my bed for a completely clandestine affair. Okay, if I'm completely honest, for more than an affair. But with the sort of wealth and power she might possess if Lenny was right, I realised that a lowly piano player could never hope to impress her.

Mrs Fuller wasn't going to let a mere man get in the way of her ambitions, although I wasn't at all sure what they might be. She obviously came from a classy background, every syllable polished to a fine patina, so it couldn't just be about money, could it? And the way some of the high rollers looked at her, I reckoned there were lots of easier and safer opportunities to get what she wanted. She certainly didn't strike me as a man hater; so what, then?

Furthermore, I was discovering that nothing went unobserved in Las Vegas. In a lurid flash I imagined the godfather's delight when he learned that Bridgett and I were lovers. Whatever protected her clearly didn't include me, and my sudden elimination would be a perfect way for him to show her who was really in control. I'd end up in the proverbial shallow grave in the desert, one hand sticking out of the sand with a sheet of music clutched in its dead fingers. I was a gambler. It would be easy to circulate rumours of an unpaid poker debt. It wouldn't be the first time a hand appeared sticking out of a sandy grave holding a card or a gambling chip. Sammy would relish the assignment.

This gory fantasy forced me to face some other unpalatable facts. An affair required mutual attraction. Bridgett had been tremendously thoughtful, kind and generous to me, even occasionally resting her hand on mine for a moment to emphasise a point, undoubtedly an innocent and impulsive gesture that invariably set my heart pumping harder. And yet, I had never detected the slightest sign that I meant anything more to her than as a good jazz pianist. Quite the contrary. A month after Lenny warned me about her no-fraternising-with-staff rule, she'd drawn me aside before I was due to play to 'her ladies'. 'Jack, you must know how happy I am about your playing. My ladies love you. There's been nothing but praise from any of them. They love your playing and, just as importantly, they are all a little in love with you, I suspect.'

I think I blushed. Hearing those words from her lips made me wonder if perhaps she might feel the same but, after a short pause, she continued, 'Jack, you're a tall, very good-looking guy and you play like an angel. You've got the ideal personality for your audience and you appear to have no hang-ups, no addictions . . .'

If only she knew she was a very serious addiction!

'. . . no faults that I can detect,' she smiled up at me and my heart lifted. 'So,' she went on, 'sooner or later, one of my ladies is going to have one too many highballs and make a move on you.'

Perhaps I looked as stunned as I felt. This conversation wasn't turning out the way I'd hoped. 'Please, Jack, I'm serious. Do not, under any circumstances, consider responding. It would break my heart to have to fire you.'

It took my fantasy life a while to recover from that blow, but I was young and optimistic and, as I was soon to discover, Las Vegas contained enough pretty young women to distract me from what appeared to be a hopeless infatuation. As time passed, one of them would drop by my apartment and sometimes even cook for me. Lenny's dishwashing machine would get a rare workout and, if I was lucky, so would my bed.

CHAPTER SIXTEEN

APART FROM SAMMY'S OCCASIONAL violent eruptions, my first six months at the El Marinero were immensely enjoyable. Fortunately, for much of that time he'd been out of town, organising the final food contracts for the Firebird and taking care of the slot-machine business. The GAWP Bar – or The Princess, as Bridgett's ladies called it – became more and more successful. Many of the women had been coming to the GAWP Bar since it opened, and regarded each other as old friends, even though they met only once or twice a year. Such was Bridgett's skill that she teamed newcomers with old hands almost effortlessly, so that the novices soon understood that The Princess was an exclusive club of likeminded women who had a thoroughly good time in each other's company.

My two sessions at the baby grand, the second ending at 2 a.m., were usually more like fun than hard work and my Sundays off were given over to The Resurrection Brothers, all of whom were nice guys. In my breaks, I enjoyed the company of good men, such as Chef Napoleon Nelson and, when he wasn't away working on the trains, the diminutive Booker T. Few members of The Resurrection Brothers were professional musicians, but it was a surprisingly good band, playing jazz, blues and gospel to a high standard. It was almost as if the music came naturally, part of the ecstasy and the agony of the coloured people. We also played to an appreciative and knowledgeable audience, and that always lifts the standard of the players.

After we finished playing, I'd usually chew the fat with one or the other member of the band or the audience and, often as not, be invited home for an early dinner. I took this as a huge compliment. Most of these folk had little or no money to spare, but they'd generously share their Sunday-night meal with me. I'd say my goodbyes with my belly full and move on, usually, to a private poker game, generally accompanied by Johnny Diamond, our pit boss at the El Marinero.

My life was full and happy and, apart from the excellent company I enjoyed when I played both poker and music, I was learning heaps. However, the longer I stayed in Las Vegas, the more I became aware of the undercurrents. On the surface it was, I guess, pretty much what you might expect of a largish town in a wealthier part of the US, apart from the unique location and, of course, the gambling and the Mob.

The workforce seemed to be divided by race: Negroes did the heavy lifting; Mexican men worked in the building trade, and women in domestic and hotel work; and families ran small businesses, such as convenience shops, bakeries, grocers' shops, dry cleaners and laundries, or small local restaurants and bars. Finally, the whites more or less took the cream of the town's work in supermarkets, gas stations, auto repairs, car dealerships, realtors and drugstores. They also did the bulk of the policing, admin, clerking, medical and municipal work.

Most of the casino employees at the tables and on the floor were white men and women; the latter, essentially cocktail waitresses in tight skirts, revealing blouses and high heels, who were referred to as hostesses and chosen for their looks. Mexican and Negro women worked as chambermaids and cleaners, and most of the kitchen staff were coloured folk.

I learned that the name Las Vegas means 'The Meadows' in Spanish, although there were precious few of those to be seen in the desert now. The permanent white residents of Las Vegas liked to boast that it was the cleanest and safest town in America and, in terms of thefts or muggings, crime was almost unknown. The Westside, or coloured section, was, if anything, even safer. You could walk anywhere after midnight without fear of being accosted.

Las Vegas lived and thrived, and still does, on the need humankind seems to have to gamble; to have a bet or take an outside chance. My addiction to poker was just one version of this compulsion, and it *was* a compulsion. Why else would people come to a nondescript desert town that baked in summer and sometimes froze in winter, often crossing the continent to bring their hard-earned money to a casino dealer, for the privilege of sitting for hours playing a game that is rigged to ensure that, in the long run, they will lose? If you play long enough, the casino will take all of your money; the numbers don't lie and the establishment doesn't even have to cheat to do it. In the end, the immutable rules of mathematics will grind you into the dust. I knew that, and yet still I gambled. It was something about the game of poker itself, or so I told myself.

Finally, the Firebird was completed and due to open in mid-January 1947, three weeks after what proved to be the premature opening of Bugsy Siegel's Flamingo on 26th of December 1946. Siegel had allowed the budget to blow out by millions of dollars, and the schedule was a joke. Perhaps he thought a gala opening would alter his fortunes and get the Flamingo off to a brilliant start.

The town was buzzing with anticipation: all the right people from Hollywood and elsewhere had been invited, and Cuban bandleader Xavier Cugat provided the music, while comedian Jimmy Durante kept everyone happy. Some big movie stars attended, but bad weather kept away many more. Alas, the premature opening of the grand casino proved a disaster and it began to lose even more money. Local journalists had a field day:

FLAMINGO CUT OFF AT THE LEGS!
LEGLESS FLAMINGO CAN'T FLY!

The headlines were pretty corny, but we loved them, at first; then, almost as quickly, we began to grow concerned. If an extravagant, hugely expensive hotel resort casino was doomed to failure on Highway 91, then what of the Firebird? Had Tony Accardo been correct all along? Perhaps a casino seven miles out of downtown Las Vegas was never going to succeed. The Flamingo certainly seemed to confirm his prediction.

Even before the Flamingo disaster, it had been arranged that I would take a two-week vacation in Toronto in the new year before returning to take over the new GAWP Bar at the Firebird. I'd been looking forward to going home. I'd been earning good money and, on top of that, I'd been lucky at cards, so when Lenny insisted he pay my rail fare, I declined. I had more than sufficient money to play the visiting hero, stopping off in New York for a day to shop, then arriving home with an armload of nice gifts for everyone; for my mom and Nick, of course, but also Mac, the twins and especially Miss Frostbite, Joe and Mrs Hodgson at the library. I'd even decided to buy a bottle of perfume for Miss Bates – Bridgett advised Chanel No. 5. After all, without her, where would I be? But I guess, one way or another, this applied to all of them, even to Old Mrs Sopworth from the Presbyterian Clothing Depot who'd supplied most of my clothes. Maybe I'd buy her a pretty hat or a nice handbag . . . a handbag was probably safer.

When I found myself recalling all the women in my life, starting with Miss Mony, with whom I'd lost touch, but who had been one of my earliest influences, I'd often think about Juicy Fruit, and whether she'd stayed on the game or become a singer. She'd been born with a pleasing voice and I'd always believed it could develop into a really good one if she worked at it.

When I imagined my return to Canada, I'd often picture myself late at night in the Jazz Warehouse, fronting Joe's powder-blue Steinway and casually playing a whole set of new blues numbers and a fair measure of really good gospel. It was all going to be very sweet, and my mom, who never ceased to worry about my being in the sinful gambling capital of America, and clearly still harboured hopes of a second doctor in the family, would stop worrying and see how happy and contented I was.

At the New Year's Eve party, there were glum faces everywhere. Fortunately, Sammy and his two hoods had returned to their families in Chicago. Almost everyone at the party must have feared that, after the Flamingo fiasco, Bridgett was in a lot of trouble. That is, everyone except Bridgett. She seemed to be making a valiant attempt to be upbeat, assuring everyone that their jobs were safe. Those scheduled to go to the Firebird could rest easy, it wasn't like the Flamingo, wasn't behind schedule, wasn't opening prematurely, was complete but for the smallest finishing touches, wasn't over budget and, most important of all, wasn't going to fail. In other words, we hadn't suffered from the Bugsy Siegel factor, we hadn't 'done a Bugsy' – the current euphemism for a complete balls-up.

At midnight we all valiantly attempted to cheer ourselves up and go through the motions with fireworks, whistles and church bells. As the old year rolled away and the new year arrived – 1947 – Bridgett had impulsively grabbed me and kissed me firmly on the mouth, and then immediately said in a flustered voice, 'Oh dear. I think I may be a little drunk.'

I smiled down at her, still feeling the pressure of those delectable lips on mine, and wished, despite my childhood experiences with alcohol, that she would drink more often.

Lenny made an upbeat speech, then got riotously drunk. God knows how many double bourbons he'd downed, but by two in the morning he had finally collapsed on a couch in a corner of the Longhorn Room and was snoring loudly. Most of the staff had departed, no doubt speculating about what the new year would bring. Bridgett and I were settled on another couch not far from Lenny. I was acutely aware of her thigh touching mine along its length, and the soft pressure of her shoulder against my upper arm.

'Well, Jack, you must be looking forward to your vacation,' Bridgett began.

'Sure, but perhaps not quite as much as I was before the Flamingo nosedived.'

Bridgett placed her hand over mine. 'Jack, despite what's happened with the Flamingo, they'll recover. There's much too much money at stake for them to fail. New York will persist in their attempts and we, down the highway, will benefit. We are not going to fail.'

'Why? Why are you so sure, Bridgett?'

'Jack, the vision persists. Also we're better managers than they are and, besides, I'm personally determined to succeed.'

'Well, yes, but is it entirely up to you?'

'As a matter of fact, to a large extent, it is.'

I certainly hadn't been expecting that, and wondered if she was more than a little drunk. It had been a fairly firm kiss, our lips parting and tongues almost touching . . . surely if she was sober, she wouldn't have kissed me like that?

'There's something I don't understand, Bridgett.'

'What, Jack? What don't you understand?'

'Well, there's obviously some sort of deal between you and Chicago. We all know that they were dead against opening on the highway. Lenny says Tony Accardo was adamant; more than that, he was certain such a project must fail. Yet, you persuaded him to change his mind.'

'You mean, what precisely caused him to change his mind?'

I nodded. 'The Mafia's attitude to women in business is fairly well known . . .'

Bridgett laughed, nodding her head in agreement.

'So, how come the switcheroo?' I asked, hoping to inject a little levity.

Despite my feeble attempt, Bridgett's demeanour grew serious. 'Jack, are you worried about your job, is that it?'

I threw up my hands. 'No, no, good God, not at all!' I protested, adding, 'You must know I get offers from other casinos almost every week.' I hesitated, then said, 'But I am worried, yes. Worried for you. What might happen to you if the Firebird goes the same way as the Flamingo?'

'Why, thank you, Jack, that's lovely.'

I ignored the fact that she might be patronising me and cut to the chase. 'Bridgett, why do you tolerate those bastards in Chicago? I've only been here a short time, but people like Manny 'Asshole' de Costa, the frequent visits of gangsters from Chicago, the presence of that vile snot-nosed Sammy Schischka . . .' I shrugged. 'How do you tolerate it? Christ, you could work anywhere you liked! Bridgett, you're a brilliant hotelier!'

'Oh, Jack, I don't think . . .'

'No, please let me finish. You're highly educated, beautiful, charming, totally professional and you ooze brains. People trust you instinctively. You know the hotel industry like the back of your hand. Staff, particularly coloured folk, adore you and trust you to take care of their interests. You're not scared to make tough decisions – Lenny tells me you'll stand up to Chicago if you need to. You've obviously got the godfather's number. Anywhere in America, you'd earn an executive salary, be properly appreciated and have a secure and glittering future. Your contacts among the very wealthy are impeccable. Why then do you put up with these ingrates, these ignorant gangsters and murderers? You're a *real* lady, you don't have to work with these low-life hoodlums!'

Bridgett laughed softly. 'Thanks, Jack, I believe that's the nicest series of compliments I've ever been paid.' She paused fractionally. 'But, concerning my background, you're completely off the mark. I was born in the heart of the Appalachian Mountains. My daddy was a coalminer, Luke Handleman Rooth. He and my mom were mountain folk who couldn't read nor write, hillbillies who belonged to the Pentecostal snake-worshipping cult. I was baptised Bridgett "Baby" Rooth, not because I was the youngest of eight kids, but because my daddy was crazy about the baseball player Babe Ruth, who played for the Boston Red Sox and the New York Yankees.'

My head was swimming. It was unthinkable that this cultivated, elegant woman had ever set foot in a hillbilly hovel. 'C'mon, Bridgett, they didn't *really* worship snakes?' I said, latching onto the most bizarre of her revelations.

Bridgett leaned back, half closed her eyes and began to speak in a solemn voice: '"And these signs shall follow them that believe: In my name shall they cast out devils: they shall speak with new tongues; They shall take up serpents: and if they drink any deadly thing, it shall not hurt them: they shall lay hands on the sick, and they shall recover." Mark 16, verses 17 and 18.'

'Jesus!'

'Yes, *he* had a fair bit to do with it in the Pentecostal Church where I came from.'

'I mean, did you actually handle the snakes?' It was a long way from Mrs Henderson and the Apostolic Church of the Pentecost in Moose Jaw.

'Of course! It's in the gospels, in the Book of Mark and there's more in the Book of Luke,' she laughed. 'But I only handled one once, when my mom said it would cure my measles.'

'Did it?'

'Of course not.' She laughed again. 'I infected the entire school. My mom said it must have been the Lord's will and accepted no responsibility.'

'Please go on,' I cried, not having ever heard or imagined such a thing could happen to a child in the name of religion.

'Well, at age fourteen I was considered to be educated. I could read and write, so my folks took me out of school and sent me to work.'

'So, what happened? How did you get away?'

'From the Appalachians? I guess it was some sort of vague ambition I probably thought was a sin. The Pentecostals don't allow anything regarded as "worldly". For instance, passing a men's toilet without closing your eyes, going to a movie; that sort of thing was wicked and a way for the devil to tempt people to become sinners. Wearing make-up, dancing in public – even if you were husband and wife – were mortal sins, blasphemy. To imbibe strong drink was undoubtedly the greatest sin of all.'

'You haven't answered my question,' I persisted.

'Oh, yes; well, my fifteen-year-old cousin Virginia Grant and I moved to Bristol, Tennessee, to work in a small hotel as maids. The hotel, more a motel with cabins and single rooms, was owned by the family of the baker in our home town, who was also a lay preacher in our church, so my parents knew we'd be safe from the devil's temptation. Well, one Saturday afternoon, filled with guilt and in fear that we'd be struck down by a bolt from heaven, we sneaked into the local movie house. The movie we saw was an old one with Clara Bow, called *It*. Clara played a shopgirl who wins the heart of the shop-owner's son by means of her 'it' quality.'

I nodded. 'Yes, of course, I remember – the movie was the source of the "It" girl idea,' I said, 'but we were only kids when it came out.'

Bridgett laughed, a deep infectious chuckle, which made her even more attractive. 'Probably a rerun. But for me it was magical. A message from the Lord himself, not the devil. I realised there was a way out for me. I took the movie literally. If Clara Bow, a shopgirl, could marry a shop owner's son and rise from rags to riches, then so could I, a hillbilly chamber maid.'

'Which, I guess, brings us to the Mrs Fuller part?'

Bridgett smiled and shook her head. 'Yes and no. Fourteen is still a bit young, even where I hail from. But I started to keep my eyes and ears open. I looked older than I was and men staying at the hotel, mainly commercial travellers, seemed to find me attractive, even though I never used make-up, of course, or showed any forbidden flesh. Nor did I allow them to touch me. But I sometimes found myself slapping more hands than making beds.

'By this time, Virginia and I, under the pretence of attending Bible class, had become movie fanatics. We went to the cinema as often as we had money to pay for a ticket.' Her eyes had taken on a remote look. 'We must have been the only girls in Tennessee who sat clutching a Bible while they watched a movie. Anyhow, I learned later that Clara Bow had been raised in poverty, too, and that her mother, eventually declared insane, had tried to slit Clara's throat to prevent her going into the movies. Such fanatical censure from Clara Bow's mom wasn't that far from the Pentecostals promising damnation if I indulged in "worldly" things. It all seemed to fit.

'When I was fifteen, I thought I was practically grown up. Like Clara, I may have been poor and uneducated, but I could learn the ways of the world. I had my hair cut in a bob like hers, even though it was out of date. Using the Singer sewing machine the hotel laundry used for linen repairs I made a pretty dress from a torn yellow cabin curtain. And, most importantly, I began to observe the ways of men.' She grinned. 'I was hoping to come across a shop owner's son. It never occurred to me to see men as romantic or sexual beings. A Pentecostal upbringing runs deep and, contrary to popular belief, mountain clansmen are not sex perverts. Not that I'd have known the meaning of such a horrible term at the time.'

'But you eventually found Mr Fuller?'

Bridgett laughed softly. 'Well, he wasn't the shop owner's son I was looking for, but – how shall I put it? – I guess you could say he was the result of a very careful selection process. Stephen Fuller was impotent, or rather sexually uninterested in women. Originally from New York State, he was an elocution teacher and an expert on etiquette. I realised even then that I needed my rough edges polished off, and so I married him in Nashville at the age of seventeen and we moved to New York City.'

'Lenny told me he passed away.'

'Yes, he died not long ago, of a heart attack. He was still quite young. He taught me everything he knew.' Bridgett paused. 'I'd discovered quite soon that he was a homosexual. That is, when I eventually realised there was such a thing as homosexuality. I thought it was something that only happened in the Bible in olden times. Leviticus 18 verse 22: "Thou shalt not lie with mankind as with womankind: it is an abomination,"' she recited in her Bible voice. 'Stephen and his friends taught me how to dress and walk and conduct an intelligent discussion. I also learned from magazines, took a part-time modelling class and, naturally, observed the manners and the ways of the educated and well-bred women who stayed at the hotel. I educated myself in business at night school while I worked in the hotel industry, eventually rising from waitress to restaurant manager.'

'And the physical side of things? Your marriage, I mean. It must have been awkward for both of you.'

'No, not really; I was growing up fast and eventually I found him a lover, not too difficult in New York when you work at the Algonquin Hotel. As the saying goes, he lived happily ever after, it's just that "after" wasn't very long, sadly. We parted ways when I was twenty, but never divorced. We remained good friends.'

'I'd never, I mean, *never ever*, have believed it!' I said, hugely impressed.

Bridgett gave a pretty little pout, glancing up at me from under her lashes. 'So, what you see, Jack, is all a fiction. I'm a complete phoney.' She touched her lips with a polished scarlet fingernail. 'The well-rounded vowels are the result of years of practice.' She grinned. 'However, this has to be our little secret, Jack.'

I nodded, suddenly serious. Bridgett oozed class – as my mom would have said, 'She's *old* money'. Her story only served to increase my admiration, especially with my firsthand knowledge of the enormous distance between poor and rich. I'd travelled part way along that road myself, and it hadn't been easy. 'Of course. Allow me to tell you about Cabbagetown, Toronto, some day.'

She laughed again. 'You're not serious? Cabbage, like the vegetable?'

'Uh-huh, though some of us managed to escape the vegetable patch. I was lucky from the start. A schoolteacher believed in me when I was still a very young kid, and I had a mother who loved and protected me from a drunken father.'

'A drunken father doesn't sound too lucky,' she said, one eyebrow arched.

'No, of course not. My mother was particularly unlucky. But here's the paradox, and you're a perfect example of this. It seems to me that happy families don't have to do a lot of thinking and planning and scheming. They don't have to leap at every opportunity that comes up. They don't have to learn from their mistakes because there's always someone to cover for them. But I grew up with a loving and determined mother fighting off a violent drunken husband, and having to support her son on a pittance from working as a night cleaner in an office block in downtown Toronto. That brings you into the real world fast, makes you realise it's sink or swim and you have to grab every opportunity. But, of course, you'd know that.'

'You're right, Jack. I'd never thought of it in quite that way.'

'Have you ever been back, to see your parents?' I asked.

'No,' she said quietly.

There were several moments of silence between us before I dared ask the question now uppermost in my mind. I concluded that she'd never have told me all this if a cocktail or two too many hadn't loosened her tongue, and I knew I'd never get a better opportunity. 'Bridgett, I have one more question.'

'Goodness, Jack, only one?' she said with that gorgeous throaty laugh. 'They say confession is good for the soul, but I've already told you more than I've ever told anyone else, except Stephen, of course. I won't answer if I think it inappropriate,' she said casually, but I knew she meant it.

'Yes, of course.'

'Well, then, Jack, what else do you wish to know?'

'What have you got over Chicago?' I blurted. Then, 'Sorry, I mean, why did they agree to build the Firebird?'

Bridgett looked momentarily bemused. 'Oh, so you know about that.' She paused. 'No, don't tell me, Lenny would have told you.'

'Yes, but he doesn't know why. And after the disaster of the Flamingo —'

'The Firebird will succeed, Jack, but you're right, there's another reason Chicago agreed.' Bridgett paused again and I waited for what seemed like an eternity before she sighed and said, 'Jack, it's all in the paperwork.'

'You mean a contract?'

Bridgett smiled. 'No, Jack, it's a special kind of paperwork. I was very disappointed when Mr Accardo said he wouldn't consider opening on the highway. I knew we had to expand, to offer more to our clients. The El Marinero was never going to be enough.' She hesitated, then said, 'I suppose this was the opportunity I'd been waiting for all my life.'

'What? Running a bigger, more luxurious gambling casino in Las Vegas?'

'No, of course not, Jack! It was my opportunity to secure my future, to own a share of something really big. Not just savings after a lifetime of hard work. I've seen how the rich live and make their money, and it isn't by opening a savings account in a bank. I wanted the same. I guess we're different, Jack; you've got talent and you'll always be safe. With my background, security is everything. Put simply, I want to be rich. Filthy rich! So, I went to Chicago to attempt to persuade them to open on Highway 91.'

'But wasn't that always going to be a gamble? Especially with Bugsy Siegel making such a mess of things with the Flamingo.'

'No, I didn't, and still don't, believe so. Meyer Lansky isn't a fool; he wouldn't have invested so much in Billy Wilkerson's Flamingo unless he was pretty certain it was going to work.'

'But getting Bugsy Siegel to build the Flamingo was not exactly a shrewd move,' I countered.

Bridgett fixed her green eyes on me. 'You're probably right, Jack. But if I had the money and the opportunity, even with all that's happened, I'd *still* invest in the Flamingo.'

'Really?' It was all I could think to say.

'Yes, but, sadly, I don't have the money. So, the Firebird was my best bet; I flew to Chicago and, I must say, it wasn't pleasant.'

'I can imagine.'

Bridgett looked at me. 'No, Jack, I doubt you can. Tony Accardo can be a very frightening man. He told me plainly that if I took my Waldorf list to another casino, I'd be "one dead dame". What's more, he wouldn't even listen to my plan for the Firebird. Said he had more important things to do than talk to some dumb broad who wanted to send him broke.'

I shook my head, hardly believing my ears. 'So, what did you do?'

'I returned to Las Vegas and called my lawyers in New York, and several days later they paid Tony Accardo a visit.'

'I don't understand? Why? Why would that help?'

'It's because of my paperwork. They presented Tony Accardo with copies of it – years of carefully documented notes, about tax evasion, mostly; that's how the FBI put Al Capone away. But more, much more: bribery of officials, state and federal; judges; police and others. The skim takings, money laundering and four cases of murder, with every detail – the why, how and when, and who ordered it – all documented. My lawyers pointed out to Mr Accardo that they felt sure killing me wasn't the wisest option, since the original documents were in a very secure place, and that building the Firebird on the highway seemed like a very intelligent idea. As proof of my confidence in the decision and as a mark of his goodwill and trust, I respectfully requested two points in the new casino, with no provisos, and the profits to be audited by an independent accountant not under Manny de Costa's supervision.'

I felt cold all over. Wasn't that blackmail? And of some of the most powerful and ruthless men in America?

Bridgett paused, then continued. 'The two points were a reward for my years of faithful service, during which I had added greatly to their wealth.'

'Two points?'

'Per cent.' Bridgett grinned. 'So, you can see, I've got a big personal investment in making the Firebird work.'

'You must be pretty sure it will.'

'Jack, I was right to tell Mr Accardo that the Flamingo would take our business if we didn't act, and act fast. My ladies trust me and I trust them but, in most things, wives don't have the final say.' She paused. 'Meyer Lansky made me an offer, but even if my paperwork prevented Chicago from killing me, I couldn't have hoped to make anything like the kind of deal I wanted. I've got nothing on New York, so points in the Flamingo would have been out of the question. Thank god Bugsy Siegel is such an incompetent fool. He allowed me just enough breathing space to get Chicago to build the Firebird in a year. So, you see, Jack, it can't fail. Every member of The Princess, every girlfriend and wife, has agreed to follow you to the Firebird.'

It was a nice thing to say, but I knew they'd really be following the beautiful Mrs Bridgett Fuller.

CHAPTER SEVENTEEN

BRIDGETT PROVED TO BE correct, New York didn't give up on the seemingly hapless Flamingo, and announced it would be closed until all building was completed. In Benjamin 'Bugsy' Siegel's words, 'It gonna make that cockamamie casino they got in Monaco look like a barn.'

This gave us the opportunity to move to the Firebird, which had been completed on time and on budget. Bridgett, determined not to 'do a Bugsy', spent a month getting the kitchens working properly and the staff familiar with the premises. She tested everything, to discover any flaws ahead of time, then tested it again. She invited white staff members and their families to test the pool and poolside bar and restaurant, and some particularly hardworking staff were invited to use the luxury suites, to iron out any problems with them. The staff enthusiastically threw themselves into playing the roles of pernickety, fractious, wealthy guests, taking great delight in giving each other a hard time. Bridgett conducted daily meetings, listening to the complaints and the reactions to them, and working out ways to avoid problems in future.

Alas, the coloured staff were not permitted to use the suites or the pool but simply played their accustomed roles; however, they did attend all the seminars. In an effort to make things up to them, Bridgett allowed them to invite their husbands, wives or parents to have dinner in the formal restaurant, with Chef Napoleon Nelson presiding over the kitchen, and the usual waiting staff and maître d'hôtel attending the tables. Although only volunteers were called for on these nights, not a single member of the restaurant staff refused to serve the black families. Furthermore, Barney, our usual bartender, volunteered to work the restaurant bar and we moved the Steinway grand in so I could play throughout the evening. For my part, I was able to invite the players from The Resurrection Brothers and their wives, as well as those other families who had so generously invited me to share their Sunday dinners.

Getting the Firebird up and running was hard work but also great fun, and allowed staff to enjoy something they might never again experience. As a result, there was a sense of camaraderie and morale was at an all-time high. No casino could have been better prepared for a successful opening. Bridgett had drawn up the guest list from America's wealthiest high rollers, their wives and girlfriends, including only *bona fide* members of the GAWP Bar. No big stars were invited, unless, of course, they'd previously frequented the El Marinero.

In a true stroke of genius, Bridgett opened on the same day as the Flamingo – now renamed the Fabulous Flamingo – without any special fanfare. The Flamingo did all the publicity work, inviting the usual list of ritzy stars of stage and screen to the week-long celebrations. Meanwhile, back at the Firebird, the high rollers and their ladies settled into their complimentary suites, feeling infinitely superior. The Firebird seemed exclusive and distinctive by comparison without the razzamatazz of the Flamingo. As for the GAWP Bar, it was simply moving into its new home, which more accurately reflected the needs and expectations of the girlfriends and wives of America's very rich gamblers.

However, Bridgett hadn't lost the common touch. The Firebird's 'slot casino', carefully separated from the high-roller section, was as brash and brassy as anything in Vegas. As Lenny put it, 'Mrs Fuller got all the bases covered, buddy. On the one hand, sheer class; on the other, sheer ass!'

Although the Flamingo was supposed to be a state-of-the-art casino, rumour had it that, under Bugsy Siegel's mismanagement, costs had finally blown out to almost six million dollars. Sadly, this astronomical sum was not reflected in the casino itself, due, no doubt, to theft, corruption and other shoddy practices. As Louella Parsons wrote in her Hollywood gossip column: *My dears, the décor reflected the personal taste of Mr Benjamin Siegel and his actress girlfriend, Miss Virginia Hill. Need I say more!*

The interior of the smaller Firebird, designed by Anna-Lucia Hermes, was variously described by newspaper and radio commentators as elegant, luxurious, intimate, and infinitely superior in tone and ambience to the Flamingo. We earned three pictorial pages plus a spread in *Architectural Digest*, the magazine that, for close to a decade, had set the standard for American interior design. This earned us points with city hall because the accolades boosted the reputation of Anna-Lucia, the mayor's wife, so that, in the next five years, she was frequently chosen to design the interiors of a number of the new casinos on what was to become known as The Strip.

The local press covered the opening of both luxury resort casinos almost equally, so that the citizens of Las Vegas and the casino patrons spoke of little else for a week. The local folk had already seen the Flamingo fall flat on its face, and flocked to the next opening, hoping perhaps to see a repeat performance. These regular gamblers were equally curious about the Firebird, still an unknown quantity, and flocked to the 'slots' section, which was only a hop, skip and jump up the highway. As one newspaper put it, gamblers could 'kill two birds with one stone'. In fact it was the gamblers who were at risk from the moment they wandered into the regular casino. Bridgett had ensured that it was completely sealed off from the outside. There were no windows and the exits all led to other areas within the complex. Once inside the Firebird, it wasn't easy to get out again. What's more, there were no clocks visible anywhere, thus insulating gamblers from any sense of passing time. There was no daylight, no temperature change, the tables operated twenty-four hours a day and the lights over the green baize tables were never turned off.

But even if the atmosphere was designed to keep the players at the tables for as long as possible, Bridgett knew that even the most compulsive gambler ultimately has to have a break. He must be given the chance to eat and sleep, and acknowledge the wife or girlfriend he brought along on the pretext of a luxury holiday with the promise of a poolside tan from the desert sun, and the chance to meet and greet her social counterparts from every state in the Union.

Bridgett had developed this concept at the El Marinero but now, at the Firebird, it came into its own. A GAWP Bar member was guaranteed a tan, entertainment, wining and dining with her husband or boyfriend; and, much, much more importantly, she was able to gather plenty of gossip, contacts, lifestyle tips, references and referrals to impress her envious friends back home. Only a woman could have figured out this heady combination. The new GAWP Bar, now known as The Phoenix, soon earned a reputation as the most glamorous, exciting and influential female meeting place in North America.

I was personally responsible for keeping the wives and girlfriends safe, happy and sentimentally romantic while their husbands and boyfriends were glued to the gaming tables. This, in the simplest terms, was my role in the vast, greedy, money-munching machinery that made up the Firebird.

With morale sky high, staff had a genuine willingness to please patrons at the Firebird, whereas at the Flamingo, there was an edgy sense of anxiety and false bonhomie. After the first week, the Firebird's regular casino, under Lenny's management, was clearly a huge success. *Mr Meet 'n' Greet Let Me Show You Your Suite* was a thing of the past; Lenny had finally discovered his civilian vocation. Next door the high rollers gambled with more than their usual enthusiasm, confident that their girlfriends and wives were happily occupied at the new GAWP Bar. For my own part, I was more than content with the new piano bar. My brand-new Steinway grand stood on a generous stage in the centre of the room, and when I first sat down to play, to test out both the instrument and the acoustics, I honestly thought I'd died and gone to heaven.

Had the godfather or any other members of the Family bothered to attend the opening of the Firebird, they would have been delighted by the profits from that first week under the joint management of Lenny and Bridgett. The joke was that they had stayed away because they were unwilling to risk facing the humiliation of a disastrous opening foreshadowed, they believed, by the calamitous first opening of the Flamingo.

Instead, Manny 'Asshole' de Costa was sent along with Sammy, under the guise of organising the renovation of the El Marinero. Sammy, forbidden by Bridgett to enter the high-roller section, was nevertheless observed strutting around the regular casino, shooting off his mouth. Lenny and Johnny Diamond, flushed with success, put his complaints and criticisms down to sour grapes. As Lenny said to me, with a wry smile, 'Jack, Sammy ain't happy with our success because Chicago ain't gonna be happy. Now the godfather gotta admit Bridgett was right and he was wrong . . . which he ain't gonna wanna do. And hey, the takings for the first week are more than we made in a month at the El Marinero.' He shrugged expressively. 'It only natural they gonna be mad as hell. Sammy's under instructions to stir . . . make trouble, you just wait and see.'

After the second stupendous week, the godfather called Lenny and, mixing his metaphors, warned him, 'Don'tcha count no chickens, ya hear? One swallow don't make no goddamn Indian summer!' However, the Firebird never looked back and, to the chagrin of Chicago, nor did 'the fucking kikes' at the Flamingo, as Manny 'Asshole' de Costa put it. Chicago took some comfort from the fact that the Flamingo was still hopelessly in debt and would likely take six years to recoup the original investment. But it was obvious after the first few months that The Strip was going to be America's premier gambling venue. It was still early days, but with the post-war boom, it was clear that Bridgett had been right to back Meyer Lansky and Bugsy Siegel's vision and that, despite some initial hitches, the concept of the luxury resort casino was here to stay. Three years after the opening of the Firebird, *Forbes Magazine* would name Mrs Bridgett Fuller American Hotelier of the Year.

One Friday, three months after the opening of the two luxury resort casinos, Bridgett and I were meeting in her office for our daily talk about the GAWP Bar. Barney, as was his custom, brought in Bridgett's Manhattan and, with a predictable sigh, my sarsaparilla, except that on this particular day he shouted from the doorway, 'Quick, turn on the radio. Bugsy Siegel's bin murdered!'

The local Las Vegas radio station kept repeating the news in flash bulletins, so we didn't have long to wait for details. Benjamin 'Bugsy' Siegel had been shot several times by an unknown gunman firing through a window of Virginia Hill's bungalow in Beverly Hills. The gangster with the movie-star looks and no head for accounting was shot several times, one bullet said to have blown an eye out of his skull and across the room.

Barney stayed to listen and then left to prepare his bar for my first session. 'Christ, what do you make of that?' I exclaimed once he'd gone.

Bridgett took a sip from her Manhattan, then said quietly, 'Jack, Mr Siegel may well have been a Mobster, a standover merchant, a thug and a womaniser, none of which is seen as a character defect, in this town at least . . .' She took a second sip from her cocktail. 'But he was also a visionary and, in a real sense, I owe him everything.'

No one was ever charged with Bugsy Siegel's murder, although it was more or less accepted that some disenchanted investor had ordered it. Given that there was so much Mafia money tied up in the casino, the order for the hit could well have originated with the Family. There was no mention of Meyer Lansky as 'accountant' (read godfather) of the New York syndicate being implicated, even though it was generally allowed that he, of all people, had not only good reason but also the authority to order the killing of his fellow gangster and lifelong friend.

In the same period that culminated in Bugsy Siegel's execution, Sammy worked like a tiger to get the *new* El Marinero up and running, with frequent visits from Manny 'Asshole' de Costa. For some unknown reason, Tony Accardo decided that Sammy should be the one to be entrusted with running the refurbished El Marinero, a decision that was seriously flawed.

While it is pretty hard to lose money running a casino, the new El Marinero lost it hand over fist, way beyond anything the Chicago accountant had estimated. Something was clearly wrong. Their publicity had been simple enough: they allowed word to get around among the local punters that they'd set their slots to pay out more frequently than those of any other casino in Glitter Gulch. Chicago had been prepared to take the lower returns involved, to gain a bigger share of the highly profitable slot-machine business known in casino parlance as 'the grind'. The plan had been gradually to raise the percentage take from the machines until it was back to the usual level.

The tactic had worked well and the new El Marinero was usually pumping, often with gamblers queuing to use the slots. But when Manny 'Asshole' de Costa temporarily lengthened the odds as a test, the losses continued. Moreover, there didn't seem to be anyone except Sammy himself to blame.

The Mafiosi knew their way around a gaming floor and how to set odds. Chicago, concerned, had sent two top lieutenants with previous casino experience to advise Sammy, but they'd mysteriously been reported as gangsters and quietly escorted out of town by two police officers. Manny de Costa knew which police were corrupt, but it seemed Sammy had employed a couple of extras.

Now the proprietor of a casino, Sammy Schischka completely lost his head, helping himself to a share of the daily take and, to the immense delight of the other Glitter Gulch casinos, losing enormous amounts in poker games. More than once, he gambled away the Mob's money in a late-night game at the Flamingo.

All of this soon became apparent to the frustrated Manny 'Asshole' de Costa, who, in an attempt to save his own butt, reported Sammy's theft to the godfather in Chicago. But to censure Sammy, his own appointment, would mean a great loss of face to Tony Accardo, so, with the Firebird making plenty of cash, the godfather simply sold the new

El Marinero and cut his losses. But then, to Lenny's consternation, he decided that Sammy was ideally suited to becoming the Family debt collector. And so Sammy Schischka, the psychopath with his two hoods still in tow, now had every unfortunate or addicted gambler in Las Vegas potentially at his mercy.

Lenny's pleas and warnings about Sammy's presence in town fell on deaf ears. In fact, they probably reinforced the godfather's resolve to keep Sammy close to the Firebird and the two cleanskins he mistrusted most of all, Lenny and Bridgett. It was a neat enough solution, Sammy would appear to be gainfully employed while keeping an eye on Lenny and the 'greedy bitch', as well as taking care of any other local Mob business.

To put it in a nutshell, we prospered hugely. Of course, the dirty little secret we all preferred not to talk about, even among ourselves, was that we were all there to help, in some way or another, separate gamblers from the contents of their wallets. But how, you may ask, can a simple piano player contribute to fleecing gamblers? How very easy it is to develop selective perception. The tiniest cog never seems important in itself but it adds as much to the smooth running of the machine as the larger cogs. My little cog in the giant, quietly humming robbery machine was playing good jazz for the wives' and girlfriends' pleasure on a very expensive Steinway piano.

Gambling is seductive – god, I should know. Unlike any other addiction, it can continue until you drop from exhaustion or you run out of cash. An alcoholic can only drink so much before he falls down unconscious. A drug addict can only take so much of a particular poison before he loses his senses or his habit kills him. But there is no limit to a gambler's addiction, provided he stays off strong drink and pills – Benzedrine (or 'Bennies') being the big temptation because it keeps you awake. The pills can also induce manic overconfidence, paranoia and other psychological problems not calculated to increase your chances of winning. The gambling bug isn't a physical addiction but it might as well be.

Arriving at a resort casino like the Firebird was all about anticipation, hope and feeding your addiction. We were more than happy to 'comp' big spenders – or, in casino terms – big losers, who came back at least once or twice a year with a wad of cash for a week of the high life. We'd supply his suite, meals and drinks free, the exception being at the GAWP Bar. While prostitution was illegal in Las Vegas, we'd also supply a special 'friend', should he need one, although this was never talked about and handled exclusively by Lenny. All it took was a nod and a wink, and the client would most fortuitously bump into his stated preference – blonde, redhead or brunette – who would ensure that his every desire was met. If you were a big enough high roller, they would even send the company Convair to pick you up and fly you home.

Around 2 a.m. when I knocked off, I'd walk through the regular casino, through Lenny and Johnny Diamond's territory, and smell the tension in the air. It's the combined smell of stale sweat, adrenaline and naked fear, and it's unmistakeable. At that hour of the morning, only the hard-core gamblers are left. It's quiet, but not because there are no people around. It's because everyone is concentrating on the game; all their attention is focused on the squares and rectangles of green baize, or the spinning of a roulette wheel, where their future will be decided.

I knew better than to find a poker game in town after completing my gig. It's never a good idea to sit in on a game that's been going twelve hours or more. I'd be in bed by 4 a.m. and up around 10 or 11 a.m. to do my chores and go for a walk, usually on the Westside, where I'd often meet some of the Sunday Resurrection Brothers and have a light brunch, and then it would be back to the casino for my regular afternoon practice.

I regarded practice as essential, for while it is easy enough as a piano player to fall into a routine you can perform in your sleep, I took my music seriously. Jazz is no different from classical music and I never forgot Art Tatum's advice: 'It jes a matter of practice, practice and more practice. Now, you remember that good, son!'

I reserved my poker playing for the Sunday-night games and an occasional one-off with a bunch of guys I knew. In these games, you could lose your shirt, but you could also have a reasonably big win. It was gambling, but the game was what counted and the skill you displayed;

greed was never the sole driving force. There were no bad players in these games, and every one of us would have good days and indifferent ones; nobody got their pockets turned entirely inside out. Even though you might go home shirtless once in a while, it was of your own choosing; there was never any pressure to stay, you were always free to pull out if you chose to do so.

Life was good. With the action moving over to The Strip, my apartment was walking distance from the casino and had doubled in value. I had installed two of those new window unit air-conditioners, one in my bedroom and one in the lounge, so I could sleep comfortably on even the hottest summer nights and through the scorching mornings. My bank balance was respectable, despite my taking the inevitable hit every once in a while. Nothing in life is more certain than that there will be someone who is better in some way or more skilful than you. This is not only true in poker but in music and everything else. But I'd always managed to stay more or less ahead of the game, even though, occasionally, I'd come perilously close to being cleaned out entirely.

Playing poker, like music, was a part of me; I wasn't Jack Spayd without it. Winning was important simply because I needed money to keep on playing, but I had no illusions whatsoever about gambling. I was perfectly aware it was never going to make my fortune. I needed it in my life to be . . . well, to keep on being me. Losing made me fear that something had gone missing in my personality, that a chunk of my awareness had disappeared and might not be present when next I sat down to play.

There seemed to me nothing more pathetic than a busted gambler, a player watching a game from the sidelines, yearning written all over his face. I could never work out why guys who'd blown every dime would hang around a game. When I was short of money and waiting to build up my bank, I'd lay low. My pride – or was it fear? – simply wouldn't allow me to look like the pathetic loser I invariably felt myself to be after a big bust.

Sure I sulked, but I did it at home, and often went to work the next evening having spent a miserable day castigating myself. I had one other rule: I never borrowed a cent to play when I was broke or entered a game if another player offered to back me in for a percentage. I wasn't going to become a poker hack or a hired gun.

Poker is notorious for breeding bad blood. Looking back, those were the two rules I believe separated me from the poker degenerates, the hopeless addicts, even though I was pretty sure I had a gambling problem. Las Vegas was full of addicts, and I vowed I'd never do business with a loan shark, or enter a pawnbroker's premises to hock something for a stake.

Las Vegas was pawnbroker heaven, the cheapest place in America to buy a classy Swiss watch, a Rolex Oyster or whatever you desired. The pawnbrokers relied for their business on gamblers who just knew, as if they'd had a visitation from the Virgin Mary herself, that their luck was about to turn. Cash in that watch or the gold signet ring, get a few bucks and get back to the tables. Who knows, maybe sometimes it worked, but I never personally saw a Las Vegas pawnbroker short of abundant stock in his bulging shatterproof steel-grid encased window.

Underpinning my poker playing was the knowledge that I had a safe job that paid well above the average. I must have been fairly good at it because in the years I worked the GAWP Bar, no casino piano bar in Las Vegas was said to compare with it. The drinks were the most expensive in town and it was claimed ours was the only casino cocktail bar that showed a handsome profit at the end of each year. Moreover, I would receive an offer almost every month, together with a generous bonus, to leave Lenny and Bridgett, and work for the now rapidly growing competition run by one or other Mob.

Some of our staff were from time to time lured away with better offers – our people were generally regarded as a cut above the rest – but I couldn't imagine leaving Bridgett, although she continued to show me nothing more than friendship. The Strip was growing up fast and there were now frequent shortages of trained casino staff. Las Vegas was no longer a hick town in the desert.

Other casinos often tried to poach Sue, the long-legged, chestnut-haired, delightful young waitress who'd originally worked the Longhorn Room at the El Marinero. Eventually, the Flamingo offered her almost double her salary to work as the senior drinks waitress on their main gaming floor. When I expressed to Bridgett my regret over her departure she replied, 'Jack, she's really bright. She wants to go to college. I hate letting her go, but the Flamingo's offer is too good to pass up.' Then she'd added thoughtfully, 'Besides, all things considered, it will be good for her to get away from here.' She didn't elaborate and I knew better than to question her further – Bridgett usually had her reasons. She was always scrupulously fair, and genuinely cared about the futures and welfare of her staff.

Money had never been my main object and, as long as I had a stake for my Sunday poker game, I was happy enough. With my vocation and my crazy working hours, I had little chance of a permanent relationship succeeding, although if Bridgett had given me the least sign, I'd have done anything to make it work.

She'd once had an occasion to visit my apartment when I'd been in Las Vegas only a short time. I forget why but, sadly, it wasn't for amorous reasons. She took one look, clearly appalled at the décor (mostly second-hand junk) and said, 'Jack, how could you possibly entertain a young lady in this ghastly mess?' She insisted on Anna-Lucia Hermes redecorating it for me, which she did without charging her usual extravagant fee. Even the furnishings and materials were purchased through the casino, at vastly reduced cost.

I must say, she did a splendid job and the following Sunday I'd invited Bridgett over to have dinner as a thank-you, offering to pay Hector, the meat chef, to cook for us. I admit I had every ulterior motive you can imagine, and when Bridgett agreed to come, my heart leapt, but then she added, 'I can only come if Lenny accompanies me, Jack. You know the no-fraternising rule. I'd love to come on my own but there are simply too many eyes and ears.' The three of us consequently enjoyed a lovely evening together as friends but any hopes I might have secretly harboured for a romantic association with Mrs Fuller were quelled, at least for the moment.

Despite my unrequited feelings for Bridgett Fuller, I had my life pretty well worked out. I couldn't envisage anything serious coming along to disturb my happy little routine. Even Sammy stayed away, busy terrorising bad debtors. Tony Accardo had appointed a dry-as-dust accountant to supervise the casino accounts and the skim, and to replace Sammy as courier. Mr Sanders, a mouse-like man who always wore a shabby lightweight beige suit, white shirt and greasy black clip-on tie, was so ordinary he could go completely unnoticed, even when he was the only other person in a room.

Sammy took his job as debt collector seriously, and was developing a reputation around town as a bad man to cross. The word was he took a bit too much pleasure in hurting people when they fell behind in their payments. He was one of the resident Mobsters the visiting hoods took pride in getting to know because he was regarded as something of a legend. If they wanted a little action, they knew to look him up. Sammy was said to love this bad-guy reputation and to cultivate it at every opportunity. He knew where to find all the bad broads, the unofficial crap games, and he'd developed a little specialty he referred to as 'nigger baiting': capturing a black man and subjecting him to threats, kicks and punches until the poor bastard, convinced he was going to die, pleaded for mercy. To the visiting Mobsters, it was a good way to let off a little steam if you'd had a bad day at the tables. In a big city, Sammy would have been a bit player, but here in Las Vegas he was an official debt collector; in other words, a gangster. He now drove the first pink Cadillac convertible in Las Vegas; a chromed, white-upholstered monster, seemingly half a city block long. Inevitably, his two cohorts sat in the back, eyes glued to the rear windows of the obscenely ostentatious machine. Incidentally, perhaps because of Sammy's choice of transport, Lenny now drove a somewhat conservative black 1948 Lincoln Club Coupe.

Luckily, Sammy wasn't my problem. He wasn't allowed into the resort side of the Firebird and I hadn't needed Bridgett's advice to stay clear. Apart from a nod or a wave when I saw him in the street, I kept my distance. I guess it was another example of selective perception, because the stories about Sammy were not only frightening but often sickening: Sammy flying off the handle and stabbing a guy at a downtown bar for trying to pick up Sammy's girl; Sammy and his ever-present goons beating up a debtor in the car park at the brand-new Thunderbird. Later there were stories about Sammy and his offsiders being behind the disappearance of a dealer sacked for cheating at the Desert Inn. Stories concerning black guys I heard from the kitchen staff and The Resurrection Brothers – they never made it onto the radar of the whites. But Sammy, as far as I could tell, didn't seem to care and none of these episodes seemed to cause any police interest. He probably knew where to leave a wad of used notes when it was needed. I doubt if there was even a slim file on Sammy in official police records. Moreover, the godfather lost no time in pointing out that Sammy's debt-collection business was thriving and that Lenny's refusal to use him as a debt collector for the Firebird was an act of disloyalty to the Family. He insisted that Sammy was the only man on the spot he could absolutely trust to keep an eye on the 'greedy bitch', whereas Lenny feared that one day Sammy would create a situation that not even the godfather would be able to fix with the authorities.

The general feeling was that the police wanted a quiet life. As long as the Mob kept things under control and stayed invisible to the public, the police weren't going to rock the boat. If respectable civilians or tourists didn't get caught up in any violence, they were happy; niggers and Mexicans didn't count. I heard rumours that the wives of judges and senior police officers had points in certain casinos, and that detectives and lower-ranking police had pockets sewn into their uniform pants that reached down to their ankles. Rocking the boat wasn't the Las Vegas way.

With the Firebird such a success, I guess we all relaxed, but then something happened that brought Sammy sharply and disastrously back into my life.

It all began not at the Firebird but at the Flamingo, when the boss of the casino retired and a new man, Louis Springer, was appointed by New York as their representative cleanskin, to run the gaming section. The Flamingo was having trouble with bad debts – mainly from mid-level regulars – but every casino experienced such problems from time to time. These gamblers were addicts who made up the bulk of the poker, black jack and roulette players and, with a few exceptions, they could usually be relied on to pay, given sufficient time. They needed their gambling fix, and the Las Vegas casinos depended on them for the bread and butter of the business; along with the slot machines, of course.

However, Louis Springer was a new broom and unwilling to listen to the conventional wisdom about these addicts. He concluded they were being allowed too much time to get their affairs straightened out. No doubt he'd heard stories of Sammy and his methods of debt collecting and, without consulting New York, appointed Sammy as the new Flamingo debt collector.

Lenny was horrified and called Springer at the Flamingo, pointing out that the Firebird wouldn't dream of using Sammy in this capacity. He tried to talk some sense into the 'Loose Spring', as Louis Springer would eventually be dubbed, but was told to butt out. Lenny then called Chicago and was told personally by the godfather to pull his head in; that Sammy was none of the Firebird's business and if the kikes wanted to hire him, it was an excellent example of cooperation between the Mobs and no different from sharing a few points in each other's casinos to prevent a breakdown in relationships. He'd concluded by saying, 'Now, you listen to me and listen good, ya hear? Las Vegas neutral – it's "golden egg" territory. We all gotta show respect, no trouble between us, not even wid the fuckin' kikes!'

Six months went by. Once or twice, I glimpsed him out driving in his pink Caddy. He'd grown enormously fat and, because of his short legs, he couldn't push the front seat too far back, so that the steering wheel was partly embedded in his great belly. It seemed a minor miracle that he was still able to manoeuvre the huge automobile. Several stories were beginning to circulate about Sammy, but Lenny said that they were the usual crap and that Louis Springer was singing Sammy's praises as a debt collector. He had earned his nickname 'Loose Spring' from the Flamingo staff for his inconsistent decisions and irascible nature, and other casino owners soon adopted the epithet.

Then, one evening, I was heading in to work as usual through the rear entrance of the Firebird, which brought me into a corridor leading to the kitchen. To my consternation, I saw Sammy and his two goons kicking a black guy who was curled up in a ball on the tiles, trying to protect his head. 'Hey, what the fuck . . .' I ran up to them and shoved the nearest goon hard. He tripped over the victim, and collided with his partner so that both of them sprawled a couple of feet from the sobbing black guy. Sammy was left standing over him.

As the two goons untangled themselves, Sammy aimed another vicious kick at the black guy's kidneys, grunting as the toe of his two-tone shoe sank into soft flesh, then stepped back and looked at me. It was eerie. His eyes were glazed, as if he were in a trance or something, and he was breathing hard through his mouth, mucus showing in both nostrils. He was like a man with a bad head cold who has just run a hundred yards and is trying to catch his breath. It was clear he hadn't recognised me.

'Sammy, stop it, will ya! Leave him alone!' I bent over to help the black guy to his feet, and was shocked to recognise that the bloody, broken face looking up at me belonged to Hector, the meat chef from the porterhouse steak incident, whom I now counted as a good friend.

Sammy shook his head and his eyes seemed to come back into focus. For a moment, he seemed surprised to see me; then he gave a grunt of recognition. 'Fuck off outa here, Jack. This ain't none of your business!'

'Hey, Sammy, take it easy, man. This is Hector from the kitchen, the meat chef.'

Something flared in his eyes and he shouted, 'This fucking nigger, he gimme a raw steak on purpose! Motherfucker don't learn the lesson

I give him when he done the same. Man, that's years ago!' He kneaded his knuckles. 'But I ain't forgot! Sammy Schischka don't forget stuff.'

The two goons were now back on their feet and moving towards me. 'Call your dogs off, Sammy, or I'll call the police. You have no right to be here in this hotel.'

'Who says? The Firebird belong to us, to the Chicago organisation.'

I ignored this comment and stood over Hector, to protect him. 'I'm not going to let you kick a friend of mine to death, so back off, all of you.'

To my surprise, Sammy grinned. 'Yeah, I heard about yer nigger lovin'. Fuckin' aroun' wid nigger women. A nigger woman fuck is worse than goin' wid a whore.' The mucus from his battered nose was now collecting on his top lip. He sniffed, then demanded, 'Get the fuck outa here, Jack. I ain't finished with this son of a bitch!'

The coloured kitchen staff, attracted by the noise, had begun to spill out of the door at the far end of the corridor and stood watching silently, afraid to interfere. Mr Joel, the second chef, pushed his way to the front.

Sammy looked up at the silent group behind me. 'Hey, fuck off, you lot. Go on, vamoose. This none your fuckin' business!'

Nobody moved and I stood my ground, my leg protecting Hector's body.

'Ah, the hell wid it, let him go,' Sammy snarled to his two minders, jerking his head in the direction of the passage that led to the parking lot. But then he suddenly stopped and, turning to me, said in his low, gravelly voice, 'You'll keep, piano boy, you'll keep. And don't think Lenny or the greedy bitch can help ya. This between you and me now, nigger lover!'

'That so?' I tapped his chest with my forefinger and grinned. 'Just you and me, eh. Happy to oblige, Sammy. How about we go into the parking lot right now?' I nodded at his two offsiders. 'Let's sort it out man to man, without these two bums.' I was too angry to care if I damaged a piano hand smacking the bastard's ugly lopsided mug.

'Fuck you!' Sammy spat, backing away from me with his two gorillas jumping in between us in case I made a grab at him. They started down the corridor walking backwards, just in case; then Sammy halted at the door and shouted, 'Hey, nigger, I ain't forgot about that porterhouse. I'll be back. Take my advice and get the fuck outa Nevada! Take that whore of a daughter, too, ya hear? I ain't forgot. Sammy Schischka don't forget!'

Mr Joel waited for the door at the end of the passage to shut, then ordered two staff members to help Hector into the kitchen. Then, with a sweep of his right hand, he asked the staff to return to their workstations.

We sat Hector on a chair, so I could have a good look at him. He was a real mess, nose bleeding profusely and clearly broken, both eyes rapidly closing and his jaw jutting to the left – almost certainly broken. I knew it might be a while before he could speak. He was pressing his right side with both hands, sobbing, obviously in real pain from the kicks to his kidneys. I guess Sammy had learned to do this stuff from experts while in Fort Leavenworth – he'd given Hector a thorough going-over. God only knows what would have happened had I not arrived. The beating was not only vicious but systematic. Sammy and his henchmen knew what they were doing.

Mr Joel was fussing around, digging into the first-aid box.

'Here, let me,' I offered, 'you've got a kitchen to run, food to prepare for tonight, early customers already coming in.' I smiled, trying to settle the staff.

'You done this before, Mr Sarsaparilla?'

'I was a medical orderly during the war.' I turned to one of the guys who had helped him in. 'Get his shirt off, Casper, I want to see if his ribs are okay.' I called over to a scullery maid, 'Georgina, bring me damp towels and ice.'

Hector didn't appear to have any broken ribs – Sammy obviously hadn't reached them yet – but he had been kicked savagely and the skin in the lumbar region had turned a deep purple. I was worried about his kidneys; from the look of his lower back, he'd be pissing blood for a week.

I turned to Mr Joel. 'He needs to see a doctor, to check out his internal injuries, set his nose and jaw. Ring emergency and get an ambulance. From the appearance of the bruising on his lower back and side, he'll have kidney damage.'

Mr Joel shook his head. 'I don't think Mr Lenny, he gonna like we call no ambulance. Maybe you be better just walkin' on by? We kin take care of Hector ourself.'

'I'm the medic here and I decide. Please get someone to call the ambulance!' Hector needed urgent attention and I'd suddenly lost patience. Sammy had so blatantly abused the hotel rules that I didn't even concern myself with checking first with Bridgett or Lenny. 'It's my call, Mr Joel,' I said, 'I'll take care of the consequences with management.'

I turned to a busboy. 'Hey, kid, go and tell Miss Bridgett I've been delayed. Tell her to cover for me in the GAWP Bar. I'll start half an hour late.' I turned to several of the helpers. 'Okay, let's go. We'll get Hector out the front for the ambulance.'

A look of sheer panic appeared on Mr Joel's big, round face. 'No, Mr Sarsaparilla. I call the ambulance, but better we take him out the back way. They don't want to upset the customers, they see somebody beat up around the hotel.' He paused. 'That number-one rule for ab-so-loot certain.'

'You know something, Mr Joel? I don't care.' We began to get Hector, who was obviously in a lot of pain, ready to move.

'Nossir, we cain't do no ambulance.'

'Where's the phone?' I demanded.

'Chef Napoleon Nelson's office,' Georgina-May said, holding the wet towels and a bowl of ice cubes.

'Clean him up as much as you can,' I instructed her. 'Go easy, his nose and jaw are probably broken.' I reached out and took a wet dishcloth, then, grabbing a handful of ice cubes, quickly made an ice pack. Hector, unable to talk because of his suspected broken jaw, was moaning and clutching at his kidneys. I lifted his hands and placed the ice pack against his side. 'Hold it there as long as you can, Hector. I'm calling for an ambulance.'

Like in every major kitchen anywhere in the world, pinned to the corkboard in Chef Napoleon Nelson's tiny cubicle was an emergency number. I lifted the receiver and dialled it and waited for a response but, before anyone could answer, it was snatched from my hand. 'Here, let me, Jack,' Bridgett said, slightly out of breath. Then she added, 'Thank you, but I'll take over from here. You have a near-full room waiting, lots of newcomers, it's a big night.' Emergency must have responded because I heard her instruct them to send an ambulance, giving the address and adding, 'It's to come into the parking lot at the back, there will be someone waiting.' Her voice, while crisp, showed no sign of anxiety. I wondered what it might take to cause this remarkable woman to panic.

'Don't you want to know what happened?' I asked.

'Later, Jack. I already know enough for now. Please hurry, you're late.'

The following morning I arrived at the Westside Hospital, the shabby institution that took care of the coloured folk who lived on the wrong side of the tracks. As I entered the ward, I saw that Hector was in a bed four from the door on the left, Chef Napoleon Nelson at his bedside. Also there was Booker T., the railway porter I'd met on that first day seemingly so long ago when I'd wandered into the bar for a hamburger and ended up in a jam session that led to my joining The Resurrection Brothers.

Hector looked a mess, both eyes closed, nose broken and, as I'd suspected, his jaw fractured. But I felt certain the worst damage lay under the sheet, with his kidneys and the internal bleeding.

After I'd said my greetings, I took my place beside Hector's bed and touched him lightly on the shoulder. 'Buddy, I feel ashamed. I've hardly slept all night. I should have insisted they call the police. They would have been forced to take note of me, together with Miss Bridgett and Mr Lenny.'

Chef Napoleon Nelson looked horrified. 'No, no, Mr Jack, don'tcha do that thing. They already bin to see Hector, take ev-ee-dence, the case already closed tight shut.'

'But Hector can't even speak!'

'I done talk for him,' Chef Napoleon Nelson replied.

'That's ridiculous, Chef Napoleon Nelson! You weren't there! It was your night off, Mr Joel was on duty.'

'Sure, Mr Joel come see me early this mornin'. We done decidin' together.'

'So, what is it Hector's supposed to have said?' I asked, my frustration beginning to make me very angry.

Chef Napoleon Nelson looked at me, his eyes sad, tired; the look you see on people's faces when they have no real power, no real say in how their lives are to be conducted. 'He say he ain't seen nothing.'

I jerked my head back in exasperation. 'Oh, I see, as usual some bullshit story, a bolt of lightning struck him several times while he was walking down the corridor towards the kitchen.'

Chef Napoleon Nelson didn't answer but simply looked directly at me and said, 'Jack, you ask him the same question. He gonna nod, use his hands, but it gonna 'mount to the same thing. He ain't seen nothin'. They knock him down, kick him, then vamoose. It all happen so quick, he ain't seen nothing 'cept somebody got black shoes.'

'Nice touch! Everybody in the whole world wears black shoes! Not black-and-white two-tone like Sammy Schischka?'

Chef Napoleon Nelson continued to ignore my indignation. 'Police, they satisfy it some coloured folk thing happen. They ain't got no interest no more.' He spread his large hands. 'Enquiry officially close. Them two policemen, they don't even open their notebook.'

Disgusted, I shook my head. 'Jesus! All this about a porterhouse steak cooked years ago!'

Chef Napoleon Nelson looked surprised. 'Who say that?'

'Sammy . . . Sammy did. I remember it clearly. "Hey, nigger, I ain't forgot about that porterhouse. I'll be back. Take my advice and get the fuck outa Nevada!" Then he mentioned Hector's daughter and said, "I ain't forgot. Sammy Schischka don't forget!"'

At this stage, Hector was shaking his head as much as he was able and making a kind of gargling sound, pointing repeatedly at Chef

Napoleon Nelson, and opening and shutting his right hand to emulate a mouth speaking, urging him to tell me something.

Chef Napoleon Nelson nodded. 'Mr Jack – Hector, he want you should know the whole real story. Ain't got nothin' to do wid no porterhouse steak. It ain't even to do wid the kitchen.'

'Oh?'

Chef Napoleon Nelson leaned back in his chair. 'You know what is a high yella?'

'Well, no, not really.'

'It a person wid light skin. Like Hector's oldest chile. She near got white blood – blue eyes, hair like red brown. You know her – Sue, she the waitress once work at the El Marinero Longhorn Room. She go to the Flamingo when we all come to the Firebird.'

'Sue? You mean Sue Stinchcombe?' I asked, taken aback. I glanced over at Hector, who was attempting to nod his head. 'You never told me that she was your daughter. Stinchcombe . . . that's not your surname, it's Brownwell.'

Chef Napoleon Nelson sighed. 'It one those things we decide best for her,' he said. 'That Hector's wife maiden name.'

'We?'

'Miss Bridgett, Hector and me also, on account I her godfather. We decide when she was fourteen.'

'What? I don't understand . . . Why?'

'Well now, Jack, it a long story. Goes back some. She come to the El Marinero to work in the kitchen when she fourteen, scullery, garbage, dish washin'. Miss Bridgett soon see Sue she got herself a bunch'a brains, got above av-e-rage in-tell-lee-gence; she don't need to be no kitchen hand. She got two more years to finish high school, but Hector and his wife Linda, they got nine other children. So, Sue gonna have to leave school and go to work help support their fambly. So, Miss Bridgett says she'll pay Sue her salary if she go back to finish high school to complete her twelfth grade. But she also arranged for Sue to sit for a trial examination for one o' them private prep school, only white folk go there, but sometime excep-tion-nal they also take one or two black chile. Sue get her a place that fancy white folks' school, two year later she graduate top the school, vale-dic-torian, and Miss Bridgett wants to pay she goes to college. But Sue say, "No, ma'am, not yet. I don't want you to pay no more. I'm gonna earn 'nough to put myself through college and also help mah fambly." She don't want no more charity.' He grinned. 'She . . . she, what's the word . . . ?'

'Headstrong?'

'Yeah, she don't take no crap from nobody. My goddaughter, she got herself a strong mind.'

'But waitresses at the El Marinero – anywhere in Las Vegas – they're all white . . .'

Chef Napoleon Nelson nodded. 'Well, that when we do the secon' decision. Miss Bridgett, she say that Sue got good manners and in that fancy school she done learn to speak like a white girl. She also very beautiful – white man's way o' seeing women – and Miss Bridgett say if Sue can be white, she kin work as a waitress at the El Marinero and get good pay, tips, so long we don't tell nobody she black. She tell us it ain't nothin' shameful, it jes prac-ti-cal.'

I thought of Bridgett and how she herself had been 'practical' and turned herself from a mountain hillbilly to a proper classy lady. This idea for Sue's betterment in this racist desert community was yet another reason to admire her.

Chef Napoleon Nelson shook his head and chuckled. 'So, now Sue come back to the El Marinero and she learn drink waitressing in the Longhorn Room, also cocktail mixing – Barney bin teachin' her as his star pupil. Then the Flamingo make her a great offer – she gonna be their head drinks waitress – and Miss Bridgett says she gotta take it because now she can save more for going to college next year.'

'Well, I'll be damned!' I exclaimed. 'I don't know whether to laugh or cry.'

Chef Napoleon Nelson shook his head. 'Jack, it ain't no laughin' matter now. What Mr Sam done to Hector, it got nothin' to do wid porterhouse. Sue the reason Mr Sam gone try to kill Hector.'

'Eh? What do you mean?' Completely mystified, I glanced at all three men. 'You're saying Sammy attacked Hector because Sue passed herself off as a white girl? Surely not!'

'Nah, that not the real reason. Like I said, Sue the boss girl and also she very popular wid the other hostesses. That because she don't take no shit from nobody and she got herself respect. She don't do no hanky-panky wid white man. Nossir, she a leader them girls do the cocktails, take care the gamblers. Now, they got themselves some problem in that waitress section, they don't got no union rights. So, Sue she go to see the union wid the other girls selectin' her so she be their re-pree-sent-tay-tif. The union man go see Mr Loose Spring. When the union man leave, he call Sue in his office and ask her about this union business. She say it Culinary Workers' Union business. She polite, but he say all the girls get tips and that's enough, then he shoo her away.

'But Sue ain't no pussycat. She say he can ban tips if he want, they just want their union rights – pension plan, medical insurance, full union rates of pay.

'He get pretty mad. "Get back to your job or you dismissed."

'Sue don't take no shit from nobody. "Am I fired or all of us waitresses?" she say.

'"You threatening me, girlie?" he shouts.'

'Jesus, what a deadshit!' I say. 'But how did all this get Hector beaten up?'

'Well, like I said, Hector's daughter, she ain't scared nobody. She go back to the union man and she say they want to go out on strike. He explain he try to talk to Mr Springer, who tell him to get his fat butt outa his office, the Mob got influence in the Culinary Workers' Union. He 'pologise to her and he say if he gonna call a strike, he a dead man.'

Chef Napoleon Nelson paused and smiled. 'Sue ain't happy, so she arrange a meeting for all the Culinary Workers' Union and they decide they gonna walk off in-def-in-ate-ly. You remember, Mr Sarsaparilla. It affect all casinos. Mr Springer, he try to call their bluff, but next shift there ain't no girls check on, also the next. Now, all the casino bosses, they angry. Croupiers, cleaners, they fetching the drinks – ain't nobody happy, least of all the clients.' Chef Napoleon Nelson smiled broadly and shook his head in wonderment. Even Hector was trying to smile, and Booker T. was shaking his head and grinning in admiration.

Of course I knew about the strike and its cause because it had also involved The Phoenix. I didn't know about Hector's daughter at the time. Besides, her name and role as the organiser didn't come up. I simply assumed it was something that had started on the Flamingo gaming floor and spread to the other casinos. I had asked Bridgett about it and she said, by some anomaly, the casino cocktail waitresses were regarded as freelance hostesses. She explained that Lenny had talked to our local union boss but he claimed he couldn't interfere in another union's business.

The girls at the GAWP Bar didn't suffer, though. I explained the situation to my ladies and they seemed happy to go directly to the bar to collect their own drinks, thinking it great fun, and they thoroughly sympathised with the striking cocktail waitresses. I guess some of them would have started life in similar jobs. Anyhow, when the gals returned to work, Bridgett and Lenny quietly paid their wages for the time they were on strike. The hostesses had won and every casino in Las Vegas had to provide proper working conditions and entitlements.

'What about Sue at the Flamingo?' I asked.

'She keep her job,' he answered. 'Ain't nobody gonna fire her case they cause another big, big problem. Mr Loose Spring, he ain't the most popular manager in town.'

'I'm beginning to understand. Someone told Loose Spring about Sue being Negro, and about her being your daughter; is that right?'

Chef Napoleon Nelson nodded. 'You got it, Jack. Why you think the police, they don't want no fuss about what happened to Hector? Mr Loose Spring knows he cain't see no harm come to Sue, but Hector a different matter. He gets Sammy to beat up Sue's daddy real bad, teach her a lesson. Sammy, he only too happy to oblige.'

'And the police have been paid to sweep the whole business under the carpet?'

Chef Napoleon Nelson shook his head. 'I cain't say, Jack. But it ain't necessary. If we tell the truth on Hector's behalf, he ain't coming out this hospital and I don't like Mr Joel's chance, nor even my own neither. Lotsa niggers buried in the desert for causin' less trouble than this gonna be, iffen it get out.'

'But this means Hector's not safe.'

Chef Napoleon Nelson glanced at Hector. 'Doctor say internal bleedin', he gotta stay here two weeks. We done decided Hector got to leave Nevada. We gonna take a collection plate in the church Sunday.' He glanced up at the railway man. 'That why Booker T. here.'

'Where will you go?' I asked Hector, and turned to Booker T. for the answer.

'We ain't decided, Mr Sarsaparilla. He kin hide someplace, maybe east. For coloured folk, that not too much a problem. But he afraid for his daughter. She want to go to college, get herself a good job. But she young, she very headstrong. When we seen her last night, she cryin' but she mad as hell. She ain't gonna do no hiding the truth now they gone hurt her daddy so bad.'

Decisions had been made and there was already the start of a plan to get the family out of Nevada. But perhaps I could help. I looked at Hector. 'Would you consider Toronto, Canada? Working in a jazz nightclub? I'm sure we can find something for Sue as well, that will allow her to go to college. The schools are good in Toronto.'

Hector was in too much pain to smile, but he nodded his head as hard as he could.

'I can arrange that – transport to Toronto,' Booker T. said, smiling. 'Ain't nuttin' but a little bitty bit over the border.'

Chef Napoleon Nelson smiled. 'So, all we gotta do is convince Sue.'

At drinks that night, Bridgett was absent and Lenny was about ten minutes late arriving. 'Hi, Jack, sorry I'm late.'

I nodded and grinned. 'That's okay. Bridgett's not here yet.'

'She's caught up. A call to New York, trying to get them before the close of business hours.' He didn't explain further and ordered a bourbon. When the waiter brought it and we were alone, he said, 'Jack, that thing yesterday afternoon with Hector. You did the right thing not going to the police.'

I didn't reply and Lenny continued, 'I told Sammy, no more. He has to stop working for Loose Spring at the Flamingo.'

'Well, that's great, Lenny; I'm sure Sue and Hector will be pleased.'

'Aw, Jesus, Jack. Just leave it, will ya?' I could see he was getting pissed off.

I held up my hands in mock surrender. 'Okay, Lenny, whatever you say, buddy.' There was no point talking about it, and I certainly wasn't going to tell him about my hospital visit; nor, for that matter, Bridgett, even though I'd trust her with almost anything. I resolved to stay *schtum* about the threats Sammy had made to me – it seemed somehow weak to be carrying tales to Lenny.

I'd decided to call Miss Frostbite during my evening break, when I knew she'd be at the Jazz Warehouse. I felt certain that once she'd heard the story, she'd agree to give Hector a job. As the best barbecue chef I'd ever known, he'd be a welcome addition to the Jazz Warehouse kitchen – good meat chefs are always hard to find.

As for Sammy and me, all this had done was to bring to the surface a problem I'd been trying to ignore the whole time I'd been in Las Vegas; or, rather, from the day I heard about the meat-cleaver incident. Sammy was a loose cannon and I had no illusions about the amount of control Lenny exercised over his cousin. His reassurances were meaningless.

CHAPTER EIGHTEEN

WHEN I NEXT VISITED Hector, Chef Napoleon Nelson was once more by his side. As soon as I'd satisfied myself that Hector was recovering, if slowly, he told me he had some news. According to a chambermaid at the Flamingo, Loose Spring – or Mr Louis, as Chef Napoleon Nelson called him – had left for New York in the Flamingo Convair.

The coloured folks' grapevine extended to all the casinos big and small and, because their welfare depended on accurate information rather than gossip and rumours, it was usually pretty reliable. Nobody knew yet whether Loose Spring's departure was permanent or simply routine, or even if his visit had anything to do with Hector's beating.

'Chambermaid from the Flamingo, she say Mr Louis, he take hisself two big suitcase, that all we know – drawers, cupboards, all empty, shoes all gone.' He paused and looked enquiringly over at Hector, who nodded. 'Also, something else happen.' Hector reached under his pillow and passed me a manila envelope torn open at the top, indicating that I should open it. Inside were twenty-five used twenty-dollar bills and a typed note:

Your hospital bill will be paid for two weeks. Use this money to take your family out of Nevada, with your daughter, Sue. Don't come back!

'Who gave you this?' I looked first at Hector, then at Chef Napoleon Nelson. 'This is evidence.'

'It be under Hector's pillow when the nurse plumpin' it up this mornin'.' He paused and shrugged. 'Hector gonna need money to settle down someplace new.' He sighed and pointed to the envelope. 'That there be a year pay for a meat chef like Hector. No evidence, no witness, Jack. Like I said, case close tight shut and that good cash money gonna give Brother Hector and his fambly a new start in Toronto, if you can arrange that job.'

I sighed. 'All right. As you wish. I called Toronto and the job is okay. Hector's family is welcome. My friend Joe will look about for suitable accommodation for them.'

Chef Napoleon Nelson's face split into a broad grin, and Hector gave me his rictus smile and nodded his head cautiously. 'That joy and jubilation! On behalf the church folk and ever-one The Resurrection Brothers, we thank you, Jack, from the bottom our heart.'

I left soon after for the Firebird. As usual, I entered through the parking lot and into the now-notorious corridor leading to the kitchen. Mr Joel called me over and led me to Chef Napoleon Nelson's office, where we could speak in private. He must have been just about due to go off shift.

'Mr Sarsaparilla, we done miss you the last two days. The staff, they jes want me to say thanks for what you do the other day in the corridor . . . and after,' he said. 'We ain't gonna forget, not never.'

'Sure, sure, Mr Joel,' I said, touching him on the shoulder; then I told him the news from Toronto.

He jumped up, stepped outside the cubicle and clapped his hands loudly several times to bring the kitchen to silence. 'Wunnerful news, folks!' he said, once they were quiet. 'Hector, his fambly, Miss Sue also, dey goin' to Toronto. All arrange by Mr Sarsaparilla!'

There was a muted cheer, every member of the kitchen staff wearing a huge grin.

'It's the least I could do. Hector will like it at the Jazz Warehouse and Susan can complete her education, as well as work there nights if she wants.'

'We mighty obliged, Mr Sarsaparilla. Sooner he gets hisself and his fambly outa Nevada, the better it be for them all.' Mr Joel sighed deeply. 'Mr Sarsaparilla, we all got us fambly. Jobs not easy to find.' I knew this was an explanation as well as a thank-you, and I reminded myself, not for the first time, how fortunate I was to have been born white, or white enough, and not an American Negro, obliged to wash dishes, scrub floors or barbecue steak, no matter how intelligent or gifted I might be. In my head I could plainly hear the worn but still-too-true lyrics of 'Ol' Man River'. The coloured people were still toting barges and lifting bales – who could blame them for feeling weary?

The nasty episode with Hector had upset me more than I was prepared to admit, even to myself. I hadn't been hurt personally, though I knew Sammy's threat to me was far from idle, but it's one thing to hear stories about bad things happening elsewhere to people you don't know and quite another to be confronted by the harm done to people you care about. I had lost the distance I had so carefully cultivated, preferring not to think about Sammy, who, until recently, had played no part in my life as a musician and only a peripheral role in my private Sunday poker games, when he tried to barge into them, usually without success. On the rare occasions when he was able to bluff his way in, Johnny Diamond and I would quietly withdraw. As I mentioned, the guys setting up private games soon got the message. As to whether Sammy took umbrage – well, frankly I didn't give a damn. Johnny mentioned once or twice that Sammy had threatened him, but there wasn't much he could do – it wasn't our game and we had no real say over who was in or out.

But I was kidding myself. The Mob really ran Las Vegas and did so with a mixture of instilling fear and inflicting brutality. Sammy was one of them and although I'd always known through the kitchen staff what was going on, I'd chosen to ignore it. Like most people, I guess, I preferred not to listen to my conscience. I told myself there was nothing I could do. But now Hector's terrible beating had involved me directly and I knew that if I'd *really* pushed it, acted like a man, made a fuss, a *real* fuss, then something might have changed. But, as Chef Napoleon Nelson had suggested, it would have been the end of Hector and his family, and possibly Mr Joel and himself, and if they lost their lives I'd never have been able to face myself again.

I thought about Hector's daughter, a truly remarkable young woman my own age and with more guts in her pinky than I had in both my big Rachmaninoff-playing hands, and I knew – *I mean, deep down I knew* – that the real reason I had kept quiet was because I was frightened of what Sammy represented. Despite Lenny's assurances, I knew Chicago would back the psychopath. I was therefore a coward. No two ways about it.

There was only one person I could talk to and that was Bridgett. Perhaps I wanted to run to Mommy, so she would make it better, tell me it wasn't my fault and what a brave boy I'd been to come to Hector's aid.

As soon as I saw her, I asked if I could speak to her in her office. I told her the whole story, starting with the first porterhouse steak, but Bridgett stopped me short. 'Jack, I know all this. What's really bothering you?'

I ran a hand through my hair and said gruffly, 'I feel like a coward, Bridgett. I know what happened, I know Loose Spring contracted Sammy to beat up Hector so he could avenge himself on Sue Stinchcombe and, yet, I've agreed not to go to the police. I'm ashamed of myself.'

Bridgett looked at me for what seemed like a long time.

'Do you *really* think going to the police would have made a difference, Jack? Take my word for it, the connection between the cocktail-hostess dispute and Hector's terrible beating could be impossible to prove. As far as the police are concerned, the girls got their union working conditions, so now it's back to normal, with only one battered Negro to show for it.'

'But at least I'd feel I'd stood up to the bastard – both bastards – Loose Spring is worse than Sammy.'

'Jack, it's time to set you straight. If you'd identified Sammy, the police would have had to act on it. But what evidence would they find?'

'Christ, I saw it happen! I'd go to the newspapers. Sue's beautiful, she's photogenic, it's the type of story they'd love. Not every American is a racist!'

'Sure, you'll force the police to ask questions. But where is the evidence? They'll make all the usual enquiries, huff and puff a bit for the newspapers, but nobody, certainly not Mr Joel nor the kitchen staff, is going to say they saw Sammy beating up Hector.'

'I know. They've already explained that to me.' I paused and looked directly at her. 'Were those your orders?' I asked pointedly.

Bridgett shrugged. 'I don't have to give orders about such matters, Jack. Coloured folk know how to react, though I daresay Chef Napoleon Nelson may have had a word to them.'

'Well, that doesn't make me feel a whole lot better.'

Bridgett was silent for a moment. 'Okay, Jack, say you went ahead. Your accusation that Hector's beating was related to his daughter's role in the strike would be made to look ridiculous in the hands of a good New York lawyer. The New York Mob may not approve of what Sammy did at Mr Springer's instigation but they'd be forced to defend him. Besides, you may be sure Sammy doesn't have a contract with the Flamingo to pursue their debtors. It would be a deal done on a handshake with cash money paid. Mr Springer would deny everything. The judge would fine Sammy for his so-called drunken attack on a meat cook, but that would be about it. Sammy wouldn't be the first drunk to take his frustrations out on a person of colour.'

I shook my head. Bridgett was only confirming what I'd told myself. I couldn't think of anything else to say. 'It just isn't right,' I said. 'And it doesn't make me any less a pathetic coward.'

'Stop it, Jack!' Bridgett snapped; then, in a more even voice, she continued, 'Castigating yourself isn't going to help. How long do you think it would be before Hector – and, for that matter, Sue – would vanish? No evidence, just gone?' She snapped her fingers, 'Pfft!'

'And you think all this is okay, Bridgett?'

'Jack, I don't think it's okay at all! But it's the way it is. If you cause a *real* problem for these guys, something that *really* affects them, they'll most certainly kill you if they have to. The Jewish Mafiosi, as a general rule, prefer to leave assassinations to the Sicilians and the Irish. They, New York, prefer to buy people off. But if they have to, they too will contract a murder. Remember Mr Siegel . . .'

I sighed. 'So, the sun comes up over the desert tomorrow morning and it's business as usual?' I said bitterly, knowing I was as guilty as anyone.

Bridgett gave me an enigmatic smile. 'Well, yes and no. I daresay New York were not *officially* informed about Hector's beating or the connection to the waitress strike.'

'What does that mean – officially? I'm told Loose Spring left for New York this morning.'

'Well, yes, that's right.'

'Does it have anything to do with Hector?'

Bridgett smiled. 'Jack, like I said, not *officially*.'

'You've lost me, Bridgett.'

'Well, let me give you a bit of background. I was pretty certain Louis Springer was clinging onto his job by the skin of his teeth. The managers and owners of the other casinos whose waitresses went out on strike have let New York know what they thought of Mr Springer and the disastrous and arrogant manner in which he handled the strike. After all, we're all supposed to be legitimate businesspeople with points in each other's casinos, in order to keep the peace. Defying the union just wasn't smart and New York would have been embarrassed. But if they'd withdrawn Mr Springer immediately, it would have shown weakness, and Mobsters can't tolerate that. They were obliged to stick by their man for the time being.'

'So, what happened to get him out of Las Vegas? I take it it's permanent?'

Bridgett nodded. 'I really shouldn't be telling you this, Jack, but I put through a person-to-person call to New York, and told them what had happened to Hector in *my* casino and the reason. I made it clear that my coloured staff were witnesses and that it would be difficult to cover things up . . . not difficult, impossible, if New York didn't cooperate by removing Mr Springer immediately.'

'You can do something like that?'

'Not usually, but I thought they'd take my call.'

I looked at her, flabbergasted. 'And you told them about Sue and the reason for Sammy's assault on Hector?'

'Like I said.'

'But how did you know they hadn't approved Hector's beating? That Loose Spring hadn't informed them?'

Bridgett sniffed. 'It would have been entirely out of character for them to agree. They only use violence as a last resort. Besides, they wouldn't want to compound the problem. Spring's was a patently stupid action and they're *not* stupid. I guessed they were only waiting for the right opportunity to pull Louis Springer out and my bluff worked. He left on their company plane this morning.'

'I suppose that's something, but Hector's still no better off.'

'Jack, like you, I'm fond of Hector. You will recall we brought him over to the Firebird from the El Marinero, to get him away from Sammy, and now . . .'

'Fat lot of help that turned out to be,' I said bitterly.

'Jack, that's simply not fair! This incident was at Louis Springer's instigation. Please allow me to continue. I also like Hector's daughter, Sue. She's a swell girl, bright, intelligent, an all-round lovely young woman.' Bridgett took a breath. 'So, I put through that call to New York.' She paused and grinned. 'It gives me another piece of insurance, and of course, they think I'm doing it for the good of the casino.' She threw back her head and gave a short laugh. 'Men seldom read a woman's motives correctly and, thank the Lord, invariably underestimate her intelligence.'

However, I knew Bridgett well enough to realise that getting rid of Loose Spring wasn't the only reason she'd called New York. 'Well, why else? You *were* doing it for the good of the casino, weren't you?' I persisted.

'Jack, I feel sure you know about the envelope under Hector's hospital pillow.'

My surprise must have been apparent. 'The grand in old notes? That wasn't . . .'

'Aha, no. It was New York. They're paying Hector's medical bills as well.'

'The typewritten note?'

'I used an old typewriter I found in a back cupboard in the storeroom. I've since disposed of it.' She grinned. 'New York were happy to oblige with the money.'

'You bluffed them into thinking it – the whole Hector thing – was going to blow up big?'

Bridgett nodded. 'Yes, but like you, I feel thoroughly ashamed. Ashamed of what happened to Hector in the corridor. Ashamed that I knew it would be just another cover-up with the police, that the coloured folk were helpless. Mr Springer had to go anyhow and the money for Hector's family will help a little to resettle them elsewhere, but it's still not right.'

'Bridgett, aren't you sailing a bit close to the wind with Chicago by calling New York?'

Bridgett nodded. 'Normally, yes, but Lenny agreed I make the call when I put it to him. Remember, they all share points in each other's casinos. Lenny immediately saw my call as an opportunity to get rid of Louis Springer, a feather in his cap with Chicago, so long as Sammy wasn't sacrificed in the deal.'

'Christ, Bridgett, doesn't that scare you, playing ducks and drakes with various Mobs?'

'Jack, I try to make very certain I never get into that sort of situation. I've got good reasons, as you know, to stay in Las Vegas and my paperwork is immaculate . . .'

'Not much good if you're dead,' I quipped.

'Killing me would be downright foolish, Jack. What I have on Chicago would allow the feds to lock them up for a hundred years.'

I felt a confused mixture of admiration and despondency; the former because she was such a remarkable woman, the latter because she would surely never look twice at a guy like me. For a moment, I considered telling her of Sammy's direct threat to me – pathetic, I know – but then decided against it and said instead, 'Sometimes I wonder whether I should stick around. Maybe it's time to pack my bags and move on?'

For a moment, a look passed over Bridgett's face that I couldn't read, and she said, 'Oh, Jack, I'd simply hate that!' Then immediately she recovered her composure. It wasn't hard to see how she'd transformed herself from hillbilly to sophisticated woman of the world; she was capable of rigidly concealing her emotions. 'Jack, that's something only you can decide,' she said, but then added, 'such a pity you don't take notes.'

'As I said before, I'm a jazz man, it's all in my head.'

'Where a bullet could so easily remove it,' Bridgett said softly, almost as if to herself; then, looking me in the eye, she said urgently, 'Please don't go, Jack.'

'Oh, well,' I laughed, unsettled by the dark turn the conversation had taken, 'I guess I'll just have to come to terms with the fact that, like you, I've done a deal with the devil.'

'Jack, I hope you can. I love having you around . . . and so do the patrons and the staff – the coloured folk, in particular, regard you as one of them, a white guy they trust with their lives.' She looked deep into my eyes and I felt my throat tighten. She really was gorgeous. 'But, *please*, if you decide to stay, if anything untowards should happen between you and Sammy, I beg you not to take things into your own hands. Will you *please* let me know immediately?'

I stood up to leave, uncertain what to say, and, quite unexpectedly, Bridgett's composure seemed to crumple. She came around the desk and to my surprise gave me a hard hug and kissed me on the cheek, then suddenly her lips were on mine, soft and very tender. She drew back almost at once, but I could see she had tears in her eyes. 'I couldn't bear it if anything happened to you, Jack,' she whispered.

I lightly touched the place on my cheek where she'd kissed me, wondering if I dared hope there might one day be something between us.

I was a gambler, after all – perhaps this wasn't the time to cut and run. 'Bridgett, I'll keep out of trouble or I'll leave. Don't worry, I got through the war with only a nick to my earlobe.'

Two weeks after 'the kiss', as I wistfully referred to it, Johnny Diamond and I were playing with a carefully chosen group of out-of-town poker players in a Sunday night game on Fremont Street. The house took ten per cent, which covered the cost of the suite, drinks and a decent tip for the barman. It was around four in the morning and I was ahead about fifteen hundred dollars.

The company was pleasant – good solid players – who always seemed to enjoy Johnny's nice laconic wit. He had a way of undercutting the town's pseudo glitz and glamour that I enjoyed. He was a realist and was always straight and true; something, I guess, we both tried to be. If, for instance, he reached his anticipated stake and it wasn't going well, he'd pull out politely. He never made a fuss, and I never saw him sulk.

We were having a break while players' drinks were refreshed, and some went to the bathroom. I got up and walked over to the window, where one of the visiting players had pulled the heavy drapes back and was looking down into the street.

You could see why Fremont Street was called Glitter Gulch – it was like a waterfall of light so bright it was like midday but with a chaotic and constantly changing kaleidoscope of colour. Nobody initially sets out to design a streetscape composed largely of neon advertising – over the years, it simply evolved to become a clashing, brashly flashing, crowded display of tubular light mixed with discordant snatches of broadcast music, and nightclub barkers shouting their invitations over the din of traffic, all of which combined willy-nilly to create a very effective lure for any sucker with a wallet who was prepared to chance his luck. While the new resort casinos on The Strip had taken most of the local action, Glitter Gulch and the older established casinos continued to flourish in Fremont Street.

The visitor, a guy named Warwick Selby, turned to me. 'This place kinda gets to you, don't it, buddy?'

'Yeah, you said it. When you see it like this, it's really something.'

'Been here long?'

'Four – maybe five – years.'

He gave a low whistle. 'And you're still ahead of the game?'

I laughed. 'I work in the piano bar at the Firebird until very late, so during the main gambling hours I'm otherwise occupied. Games like this one on my night off are pretty much it. So far,' I jerked my head in the direction of the card table behind me, 'playing this way, I have a fluctuating bank balance, though, for the most part, it's in the black.'

'Wise man. A friend is staying with her husband at the Firebird and invited my wife to hear you play last night. I think she fell a little in love with you – they both did. They want to go back and hear you tomorrow night.'

I smiled. It was a common compliment and I'd learned to deal with it by pretending to be slightly embarrassed.

'She says you're very good, I mean *very* good.'

'Why, thank you. It's always nice to hear about happy customers.'

'So, how long do you plan to stay?'

The question was one I had been asking myself ever since my talk with Bridgett. Deep down I knew the answer but wasn't sure I wanted to admit it, even to myself. 'I'm not sure I know. Why do you ask?'

'Oh, my family have various entertainment interests in Houston; among them, a club my dad started way back in the twenties. It's small but classy. I thought you might like a sea change. We'd pay you well and build you any piano-bar setup you want – good clientele, no jerks, your kind of music.'

I feigned astonishment. 'You're making this offer on your wife's recommendation? Don't you know the GAWP Bar – I mean, The Phoenix – is famous for the strength of its highballs?'

He laughed. 'No, but she was a pretty good jazz singer in her day – still is, I guess – but now she's on the other side and helps with our business, mostly with the hiring of talent; and, believe me, she knows a good piano player when she hears one.'

'That's a very nice offer and I thank you, Warwick. I confess I have two addictions, jazz and poker, and both are available here and in about the right combination and, alas, nowhere else in America.'

'I like a serious game of poker myself.' He jerked his head to indicate the interior of the room. 'Games like this one.'

'So, you don't come to Las Vegas to play in a casino?'

'Yes, occasionally, but playing poker without having to win at all costs, with guys like you and Johnny Diamond, that's one aspect of this town I love. If you have any other friends, next time I'm in town let's get together for a private game.'

'You're right, Warwick. We all know when we're in a casino it's going to end up in a Mobster's pocket. I prefer to think I can win or lose to someone who plays to enjoy the game. I admit I'm addicted to poker and the piano, like I said.' I gave a short laugh. 'I guess they're going to have to carry me out of Las Vegas in a box.'

Warwick Selby nodded. 'I'm not a hood, nor was my daddy, but he knew just about every big Mobster in America. You don't get through Prohibition as a nightclub owner without meeting a few less-than-honourable men on the way. Las Vegas has more than its fair share. I should know; my family are among the few honest investors in two casinos in this town and we see the names behind the names, if you know what I mean.' He gave me a steady look. 'Jack, you could well end up leaving Las Vegas in a box. Think seriously about a sea change. Take my advice, my offer of a piano bar in Houston stands any time you want. My daddy always maintained that the company you keep defines you, and if it involves the Mob, in the end it may eliminate you.' Before I could think of a suitable answer, or even thank him for his advice, the call went out that the game was about to recommence.

I won a reasonable amount – no fortune but well worth my Sunday night. I crawled into bed with the air-conditioner rattling its usual breathless lullaby and got to thinking about what Warwick Selby had said about the company you keep defining you. Maybe it was time to move on. But, as soon as the thought entered my head, I pictured

Bridgett. How could I leave her? How could I ask her to leave with me? It was hopeless. With her points in the Firebird and the essential role she played in the success of the GAWP Bar, she was stuck for years if she wanted to become filthy rich.

Although she worked with Lenny and frequently met with the other casino owners on business, when she attended a social occasion, she always went alone, even though almost everyone else brought a spouse or a friend. Those who didn't know her regarded her as a cold, over-efficient harridan. But among her staff, Mrs Fuller had, at the very least, total respect and often absolute love; in fact, the lower down the hierarchy, the more love and trust she inspired. But her ability always to keep just the right distance meant that nobody had the courage to tell her how much they admired, respected, trusted and loved her. She'd mentioned that the coloured folk liked and trusted me; by comparison to the way I knew they felt about her, I would have been considered a poor second.

I'd mention their regard for her from time to time but I don't think she believed me and wouldn't discuss the subject, dismissing my passed-on compliments with a click of the tongue and a flick of her elegantly manicured fingers. 'Jack, it's my job,' she'd finally conclude.

Perhaps she thought no man would want her, but if this were true she was mistaken. I saw the way guys looked at her, and I knew how much I wanted her. I longed to hold her, make love to her, and she'd figured in my fantasies from almost the day I met her. But she was my boss, four or five years older than me, and in those days that was supposed to count. In truth, I simply didn't have the courage to make the first advance. I analysed that kiss, the one on the mouth, and told myself it had lasted longer than necessary, and her being near tears; surely that meant something? But her startled withdrawal after the kiss and the speed with which she regained her composure seemed to warn me not to make any assumptions.

I was deeply honoured that she'd chosen to tell me about her hillbilly past. Humans are by nature social animals, even those who draw into themselves almost completely. Eventually they all need to talk to someone. The idea that confession is good for the soul underpins many religious faiths and, as Joe once said to me when I'd confessed some deep, dark secret of my childhood, 'Jazzboy, we all gotta carry dat bag o' beans on our back. Ever' day more beans goin' in and if no beans comin' out ever, it gonna get too heavy. Dat why ever once in a while we all gotta spill da beans.'

I'd seen the effects of low self-esteem in Cabbagetown innumerable times; known them myself, on more than one occasion. People from dirt-poor backgrounds, the so-called white trash of society, no matter how successful, never feel they're quite good enough to make the grade. Bridgett was one of us and I felt honoured that she'd chosen 'to spill the beans' to me. Despite going over things for an hour or more, I was none the wiser, and eventually descended into a troubled sleep.

Nothing was said to me officially about not talking to the police, and Sammy was still driving around Las Vegas in his pink Cadillac convertible with the two goons in the back seat manning the rear window. He'd relocated his debt-collection business from downtown to almost next door to the Firebird, so I'd now often see him on my way to work as I crossed the road to go through the parking station and into the kitchen entrance. In fact, it soon became obvious that just before three o'clock, when I came in to practise piano, Sammy and his two henchmen made a point of being on the sidewalk outside his office. He would stand, legs apart, his arms crossed above his increasingly enormous belly, and stare at me, his two goons adopting the same stance and stare. I could always have taken a longer route but I told myself no one had ever been killed by a stare and I was damned if I were going to give the fat little fart the pleasure of upsetting my routine.

As for Loose Spring, he never returned from New York. He was probably wearing an apron and selling bagels and lox from a pushcart in the Bronx. The Flamingo replaced him with a seemingly nice-enough guy named Michael Solomon, inevitably known as 'Mr Sol'. Although I had little or nothing to do with him, Lenny, who didn't share Chicago's attitude to Jews, said he was on the ball and a real nice guy who'd made a point of offering his cooperation, should it become necessary.

There wasn't much I could do about the daily appearance of the threesome, but I admit, after a bit, it was making me increasingly uneasy. This wasn't Bridgett's territory, so, after several weeks of ignoring the intimidation, I decided to raise my concerns with Lenny.

'Come!' Lenny, ever the master sergeant, called without glancing up when I tapped on the open door of his office.

I walked in and sat down facing him across his over-large desk, the surface of which was spotless except for an immaculate blotter with scarlet leather trim, on which lay a copy of Sports Illustrated open at an article he appeared to be reading.

He'd recently redecorated his office in scarlet and gold, the colours of the US marines. There was no hint of Anna-Lucia Hermes' influence and, I must admit, the effect was more Chinese New Year than US military. Heavy gold drapes with scarlet tassels framed the large window, the carpet was scarlet and the ceiling was gold; although, thankfully, the walls had been left a deep cream. On one wall was an enormous colourful painting in an ornate gold frame, inspired by Joe Rosenthal's famous black-and-white photograph of the US marines raising the flag at Iwo Jima. Miss Frostbite would have referred to it as being 'in truly appalling taste' and I feel sure even my mom would have agreed with her.

'Oh, hiya, Jack!' Lenny exclaimed.

'Have you got a moment, Lenny?'

He spread his arms and smiled. 'Hey, Jack, buddy! For you . . . always!'

'It's Sammy, Lenny,' I began.

Lenny frowned. 'Whaddaya mean? He say somethin' to ya? Somethin' outa line?'

'I didn't tell you at the time, but he threatened me in the passageway when I stopped him beating up Hector,' I said, and Lenny's frown deepened. 'And now . . .' I explained the regular sidewalk routine with Sammy and his two minders.

Lenny immediately relaxed and leaned a long way back in his new scarlet executive swivel chair, his hands thrown wide above his shoulders. 'Jack, take it easy, old buddy. You know Sammy. That a matter o' pride, him tellin' ya he ain't forgot. But, listen up, he ain't gonna start nothing, ya hear?'

'Lenny, I kept my side of the bargain. I kept my mouth shut. For Sammy, it could have turned out a whole lot worse.'

'Let's not go there, kid. I'll talk to him. I know it ain't easy for you. Even if Hector is only a nigger, it happened on the casino premises and coulda maybe come to something if you hadn't stayed *schtum* and Bridgett hadn't stopped the kitchen staff talkin' to the cops. Sammy ain't stoopid enough to shit in his own nest a second time!' He then added, 'The godfather glad Sammy stayed outa trouble. Sammy don't want to get into no more shit like that.'

'Thanks, Lenny. I appreciate your help.'

'Jack, Sammy's just being himself – fat little guy, gammy leg, fucked in the head. Jesus, he's a debt collector! Intimidation is all he's got goin' for him. That Loose Spring strong-arm stuff, it all over now. Ain't nothing gonna happen between the two of you, buddy! Nigger's one thing, beating up you – white guy, big money-spinner for the casino – that's somethin' else. You know what I mean? Chicago gonna tear him a new asshole if he try something like that.' He shook his head slowly, then added, 'It don't make no sense. My advice, take no notice.'

Though he'd inadvertently put me in my place as a mere money-spinner, I knew it was just Lenny's clumsy way and that he regarded me as an old friend and wartime buddy. Although I wasn't entirely convinced Sammy would behave himself, I accepted Lenny's reasoning and his promise to talk to his cousin and, almost at once, the sidewalk intimidation stopped. Three months passed and I'd only occasionally see Sammy; usually on The Strip, driving his pink Caddie convertible with his two hoods in the back seat.

What I didn't suspect was that the sick puppy in Sammy was steadily growing into a mad dog, and that he'd developed a dangerous addiction to Benzedrine. As a medical orderly, I'd issued Benzedrine during combat and was aware of the drug's dangerous side effects, such as paranoia, aggression, agitation, anxiety, grandiosity and even psychosis. Had I known he was hooked on Bennies, I'd have taken my own advice and left the night Bridgett and I talked and she ended up kissing me. I should have taken the memory of her kiss with me and run for my life.

I've mentioned before that Sammy was, at best, a poor poker player, but the drug exacerbated his delusions of grandeur. There were rumours around town that he insisted on playing poker with the rich and famous in other casinos, and that, as usual, he was losing hand over fist. None of that was my concern, although it made me anxious about the private Sunday games I played with Johnny Diamond and various acquaintances. Sammy hadn't given up on these and, once or twice, he'd cost us a night's poker when we'd had to turn down an invitation from an outsider who didn't know what he was getting himself into when he invited Sammy.

I had my fair share of poker games with the rich and famous, too, mainly through the GAWP Bar. Bridgett would tease me about whenever some movie mogul or star, or mega-rich oilman, requested a private game be set up because his wife or girlfriend had sung my praises the previous night, having imbibed one too many Manhattans. When the husband or boyfriend heard that I knew my way around a poker game, he'd request a private one, either to check me out or show off to the little woman. Bridgett would pass on the invitation with a twinkle in her eye. 'Women love you, Jack, and it's not only for your piano playing . . . or your poker!' Sometimes I'd be invited to play a game in a guest's suite, organised by the Firebird. It might be with a visiting high roller or big-time musician or movie star, who, for whatever reason, had requested I be included in a game. Bridgett had little choice but to agree to such requests, and the casino supplied my stake. It was usually nice work and I'd often end up with a little bankable money. I kept my winnings and the casino carried any occasional losses. It was, in a sense, public relations.

I was practising in the GAWP Bar at around four on a Wednesday afternoon, some six months after the Hector incident. Hector, by the way, had almost completely recovered and had started work at the Jazz

Warehouse, while Sue was attending college and working three nights a week in the club as a cocktail waitress. Anyhow, I was fairly well into my practice session when I felt a tap on my shoulder. It was Johnny Diamond. I offered him a drink, but he said, 'No, thanks, I won't stay, got to get back to work; just wanted to have a quick word.'

'So, what brings you here, buddy?'

'Hey, Jack, you remember we played poker with those guys from Houston and Dallas?'

'Yeah, Warwick Selby, the nightclub owner from Houston; and a bunch of other guys, mostly from Dallas, Texas – nice guys, played good poker.'

'Right. Well, a few oil guys from Louisiana are here, along with some of the old Dallas guys. They're staying at the El Cortez for the 101st Airborne reunion dinner. It's on Friday night at the Desert Inn. They want us to join a game tomorrow night. Do you think you can get an early mark; say, just before midnight?'

'Probably be okay. I'll ask Mrs Fuller.' I laughed. 'She owes me six hours. Two groups from Atlanta, Georgia, wouldn't budge until near dawn most of last week. Those southern gals sure know how to party.'

'Can you let me know soon? Warwick Selby, especially, asked that we be included. Jack, it's only two hours off your shift. Be fun, buddy.'

'Hey, wait, did you say it was at the El Cortez? We don't play in casinos, unless it's something special.'

'Hey, no, man – it's the hotel across the road, same as last time.' He grinned. 'Yeah, good money burning a hole in their pockets. It seems they been wildcatting down in Louisiana, gas and oil. Struck it rich, but you know those guys; rich Monday, broke by Friday. Mad gamblers. They warned me as a joke – a serious one, I guess – not to bother coming unless we had a roll that would choke a horse. They've come to play serious poker. We did okay last time, though. Never know your luck, eh? When can you let me know?'

'Do it right off,' I said, rising. There was a phone at the bar, and I walked over, dialled the switchboard and had Bridgett paged. A minute or so later, she answered. I can't say she was ecstatic but she agreed to let me leave two hours early the following night. 'Okay, Johnny, keep me a seat,' I said, replacing the receiver.

'Great, Jack! Let's hope we get lucky again. See you there.'

By the time I got to Glitter Gulch the following night, it was fifteen minutes past midnight and the game was already underway with a vacant seat left for me. Johnny Diamond had been on afternoon shift at the Firebird, which ended at 10 p.m., so he'd arrived earlier and had been in the game for an hour or so, getting to know the competition. But arriving a bit late didn't bother me unduly. I knew Johnny's game and Warwick Selby's, and I'd played with one or two of the oilmen before. It was unlikely the new guys would be anything out of the box. Poker players usually find their level.

Most of the men were smoking, two of them big Havana cigars, so the air was the usual fug. Even the best air-conditioning can't cope with the heavy smoke you get around high-stakes poker games. There were always those players who felt having a drink or two beforehand helped them to concentrate, but no good poker player would play with real drunks. Occasionally even a good player would be dealt out if he were thought to be a tad too inebriated. It was part of the code of honour among decent poker players. In my experience, any more than one or maybe two drinks impairs a man's judgement in a high-stakes game, and I was often glad that I'd sworn off alcohol as a child. Seeing the mess it made of my father's life, and my mother's and mine, it was an easy decision. However, I'd become weary over the years of explaining why I didn't drink, so these days I'd simply order myself a tonic on the rocks and pass it off as either a gin or vodka mix. It meant that I could blend in in the capital of American hedonism and not be looked at as some kind of puritan freak.

After the usual chiacking – 'Hiya, Jack' and 'Welcome back, buddy' and 'Ready to lose your shirt?' – from players I knew, together with introductions, greeting and laughter around the table, I took my seat. They were a friendly bunch and every visiting player wore on his lapel the eagle badge of the 101st Airborne. All were there for a good time and, to their obvious delight, they had given the El Cortez casino floor a huge flogging earlier in the evening. They were awash with cash and they'd set the stakes as high as they thought they could without frightening us away. Easy come, easy go, I guess.

'You shoulda seen it, buddy,' one of them told me during the settling-in period. He had a slow Texan drawl and had earlier been introduced to me as Kid Lewis, and thereafter simply referred to as the Kid. 'Frankie here was playing craps and after three wins we all gave him some cash and, ya wouldn't believe it, he made his point nine times in a row. We *really* cleaned up, bigger than fuckin' Texas!'

Frankie, the lucky craps player, was obviously having a good night. Winning a lot of money for your friends was always going to make you popular and I decided to keep an eye on him. Feeling lucky and overconfident is a bad combination.

We started to play and, after three hands, Johnny Diamond threw in his cards and rose from the table. 'What's up, Johnny?' I asked.

The Texans laughed at the question. 'You shoulda seen him before you came, Jack. He couldn't buy a card to save his life.'

Johnny shook his head. 'Some nights a guy should just stay home. I'll hang around and watch, serve the drinks, maybe go for a walk later.' He was smiling, though. As I said, he was a careful player who seemed always to stick to a pre-set limit. Once that was gone, he would stop. I guess a pit boss sees enough not to be careless with his own money. The Texans, flush with the earlier injection of cash from the craps win, had, as I mentioned, set the stakes high and Johnny, having a poor night, had obviously quickly lost as much as he cared to lose, but he never bitched or whined about it. Johnny was a regular guy.

After a couple of hours of play, I was up about eight hundred dollars, and one of the other locals, Jim Bragg, was also up a couple of hundred. The Texans were winning and losing, largely to each other, with a nice little share here and there for Bragg and me, but Frankie was taking a beating. 'Big money brings few smiles into a game,' as they say. But the company was good, we were all about the same age and most of us had been in the services, so, naturally, there was a fair amount of talk about the war.

Younger people don't realise just how all-enveloping the Second World War was. If you were in the right age group, you were in it, unless there was something pretty seriously wrong with your health. Swapping war stories was always interesting. When my turn came, I explained that I'd served overseas too. 'Most of the time I was in England. We were based near Gatwick airfield for a while and later I had a soft number in London.'

'Goddamn, how about that!' Frankie said. 'We were there for a while in 1944, after the landings in Normandy.' It was surprising how often ex-military people had been in the same places at the same time.

'What happened between Gatwick and the soft posting in London?'

'Ah, in between was a very short stint in Dieppe.'

'We heard about that,' the Kid exclaimed. 'Nasty. Were you taken prisoner?'

'No, I was lucky. Our LCM broke down a mile or so offshore and we arrived late. Some of our guys jumped in when they let down the ramp; then we realised we'd landed right in front of a German pillbox and the navy guy in charge pulled us back off the beach. We lost a lot of guys that day.'

'Yeah, we were always glad we were jumping through air and not into water when we went in,' Frankie commented. 'Wading through water up to yer thighs and then running across wet sand in army boots musta been like being on the wrong end of a kraut shooting gallery. Don't appeal to me at all.'

Several players nodded their agreement.

'Funny you'd say that. I felt that way about people jumping out of a perfectly good aeroplane. Strange, isn't it? We all reckon we had it better than the other guy.' I grinned. 'As far as I was concerned, the poor bastards in the navy had it the worst. We went over on the Queen Mary and I practically shat my pants the whole time I was aboard. I don't know how those navy guys did it year after year, never knowing when you were going to get a torpedo slap bang in the guts.'

This drew agreement, except from Jim Bragg, who, it turned out, was ex-navy. 'Ah, you'd all get sick on wet grass! There were always lifeboats, not like having someone taking pot shots at you on a beach, or tumbling out of the back of an aeroplane with a kraut farmer waiting to catch you on the end of his pitchfork.'

It was that sort of night.

By 4.30 a.m. there was a general feeling we should finish up. I was up around $1000, and I was feeling particularly relaxed and couldn't remember enjoying a poker night so much in a long time. I was getting ready to take my leave, when Kid Lewis, who seemed to be one of the leaders, called over, 'Now, Jack, we wanna see you again Friday night. We're flying back to Dallas day after.'

'Hey, but it's your reunion dinner, isn't it?'

'Well, yeah, but we've organised a game after.' The Kid pointed to Johnny, who stood across the room, talking to two of the other guys. 'Sergeant Johnny booked the room at the Desert Inn a month back.'

'Johnny Diamond, he one of yours?' I asked, surprised.

The Kid looked genuinely astonished. 'Yer mean ta tell me, yer didn't know he was 101st Airborne? Sergeant Diamond, fuckin' living legend during the Normandy Invasion – Distinguished Service Cross. He was with us all the way from our first training camp to the finish in Germany.' The Kid turned and shouted, 'Hey, Johnny, come on over here for a moment, will ya?' Johnny Diamond excused himself from the two guys he'd been talking to and came over. 'Tell Jack we want him in Friday night's game, buddy.'

Johnny shrugged. 'I thought it was strictly 101st Airborne, but it'd be real nice if you could make it, Jack.'

'I don't know if I can,' I said.

'I know Friday's a big night at the GAWP Bar.' Johnny grinned. 'I applied to Lenny for the day off three months ago.'

I hesitated. Bridgett wouldn't be happy and, besides, it's never a good idea to 'play the same pack' too soon after a high-stakes game. I'd won a fair bit, certainly ending ahead of any of the other players, and if

I did that two nights in a row, the group might decide I was 'a cut above the pack' (another poker term) and I'd be excluded from future games.

'I'll have to check with my boss. Like Johnny says, Friday's one of our big nights.'

The Kid stabbed his forefinger into my chest. It was obvious he wasn't going to accept no for an answer. 'Try real hard, Jack, will ya? A friend of Sergeant Johnny Diamond is automatically considered one of us.' He called over to the others, 'Right, fellas?'

'Right!' they all chorused.

'Great, buddy; see ya Friday, midnight, eh?' the Kid said.

'Come on, I'll give you a lift home, Jack,' Johnny offered.

Once we were in his car, I said, 'Hey, you never told me you were with the 101st Airborne in Normandy.'

'You never told me you were at Dieppe,' he replied.

When we reached my apartment, I thanked him for including me in the game and said how much I'd enjoyed his wartime comrades. 'Sorry it wasn't a great night for you,' I added. 'Perhaps tomorrow night, eh? Goodnight, buddy.'

He shrugged. 'Some nights are great, some not. Nobody knows that better than you, Jack.' He then said, 'Be nice if you can make it, but I understand if you can't. Call me either way.'

I nodded. 'I'll talk to Mrs Fuller.'

I slept well and woke after midday – winning tends to be the best sleeping pill of them all. I showered, dressed and walked directly to the Firebird to see Bridgett at 2 p.m. After a bit of 'umming and ahhing', and a nudge about the gals from Atlanta the previous week, she agreed – probably the worst decision on my behalf she ever made. 'You owe me, Jack,' was her final comment. Not strictly true but, what the hell, she was pretty particular about whether a new intake had a great night at the GAWP Bar.

I called Johnny and told him.

'Great news, Jack, the guys'll be pleased. I'll meet you at quarter to midnight sharp.'

I had my customary late lunch, or early dinner, and settled into an hour-and-a-half's practice in the Phoenix Bar, while the staff set up the room for the evening and Barney prepared the bar. Bridgett permitted any member of staff who had a birthday to have fifteen minutes off to allow me to play a special request or two in their honour. Then I was due to meet Bridgett and Lenny for a drink; although, on Fridays, Bridgett was often run off her feet, and sometimes couldn't make it. After this, I'd have a little time to relax, and read a book in my dressing-room before changing into my tuxedo for the early show.

I was just thinking about finishing practising when I sensed someone standing behind me. Completing the short exercise I was running through, I turned around and realised with a start that Sammy Schischka was directly behind me.

I attempted to conceal my surprise – we hadn't spoken a single word since the Hector incident and his subsequent threat.

'Oh, hi, Sammy. What can I do for you?' I asked. Bridgett had assured me he was banned from The Phoenix Bar, making his appearance even more startling. As usual, he was with his two scowling retainers, who stood below the platform on either side of their master.

'You're playing in a poker game over at the Desert Inn tonight.' It wasn't a question but a statement.

'Yeah?' It was none of his business but I wasn't looking for trouble.

'Well, I wanna play. Get me into the game.' It sounded like an order.

The room was silent; the cleaners had stopped working, no doubt as shocked as I was to see him.

'Sammy, this is my practice time. You're not supposed to be in this part of the hotel and the answer to your question is simple, I do not have the authority to invite you to tonight's game.' I paused. 'That is, even if I wanted to and . . .' I now realise I should have left it at that but I added, '. . . even if I could, I'd be damned if I would.'

'What's that supposed mean?' he asked, his voice the sound of a barrow upturning a load of gravel.

I was already beginning to regret not keeping my reply straight and to the point, simply explaining that I was a guest myself, and that this was a reunion of the 101st Airborne and, therefore, strictly private. But instead, I said, 'Sammy, these are war buddies at a reunion. They want to play a late game together. You'd be way out of your depth. They're very good, they take poker seriously and they're cashed up. This is not your sort of game.'

'Oh, yeah, but it's yours, is it? Who the fuck you think you are? I've played *you* before! Remember Gatwick?'

I was trying very hard to keep my cool. 'Yes, that was a long time ago and you always lost. But listen, Sammy, that's not why I can't invite you. Johnny Diamond, the pit boss, was in the 101st Airborne and it was one of his wartime buddies who invited me.' I then added, 'Johnny and I are friends, and I've played with some of them before; they're buddies.'

To my surprise, Sammy actually stamped his foot. 'Well then, fuckin' ask Johnny to get me in!' he shouted.

The little-boy-style tantrum was almost funny and allowed me to collect my thoughts. In a reasonable voice, I said, 'Now, I can't do that, Sammy. It's not Johnny's call. Besides, you could ask him yourself.'

'Can't!' he snapped.

I then remembered he was permanently banned from the gaming floor, where Johnny was the pit boss; a ban he seemed to accept. I sighed. 'Be sensible, Sammy. Even if Johnny could, and he can't, you'd get rolled! Cleaned out. Like I said, this is a high-stakes game but it's still friendly.'

'What yer fuckin' mean? I haven't got that kinda dough?'

'Hey, steady on, ladies present!' I indicated the cleaners, then said with a sigh, 'No, I didn't suggest that. But if you have, then you'll lose it!'

I hadn't given much thought to the gossip about Sammy's Benzedrine habit – these sorts of rumours were always flying around and Sammy attracted more than his fair share of them – but now, glancing at him, I could see he looked jittery and hyped up, with a heavy sheen of sweat below his hairline, even though the piano bar was air-conditioned. *Careful, Jack, this guy's high*, I warned myself.

'Well, ya gonna fix it?' he asked, as if he hadn't heard a word I'd said.

'Sammy! Ferchrissake, I just told you, I can't! It's not my call. The guys from the 101st invited me but they definitely didn't say I could bring anyone.'

'You fuckin' war heroes all think yer something special, doncha? Well, you can shove your game up your ass. Mark my words! You'll be fuckin' sorry, punk! And you can tell your friend Johnny Diamond the same. Asshole wouldn't allow me onto the gaming floor last week. My fuckin' family owns the fuckin' joint! Who the fuck does he think he is!' He turned and stomped off across the lounge, trailed by his twin shadows, who, it occurred to me at that moment, I had never seen without their hats.

Too late, I realised I had hit a nerve: Fort Leavenworth and Sammy's prison experience. The 101st Airborne was army and here they were, punishing him once again with another dishonourable discharge, treating him like shit. Could it be that simple? I was no psychiatrist but who could say what went on in Sammy Schischka's warped mind? I wondered whether I should mention the incident to Johnny, but decided to hell with it; if Johnny, as pit boss, hadn't allowed him on the gaming floor, he was only following management's instructions. Sammy would get over it. I didn't need to worry Johnny with this one. Benzedrine eventually wears off, and by morning, even Sammy would most likely have forgotten the episode or decided it never happened. To hell with the fat little psychotic jerk.

I continued practising for another fifteen minutes, just to calm down a bit, then left to have my usual drink with Lenny and Bridgett, deciding to say nothing about Sammy's visit. I then played my one- and three-quarter-hour shows and, without bothering to change out of my tuxedo, left to meet Johnny Diamond out front.

He was waiting for me in the foyer. 'Hey, Jack, how was the show?'

'Good, Johnny. House full and they seemed to enjoy it.'

'That's why the Firebird loves ya, Jack. It's the dearest place to have a drink in Las Vegas and it's still packed out every night you're on.'

'It's Mrs Fuller,' I replied. 'She works the magic. I simply play piano.'

Johnny pretended to fire a shot at me, forefinger pointed, fingers curled. 'Bullshit, buddy. You the man!'

We'd reached the front doors. 'Where's your car?' I asked.

'Flat tyre. I've left it in the parking lot. I'll get a new one tomorrow. It's a nice night; I thought we might walk, eh? The dinner's over but just about everyone at the reunion has moved to the Sky Room for drinks. We've got time.'

'Great, I missed out on a walk today.' It was a dry night in late fall, desert-dry and clear, although the flashing neon along The Strip overpowered the starlight. Stars in the desert are like no others and I'd sometimes stroll out beyond the city lights after completing my shift, just to enjoy them. Of all the things about Las Vegas, a clear, cold, star-filled night would be among the very best.

'Remember when we were the only place out here, apart from the Flamingo and a few burger joints and used-car lots?' Johnny asked me.

'Yeah, you can't keep a good gangster down. They say there are another four or five places going to go up in the next year or so.'

'I sometimes think the action is getting a bit heavy. Time to move on, maybe.'

'Yeah, I know just how you feel,' I said.

'Jack, you're a musician, you can get a job anywhere – good-looking white guy who plays jazz better than most coloured folks . . .' He spread his hands. 'What does a pit boss in a casino do? There ain't many jobs beyond this burg and, with the gambling business expanding every year, it makes sense to stay put. It's good dough, and there's always a dame when you need one and no complications afterwards. But it gets tricky sometimes. I just feel I've stayed too long with the bad guys and want to get back to normal people. By the way, talking about lying, cheating and thuggery, did Sammy Schischka come and see you?'

'Yeah, I wasn't going to mention it to you. He wanted in on tonight's game.'

'Sorry about that, Jack. As you probably know, Lenny's given me the nod to keep him away.'

We walked on in silence until we reached the Desert Inn, neither of us wanting to talk about Sammy and spoil the night.

'Pity you missed the get-together after the dinner,' I said.

Johnny laughed. 'No way, buddy. Saves me having to glad-hand two hundred vets and their wives and girlfriends.'

'You mean, you know them all, the entire division?'

'No, of course not. I know the guys in my company.' He laughed. 'I won't recognise most of them, guys change shape, but they'll know me. I had the misfortune to get a decoration for something any of us could have done in Normandy. Kind of the right guy in the wrong place at the right time.' Johnny laughed. 'Five minutes later and I'd have been spared five hundred thousand future handshakes with strangers. Everyone wants to shake the hand that shook the general's hand that pinned the medal to the breast of the so-called warrior, and then it's compulsory to introduce the wife or girlfriend.'

'I think I understand a little how you feel,' I said as we walked into the Sky Room.

It was pretty packed, but the guys were fairly relaxed, and I ordered my customary G and T without the G, which I could nurse until the game started. But, what with one thing and another, it wasn't until after 2 a.m. that the poker game was mentioned, and by that stage most of them were half tanked. The Kid did a quick head count and decided to call the game off.

'Damn,' Johnny said into my ear. 'Tonight I'm really feeling my *cojones*.'

I wasn't really sorry – a relatively early night would help settle me after Sammy's visit, which had upset me more than I was prepared to admit even to myself.

About a dozen guys and their wives spilled into the foyer to see us off, and, as we moved towards the entrance of the Desert Inn, I was surprised to see Sammy and his two shadows coming towards us through the entrance.

'Where's the game, Johnny?' he demanded while he was still some way off. 'I know ya bin in the fuckin' Sky Room. Game ain't started yet!' His lips were spit-flecked as he fronted Johnny Diamond, ignoring me completely.

'There's no game tonight, Sammy; it's off. And mind your language, buddy, there's ladies present!'

Sammy didn't look right; he was sweating heavily and was very agitated, like a man who's worked himself up for an argument and was determined to have one. 'Hey, you okay?' Johnny asked.

'You fuckin' liar,' Sammy yelled. 'You and Spayd are fuckin' *employees*. You'll do as you're fuckin' told or else.' He stabbed his finger at the two of us. 'Now, where's the fuckin' game?'

'Hey, whoa . . . Sammy, take it easy, man,' Johnny said, placing his hand on Sammy's shoulder.

Sammy shrugged it off. 'The game, asshole! Where is it?' he yelled.

The whole group had fallen silent. A couple of the women had moved closer to their partners.

'We don't like that kind of language in front of ladies, sir,' Kid Lewis said in his slow Texas drawl. 'Perhaps you should just go home, eh?'

Sammy swung around to face him and saw a small wiry guy. 'You shut your fuckin' Texan mouth or me and my guys will shut it for you.' Sammy's thugs moved in quickly to stand on either side of him.

Once his backup was in place, Sammy swung a wild haymaker at the Kid, who almost lazily swayed out of its path, the punch missing by inches. 'Hey, take it easy, sir.' He waited for Sammy to recover his balance.

One of Sammy's helpers stepped forward and Sammy pulled his arm back to have another crack at the Kid. After that, everything happened very quickly. The Texan hit Sammy flush on the nose, with a brutal straight left. It had all his weight behind it, and I heard the crack and a sickening crunch as the cartilage in Sammy's nose was crushed. It was one of those perfectly timed punches that spreads a nose halfway across a face. Sammy dropped to his knees, cupped his face in his hands and started screaming like a little kid.

The bodyguard on his left reached inside his jacket, which was a mistake. Warwick Selby grabbed his arm at the elbow and wrist, and began to rotate it rapidly skyward as a gun clattered to the foyer floor. Warwick then kicked the hood's feet out from under him, rolled him over his hip and used his grip on the tough guy's arm to fling him hard against the marble floor. The second thug had seen enough, and took off through the entrance and into the night. I started after him but Johnny yelled, 'Jack, let him go!'

Sammy was still on his knees, sobbing, both hands covering his face. 'Who is this pussy, Johnny?' the Kid asked, only breathing a notch or two above normal.

'He's a debt collector,' Johnny said, 'one of the Chicago Mafiosi behind the Firebird.' Most of the guys were shepherding their wives and girlfriends away from the pool of blood spreading over the floor. Several late-night staff from the Desert Inn came running up.

'Say, Jack . . . Johnny, I sure hope we ain't got you two *hombres* in trouble,' Kid Lewis drawled. 'Down home, we don't tolerate this sort of behaviour in front of the ladies.' His slow drawl and old-fashioned, almost courtly, manner were in stark contrast to the brutal efficiency he and Warwick Selby had used to dispatch the pair.

Sammy was still keening like a wounded animal and his offsider was doing a damn fine job of pretending to be unconscious.

By this time the casino security had arrived, and a guy who was obviously the night manager assured us he'd take care of everything if we'd be kind enough to leave immediately. 'There are plenty of witnesses, ladies and gennelmen,' he said, smoothly. 'Nothing for you to concern yourself about; we saw it all.' The security began to move the wounded pair from the foyer towards the rear of the hotel.

Johnny and I farewelled our hosts, and assured them that they needn't worry about us. I mentioned that Sammy was almost certainly on Benzedrine, and we said our goodnights and set out to walk back to his car at the Firebird. Alone at last, Johnny let out a long sigh. 'Jesus, what an almighty fuck-up!'

I couldn't have put it more succinctly. 'That night manager at the Desert Inn is going to get the shock of his life when they clean Sammy up and he sees who he is,' I replied. 'By the way, did you ask his name; get a good look at him?'

Johnny shook his head. 'Jack, we've screwed up big time. Chicago almost certainly has points in this casino.'

We continued to walk, not entirely sure we wouldn't be followed or jumped in some dark corner. After a while, Johnny said, 'Jack, I can't see Sammy just letting this go.'

'Christ, Johnny, he had it coming to him.'

'Buddy, you play The Phoenix Bar. I work the floor – I see more hoods in a day than you see in a month; investors, owners, bad guys checking on their assets. Sammy's a bad bastard but so are they; they may not want him on the floor, making trouble, but he's still one of them, he's Tony Accardo's man in Las Vegas.'

'But he's also a psycho. They know that?'

Johnny laughed. 'The Mafiosi are the official employment agency for psychos, as you so nicely put it. To be a sick fuck is almost a condition of employment, Jack!'

'What are you suggesting . . . that we report this incident to Lenny?'

'For fuck's sake, Jack, wake up! Can't you see what happened tonight? It's all over, man. I'm outa here. I've got a bit tucked away. I'm a damn good motor mechanic by trade. It ain't glamorous but I'll stand half a chance of growing old. I'm off, back to the East Coast.'

'C'mon, Johnny, aren't you being a bit melodramatic? Sammy and his help simply got what was coming to them.'

'Whaddya mean, melo . . . ?'

'Exaggerating.'

'Jack, Sammy's fucked up big time tonight. The whole of Las Vegas is going to know about this. Tony Accardo made the New York guys bleed over Louis Springer. You don't think New York will grab the chance to do the same? Chicago can't let that happen.'

'What's that supposed to mean?'

'Can't you see, they'll claim we set it up. That business with you in the kitchen hallway and me goosestepping him off the gaming floor in front of some very high rollers. He got really abusive, using foul language, claiming he owned the Firebird, and generally upsetting the other players. He grabbed a tray of cocktails from one of the hostesses and hurled it against the wall, then yelled at her, "Are you a fuckin' white nigger bitch too?" He stopped the floor dead.' Johnny shook his head and we walked on for a while in silence.

'Do you mean it, buddy?' I asked him eventually. 'You really thinking of leaving?'

He stopped and grabbed me by both shoulders. 'Jack, you're not 101st but you're like my brother; listen ter me, buddy. I'm going to the Firebird right now to fix that puncture. Then I'm gonna go home and pack the car, and I'm leaving tonight. I'll be across the state line by dawn, before that prick Sammy is in any condition to retaliate. We were taught to hit and run, so that's what I'm gonna do. Sammy won't see me for dust.'

'C'mon, Johnny, Sammy hasn't got the brains to get himself out of this jam.'

'Maybe not, but Chicago has. By noon tomorrow, Sammy will have their instructions, the story he's gonna tell.'

I was finding all this pretty hard to believe. 'But we didn't lay a hand on him, neither of us,' I protested.

'Exactly, we imported the muscle from out of town. That'll make perfect sense to the Mob. They do it all the time. It would have been far better if we'd laid into the three fuckers ourselves; at least it would have been two on three. Everyone knows his twin hats carry guns – we might have maybe won the sympathy vote.'

'But what about the witnesses?'

Johnny actually laughed. 'The manager of the Desert Inn, who the fuck do you think pays him? Security is gonna say what they're told to say. The vets in our party who saw what happened will all have gone home. The Mobsters may privately hate each other but they're all in this together, swapping points, scratching each other's backs . . . you've seen enough to know it's the way it goes here in Las Vegas.'

'Johnny, this isn't the first time Chicago has had to worry about Sammy. Heck, there's dozens of bashings around town for debts not paid on time, the thing with Hector and me . . .'

'Yeah, all of them covered up.' Johnny turned and grabbed me by the lapel of my tuxedo. 'Jack, there are plenty of places in New York for a top piano player. Let's scram. Come with me tonight, buddy, *please*.'

'Thanks for the offer, Johnny, but I don't think I could let down Lenny and Mrs Fuller. We've been friends for a long time, Lenny and I, from way back in London during the war. Besides, I've got an apartment and a bank account I can't operate until they open this morning. By the way, what are you going to do for money, Johnny?'

'Never did believe in banks, Jack. The Depression, I suppose. I've got my stake for tonight's game intact and a bit under the mattress at home, and I'm up to date on my rent. I've got enough to get me to New York, with a bit leftover. I need a new rear left tyre but that's no sweat; get one when I cross the state line. Been meaning to adjust the brakes for months, too.' Johnny, it seemed, was already in mechanic mode. 'What about you? Won't you change your mind? You can get Bridgett to sell your apartment and it's only money in the bank – you can have that transferred, can't you? And, in the meantime, you've got tonight's stake.'

'I'd rather wait until the banks open, then make up my mind; there's a fair bit involved,' I said to appease him.

Johnny Diamond sighed. 'Okay, then, Jack, if you're that confident. I hope you're right, buddy. It's been real nice knowing ya.'

We'd reached the Firebird parking lot.

'Just stay safe, Johnny, look after yourself.'

'You too, little buddy.'

'I'll be okay, I'm Canadian. I have a border I can cross. Need any help with that tyre?'

'Nah, I'm a mechanic. Do it with my eyes closed. You'll only get in the way, old son.' He grinned in a valiant attempt to cover his concern and we shook hands. 'Do it soon, Jack. These guys don't fuck around. Be seein' ya, buddy. Just remember to watch out for Sammy; he ain't gonna leave this one alone.'

Then, somehow, we both started to laugh. 'Christ, Johnny, the Kid hit him so goddamn hard. You guys must have really been taught by experts in the 101st. The Kid's punch damn near buried Sammy's nose.'

'Yeah, I guess we were all pretty handy. You never knew what was waiting for you when you hit the dirt. But the Kid is something special. He was runner-up in the middleweight Golden Gloves in Fort Worth in 1940. If the war hadn't come along, he probably would have turned pro, he was that good. He also boxed for the US army. Sammy made the mistake of thinking he was easy because he's not a real big guy.'

We laughed some more, then I gave him a wave and started to walk home. I'd only gone maybe thirty yards when he called, 'Jack, get the hell outa here. Don't trust Lenny . . . even Mrs Fuller. Go home, pack your kit and we'll hit the road, brother.'

'Thanks, Johnny, I promise I'll think about it, but not tonight, buddy!' I called back.

I was real sorry to see him go. Good men were hard to find in Las Vegas. I felt a bit shattered, now I was alone, as if a piece of my life had dropped away. It wasn't just that I was going to miss a regular guy I liked. We all adjust to farewells and arrivals, exits and entries. It was something else, something about final outcomes. I was rejecting an opportunity that might well have changed my life and I still wasn't certain I'd made the right decision. New York was an option that I knew would probably lead to musical success. Of course, there were better musicians than me, but I was by now highly experienced and near the top of my profession as an entertainer. Deciding to forego this next step in my career because of a game, a simple card game a child could learn to play in a single afternoon, a game that had nothing to do with making a unique mark in life, didn't make sense. Some epitaph, 'Jack Spayd – a damn good poker player'. Johnny Diamond, perhaps unknowingly, was telling me not to cheat myself out of a good life, especially not for the sake of sitting in a smoke-filled room around a table with five cards in my hand. In real-life terms, it was no jackpot.

The air-conditioner didn't sing its usual lullaby as I lay in bed, unable to sleep. Over the months and years, I had begun to think I might never leave Las Vegas, but now I wasn't sure. At first light, I rose and went for a long walk over to the Westside. There were a few people on the streets, mainly coloured folk going to their jobs, and I realised I'd never thought about the hour they had to leave home to cook our breakfasts or polish our shoes or scrub our kitchen floors.

I walked beyond the last of the houses and into the desert, going over things in my head, telling myself that I was a gifted piano player and that my musical life transcended everything else. If I left Las Vegas, my world wouldn't come to a grinding halt. It wasn't like being in Toronto, where nothing ever seemed to happen. In New York, LA, Houston, wherever I found myself, I'd be okay; it would be possible to find a regular poker game, even a good one. I wasn't the best in the business, and there would be guys who could match me in almost every big city, so what was stopping me? A fleeting memory of Bridgett pressing her mouth to mine came to me, but I forced myself to ignore it. Bridgett would want no part of my life, either here in Las Vegas or anywhere else. I had to face the facts.

I walked for six hours and went over Johnny's argument a hundred times, and each time it made more sense. Sammy was going to want payback from someone for what had happened to him and I would almost certainly be that someone. I realised I was frightened of the sort of violence this might involve if, as Johnny suggested, Chicago gave Sammy the go-ahead this time. I could still remember, as a child of eight, waiting for my father to come home from the tavern to beat up my mom and me, and I wasn't prepared to live with that kind of fear again. A child's fears never completely fade, even well into adulthood. Nothing was worth living like that once more.

My mind was finally made up. I went directly to the Firebird without returning to my apartment, so I could catch Lenny before too many other people gave him their version of what had happened.

He was in his office, swinging back and forth in his new office chair, and playing with a fancy new gold pen. Lenny always wanted the latest anything, as long as it was expensive and others could see it and appreciate its value.

'Jesus Christ! Jack! Thank god you've come in. We went over to your apartment but you weren't there.'

'Oh?'

'What the hell is going on? What the fuck happened at the Desert Inn last night?'

'No, Lenny, you tell me your version. What've you heard? Has it reached Chicago yet?'

He seemed surprised by the question. 'Why? Why should it?' he asked.

I could tell Lenny was bluffing. 'No, answer my question first, please,' I insisted. 'Has it?'

He'd recovered from his initial relief at my appearance and nodded slowly. 'There and back, Jack. What the hell happened?'

'Sammy took a sock at the wrong guy over not being allowed to play in a poker game at the Desert Inn, which never, in fact, transpired. Have you heard from the manager of the casino? He saw it all.'

'Transpired? Ya mean, the poker game, it didn't happen?'

'Yes.'

'So, Sammy starts a fight at 2.30 a.m. in the foyer of the Desert Inn over a poker game that didn't happen. Is that what you're saying, Jack?'

I didn't like the inquisitorial tone he seemed suddenly to have adopted. 'The manager of the casino would have told you that, Lenny.'

'No, not at all, that's not what he said he saw.'

'What?' I cried, startled. 'What did he say?'

'The version he gave me is that two hit men attacked Sammy and his helpers, and Johnny Diamond stood by laughing. It was obvious Johnny had set it up, he said.'

I almost laughed. 'Yeah, two guys using bare knuckles against two, possibly three, men carrying guns – seems like a well-planned attack,' I said, not without a fair amount of irony. 'What about me? If Johnny's falsely implicated, then so am I.'

'I'll get to that later. Just tell me what you know, Jack.'

I then told Lenny the whole story.

He didn't reply for a long moment, then said quietly, 'So, why did Johnny Diamond fly the coop?'

I kept my face impassive. 'Has he?'

Lenny nodded. 'It seems Johnny Diamond has packed up and left town. Did you know he was on with Sue Stinchcombe? It was Johnny who was the secret force behind that strike,' Lenny said with a completely straight face.

'Johnny, on with Hector's daughter? That's a laugh. Why, you know that's crap, Lenny. Complete bullshit! He used to play around a bit but he's been with that chorus girl, Gina, for over a year. As for him being the main force behind the strike, that's crap too. What did he have to gain? Everyone knows Sue had the guts to run that strike all by herself. If what you say is true, why didn't Louis Springer send Sammy after Johnny instead of Hector?' I was growing more and more angry. 'Lenny, do you *really* believe all this horseshit?'

Lenny sighed. 'Jack, old buddy, not a single word. I believe everything you've told me. But I've got my instructions. Be sensible for a moment. All's well that ends well. Think this through. Whoever does the thinking for Tony Accardo is fuckin' brilliant. Think consequences.'

'Tell me.'

'Well, in a nutshell, Johnny throws Sammy off the gaming floor.'

'He was acting under instructions . . .' I interjected. 'You agreed to it yourself.'

'Yes, but . . . what's the word, he was over . . . overzealous! He roughed Sammy up in front of the girls and some of the high rollers.'

'Wait on, what's this got to do with last night?'

'Sammy was pretty upset. He obviously knew about the reunion and waited for Johnny to come down so he could demand an apology for the way he was treated. Johnny eventually arrives with his old war comrades, they're all drunk and they don't like Sammy's style. Johnny refuses to apologise and Sammy takes a swing at him. Johnny's buddies come to his aid and go too far.'

I could see what was coming. 'So, Johnny sobers up and realises his thugs have beaten up one of the chosen few and that the Chicago Mob isn't going to accept his apology. So, he gets the hell out of town?' I concluded the story for him.

'Ya got it in one, Jack. By the way,' he held up an envelope, 'this was tucked under my office door when I came in this morning. It's Johnny's resignation.'

'Well, does it say what happened?'

Lenny opened the envelope, unfolded a single sheet and read: '"*Dear Mr Giancana, I hereby resign without notice. There's only one Sammy Shishka in town but it's one too many. Look after Jack Spayd.*"' Lenny glanced up, then added, '"*Yours sincerely, Johnson 'Johnny' Diamond.*"'

I reached out. 'May I see that please, Lenny?'

'Sure, buddy.' He handed me the letter. It was in Johnny's handwriting and, unsurprisingly, he'd spelled Sammy's surname incorrectly. It looked genuine.

'Jack, you haven't spoken to anyone, have you? The cops? Anyone else? Bridgett says she hasn't seen you.'

'No, not yet. But I think I should . . . maybe there's one or two honest ones left in town. But after I've resigned. That's the reason I'm here.'

Lenny jerked violently in his fancy new chair. 'Jack, Jack buddy, whaddaya talkin' about?'

'Lenny, I agree with Johnny Diamond. There's one Sammy Schischka in town and that's one too many. Time to go. Vamoose.'

'Jack, you make up you own mind but, before you do, just lissen to me for a moment, will ya?'

'Lenny, it's been six years and you've kept your word – Sammy's never laid a hand on me. But it's only a matter of time. I know that and so must you.'

But Lenny didn't appear to be listening. 'Jack, you have nothing to fear from Sammy for the next month, maybe two. Pretty funny coincidence – his injuries much the same as that nigger's were, busted nose, jaw, eye socket . . .'

'Lenny, stop right there! You're no longer my boss and I take exception to you calling coloured folk niggers. The guy's name was Hector and he was Sue Stinchcombe's father – a more decent guy would be hard to find.'

Lenny spread his hands apologetically. 'Buddy, it's a habit, I don't dislike coloured folk. No harm meant.'

I could see that he wasn't particularly sorry at all, I'd simply interrupted his chain of thought. But I felt better speaking my mind.

'Sammy's off the air for a month and his offsider has a fractured skull,' Lenny concluded.

'Nothing trivial, I hope?'

Lenny actually laughed. 'The point is, as far as Chicago's concerned . . . and, by the way, I agree with them, Sammy's had his comeuppance. He's gonna live. The goon with the cracked skull is out of his coma, calling for his mama. The vets have all gone home. Johnny Diamond has fled the coop and is smart enough to keep his mouth shut. The Nevada police can be kept out of this and you're in the clear.' He paused. 'That's if you keep your mouth shut.'

I sighed. 'Christ, not again! What if I don't?'

'Jack, take my advice; this time someone in the Family has been hurt, hurt bad.'

'Not just some poor coloured bastard in the kitchen, a father with nine kids to support, eh?' Lenny ignored this and I knew it would be pointless to continue. He wasn't listening. 'So, what about the other hood, and the night manager of the Desert Inn – what if one of them talks to the cops?'

Lenny picked up the gold pen again. 'The night manager has . . . how can I put it . . . the right background, comes from Atlantic City. The promise of a nice clean envelope with a couple of used C-notes will make him say whatever we please.' Lenny paused. 'And, by the way, they've both already been briefed. You were never there, Jack. And now it's even better. You're not a veteran of the 101st Airborne and there never was a poker game. There was no logical reason for you to be present.' Lenny pointed the pen at me and looked somewhat smug. 'All taken care of, Jack.'

'You know, Lenny, there is only one person capable of putting together this scenario.'

'Oh, and who would that person be?'

'Why, Mrs Fuller, of course.'

Lenny looked up slowly. 'Does it matter, buddy? Nobody's hurt, except Sammy and his helper and that's no tragedy.'

'Okay, but how did she know I hadn't left with Johnny Diamond?'

'One of the early morning nig— er, coloured maids in the kitchen told her she'd seen you walking Westside on her way to work; that's when we checked your apartment.' He paused. 'We'll pay for a new lock.'

'Does this at least mean Sammy's going back to Chicago forever?'

Lenny placed the pen down carefully, then spun it, so that eventually it came to rest pointing at one side of his desk and away from either of us. 'I don't know, but I doubt it. My guess is that he'll stay for a while anyway. A few months, then we'll get Bridgett to recommend that he leave town for health reasons.'

'Thanks for not lying to me about Bridgett's involvement, Lenny.'

'Jack, she's going along with this because she doesn't want to lose you.'

'I see. The best pit boss in America is lost to the industry, but the Firebird doesn't want to lose their piano player,' I said, not without a tinge of bitterness.

Lenny looked genuinely shocked at this statement. 'Jack, you ain't serious? You and Bridgett, don't you know it's much, much more than that?'

CHAPTER NINETEEN

I LEFT LENNY'S OFFICE and made my way home, to find that the door of my apartment had been smashed in, then jammed shut with a wad of paper. Removing it, I saw it was a note. *Jack, sincerest apologies, locksmith will make good later this morning. We are worried about you. Will you please contact Lenny or me urgently about last night at the Desert Inn. Bridgett.*

I was too confused to ask myself what I thought about Bridgett going to the lengths she had to keep me safe. Fuck everything, I was getting out. I'd have to try to warn Johnny that the Mob might be after him, but how? He was on the road and I knew he wouldn't have left a forwarding address.

The doorbell rang and I jumped, but it was only the promised locksmith. He gave me a cheery good morning and mumbled his name, Victor something, and immediately began to examine the damage to the door. 'Lose your keys, eh?' I nodded, too exhausted to want to talk. 'Typical. Pre-war, made in Japan, burglar's gift. I can replace it with a Yale-reinforced steel one, the latest two-click lock; cost a bit more, though . . .'

'Go ahead, but can you hurry, please? I have to go out.'

'You don't want a quote? Lady called to say to send the invoice to . . .' He began to rummage in his tool bag.

'I'll pay you myself. Just fix it, please. *Fast!*'

My obvious impatience got him off his ass and I left him to get on with it while I shaved, showered and changed into a lightweight suit I'd only worn a few times, a white shirt and navy blue tie. I'd bought the suit on a shopping expedition with Bridgett after she'd agreed to an afternoon charity performance two years previously for Anna-Lucia Hermes, in aid of the Mormon Missionary Training Centres and some orphanage in Africa. I have no doubt that, at the time, it had important political implications for the Firebird, no doubt involving the mayor, Lucan Hermes.

Though I can't explain why, something from my boyhood prompted me to wear the suit to resign in – it seemed the right thing to do. Although Lenny would undoubtedly have told her of my intention to quit, Bridgett was my boss and I felt I needed to formally resign to her as a matter of courtesy.

I sat down and wrote out my letter of resignation, saying simply that I felt the need to move on, and that my resignation would be effective in two days. I'd never signed a contract, so there was no need to give a month's notice. I thanked Bridgett for her unfailing courtesy and help, and signed the letter, using the new, very expensive, very fancy Reynolds Rocket ('it will write on wet paper') my mom and Nick had sent me for an early gift for Christmas, two weeks away. My mother still regarded America as some distant land where it took weeks for anything to arrive by mail. I think she imagined the parcel travelling by mule train, the poor beasts trudging for days through endless desert wastes.

I was suddenly ravenously hungry. I fried a couple of eggs and rummaged around for some bread, but there was only one slightly mouldy slice. I cut off the mottled crust and stuck the bread in the toaster.

Apart from being exhausted I was overwrought and jumpy, especially after Johnny Diamond's lightning exit. Johnny was nobody's fool. He was a war hero and no fly-by-night character – he had a good job he enjoyed, he loved playing poker – and if he felt the way he did about possible retaliation from Sammy and the Mob, then I ought to take it seriously too. But I needed a couple of days to fix my affairs and put the apartment on the market. Sammy had taken a bad beating and was in hospital; surely that would buy me some time.

By now the entire domestic workforce at the Firebird would know what had happened in the early hours of the morning. The night security staff at the Desert Inn were white but the coloured cleaners would have seen everything. Although the cover story would be widely circulated, the real story of what had happened would be known to one and all. Duplicity is yet another name for Las Vegas. News of Johnny Diamond's departure would be spreading equally fast. No doubt someone would have been finishing up or starting the dawn shift and would have seen him drive off in the somewhat battered light-blue Chevy. He may have been a skilled mechanic, but his car was a case of the shoemaker's children going unshod.

I ate my two greasy eggs slowly, spreading the yolk over the toast to conceal any vestiges of mould. The food helped settle my nerves and I tried to see things a little more clearly. The fact that Bridgett had been in a large part responsible for the story of the Desert Inn incident, which was to get me off the hook with Chicago, strengthened my resolve to leave. Bridgett, of all people, would know the likely consequences of Sammy's beating.

By the time I'd fixed myself a cup of black Java – the milk in the fridge was off – the locksmith was all but done.

'What do I owe you?' I said.

'Lady who called said to send the account to her, sir.'

'Damn, I *told* you I'd pay.' I reached for my wallet. 'How much?'

'Five dollars, sir, the carpen—'

'Thank you, I don't need to hear the details.' I gave him a five and added a buck as a tip, and stuck out my hand for the two keys.

He thanked me. 'Better keep one in a safe place, sir.'

'Thank you,' I said, pocketing the keys and ushering him out ahead of me, before slamming the door and brushing past him down the stairs.

'No, sir, you lock the door a second time, using the key. It's the double click I told you about. You have to turn it twice, the key; there and back!' he called down at me. If I hadn't been so far ahead of him I'd have returned and punched the stupid bastard.

It was windy and I was fairly chilly in the lightweight suit, and I momentarily considered going back for a sweater, but the thought of facing the double-click locksmith on the stairs decided the matter and I hailed a conveniently passing cab instead of walking to the casino.

I knocked on Bridgett's office door even though it was, as always, ajar and I could see her seated at her desk. She glanced up, leapt out of her seat and rushed to hug me. 'Thank god you're safe, Jack,' she exclaimed, her voice cracking. She pressed her body hard against mine and I could feel her trembling. I tried to understand what this could mean, but the pressure of her breasts against my chest, the feel of her in my arms after so long, made it impossible for me to think straight. I simply made the most of it, breathing in the perfume of her hair and feeling its softness against my cheek. 'Lenny told me you'd been to see him earlier,' she said and abruptly released me. I watched her struggle to regain her composure – why do women tug at the sides of their skirts to adjust their emotions? – and saw that iron control reassert itself. 'Please sit, Jack,' she said, indicating the chair facing her across the desk. My heart sank to my boots as I settled myself into her stiff-backed chair. We were back where we always were.

I handed her my letter of resignation and sat back, gazing around the room while she opened it. In contrast to Lenny's enormous scarlet and gold 'Chinese New Year' office, Bridgett's could barely contain her desk and a couple of chairs. She read my note almost at a single glance, then looked up at me. It was business-as-usual Bridgett who now confronted me. 'Jack, Sammy's taken a terrible beating and won't be out of hospital for six weeks at least. Please don't leave immediately.'

I'd been rehearsing my words all the way to the Firebird and, to my surprise, they came out perfectly. 'My mind's made up. I'll just collect my music and be gone by tomorrow afternoon.'

Bridgett was too smart to tackle me head on. 'Jack, Christmas is coming up in two weeks and, as you know, the GAWP Bar is booked out for the month leading up to the festivities, and beyond until New Year's Day. You're right about Sammy; we can't stop him doing something stupid, no one can. To add to the danger, I believe he's on Benzedrine tablets.' She paused. 'I have a hospital report. He can be no possible threat to anyone for a good while yet.'

I shrugged. The temptation to give in to this beloved woman was almost too much for me; I *had* to stick to my decision to leave. 'Bridgett, I've loved being here, but Lenny read me Johnny Diamond's letter before he burned it and I agree with him. Sooner or later, Sammy's going to go berserk and I'm the obvious choice of victim. As you've so often said, he's Chicago's man. That makes him more than just a man. Sammy's on Bennies, and I know all about them and what they can do even to a normal man. I'd like to get a head start – to be long gone before Sammy comes out of hospital.'

'Yes, yes, Jack, I understand. The man is mad, and belongs in an institution, locked away for life somewhere. Why the godfather wants this monster around is inconceivable. As a loan shark or debt collector, or whatever he is now, he's even worse than he was. Rumour has it – and it's via the coloured staff, so it probably has substance – if a client doesn't pay up on time, they get taken to a basement Sammy has in a derelict house on the Westside and severely beaten. Lenny's tried to warn Chicago but they've made it clear that the loan-shark business isn't part of our operation. At least he's not *our* debt collector.'

'But Sammy hates the Westside. Calls it Nigger Town.'

'Perhaps that's why he goes there. No white faces and the police don't care.'

'Did Lenny check out this basement? I mean, it could be real evidence.'

'I can't say, probably not, but the busboy, the kid who you sent to fetch me when Hector was hurt, knows where it is. He lives in a tenement close by and has seen the Cadillac parked outside several times.'

'That means they all know . . . the coloured staff, I mean. Bridgett, all this is doing is making me more determined. It's no good, I've —'

She raised a hand to stop me. 'Please, Jack, just hear me out first.

Whatever Sammy's intentions, for the moment he's harmless. You'll be okay for at least six weeks. I'm told he will be wearing a cast on his ugly face for at least that long. He's got a broken nose, a crushed cheekbone and a broken eye socket. His minder is in the room next to him, although, I'm told, he slips in and out of consciousness and speaks gibberish most of the time, then calls for his mama. That fractured skull means a protracted stay. Sammy's second minder, it seems, has disappeared with the pink Cadillac. Pretty stupid – there can't be that many pink Cadillac convertibles driving around Nevada.'

'Have the police been alerted that it's been stolen?' I asked, alarmed, knowing one thing inevitably leads to another.

'No, Jack, of course not. The Mafia do things their own way. But I have no doubt they'll find him. The point is, Sammy is a coward without his two henchmen at his side. Even if he could – and he can't for several weeks – he wouldn't attempt to tackle you on his own.'

'That's great, Bridgett. So, that gives me six weeks to get as far from here *and* Chicago as possible.'

Bridgett paused and seemed to be thinking. 'Jack, you've had quarterly wage rises ever since we moved to the Firebird.' She gave me one of her knockout smiles. 'I daresay you're the highest-paid piano player in any bar in America. No, don't worry, you've earned each and every cent, and the exorbitant price of cocktails in the GAWP Bar more than covers your salary. Our bar takings are up a staggering four hundred per cent. That's unheard of. We sell the most expensive drinks in America, while the opposition has to give them away to woo the high rollers. I know money isn't everything to you – you've never once asked me for a tide-over loan, even when I knew you'd been cleaned out at poker – but we really can guarantee your safety for the next six weeks if you'll agree to stay until New Year's Day. That's less than three weeks, then you've still got three weeks to find somewhere safe. A new life . . .' she said – somewhat wistfully, I thought. Then, in a more businesslike tone, she continued, 'You'd not only be doing me a great personal favour but we'll give you three months' salary as a Christmas bonus.'

I threw up my hands. Did she think the only thing I cared about was money? It was hard enough telling her I was walking out of her life, without her insulting me as well. 'Bridgett, you should know better than that,' I said. 'If you were Lenny, I'd tell you to stick your money where the sun don't shine. And, by the way, part of why I'm out of here is that I've never told a single soul when I've been busted in a poker game, yet somehow you knew. Everyone knows everyone's business in this place. It's high time I regained a semblance of a private life.' I tried for a lighter tone. 'Jack Spayd, sometime jazz and not bad blues player, himself at last.'

Bridgett smiled. 'That's why you're the success you are, Jack. You're always yourself.'

I shook my head. 'If only you knew.' I'd be round that desk and gathering her in my arms in a second if I thought I stood a chance.

'Jack, I apologise for trying to . . . well, to put it bluntly, bribe you. You were going to get a bonus anyway. You're right, this place is incestuous. And it leaks like a sieve. So, before I say what I'm about to, I want you to know that if you leave tomorrow morning, you owe me nothing. I've loved working with you and I do understand why you're leaving.' She smiled again, although I didn't think it was the happiest smile I'd ever seen light up her attractive face. 'So, what I'm going to ask is purely selfish on my part and if you decide against it . . . well, that's okay too. There will never be any hard feelings between us.'

'Okay, go ahead, but, before you do, if it's about staying, I really don't like your chances, Bridgett.'

She nodded. 'I've never told you, or anyone this, but there was a price to pay for my two points in the Firebird. I signed a contract with the godfather that I would guarantee we'd increase our takings by fifteen per cent each year for the first five years; that way, the Mob had nothing to lose.'

'You mean the profits for your part – the high rollers and the GAWP Bar?'

'No, I mean the regular casino as well, Lenny's part, too. On paper it was a pretty stupid agreement, I admit. But for a girl from the

Appalachians, whose parents believed stroking a snake could cure measles, it didn't seem too farfetched. America was getting back on its feet after the war, and the numbers of very rich people were steadily increasing and would continue to grow. My hotel experience taught me that it's not possible to overindulge the wealthy. A grand resort casino was the way of the future. Besides, this way, it wasn't blackmail; I could always tell myself I'd earned every cent.'

'But what about the skim?'

'Well, I was growing up pretty fast. I could see myself being cheated, my profits being carried off in a black briefcase every month so that I couldn't meet my fifteen per cent increase each year. I got the godfather to agree that my figures were above the line – before the skim. Then I demanded two per cent of the skim as well, so that I knew what they were taking out tax-free. They squirmed and threatened but they were forced to agree in the end. To be truthful, Chicago never dreamed the Firebird could show the kind of profit growth each year that it has up until now.'

I shook my head in disbelief. 'Bridgett, you're amazing.'

She smiled. 'Jack, this is the fifth year and my contract ends on New Year's Day and, well, with new casinos on The Strip, each year it's been a little harder. This one,' Bridgett shrugged, 'we're skating pretty close to the line. I'm not saying we won't make it, but I can't take any chances. If I'm one dollar short, those bastards will make sure I don't get my points.'

I wasn't used to hearing her swear. Clearly she was under pressure, but did she take me for a fool? 'What are you saying, that my leaving three weeks early could affect your annual result?' I looked at her. 'Bridgett, that's very hard to believe. The GAWP Bar is booked out.'

It was as if she'd read my mind. 'No, Jack, you're not a fool, far from it, but you *are* a male.'

'And that means the same thing, does it?'

'No, not at all, just that you don't always think like a woman.'

'Well, thank god for that.'

She looked directly at me. 'Jack, perhaps you don't realise, but you're the main attraction.'

I threw back my head and laughed. 'Give me a break, Bridgett! With respect, any good pianist could fill my role. The wives and girlfriends come to gossip and to drink and to have a good time. I just provide the background music.'

'You're right, playing the piano is only incidental, but *who* plays it isn't. Jack, it's *you*! Anyone can start a GAWP Bar, it's not rocket science. They come for the total mix and a big part of that is you, your personality, your looks, your easy manner, modesty, talent, charm . . .' Her smile grew as she ticked these off on her fingers.

'Thank you, Bridgett, but that's very hard to believe.'

She ignored me. 'We're booked out until the new year with America's wealthiest gamblers and their wives. I had to turn down nearly fifty applications. Putting it bluntly, if you're not playing in the GAWP Bar the girls will go elsewhere and take their husbands with them. They can gamble anywhere. The Desert Inn has their new ritzy curved swimming pool; Michael Solomon is doing wonders at the Flamingo – he's got an entertainment list over the Christmas break that's like a who's who of American entertainers; most of the new casinos have suites bigger than ours and just as luxurious or even more so. The moment they get a whiff of this, they'll do everything they can, legal or otherwise, to steal our business, make our high rollers an offer they can't refuse.' Bridgett paused. 'It could be an absolute disaster for me. We lost a fair bit during the waitress strike, but that will be nothing compared to what could happen when people learn you've left town. I'd have to write and tell them – they'd never forgive me if they arrived and found you gone. The competition from the newer casinos has been fierce this year and there's a chance I won't make the percentage in my final year. As I said, one dollar short and the godfather will withhold my dividends and cancel my points in the Firebird. It could well be the happiest day of his life.'

'Jesus!' was all I could think to say. I'll give Bridgett credit, she didn't burst into tears the way women usually do when they desperately need something from a guy. She simply sat, looking down at her hands in her lap. Then she looked up and said, 'Jack, if you decide to leave today I'll understand. This is my problem, not yours, but I wanted you to have all the facts before you decided.'

What could I do? I sighed, perhaps a little melodramatically, then tried to cover it with a grin. 'Mrs Fuller, come January the 2nd I'm outa here. It gives me time to sell up and sort out my affairs. "*Apartment for sale, brand new Yale lock fitted*",' I quipped.

'Yes, I'm sorry about that, Jack. I told the man at the locksmith to send me the invoice.'

I brushed this away. 'I paid him. And I get the Christmas bonus, three months' salary?' I asked cheekily, to lighten the moment.

Bridgett smiled. 'I'll personally see to it you get it the day after Christmas.'

I did a quick calculation – three months' extra salary would give me a handsome sum. 'I'm not short of money – been on a lucky streak, I guess – but I'll give you the name and address of a friend of mine in Canada, Mac McClymont, who wants to start a small guitar factory in Toronto. Could you make the cheque out to him, please, Bridgett?'

Bridgett rose from her chair and, for a fleeting moment, I thought she was going to kiss me, but she looked me straight in the eye and extended her hand. 'Thank you, Jack,' she said quietly.

'You're welcome,' I replied, a little embarrassed, but also pleased she hadn't made a big deal of it. 'Glad you're going to get your points. I may need a loan some day.'

'We'd have to discuss what I get in return, Jack,' she laughed.

Christ, this lady had a lot of class. Sometimes I wanted her so much it hurt, but once she had her points she would be so far outside my league she wouldn't look sideways at me.

I needed sleep, just a couple of hours, before I had to play, so I went straight to my dressing-room, set the alarm clock for 5.30 p.m. and passed out on the couch.

Bridgett was right about the week leading up to Christmas – I was damn lucky if I got home before sunrise each morning. The rich had come to play – to gamble and gambol. I barely had time to think about selling my apartment and furniture. I thought about my departure in snippets, while shaving, or washing my hair under the shower, or just after my afternoon practice when I had ten minutes to relax before changing into my tux for the late afternoon session. I couldn't see myself being content to settle down in Canada. I was pretty confident that, despite Sammy's threat in the kitchen corridor, once I got out of Las Vegas that would be the end of the whole business. Surely even the paranoid Sammy Schischka would get on with his ugly life, and why should the Mafia worry about one lousy piano man? I couldn't believe pursuing Johnny or me made any sense, even to a sick-head like him. After all, he would have achieved his purpose – we'd have both been sufficiently scared of him to get the hell out of town. Game over.

The point preoccupying me was where on earth I would go. Certainly a long way from Chicago. Perhaps that's why Johnny had chosen New York. It was an excellent choice if someone wanted to get lost. I'd never quite forgotten staying at the Waldorf with Miss Frostbite, visiting the World's Fair and, best of all, meeting the great Art Tatum with Joe. Whatever else, the USA offered plenty of excitement – maybe even a bit too much at times. But New York, well, if you made it big as a jazz musician in New York . . . then I'd stop short and not allow my mind to go past this seemingly impossible aspiration.

I longed to get back to fundamentals. New Orleans jazz, blues, the fundamentals on which all jazz is built. I was aware that even the jazz music I was playing in the GAWP Bar wasn't what I called 'Joe jazz'. I recall him saying once, when he heard me doing a little choppy phrasing, 'Hey, Jazzboy, yo never gonna stop lovin' yo mama, likewise yo never gonna start being a smart-ass wid jazz and da blues.' There was another good reason to listen to Joe's advice. Our black audience at the Sunday basketball stadium might dig cutting-edge modern jazz, but the GAWP patrons didn't. The new jazz style referred to as bebop seemed to leave them cold, however much it excited the kids. The introduction of extended harmonies and highly syncopated rhythms simply didn't seem to work for the rich folk, even though it had the coloured kids jumping. You could almost feel them starting to drift away. Besides, it wasn't where I wanted to go. Jazz is endless innovation, but this wasn't a direction I wanted to take. I tried to keep an open mind and I'd done a bit of bebop at The Phoenix; that is, until one afternoon one of the coloured cleaners summoned up the courage to interrupt me. 'Mr Jack, we all done agreed that stuff you playing, it ain't no good jazz. Nobody jumpin' inside demself when you play dat thing. Lordy, lord, it jes don't swing.' I finally decided I was conning myself. 'Esther, you're right,' I said, easing into a blues number I knew they especially liked. Perhaps it was a generational thing.

I guess it was presumptuous of me to spurn bebop. I admired the virtuosity and dazzling inventiveness of Charlie Parker, clearly a genius, of Charles Mingus and Miles Davis, but I thought their music was too rarefied, too esoteric, too far removed from the original jazz roots and mainly appealing to a small, trendy audience. But who was I, a piano player in a casino, to say they were wrong? Joe's words came to me once more: 'Jazzboy, we all got a right to do the music we love. But, likewise, iffen we gonna call ourself pro-fession-al, you gotta give the audience enough of the music dey want.'

My biggest regret was that I was often too exhausted after a Saturday-night gig to attend the Sunday morning gospel services. How very different they were from Moose Jaw and Mrs Henderson's Pentecostals with their 'Praise the Lord, praise His precious name!', its single piano and carefully syncopated hymn singing and hand clapping. Chef Napoleon Nelson had told me, 'Jack, them Pentecostal cats, they really crazy, crazy, man. They kin really sing and holler. They go jumpin' and praisin' and cavortin' for the Lord Jesus. I don' hold wid everythin dey gone do, like speakin' in tongues, some other things also, castin' out the devil, evil spirits, but we da Southern Baptists, why we jes pussy-footin' dat gospel music compare to dem lot.'

'Don't they worship snakes?' I asked, perhaps stupidly.

'Hell, no. That white hillbilly nonsense. Some, not all, done do dat.

Coloured folk know better than doin' somethin' blas-phee-mous like bringin' a snake into church. Everbody know da serpent, he come to Eve wid a nice big, shiny red apple. He da devil's chile turn serpent hissin' in her ear, makin' promises and causin' mischeef.' He threw back his head and laughed a big, hearty Chef Napoleon Nelson laugh. 'All the problem men dey have wid women, for sure dat serpent in dat Garden of Eden, he gotta be the one we done have to blame. Why, before he come hissin' with his fork tongue, women dey just a piece of Adam rib – dey know der place. Like good barbecue spare rib, dey gotta stay juicy an' tender.'

But somehow the visit to the Assembly of God prayer meeting never happened. What I learned about church music – Negro gospel music – from The Resurrection Brothers nevertheless gave me new ways of seeing into the heart of things. Jazz, gospel and blues can't be separated if you are serious about playing American music. It was time to get back into something real, back to the fundamentals. The GAWP Bar had taken my eye off the ball, and I'd let poker interfere with my musical life. If it wasn't for The Resurrection Brothers, I guess I'd have eventually ended up a casino entertainer with a cummerbund to flatten my gut, dyed hair and a capped-tooth smile.

Christmas came and went and I barely had time to notice. Bridgett gave me a gold Rolex watch inscribed with *Jack Spayd, the piano man. Thanks, Bridgett*. Like her, it wasn't in the least sloppy or sentimental, but I could read between the lines. She also told me she'd had the bank send off the cheque to Mac. To my eternal shame, it hadn't even occurred to me to buy her a Christmas gift.

Until 30th of December, everything was fine. I'd finished early, an hour into New Year's Eve, explaining to the ladies in the piano bar that we'd be open from 6 p.m. until sunrise on New Year's Day. I intended sleeping in until after lunch to prepare myself for the long musical night to come. They'd taken the news well. There comes a stage in a night of drinking and carousing when music isn't strictly necessary and may even get in the way of lively inebriated conversation. I always played soft sentimental numbers towards the end of the evening. When you work a piano bar, you learn to go with the flow; it's no place for a prima donna.

I changed into my street clothes and shrugged on an overcoat for the chilly walk home. As usual I strolled through the regular casino to check the action before leaving via the kitchen corridor. As I passed the snack and drinks bar, I heard Lenny call out to me. He was still up, having a drink and a bite with a couple of men, probably pit gamblers. I was tired and the last thing I felt like was a meet and greet, but with only two days before I left Las Vegas for good, it would have been churlish to refuse, so I approached their table. To my surprise, Lenny rose and met me halfway.

'Jack, glad I saw you before you left.' He nodded his head towards the two guys at the table. 'Doctor says Sammy is well enough to travel, and these two guys have been sent from Chicago to take him back on the company Convair in the morning.'

'Are they medics?' I asked, looking them over more carefully.

'Yeah, one is trained, but both are in the Chicago Family.' He clapped me on the back. 'Just thought you'd like to know, Jack. Sort'a like a New Year's gift from your uncle Lenny.' He laughed. 'Sammy is finally away and out of our life, our lives, for fuckin' good! How about that, buddy?'

'Great for you, Lenny, but I thought he'd need at least another two or three weeks in hospital, and his offsider even more.'

'Sammy can walk and sort'a talk. As for the other guy, who the fuck cares? He's goin' anyway.' He shrugged. 'If he dies on the plane, so what. Life's short. Doc says he can walk and is strong enough, just a little nuts. Got his head bandaged like one'a them Egyptian mummies. We'll put them both back into hospital in Chicago.' He paused and chuckled, head to one side. 'You wouldn't consider changing ya mind and stayin', would ya, Jack?'

I shrugged, then patted him on the shoulder. 'My time's up, Lenny, but we're always going to be buddies. I'll stay in touch. I intended to come around and see you New Year's Day, have a drink. I'm off on the early train the next day. By the way, thanks for the generous bonus.'

'Jack, you earned it, every red cent, buddy. Call around, say goodbye, we'll have that drink together. Walking home as usual, are you?'

'Yeah, nice and brisk.'

'Get used to it, Jack. Toronto'll freeze ya balls off,' he laughed.

I retraced my steps and took the kitchen corridor, which led into the parking station, and had just stepped through the open doorway into the street when I saw a pink Cadillac parked directly opposite the entrance and a dark shape leapt at me from behind a parked car. I felt a terrible pain in my head and then everything faded to black.

When I woke up I was in a scene from a horror movie, in a windowless concrete basement with a plain table like a narrow carpenter's bench, and the hard wooden chair I was sitting in facing it. I was tied to the back of the chair with ropes around my chest, and my wrists were lashed to each wooden arm. When I tried to ease my back I discovered that my ankles were tied to the chair legs under the narrow bench. I could see the door through which they must have brought me, and out of which I'd probably be dragged as a corpse.

The pain in my head was severe and I felt sick whenever I tried to move. There was an unfamiliar grunting, gargling sound nearby, and when I began to focus, I saw a figure, its face almost completely covered by a plaster cast, pacing around the room. One feverishly glittering eye was exposed, the other covered by a padded bandage. It was Sammy: the fat gut and limp were unmistakeable. 'And . . . a-a-and remember . . . and . . .' Curiously, his gravel voice had become a squeak.

'He's waking up, Boss,' I heard someone growl to my left and turned to see the minder who'd run for his life during the Desert Inn altercation. Then I saw the second minder. He was seated on a wooden box, snuffing and snorting, wringing his hands and occasionally whimpering, 'Mama, Mama!' His entire head was covered in bandages, except for two slits over his eyes.

Sammy came over to me and punched me on the side of the head. He may have looked sick and frail, but this didn't extend to his fists; the blow caught me on the cheekbone and hurt, but nowhere near as much as the blow to my head that had knocked me unconscious in the car park.

'Thaz . . . f' tha' piece o' shit, Jo . . . nee . . . Dia . . . dia . . . min.'

His voice was slurred as if he had a cleft palate, and the effect was chilling. I was absolutely petrified, my heart racing, sweat prickling all over me despite the freezing temperature in the cellar.

'Thought ya were gonna walk out on Sammy widout payin' for what happened, did ya? Huh, piano player?' (I won't attempt to recreate the mangled way he spoke with a broken jaw. It was clear enough for me to understand exactly what he was saying.) 'Well, ya guessed wrong, ya prick, and now it's my turn, Sammy's turn.'

'You get out of hospital?' It was a stupid and, of course, obvious thing to say. 'With your pal,' I added, nodding at the bandaged monster calling for his mama. 'I see Chicken Shit has returned,' I continued, glancing at the second minder, who must have played a large part in their escape from hospital. This was not bravado – I was terrified – but, rather, the first words that came to me. I could think of nothing to say and didn't have the sense to remain silent. The back of my head throbbed, and I could feel blood sticky against the collar of my shirt and realised my overcoat had been removed. I had no idea how long I'd been unconscious, but it was at least as long as it took to truss me up like a Christmas turkey and drive me to this dive.

'No point lookin' around, Piano Prick.'

'Piano Prick, that good, Boss,' Chicken Shit chortled.

I don't suppose Sammy's plaster cast allowed him to grin, but he nodded his head, accepting the compliment. 'Dis is where we bring da wise guys who don't pay what dey owe Sammy for saving der butt wid a loan they swear'd on der mama's grave dey gonna pay back on time wid interest. Also the ones who think dey can cheat the casino. Dem smart-ass dealers who try and palm a part o' the drop, thinkin' nobody ain't lookin'. People, dey greedy, dey gotta be reminded it not der money. We got the right ta be greedy, not those suckers. We bring dem ta this nice cellar Westside, where nobody can hear dem screaming and pleadin', leastways no white folks. Niggers hear, and it good dey hear, den dey know what happen if dey step outa line.' He paused, using the back of his hand to wipe away the fine line of white spittle that had formed around his mouth. 'Now ya gonna do me some pleadin', Piano Prick? Maybe we gonna listen, maybe we not.' He turned to Chicken Shit. 'But I don't think we in no listenin' mood tonight, hey, Rufus?'

'I don't think we doing no listenin' tonight, Boss,' Sammy's minder agreed, shaking his head melodramatically. It was the first time I had ever heard his first name.

Sammy turned to the bundle of bandages. 'Hey, Groucho, ask yer mama if she in a listenin' mood. She wanna hear da Piano Prick pleadin'?'

A gargling sound came from the bundle of bandages I now knew went by the name of Groucho.

'Yeah, seems der ain't no one here wanna listen, Piano Prick. Ain't none of yer tough-guy war hero buddies gonna help you now, ya piece a' Canuck shit.'

'Canuck shit!' This with a sycophantic chuckle.

Sammy was obviously on Benzedrine or perhaps something even stronger, no doubt supplied by Chicken Shit, and was sweating like a pig, working himself up into more of a frenzy. He bent over me, his mangled face an inch or so from my own, spraying spittle as he spoke, his breath rancid. 'All ya fuckin' war heroes, laughing at poor Sammy. Poor Sammy, only a kitchen hand in the fuckin' US air force while dem dumb fuckers are jumpin' outa the back o' planes to get demself killed. Who da dumb ass now, hey?' It was a rhetorical question and he raved on in his squeaky broken voice. 'Yer asshole buddy hit me when I wasn't lookin'. I coulda taken him out but he hit me when I wasn't lookin'. Dumb fuck coward prick, he hit me when I wasn't lookin' . . .' he paused, perhaps remembering. 'Ya all standin' roun' laughing at me when I bin hit blind.' His voice had become an hysterical shriek by now. 'Who's laughin' now, Mr War Hero Piano Prick tough guy?'

I had the sense to keep quiet this time.

'Ya allowed ta answer!' he prompted.

I felt so sick with fear that if the ropes around my chest and ankles hadn't held me to the chair, I'd have fallen to my knees. As it was, I could feel myself quaking. 'Untie his hand,' Sammy commanded. 'That one,' he pointed at my left hand. 'Then hold him tight, Rufus. You too, Groucho – both of ya.'

Bandages rose from his box, his lips slobbering, but he walked steadily enough. He grabbed me by the upper arms. I couldn't believe how strong he was. They say the insane gain strength but his hand felt like a steel clamp. Chicken Shit held a small filleting knife, which they probably used to threaten their debtor victims, and began sawing through the rope tying my left wrist to the chair. Once the rope was severed, Chicken Shit dropped the knife and grabbed my arm just above the wrist. 'Put his fuckin' hand down flat on'a table,' Sammy screamed.

I was straining every muscle in my body to resist but it was useless. Bandages seemed to possess the strength of five men. He had stopped calling for his mama and had his tongue sticking out of the corner of his mouth as he concentrated on the task of holding me; mucus drained from the bottom of the bandage covering his nose and into the damp, dirty bandage around his chin. They lifted my arm and slapped my palm against the table.

'Move it forward, and hold his wrist on'a table,' Sammy commanded, then walked around behind me as they pinned my forearm down on the rough surface of the wooden table.

When Sammy reappeared he was carrying a hammer and stood directly in front of me, with the narrow bench between us. I curled my hand into a fist and Sammy tapped it not too hard with the hammer. 'Stretch it or maybe ya never gonna open it again, shit f' brains!'

I opened my hand, fingers spread.

Sammy tapped the hammer head down on the edge of the bench. 'See dis, piano player? Dis a five-pound ball-peen hammer.' He weighed it thoughtfully in his hand. 'When I've finish wid you, you ain't gonna be playing the piano no more for all dem rich ladies who wanna fuck ya.'

'Please, Sammy, I beg you, don't! Please, please! I'll give you anything!' I cried.

'What ya gonna give me, Piano Prick? Hey, ya piece'a dog shit. Tell Sammy what ya got dat gonna rub out da insultin' way ya treated me.'

'My apartment! I've got ten grand in the bank, you can have it all!' I blubbered.

'What's dat, maybe fifteen grand tops?' He seemed to consider the offer. 'Dat's a lot of money for a hand ya use to jerk yerself off.'

'Please!' I begged, sobbing.

'I got enough dough and I ain't stayin' in this shit hole no longer.' He suddenly bent close over the table so I could smell his foul breath and screamed into my face. 'No fuckin' deal! Ya hear? NO FUCKIN' DEAL!' Then, suddenly, he pulled back, fingering the hammer, seemingly in control again.

There comes a moment, I discovered, when fear leaves you. 'Sammy, kill me! Go on, do it now, please.' I was quite calm. With my hands gone, what was the point of living?

'Kill you? Why dat murder, man! Besides, how you gonna suffer when ya dead, dumb ass! Dat ain't no Sammy Schischka-style revenge, ya hear?' He turned to the two goons. 'Hold tight, boys.'

I saw the hammer rise and I thought for a second, watching it, that this was some sort of a nightmare and wasn't – couldn't – be happening to me. I tried to look away but found I couldn't. I was like a bird in front of a snake, frozen with fear.

The hammer swung down and I was thrown into hell. Pain washed over me like a black wave. My eyes were screwed shut as more blows thudded into my flesh, but I was still overwhelmed by that first fierce wave of pain. I could hear myself grunting, then screaming, as my body struggled to cope with the shock. Somewhere above it all, I was aware of Sammy's shrieking giggles as he continued to pound my hand. Then, mercifully, I was gone. My mind must have given up.

I must have been out of it for only a short time, because when I came to, they had my right hand in position. Only Rufus was holding it down while Bandages lurched around the room whimpering, 'Mama! Mama!'

Sammy's face appeared, checking that I'd regained consciousness. I'm a big guy but I shall never know where I found the strength for what happened next. Rufus was no match for me – I brushed him off like a fly and sent him tumbling to the cement floor, then grabbed Sammy by the throat and I squeezed, at the same time pulling him across the narrow table so his legs were off the ground. I was still tied to the chair by the ropes around my chest, my left hand a mess of bloody meat in my lap. I tightened my grip, shaking him like a dog. *Squeeze, Jack, squeeze. Kill him*, was all I could hear in my mind.

Rufus scrambled to his feet and must have reached for his pistol. I think I saw all this, but I can never be sure. I had Sammy on his stomach on the bench, his head straining backwards as I throttled him, and I must have turned him just as the gun went off, and the bullet that had been meant for me went straight through Sammy's back. He dropped like a sack of potatoes onto the bench with his head in my lap. Bandages suddenly stopped his wandering and, with a fierce gargling cough, ran at Rufus, who was about to take a second shot, certain to hit me in the head this time. Weeping 'Mama! Mama!', he cannoned into Rufus, who lost his grip on the pistol, which clattered into a corner. Rufus recovered quickly, scrambled to his feet and made a run for the entrance just as the door crashed open, and he ran straight into some guy's arms. That's all I remember before I passed out a second time.

After who knows how much time, I sensed a bright light shining directly at my eyes. 'Mr Spayd? Mr Spayd?' It was a female voice. Female. What did that mean? I had a terrible pain in my left hand.

'Are you awake? You're in hospital, Mr Spayd. We don't like giving you morphine until you're conscious.'

The light moved away and I cautiously opened my eyes.

My mouth felt like it was full of cottonwool. I tried to lick my lips.

A cool, wet cloth was wiped over my face. I sucked desperately at the cloth to moisten my lips and mouth, until a hand dropped a single small ice cube into it. 'Mr Spayd, are you awake?'

A woman's face swam into focus, looking down at me. Behind her was a white ceiling. I felt sure white ceilings had nothing to do with the hereafter. I was alive.

'How . . . how?' My voice was a croak.

'You've been asleep for nearly twenty-four hours, Mr Spayd. How do you feel?'

I tried to look down at the bed covers. I could feel my left arm lying next to me. Raising my head slightly I could see a huge mound of bandages. I looked over at where I thought my right hand should be and there it was, unharmed. I moved my fingers slightly. It was intact. There were bruises from the ropes on my forearm and wrist, but nothing worse than that.

'They didn't cut my left hand off did they, nurse?'

'No, Mr Spayd. Your hand is badly injured. Now you're conscious, we'll . . . the doctor will administer a painkiller immediately. We've been waiting for you to wake up.' At that moment, a man in a white coat – a doctor, I guess – entered with a second nurse, carrying a tray with phial, syringe and swabs.

'My name is Dr Freeman, Mr Spayd. Good to see you awake.'

I felt totally exhausted, hazy and confused, but managed a nod.

'I'm going to give you a jab, then we'll administer morphine by intravenous drip.'

I still felt very groggy but tried to concentrate. 'Sure, doc . . . medical orderly . . . the war,' I managed to slur.

'Oh, good, then you'll understand we need to keep you fairly well sedated. When you were admitted, you were in deep shock. We were pretty concerned.'

'My, my . . .' I pointed to my bandaged left hand.

'Your injuries? Well, you've obviously got a badly damaged left hand, and concussion from a severe blow to the back of the head as well as bruising around the arms and face. The main thing is, your skull is not fractured and there appears to be no bleeding of any consequence inside your cranium.'

'My hand; how bad, doctor?'

'Mr Spayd, it's best to be frank in these matters. It's not good. Your hand's been injured by a series of very heavy blows and there's severe skeletal damage, as well as soft tissue trauma. Do you recall what happened?'

'No, I was heading home . . . something hit me . . .' I mumbled. It wasn't a lie, but I had the wit not to say anything more until I knew a bit more myself. 'Does anyone . . . know anything?'

'Not much, I'm afraid. It's compulsory to inform the police in such matters and they've concluded it was a mugging. The blow to your head indicates that much. You were left on the steps of Emergency. Someone rang the bell and the vehicle that brought you here evidently raced off before anyone could get the plate number. Your head injury is consistent with a mugging but your hand injury is a mystery.'

'My watch?' I said.

'That's a lot of damage to inflict for a watch, but the police found no wallet and they think it unlikely they'll ever find the culprits. But they'll want to interview you. It's pretty routine. Don't worry about it now. Sometimes details return with time.'

'Today?'

'No, no, of course not. We've told them you'll be sedated and we don't expect you'll be able to tell them anything useful for quite a while. We don't want you grilled when your system's full of painkillers, do we?' Then, glancing at my left hand, he continued, 'We have a specialist surgeon here who set some of the broken bones and did what he could, but the hand will require a fair bit of work down the track.'

'Can you fix it?'

'You'll have to talk to the surgeon about that, Mr Spayd. For the next few days anyway, you'll have to rest. You have a concussion and we will need to keep you sedated, give your body a chance to heal. I'm afraid that hand is going to give you a good deal of pain for quite a while, but we can help with that.'

They must have been doping me up pretty heavily because the next few days were a blur. I would wake up, then fall back into a doze. I never felt fully awake, and I had great trouble staying alert. I know I had some visitors. Several serious-looking men in suits appeared at my bedside from time to time, and one day I came to and found Bridgett sitting by my bed. She looked like she had been crying but I was too woozy even to greet her.

When they first reduced the level of morphine in my system, I became more alert, but the pain in my hand steadily increased. It would start as an ache, like the first pangs of toothache, then build and build to a throbbing misery that wouldn't go away until the nurse appeared to 'fix' my drip, sending me back into woozy semi-consciousness. I refused to think about the morphine. I'd seen what opiate dependency could do to a soldier, and I didn't want to end up like Charlie Parker, with a raging heroin habit. He wasn't the only prominent jazz musician hooked on horse either.

They must have been fiddling with the dosages because they seemed to reach some sort of balance where I began to feel more alert for longer periods without the crippling pain.

One day I opened my eyes and Bridgett was sitting beside the bed again.

'Jack, you're back.'

'Hello, Bridgett,' I croaked. 'Wha'za date?'

'Saturday, 10th of January.'

'You get your points?'

She smiled sadly, bent over and kissed me on the mouth. I wish I could say it was lovely, but my lips were so dry, there was almost no sensation. 'Only you would ask, Jack. Yes, thank you. Thanks to you, we made the profit we needed.'

I wanted to ask her a whole heap of questions but found I lacked the strength. 'Get me a drink, Bridgett. My mouth . . . like paper.' I forgot to say please.

She left and, moments later, returned with a glass containing a straw and held it up for me to take in my right hand. I sucked greedily, the water cleaning and loosening my tongue so that I was able to speak normally. 'Thank you,' I grinned, 'for the kiss.'

She reached out for the glass and put it on the bedside table, then took my right hand. 'Oh, Jack, if only you knew how worried I've been,' she said, struggling to keep control. 'You seem to be a bit more awake today. It's the first time you've spoken coherently in nearly a fortnight.'

'I think they're adjusting the drug dosage, and starting to get it right. So, what happened? Tell me what you know, please.'

She began to tear up and dabbed her eyes with a handkerchief. 'Jack, what do you remember?'

I'd had plenty of time coming in and out of consciousness to recall what had happened and over the next half hour, pausing every once in a while to gather my strength or to make sure I got it right, I told her what happened to the point when Chicken Shit ran for his life, and the door crashed inwards and he ran into some guy's arms.

'Are you sure you feel up to hearing the whole story? Or the part of it I know?' she asked.

'Yes, yes, please. Not knowing is starting to drive me crazy. Sammy, Chicken Shit, Bandages, what happened to them?'

Bridgett looked bemused. 'Pardon? Sammy I understand, but *who* else?'

I explained. 'In my head I named Sammy's offsider, the guy who took off with the pink Cadillac, Chicken Shit, and the minder with the fractured skull and obvious brain damage Bandages. Their actual names, I've discovered, are Rufus and Groucho, but somehow the nicknames are permanently embedded in my mind.'

'Well, let me begin at the beginning as I try to recall the sequence of events. The person who saved your life was one of the kitchen hands, Jim-Jay Bullnose.'

I must have looked blank because she went on, 'You remember, the busboy you sent to alert me when you were in the kitchen attending to Hector? Well, he was on late nights – I know I shouldn't let a fifteen-year-old be on duty past midnight but that's Las Vegas; his family needs the money, and all staff volunteer for that shift work to get the extra pay, especially at this time of the year.'

'Gotta do something for the boy,' I said.

She nodded. 'Well, it seems one of the other coloured people in the parking station saw what happened and came running into the kitchen. With New Year's Eve coming up, I'd gone to bed early and nobody wanted to be responsible for waking me and they were too scared to tell Lenny.' She shrugged. 'They regard you very highly, Jack, but associate Lenny with Sammy, whether we like it or not, and he was with two guys in the twenty-four-hour café over in the regular who obviously weren't guests. But someone remembered Jim-Jay Bullnose was on duty out front and had been the one who'd initially told them all about Sammy's Westside basement and also called me the night Hector was hurt. He lives with his family in the tenement next door to that dreadful place. By the way, among the coloured staff, it is, or was, known as Mr Sammy's torture chamber. And, well, he'd previously fetched me for Hector, so he volunteered to phone me, to dial my apartment number.

'Thank god Lenny was still up with the two men from Chicago. I immediately alerted him. Jim-Jay Bullnose then took them in a car that the two men had hired, Lenny having enough presence of mind not to take a company car to the basement on the Westside.' She paused. 'Lenny forbade me to accompany them . . .' Then suddenly she burst into tears. 'They arrived too late to save your hand and . . . and it's . . . it's all my fault you stayed on! Oh, oh, Jack!' she wailed.

I patted her on the shoulder with my good hand for some time while she had a bit of a weep – more than a bit. 'Bridgett, stop it!' I kept repeating as firmly as I could with my failing voice. Then, finally, when she seemed a little more in control, I asked her, 'Who knows about this; I mean, apart from the coloured staff?'

'You mean the police?' she sniffed.

'Well, no, the hospital told me they've settled for a mugging by parties unknown who stole my wallet, but they'll want to interview me at some stage.' I didn't mention the stolen Rolex, in case this set off a fresh bout of weeping.

Bridgett finally wiped away her tears. Her mascara had run and her eyes were bloodshot, but she still looked beautiful. 'Sorry, Jack, I feel so guilty . . .' But eventually she composed herself, realising perhaps that this was no time for confessions, which would change nothing. 'The two men from Chicago took over. It was close to dawn on New Year's Eve by the time I'd made all the arrangements; private ambulances, getting the company Convair prepared to take a stretcher and ready to fly. They wanted nobody to know what had happened and insisted I do the organising, as usual.' Bridgett sighed. 'I don't get it with these hoods – they must think coloured people can't think or act. The entire hotel staff would have known every detail by noon at the latest. They gave Jim-Jay Bullnose a hundred dollars the previous night when he took them to the basement and said they'd kill him if he ever went to the police. He brought it to me and asked if he should keep it. It was, of course, a veritable fortune for his family. I told him he had no choice, he couldn't return it or they'd get suspicious. He then told me the story of what happened in the basement. I've sent him on the Greyhound to his aunt and uncle in Alabama, just in case. I've spoken to his parents and they've agreed I can see he gets a proper education.'

'What about the hospital; they didn't question Sammy and Bandages leaving the day before they were expected to?'

She gave a grim laugh. 'The hospital . . . well, they, whoever was on duty, is evidently prepared to say that Sammy and whatshisname, Bandages, had been officially signed out that night. I guess by your Chicken Shit guy.'

'Seems strange, though, the two guys arriving from Chicago. Sammy must have known they were coming and this was his last chance to get at me. Lenny told me they were taking him and Bandages back to Chicago the following day.'

Bridgett looked serious for a moment. 'Jack, I simply don't know. If money changed hands, and it always does, the ward supervisor or head nurse or whoever . . . I really can't say.' She paused. 'The remainder comes from Jim-Jay Bullnose. When the men broke down the door of the basement, they forgot all about him. One of them had lifted the door back to cover the entrance but it left a crack that allowed Jim-Jay to see into the room. The guys from Chicago wrestled Chicken Shit to the ground but Bandages was squealing and pointing at him, 'He kill Mama! He kill Mama!' He showed them the gun lying in the corner, then ran over, grabbed it and fired two bullets into Chicken Shit, evidently killing him instantly. He then pointed the gun at you, but one of the men from Chicago had his gun out and shot him dead.'

'Christ! That's two citizens America isn't going to mourn,' was all I could think to say.

'Anyhow, Jim-Jay Bullnose knew better than to hang around and fled for his life. It seems, according to Lenny, they carried the near-dead Sammy out of the basement to the pink Cadillac parked around the corner, having retrieved the keys from Chicken Shit's pocket. They laid Sammy in the luggage compartment, and the two men drove it back to the Firebird while Lenny drove you in the hired car to Emergency and carried you to the entrance then left before he was seen.

'I arranged for a private ambulance and a doctor whose lips are sealed. Occasionally we need him, and we reward him very well. He's a compulsive gambler who usually gets his gambling debt wiped out. It seemed the bullet hadn't entered any of Sammy's vital organs but had smashed into the bone in his hip. He, the doctor, patched him up and gave him a stiff shot of morphine with further supplies for the journey and said Sammy was okay to fly. It was decided that one of the Chicago men, a trained medic, would accompany the ambulance to the airport and travel with him. The other was going to stay and help clear up the mess in the Westside cellar. Because, of course, Lenny couldn't be seen anywhere near it. By sunrise the Convair was in the air with Sammy on a stretcher on the way to Chicago. The pink Cadillac has since disappeared.'

Even by Nevada police standards, you could walk a circus elephant through the holes in this case, though, no doubt, some deep pockets would be filled to the brim with untraceable, used large-denomination notes. 'What happened to the two dead guys in the basement? They disappear with the Cadillac?' I asked.

'No, the Chicago guy must have hidden their bodies in the cellar; then it was boarded up. Lenny was back at the Firebird on the phone, calling all the right tradespeople and anyone else he needed to cooperate.' Bridgett paused then explained, 'He may be a cleanskin but he's still Mafiosi and he knows who to call.'

I nodded. 'Yeah, keeping that skin clean must sometimes get pretty tricky.'

Bridgett nodded, then continued. 'White security guards were hired before the plane had even taken off, and the derelict two-level tenement containing Sammy's torture-chamber basement was roped off with a 'Danger. Building Unsafe' sign. By noon the wooden building had been bulldozed and the basement filled with concrete to a depth of twelve feet. According to staff, informed by Jim-Jay Bullnose's parents, twenty big concrete trucks arrived during the morning. By lunchtime the basement was filled to street level with cement. They let it set and the next day they removed the wood and bulldozed the rubble back over it. Lenny is one of the few people in Las Vegas who could have made all this happen on New Year's Eve and New Year's Day!'

I smiled. 'I know one other!'

'No, Jack, there are some things . . . I knew you were safe in hospital and were not going to die. The rest was Mafiosi business. I refused to cooperate; that is, beyond arranging for the private ambulance and the doctor for Sammy, and that was always going to happen with his release from hospital that day and could be explained. Lenny did it all himself, even arranging for a case of beer to be sent to every truck driver and workman involved, with an extra little envelope attached. The envelopes, he got Mr Sanders to do.'

'And through all of this not a policeman in sight?' I suggested.

Bridgett gave a bitter laugh. 'No, you're wrong. According to the staff, two motorcycle traffic cops directed traffic, to allow the trucks to turn onto the site. I daresay they'll have no trouble taking their kids to California for the holidays.'

'Well, thank God you kept your nose clean, Mrs Fuller. I should have known better than to suggest . . .' I didn't complete the sentence.

Bridgett looked serious and, once again, on the edge of tears. 'When I was forbidden to accompany the three of them to Sammy's basement, I became terribly distraught. Jim-Jay Bullnose was the only one who knew where it was or, I swear, I would have tried to get to you. Jack, *please* believe I would have happily implicated myself, thrown caution to the winds and gone with them in the hope of finding you safe and sound.'

'No, no, I'm glad you didn't,' I said; then, seeing her distress, I fell silent, gulping back my own tears, though I could feel one errant teardrop sliding down my cheek. 'Oh, shit!' I muttered, reaching out and taking her hand. She bent over as if to hold my hand against her cheek but then suddenly pulled back. 'Jack, I'll resign, I'll look after you forever, if you'll have me. We'll leave. I've got my two points. Oh, Jack, how can I ever —'

'Shush! I'm a big boy. No, no, Bridgett. That wouldn't work. Don't even think about it! I made the decision to stay, all on my own,' I said, recovering. The last thing I wanted was for her to settle for me out of a sense of obligation.

'Jack, I've thought of nothing else. I was in a terrible state, thinking I was letting you down by not coming to find you. I had no sleep that night. I'll do anything —'

'You'll do nothing, you hear? Nothing of the sort! How do you think I'd feel?'

'Oh, Jack, this is too awful for words.'

I had never seen her like this. 'Bridgett, pull yourself together. Tell me what you did New Year's Eve without me there.' Perhaps that would distract her.

She sniffed and reached into her sleeve for a handkerchief, and blew her nose. The composed Mrs Fuller emerged almost at once. 'I can't say it was easy preparing for New Year's Eve, acting as if nothing had happened.' Bridgett brushed at her tears and smiled, now looking at me in a distinctly mischievous way. 'But the joint was jumping!'

'Oh, so you found another piano player, did you?' I said, pretending to be miffed.

'Oh, something much, much better than that,' she teased. 'I paid Chef Napoleon Nelson for his usual shift and then gave him the night off from kitchen work. His staff could manage – he'd prepared absolutely everything.' She paused, and I wondered where this was leading. 'And then I rehired him with The Resurrection Brothers for the GAWP Bar.'

I stared at her blankly. 'Bridgett, you didn't! You did that?' I exclaimed.

'Well, there have been headline acts with coloured musicians before.'

'Yes, but these are kitchen staff or the equivalent, all amateurs and all black. You must have known you were taking a chance. What if some of your ladies objected?'

'On the contrary, you've talked about The Resurrection Brothers so often, I had very few doubts. I figured you don't fill the basketball stadium Westside every Sunday afternoon unless you're pretty good.' Bridgett hesitated. 'I told the ladies that you'd had a bit of an accident and hurt your hand and had to go to hospital overnight.' She looked down at her own hands. 'Not a complete lie, but then I added that you had asked me to get The Resurrection Brothers to take your place, as you'd been playing with them every Sunday for years, and you had assured me they would prove to be a special treat.

'They were sorry to hear about your hand but they took it well, and the free Krug champagne – compliments of Jack Spayd – helped put them in a party mood. By the way, fifty-six large bunches of roses arrived for you from the GAWP ladies on New Year's Day. I guess Las Vegas ran clean out of red roses. I'm sorry you weren't able to appreciate them.'

Bridgett continued, eyes dancing. 'Some GAWP members, I admit, were a little surprised when they discovered the band members were all black. But it didn't last. Nobody walked out and they simply loved the music. As you know, other casinos have headline acts with Negro stars and musicians, but this is the first time in Las Vegas an all-coloured band of local church musicians has ever played at a casino. They especially loved Chef Napoleon Nelson. My goodness, you'd have thought he was Count Basie with his big band, the way the ladies carried on. They simply lapped it up.'

'Bridgett, that took a lot of guts.'

'Not at all; it was fun and took my mind off you, Jack.'

'And, in the process, you thumbed your nose at Chicago!' I laughed.

'Well, maybe. I acted as MC and pointed out that the members of the band were all working folk who'd come at short notice as a special favour to you, many giving up overtime jobs on New Year's Eve to do so. We passed around a silver champagne bucket and it filled three times over with folding money,' Bridgett laughed.

'Then, at the very end, Chef Napoleon Nelson stood up and thanked them for their generosity. "The Lord is good," he said, and made a little speech. You could have heard a pin drop as he told them how he'd first met you in a bar on the Westside when you'd come in and ordered sarsaparilla! This got a good laugh from the ladies, who were full of vintage Krug. He then went on to say how you'd jammed together, with you demanding he stay at the piano while you played the harmonica.' Bridgett hesitated. 'He had the room in tears with his story of how you played, and the people came and filled the café and the street outside. Then he said, "And now, we gonna play for Mr Jack Spayd the same number we played that first time. Ladies . . . 'Saint James Infirmary Blues'."'

Bridgett began crying again, and I confess I was pretty choked up myself. 'French champagne and "Saint James Infirmary" with me in hospital, that's neat,' I managed to say with a choked kind of laugh, trying to keep it light. 'Well done, Bridgett. Is it any wonder the coloured folk love you?'

'Jack, they feel the same about you,' she said quietly.

'Bridgett, what now?' I asked, feeling a little uncomfortable. 'Are *you* going to be okay?'

'Jack, if anything, I've got more paperwork. Yes, yes, I'll be okay.'

I lifted my bandaged hand. 'Well, you'll have to find a new piano man now. Your GAWP ladies will understand.'

Bridgett burst into tears again. 'Oh, Jack, what have I done! How can I ever —'

'Shhh! That's enough. These things happen. Just make sure you end up filthy rich out of all this!'

The senior nurse came in and announced that they were about to change my dressings and that visiting hours were over. She stood by while Bridgett gave me a chaste kiss on the cheek and promised to be back the following day.

I had to keep up some semblance of optimism, hope and good humour with the constant stream of visitors to my bedside. Chef Napoleon Nelson came every day and so did Lenny. He told me Sammy would probably need crutches, or at least a cane when he came out of hospital. Can't say I was sorry. Lenny wanted me to delay my resignation, saying the Firebird would then be able to pay my hospital bills, but I'd had Bridgett update my original resignation to 2nd of January, then type it out so I could sign it. I wanted to be clear – not of Lenny, I explained, but of Chicago. I wanted no favours.

I groaned inwardly every time I saw a figure at the door, with the exceptions of Bridgett, who came every day, Lenny and Chef Napoleon Nelson. All the members of the band came in one day, plus a heap more of the casino staff and the parents of Jim-Jay Bullnose. Even Booker T. visited when he was in town.

The only good thing was that the constant throng during the day did stop me from dwelling on the condition of my left hand and what it might mean for my future. However, the nights – the endless nights after everyone had left, with only a dim half-light surrounding me – were like being in Hell's waiting room.

CHAPTER TWENTY

EVERY MORNING, DR LIGHT, the surgeon who first operated on my hand, would personally supervise the changing of my dressings, and every morning my wounded hand filled my heart with despair. It was a horrible purple colour, almost twice normal size and, covered in fresh scars and stitches, it only vaguely resembled a human hand. The very sight of it reduced me to tears. While he was careful to make no promises, Dr Light would inevitably conclude each examination with words such as, 'Jack, you're young and fit and the hand is mending well, but it's much too early to tell what the outcome might be.' It wasn't exactly encouragement, but it gave me the tiniest sense of hope.

As I've mentioned, I have big hands – Rachmaninov hands, as Miss Bates used to call them – good piano hands, anyhow. Now the left one looked as if Hector, the barbecue chef, had tenderised it with a meat mallet. Even after I got used to the way it looked, the sight of it still filled me with a sick terror.

The piano was my life and, despite the tiny ray of hope Dr Light always left me with, it didn't take much imagination to see that my career as a pianist could be over. Then, one afternoon, Dr Light entered wearing a broad smile, and accompanied by a tall man of slightly foreign appearance. He hung the 'Do Not Enter' sign on the door and closed it behind them. 'Jack, may I introduce you to Dr Haghighi. You wouldn't believe it, but as luck would have it, there is a medical convention at the Last Frontier casino. It occurred to me to check through the list of visiting surgeons and I discovered Dr Haghighi was giving a paper.' He glanced up at the tall, smiling man. 'Dr Koroush Haghighi is originally from Persia but is now considered one of America's best hand surgeons. He is from back east and operates out of Albany General Hospital, New York State. He has generously agreed to examine your hand.'

It says a lot for Dr Light that, as a surgeon himself, he was prepared to defer to a colleague with presumably near identical qualifications.

'Good afternoon, Mr Spayd,' the visiting surgeon greeted me.

'Hi, Doctor; please, it's Jack.' I couldn't be sure I'd pronounce either of his names correctly. I figured if he called me Jack, I could then simply refer to him as 'Doctor'.

'I've looked at your x-rays, Jack. I suspect there's not much more that can be done here. Dr Light has done a remarkable job, considering the facilities available. But let me have a look for myself. X-rays don't always show everything.'

Dr Light proceeded to remove the dressings, a process that took a fair amount of time. It sometimes seemed I had more linen wrapped around me than an ancient Egyptian mummy. Meanwhile, Dr Haghighi went over to the porcelain basin in the corner of my room, removed his jacket, and proceeded to scrub his hands and arms up to the elbows with antiseptic lotion.

'Jack, you may have noticed there are no nursing staff present. I'd be obliged if you didn't mention this visit by Dr Haghighi to anyone. He isn't licensed to operate in Nevada and is doing me a great personal favour by looking at your hand. I must emphasise, please don't mention it to any of the hospital staff – or anyone else, for that matter,' he repeated.

'Of course, I understand. Thank you both,' I said, wincing despite the morphine as the last piece of dressing was removed, and the second surgeon, freshly scrubbed, appeared at my bedside.

Dr Haghighi spent a good while looking at and probing various parts of what passed for a human hand, once in a while asking me to attempt to move a finger or turn my hand. Despite the painkiller, this often proved acutely uncomfortable. 'Jack, you have lost some of your fine motor functions. There are also issues with the repair of the many fractures. I have the honour to head up a specialist hand injuries' centre at the Albany General Hospital. It's a very fine facility and I'm sure I can find you a bed if you're willing to come east; though, I suggest, the sooner I operate, the better. The convention runs for a week, so it would be good if you could come to us as soon after that as Dr Light thinks it safe to move you.'

'Can you fix it so I can play the piano again, Doctor?'

He looked at Dr Light, who nodded. 'Mr Spayd – ah, I beg your pardon, Jack – I can't promise anything at this stage. This is an accident no surgeon can fully repair. The human hand is an extraordinarily complex physiological device, and it can often adapt remarkably to injuries but seldom to the sort of damage yours has received. I doubt we can fully restore it to its former capacity.' He indicated my hand. 'These are among the worst injuries I have personally witnessed. For a pianist, even a lesser injury would likely cause problems.' He sighed. 'I'm very sorry but it's better to be truthful than to raise your hopes. However, I feel sure we can restore much of the use of your hand if you come to us.' He shrugged. 'But there is only so much we can do.' He spoke English with only a trace of an accent and with perfect grammar.

I closed my eyes for a moment, and suddenly saw that hammer swinging down again and the madness and delight in Sammy's single exposed eye.

'What do you mean by "much of the use"?' It was a desperate question.

'Depends on what we find when we get inside for a second look. I think we can get you back to normal strength but the articulation of your fingers will not be the same as before. I'm not sure about the degree of feeling either. In your profession, I imagine, touch is essential. Also, I'm afraid arthritis later on is almost inevitable.'

'So, no piano?'

He thought for a moment. 'Well, Jack, it's a question of how well you formerly played. If you give us the opportunity and you do the post-operative exercises, I'm sure we can effect a reasonable outcome, but I very much doubt you'll be able to play at the level you once did.'

'I think I'd like to be left alone for a bit now, thanks, Doctor.' I could no longer contain my emotion and quickly turned away from them, gulping back my sobs while Dr Light replaced my dressings and bandages. The words Joe had once spoken to me floated back into my mind. I'd been suffering from a dose of flu and was unable to compete in a piano competition I was fairly confident I could win, and was whingeing about how unfair everything was. Joe said, 'Jazzboy, life got a way of cheatin' on everybody. Sometime we jes got to harden up some.' I was still a long way from 'hardening up some' and continued to weep pathetically.

'Get in touch with me if you decide to come east, Jack. To the Albany General Hospital,' I heard the visiting surgeon say in a quietly sympathetic voice. With my face turned away, I was unable to respond or even to thank him, except to nod my head.

Some days later, the police arrived. My heart sank when they introduced themselves – they were the same two detectives who had been at Hector's bedside taking evidence. Or, to put it more accurately, taking a statement that allowed them to sign off on the case. Chef Napoleon Nelson had told me their names: Detective Myles Stone and Detective Hank Gillespie. How could you possibly forget a name like Myles Stone? Sometimes you have to wonder what the heck parents are thinking when they name their children.

Messrs Stone and Gillespie got straight to business after a perfunctory introduction that included a display of their badges.

'We have seen the hospital report, Mr Spayd. Your injury appears to be a result of an accident or assault in the early hours of December the 30th when you were on your way home. Do you recall what happened?' Stone asked.

I'd given a good deal of thought to what I was prepared to say and decided that there was no way I could tell the police what happened without implicating Lenny. From Chef Napoleon Nelson's description, I knew enough about these two not to run off at the mouth. 'What sort of protection would I get as a witness?' I asked.

'Oh, are you telling us it wasn't an accident, sir?' Stone asked.

'I'm not saying anything more until you answer my question, officer.'

The second cop, Gillespie, then said, 'Well, if the sheriff authorises it, we could provide police protection leading up to and during any subsequent trial, sir.'

'And afterwards?'

'Ah . . . well, I guess that would be dependent on the circumstances, sir,' Stone replied.

I knew what that meant. I would be on my own if I gave evidence against Sammy. It would be a miracle if I lasted long enough to see any trial.

Then Gillespie asked, 'In your case, are there any other witnesses, sir?'

'No.'

'No witnesses at all?' Gillespie repeated, his tone a clear warning.

'No.'

'Did you have any previous cause to suspect this person's motives?' Gillespie asked. They'd obviously done their homework and had quite clearly received a detailed briefing. I warned myself to be very careful with my reply.

'Yes.'

'Are you saying he had previously caused you trouble or harmed you personally?' This time it was Stone. They were a well-trained duo.

'No. He threatened, but never actually harmed, me.'

They looked at each other. 'And you didn't actually see your attacker?' Stone said with emphasis.

'Better find yourself a very good lawyer and have a long talk with him before you start accusing anyone, sir,' Gillespie warned.

I sighed. 'I think I'm getting the message.' There was no point in telling them about Sammy's pink Cadillac; it hadn't been reported missing and with the night staff paid off, they could prove Sammy was in hospital at the time.

Both tried to remain looking deadpan but I could see they were relieved. 'Sir, we have the hospital report and we know you lost your wallet.'

'And a gold Rolex watch,' I added.

Both wrote this down. Then Stone said, 'It doesn't explain your hand. The felon wouldn't damage your hand to remove a watch. By the way, was there an inscription on the watch? If we apprehend someone in the future, it may prove useful,' he explained.

'Yes.'

They waited, notepads poised. I realised I'd made a mistake mentioning the watch. Damn, damn, damn! Now I was going to have to involve Bridgett.

'Yes, it simply said: *Jack Spayd, the piano man. Thanks, Bridgett.*'

'Is that Mrs Bridgett Fuller from the Firebird?' Gillespie asked.

'She was my boss and she gave it to me as a thank-you for five years of playing piano in her casinos.'

'Expensive gift, ain't it?' Stone remarked.

'Well, perhaps. What are you trying to say, officer?'

'You and Mrs Fuller, you weren't . . . ?'

The implication was obvious. 'I take exception to that, officer,' I said in a cool voice, so they couldn't accuse me of being angry. 'The inscription is semi-official; she refers to me by my full name Jack S-P-A-Y-D,' I spelled it out, 'then simply thanks me, as any professional manager might do. Anyhow, a gold watch is not an unusual retirement gift.'

They duly wrote down the inscription and I felt I'd scored a rare point. 'Will you read it back to me, please?' I asked. They did so and it was correct. 'Thank you,' I said coolly.

'Mr Spayd, please,' Detective Stone said in what I think was intended as a conciliatory tone, 'You must understand we're trying to get to the bottom of what happened. Right now we can only surmise that you were attacked with a blunt instrument by a person or persons unknown, rendered unconscious and robbed. Your wallet and, we now know, your watch were taken. Maybe you were lying on the road and they drove over your left hand in their hurry to escape?'

'And then I miraculously landed in the emergency department?' I said, not without sarcasm.

The two detectives may have seemed like routine hacks but I hadn't the least doubt that, along with a whole heap of other Las Vegas cops, they were on the Mob's payroll. They had not been chosen for their stupidity and were certainly not following the usual procedures.

'Yeah, it doesn't seem likely the perpetrators would do that,' Gillespie admitted. 'Perhaps the original perpetrators left you lying in the road in the dark, and a second motorist came along and didn't see you until it was too late and drove over your hand. He is a good citizen, but doesn't want to get involved.' He paused. 'If he called an ambulance he could get caught up in a possible future court case, always a long and thankless process.' He paused again. 'But, thankfully, he, or they – we expect it was more than one person, as you are a big man to lift – had a conscience and, instead of driving off and leaving you, dropped you off here, at emergency.'

Stone then reminded me, 'There are no witnesses, sir. The doctor who examined you in emergency says in his report . . .' he flicked several pages of his notepad, 'Yeah, here, "*The damage to the patient's hand is consistent with it having being run over by the wheel of a motor vehicle*".'

I sighed, knowing it was pointless to carry on. There was nowhere to go, I was caught between the proverbial rock and a hard place. I shrugged. 'What can I say? I guess it was a car that ran over my hand, after all.'

The two detectives remained poker-faced. 'We will prepare your statement, sir,' Myles Stone said in an even voice.

'Thank you for your cooperation,' Gillespie added, turning to his partner with the merest hint of a smile. I was forced to silently congratulate Manny 'Asshole' de Costa on his choice of policemen to bribe – Sammy would never have had the sagacity to pick these two. 'We will return in two or three days to have you read and sign your statement, Mr Spayd,' Gillespie concluded.

With a permanently damaged left hand, my musical career was effectively over and there wasn't anything I could do to change that. Sammy had kept his promise to get even. I tried to tell myself I was a near-professional poker player and as long as I could hold a hand of cards, I'd have something going for me. But if poker was an addiction, then music was an overwhelming obsession; one could never replace the other. Perhaps a medical miracle at the hands of the Albany surgeon with the unpronounceable name? It was worth a try; that is, if I ever managed to get to Dr Haghighi at Albany General Hospital. With Sammy still alive, I convinced myself, Chicago would want to clean up the mess. It made perfect sense; this was no longer just about Sammy, there were too many loose ends, too much that could go wrong and too much at stake, and that would mean getting rid of the prime witness. I was the big red bullseye on the target.

I thought constantly of Bridgett's offer to resign and be with me, and about the irony of this. With an undamaged hand I'd have done anything to be with her, accepted any terms she cared to nominate, but now it was impossible. Mrs Bridgett Fuller was an exceptional example of the human race and if I – I mean, Sammy – hadn't . . . I couldn't take the thought any further. I asked myself who would want an ex-pianist for a husband, one who was addicted to poker playing and who lacked any other means of gainful employment. A great catch, I don't think! Mrs Fuller, with her potential wealth from the two points in the Firebird, giving me my pocket money, my stake, to play cards with my pals. Pathetic thought. I could still go back home, and maybe reapply to take up my vet scholarship and eventually become a suburban doctor. I knew I'd have to give that some serious thought but, I must admit, it still didn't appeal. Writing prescriptions for people with sniffles hardly compared with the life I'd been living . . .

Bridgett Fuller was an intelligent, clear-eyed, pragmatic and – using the word in its best possible sense – calculating woman. If she hadn't been, she could never have survived all those years working with Chicago. The idea that she'd give up her career to care for me was unreasonable and I simply wouldn't allow my imagination to go any further.

You may laugh at me, after my cowardly acceptance of the police version of my 'mugging', but I still had a scrap of my tattered pride left. To have her in my life because she felt guilty about my hand was simply out of the question.

In the weeks since my ordeal she'd proved herself a loving, thoughtful and kind friend. Now it was time for her to leave my life forever and get on with her own; one that would prove peaceful and guilt-free and in which her hard-earned two points would soon allow her to live in luxury.

I admit, I felt sorry for myself and I had a second great howl into my pillow after the two cops left.

Bridgett turned up the next day, as usual. Being Bridgett, she'd somehow managed to persuade the hospital staff she could visit outside normal visiting hours. 'Jack, your room gets too crowded; I don't like to share you,' she laughed. If my days could be said to have a highlight, it was certainly when she was by my bedside.

I guess I couldn't help myself; I needed a mother confessor after the police interview and I told her everything. She didn't comment except to say in that practical way she had, 'Jack, you were right to agree to their terms. Have you signed the statement they've prepared?'

'No, they haven't returned yet, they said it might take two or three days.'

She gave me a suspicious look. 'They said that . . . two or three days? Hmm.' Then she advised, 'Sign it, but read it through carefully first, every comma, every full stop.' There had been no criticism and no judgment, just sound advice. 'As soon as Dr Light says you may leave, I'll make the arrangements to get you safely back to Canada.'

I felt like a complete heel; worse than that. I hadn't told her about

Albany and Dr Haghighi's offer, which I'd accepted. I was afraid she'd insist on accompanying me.

A few days after the surgeon from Albany had departed, Dr Light finished examining my hand and said, 'Jack, it's coming along nicely. I'll release you to go to Albany General Hospital as soon as you're well enough to travel by air. You okay for funds?' I assured him I was. I'd asked Bridgett to sell my apartment, using this as an additional ploy to stop her insisting on accompanying me east. But, of course, when I did mention Albany to her, she wanted to come and took a fair bit of dissuading not to.

To my delight, she had decided to allow Chef Napoleon Nelson to take my place in the GAWP Bar. I used this as a further reason for her to stay right where she was. 'Bridgett, despite your new year's triumph, not all your GAWP ladies will be thrilled. He'll need training and he'll need you.' It made sense and she agreed.

After three more nights, nights in which I'd wake with a start, my mind fuzzy but nevertheless filled with terror, I'd still heard nothing from the two cops. I tried to convince myself that they were busy and that my pathetic performance had put them at their ease. Directly after their visit I'd asked not to be given any sedation other than my normal drip, which was now down to the very minimum. I was by no means pain free, but there was a reason for this. One kind of addiction is bad enough; two, a disaster in the making. Being a poker addict without a stake combined with having a morphine addiction would likely lead to heroin, an even more addictive opiate. I was aware there would be times when I needed to get away from my depression, but 'horse', as it was known in my world, could make my future life impossible and destroy anything creative I may have left in me. The physical pain was bearable – you can grow accustomed to pain – but I was finding it almost impossible to adjust to the mental anguish I felt when its effects started to wear off. This was the real fight that lay ahead of me.

However, I was determined to endure both the physical and mental torment. Dr Light, that very afternoon, had said that in another few days, a week at the most, I'd be fit enough to leave for the East Coast.

Two nights before I was due to leave, the nurses had settled me down, almost begging me to take a painkilling injection or at least sleeping tablets. I had resisted both and lay awake, trying to cope with the pain as all the familiar hospital sounds died away and I was left with the extra tyranny of almost complete silence.

It was after midnight when I heard a *squeak, squeak* coming along the passageway leading to my own and the other private rooms. For god's sake, you'd think the night cleaner would have the brains to oil the wheels of his trolley, I thought. Then my door was slowly eased open and a thin shaft of light penetrated from the passageway. Moments later, Bridgett appeared in the doorway. She was holding a finger to her lips and beckoning someone behind her to follow.

She came quickly to the bedside. 'Jack, are you awake?' she asked, just above a whisper.

'Bridgett? What the hell? It's past midnight. What's going on?'

'We've got to get you out of here tonight, Jack.'

'Tonight?'

She was carrying a small canvas bag, which she placed on the bed. 'Lenny's been killed.' Her voice cracked, but she quickily regained control.

'No!' I couldn't believe my ears. 'How?'

'He was shot some four hours ago in his quarters. Someone from the late-night kitchen staff came to my quarters to tell me; they thought I might be in danger. Jack, if they'll murder Lenny, one of their own, you're certain to be next in line.'

I looked past her and realised the person who had followed her in was Chef Napoleon Nelson.

'They're tidying up, Jack, getting rid of the evidence. Time to go,' Bridgett said firmly. I knew she would have been as shocked as I was by Lenny's murder but for now her feelings were in lockdown.

Thank Christ I hadn't taken any sleeping tablets or morphine. My heart was thumping but my mind was more or less clear; nevertheless, I was still attempting to come to terms with what she'd just told me.

'Lenny? Jesus! Yeah, right. But where do I go? They wouldn't . . . ? I mean, Chicago? Lenny's their —'

'Jack, listen to me!' Bridgett said urgently. 'This is serious. The police have obviously told Chicago about the interview with you, and they, just as obviously, don't trust the signed statement the police prepared.' She paused momentarily. 'You have signed it, haven't you?'

'No, they haven't been around. But Lenny, killing Lenny, how is that tidying up?' I asked.

'Mobster mindset, it's how they think. They want Lenny to look like another Bugsy Siegel. Money, Jack, it's always about money. Lenny was the old Giancana side of the family that Accardo never trusted; he was also your friend and had gone to your rescue.' Bridgett began to unzip the canvas bag. 'Jack, it's no longer just Sammy. He couldn't have authorised Lenny's murder and he couldn't have done it himself. Both his thugs are dead. He couldn't recruit new muscle so quickly, not from hospital. This is the godfather himself and the Chicago Mob. If Chicago thought it necessary to have Lenny killed because of his involvement in your rescue and for organising the cement to fill the basement, they'll see you as a lot more dangerous to them as a hostile witness than Lenny ever could have been.'

'Where can I go? I'm due to go to Albany.'

'Go to Albany. Only Dr Light and I will know, and now Chef Napoleon Nelson and Booker T. Dr Irwin Light and his wife Erica are among my few friends in Las Vegas. They've long known about the Chicago Mob and the casino, which isn't exactly a state secret.'

The door was closed so I switched on the light. Almost immediately the door eased open again. It was Dr Light, carrying a small tin box with a red cross on the lid and looking decidedly concerned. He acknowledged me with a nod and a single 'Jack', then turned and spoke directly to Bridgett. 'I'm worried. The night sister just told me there were two guys downstairs ten minutes ago, asking about Jack. They said they were old school friends from Toronto, Canada, and were travelling to San Diego by car overnight. They knew it was late but hoped an exception could be made, as they had heard Jack was in hospital. Lynette – I mean, Sister Barry – knows a Chicago accent when she hears one. She was born and raised in K-Town, a poor area of Chicago. She claims she'd recognise the accent in her sleep. She told them to go away and come back during visiting hours on their way back from San Diego. She said she didn't like the look of them one little bit; both were thoroughly nasty pieces of work, in her opinion.' Dr Light was over-explaining to hide his nervousness.

'So soon!' Bridgett whispered.

Chef Napoleon Nelson stepped forward. 'Jack, we can get you out o' here widout you bein' seen. I got two of my church buddies outside who work here in da hospital laundry. Dey waitin' in da hallway and dey gonna remove you by da magic of da unseen basket trolley.'

I rose from my bed. 'I haven't got any street clothes; they were too bloodstained to keep.'

Bridgett drew the canvas bag towards her and managed a wan smile as she pulled out a blue tracksuit. 'I found this in your dressing-room. I know you sometimes change into it to walk home. But I haven't got any undies . . . er, Jockey pants,' she corrected. She placed the tracksuit on the bed and lifted the top. 'I've cut out the left arm . . . .to make it a bit easier.' She helped me into it, then turned to Dr Light and handed him the pants, and turned her back as he helped me out of my pyjamas and into the tracksuit pants.

'Jack, I've got to go,' Dr Light said nervously, 'but I'm giving you a small shot of morphine now. I've given you plenty of morphine sulphate in one-use syrettes. As a medic, you're familiar with them, right?'

I nodded.

'There's also plenty of bandages and dressings, and some analgesics as well. There's iodine for when you change the dressings. There's also penicillin in vials and some hypodermics for if you get an inflammation. Do you think you can handle the dressing and medicating yourself?'

I nodded again. 'Yes.' There didn't seem any point reminding him I was off morphine. He hastily prepared a syringe and administered the drug. Within moments it kicked in and I can't say it didn't feel good. 'Thank you, Doctor. I don't suppose I'll ever be able to repay you.'

'Stay safe and get to Albany, Jack.' He grinned; partially, I suspect, to hide his nerves. 'It's been a real pleasure. Give my regards to Dr Haghighi. I'll send him a message in medical code, in case someone around here is snooping.' He turned, opened the door and left, his hurrying footsteps echoing down the hallway.

'It be okay now, Miss Bridgett,' Chef Napoleon Nelson said softly. 'Now we gon' move, Jack.'

'How is this going to work? They must be watching the hospital exits,' I said.

'Like I sayed, Jack. We got the wicker laundry basket on wheels outside your door. Ain't nobody even looks at us black folks when dey lookin' for a white man. We just go right past dem, up the ramp and into da laundry van.'

'Jesus! What about you, Bridgett? If these guys are waiting outside and see you, they'll know something's up.'

'He right, Miss Bridgett. You all better go in de basket also. Don't worry, it plenty big enough, so long you be good friends,' he chuckled. 'We drop you off later. My niece, Lizabeth – she bin named after da queen o' England, because she born da same day – she grow'd up woman now and kin take you all up to Fremont, to catch you a cab this late time o' night. Jack, you be stayin' Westside while we get ourself organised. We be taking you to stay wid Pastor Jake Moses, his res-e-dence. You already met him at Sunday meeting. Booker T., his wife say he be arriving tomorra afternoon, leave to go back east last train night-time da day follow. Let's go, people,' he commanded. He wasn't a head chef for nothing and had assumed complete control.

He helped me through the door and there stood the biggest wicker laundry basket I had ever seen. It looked to be about four feet wide, seven feet (or a little more) long, and must have been four feet high, with a wicker lid and a big LAUNDRY sign on each side. Two coloured men with LAUNDRY embroidered in red on the backs of their white coats were waiting. Other than them, the corridor was completely deserted. The two men helped me over the side of the basket and into it. I bumped my hand but it caused little pain, the morphine having blessedly already kicked in. I would have to be more careful, though; I wasn't going to use Dr Light's kit unless I had to. They'd placed a couple of doubled-over blankets and a pillow on the floor of the basket and now eased me down onto my back. Then Bridgett climbed in and squeezed beside me, lying on her side against my body, one arm draped loosely over my stomach. The laundry guys then placed a sheet over us and we felt the basket begin to move, the squeak of wheels marking our departure.

Bridgett kissed me on the side of my face. 'God, Jack,' she whispered, 'you didn't have to go to all this trouble just to get me between the sheets. All you had to do was ask.' As the basket rolled along, and despite the desperate situation I was in, we tried unsuccessfully to stifle our giggles.

'Now you tell me!' I whispered back.

'You two be quiet now, you hear?' Chef Napoleon Nelson ordered as we squeaked along in the dark. I was very aware of Bridgett beside me, and of the perfume she always wore.

I was on my way to god knows where, Chicago's thugs were outside, waiting to finish off the job they'd been sent to do, and I had a raging hard-on. Bridgett's arm was too close to the offending erection for comfort; all she had to do was lower her hand six or eight inches and I was a goner.

Thank Christ it was dark inside the laundry basket and we were covered by the sheet. A woollen tracksuit with no Jockeys doesn't exactly conceal the only male part below the neck that has a mind of its own.

We were jolted up what seemed like a ramp and I heard the van doors slam. The basket lid was lifted and Napoleon asked, 'You two be okay down dere?'

'Sure, Chef Napoleon,' I said. It wasn't quite pitch dark, as the driver had his cabin light on. Bridgett must have felt insecure going up the ramp and her hand clasped my arm just above the wrist. She was now even closer than previously. Thank god Bridgett wasn't Juicy Fruit or she'd have twigged immediately and embarked on an exploration. But, then again, the result might have been even better than the shot of morphine. 'I gotta sit in the front wid da driver, Luke. You holler you want something, you hear now, Jack, Miss Bridgett,' Chef Napoleon Nelson said, barely above a whisper. 'But only when maybe we be gone some.'

He replaced the lid, and the back of the stationary van shook slightly as he moved forward and climbed into the front seat. A few moments later, the engine fired and we moved away. After a short time, Chef Napoleon Nelson called out, 'Okay, folks, we now headin' Westside. Road gonna get a little bumpy.'

Moments later we hit a fairly big bump and Bridgett said, 'Oops!' and at that moment her hand slid down and brushed the tracksuit pants, bumping against the veritable tent pole under the sheet. Her fingers remained motionless for a few seconds, then came to life and curled around the sheet that covered my erection. 'Oh, Jesus,' I said softly.

Bridgett giggled. 'No, Jack, not even the Virgin Mary,' she whispered. 'I . . . I . . .'

'Shhh!' she whispered again, and kissed me. 'What a lovely surprise, Jack.' Then she removed her hand and, next thing, she'd removed the sheet covering us. 'Keep your bad hand above your head, Jack,' she whispered. 'Does it hurt? The hand, I mean.'

'No, er . . . it's fine. Morphine . . .'

I felt her leg move across my body until her knee was cushioned between me and the side of the laundry basket, and then she was suddenly straddling me. With her arms pressed down on either side of my body, she started to slide downwards. 'Close your legs, Jack,' she whispered. Moments later I felt her thighs rub against my belly and then meet the rampant pole, pause a second, then lift to pass over, just brushing the tip straining at my track pants. She kept moving downward a little and I felt her straddling my legs. I hadn't said a word. I thought I knew what was happening but couldn't think of anything appropriate to say, or perhaps remaining silent *was* the appropriate thing. I felt her grab the elastic around the waist of my tracksuit bottom, my penis bending at the base then jerking erect. I raised my butt to allow her to pull the track pants further down. Moments later I felt Bridgett's sweet mouth and soft lips come into play.

'Oh, oh!' I gasped softly. This was something I'd imagined happening with her a hundred times. Sex is one thing, sex with the object of your desire, lust, love, is quite another; making love with the person you absolutely crave and secretly love is a completely overpowering physical and emotional experience. Moreover, Bridgett was no amateur. While I'd been in Las Vegas I'd developed into a competent lover; as Johnny Diamond had remarked, it wasn't difficult to find a chorus girl or some other gorgeous creature happy to oblige without complications afterwards. But I had always been in control. As Juicy Fruit had once advised me, 'Be generous and patient, Jack, and women will reward you.'

However, now I was completely helpless and felt myself starting on the certain road to the disgrace of a premature ejaculation. I'd desired Bridgett too often to control myself now. The truck had turned into a more than usually rutted road, and we were swaying and squeaking on old springs. This didn't help one little bit as Bridgett's mouth and generous lips worked the length of my raging erection. My febrile mind screamed, *No, no, Jack, don't! Stop it! Get control!* 'Darling, inside . . . take me inside you,' I gasped in desperation.

Bridgett had her hand around the base of my erection, continuing to hold it as she raised her torso, and I heard the creak as her head brushed against the lid of the laundry basket. Then she moved forward and I felt her buttocks rise and her hand inserting me, then the slide into glorious smoothness as she engulfed me to the hilt. There wasn't much I could do to help, as I was on my back. But that wonderful derriere I'd so often admired turned out to be not simply for show and I clung onto her wrist with my right hand for the ride as her breathing became more rapid until, finally, she was panting violently. Then, letting out a moan, she cried, 'Oh, oh . . . I'm coming . . . I'm coming! Jack, oh, fuck me, Jack, darling . . . oooooh!'

Her urgent thrusting made the laundry basket shake and creak as I lost it at the same moment. With a moan of my own I ejaculated deeply within her, my hips lifting and holding her torso in the air until I finally allowed it to sink back onto my thighs. 'Thank you, thank you, darling,' I said, at last.

'Oh, Jack, I have waited so long for this,' she whispered.

Still panting, I hoped that the dull roar of the engine and the squeaky springs of the van had covered our mutual ecstasy. But suddenly Chef Napoleon Nelson called out, 'You folk be okay? Westside road here got itself lotsa bumps, eh? We be there soon. Maybe five minutes.'

'Thanks, yes,' I gasped, my breathlessness obvious.

There was a moment's silence, then Chef Napoleon Nelson said, 'Maybe it take ten minutes before we gone arrive, Jack.'

I have absolutely no idea how Bridgett managed to get my tracksuit pants back on, and do whatever else was necessary to restore some kind of normalcy for when the laundry basket was opened at our destination.

'Okay, peoples, we be here,' Chef Napoleon Nelson called loudly several minutes later. The van had slowed and turned, then come to a stop. 'Just wait a minute and I get us everything organised.' We heard the doors open and his footsteps moving away.

The van settled on its springs as he jumped back in a minute or two later. 'Okay, Jack, Miss Bridgett, all clear. We can go in the house from here and no one see. Nobody up this time anyhow.'

Napoleon and the guys from the hospital helped us out of the basket. We were in a lane behind a row of identical single-storey houses. Chef Napoleon Nelson spoke briefly to Luke, the driver, and the laundry van moved off before I could offer my thanks; then he ushered us through a gate in the paling fence and across a small tidy backyard onto the back porch of the house.

We were greeted by an old balding Negro in dark trousers and an open-neck white shirt, whom I recognised as Pastor Jake Moses of the Southern Baptist Church.

'Mr Spayd, welcome to Westside,' he said in a grave, courteous voice.

'It's Jack, please, Pastor Moses, and this is Mrs Fuller,' I said, introducing Bridgett.

'Please call me Bridgett, Pastor Moses.'

'Miz Bridgett, I am dee-lighted!' Pastor Moses chuckled. 'On the Westside, there are folk who consider you a saint. I feel I've known you many, many years. Come, come,' he urged us forward, leading us down a hallway into the parlour at the front of the house.

'Sit down in here, please. My wife is in the kitchen, making Java. She be here soon.'

'I'm very grateful to you for helping me, Pastor, and I realise this could be dangerous for you and your friends,' I said.

He drew his head back and said, 'For Chef Napoleon Nelson, there ain't nothing we won't do. But there be other, many other reason, Jack. Hector Brownwell, he be my cousin and but for your help with settlin' him and his family in Canada, he be a dead man now. Maybe even beautiful Sue, also. Not just him but lots of the folk who work in the casino kitchens, they be helped by your advising of Miz Bridgett here when that prince o' darkness, Mr Sammy, come to torment. To be a small help, be my pleasure. My wife Martha, her brother, be the local head of the union for the Brotherhood of Sleeping Car Porters and already you know Booker T. Once we get you on the train, you be safe,' he said. 'Snug as a bug in a rug! Chef Napoleon Nelson, he gone organising a second transport for you right to the railway car in one o' them Pullman Company linen baskets, jes like you been tonight. No white man gonna see you, not Mafia, not anyone. Same the other end.' His rich voice with its rolling cadences, perhaps not as pronounced as those of Chef Napoleon Nelson, carried over as if from the pulpit and seemed to be the natural mode of expression of this kind elderly man.

'I'm very grateful, Pastor.'

'The boot on the other foot, Jack. Coloured folk paying back some. I heard you plenty of times playing wid The Resurrection Brothers. You a mighty fine piano player, sir; maybe someday you come back and play for folk in my church, eh?'

I held up my bandaged hand. 'I think those days are over for me, Pastor Moses.'

'We gonna do a whole heap o' prayin', Jack. The Lord will look after you. Have faith, my brother, His healing power is beyond anything; the heavenly surgeon, he gonna take care of you, son.'

At this point, his wife Martha appeared, carrying a tray. 'Coffee ain't right this time o' night, so I made up some hot lemon tea.' We introduced ourselves and she said, 'Nice to meet you folk at last. I bin hearing good about you both a long, long time. It's a pleasure, to be sure.'

I sipped at the hot lemon drink and suddenly felt completely exhausted. Everything was catching up with me. 'I think you should get some sleep now, Mr Jack,' Martha said. 'I've made up a bed for you across the corridor.'

'When does Jack leave; I mean, what time?' Bridgett asked.

I was shocked by the question. 'Bridgett, don't you be anywhere near that railway station!'

'No, Jack, of course not, I just want to be thinking of you,' she said softly and gave me such a loving look I knew immediately I would carry it with me for the rest of my life. So near and yet so far, so little and yet so much; I knew, with absolute certainty, that whatever happened to me, I had, if only once, consummated the love of my life.

Pastor Moses then said, 'My brother-in-law sent a railway telegraph, sayin' we gonna put Jack on the through train to Chicago, most probably on Thursday afternoon. Dat three days from now. Booker T., he rostered for that trip, and my brother-in-law, he says he'll make sure some other people he can trust are on dat train as well.'

'Jack, you be perfectly safe,' Chef Napoleon Nelson added.

The pastor spoke again. 'You want him to get to Albany, New York State?'

'Yes, sir, the Albany General Hospital.'

'He's to be under the care of a Dr Koroush Haghighi, the senior surgeon,' Bridgett added. She'd heard the surgeon's name only once but already she had it down pat.

'Fine, Miz Bridgett. Better write that down, how you say it by way of pronouncing, because we'll use the railway telegraph to set everything up.'

'Is that safe?' Bridgett asked.

'What colour you think all the telegraph operators they are, ma'am?'

'I'm sorry, I didn't think it through,' Bridgett said.

'Ha! Ain't nobody do, Miz Bridgett, that's why it safe. We'll get a most discreet message to Doctor Hag . . . whose name and pronounce- ment you gonna write down.'

Martha appeared with a pencil and paper and then left the room as Bridgett wrote 'Haghighi' then, phonetically in capitals, HAG-HIG- HEE, and handed it to the pastor.

Martha returned almost immediately. 'Lizabeth come to take Miz Bridgett to the taxi,' she announced.

'Do you think we could have five minutes privately?' I asked, suddenly stricken. The time had come and I began to fear that I might never see Bridgett again. 'Some personal instructions,' I said lamely.

Martha showed us through to the bedroom I was to use and shut the door behind us. 'Oh, Jack,' Bridgett cried, 'whatever shall I do? I can't come to Albany in case I lead them to you!'

I clasped my right arm around her and we kissed deeply, and then I held her head against my chest while she sobbed. 'Bridgett, we'll find a way. I love you more than I can possibly say.'

'Jack, I want you! I want to look after you,' she cried, 'I've loved you for so long.'

'Bridgett, you must stay away from me. I'm bad news now.'

'No, no, don't say that, Jack!'

'Let me get through Albany and then I'll have to lie low for a bit. I'll send Dr Light my mother's address in Toronto.'

Bridgett nodded her head against my chest, then stepped away from my grasp and knuckled the tears from her eyes. I could see her pulling herself together and, moments later, Mrs Fuller appeared. 'Jack, I love you.' She smiled. 'How am I ever going to be able to tell anyone that I found the love of my life in the back of a van at the bottom of a hospital laundry basket?'

I was choked up but managed to say, 'Oh, Bridgett, darling, we'll . . .

we'll find a way of getting together, somehow, somewhere, I promise.'

Bridgett nodded. There wasn't any more to say. She knew she had to stay away, have no contact with me in Albany in case she inadvertently led the Mob to me. 'Write out a simple power of attorney and have the pastor witness it, that way I can sell your apartment and send your things on, clothes and anything else you want to keep, via Booker T. Will that be safe, do you think?' I knew she meant my music but was being tactful. 'Jack, we'll use Pastor Moses as our post box. I'm sure he won't mind.'

'Better not go to my apartment yourself, Bridgett. They're bound to be keeping watch. Don't worry about my clothes and stuff, give them to Pastor Moses for the poor in his congregation; just fix the bank, my apartment and . . .' I hesitated, 'send my music.'

Bridgett nodded. 'Don't worry. I'll send one of Chef Napoleon Nelson's invisible kitchen clan. Being black in America does have some advantages, if only a very few. It had never occurred to me before that the perfect way to hide is by being entirely invisible.' She came over and kissed me deeply. 'Let me go first, Jack. Stay here for five minutes so I can leave with Lizabeth.'

A single tear ran down her cheek, and I felt my own eyes prickling. She turned and opened the door. 'Jack, oh, Jack,' she whispered.

'Bridgett!' I cried. But she'd gone.

I was forced to use three of the syrettes over the next three days while I waited to board the train. I could manage the pain during the day, but needed the morphine to sleep. On the morning of my departure on the afternoon train to Chicago, a letter arrived from Bridgett via Mr Joel, who informed me he was now referred to as Chef Samson Joel, having taken over from Chef Napoleon Nelson, who was now performing at the GAWP Bar.

Darling Jack,

As you will have guessed it is chaos here, with the place crawling with police and the FBI. Predictably, Manny 'Asshole' has taken over Lenny's side of the casino and is demanding justice from the police and the FBI. (Oh, my, what a joke!) Somehow I've managed to keep the GAWP Bar going and Chef Napoleon Nelson is doing a splendid job, though your place is going to take a lot of filling. I don't think it wise for him to see you on your departure and have told him so.

As I'm sure you've been told, your abduction is also in the news. At this stage Lenny's assassin is unknown, but the two men who visited you earlier are the prime suspects and the FBI has issued a nationwide description of them based on Sister Barry's description. Please don't worry about me. I am completely safe (paperwork) and my two points are intact even if Chicago lose their casino licence, which seems highly unlikely.

Manny 'Asshole' is said to be spreading money around like confetti at a wedding! Darling, it is unsafe to go near your apartment (police watching) and I suggest after a month or so your mother sends me her bank details so I can transfer the money and your bank balance to Toronto. Tell Booker T. if this is okay. I have your power of attorney, thanks to our invisible friends.

Please, darling, you have simply got to disappear. Chicago are most definitely after you! Also, it will be necessary to change your name. I have phoned your surgeon to admit you in the name of Jack McCrae and to note your hand injury as 'auto accident'. Hope that's okay. Dr You Know Who will destroy all paperwork here regarding your transfer.

Jack, darling, I'll try to find a way, but in the meantime I guess we shouldn't make any contact under <u>any</u> circumstances, not even through the pastor. Know only that I love you with all my heart and always will.

Bridgett 'Love in a Laundry Basket' Fuller X X X X

P.S. Be sure to burn this letter.

I borrowed a pair of scissors from Martha and carefully cut out the lines *Know only that I love you with all my heart and always will. Bridgett 'Love in a Laundry Basket' Fuller X X X X*. These I carefully folded into a compartment in my wallet before burning the remainder of her letter.

That afternoon the laundry truck arrived with the blanket-lined linen basket. I said my thanks to Pastor Moses and Martha, adding, 'I wish there was some way I could repay you, sir, ma'am.'

'Jack, you already done that many, many times before. Black folk, dey love you.' He gripped my hand and smiled into my eyes.

Booker T. consulted his railway timekeeper, a large silver fob watch. 'Better we be off now.' He then handed me a small parcel. 'Miss Bridgett says to give you this; she says you open it only when you on the train, Jack.'

'Booker T., when you get back, please tell Miss Bridgett her plan about my apartment and bank deposit is fine.'

'Jack, that already changed, only because maybe somebody get that letter by mistake. She gonna bide a while, then she gonna send that money through me and the Brotherhood of Sleeping Car Porters. That be by far the safest. Then it go hand to hand, nobody know nothing, jes delivery to Mr Jack McCrae.'

As usual and despite the chaos at the Firebird, Bridgett had all the bases covered. The driver and Booker T. then helped me into the basket and lowered the lid. And that was how I left Las Vegas.

The first thing I did was open the parcel from Bridgett. Inside was a small black leather case with the initials J. McC. in gold on the outside. Inside was a gold fob watch. I opened the lid and read the inscription in tiny letters covering the entire back of the watch:

Love bears all things,
believes all things,
hopes all things,
endures all things.

Bridgett may have left her hillbilly past far behind, but when she needed to express her deepest feelings, she turned back to the Bible, the first poetry she would have heard as a small girl. I stared at the watch for a long time, then tucked it away in my breast pocket.

We eventually reached Chicago, and I was wrapped in a railway man's overcoat and transferred into a private compartment on the Commodore Vanderbilt's premium service to New York via Albany. In that city I felt everyone was a potential assassin.

I dozed when I could, but the pain kept me from becoming too comfortable. The service was splendid; nothing was a problem. I felt a bit like the legendary 'man in the iron mask', kept in total seclusion while I was being transported, so no one else knew I was there.

It made me realise I was benefitting from a parallel black universe that I never knew existed. No doubt it had helped Hector and Sue escape safely, too. Miss Frostbite had previously written to say Chef Hector was an absolute blessing to the Jazz Warehouse kitchen and he'd been elevated to head chef on the retirement of Mr Charlie Blinker. Sue was also proving a great success as a waitress three nights a week and was being put through a modelling course as well as going to college. At the time, a black model in a white fashion magazine would have been unthinkable anywhere in North America and, I'm ashamed to say, possibly in Canada as well, but Sue's blue eyes and fair skin disguised her Negro parentage.

I arrived in Albany very early in the morning, the city I had mistaken for New York when I was still a boy. Wrapped up again in a long railway man's overcoat, head covered by a warm scarf, I was hustled down onto the tracks when the train stopped just before Albany station. I crossed two sets of tracks and was handed over to two young Negroes, who nodded silently and escorted me to a waiting car. 'Hello, Jack. Welcome to Albany,' Dr Koroush Haghighi called from the driver's seat.

I got into the passenger seat and turned to thank the two young guys who'd escorted me but they'd disappeared. We watched as the train drew away, then drove off.

'Jack, I've booked you in under my care using your assumed name, as

Mrs Fuller instructed. From now on you'll be known in the hospital as Jack McCrae. You'll be safe here for as long as we need.'

'Thanks, Doctor. I've got enough money to pay you for all this,' I hastened to say.

'Good. I'll do my part *pro bono* but if you can cover the hospital costs, it will mean there's less paperwork and fewer questions asked.'

I was to spend a little over three months in Albany and undergo several operations under Dr Haghighi's care. I left the hospital after two weeks and stayed at a small boarding house close by. My hand was still painful but most of the time it was bearable. Gradually I began to get back limited movement in my fingers. For instance, I could grip things, such as a cup or a spoon, but I couldn't imagine sitting down at the piano. I bought a kettledrum and used it to exercise my hand and wrist, slowly increasing the speed of my movements, but using my fingers separately was a major problem. I was still a musician only in my head.

Fortunately, my thumb had been damaged less than my hand and fingers. The one-eyed Sammy Schischka was probably concentrating on the easy target of my palm.

'The thing now, Jack, is to build up the strength in this hand. Work it until you want to cry from the pain and it will reward you. The more exercises you do, the better.' Then Dr Haghighi would ask, 'How is the feeling in your fingertips?'

My reply was always the same. 'What feeling?' But gradually I started to get a little more sensation in my three middle fingers, although my little finger was still numb. For a piano player, that's a bit like being a baritone without his lowest note.

'I was afraid of that,' the surgeon said. 'There is nerve damage and I can't do much about it, unfortunately.'

The other thing exercising my mind was the future. Bridgett kept silent for six weeks, then a typewritten letter arrived via the Brotherhood of Sleeping Car Porters. It opened with 'Dear Mr McCrae' and ended 'Yours sincerely, H. Billy', without a signature. I smiled fondly over the reference to her childhood. It was wonderful to hear from her, although she was forced to write about 'Mrs Fuller' in the third person. She explained that 'Mrs Fuller' now ran the entire Firebird, after the death of Mr Lenny Giancana, and I had no doubt that her paperwork regarding the basement full of cement would have helped. Miss H. Billy never signed her letters or expressed any loving sentiments but, even so, it wouldn't have been difficult to trace the letters back to her if one went astray. At least if it fell into someone's hands, they wouldn't know of our love.

H. Billy informed me that she had sold my apartment and deposited the money in a local Albany bank under the name Jack McCrae, as well as the balance in my Las Vegas bank account, which gave me a total of $15,600; a very pleasing sum. She must have decided it was too risky to send that much cash via the Brotherhood. Included in the letter was a new ID card and social security number in the name of Jack McCrae, 'compliments the interior decorator'. She'd obviously used Anna-Lucia Hermes and her husband, the mayor, to obtain it.

After I'd been in Albany for three months I received a letter from H. Billy, via the usual means, with distressing news. Johnny Diamond had been shot and killed outside his parents' home in Ohio, hunted down by those animals, basically, because he had been in the wrong place at the wrong time. The murder had been reported in the local newspaper, simply headlined: EX-PIT BOSS MURDERED. In her note she cautioned me that Sammy was back on his feet, although with the permanent support of crutches. The article repeated the usual no-suspects line, but told of the fight at the Desert Inn and Johnny Diamond's hurried exit from Las Vegas. Shortly after Johnny's death, a frightening note had been slipped under Bridgett's door: *The Diamond has hit the deck. The next card to go will be the Jack of Spayds.*

It didn't sound like anything Sammy could possibly have composed and I guessed it was sent from the Chicago Mob, warning that godfather Tony Accardo, and his big guns were out to get me, and that, unlike Sammy, they were not a bunch of Chicago hicks carrying meat hooks. My unsigned statement to the police was worthless, and I suspect a signed one would have made little difference. I was still a loose end that needed to be snipped off. Slipping the note under Bridgett's door meant they suspected she was keeping in touch with me, so I wasn't surprised when H. Billy ended her letter: *Mr McCrae, future contact will now cease,* but I felt my heart sink.

I suddenly felt very lonely. I had contacted my mother and Nick Reed via the porter network, which carried over the Canadian border. It was complicated, though, and Booker T. insisted they couldn't guarantee it. I had warned my mom and Nick not to contact me and told them about my hand and that the Mafia were involved. If I came home, it wouldn't be safe for me or anyone involved with me. I didn't give them my address or even tell them I was in Albany but simply said that I was being treated by one of America's best hand surgeons, and that I'd be in touch as soon as I felt it was safe to do so.

Several days later, Dr Haghighi surprised me, after a regular check on the progress of my hand, by saying, 'Your stepfather will be here tomorrow, Jack. He's officially here to consult on some burns patients. While he's not aware of being watched, he doesn't want to expose you to any more danger.'

'How the hell —?'

He cut me short. 'Surgeon's network.'

Nick arrived and I spent the day telling him the whole story, after Dr Haghighi had filled him in on the details of my hand injury. Nick thought about it for a few minutes before saying, 'Jack, your treatment is all but finished, the dressing is off and you know how to care for yourself. Dr Haghighi says that, with time and exercise, you'll get more movement in your hand, and that the movement you've got already is pretty remarkable. As one surgeon to another, he's done a great job.'

'Yeah, but no piano,' I said softly.

'Afraid not, son; not as a professional, anyhow.' He didn't carry on – there was no point – and how could I tell him that life as a musician was everything to me, and that without jazz, the blues, my life was finished as far as I was concerned? He hadn't told me anything I didn't know. 'What seems obvious to me, Jack, is that you need to get the hell out of North America for a good bit.' He paused. 'And that includes Canada.'

'The Mafia has a very long arm, Nick. I'm not broke, but it's a question of where? I imagine Jack Spayd is not a common name on a passport.'

Nick, as usual, was pretty calm, almost laconic, but I knew his manner covered deep concern; he was, by nature, a man of few words. 'I'll come back next week . . . see what can be done.'

He was back six days later. 'I've had a quiet word to a friend or two in the Royal Canadians, permanent brass in our old regiment, and they connected me with some friends of theirs in the Mounties who run Canadian Intelligence. As we discussed, they recommend you leave the country, get away someplace where they'll never look for you.'

'Yes, but where, where the hell do I go?' I said. 'I'll need a passport under another name if I want to do that safely . . .'

'I guess we're thinking alike. Canadian Intelligence have come up with a legal trick. They've arranged for your passport using my family name, without any of the usual adoption paperwork. No need for any complicated legal stuff. Your mother has found a snap of you that can be made to work as your passport photo. That should be enough to throw anyone off your trail.'

'They did that?'

'Well, normally it would be a bit tricky. The guy involved is pretty high up in the security section of the Mounties. He's repaying what he says is a favour because I saved his brother's life. Guy received burns to fifty per cent of his body after being rescued from a burning tank at Normandy.' Nick shrugged. 'Just doing my job, I guess, but he insists he owes me this one. Your medal didn't hurt either.'

'Missing earlobe pays off at last,' I laughed. 'Thank you, Nick,' I said simply. There wasn't much more I could say, anyhow. I'd become the owner of a new Canadian passport in the name of Jack Reed, a new man with a new life.

'Africa, Jack; for a while, anyway – somewhere in the middle or to the north, that's what the Intelligence guys say. That's where a lot of the German SS disappeared after the war. Just one more thing and I stress that it's very important: you cannot, *must not*, contact anyone in Canada or tell any person who may have previously known you your new surname. The same goes for any friends in America. Not a word until you're settled. You have simply disappeared . . . gone, vanished for the time being.' He looked at me sternly. 'No Miss Frostbite, no Joe, no Mac. Please, Jack?' He paused, then said, 'and no one in Las Vegas. You're not the only one involved in this.' He stood up, and removed a new Canadian passport from the inside pocket of his jacket and handed it to me. 'It's got all the right visas you're going to need from the bottom of Africa to Ethiopia. I've also prepared a set of papers on regimental notepaper outlining your career as an army medic; the courses you've passed, medical experience while in action. I've signed these but also got your old CO, as well as the battalion commander – now a major general – to do a reference for you. You never know when they may be useful,' he concluded. 'Now, I've got a train to catch. Good luck, son.' We shook hands (he wasn't the kind of man who hugged) and he grinned, but it wasn't one of those grins intended to indicate mild humour. 'Only one other person can know any of this, so my next concern is how I am going to explain all this to your dear mother.'

'Do your best, Nick,' I said fervently, 'and give her my love.'

Nick left without a nod. The more I saw of this remarkable man, the happier I was for my mom.

I'd done my blubbing. Until this moment I'd hoped to get back to my beloved Bridgett but now I felt certain I'd lost her, possibly forever. I dared not tell her my new name. Nick had emphasised that I couldn't even tell my surgeon because it could compromise Canadian Intelligence, who'd gone out on a limb for me.

I sat silently for a long time, my left hand resting in my lap. It still looked a mess, but the bones had knitted, the skin had healed and, although it was pretty ugly to look at, it had movement. Perhaps one day the feeling would return to my pinky.

I rose and reached for the soft yellow polishing cloth that contained the second-hand harmonica my drunken father had won from a friend at the tavern and given to me as a belated eighth birthday gift. I picked up the battered old instrument and began to play 'St James Infirmary Blues'. Softly, tentatively at first, then with more confidence.

What the hell! What was to stop me, a guy named Jack Reed, becoming the best jazz and blues harmonica player in the entire world?

PART FOUR

—◆—

AFRICA

CHAPTER TWENTY-ONE

AFRICA! IN MY CHILDHOOD the map of Africa was fairly well covered with red colonies belonging to the British Empire. Perhaps it would be more correct to say the red bits were members of the empire, but as a kid I saw the Union Jack as the proprietorial flag and, in my mind, wherever it fluttered, it signified absolute ownership.

Starting with the books Miss Mony first taught me to read and later with those suggested by Mrs Hodgson at the library, I was able to conjure up the vast African continent from stories of derring-do and adventure. In them, square-jawed men with steely blue eyes served as exemplars of white Anglo-Saxon manhood, willingly giving selfless service, their energy, prowess and knowledge, to bring primitive people those quintessentially British gifts of sound governance, justice, medicine and education.

Alas, very few women seemed to feature in this childhood pantheon of heroes, my notion at the time being that by remaining in their homeland, they were protected from the rampaging lusts of the dark races who had, as a matter of tribal law and absolute entitlement, treated the opposite gender as a possession and, in all senses, as inferior. That white women were oppressed never occurred to me; nor did I ever think that all this spreading of cartographical red ink was largely motivated by greed, natural resources being plundered solely for the enrichment of a nation that then demanded respect, subservience and sycophantic allegiance from the indigenous people they regarded as inferior in every way.

I was taught at school that our white man's duty was almost a part of the Darwinian struggle; that British law, medical science and industrial might combined with the Christian faith were, in effect, part of a relentless evolutionary process that was necessary, even by the use of force, to overthrow the superstitious, ignorant, heathen tribal ways of the primitive natives wherever they were to be found, and 'wherever' often meant Africa.

Patently the motivation of the greatest empire on Earth wasn't benign, and yet, as a consequence of it, some order was brought to the former chaos, some enlightenment to the indigenous mind, some progress made against ravaging disease and some small steps towards social justice began to appear.

This could not be said for all European conquests of the African continent. The Belgians brought with their possession of the Congo the greatest reign of murderous terror Africa had ever experienced. And yet, until they finally banished slavery in 1807, Britain was second only to Portugal as the nation controlling the slave trade to North and South America. It was Britain that had brought the forebears of Hector and his lovely daughter Sue, Chef Napoleon Nelson, Booker T. and the members of The Resurrection Brothers to America. It should be noted too that the French, Belgians, Portuguese, Germans, Italians and Dutch were also deeply involved in African colonisation.

To all my fanciful fictions of benign British colonial rule had been added the stories of the 1914–18 war, where men had willingly sacrificed their lives in countless numbers to uphold the traditions of the glorious empire. Despite the fact that my own country was not under threat from Germany or Japan in the Second World War, this same sense of duty prevailed when I joined up to fight for the greater good of the far-flung empire. I regarded my tiny contribution as a part of the ongoing tide of good sweeping away the tyranny of evil. The war was a rite of passage for me, as it was for many young men, but it had not changed my life as much as the psychopath Sammy Schischka wielding his ball-peen hammer had.

Even without Sammy, my life would have been changed by the cruel twist of fate that had allowed me to find true love and, almost in the same breath, lose it. I told myself she would forever dwell in my heart and perhaps someday . . . but even before Nick Reed's warning not to contact her, I'd pretty well decided that my pride simply forbade me from doing so. To become dependant on her love, to try to salvage what was left of my shattered ego, was unthinkable. I was once again on my own and, in effect, scuffing. I was no longer Jack Spayd, or Jack McCrae, but Jack Reed, ex-piano player, now jazz harmonica player and sometime medic, on my way to Africa with a deck of playing cards in my hip pocket, ready to start all over again but with very little idea of where or how to do it.

If all this sounds pathetically melodramatic, then you're probably right. But at least I had long since given up feeling sorry for myself for my physical condition by the time I set off to build a new life from the smoking ruins of the old one. I'd done my weeping in private and, to be truthful, was somewhat embarrassed by the scale of mine when compared with those I'd witnessed in the physical therapy department of the Albany General Hospital. People recovering from motor and industrial accidents, with arms and legs missing, faces smashed into permanent and nightmarish Halloween masks; people in wheelchairs, their backs broken, who would never walk again. They too had lost their careers and dreams and much more besides, while, I told myself, the sum total of my disabilities was a numb left pinky, a missing earlobe, and fingers that no longer moved sufficiently swiftly for a keyboard virtuoso. I could almost hear Joe saying: 'Jazzboy, it be time to harden up some. Time to go back to dat harmonica where you done all yo jazz 'n' blues startin' out. Time to go forwards by goin' backwards. Time to meta-phor-i-cally crawl under dem Jazz Warehouse steps once more.'

I wondered if I would ever see Joe again or Miss Frostbite, or Mac and the twins, or even Mrs Hodgson, but, most of all, my darling mom and Nick Reed, whom she loved so dearly. Then, of course, there were the coloured folk, Chef Napoleon Nelson, Hector, Booker T., the people who had worked in the kitchen or as cleaners, and The Resurrection Brothers – people who had given me so much joy and happiness and, as Bridgett and Pastor Moses had pointed out, so much love. I couldn't bear to think I might never see Bridgett again.

I took the train to New York, booking a private compartment in the name of Jack Reed; my first public act using my new name. I found a small, cheap and essentially nondescript hotel in the East Village, then spent the next two days in the New York Library, getting rid of the crap in my head about Africa and replacing it with some facts that might help me find useful employment in a place where I could remain well hidden.

I wasn't sufficiently foolish to think that Africa needed a harmonica player of jazz and blues, but I was equipped for little else. Barney de Andrade, the bartender in the GAWP Bar, had taught me how to mix cocktails but it wasn't a skill that I imagined would be in demand at my level of proficiency. Perhaps in South Africa, in some second-rate cocktail bar in Cape Town or Johannesburg, although I'd already decided that the attitude of the whites to coloured folk in Africa was even worse than in America and, besides, large cities would not be sufficiently remote to keep me safe from the Mafiosi.

Then, purely by chance, my eye caught an article that was buried in the business section of the *New York Times* and had the headline: A PLACE IN THE SUN FOR SHADY PEOPLE. It explained that the world was seriously short of copper, due to demands during the Second World War, and now the Korean War. The 'Copperbelt', situated in Central Africa and incorporating the mines in the Belgian Congo and Northern Rhodesia, was a major source of supply outside of Chile. Professional South African goldminers could triple their income in the copper mines, where few questions were asked and skilled men were well rewarded. This also attracted men who kept their past a secret and had felt the need to leave their country of origin, among them war criminals and other white men with no mining experience. The article mentioned a mining company called the British American Selection Trust, an American-financed mining group that operated the Luswishi River Copper Mine in Northern Rhodesia, the richest of its kind in the world.

Bingo! I'd found my red patch, almost plumb in the centre of Africa. It didn't take me long to locate their New York office and telephone to ask if I could see someone about employment opportunities in Central Africa. To my surprise I was put through to a Miss Truscott, the personal secretary of a Mr Leslie, Global Vice President of Mining Recruitment. She had me wait a few minutes, then came back and made an appointment for three o'clock the following day, asking me to bring my resumé with me. So much for no questions asked or skills required.

I spent an hour that evening preparing my resumé or, rather, trying to improve it, for the preparation took less than fifteen minutes. War medic and piano player just about summed it up, unless I included my skills as a poker player or cocktail mixer, but somehow that didn't seem appropriate. The result was pretty pathetic. I most definitely fell into the unskilled category mentioned in the newspaper article. Perhaps the only thing I had going for me was the set of papers my stepfather had prepared detailing my career as an army medic, including several references to courses I'd undertaken, some of which I barely remembered, involving medical knowhow I'd long since forgotten. Still, emblazoned with the regimental insignia, and with Nick's signature and impressive qualifications as well as that of the regimental commander, they looked reasonably professional and impressive. Among them was the recommendation that I study medicine at the conclusion of the war and the fact that I'd qualified for an ex-serviceman's grant to do so.

To my surprise, Mr Leslie seemed impressed after reading the top page outlining my pathetic employment history. 'Your medical background in the Canadian army could be very useful to us, Mr Reed,' he said enthusiastically.

'Oh? I'm not a doctor, sir,' I hastened to say.

'No, man, that's not important.' He spoke with a fairly guttural South African accent. 'Are you prepared to work underground?' he asked.

I shrugged. 'I guess we're all going to end up there one day,' I quipped.

'Hey, man, that's very funny! *Ja*, I guess you're right. The pay is good. I guarantee you can't make this sort of money as a medic anywhere else in the world.'

'What would I be expected to do?' I asked, adding, 'For instance, will I work under the supervision of a doctor?'

'Mr Reed, I'm going to be honest with you. This is the *bundu*, man!'

'The *bundu*?' It wasn't a word I knew.

'The backwoods, the bush,' he explained. 'The Copperbelt is mining country – nothing else there, no farming, no industry – everything depends on the mines. Yes, there are some small towns – Ndola, Luanshya, Chingola, Kitwe, Luswishi River – but this is a British protectorate, so, apart from the civil servants and public utilities, police, hospitals, that sort of thing, everything else is linked to the mining industry. In Ndola, there is a proper hospital – even looks after blacks – and in the other towns, there are cottage hospitals for whites only. We have one with twelve white beds, run by a nursing sister who is also a midwife. Some of the miners, the professionals – diamond drillers, engineers, hoist drivers, administration – they have families and we have a special section on the mine where they live, and that's where the cottage hospital is situated.' It was all said with hardly a pause.

'Oh, I see, so the white miners are in the majority, then?' I made a mental note to ask him what the hell a diamond driller was doing in a copper mine.

'No, man, don't be silly; we have ten thousand black mine workers, only about four hundred white miners.'

'No black cottage hospital?'

'*Ja*, man, like I already told you; in Ndola they got one, a proper hospital with a section for blacks that's used by all the copper mines. Doctors, too, three from India. But Ndola, it's 40 miles away. In the wet season, you sometimes can't get in by road. We have a mine ambulance and we take them there if it's a bad accident. In the big wet we load the ambulance onto an ore truck and it goes by rail. But we've got a clinic for them at the mine, and the Indian doctor comes twice a week from Ndola.'

'And I'd work in that clinic?'

'*Ja*, dressing wounds, cuts, they happen a lot, but your first priority is the white miners and the accidents that happen to them underground.'

'But . . . but doesn't it stand to reason, with the black-to-white ratio, there'd be a lot more accidents with the black miners?'

'*Ja*, of course, man, you're right but also wrong. You see, they're not so valuable. You must understand, a white man on the Copperbelt is a valuable commodity. Don't you worry, we look after *all* the workers. The blacks even got their own union now. But injuries cost money; a black man we can always replace. It doesn't cost a lot of time and money to train a black from the bush to use a pick and shovel or a crowbar, or even to handle a jackhammer or pneumatic drilling equipment for the stopes.'

'So, the black guys don't do any of the more skilled jobs?'

Mr Leslie looked surprised. 'Of course not, man! The Northern Rhodesian Mine Workers Union made an agreement with management before the war. Black workers are locked out of all management and skilled worker categories. There was some nonsense during the war about bringing the blacks into the union, but it came to nothing.'

'You mean, even if they could do . . . be trained to . . .'

'Ah, let me interrupt you right there, man. I know what you're going to say. But let me tell you something for nothing, those blacks, they *can't* do it, they don't have the intelligence, they not like us white men, these *kaffirs* – natives, I mean. They're straight from the bush, half wild. Even after we train them, they do stupid things, they not like white men, they don't see consequences. They're mainly bush blacks from remote African villages, just a few mud huts deep in the bush. When our recruiting gangs go out for the mines, the blacks they bring back, some have never seen a train or been in a town with electric light. They're primitive, ignorant. And these the ones the stupid British allowed to form a union! Nothing but a bunch of black communists!' He was getting pretty het up. 'It's a training ground for black politicians in case one day they're granted independence. Can you imagine, they just ten minutes out of the trees, eating mielie pap with their hands and already they're demanding independence!'

'Mielie pap?'

'Like porridge made from corn; it's made stiff so you can eat it in lumps.'

I decided that the state of the local black population wasn't a topic I should pursue, so I asked, 'Would I receive any additional medical training, sir? It's been quite some time and I guess I'm a bit rusty.'

He grinned. 'Agh, rusty is nothing. Don't you worry, man. Like I told you, we'll let you practise on the blacks before you touch a white guy, except maybe in an emergency.'

I winced inwardly. 'Who would I report to? As you can imagine, I know nothing about mining or treating accident victims in underground conditions.'

'Maybe Sister Hamilton can help a bit but, you must understand, women don't go underground.' He shrugged. 'I dunno, man. You'll find out soon enough. The other medics will help you.' He began to read through the papers Nick had prepared for me, laying each sheet aside until he'd gone through them all, by no means a lengthy task. Then he stabbed his forefinger onto the pile and looked directly at me. 'What are you talking about, man? What you've done here is perfect. You're trained in combat conditions. You're used to open wounds, bad accidents . . . just like in a mine. You can stitch up cuts, set bones, stop bleeding, inject, clean wounds, do bandages, splints, resuscitate . . .'

I hesitated, uncertain. 'Well, yeah . . . but it was a while back now.'

'You don't forget that stuff, man.'

'I guess,' I said, my tone uncertain.

'Well, then, no worries, anything else can be done on the surface when the doctor visits or we can send our ambulance to Ndola. Most of the time you'll be patching up the blacks – but they don't feel pain like we do. These mine blacks sometimes just lie down and die of something that's no bother to the white man. Just lie down an' croak.'

I was shocked by these remarks and felt compelled to say something. 'Is there any scientific support for this idea that black people have a higher pain threshold?' I asked, immediately realising I'd probably gone too far and blown the interview.

'No, man, you don't need scientists to tell you that. Just you wait and see. All I can say is, you are in for a few surprises.'

'Sir, I guess I've blown this interview but, if I am to work as a medic, the colour of a man's skin won't concern me when I'm treating him.'

Mr Leslie seemed to be thinking for a moment. 'That's your business, Mr Reed, but I wouldn't go saying that too loudly. You love the blacks by all means, but keep away from the women. That's a definite no-no; go there and you're as good as dead. It won't be tolerated, you hear?'

'And white women?' I asked.

'Big problems there. They're all married, and if you touch a miner's daughter, I got to warn you, you're *worse* than dead!'

While I couldn't imagine anything much worse than death, I asked, 'But you said there are men from all over the world. Surely they have . . . er, needs?'

'We got an arrangement. You'll see when you get there.'

'A brothel?'

'No, man, the British don't allow that in a small mining town. All I can say is, you'll see.'

'Sounds intriguing, sir.' I realised it was time to shut my big trap.

Mr Leslie picked up a pencil and tapped the blunt end two or three times against the surface of his desk blotter, then pointed the sharp end at my left arm. 'Tell me about your hand. I noticed it when you came in. Accident, was it? Is that why you're looking for employment in Africa? Have you got normal movement?'

I lifted my left hand above the surface of his desk and opened, then fisted, it several times, spreading my fingers. It still hurt like hell to do this, but it was a routine exercise I did fifty or so times a day to try to regain full use of my hand. 'Doesn't look too great but it works fine, sir,' I grinned. There didn't seem to be any point in mentioning the numb pinky. 'Yes, it was an accident. As you would have read, I used to be a professional pianist. The hand works well, but not quite well enough to continue to play piano.'

He smiled. 'You can count yourself lucky, Mr Reed. I can tell you something for sure, the one thing we're *not* looking for in the copper mines is a professional piano player, unless you want to play at the club sometimes for a singsong.' He paused, then said, 'I can see you're worried about working as a medic. The other option is to train you to be a miner, but I don't recommend that, not with . . .' he tapped the papers with the pencil, 'these excellent credentials.'

'Oh, what would that entail?'

'*Ja*, okay, you go to the School of Mines for three months to learn general mining and to qualify for your IBL – international blasting licence. But, I have to be frank, it's miserable work, wet and dirty, and after you qualify, it's still wet and dirty but then you go onto night shift, using high explosives. You'll do that for a year . . . if you survive.'

'Survive? You mean, prove I can do the job?'

He laughed. 'No, Mr Reed, if you don't kill or injure yourself.'

I gave him a quizzical look. 'If I may say so, sir, you're being extraordinarily honest. Do you make these comments to everyone applying for a job in the mines?'

He laughed uproariously. 'Good heavens, no, man!'

'Then why me?'

He leaned back in his chair, twiddling the pencil. He was a big man with a bit of a paunch, his short dark hair beginning to thin on top. A bulbous nose and ruddy complexion suggested a fondness for spirits. As Barney had told me, beer builds a gut but seldom a nose to go with it. 'Mining is something I know. I was once a miner, I still am, I suppose. But my leg is finished, no good. I worked underground in one of the company's gold mines in South Africa, where I was a mine captain; that's like a supervisor. I had an accident underground. A big rock fell on my hip and leg when I was examining a recently blasted section of a ventilation shaft,' he explained. 'I was on all fours when the rock hit. Luckily, it missed my spine but my left leg was trapped. I couldn't reach my two-way radio or the battery for my miner's lamp. The light on my hard hat went out. Eleven hundred feet underground is so dark you can feel the air around you, like you're being smothered in black cotton wool. No one could hear me shouting. I didn't know it at first but the rock had sliced into an artery at the back of my knee and eventually I passed out from loss of blood.'

His explanation was rapid and it was obvious it was well rehearsed; over-rehearsed, and so familiar he was barely hearing himself. 'So, what happened next?' I asked, in the hope that he'd get to the point.

'What happened next? Let me tell you, man. The radio was squawking – they're calling from the surface. I'm supposed to call in every hour and I haven't. But I can't do anything, man. I'm unconscious. They've sent down a team to find me. You see, they know from the logbook what part of the mine I'm in. But they don't look in the ventilation shaft and they've gone way past it by now. Then a timberman who's coming off shift hears the radio as he's passing. John Adamson; that was his name. There's nobody supposed to be in the air tunnel. So, he looks in and he hears it again, crackle-crackle, radio voices calling. He shouts into the shaft. Nothing. I'm unconscious, bleeding to death. So, he crawls in to take a look and, thank the good lord, he finds me.'

'Wow! Lucky for you,' I remarked, unable to think of any more suitable comment.

'Hey, man, let me tell you something for nothing, the Lord God was definitely on my side that day. I don't know how Adamson shifted that rock but he did, then he tied the artery. By now, man, I'm more dead than alive. He makes a splint using some planks and his shirt, and then carries me on his back a quarter of a mile to the underground cage and up to the surface.' Mr Leslie paused and at last took a deep breath. 'Now, it turned out he's a Canadian and also he's been a medic in the war, just like you, Mr Reed. I couldn't believe it just now when I read your papers and saw that you were a Canadian and a medic. I owe him big time, man. I walk with a stick and I've got a built-up boot, but it's nothing. I'm alive and I'm very grateful.' He paused. 'When I came out of hospital a month later, I tried to locate this guy who saved my life but he had left the mine, no forwarding address.' He shrugged. 'It's not much repayment for what he did for me, but now I can help you, Mr Reed.' He tapped my papers with the end of the pencil. 'Take my advice, don't make a stupid decision; don't go to the School of Mines.'

'I'm sorry to hear about your accident, sir.'

'No, man, there's nothing to be sorry about, accidents happen. Mining is mining. British American Selection Trust, they look after their people very well. They needed someone who knows mining like the back of their hand, specially copper and gold, so I became their American-based recruiting officer.' Almost without catching his breath, he announced, 'Now, I advise you to apply to work as a medic. Don't work underground as an ordinary miner. There are bad guys in the single quarters, riffraff, even some ex-Nazis, SS types. Not everyone, you understand; some guys are just trying to get a little money so they can go back home and start something for themselves. But if you're a medic, they have to respect you. They never know when they're going to need you.'

'Thank you, sir, I really appreciate your advice.'

'No, a pleasure, man,' he said with a flick of his hand. 'So, let's get down to business, eh? Would you like to make an application? We can process you here in New York and if you'll sign a contract of employment, we'll pay for your transport to the mine. We don't do this for everyone, you understand, but medical staff are different. It's hard to find anyone with good accident experience. Twelve months is minimum for the contract. I'm sorry, man, I can't do better.'

I thanked him again, then said, 'I take your advice and your offer seriously, sir. But I have the means to get to Central Africa on my own and once there I'd like to see what my options are. If I'm tied to a one-year contract in advance, that wouldn't be possible.' I'd been in Las Vegas too long not to know that to be 'comped', however good the deal sounds, almost always favours the person making the offer. A year was a long time to be locked into a strange place and a new job. I was still a man on the run and moving quickly could well turn out to be important.

But I understood that Mr Leslie had made me a generous and genuine offer and I'd be foolish and ungracious to simply overlook it. 'Sir, if you'd be kind enough to give me a letter of introduction to the Luswishi River Copper Mine personnel manager, I'd be more than obliged.'

'Of course, I know him well. I'll add a personal note.' He rose from his chair with some difficulty, clutching the edge of his desk to support his weight, and called to his secretary. 'Miss Truscott, bring your pad! Dictation!' He settled back into his seat with a pronounced sigh, and I wondered if he was in pain. 'Make sure you go see us first when you arrive. We are the biggest, you hear? The pay for a white medic is good, very good, and also you get a copper bonus.'

Miss Truscott entered and took the seat beside me, her slim ankles crossed, shorthand pad at the ready on her lap. I caught a whiff of her perfume and my heart suddenly beat faster. It had been over three months since I'd made love to Bridgett in the laundry basket and, while I felt guilty at my response, I couldn't help feeling horny as hell. Jack Spayd, who had been surrounded by women all his life, was suffering withdrawal symptoms. It wasn't just the lack of sex, but the lack of the deeply enjoyable presence of women around me. My nights in the piano bar were over forever. Moreover, Central Africa and the copper mines promised to confound my desire to meet this one great need within me. Where would I find women's laughter, smells, flirtatious glances . . . I suddenly felt very lonely.

Mr Leslie proceeded to dictate a very friendly letter to the appropriate department at the Luswishi River Copper Mine. 'Look up his title, Miss Truscott. Make sure it's the personnel manager, you hear, Coetzee is a very common Afrikaans surname,' he instructed.

I watched Miss Truscott walk from the room, her perfume lingering – she was so very pretty. 'Thank you, Mr Leslie,' I said. 'I'll make a point of presenting your letter of introduction to Mr Curtsy.'

He laughed, 'No, man, it's pronounced Koot-see, to rhyme with look-see,' he said.

I thanked him. 'May I ask one more question?'

'Ask away, that's why I'm here, man.'

'Well, can you tell me about diamond drillers? It seems curious that there would be miners who drill for diamonds in a gold or copper mine.'

He chuckled. 'No, man, the diamonds are on the drills they use in the stope – that's a big hole, sometimes fifty yards across and nearly as deep. There are dozens of them underground where they extract the copper ore. The tungsten steel bits in the big pneumatic drills are tipped with industrial diamonds to make them harder than the surrounding rock. They drill holes in the walls of this big hole and pack them with gelignite; that's like dynamite,' he explained. 'Then they blast out the rock and ore. We call these men diamond drillers because of their drills. They're the aristocrats, the most highly paid men underground, not the riffraff from here there and everywhere, like the grizzly men. They're mostly from South Africa, but some come from Wales.

'Working a grizzly is very, very dangerous, Mr Reed. Most of the accidents happen on a grizzly. You're supposed to have procedures, go by the book, but often – in fact, mostly – it isn't practical and you have to take risks, huge risks. For instance, the rocks jam at the entrance to the grizzly shaft that drains the ore from the stope – maybe two or three hundred tons of rock jammed sixty feet above the grizzly bars – and you have to somehow climb up to it and lay a charge to break it up, so it will flow again. Maybe it's all being held by only a small rock, and it comes loose and you're up there and that's the end.' He shrugged. 'No more grizzly man.'

'I'm having trouble understanding what a grizzly is,' I said. 'How does it work?'

'Hard to describe – you really need to see one. It's a grid that sieves the ore so that it's the right size before it's carted off to the surface. The bigger chunks get stuck on the bars of the grid.' I must have looked blank because he went on. 'Imagine lengths of railway line laid side by side with good-sized gaps in between across the mouth of the shaft below a slope where the diamond driller is working. The grizzly man balances on the bars and breaks up the rocks with a sledge hammer or, if that doesn't work, he blasts them. It's dangerous, even with a safety chain, and lots of them don't bother, so there's always the risk they'll fall through the bars. Grizzly bars are banned in other countries but up there on the Copperbelt they're still the most efficient way to extract ore.'

'But why would a grizzly man take risks like that?'

'Agh, man, there's huge pressure on him to empty the stope. If it isn't empty the diamond driller can't drill and he doesn't get his full ore bonus, which is calculated on the number of ore trucks filled from the night shift. And then the grizzly man doesn't get his share of the bonus. All grizzly workers are young guys like you, willing to take risks but also proud. They don't want to look like fools or cowards in front of the diamond drillers.'

'But why wouldn't they wear a safety chain?' I asked.

'Because if they slip and fall through the bars, the chain will snap them to a halt twelve feet down, and sometimes that can break your spine or a rock falling from the stope can smash you to pieces.'

'So, grizzly men are more or less forced to break the rules?'

'Ja, man, all the time, with everyone turning a blind eye. When someone gets injured or killed, the mine management points out that he broke their very strict operating rules. If you come off the grizzlies after a year and you haven't been badly injured, it's a miracle, man.'

'I can see why they need medics.'

Miss Truscott entered with the letter and waited by the desk while I enjoyed the sight of her slim figure. 'Thank you, that will be all, Miss Truscott,' Mr Leslie said.

I thanked her and wondered for a moment if I should invite her for lunch, or a drink after she finished work, but then I remembered I was on the run, and squiring a pretty girl in a New York cocktail bar was hardly inconspicuous. Miss Truscott gave me a gorgeous smile as she left, and I knew under normal circumstances I would definitely have followed it up. After five years at the GAWP Bar, I guess I could read most female body language. The smile, the slight turn of the shoulders, the second glance, the hardy perceptible increase in the swing of her hips and the slightly mincing steps she took to make her derriere move in an even more deliciously suggestive manner were all words in that unspoken female language.

Mr Leslie reached for his fountain pen and signed the single page, then rolled a blotter over the wet ink before folding the letter and sliding it into the envelope. 'I haven't sealed it, Mr Reed, so please read it if you want, hey.' He extended his hand. 'I hope you take up our offer.'

I shook his hand. 'You've been extraordinarily generous with your time and advice, sir. Please be assured I am most grateful.' I held up the envelope and repeated. 'Thank you. You may be sure I'll use this.'

'It has been a pleasure, Mr Reed.' He held onto my hand a fraction longer than might have been necessary. Releasing it, he said, 'Whatever you're running away from, Jack, I hope it all turns out well for you in the end.'

I stepped out of Mr Leslie's office and was about to smile at the delectable Miss Truscott, thank her and stroll past her desk, when I stopped. What the hell, I was headed into purgatory anyhow, and the closest I'd been to a woman since darling Bridgett had been the nursing staff at the Albany General Hospital, who were capable, cheerful and efficient older women.

'Miss Truscott, I'd love to buy you a drink,' I said quietly, 'then, if you're free, perhaps dinner? I'm ravenous. I was too nervous to eat today.'

She was silent for a moment, her eyes lowered, and I noted she was wearing light grey eye shadow. Finally she looked up, her lovely grey eyes amused. 'As long as that's the only thing you are ravenous for, I'd love to accept, Mr Reed,' she laughed, adding, 'I finish in twenty minutes.'

I knew that kind of laugh, too, with its hidden meaning. *Never know your luck in the big city, Jack Spayd . . . er, Jack McCrae, oh shit, Jack Reed*, I thought to myself. *Maybe later, after dinner, a little serenade on the harmonica . . .* 'It's Jack. I'll be waiting in the foyer, Miss Truscott.'

'It's Stacey, Jack.'

CHAPTER TWENTY-TWO

WHEN STACEY SUGGESTED WE go to her favourite trattoria I swallowed hard. In my imagination any Italian restaurant was likely to be swarming with members of the Mob. Clearly, I was more paranoid than I'd realised. But she was so pretty I couldn't refuse, and I told myself that a familiar restaurant would mean she'd feel at ease, always a good start to an evening.

Barney's champagne had worked like a charm – 'good liquor makes seduction quicker, Krug Rosé is the perfect way!' and when the lovely Stacey invited me home to her tiny flat, my 'lullaby' on the harmonica added the finishing touch to the pink bubbly. 'You're a real classy guy,' she'd said happily after two glasses, which had been a great boost to my faltering ego.

Yes, I did feel guilty about Bridgett, but I'm a man and I told myself the evening was part of a deliberate attempt to forget and move on. Also, I guessed that it could be a long, long time before I was fortunate enough to meet a suitable woman in Africa. Mr Leslie had made it clear that even looking at a woman of colour would not be tolerated and that all white women were either wives or daughters, both out of bounds.

Despite this, and the many pleasures of Stacey's company, I realised that the sooner I got out of New York, the better. It's a big city in which to get lost but all it would take was one slip, one unlucky sighting. I knew that the Mafia's tentacles could reach me wherever I tried to hide – Johnny Diamond had never mentioned the name of his home town, and yet the Mafia had discovered him in Oak Harbor, Ottawa County, Ohio, a village of less than eight-hundred souls on a tributary of Lake Erie. He was practically on the Canadian border and yet it wasn't far enough away to keep him safe. As Lenny would have said, 'Vamoose, Jack!'

I knew better than to travel by passenger liner – too many people with time on their hands, curious about other passengers. I had heard somewhere that some of the freight lines carried a few passengers as well as cargo. Rather than visiting the various shipping lines I went back to the New York Library. Mrs Hodgson had taught me well and I knew my way around a library; although, of course, the New York Library was something else, and would have given the British Library a nudge. Regarded as the greatest library in the world, when I'd visited it during the war the British Library had been boarded up, with all of its valuable books and manuscripts removed to a safer location, so I hadn't seen it at its best. Often I'd instead repaired to Foyles Bookshop in Charing Cross Road for the steady diet of books I needed. Despite its eccentric and old-fashioned practices, it was a wonderful shop, stuffed with books from every writer published in English, or so it seemed.

It didn't take me long to discover what I needed to know about shipping lines. The English Bank Line was one that carried a mere handful of paying passengers and shipped cargo to all points of the globe from American and Canadian ports.

I called the shipping agents and learned from an English clerk that the *Lossiebank* was due to sail in about three days from New York for the port of Liverpool in the UK. 'She's a very comfortable ship, sir. You'd have your own private cabin and I'm told the Khalasi cook is excellent.'

'Khalasi?' I asked.

'The cook is an Indian. The Khalasi are mostly dockworkers, porters and sailors, but I guess he's been elevated to the galley.'

'So, curries . . . ?'

He laughed. 'Of course, but not exclusively, I'm sure.'

'Sounds perfect,' I said. 'Can you tell me the exact date and time of departure?'

'I'm afraid not, sir. You have to understand that these are cargo ships; they leave when all the cargo is aboard. That can vary by a couple of days, depending on the dockworkers and their workload. You'll need to call me every morning after ten. When she leaves, she sails on the evening tide for Liverpool. Shall I book a cabin, sir?'

Sails on the evening tide . . . only an Englishman would use an expression that dated back to the days of sailing ships. 'My final destination is Africa, as I said, so is it possible to find a ship in England that will take me there?'

'Why, yes, sir, our ships sail to just about every part of the world with the old red duster.'

'The red duster?'

'The red ensign, the flag of the British merchant navy. The Bank Line has cargo ships sailing regularly from Liverpool to the west coast of Africa.'

It wasn't a hardship to wait a couple more days. Stacey Truscott had succumbed to 'Tenderly' by Walter Gross, played soft and low on the harmonica, and I felt fairly certain that until the call came to go aboard there was room in her bed for two. Stacey was open-hearted and affectionate, and when I explained that I was leaving America, she'd generously offered to take me back to her place for 'my farewell gift'.

Now, with the *Lossiebank* due to sail in three days or so, I hoped my farewell celebration might extend a little if I were lucky, so I found a top perfumery on Fifth Avenue and bought a bottle of Chanel No. 5 *Eau de Parfum*. Working in the GAWP Bar I'd smelled almost every type of French perfume and been assured by many of the women that Chanel No. 5, Joy by Jean Patou and Shalimar by Guerlain, were by far the most popular perfumes among the very rich. I hoped it might cement my 'classy guy' reputation and, I'm happy to say, it worked wonders.

I wasn't sure what, if anything, I'd need in Africa, but I visited Sam Ash Music in Brooklyn and purchased two sixteen-hole chromatic Hohner super harmonicas.

Four days later I was told the *Lossiebank* would sail that evening on the tide. I'd paid the $120 for my passage to Liverpool, and gave thanks that, at least during this crossing to England, I wouldn't be lying in my bunk having nightmares about German torpedoes.

So, the die was cast. I stood at the stern of the MV *Lossiebank*, having waved farewell to the generous, pretty and tearful Stacey, and then watched as the old cargo boat nosed her way out of New York Harbour and began to roll gently on the Atlantic swell. As the Empire State Building receded, I wondered whether I would ever see North America again. I glanced down at my hand on the rail; it wasn't a pretty sight. Perhaps I should have worn a leather glove to cover it, but then people would ask about it, which would lead to more explanations. Usually when anyone noticed my left hand, they didn't comment. It was better that way. I'd learned from having a missing earlobe that explanations soon became tedious. I thought of Mr Leslie, who obviously enjoyed recounting the story of his underground mine accident, but I was different; I'd always preferred to grandstand from the keyboard.

'Mr Reed, sah.' I turned to see the owner of the voice, an immaculately white-jacketed Indian steward, standing to rigid attention and looking up at me. 'Captain Irvine invites you for a drink in the saloon with the other passengers, sah.'

I followed him into the interior of the ship, noticing as I went the beautiful old-fashioned teak panelling in the corridor, and the heavy reassuring 'thunk' of the teak door as it swung shut behind me, in effect cutting me off from my past.

There were four other passengers at dinner: an American Episcopalian bishop and his English wife; and two American women who appeared to be in their late sixties, both ex-schoolteachers. The bishop had been invited to attend the coronation of the new queen, Elizabeth II, and was taking an extended holiday prior to the ceremony at Westminster Abbey. The captain, a Lancastrian, proved to be a man of few words who left the conversational work to his first officer, Alastair MacIntyre, and another Bank Line officer called Peter Adams, who was hitching a ride back to the UK to take up a position on one of the company's cargo boats. We proved to be, as the bishop's wife, Mrs Shillington, put it, 'a jolly nice lot', although I saw very little of the other passengers during the daytime, which they spent playing bridge. At meals, they discussed the relative merits of the different bidding systems used in the game, the two Americans, not surprisingly, favouring the American system, while Mrs Shillington insisted the British system was superior.

The bishop, who started on his first glass of claret at midday, abstained from expressing an opinion on either system. By the time we gathered for a 'sun-downer', he'd finished his first bottle of claret and took what remained of his third back to his cabin after dinner. A chubby, greying and undistinguished-looking man, his claret nose made Mr Leslie's look relatively normal.

I spent most of my time reading, or in the company of Peter Adams, another bibliophile and a keen amateur photographer; or 'snapographer', as he modestly called himself. I'd seen some of his photographs and they were a lot more than mere snaps. Apart from our love of books, we had the war in common and Peter proved to be excellent company, as did Alastair MacIntyre, when he wasn't busy on the bridge.

The crossing was comparatively calm compared with my first experience of the Atlantic, and one day blended seamlessly into the next, as they often do on voyages. We arrived in Liverpool and I took the train to London, the name of a decent small hotel in South Kensington, recommended to me by Peter Adams, tucked into my pocket. Almost the sole purpose of my trip to London was to visit Foyles Bookshop to stock up on Penguins, the famous paperbacks that had been popularised in the 1930s, and were orange for fiction, green for crime fiction, blue for biographies, and so on. I quickly filled the large canvas bag I'd brought along and saved on weight and also a small fortune. I also bought a copy of *Gray's Anatomy* and two large books on industrial first aid, and emergency first aid, to study on the voyage out.

A day later, Peter Adams phoned me at my hotel.

'Jack, I've been appointed first officer on the *Roybank*, a cargo ship, sailing to Lobito in Angola, and assorted other African ports. She sails in four days' time – interested?'

'Definitely.'

'She's a nice ship, I'm sure you'll be comfortable. Captain Paul Eggert's the man in charge . . .'

I jotted down the address of the Bank Line head office in London where I could purchase my passage.

My remaining three days in London I spent looking around. To my surprise, there was still a lot of bomb damage, and Londoners, generally speaking, looked drab and disconsolate in the late winter gloom. Perhaps it was the food rationing, which continued to make their lives joyless. They'd been required to show their stiff upper lips for way too long, and I couldn't help wondering whether winning the war was all we'd thought it would be. The British certainly didn't seem to be reaping any rewards for their courage and grit, and there was no sign of the brashness and optimism epitomised by Sammy's pink Cadillac convertible. Instead of getting back on their feet, it seemed, they were still making an effort to rise from their knees. London in 1953 was a long way from the brassy neon-lit greedy opportunism of Las Vegas or the bright confidence of New York.

At one stage on the crossing from America I'd toyed with the idea of 'disappearing' in England, but the dull weariness of London had left me depressed and I thought it unlikely that the British wanted jazz and blues harmonica playing to cheer them up. Africa, here I come.

My fellow passengers on the SS *Roybank* were an Ethiopian diplomat, Berihun Kidane, and his wife, Fenet, who were on their way to Lagos, where he would take up his position as the new consul at the Ethiopian consulate in Abuja. The former consul had died suddenly of a heart attack and Berihun was being transferred from London. It was technically a promotion, but, as Fenet pointed out, a doubtful one. When I'd suggested that I didn't know diplomats usually travelled by cargo boat, she'd admitted that she had a fear of flying and the *Roybank* had been the first ship leaving for Nigeria. They were a handsome young couple and she was an absolute stunner.

I confess my ignorance at the time. All I knew about Ethiopia was that it was originally known as Abyssinia and was situated somewhere left of the Red Sea, occupying part of the Horn of Africa. What I learned from Fenet was that the ruling class, she and her husband obviously among them, came from the ancient Amhara people of the central highlands. Moreover, they are often very tall – she must have been close to six feet, elegant and slim as a pencil. Fenet told me she could trace her ancestry back to King Solomon and the Queen of Sheba. Like most people, I knew a little about the queen from Bible references, but I'd never considered her appearance. Now, looking at Fenet, I suddenly understood that she could well have been a beauty.

As we steamed south, the weather seemed to control its temper and the air over the Bay of Biscay was warm. By the time we reached Gibraltar, we were in our shirtsleeves and the ship's officers had donned their white shirts and shorts. As we sailed down the African coast, the weather remained benign, the nights dream-like as the familiar northern stars changed to strange new southern constellations.

We went ashore in Dakar, the capital of Senegal, and I was surprised to see how European the whitewashed colonial buildings were, and how smart – what is it about the French? Freetown, in Sierra Leone, on the other hand, was more like I'd imagined Africa, and was just as Graham Greene described it: a place where nothing happened in a hurry. Lots of black folk stood around, stray dogs panted in the blazing sun, and a few rattling pre-war trucks hooted at nothing in particular. I wished Joe could see the huge cotton tree under which freed slaves had gathered in the 1790s. Curiously, fruit bats slept in the tree during the day, seemingly undisturbed by the noise or traffic.

When we arrived in Lagos, in Nigeria, it was pouring rain, which lasted the entire time we were in port. A black Citroen awaited Berihun and Fenet, but before going ashore, Fenet handed me a letter.

Jack, we've loved your company on the voyage. This is to my father in Addis Ababa and is on diplomatic letterhead. If you ever come to Ethiopia, look him up. Who knows, we may be back home as well. Hopefully this posting isn't forever and we'll meet again.

I looked up at her, thinking, *Oh, God, why aren't you single!* 'Surely you won't be there forever?' I said.

'Ah, Jack, it depends on our families.' She smiled. 'If we're all in favour with the emperor, good things will flow from on high; if not, Lagos may well be where our future children grow up.' She spoke with a very posh English accent, and she, in particular, had been good company. I knew she'd fled Ethiopia at the age of five with her family and other elite Amhara families, following His Imperial Majesty Haile Selassie I, Conquering Lion of the Tribe of Judah, King of Kings, Emperor of Ethiopia, Elect of God. Her family had gone into exile after the Italian invasion of Ethiopia in 1936 and settled near the emperor in Bath, in southern England, where Fenet received an excellent education, culminating in a first-class degree from Cambridge. I forget her husband's exact credentials, but they were just as impressive.

Peter Adams was as enchanted by Fenet as I was, and couldn't stop taking photographs of her. I implored him to send me one and gave him the address of Mr Coetzee, the personnel manager of the Luswishi River Copper Mine, where I presumed I'd end up. It's not often you want to keep a picture of a woman you can never have and may never meet again, but she was *that* good-looking, and I think I was missing Bridgett badly. I wished now, too late, that I had asked her for a photograph to console me through the next part of my life, which Mr Leslie had indicated would be a sexual desert.

In the three days we were in port in Lagos, I didn't venture ashore. Peter Adams claimed it was one of the few places on earth where he hadn't taken a bundle of photographs, and described the mangrove swamps, biting insects, malaria, featureless buildings, lethargic people and endless rain and heat. 'In other words, Jack, a shithole; the quintessential white man's grave in Africa.'

We arrived at Lobito in Angola – my destination – at about seven in the morning. I'd done my Angola homework in the New York Library, swotting up on its history. Apparently the Portuguese had been in Angola since the sixteenth century, exporting African slaves to Brazil, another Portuguese colony.

I said my fond goodbyes to Peter Adams, who had been a generous companion and host, and stood on the wharf alone, with the *Roybank* towering over me and affording a little shade from the already blistering early-morning sun. It must have been around ninety degrees and the humidity one hundred per cent. Within a few minutes my starched white shirt was soaked and clinging to my back and chest. Jack Spayd, alias Jack McCrae and now Jack Reed, had arrived in Africa more or less intact, if you didn't examine his left hand too closely.

The plan, as I recall, was for the ship's agent to transport me to the town of Benguela some twenty miles along the coast, from where the weekly train was due to leave in a few days for Elisabethville in the Belgian Congo, situated as far from the east coast of the African continent as it was from the west. It would be a long journey back, should I ever wish to see the ocean.

I heard a toot and then a voice calling out, 'Mr Reed, your car. Mr Reed?' My escort had arrived. I turned to see a short, thin guy in his mid-thirties jump from yet another black Citroen. His skin was dark but not the really deep black I'd seen in the other African ports, and he wore a white shirt and linen suit at least two sizes too big for him. 'I am late, *senor*; a thousand apologies!' He adjusted his jacket by wriggling his shoulders, an action he'd obviously perfected, then hastened to open the rear door.

'Not late,' I replied, smiling. 'Your name, *senor*?' I asked, then added, '*Obrigado*, but, please, may I sit in the front?' I had learned the word *obrigado*, Portuguese for thank you, from Peter Adams before going ashore as well as a few other useful phrases.

'Luis de Silva,' he replied, undecided about whether to close the door first or pick up my kitbag. I stooped to grab the kitbag in my right hand, then reached down with my left for the canvas bag of books. He must have seen my scarred hand because he exclaimed, 'No, *senor*, I must carry!' He looked shocked. 'Front seat not good, spring not okey dokey, but if you want.'

A spring had pushed up through the worn leather, but I pressed it back into place and slid onto the seat.

'Don't worry,' I said with a grin. 'Big bum!'

He laughed, shaking his head. 'No, no, *senor*, not big bum! You will see my fadder!'

'You speak good English, Luis. I'm afraid I know no Portuguese.'

He seemed pleased. 'I am trying always, *senor*. Now we must go manager office before we go Benguela. Is okay?'

I nodded. He was obviously making a big effort, treating me like some bigwig. I'd wondered about the customs officer coming aboard to stamp my passport. Captain Eggert must have exaggerated my importance on the ship's wireless as we came into port.

We drove no more than a couple of hundred yards, though in such oppressive heat I was glad we hadn't walked. 'We are coming here now, *senor*,' Luis de Silva announced as we drew to a halt outside a nondescript single-storey brick building. A painted board on the wall beside its front door announced 'S.L. de Silva – Shipping Agents', followed by a lot of other information in Portuguese.

'Oh, also de Silva?' I said, pointing to the sign.

'My fadder, Senor Reed.' I followed him into the building, where a rattling, squeaking electric fan stood on a single leg several feet from the front door. It must have been a primitive form of air-conditioner, the fan blowing air past a large block of ice resting on a stand in a tin tub. The cold draught caused Luis's oversized suit to flap as he stepped aside to allow me the full benefit of the ice-cooled blast. 'Air-condition

Angola,' Luis announced earnestly. He then led me into an office at the rear, where a very fat, short man wearing a similar loose-fitting white linen suit and a red tie was seated at a large, untidy desk. He heaved himself out of the chair and made his way ponderously around the desk to greet me. He was a dead ringer for Sydney Greenstreet in the movie *Casablanca*, though without the fez. 'Mr Reed!' he boomed. 'Welcome, most welcome to Angola. We are very, very honoured to be of service to you and the esteemed British Bank Line.' He clasped my hand within both of his own and shook it vigorously several times, then announced, 'S.L. de Silva at your service, no wish too big.'

I wasn't sure whether he customarily referred to himself by his initials or whether he meant the company, so I replied, '*Obrigado*, Senor de Silva.'

He threw his arms wide and beamed at me, then glanced at his son, Luis. 'Five minute and already he speak Portuguese! A cool drink for you, Mr Reed?' he asked. Before I could reply he said, 'Luis, Coca-Cola for the *senor*!'

'Thank you, but could I have a bottle of water to take in the car instead, please? I'd like to get to Benguela and to my hotel as soon as I can,' I said.

With Luis again at the wheel we left a short time later for the thirty-mile trip to Benguela. The town, which didn't seem large enough to be called a city, had a vaguely Mexican or Spanish air, with plenty of white stucco and red tiled roofs. There were several quite imposing stone buildings, including my hotel, which had recently been renamed The Salazar, in honour of the Portuguese prime minister, whom Luis referred to as '*our* prime minister'.

I was surprised at the number of people I assumed were Portuguese and questioned Luis about them. 'Oh, *senor*, we have been here a long time, but still lots of people come from Portugal. My family are here long, long time. But still we are European. Here also, Europeans run everything, the government, soldiers, army.'

'No African soldiers?'

'No, *senor*.'

I soon got the idea: Europeans were those who ran things and owned land, no matter their colour. Still, as Mr Leslie had indicated in New York, black people were at the bottom of the social ladder here, and, as I was soon to learn, pretty well everywhere in colonial Africa.

After I'd checked in, Luis drove me to the bank to change sufficient currency to buy a train ticket to Elisabethville, and pay for my hotel and some appropriate clothes. 'Can you take me to a good tailor, too, please? I need a couple of tropical suits made,' I said.

'I will take, there is one who makes clothes for where you are going, *senor*.'

The tailor, a Senor Candido, spoke tolerable English and had evidently made it his business to outfit Europeans heading to the centre of the continent. I asked him to measure me up for two white linen suits; not too baggy, I stressed. He politely enquired where I was going and, when I said the copper mines near the border of Northern Rhodesia, shook his head vigorously and tut-tutted, explaining that white linen suits would be entirely unsuitable, and that he would make me three khaki bush jackets with long khaki pants for formal wear, and at least five pairs of khaki shorts and short-sleeved shirts. 'It will cost the same, *senor*,' he offered. He looked down at my shoes. 'Shoes good,' he announced, then, indicating a point just below his kneecap, added, 'Long sock khaki pulled up so, you also must have.'

My clothes would take three days to make, which was fine. If I missed a train to Elisabethville, there would be another, and I would enjoy regaining my land legs exploring Benguela and trying to spot as many of the local birds as I could. I knew nothing about African birds other than the flamingos I'd seen long ago in the Riverdale Zoo in Toronto. Once I'd been in the town for a few hours, Noel Coward's 'Mad Dogs and Englishmen' sprang to mind, because from noon to three o'clock in the afternoon the town shut down, all businesses having closed for siesta, and everyone went home for a nap; a very sensible idea, if you ask me.

Each evening, Luis would drive from Lobito to take me back to meet his friends, then drive me home to The Grand, now known as The Salazar, around midnight. Luis's friends were a pleasant lot and I decided that, unlike Fenet's posting to Lagos, a few years spent in Lobito might be quite pleasant. However, I was reminded of how things really stood one evening, when I returned with Luis de Silva to The Grand. 'Jack,' – he had finally gotten round to using my first name – 'that man in the hotel when we came in, he the PIDE, the secret police.'

The Irishman John Philpot Curran is credited with the phrase 'the price of freedom is eternal vigilance', but, in this case, it was 'the price of tyranny is eternal vigilance'. I wondered why the authorities needed to keep the people under surveillance when, as far as I could tell, Angola was a peaceful and law-abiding place, but I couldn't know what might be concealed under the seemingly benign social surface.

The weekly train left on my fourth day ashore. I was informed that the train trip to Elisabethville could take three days; an inordinate length of time, I thought, for continuous travel over a distance of 1200 miles. 'Why does the journey to Elisabethville take so long?' I asked one of Luis's friends who worked on the railway. He explained it was a single line, and nothing was allowed to interfere with the ore trains coming from Katanga province in the Belgian Congo and the Northern Rhodesian Copperbelt. The weekly passenger train was obliged to pull off into sidings at fixed times to let the ore trains through. 'Sometime if the ore train is late, you must wait three, maybe four, maybe even more hours,' he explained. 'Also, the mountains. Sometime you have to change to the big locomotive. Very slow, and burns a lot of wood.' It had never occurred to me that a locomotive might burn wood instead of coal, but this was Africa and the tropics, and wood was in abundant supply.

Ah well, I thought, *I'm travelling first class, I've brought lots of books, and I'll have plenty of time to read. Maybe* King Solomon's Mines *by Rider Haggard? A corny thought.*

The railway station at Benguela had a distinctly European look, with a raised platform, which was hardly surprising, given that the railway was developed by a Scotsman, Sir Robert Williams, who was an associate of

Sir Cecil Rhodes and largely responsible for the discovery of the copper deposits in the Katanga province. The railway line followed the old slave and trade routes through from the centre of the continent to the coast.

I only mention Benguela station because it was the first place where I saw a definite division between the races; or, at least, the classes. White-jacketed porters stood on guard at either end of the two first-class carriages, beyond which stretched the other, somewhat battered-looking, carriages with rows of hard seats to accommodate those folk not entitled to call themselves European. They seemed a far happier lot, laughing and calling out to each other, every carriage window crammed with black people reaching down to buy food from vendors and chatting excitedly with the folks who'd come to see them off. I noticed several people boarding the train carrying baskets of live chickens.

Sitting primly in my first-class compartment I realised that happiness and laughter could be found in abundant supply just two carriages beyond my own. I felt suddenly very lonely and miserable.

The trip to Elisabethville in the Belgian Congo took three stop-and-start days to cover a distance of 1200 miles or, if you like, we averaged less than twenty miles an hour. Tedious wasn't the word.

Finally we arrived in the Congo, a country of roughly fourteen million people, once regarded by the king of Belgium as his personal estate, but now a Belgian colony and the treasure house of middle Africa. Rich in copper, of course, it also had huge deposits of cobalt, zinc, tin, silver, gold, manganese, coal and uranium ('Little Boy', the atomic bomb dropped on Hiroshima, used uranium from a mine in the Belgian Congo). There were also gem and industrial-grade diamonds. Any African caught mining for alluvial diamonds was summarily shot, according to a fellow passenger I met in the dining car: a Belgian, who referred to himself as a *colon* or settler. There was no trial or warning, simply a revolver to the forehead. Bang!

It was early evening when I arrived in Elisabethville. I booked into a cheap hotel and then went out for a walk. Some of the buildings seemed to owe more to Europe than Africa, although I really couldn't say with authority, as the closest I'd been to France or Belgium was nearly landing on the beach at Dieppe. Other buildings seemed more colonial, but all of them looked exotic and interesting to a boy from Cabbagetown.

However, as Northern Rhodesia and the Copperbelt were only about 150 miles away, I decided to push on the following morning, arriving in Ndola just before noon. I had barely stepped onto the platform when two teenage boys ran up to me, pushing several other kids aside. One pointed to my bags and said, 'Bwana, we carry for you, only one shilling.'

'Can you take me to a bank first?' I asked.

'We take,' the smaller of the two African lads said.

'Do you know the offices of the Luswishi River Copper Mine?'

Both shook their heads; then the taller one said, 'No, not here, Ndola this office, bwana.'

'We show you bus to that mine,' the smaller one said, then, flashing a brilliant smile, 'maybe go bank, show bus.' He pointed to my luggage and said, 'All one and six?' I could see the extra sixpence was a try-on. They knew a sucker when they saw one.

I changed twenty-five US dollars into Rhodesian pounds at Barclays Bank and the two lads, lugging my kit, escorted me to the mine bus terminus. I gave them each a shilling and they seemed well pleased, racing away down the street, shouting happily. It was a nice cheerful welcome.

The bus to the town of Luswishi River turned out to be a Volkswagen Microbus owned – as I was to learn – like just about everything else, by the mine. On the driver's door was painted 'Rhodesian Selection Trust' and under it 'Luswishi River Copper Mine'. I'd never before seen anything like this vehicle, where the driver sat right up against the windshield with no engine between him and the road ahead. I glanced through the rear window to see eight seats, all but two piled high with parcels and bits of equipment, obviously collected in town to take back to the mine. The engine was presumably situated somewhere under the floor at the back. There was no sign of the driver and when I tried the door it was locked. I was beginning to wonder if the two young black guys had conned me when a white guy stepped out of a nearby shop and paused to light a cigarette.

'Excuse me, can you tell me if this is where I catch the bus for Luswishi River?'

He drew on the cigarette, exhaled, then, squinting through the smoke, answered in a twangy Australian accent, 'No, mate, that's the old Bedford, but it's for the black blokes. Need a ride?'

'Well, yes, and thank you.'

'No problems.' He reached the van and unlocked the driver's door. Turning to me, he said, 'Noel . . . Noel White, I work for the mine – communications.' He extended his hand.

'Jack Reed,' I said, shaking it.

'You a Yank, Jack?' he asked. 'Don't get too many Yanks here.'

'No, Canadian.'

'That right? Well, yer welcome anyway. I'm Australian. Come to join the United Nations, eh?'

He unlocked the other door and said, 'Stow yer gear, then hop in the front. I've got one or two calls to make, then we'll be off.' I threw my kit in the rear and hopped in the front.

'Never been in one of these,' I remarked as he climbed in behind the wheel.

'Yeah, German, not bad; useful but no fuckin' good in the rainy season. Starts next month. Wheels get buried in red shit and won't budge.'

We set off and I soon got used to the road rushing towards me. After one or two quick stops to collect parcels, we headed out along a dirt road for the Luswishi River.

'You said you work in communications, Noel?'

'Yeah. Well, you could say I'm the guy who has to tell everyone when the shit hits the fan.' He laughed. 'You know, make sure everyone knows what's going on underground and above, sort of liaison with all the various working groups, surface workers, hoist drivers, office, maintenance; then underground, diamond drillers, grizzly-bar workers, pipe fitters, train drivers, main haulage guys, you name it.'

'Medics? They're included?' I asked.

'Yeah, of course, bloody important.'

'So you'd know Mr Coetzee?' I pronounced it 'Koot-see' as Mr Leslie in New York had suggested, then added, 'I have a letter of introduction to him from New York.'

'To Jannie Coetzee? South African? Nice bloke. So, a letter from New York, eh? You must be someone important then, Jack. Why wasn't I told to meet the train?'

I grinned. 'On the contrary, I'm simply hoping to get a job, possibly as a medic.'

He seemed relieved. 'No problem, they'll welcome you with open arms. Speaking of arms, I noticed . . .'

'My left hand? Yeah, injured in an accident. I was formerly a professional piano player. I got my experience as a medic in the Canadian army during the war. It isn't much of a qualification but the guy in the New York office seemed to think it was okay.'

'Yeah, he's right; it will be, mate. Lemme offer you some advice.'

'Sure, of course.'

'I didn't hear any of that. You're a qualified medic, that's all. Get that into your skull. There are men from over forty-five different countries in the single quarters and they're run by a bunch of thugs who call themselves Polish resistance fighters or Jews that survived the concentration camps. Poles, Jews, my fucking arse; they're all ex-SS officers and think we're stupid enough not to know the difference between Polish and German. Jack, don't tell anyone a bloody thing. Yeah, okay, you're a Canadian and a medic, highly fuckin' qualified, and that's it. Mate, in the mines it's bullshit bullshit über alles. I take it your crook hand works okay.'

'Crook?'

'Bad hand . . . it's okay?'

'Yeah, fine, but not for playing piano.'

Noel White glanced sideways at me. 'Jack, fer cryin' out loud, no fuckin' details. Accident, it was an accident; you're a medic, there's no need for more. And lock your hut door when you're in it and when you leave, even to go to the *cimbush*. It's steel reinforced and that's not for nothing.'

'Chimboose . . .?'

'Shit house, lavatory, single quarters' shower block.'

The road was dusty and rough, and the flat country we were passing through was largely covered in open woodland, the leaves in various shades of yellow, maroon, deep purple, rust, red and occasionally green. It looked more like the Canadian fall than how I'd imagined Africa. Every once in a while, a red anthill six to eight feet tall rose up among the trees.

'Thanks for the advice, Noel, I'll keep quiet.'

'Play poker, Jack?' he asked.

'No,' I said, taking his recent advice.

'Good. Every month the Krauts organise a game with a couple of blokes, French or Belgian, not always the same guys, but they all come across the border. I'm sure it's a scam. Some of our guys win a bit but the visitors seem to clean up most of the time. Been caught once or twice myself. A man feels a bloody fool, but that's poker, I guess. You're lucky the bug hasn't bitten you, Jack. We all know there's something going on. These blokes from across the border are professional con artists, and the Nazis bring them in and then set up the game in the single quarters' recreation hut to suck us in. Several of the married blokes, myself included, have been stupid enough to think we'll win. Best I've ever done is win fifty quid, but it was enough to bring me back. Not every time but once in a while when the urge gets to me. I guess I'm a weak shit.'

'Can't you – I mean, the mine – do anything about these ex-SS guys?'

'Mate, like I said, there's blokes from over forty-five different nations and all – or most, anyway – are single. The Krauts know how to keep the peace; they're experts, trained in the war to be bullies. Jannie Coetzee, the personnel manager, isn't gunna interfere if some bloke gets his head kicked in. As long as it doesn't go beyond the gates of the single quarters.' He shrugged, then gave a sardonic grin. 'Three monkeys, mate, that's mine management. Just stay clear of the Krauts. They ask you something about yourself, tell them bugger all. By the way, Jannie Coetzee is also a bit of a poker player, and so are some of the diamond drillers.'

'I got the impression in New York from Mr Leslie that the diamond drillers are the top dogs.'

'Dead right! But that's underground. They're mostly married and live in town, in houses owned by the mine. They're not all South African but most are, they're the professional miners. If you interfere with them on their patch – underground, I mean – they can be real cranky bastards. The miners union committee is made up almost entirely of diamond drillers – they fuckin' rule the roost, mate.'

Noel White was being pretty open with me and so I thought I'd ask him about the opposite sex. 'Noel, what does a guy do about, you know . . . sex?'

He threw back his head and laughed uproariously and in the process nearly drove off the road. 'Mate, your donger's a goner! No naughties for free unless you want ya balls danglin' from the nearest tree.'

'So, the outlook isn't good, then?' I laughed.

'Well, there's several known turd burglars run by the Germans in the shower block. I'm told it'll cost you a tenner, six to the guy bending over and the other four to the Kraut running the hole in one session.'

'Jesus!'

'Then there are the birds from the Congo.'

'I don't understand . . . ?'

'Well, sort of temporary prostitutes.'

'Are they black?'

'Jesus, Jack, don't go there, mate. Black velvet, that's the ultimate no-no. Get caught fucking a nigger woman, you'll be very lucky to get out of town alive!'

'So, "temporary prostitutes"? I gather there's not a brothel in town . . .'

'Jack, Jack, Jack, this is a British protectorate! Luswishi River has an Anglican church that practically nobody attends, but a brothel that could stay open twenty-four hours a day? Jesus, no, mate!' He paused. 'But the Brits, the police, local civil service, all turn a blind eye to the birds flying in across the border for a twenty-four-hour shift at each of the six mines.'

'Six mines?'

'Yeah. You probably know the Copperbelt extends into the Katanga province, where you would have got off at Elisabethville to get the train here. They have the same problem, lots of single white miners. But, unlike the Brits, they understand the needs of young blokes, or single men. But here? You lay a finger on a married woman and you're dead meat. She can be a married sheila who gets pissed at the club and takes a fancy to some young bloke and wants a knee-trembler out the back, a schoolgirl or a miner's daughter; even if she's eighteen and past the age of consent, you're still dead meat. So, every month they fly a DC-4 packed with ten young sheilas, birds, women, whatever you like to call them, who arrive from Brussels. Two or three are your genuine whores – lots of the older miners like it that way – but most are young Belgian girls looking for a dowry; not virgins because they don't tolerate that, but just young girls, not professional whores. Pretty good sorts, actually, none of your rubbish. They're picked for their looks. Because of the war there's a shortage of eligible blokes everywhere in Europe, and these girls, if they want to get hitched, they're gunna need a dowry to get a good bloke back home. Well, a coupla tours to the Congo and they're set for life, got enough dosh to buy a house and nobody back home knows a damned thing. Far as the bloke they marry is concerned, they're pure as the driven!'

'Sounds reasonable.'

'Yeah, I agree, it is. If we can't have a brothel, it's very sensible. But I object to the fact that we have to get the leftovers. By the time the sheilas arrive in the DC-4, they've been banged senseless by the miners in Katanga, too buggered to even pretend for our young blokes. They've already made a fortune over the border and we're the bonus, the raisins in the Christmas cake. When the DC-4 arrives, I drive out to "fetch the mail". The sheilas spend twenty-four hours here every month by special arrangement with —'

'The Nazis in the single quarters?' I suggested.

'Bang on, Jack! Got it in one. The sheilas are cleaning up big time. They fly off with a suitcase full of money, having left behind one or two blokes with a nasty reminder, if you know what I mean, and taken home a bit of a souvenir themselves, some of them.'

'But you said they were all amateurs? The er . . . reminder, that from the whores?'

'No way. Whores – well, the ones they send – are pros. They don't carry venereal disease. Nah, it's the amateurs. You see the miners in Katanga, some don't like to use frangers. Same here with some of our own young idiots. It costs double to ride bareback, but some blokes – young grizzly men usually – well, they've got more money than sense and they like to boast about it afterwards.'

'Until they wake up one morning with a nasty itch?'

'Yeah, Jack, right on. Someone here or over the border may have the pox and the girl they've banged transmits it to the next cowboy who wants to ride without a saddle.'

'But what about the girls? What if they get pregnant?'

'Nah, their contract allows them full medical treatment, even an abortion if they're up the duff.' Noel laughed, then glanced across at me. 'Jack, if you get desperate, always use a franger – a rubber – won't you?'

'Sure,' I said laughing.

'So, welcome to the Northern Rhodesian Copperbelt, and don't forget to keep your rondavel door locked at all times.'

'Rondavel?'

'Yeah, it means round hut, you'll be allocated one. Check the window bars as well. Never know what to expect from those reffos.'

We'd entered the one-street town, and passed a few Indian shops, a petrol station, a small stone church, a school, and then we were travelling through a residential area, several hundred identical-looking houses in streets laid out in alphabetical order, so that an address might be 12 Z Avenue, or 15 N Avenue. I noticed a social club, tennis courts, a squash court, swimming pool and football field – not too bad, really.

'The single quarters, where are they?' I asked Noel.

He jerked his head towards the driver's window. 'Way the other side near the mess where you single blokes eat. It's as far from the married section as possible, which is fenced off with only one gate.'

'You mean you're locked in?'

'No, nothing like that. It's sort of like a symbol; the Krauts like it.' He gave a dry laugh. 'They're good at running concentration camps.'

We'd come to a halt outside a large white building with a red corrugated iron roof. 'We're here, mate. Mine administration offices. I'll take you in to see Jannie Coetzee. Decent sort'a cove, but remember, tell him *only* what you have to. He isn't gunna ask too many probing questions anyway. Maybe about your hand, but tell him it's fine and you're a qualified medic and prepared to work underground. He may want you to go to the School of Mines and train to be a grizzly man. Take my advice, don't. It's bloody dangerous and they like to recruit young blokes like you whose reactions are fast.' He paused, then added, 'Hey, tell him your hand's good, but not good enough; perfect for a medic, though.'

'Noel, thanks for the lift, buddy – especially the talk. I owe you.'

'Pleasure, mate. Shout me a beer at the club next time you see me. Come on, Jack, I'll introduce you to the personnel manager.'

CHAPTER TWENTY-THREE

NOEL WHITE ESCORTED ME through the building to the personnel department, where he introduced me to a Mrs Dulledge, Jannie Coetzee's secretary.

'Afternoon, Marie. This is Jack Reed. He's here to see Jannie Coetzee.'

She neither returned his greeting nor looked at me. 'Has he got an appointment?'

'Well, no.' Noel looked around. 'But, hey, there's nobody else waiting.'

'He's busy,' she replied, her lips pulled tight. 'We're not here for just anybody's convenience, you know!' Explaining no further she went back to her typing, then stopped momentarily and pointed to a row of chairs against the wall. 'Sit, please.'

Noel glanced at me, one eyebrow slightly raised. 'Personnel manager not here for everyone's convenience? That's a flamin' new one.' Then, turning to me, he said, 'Jack, afraid I can't stay. Sorry about the welcome. Have to go, mate.'

'Yes, of course, Noel. Thanks, buddy. I won't forget your kindness, and thanks for the lift.'

Noel White looked down at Mrs Dulledge. 'Jack's one out of the box, Marie. Look after him, please.'

Mr Coetzee's secretary didn't even blink, much less smile or nod her head. '*Ja*, I already heard you,' she replied, then glancing down at her spiral shorthand notebook, she continued to type. I guess she must have seen a few nasty surprises coming out of the box in her time.

'See ya, Jack. Pleasure meeting you,' Noel called from the doorway. 'We'll get together for that beer, mate.'

'Sit, please!' Mrs Dulledge commanded. 'You are not expected, Mr . . . ?'

'Yes, I apologise, I've only just arrived. It's Jack . . . Jack Reed.'

'Oh,' she said and wrote it down. 'You'll have to wait. I don't know how long, Mr Reed.'

'Of course,' I said, smiling. 'I have a letter from Mr Leslie, from the New York office, for Mr Coetzee,' I pronounced his surname carefully. A sudden look of surprise crossed her face, and she reached for the letter I held out. She smelled vaguely of rose-scented talcum powder, like my mom used. 'Do you have anything else? References?' Her expression suggested she'd be very surprised if I produced anything of the kind.

I handed her the manila envelope containing Nick Reed's impressive army letterheads that lent authority to my far-from-impressive credentials. 'I have these, ma'am. At my previous job, they didn't hand out references; it was all hands-on stuff, direct demonstration.' I smiled. 'You either could or you couldn't,' which, I guess, wasn't a lie.

'Just a moment.' She marched towards the door behind her desk, opened it without knocking, and walked in. Before she closed it, I caught a glimpse of a very large blond guy with a crew cut, leaning back in an office chair and talking on the telephone with his feet on his desk. He wore polished brown boots that had recently been re-soled, the leather only slightly scuffed.

Mrs Dulledge returned a few minutes later. 'Mr Coetzee will see you now . . . er, ' she glanced down at the pad on her desk, 'Mr Reed.'

Jannie Coetzee, his feet no longer resting on his desk, rose as I entered. He was at least four inches taller than me and a lot bigger around the girth. 'Hey, man, all the way from New York. What brings you here, Mr Reed?'

'It's Jack, sir.' It was a curious question, since he must have read Mr Leslie's letter of introduction and the contents of the envelope. Then, remembering Noel White's advice, I held up my left hand. 'I injured my hand in an accident.'

'*Ja*, I understand.' He tapped the letter from Mr Leslie. 'It says here you're a medic, highly qualified in combat conditions. That's good, man. Your hand – it doesn't interfere?'

'No, sir, almost good as new; it's just that my previous work required absolute precision.'

'Combat, hey? You've come to the right place, man. That's for sure. Are you willing to work underground?'

'Yes, I guess that's where most of the emergencies occur, sir.'

'Definitely. Will you go permanent night shift?'

I almost laughed. After the years at the GAWP Bar, I still hadn't quite adjusted to waking up early. 'Sure.'

'Well, then, you've got the job. When can you start?'

I shrugged, hoping I looked unconcerned. 'Whenever it suits, sir.'

'Now, you a senior medic, you can call me Jannie,' he offered.

'Senior?' I asked, surprised. 'But I've only just got here.'

He looked momentarily embarrassed, then cleared his throat. 'Our last medic left unexpectedly last week. You him now, man. You've got his position. You see, we have three white medics, one on each shift.' He counted them off on his fingers: 'There's morning shift, that's eight o'clock till four o'clock; then afternoon shift, from four till twelve; after that, it's you on night shift, eleven till seven o'clock in the morning. It's the grizzly workers' shift and it must go to a senior medic because that's when most of the accidents occur.'

He didn't offer an explanation for what was obviously the unexpected departure of my predecessor. Heeding Noel White's advice, I didn't ask. 'Shouldn't I be given some sort of test? Senior medic sounds pretty serious.' I'd bluffed my way to this point but now my conscience overcame me.

'See, that's nice, you modest as well. I can tell from these papers, man. One of them is signed by a general. Jesus, what more do you want?'

'Major general,' I corrected, not explaining that he'd only been a colonel during the war.

He shrugged. 'No diff, he's high up. Besides, the other two medics, they don't want to do it, even though it's a promotion. I've already spent four days on the telephone to our head office in Jo'burg to send us a new senior medic urgently. I just got off the phone now.' He shrugged. 'But they say they don't have anyone on their books. Have to advertise. But hey, man, now you here!' He tapped Nick's papers. 'And with experience in combat conditions. I can't hardly believe it.'

Then, seeing my expression, he added, 'Agh, man, don't worry. The boss boy on the night shift team has been here three years already; the other three *kaffirs*, more than one year. Then there's Matron Hamilton at the cottage hospital. She can be very useful, but of course she can't go underground and she's only on day shift. But she can give you medical advice any time you need. Just go and see her. I'll let her know you maybe call around, hey?'

Senior medic on night shift, the dangerous shift. It wasn't at all what I wanted to hear. I'd never conned anyone in my life, I'd always let the keyboard speak for me, perhaps not always with eloquence, but, I hoped, with honesty. Now I was being put on the front line, in charge, under who knew what conditions. I simply didn't believe myself sufficiently in practice after so long out of the army. I'd read *Gray's Anatomy* and the first-aid books from Foyles at least twice until I thought I knew every bone in the human body, and just about every industrial accident that could occur and how to treat it. As a general rule I trusted my memory, but it isn't the same when someone's brains are spilling onto your lap or a leg has been severed; my imagination was suddenly running riot. 'But, but, Mr Coetzee – I mean, Jannie – I've never been underground; I simply have no idea of the conditions, or what it's like working in the dark . . .'

He laughed. 'Agh, don't worry, Jack, you wear a hard hat with a light on it, and a wound is a wound, above or below ground, what's the diff, hey? It's mostly only natives – you'll soon learn, man. If a *kaffir* dies, he dies. We don't do post mortems or make any official enquiries with black mineworkers.' He paused. 'You have to understand, they're not like us.'

There it was again. *They're not like us.*

'In what way?'

'They don't cost so much to train. Pick and shovel, crowbar, jackhammer, easy stuff.'

Of course, I should have called it quits right then and there. There would be times in the future when I dearly wished I had. In fact, I should probably have quit during the interview in New York when Mr Leslie made similar comments about black folks' lives being expendable. I'd been trying to save my own ass from the Chicago Mob rather than stick to my convictions. And here it was all over again, '*They're not like us.*' It occurred to me that I should use Fenet's letter of introduction to her family, which she'd given to me on board the *Roybank*. Push on across the centre of the continent, find a ship sailing up the east coast to the Horn of Africa. But instead, all I did was say, 'That's not how I see it, Mr Coetzee. Every life counts.' It was a pathetic rejoinder.

He looked at me as if he vaguely understood. 'You Canadians don't have many black people, so I appreciate what you saying, man, but you'll find out.' He leaned back slightly in his chair. 'So, Jack, will you give it a go?'

Suddenly I felt weary. Where else was I to go if I knocked back this job?

'As a senior medic on the grizzly shift, you also get a bigger copper bonus.'

I didn't care about the money, but I agreed to take the job. I guess it was about as far away as I could run from the Chicago Mob. *Joe, Hector, Chef Napoleon Nelson, Mr Joel, Sue, Pastor Moses and his wife, Booker T., Jay-Jay Bullnose, the kitchen staff and the women who cleaned the GAWP Bar at the Firebird, The Resurrection Brothers Band, the immortal Art Tatum, all the coloured folk who had been good to me in the past, can you forgive me?* I know I should have told the personnel manager to stick his job up his ass but, alas, I didn't.

The single quarters were just as Noel White had described them. Nobody was officially in charge; everyone had an identical rondavel with a polished red cement floor, containing a washbasin, cupboard, chest of drawers, small writing table and upright wooden chair beside a basic iron bed with bare mattress and pillow. It seemed the workers supplied their own linen. All the furniture except the mattress and cushion was pretty scuffed or battered. The round hut also featured a small verandah that stretched halfway around its circumference on either side of the reinforced steel door. The previous occupant had left a couple of battered wicker easy chairs behind.

It didn't take long for one of the Krauts, as Noel had termed them, to visit. In fact, an hour after the personnel department had allocated me a rondavel in the single quarters, there was a knock on the steel door. I opened it to see a guy standing outside whom I guessed to be in his mid-twenties. 'You are Jack,' he declared, stabbing a blunt finger at me.

Hearing his accent I was immediately on my guard. 'Yeah, that's me. Who wants to know?'

'*Meine* name is Hans, Hans Meyerhof. Ve have some rules I must explain, rules you must obey.'

'Oh? The personnel manager explained some of —'

He didn't allow me to finish. '*Ja*, that is mine rules. Here is single quarters' rules. Here ve must have some rules also, so everybody can understand.'

'Understand what, Mr Meyerhof?'

He looked momentarily confused. 'Of course – the rules.'

'And who makes these rules everybody has to understand?' I asked, a tad churlishly.

'The rules ve make by the committee.'

'Oh, I see! It's a committee elected by the guys who live in the single quarters?'

'Already I think maybe you ask too much question, Jack,' he said, looking directly at me and shaking his head; then, with a cluck of his tongue, he added, 'Ve have rules you *must* obey. That is all you must know now.'

It was clear our discussion had come to an end. 'And these rules are . . .?'

He looked a little less stern. '*Ja*, the rules, so now I must tell you. No voomen, but also ve can supply every month one, twenty pounds short time. No *schwartze . . . kaffir* women *verboten!* You vant man, you see Holz at the *cimbusu*, ze shower block, he can arrange. You want to drink something, beer, whisky, schnapps maybe? You buy from ze recreation hut. We got there *gut* bar. Shower block, for hot shower one time, one shilling; cold shower, you don't pay. When you are drunk, you go your rondavel, ve lock you in; morning again, ve come and open. You vant your hut cleaning? *Ja*, ve get you cleaning boy. You pay us two pounds for za month and we pay zat boy also.'

'That's okay, I prefer to do my own cleaning, thanks.'

He shook his head. 'Not permitted.'

It was just as Noel White had said. 'I see. Hans, you guys control everything, is that it?'

'*Ja*, it is better so.' He suddenly switched subjects. 'Vhat job you do in ze mine, Jack? You go underground? Learn mining, take blasting licence, then go work grizzly?'

'No, I'm the new night-shift medic.'

His attitude seemed to change and his eyes widened. '*Ja*? That is *gut*, maybe sometime you can help us. Maybe zere is some fighting, somebody drunk, maybe zey are hurt?'

'I'm on night shift. I don't suppose too many guys get drunk during the day and fight.'

He laughed. '*Ja*, it is true, but night shift begin late, and before zat, lots of time for guys, they getting drunk, *ja*? If you say you can help, you don't pay *cimbusu*, you don't pay shower block.'

'What? The shilling for a hot shower, or the other, with whatshisname?' I was getting annoyed. 'By the way, is a shit free?'

He didn't laugh. '*Ja*, is free. Hot shower also, if you help somebody hurt, so ve don't go Frau Hamilton . . . Mrs Hamilton.'

'What's wrong with them going to the cottage hospital?'

'Mrs Hamilton, she makes always trouble. She don't like za committee; ven somebody get hurt, she vant to know always what happen, everything.' Hans looked at me. 'We must have discipline! *Ja*, it is necessary always.'

Observing my doubtful expression he changed tack once again, pointing to the bare mattress and pillow. 'You vant to buy sheet, blanket for bed? Ve have *gut* one, second-hand, but also clean. One blanket, two sheet . . . but you must have four, also two pillow cover, for vashing, one pound ten shilling. The cleaning boy vash them, two sheets, pillow cover, every veek. You *must* be clean.'

I finally agreed I'd lend a hand if someone got hurt in a fight in the single quarters, then handed over the money for the second-hand bedding and the wage – with, no doubt, a percentage taken out by the committee – for the cleaner. I would later learn that I'd made the correct decision and that any newly arrived guy who hadn't had the benefit of a Noel White to advise him and so objected to the rules found himself dealt with by the committee in a cruel way.

The Nazi thugs would wait until he was under the shower, then grab him and hold him down while he was raped by one of their homosexual prostitutes. It was a way of warning the victim without leaving any outward signs of his ordeal. They also knew that he'd be too ashamed to go to mine management to complain.

With so many young guys locked up together without an outlet for their energy, drink was the usual form of relaxation and brawls were frequent. The committee possessed all the latest first-aid gear, to keep patients away from the redoubtable Matron Hamilton, and I would usually stitch up or bandage at least half a dozen young guys every few nights.

By agreeing to be the single-quarters medic, I'd once again taken the easy way out but, as a consequence, I was treated with respect by the greedy Nazi thugs and bullies I loathed. I guess the Las Vegas habit of not asking too many questions and keeping a low profile was hard to break.

For the first three weeks I attended the morning shift at the underground School of Mines under the direction of a tough-as-teak Welsh miner named Russell Howell – or Mr Howell, as he insisted on being called. He was a stern and uncompromising instructor, and I was glad I was only there as an observer to familiarise myself with the various underground activities in the mine. For some of the young foreign guys who didn't speak English all that well, his Welsh accent made it pretty tough going. However, I could see that after this ordeal they'd either leave or be sent packing, or they'd sit for their international blasting licence and then be thoroughly capable of running a grizzly, a job so dangerous that never a week went by there wasn't an accident or even a fatality. These guys, usually no older than twenty-three, couldn't wait to get onto a grizzly with a box of gelignite, a roll of cortex and a box of fuses and start making money. Next to the true professionals, the diamond drillers, engineers and shift bosses, working a grizzly was the highest-paid job in the mine and a young guy could earn some serious money.

I hadn't been with Mr Howell long when he approached me and said, 'Boyo, I've watched you and you're a good lad. Let me train you to be a grizzly man. You'll make three times the money.'

Grizzly men were paid a nominal salary and then a copper bonus on the amount of rock they emptied out of the stope and through their grizzly; the ultimate achievement for a grizzly man being to leave his diamond driller's stope empty after the night shift. This meant both he and the diamond driller got the maximum copper bonus for the shift. The South African diamond drillers would refer to their grizzly men as either 'eerste klaas [first class]' or 'kakhuis [shithouse]', cherishing the 'good' grizzly men and often seeing to it that the 'bad' ones were 'relocated'.

A grizzly man always worked the same grizzly, because each set of tungsten steel bars was said to have its own peculiarities; you learned to 'read your grizzly' and understand its personality. The men also believed they had to become attuned to the 'groan' of the surrounding rock, the particular sounds it made, which could be a matter of life or death. Unfortunately, a good grizzly man was often a young guy who would take chances and break the rules, and a bad one was someone inclined to be more cautious.

Like most young men, the so-called 'good' grizzly men believed they were bullet-proof. The war – especially the aborted landing at Dieppe where I'd lost my earlobe – had cured me of any such foolish notion, and every morning as I looked in the shaving mirror I was reminded that if the bullet had been an inch or two to the left, I'd have been dead as a dormouse, or worse, brain damaged or quadriplegic, with a face not even my stepfather could have reconstructed. My maimed hand, courtesy of Sammy Schischka, was another reminder of how easily you could lose what you valued most. But as a medic I'd seen plenty of bravado and foolish heroism, and often had to patch up the results.

I thanked Russell Howell for the compliment and then politely refused his offer to train me as a grizzly man. The Mafia murders of my old buddies Lenny and Johnny Diamond – the main reason I was in the middle of nowhere, buried deep underground – gave me more reasons to cherish the idea of remaining alive.

Nobody talked about it, but a grizzly was a potential killer, the most dangerous way to mine copper. But with the Korean War dragging on and a world greedy for the essential metal, it was also by far the most efficient way of extracting ore from a stope. I'd seen a diagram of the layout of a stope, with the grizzly bars at the bottom like a giant sieve, allowing only the smaller rocks to fall through to the shaft beneath, but nothing prepared me for the reality.

The stope was a huge hole blasted out of solid rock. Diamond drillers forced their diamond-tipped drill bits up to twenty-five feet deep into the walls of the stope, then packed the holes with gelignite. The ensuing blast would enlarge the stope, and cause an avalanche of ore and rock to fall to the bottom, where it passed through or jammed in the bars of the grizzly. The ore that fell through to the shaft beneath would be transported away from the stope; the remainder had to be forced through the gaps between the bars by the grizzly man's four black workers, using crowbars or mallets and balancing precariously on the bars. If that failed, the grizzly man had to clear the bars by blasting the rock with sticks of gelignite. After he lit the fuse he would have to scramble into a safety tunnel and hope for the best. When the shaft below the grizzly bars filled with ore, it was emptied in stages through a large steel bucket-like door that allowed through only enough ore to fill a single truck, one of fifty or so drawn behind an electric ore train, which would then shunt forward until the next truck was in position.

When full, the ore trucks were hauled to a vertical shaft to the surface, some eleven hundred or so feet above. The ore and rock were then fed onto a conveyer belt leading to the crusher, which pounded them to the consistency of coarse gravel. This was then loaded once again into trucks and hauled by train to the copper smelter. Here, the ore within the 'crush' was refined into copper ingots. The entire process was dangerous, but a miner's best chance of being killed or badly injured was working the grizzly.

The midnight-to-dawn shift kept me as 'busy as a blue-arsed fly', as Noel White would say. The mine employed about four thousand African mine workers, around a thousand of whom worked on one of the various underground levels on my shift. Only a very few of them worked the grizzlies, but it was during the night shift that rock that had been blasted during the afternoon was cleared. During these shifts I would have to treat injuries of varying severity, ranging from bad lacerations, muscle sprains and tears to fractures, and there would even be an occasional death.

The medic who had preceded me, Koos Dippenaar, had trained my medical team extremely well; there was very little they hadn't coped with in the past and I quickly grew to trust them implicitly. But here's the paradox: while they were perfectly capable, the white miners' union would not allow them to perform certain procedures; only white medics were deemed sufficiently skilful for these duties. Sutures, inserting a needle into a vein for a transfusion, using a hypodermic needle, administering aid in any way to a white man were all forbidden. This last one was the most stupid rule of all, and I decided that, should the situation ever arise where I was unable to supply the help needed, I would instruct one of my medics to do so in my stead. However, I was not naïve enough to let this be known among the white miners, particularly the diamond drillers, who, fortunately, seldom worked underground on the night shift.

My senior black medic was an impressive-looking man of around thirty named Daniel Mwanawasa from the local Bemba tribe, who was far more experienced and capable than I was, especially at the beginning when I had a great deal of trouble communicating with my medical team. One of my tasks at the School of Mines had been to study Cikabanga (pronounced Chi-ka-banga), a *lingua franca* used in the mines, consisting of words derived mainly from Zulu, with a sprinkling of English, Afrikaans, Portuguese and a few words from local tribal languages such as Chibemba. It was similar to Fanagalo, the pidgin used in mines in South Africa and the Belgian Congo. The name Fanagalo means, roughly, 'to be or do like this' in the Zulu language. Both have about two thousand words each.

For novice miners to develop a reasonable working knowledge of Cikabanga usually took all of the three months in the School of Mines and then some. Young miners generally had a minimal grasp of it, sufficient to get by underground, but the paucity of the communication between them and their gangs could be dangerous, leading to confusion and sometimes accidents. The professionals – diamond drillers, engineers and shift bosses – were, for the most part, fluent. I guess I was blessed with a musician's ear, and my ability to speak Cikabanga fairly well in just a few weeks was probably one of the reasons I impressed Russell Howell at the School of Mines.

But for the first six months or so, until I could speak quickly and easily, it was very difficult to work efficiently with my fellow medics. Still, I always enjoyed working with my team, who were generous in sharing their knowledge, anxious to acquaint me with local conditions. When we weren't working – bandaging, stemming haemorrhages, stitching wounds, resuscitating, injecting, stabilising fractures – we laughed a lot; nice guys, all four of them. They'd given themselves European names for their white bosses, and were known as Daniel, Samson, Milo and Jacob. Jacob was a Luba, from the Katanga region across the border in the Belgian Congo, and when things got difficult he would curse in French, oblivious to the fact that I had studied French to a fairly proficient level in high school and could understand most of what he said, some of it directed at white guys when they were being difficult: *branleur* – wanker; *casse toi* – piss off, get lost; *débile* – idiot; and of course the well-known *merde* – shit. I never let on that I understood these less-than-complimentary expressions, and when they were directed at me in the beginning, after I'd made some fundamental mistake, I took the criticism as part of my education.

What the other three may have said in their own language I shall never know. But after a while, all my training as a medic came back to me. With my eidetic memory, the various courses I'd taken under Nick Reed's direction during the war came back to me in detail, so that I was able to cope reasonably well. When there were no white guys about, I taught my team stuff I knew and that they were not permitted to do. The idea that someone should be banned from potentially saving a life because of the colour of their skin was anathema to me.

Life on the night shift wasn't all that different from working at the GAWP Bar at the Firebird, except that I had the early evenings to myself. Noel White and his wife, Judy, would often invite me to dinner. I made a few friends at the Club, not the recreation room and bar in the single quarters run by the Krauts, but the social club for all the miners and their wives. I'd spend a couple of hours at the pool (referred to as the 'swimming bath') or in the Club gym, but mostly I read my Penguin paperbacks or something I'd taken out of the Club library, or I'd study medical stuff.

When I'd settled in, I bought a record player in Ndola and ordered a stack of the new long-playing records – classical, jazz and blues – plus some sheet music by mail-order from a catalogue I found in the Club. The firm that produced the catalogue, Polliacks, had stores in Johannesburg, Cape Town and Pretoria, and claimed to be the biggest music shop in

Africa. They even featured a Steinway grand in their catalogue, though I couldn't help wondering who would buy such an expensive instrument by mail-order. I'd asked them on the order form if they stocked jazz and blues sheet music, and when the records arrived, they'd included the score for George Gershwin's opera *Porgy and Bess*, 'With compliments'. It wasn't exactly what I'd had in mind but I was to find that much of it could be adapted for the harmonica.

I was corresponding with my mom and Nick through using a private post-office box, and I'd often ask Nick for detailed medical information. With the doctor only visiting twice a week to attend to white patients, and the African hospital for black patients thirty miles away in Ndola, I was having to do rather more than I was trained to. Matron Suzanna Hamilton was a marvel and seemed to have every certificate a nurse could possess. But sometimes, when it came to a black miner, it was a choice between doing what I could and his certain death.

Of course, some miners died despite my attempts to save them and this caused me a great deal of distress, whether it was my fault or not. In some cases they'd have died even if we'd had a surgeon standing by. I can't tell you how bad it feels to see a man die in front of your eyes, just because you lack the necessary skills to save his life and you know he'd never have reached the hospital in Ndola in time.

As the year drew on, the wet season began, with constant rain, mud and slush. There was mould everywhere, and everything felt damp. It was the time of year when the ambulance had to be loaded onto a train because the road to Ndola, or anywhere else, was impassable.

I'd been underground about six months when one night, at about 2 a.m., a call came to attend an accident on a grizzly on the eleven hundred level; that is, 1100 feet down. When we got there, the grizzly man's leg was trapped between the bars, jammed between rocks. He explained that he'd been crossing the rocks to lay a charge to break up several large boulders at the far end of the grizzly when they'd suddenly shifted and he'd slipped, trapping his right leg. His black gang were unwilling, or too frightened, to use crowbars to attempt to free him. It was a dangerous situation because, while rocks were not as yet coming down the funnel from the stope, there was always a chance that one would. A rock the size of a football falling sixty feet would kill a man if it landed on his head, or rip his arm off if it hit his shoulder. In a great deal of pain, the grizzly man had sent one of his 'boys' to fetch me.

I could see he was losing blood from what might have been a compound fracture. Without my having to ask them, my three medics grabbed crowbars. We were supposed to wear safety chains but the accident had occurred at the far end of the grizzly, and the chains barely stretched that far, which was dangerous if we needed to move quickly. The grizzly man himself had decided against using his chain when he'd gone to lay the gelignite charge. So, we walked the bars without chains. Straddling two bars eighteen inches apart, my medics set about trying to lever the rocks apart sufficiently to free his leg. The grizzly man's name was Karel Pretorius, and while he was pretty stoic, it was, of necessity, a crude procedure and he screamed in agony as I finally pulled his leg free.

Daniel and Samson then carried him off the bars – a dangerous manoeuvre – as Milo followed, hovering anxiously. I was ahead of Jacob, who was holding the, now bloody, crowbar. There was a sudden scream and I turned in time to see Jacob disappear between the bars. A small rock the size of a tennis ball had fallen out of the stope and down the grizzly shaft. It hit him on the shoulder blade, knocking him off balance and sending him tumbling down through the bars to fall some thirty feet, landing on the rock half filling the shaft below. Somehow he'd landed on his heels and butt before tumbling, but at the same time more material fell from the stope, creating a small rain of rocks. Fortunately, I was able to jump clear of the bars just in time, having been afraid that the small rock might have been holding up a mass of larger ones that were about to come crashing down on us. Such a blockage was known as a 'bunch of grapes', and this is what had occurred.

Fortunately, Jacob had tumbled down a slope until he landed directly under the large rocks from which we'd extracted the grizzly man's leg, so that these now acted as a roof to protect him from the small avalanche of rocks as he lay thirty feet below us. Miraculously, despite the nasty fall, he seemed okay at first, though I could see his left shoulder had been dislocated when the small rock struck him. Then he tried to sit up and it immediately became apparent that his left arm was wedged under several rocks and he was unable to move it, no doubt because of the intense pain of the dislocation.

I instructed Daniel to give Karel Pretorius a shot of morphine and then, with Samson and Milo, to apply a tourniquet to slow the bleeding and apply a splint to the broken bone. Black medics were forbidden to perform some of these procedures, of course, but fuck it, Karel Pretorius wasn't going to be allowed to die and Jacob had every chance of being killed if a big run started in the stope ninety feet above him.

It never occurred to me at the time that it was forbidden to rescue a black miner if he fell down a grizzly shaft and wasn't able to be pulled free using a rope or safety chain. In effect, if he were partially buried under rock, even if he were still alive, like Jacob, it was, as Noel White would say, 'All over Red Rover, poor bugger'll soon be pushing up clover!' A white medic climbing down into the shaft below the grizzly bars to rescue a trapped black miner was unthinkable to mine authorities and, apart from being forbidden, was plain insanity.

I know it was stupid of me but, at the time, with the adrenalin still running from having rescued Karel Pretorius, this didn't occur to me, and what other choice did I have, anyway? I clipped three safety chains together, anchored one end around a grizzly bar and lowered myself the thirty or so feet to where Jacob lay. When I reached him I tried to extract his arm, but it was clear that, even with the crowbar Milo lowered to me, this wasn't going to work. Jacob's shoulder was dislocated, and almost half of his arm was trapped in rock I had no hope of moving. Nothing short of blasting would work, and Jacob would have been killed in the process. I had to face the fact that the only way to free Jacob was to amputate his arm. His forearm was crushed and the bones protruding from the skin, the entire arm bent at an unnatural angle. Disastrous as it sounds, this came as a relief; it meant I wouldn't have to use the bone saw.

Thank God for the hours I'd spent pouring over *Gray's Anatomy*. I had a medical bag lowered to me containing tourniquets, hypodermic syringes, morphine, scalpels, iodine solution, swabs, clamps and sutures. It was one of our special medical kits we hoped we'd never have to use.

Jacob had lapsed into unconsciousness, but I injected the morphine just in case, my mind trying desperately to recall the three demonstrations I'd attended as a medic in the army. I secured a tourniquet around his upper arm to stop further blood loss, and washed the arm liberally with iodine solution, dousing my hands in it as well, in an attempt to protect the wound from contamination while I made the incisions.

The brain is an amazing organ. If you've seen, heard, experienced or read something, the knowledge remains tucked away in some tiny crevice of it, and, although I seemed to be working almost by instinct, I knew that I could trust my poker-player's memory. My main task was to ensure that I made the incision as close as possible to the break, and that I left sufficient skin and muscle to form a pad over the severed bones so that when Jacob got into the operating theatre, the surgeon could tidy him up. That is, of course, if he survived the shock of the injury and what I was preparing to do to him.

I made the first incision, cutting around the circumference of the arm and into the muscle, then angling the cut upward towards the elbow to expose the broken ends of the radius and ulna. Fortunately, the breaks were clean, which would, I hoped, minimise the need for further bone removal. Once I had removed the forearm, I clamped off the radial and ulnar arteries and the two main veins, then tied them off. The minor blood vessels still oozed a little blood but there wasn't much more I could do, apart from sloshing on more iodine and placing a large dressing over the stump.

It was only then that I realised what a desperate situation we were in. I looked up, and the torch on my hard hat illuminated the bottom of the rocks that had trapped the grizzly man's leg and protected Jacob and myself so fortuitously. I couldn't imagine how either of us would get back up safely to the grizzly bars, but somehow we did, Jacob still blessedly unconscious as he was jolted back up. I shall never forget the faces of Karel Pretorius's black grizzly gang. One of them was grinning fit to burst, clapping his hands and almost dancing with delight. Sometimes you are forced to accept that there is a god in heaven. If we could get Jacob out safely and I could minimise the time the tourniquet remained on his arm, he was young enough and fit enough to make it. Later, Daniel would inform me that the grizzly gang claimed to have seen the impossible, and that I had become known across the Copperbelt as a white man who had risked his life for a black man. Apparently, I was no longer known as Bwana Jack, but as *Ingelosi*, or Angel, Doctor Canada.

My own indelible memory of that night was of the severed part of Jacob's forearm – crimson, ivory and black – sticking out of grey rock.

I won't recount the tedious and difficult process of getting both men back to the surface, but when eventually we did, I insisted they travel in the waiting ambulance to be taken to the cottage hospital. There they could be cared for by Matron Hamilton until the doctor arrived to perform the necessary surgery and decide when Jacob would be fit enough to travel to the Ndola Hospital.

I would be censured for this later, but not by Suzanna Hamilton. She refused to relinquish Jacob for three days until Dr Patel, the Indian doctor, pronounced it safe for him to travel to Ndola Hospital for more specialised care.

Whether Karel Pretorius knew that Daniel and Samson had performed forbidden procedures to effect his treatment at the grizzly, I can't say, but he had nothing but praise for the way he had been rescued. And, although he was white, and an Afrikaner to boot, he made no fuss about having to recuperate in the bed opposite Jacob's in the cottage hospital, even demanding that the sheet someone had hung from the ceiling between their beds be removed.

In addition, Daniel and Samson received a certificate of merit from the Red Cross and a commendation from the mine management. They were proud to receive these marks of appreciation, and I was glad there'd been no unpleasantness. I guess I shall never understand how race relations work in Africa. We'd done dozens of procedures on black miners underground, but everyone decided to acknowledge this particular one; I suppose to be seen to be promoting harmonious relations between blacks and whites.

For my part, I confess I was rather pleased when the surgeon at the Ndola Hospital phoned to tell me I'd done a commendable job on Jacob's arm and that there was no gangrene or other infection. I suspect Matron Hammond should have taken the credit for that, but I was pleased to hear that the surgeon was fairly confident Jacob would eventually recover without any complications beyond a missing forearm.

Life continued and I visited Jacob in Ndola Hospital over several weekends until he was fit to be sent home across the border, with a ten-pound accident gratuity payment, and a train ticket back to Katanga province, from the mine management. As he boarded the train to Elisabethville, I said my farewells in French, 'Merci mille fois et je vous bénis [A thousand thanks and bless you].'

Jacob's eyes widened. 'Vous avez compris tout le temps, bwana? [You understood all the time, bwana?]' he replied.

'Bien sûr [Of course],' I answered as the guard blew his whistle and the train began to move away. He was a bit of a character and I was going to miss him. Poor bastard, with one arm and a shoulder that would never again work perfectly, he was in for a tough time.

One of Karel Pretorius's grizzly gang, who called himself Jackson, applied for Jacob's job on the medic team, which came as something of a surprise. Working on a grizzly paid considerably more than working as a medic, even a fully trained one, but he'd been the one with a smile as big as a slice of watermelon who had almost broken into a dance after Jacob's rescue.

I managed to negotiate Jackson's transfer with the help of Jannie Coetzee in the personnel department, even though he didn't handle native recruitment. When I went in to see him about it, Jannie drew me aside to warn me. 'Jack, the union is furious, very, very upset, man. They told me in confidence it's only because Karel Pretorius refuses to make a written complaint that they're letting it go this time. But I'm warning you, man, don't do anything like it again. That grizzly incident was stupid, you hear?' Then he added, 'I'm talking to you as a friend, Jack. Remember, it was only a *kaffir*. With one arm he might as well be dead; he can't earn a living for himself or his family now.'

'He was a good guy,' I replied, 'I'll miss him.' I suddenly recalled one occasion when I'd visited him in hospital, which in itself had caused a few raised eyebrows. Jacob had pointed to my hand and said, 'Now we are brothers, Bwana Ingelosi Doctor Canada.'

'That's enough, Jacob,' I'd said, trying to sound stern, 'the name is absurd. I've told the team simply to call me Bwana or Bwana Jack and that includes you, my friend.' But I was touched by the idea of Jacob being my brother.

Jannie Coetzee shook his head. 'You Canadians, you don't understand, do you?' He paused. 'But I got to hand it to you, Jack. With the *kaffirs*, you're now a god, man. Bwana Ingelosi Doctor Canada, that's a *blerrie* big compliment man, *kaffirs* don't just hand out names like that.'

And so, another six months went by, with numerous medical incidents but nothing out of the ordinary – lacerations, sprains, fractures – with the exception of a young Czech grizzly man who fell through the bars while wearing his safety chain, which jerked him to a stop and snapped his spine, putting him in a wheelchair. So much for working to the rules. Everyone knew that wearing a safety chain on a grizzly was potentially as dangerous as going without one. The rules were only there to cover management's ass should a white guy be badly injured or killed and there was a coroner's enquiry.

Then one day Daniel approached me and asked if he and the team could visit me at my rondavel in the single quarters the following Saturday. Technically, there was nothing to stop them, but the Krauts forbade anyone but cleaning staff and servants from entering the area without permission. I hated the bastards but knew it was pointless protesting and went to see Hans Meyerhof, who seemed in a good mood. Thank Christ news of Jacob's rescue hadn't reached the Nazis. Before I'd opened my mouth, he said, 'Jack, you like to play cards?'

I remembered Noel White's warning about the poker professionals who periodically came into the single quarters to skin the unwary. It wasn't quite how he'd put it but, nevertheless, I was pretty sure such a game would be rigged in some way. 'Why do you ask?' I replied.

'In two weeks, Saturday night, is coming some friends. They wish to make poker school. Maybe you want to play also?'

'For fun?' I asked.

'*Ja*, maybe a little money, only a few pounds, but maybe you win some.'

'I'll think about it,' I said, then asked him about my medic team visiting. I'd bandaged a few heads after drunken Saturday-night fights and figured I was in the Krauts' good books.

'Maybe it is okay, but maybe also you want to play with our friends some poker, *ja*? You will enjoy,' he assured me. He was obviously indicating that one favour deserved another.

'When?'

'Saturday two weeks; six o'clock at the recreation hut, drinks are on the house, compliments za committee.'

'What are the stakes?' I asked.

'Okay. We start five-pound limit; zen after zat, the school, zey decide.'

I whistled, feigning shock., 'Five pounds. Jesus, I dunno if I want to risk that much, it's been a long time since I played. Sounds way out of my league, Hans.'

'*Ach*, no, don't vorry, ve are all friends togezzer, Jack.'

Yeah right, I thought.

From what Noel White had told me, together with the odd bit of gossip I'd picked up around the place, the visiting players seemed to clean up regularly. Funny that. Two weeks gave me time to make a few enquiries. In fact, maybe, just maybe, I could get a little of our own back, I mean, something for the guys in the single quarters, who, like me, were kept firmly under the thumb of the Germans. 'Can I think about it, Hans?' I asked.

'For sure, Jack. But ve *must* see you, Saturday, two veeks, okay?' There it was . . . *you must obey!*

Even better, I thought. I've been nominated as the sucker. 'Any other locals playing?' I asked, my expression a mixture of wariness and uncertainty.

'*Ja*, always some,' Hans replied. 'You vill like zem, Jack.' As always, liking them sounded compulsory.

I sighed. 'Okay, count me in, Hans.'

'*Gut. Ja*, okay, you can bring your *kaffir* gang zis Saturday, but only one hour.' Hans Meyerhof was smiling like a fucking Cheshire cat or whatever the German equivalent might be.

If I'd been offered a million pounds to guess what would happen next, I wouldn't have even gotten close. As arranged, Daniel, Samson, Milo and Jackson arrived outside my hut that Saturday, accompanied, to my astonishment, by Jacob.

'*Bonjour, Bwana Ingelosi* Doctor Canada!' he said, laughing at my obvious surprise.

'Jacob! *Je n'en reviens pas* . . . [I can't believe . . .]'

And then I saw it. Perched on what remained of his severed arm was a parrot, a grey parrot that stood about twelve inches high, with red tail feathers.

I changed to Cikabanga for the benefit of the others. 'What have you got on your arm?' I exclaimed.

'It is a gift of thanks from my people, *Bwana Ingelosi* Doctor Canada.'

'Jacob, his father, he is chief,' Daniel explained. 'Many, many peoples, this tribe, *bwana*.'

I was incredulous. 'A parrot, a gift? But how will I look after such a nice gift?' I asked, trying hard to look pleased, so as not to hurt Jacob's feelings. He'd obviously slipped over the border with the parrot and walked god knows how far to get to Luswishi River.

This produced laughter all round. 'No, *Bwana Ingelosi* Doctor Canada, you must kill the parrot.'

'What!' I cried, taken completely by surprise. It wasn't the most attractive bird I'd ever seen, but even so . . .

Jacob stroked the parrot's breast with his forefinger and ruffled its neck feathers, then indicated the crop. 'Inside is the gift, *bwana.*' Then, in French, he said quietly, '*Diamants . . . bijoux* [Diamonds . . . jewels].'

'Diamonds! You mean there is a diamond in its crop?' I couldn't believe what he was telling me.

'Many *bwana*, many *diamants,*' Jacob said, grinning.

They all nodded happily, the French word for diamond too similar to the English one for them not to understand. 'You will be rich, *bwana,*' Jackson laughed, then added, 'I will kill for you this bird.'

In the meantime the parrot had hopped onto Jacob's shoulder. I knew that in the Congo Africans who were caught mining alluvial diamonds were instantly shot. Jacob had risked his life, or those of some of his father's tribe, to repay me for saving his own.

'No, no, I cannot kill it!' I protested.

'It is only a bird, *Bwana* Jack. Inside is the gift,' Jacob said.

'Ah, is that like "*It's only a* kaffir, *let him die?*"' I mimicked.

There was a roar of approval from the team and Jackson broke into a handclapping dance. 'Maybe, one day when you need help, like you helped me, *bwana*, then the diamonds will be there,' Jacob said, laughing, accepting my point.

'But how old is he? When will he die naturally? Perhaps then?'

Jacob laughed again. 'We have him in the village, in my father house, since he was a little baby, but he is two-and-a-half years only. He will live many, many years, more than you even, *bwana.*'

The little parrot had cocked its head and I swear was looking at me. Then suddenly, almost as if making up its mind, it took off and landed on my right shoulder. 'See, *Bwana* Jack, he knows you already,' Jacob cried happily.

'I shall call him Diamond Jim,' I said, reaching up and stroking the parrot with my damaged hand. The little fellow immediately nibbled my hand and then nuzzled his head into my hand. It was mutual love at first sight.

After my team had gone and I'd thanked Jacob profusely, I procured a cardboard box from the mess kitchen, knocked holes in it, so Diamond

Jim could breathe, then phoned Noel White and asked him if I could borrow his family car to go to Ndola. 'Of course, Jack,' he replied.

'I need to buy a big birdcage. Where would I find one?' I asked, aware he knew the town inside out.

'The town's closed, mate . . . I mean, the shops. Saturday arvo, everything's shut tight as a duck's arse. Don't worry about the car. My neighbour's kids used to keep half a dozen budgies but they're down south, the kids, not the budgies, at university, so he gave them away to another family. I'm sure he's still got the cage. Wait on, he's working in his shed, I spoke to him half an hour ago, I'll ask. Can you hang on a mo?'

Noel returned a couple of minutes later. 'Sure thing, mate, you're welcome to it. I'll bring it around in the van. Gimme an hour or so.' As usual, Noel didn't question me. Why I wanted a birdcage was my business and he stuck, as always, to the three monkeys code.

I was somewhat apprehensive that the cage might be too big for my rondavel but, as it turned out, it fitted nicely. It was a large wooden and mesh box on four legs, just the right size for a parrot. 'Perfect!' I exclaimed. 'How much do I owe your neighbour?'

Noel looked surprised. 'He's happy to get rid of it out of his shed, mate. Carpentry's his hobby, he made it himself.'

'No, I must,' I insisted. 'It's a nice cage and he must have paid for the timber and wire mesh, never mind his time.'

Noel didn't argue. 'Gimme a quid and I'll buy him a case of Lion Lager, he likes South African beer,' he said. Then, seeing Diamond Jim perched on the windowsill, said, 'Shit, that's one ugly bloody bird!'

I laughed. 'He's a male.'

'Thank god for that. Wouldn't want a sheila lookin' as bad as that! You gunna teach him to talk, Jack?'

'Yeah, I hope to, but I know nothing about parrots.'

'Me neither, except that he's a Congo African Grey.'

'Oh, thanks; that's a start, anyhow.'

But, I must say, I wasn't at all sure what I was going to do with a greyish-green and, I admit, far from attractive African Grey parrot with a purported stash of diamonds in his crop. Or, for that matter, what the Krauts might have to say about the possibility of parrot shit in my rondavel. *Ziz bird kak on za floor everyvere, you must kill him! Ja, ve must have clean!*

With the poker game in two weeks, maybe I could negotiate, insist I do my own cleaning. But what about afterwards, if I managed to achieve what I had planned? Diamond Jim's life might well prove to be a short and far from happy one.

CHAPTER TWENTY-FOUR

FROM THE GOSSIP I'D picked up in the months I'd been at Luswishi River Copper Mine, I'd decided the poker games organised by the Krauts had to be rigged. The 'visitors' from across the Congo border cleaned up the locals way too frequently. They were either the best players I'd ever heard of or they were running some sort of scam. Even the best players don't always pocket the cash. Moreover, as with most con men and cardsharps, they always left a little butter on the bread, allowing a few bucks . . . sorry, pounds . . . to fall into the laps of the locals; twenty-five or fifty pounds, certainly no more, just sufficient for the winners to boast about their win and make the game look straight.

While living in Las Vegas, and like most gamblers who take their game fairly seriously, I'd developed an almost obsessive interest in how the odds worked in just about every game of chance ever invented. Knowing guys like Johnny Diamond, I'd been exposed to what went on behind the scenes, and learned the immutable rule for gambling professionals: that if someone is defying the odds over time, then it isn't luck. They are not beating the odds, they are simply altering them. This applies to any game of chance. Sure, casino games and the slots were designed so the punter would eventually lose, or rather the house had to win. But even in poker, a card game that involves a fair degree of skill, players are still subject to the same rule. Nobody, not even the best player in the world, wins constantly; everyone has bad days. Sometimes the cards just don't fall the right way. You don't get the card you need to fill an open-ended straight, the diamond doesn't fall for a flush, or the third king doesn't come to make three of a kind. Worse still, your opponent gets the cards he needs all damned night. That's poker, always has been, always will be.

However, I know one more immutable human rule: if a school of poker players feels they've been cheated, then they'll make sure the cheats get what's coming to them, usually a very painful experience. The saying, hell hath no fury like a woman scorned, pales into insignificance compared with when a bunch of 'bunnies' find out they've been cheated at cards.

I approached Noel White and asked him if he'd let me have the names of any guys who'd played in poker games organised by the Krauts against the visitors from across the border.

'Jack, you know the rules. No names no pack drill. Besides, you told me you don't play cards.'

I came clean then and told him the truth. He nodded. 'And they've invited you to play and you've agreed?' I nodded too and then told him I planned to find out if they were cheating. 'Shit, Jack, are you sure you know what you're doing? We've all thought like you but none of us has ever been able to find anything wrong. Sure, the French . . . er, Belgian guys clean up, but that's because they're good.'

I then explained. 'If they do it every time and allow one or two of the local players to pocket a bit of a win, always one or two guys in a game who get ahead of their stake by twenty-five or fifty quid, then they're cheating. Nothing more certain, buddy.'

'Well, there's Jannie Coetzee, of course. That's why he's pretty lenient with the Kraut fuckers in the single quarters. They keep quiet about him playing a game that's illegal to play for money in the colony, so it doesn't get to mine management.' He shrugged. 'And in return . . . well, you know the rest.'

'What are you saying? Jannie Coetzee is in on the scam?'

Noel looked askance. 'Jesus, no way! Jannie Coetzee is straight as a die. Most of the Afrikaner diamond drillers are; it's just that they're Afrikaners, a stubborn breed. They hate *kaffirs* and get angry when they're conned or even contradicted. They're what you'd call a *definite* bunch of blokes. You don't want to get one who's religious, he'll tell you they're one of the lost tribes of Israel or some such bullshit, but don't try changing their opinions if you know what's good for you. Know what I mean?'

'Well then, what about getting a group we can trust into the game? Guys who've played before, so the Krauts don't suspect anything.'

'What, and you'll brief us? Mate, I know about the black bloke's amputation; you don't want to go shitting in your own nest again.' His eyes narrowed. 'Jack, how fucking good are you?'

I shrugged. 'Good enough, I reckon.' He looked doubtful. 'Noel, I'm very, very good.'

'Righto, Jack, if you can pull this off, even the diamond drillers in the union will forgive you for saving that black guy. Jesus, mate, I don't think you know how fortunate you are that Karel Pretorius stood up for you. You're lucky you weren't on the next train outa Ndola, carrying a very bruised body and a bone or two out of position, mate. You sure you know what you're doing?' His concern for me was genuine.

'Noel, I wasn't a full-time professional in Las Vegas but I played with some of the best players in America and won my fair share. If these Congo guys are not fixing the game, I'll take what's coming to me. But we'll try to set it up so that if the game is straight, we all go home knowing we were beaten by better poker players and not by a couple of cheats.'

'I can see you doubt that's gunna happen,' Noel replied.

'Well, put it this way, I'd be very surprised; delighted, in fact. It would mean I could play whenever I wanted. The only reason I haven't played is that I loathe those Nazi bastards. Every one of that so-called committee says '*Jawohl!*' to Hans Meyerhof and practically clicks their heels together. It's always a bad idea to play with someone you dislike intensely – too easy to let your emotions cloud your vision rather than playing the cards you're dealt well.'

He nodded. 'Fair enough. Tell you what, I'll invite a bunch of blokes I know have played in the past.'

'No, Noel; ask guys who've been several times, played often enough to have won a bit once or twice.'

'Sure, I get the drift, Jack.'

He arranged a meeting at his home for the following Saturday and Judy turned on a *braaivleis* – that's a barbecue to the uninitiated, but even Noel had learned to use the South African term. Jannie Coetzee was there with three diamond drillers I'd met once or twice, Russell Howell from the School of Mines, and two other drillers I'd seen around but hadn't actually met. If I could convince the guests at the barbecue – sorry, *braaivleis* – then, together with the two guys from the Congo, that would make ten, enough for a poker table with a couple of guys to spare.

Noel, while cooking sausages, outlined why we were there, although I think he'd already given everyone a fair idea. Then he introduced me and mentioned my experience in Las Vegas; just that I'd lived and played poker there and knew what's what.

'Thanks for coming, guys,' I said, then explained why I was convinced that the game with the Congo guys was rigged.

Jannie Coetzee interjected. 'But hey, Jack, the German guys don't even play. So, what's in it for them?'

I realised that I was going to have to be very careful with my answers. 'Jannie, I'm guessing they take a share of the winnings from the Congo guys, which would make it well worth their while to set up these games.' I looked around at the group. 'Someone here take a stab. What do you think they would take out of a game, the two guys from over the border?'

The men looked at each other. 'Jesus Christ, boyo, two thousand pounds, maybe a little more? I've been known to drop a couple of hundred,' Russell Howell admitted. Several in the group nodded.

'*Ja*, maybe, man. I never thought of that before,' Jannie Coetzee admitted. 'That's why they're so keen on putting on a game. They always say it's just a friendly game with the guys from across the border.'

'Why would you suspect their motives?' I said, in an attempt at appeasement, although I was surprised they hadn't questioned these games a lot more closely before this. 'Look, you guys are professional miners, not professional poker players. You may know everything about drilling a shaft or a stope or blasting ore, but you play cards to relax, have a bit of fun, win a bit, lose a bit, it's just recreation.'

'It's been fucking expensive recreation, boyo, if that's what you want to call it,' Russell Howell ventured again to general laughter as we helped ourselves to bread and meat.

'You can say that again!' Piet Wenzel shouted.

'Well, what's the decision?' Noel asked, looking at the guys, who now had plates of charred meat on their laps.

There was a general mumble of acquiescence. 'Count me in,' Jannie Coetzee cried, waving a half-eaten sausage.

'Me too, boyo,' Russell said. And all the others followed with nods or 'Yeah, me too, man!'

'How many of the Germans usually attend a game?' I asked.

'They generally make it a bit of a party. The twenty guys on the committee are usually there,' said Bokkie Prinsloo, one of the diamond drillers.

'Then we'll need some backup in case things go wrong,' I suggested. 'But choose guys who can play poker, so if they're needed they can sit in on the game, as well as break a few heads.'

'Leave that to me,' Jannie Coetzee volunteered. 'Jack, are you going to cheat? Show us how, then we can give them a taste of their own *mutie*?' *Mutie* was the Cikabanga word for 'medicine'.

I shook my head. 'Nah, we'll keep it straight. If we can screw up their scam, they're going to be thrown off their natural game anyhow. The very fact they may be cheating means they can't be that good in the first place.' I paused and looked around the group. 'I'd like to think we can play the game straight, but why not take the opportunity of getting back some of the money you've lost in the past?'

There was cheering all round. 'And you think you can do that, Jack?' Noel asked.

I grinned. 'We can give it a damn good try.'

'*Heere*, man, I lost two weeks' copper bonus last time I played,' Piet Wenzel said. 'Let's go get the fockers.'

'I'm going to need one of you to liaise with me, someone the Krauts absolutely trust.'

They all looked at Jannie Coetzee. 'Jannie, you?' I asked.

'*Ja*, that's okay by me, Jack. What do I do?'

'Well, for a start, I want you to come with me to buy four packs of new cards, brand-new sealed packs from the Club. Then, should we decide to introduce new packs into the game, you can tell them you were with me when we bought them and that they're legit, haven't been tampered with. Oh, and by the way, I guess you all drink a fair bit during the game? This time, bring just one drink to the table, and nurse it, don't have a second. Please, it's important.'

They looked at each other. 'Jesus, no grog?' Noel cried.

'Just one drink when we start the game, so they don't suspect anything. But it's important to stay off the booze if we're going to pull this off.'

'The Congo guys do a lot of talking, but it's in their lingo. What if that's how they're, you know, cheating?' Noel said.

'That would be great. I'm a Canadian. A lot of us speak reasonable French.'

This brought a general laugh.

'But . . . but, Jack, lad, the Jerries, they'll close the game down if they realise we've found out they're cheating,' Russell Howell said. 'They're ex-SS, they're not stupid. Well, Hans Meyerhof isn't.'

I shook my head. 'That's precisely why he won't close it down. He knows if the story gets out that they've been cheating, he and his committee will be torn limb from limb.'

'You're focking right there, man,' Piet Wenzel growled.

'So, as they say in Las Vegas, Hans Meyerhof will be made an offer he can't refuse. We'll give him an out. How much have you guys lost in the past? Counting the guys you're going to bring as backup – four, five thousand pounds?'

'Make it six, Jack,' Noel laughed. 'Just to be on the safe side.'

'Okay, you can have a private chat with Hans Meyerhof, Jannie. Tell him we're onto him and we want him to keep the game going until his two Congo stooges have lost six grand, then they can get out and we'll keep our mouths shut about the cheating.'

Jannie Coetzee started to laugh, and the others joined in; the prospect of revenge was truly sweet.

'Okay, gentlemen,' Noel said, 'I guess that's it. Let's have a drink or five. Let Jannie here know if the Krauts invite you to play next Saturday and, of course, if you've accepted.' They all nodded. 'Show a bit of reluctance – not too much, just something like "Shit, last time I lost my shirt. But okay, what the hell . . . " That kind of thing. In other words, act normal.'

I could see the union guys had changed their opinion of me. I wondered how any of these men would feel if they knew what was contained in Jacob's gift. 'See you all at the game next Saturday. Jannie, you and I will have to talk before then.'

'My office, any afternoon, Jack; I'll tell the dragon you're coming,' he laughed.

I spent the next week getting to know Diamond Jim. He liked several types of grain and lots of fruit, and we quickly took to each other, getting on like a house on fire. Maybe I was just imagining it, but it struck me he was pretty intelligent. For instance, he only shat in his cage, which had a removable tray and was easy to clean.

I wrote off to the Audubon Society in New York and, of course, Foyles Bookshop, asking each to send me any information they had on the African Grey Parrot and enclosing cheques I hoped would cover costs. I had a half-formed idea about Diamond Jim, so every afternoon

I practised the harmonica for two hours with the little guy perched on my shoulder, swinging my body in time to the music and bobbing from one foot to the other. It was good exercise, even if it didn't teach my parrot a thing. Then I decided to buy a mirror so that I could check if my new partner was reacting to any of the stuff I was playing. In the week leading up to the big poker game, Diamond Jim simply cocked his head at me and blinked his big, intelligent eyes. But I told myself to be patient; poor little guy must still be unsettled by the move.

On the Thursday afternoon before the poker game, I dropped in to see Jannie Coetzee and got what passed for a smile from Mrs Dulledge. *If ever anyone was well named*, I thought. Jannie Coetzee suggested his secretary go to the staff canteen for a cup of tea. He had a big voice that carried through walls, so after she left, with a toss of her head, Jannie noted, '*Ja*, just in case, you never know. Noel White's got this expression, "stickybeak"; that's her, man. So, now we can talk, Jack,' he continued, adding, 'afterwards we'll go and buy those cards.'

'Jannie, there isn't a lot to talk about. As you know, it's usual to change cards a couple of times during a game, so if I find out they're cheating, I'll get up to take a piss, and shortly afterwards you do the same and I'll brief you on what to do. It's best the others don't know what's happening, so they'll play their normal game. You'll call the shots to my directions, okay?'

'*Ja*, that's fine by me, Jack.'

'So, when it's time to bring the new packs into the game, you'll do it.'

'*Ja*, okay, but you know, in the past when they present new packs, they're always sealed, they break the seals in front of our eyes.'

'Buddy, any cardsharp worth his salt knows how to reseal a pack of cards so not even an expert can tell they've been opened and marked. Just grin and say you bought them at the Club on a whim, you thought it might change your luck . . . something like that.'

'And we don't do the same, mark ours?'

'No. If I'm right, we can do this straight, Jannie; no fancy tricks.'
I hoped to hell I *was* right, otherwise I was going to have a lot of

explaining to do. My guys would be bringing big bucks to the table, hoping to win back some or all of the money they'd lost.

We left to purchase the cards and Jannie Coetzee took charge of them. 'So long, Jack, see you at the game, Saturday, six o'clock sharp.'

'Jannie, for Chrissake, tell the others not to have a free drink or two at the bar before the game, it's very important they're sober.'

'*Ja*, understood, I'll tell them all. Thanks, Jack.'

Saturday night came and I put Diamond Jim into his cage and stroked the tiny soft feathers on his head. He nuzzled his beak and face into my hand and made a sort of throaty rattling sound. 'Wish me luck, buddy,' I said, closing the door of his cage. Then, almost on cue, he gave out a loud chirp. 'Thanks, buddy,' I called back. Diamond Jim was the nicest thing to happen to me in a long time, and I couldn't help but wonder in what condition I might be when next I opened his cage.

Apart from my intense dislike of the Germans in the so-called committee, they frightened me. I was familiar with men who made their own rules. Las Vegas had taught me to keep quiet and knuckle under and when I hadn't done so . . . well, you know the result. Now here I was again, facing up to men who had all the power they needed to do me a lot of harm. *What is it with you, Jack Spayd? Don't you ever learn?* I told myself. But then I could almost hear Joe saying, 'Jazzboy, sometime we got to shut our mouth even when we be right, but sometime we also got to do ourself a deal o' yellin' out.' I could only hope tonight was the night to start yelling.

After coming off night shift on the Saturday morning of the game, I lay awake going through all sorts of methods of cheating – shaved decks, cold decking, crooked shuffles and dealing off the bottom, selecting cards from below the top card, but all of those were hard to sustain throughout a game without being caught out or, at the very least, raising suspicion. I'd gone over and over every possibility a dozen times in my head and it was pointless; I needed some sleep, preferably extending well into the afternoon before the game.

When I woke, I showered, dressed and had an early light meal at the mess before turning up for the game, where the others were already seated around the poker table, everyone with a drink beside them. Hans Meyerhof introduced me to the two guest players from the Congo, Jean Dubois and Pierre Laurent. 'Jack Reed is tonight for his first time here, chentlemen. Ve velcome him; *ja*, ve vill all have fun togezzer.' I almost expected him to add, 'It is compulsory!'

The recreation hut was packed: the entire Kraut committee was there and a heap of miners and other guys, most of them past players invited by the men around the table. It may have been my imagination but the atmosphere in the recreation hut seemed almost electric. *Jesus, what if our plans have been leaked and reached Hans Meyerhof?* I comforted myself with the thought that while the Krauts might be clever, subtlety wasn't their strong suit. They were ex-SS after all and would have seen to it that I never got near the game if they thought I was a threat. What was the German equivalent of a hand sticking up out of the desert? Perhaps a pile of well-chewed bones left by the hyenas in the veldt, as the woods were usually termed.

The game took place in a roped-off section of the recreation hut. Everyone was already seated, as I said, and I'd learn later that they hadn't cut cards to decide our positions around the table. Hans had simply pointed to a chair and called out a player's name – so far, so bad. The two Congo guys sat opposite each other. The dealer didn't even look up or nod. He was, to say the least, a pretty poor example of the master race, fat and short with a bald crown sparsely covered by strands of dark hair he'd combed over from the side of his head. The scalp showing through the pasted strands of hair was an even baby pink. I could not imagine him storming Stalingrad or anything else. I decided to call him Colonel Comb Over.

Grunting, he dished out our chips, storing the cash in the drawer of a small table on wheels, on the top of which he kept several decks of cards and a box of chips. The Congo guys spoke reasonable English but always spoke to each other in French. We didn't object, and I was interested to hear Jean Dubois say in a deadpan voice that they hadn't been pulled up for speaking French. It was all he said, but the little smirk that went with it, and the slight nod from Pierre, spoke volumes. These guys were about as straight as a somersault.

We began to play, and almost at once I could see how they'd worked the scam. The whole thing was so obvious I couldn't believe it. Over the past few days I'd been mulling over everything I knew about card scams, and trying to remember what Johnny Diamond had told me about how a game of poker could be fixed. In every case, if you're going to cheat well and win consistently, the best way to do it is to know with certainty what cards your opponents are holding: then you can fold whenever they hold the better cards, only risking your ante; or, when you hold the stronger hand, you can keep raising – the more your opponents bet, the more they lose. Often you don't even need to show your hand if your opponents can't afford, or don't want, to match your raises. I know that sounds obvious but there are some very sophisticated ways of going about it. The one the guys from the Congo were using wasn't brilliant or even clever.

Colonel Comb Over dealt the first round of cards, face up to see who got the highest card, and thus became the first to place a bet. It was then that the visitors reached for their spectacle cases, opened them casually, almost absentmindedly, and put on their specs. One pair was round and gold-rimmed, and the other horn-rimmed; just your average spectacles, with the exception that both sets of lenses had a red tint.

I very nearly fell off my chair. *Jesus, it can't be that simple, surely?* There was no way a cheat in his right mind would try this one on in even the smallest roadside casino in Nevada. In fact, it was almost an insult, the sort of cheap trick any casino manager would pick within thirty seconds of the start of a game. The red-tinted lenses filtered out red light, highlighting faint green markings invisible to the naked eye hidden among the red pattern decorating the back of the Bicycle-brand cards. These markings showed the value of every card. The trick was for the dealer to lay each card down before each player picked up those allocated to him. In other words, they didn't need to be great poker players, just have a reasonable memory, which is common among good card players. I was pretty sure they'd be competent players at the very least. The two Congo guys would know what every other player was holding almost before they did.

It was an old trick and initially I doubted what I was seeing, thinking that they'd donned the tinted glasses merely to mislead, and that something truly subtle might be taking place. In all my time in Las Vegas I had never heard of anyone stupid enough to attempt to get away with such an old card-marking scam. It was one of those cheap tricks you might have gotten away with twenty or thirty years before, but not since. Still, this was the boondocks, after all; literally the middle of Africa, what Lenny would have referred to as the asshole of the world or, in the local parlance, *arse*hole of the world.

I decided to let things go for a while, to see what transpired as I watched Jean and Pierre play. There was no need for an exchange in French now, it was simply too easy. The dealer, Colonel Comb Over, wasn't pulling any fast ones either: his was a slow, steady shuffle and deal, no 'mechanic's grip', no false shuffles. His side already had all the advantage they thought they were going to need.

My fellow players were, certainly by Las Vegas standards, pretty average, a notch above a game on a Saturday night at a friend's house. After an hour I'd won a small pot; Jannie Coetzee was down about twenty pounds; Piet Wenzel had been sighing for twenty minutes, slapping his cards down hard as he threw in his hand – he was down about fifty pounds. I noticed he was glancing at me as if to say, 'When are we going to make our move?' I could only hope Hans Meyerhof wasn't watching him. The others were barely holding their own; at this rate, by the end of the night they'd be broke, skint. I was now confident I knew the extent of the scam. The Congo guys were biding their time, each winning a small pot once in a while. But then one of them scooped in a pot worth about ninety pounds. I guess we'd both decided it was time to move the game along. In fact, Pierre glanced briefly at Jean and, as if talking to himself, mumbled, '*C'est le temps* [It's time].'

Yeah, dead right, you bastard, I said to myself. Pushing back my chair, I stood up and announced that I needed a piss.

'*Ja*, not a bad idea,' Jannie said, getting heavily to his feet. It surprised me that Hans or the German guy behind the bar hadn't noticed that no one around the table had replenished their drinks. Jannie Coetzee and I were alone at the urinal. 'So, tell me, man, what's going on?' he asked.

'They're using marked cards, buddy,' I replied, with a snort. 'It's one of the oldest tricks in the book. I almost feel insulted.'

'Bending the cards? Scoring them? I've looked for that, there's nothing like that going on, man,' Jannie replied.

'No, the glasses, the red-tinted lenses; they filter out the red pattern and let them see faint green markings on the backs of the cards as they're dealt. They might as well be dealt face up.'

'Jesus, are you sure?' he exclaimed.

'Jannie, concentrate on one thing at a time, you've pissed all over your nice brown boots.'

'*Heere*, Jack,' he tucked himself away and buttoned his fly, 'you sure? Certain?' He pulled a square of newspaper off a hook near a washbasin and cleaned the toes of his boots. 'We'll kill those fockers. The men are going to be pretty focking angry!'

I placed a hand on his shoulder. 'Take it easy, will you, buddy? The *real* action is about to begin.'

'I can't wait, man.'

'When we get back, we insist on a change of deck. Give them one of the packs we bought at the Club. Now Hans Meyerhof is certain to object, so stay cool, smile, ask him for a quiet word in his office.'

'Will you come with us?'

'No, Jannie, you go alone. You're the guy who holds the key to their dominance of the single quarters. He won't refuse. If I go with you, he's going to smell a rat.'

Jannie smiled. 'That's two rats then. *Ja*, okay, I understand. What do I say?'

'Tell him you're obliged to demonstrate to everyone in the room how the glasses our visitors are wearing help their eyesight. Oh, then smile and remind him that there's enough muscle in the room to do him and his committee a great deal of harm.'

'*Wragtig*, Jack, if the room knows what's going on, I'm telling you, they'll kick the bastards to death, right there on the spot. I'm not joking, man.'

'He'll know that. Next, you inform him how much his two friends across the Congo border are going to lose.'

'So, six grand . . . six thousand pounds?'

'That's what we decided at the *braaivleis*, wasn't it? Oh, and every deal has to have a sweetener; tell him if he complies, not a word will be said about the glasses, but after the game is over, they'll be confiscated and kept as evidence, "just in case", along with the marked deck.'

Jannie nodded. 'Good, Jack. I'll go first, then you follow me a bit later, hey?'

I had a sudden thought and called after Jannie. He came back to me. 'When you hand over the new deck, just collect any of the marked deck on the table and put them in your pocket.'

'Jack, you'd make a *blerrie* good diamond driller. You got detail in your head all the time.' He laughed.

I left the toilet block and waited outside. The stars in that part of Africa are spectacular, so myriad that you'd sometimes wonder if there were any black sky between them. I wondered whether if 'everything went apeshit', as Noel White would put it, I'd live to see another night sky like this one. *What would happen to Diamond Jim?* Perhaps I'd been away from women for too long.

I returned to the recreation hut and resumed my seat. Jannie emerged from Hans Meyerhof's office shortly after, followed by Hans. Without even glancing at me, he handed Colonel Comb Over a deck of cards. The fat little man glanced towards Hans, and I looked up in time to see the German nod. Hans Meyerhof then walked over to Jean Dubois, and asked if he could see him and Pierre Laurent in his office for a moment. 'Some telephone call is coming from Katanga,' he said, by way of explanation to the table. 'Maybe you play on?'

'They're not coming back?' Noel White asked.

'Certainly, they are coming,' Hans replied. He removed a handkerchief from his pocket and wiped his brow. Whatever Jannie Coetzee had said to him, I could see he was afraid.

In the meantime, Colonel Comb Over had opened the sealed pack Jannie had passed over to him and, grunting to himself, was going through his deliberate, almost ponderous, shuffle. 'What say we wait for our friends from across the border before we resume?' I suggested.

Noel White lifted his empty beer glass and showed it to me, the meaning obvious. I shook my head. He grinned a little sheepishly.

It was not till later, after the game, when Jannie invited us home for a drink, that we learned what he'd said to Hans Meyerhof. Everyone was too worked up to go home, and Jannie's wife, Anna, had already gone to bed, so we had plenty of time to talk. He stood facing us as we sat on his porch, having a nightcap.

'We went into Hans's office and he locked the door. I dunno why, but then he said, "Jannie, you vant to borrow some money? How much you vant?"

'"No, man, I'm okay," I said. "It's not that."

'"Ve all frens here, Jannie. You tell me I fix?" he said. Had no idea.

'"Hans," I said, "this poker game, you're cheating us. You and the two guys from over the border."

'He holds up his hand so, in front of his face and shakes his head. "No, no! You talk crazy, Jannie. Zey *gut*, zey know zis game poker, very *gut* player. That's all vot happens."

'"Hans, don't bullshit me, man," I said. "The cards are focking marked!"

'"Hey, Jannie, what you say? Mark cards? No vay!"'

Jannie looked at us, then said, '"Hans, the focking game is up. We know about the red glasses, man, and the green marks!"'

He shook his head. 'The foxy bastard is no fool. "Vot you say, ze glasses? I don't understand?" he says to me.

'"The eye glasses, spectacles, *brille*, those Belgian buggers can see green marks on the back of the cards."' Jannie laughed. 'Hans throws up his hands, "I am *schwachsinniger* [an imbecile]! Always zey are saying ve must use the card zey bring from Congo."'

Jannie Coetzee looked over at me. 'For a moment there, I thought he had me, man. Then I remembered how you'd asked the guy at the Club sports shop if he sold playing cards to Hans Meyerhof and what make they were.' Jannie grinned. 'You remember what he said?'

'Yes, of course, Jannie. He said Hans Meyerhof bought them himself and they always had to be Bicycle brand from America. He gets them specially sent in. He said he'd sold him ten packs three weeks ago.'

'*Ja*, dead right, then remember he said he might have a couple of decks left he could let us have? But you said, no, you wanted another brand.' Jannie took a mouthful of brandy. '*Heere*, man, thank God I remembered all this in time and of course the brand Hans used in our game tonight was Bicycle.' Jannie swirled his brandy thoughtfully before he went on. 'Now he's beginning to sweat, his *sakdoek* is already wet from mopping his brow.'

'"Zose cards I buy from Club shop, zey for anusser game not the vun in ze recreation hut," Hans says to me. So I take a big chance. "Hans," I say, "tonight we used Bicycle and we checked, they don't sell them in Katanga, not anywhere in the Belgian Congo." I'm telling a lie, how would I know what cards they sold in the Congo; but hey, man, what can he say?'

'Good one, Jannie,' Noel called out. 'All over Red Rover! So what'd he do next, mate?'

'He asks me what I want. So I say to him, "Simple." I take a clean deck from my pocket. "We want to play with our own clean deck."'

This was greeted with a roar of appreciative laughter. 'Well done, boyo,' Russell Howell called.

Jannie, enjoying himself, continued. '"*Jawohl!*" Hans says to me. "Ve go back now, ve can change za card, no problem."'

'"No, that's not all, Hans. I want your two Congo boys to play to lose. That is, until we decide we've got enough money back to repay us for what we lost in the past."' Jannie shrugged. 'I got to say, man, he doesn't panic, he just says, "So, tell me also, you can keep quiet the Bicycle card?"'

'"You mean about cheating all this time? Marking the cards? *Ja*, that's the deal, only two other things. The two guys hand over the glasses and the Bicycle deck we used before as evidence, in case you try to *verneuk ons* [cheat us] again."

'"No, no, ve vill not have zem come again, zese Congo." He's shaking his head like his neck is on a spring. I point at him and say, "Hans, if you or your Nazi friends ever try anything like this again, I want you to understand, the union boys will escort your whole focking committee underground for a tour, and I'm sorry to say there'll be a blasting accident – twenty dead Germans."

'"How much you vant ve lose?" he then asks me.

'"Six thousand pounds."

'He throws up his hands. "No! Zat is too much!"

'"Too bad, Hans. Six grand, man, not a penny less, you hear?" I tell him.

'"But zen, Jannie, you keep everything quiet, *ja?*"

'"You have my word, Hans. *Ek is n regte Boer* [I am a true Boer], I tell him."'

All the diamond drillers nodded their heads, their expressions serious. I would later learn that to an Afrikaner, this is akin to a blood oath, although the original meaning of *Boer*, and the literal translation, is 'farmer'.

Curiously, once we started to play with the new pack, I began to get the best cards I'd seen since that long night in Moose Jaw at the end of my scuffing tour. In fact, these cards were even better. In no time at all, I was up three hundred pounds and I hadn't had to show my hand once.

However, even without Lady Luck's smile, it soon became obvious that I was several pegs above my opposition, including the so-called cardsharps from the Congo. At three hundred pounds, with no losses to regain from previous games, it was time to get out and give one of the other players a chance to win back what he'd lost to the guys from the Congo.

I leaned towards Jannie while Colonel Comb Over was shuffling. 'Time I gave up my seat, buddy.'

'How much you up, Jack?'

'Enough, about three hundred.'

'No, man, you play till you're up five hundred, then come and sit behind me, keep an eye on these two Congo fockers.'

It was generous of him to let me take out another two hundred quid, and the right cards just kept coming. The paradox was that, for once in my life, I didn't need particularly good hands. I could have played with quite ordinary cards and still won.

I was getting close to my cut-off point when it happened. I had four diamonds, open both ends, ten to the king. I very nearly pooped my pants. This was the perfect launching pad for a running flush, or even a royal flush. My turn came and I discarded one and asked for a card, my heart thumping.

There are moments in your life you never forget. The new card was the ace of diamonds. I'd just reached the pinnacle of the card-player's Everest. In all my years of playing, in all my time in Las Vegas, I'd never even met anyone who could claim to have seen a royal flush. In a game where I couldn't lose I'd achieved the impossible. I took the lead and began to bet so the others quickly dropped out, except for the two Congo guys who were obliged to stay in the game. I hoped they wouldn't notice the tremor in my hand.

I raised them until there was nearly two hundred in the pot, a third of which I had put in. Instead of waiting for Jannie to tell them to fold, I called them. Both looked at me like they'd been shot. Technically, they were in a position to win.

Jean Dubois looked at Pierre Laurent and said in French, 'Shit, what now? He wants to see our cards.'

'*Merci beaucoup, monsieur, s'il vous plait* [Thank you very much, sir, if you please] . . .' – I was being sarcastically over-polite.

'*Vous parlez français* [You speak French]?' Pierre Laurent exclaimed, appalled. If I translated the things they'd been saying about us all evening, the guys would have taken them behind the toilet block and beaten the shit out of them.

'*D'accord* [Of course],' I replied. Their fear and embarrassment were almost palpable.

'Do what he says, man!' Jannie Coetzee barked at them, not understanding what was transpiring.

Both laid down their cards. Laurent had three kings and Dubois two pair. Not bad hands. They were probably shitting themselves that they might win.

I placed my cards down delicately and slowly. There was a gasp from everyone around the table.

'Jesus! A royal flush, a focking royal flush!' Jannie Coetzee roared as the guys watching leaned forward to see it for themselves.

I sagged in my chair. 'Cash me out, Kurt. Cash me out.'

We all left Jannie Coetzee's home late that night in a happy mood, the guys having more than made up for their earlier abstinence during the poker game. In the days and weeks following the game, a curious change came over Hans Meyerhof and the committee. They dropped their former domineering ways, smiled whenever we crossed paths and made no demands whatsoever. It was as if I had proved myself the better man, and they were forced to respect it. As for the diamond drillers and the union guys who had previously ignored me, now they'd acknowledge me with a smile and familiar 'Howzit?', the South African equivalent of Noel White's 'G'day'.

Another six, uneventful, months went by. Mining is routine work; dangerous routine in some respects but nevertheless predictable, as were the injuries the men sustained. I could almost anticipate what every night shift would bring, but even so, a catastrophic accident was always on the cards – the chances were a lot higher than those for a royal flush.

I spent much of my time in my rondavel, reading or talking to Diamond Jim. He was such a clever little fella and I soon came to regard him as a dear friend, in much the same way as someone might regard a beloved dog. Luswishi River was a lonely place, despite, or perhaps because of, there being people from just about every nation in Europe. Some would have us believe they were perfectly respectable, but there were others, and I guess I'd have to include myself among them, who wanted their past lives to remain secret. As a result, it was difficult to make friends; you had to be constantly mindful that you could be treading on toes, and so you walked on eggshells.

However, Diamond Jim had no past I knew about, except having his crop stuffed with diamonds, which can't have been a pleasant experience. I saw him not only as a companion but as a work in progress. He was still young, so he had every chance of learning to talk. The Audubon Society had sent some useful material, from which I learned that this particular parrot species was mentioned in the writings of both Dr David Livingstone, the famous missionary explorer, and the man who was sent by the *New York Herald* to find him, Welsh-born American, Henry Morton Stanley, whose first words were, apparently, *'Doctor Livingstone, I presume?'*.

According to the Audubon Society, my African Grey Parrot, *Psittacus erithacus erithacus*, was considered among the most intelligent of birds and known to live to the age of fifty years or more. Wild African Grey Parrots are able to mimic many other animals. Those raised by humans can often learn to speak. The sub-species was described as 'handsome', which I guess is a nice way of saying they were not beautiful, the description usually accorded more colourful parrots. Fully grown, they weighed a pound or so, with a body length of fourteen or more inches, and a wingspan of up to twenty inches.

Diamond Jim wasn't yet that tall and I'd never weighed him, but according to the Audubon Society, a mature bird has a pale yellow iris surrounding the black pupil. Diamond Jim's iris had changed from grey to yellow and he stood just a fraction under thirteen inches, so I assumed he'd reached maturity.

The notes I'd received suggested that his species don't start to mimic, or 'talk', until they are two or three years old, and certainly for the first three months he merely chirped noisily with an occasional sharp exclamatory squawk, or made that strange throaty sound I mentioned. I'd often reply with a short whistle, then I'd pick up the harmonica and play through the first verse of 'Love Me or Leave Me'; then I'd sing the lyrics and finish by saying clearly, 'I love you, Bridgett'. It was hopelessly sentimental, I know, and of course way beyond anything I could possibly expect a parrot to achieve. I'd tried to forget Bridgett but still thought about and missed her every day and night of my life. The lyrics were appropriate: night-time really was the worst time for me, when I remembered Bridgett most vividly, and I was afraid that the song might also prove to be prophetic: perhaps I'd never be happy with anyone else. So often did I perform the song with Diamond Jim, that, for Bridgett's sake, I'm glad she wasn't around to witness my ridiculously repetitive and, I guess, mawkish behaviour.

As for Diamond Jim, I convinced myself that he was developing a sense of rhythm from mimicking me as I rocked from one foot to the other, playing the harmonica. He'd do the same, nodding his head and lifting his legs in perfect time . . . well, in reasonably good time. It was, I thought, a pretty impressive beginning to his training, and he'd keep it up for the two hours I practised jazz and blues every afternoon in my rondavel. It soon became clear that he was a very social animal and disliked being in his cage, clearly preferring to be near me, usually perched on my shoulder as I played. Furthermore, he never seemed bored with the music.

I'd wondered at first why nobody ever mentioned hearing the music, and I suppose I was slightly miffed until I realised that none of my near neighbours worked the night shift, so I was surrounded by empty rondavels. Given Noel's warning, it may well have been for the best.

Diamond Jim loved having a shower and I'd take him with me into the shower block. After I'd showered I'd run the cold water and let him have a shower of his own, watching as he danced from one leg to the other and squawked happily. I'd let him out to fly, for exercise, and he seemed to want to stay in sight. After about fifteen minutes he'd return to my arm. He loved toys and I'd bring him blocks of wood, branches, tennis balls and rattles, most of which he managed to shred with his sharp beak. I also learned that, because he was such an intensely social creature, if left alone for too long he would become self-destructive, plucking out his own feathers. During the day I seldom left him alone, and working at night, when most birds sleep, meant that he was rarely aware of my absence. Diamond Jim – or DJ, as I sometimes called him – became a familiar sight on my shoulder when I left the single quarters to go anywhere during the day or the early evening. It was a bit like having a very bright but very demanding four-year-old in your life, and he taught me a great deal, usually with the help of information from Foyles or the Audubon Society. It seemed the friendship between African Greys and humans stretched back into antiquity, with the birds being mentioned or depicted by the Egyptians, Ancient Greeks and Romans. These parrots were the playthings of royalty: Henry VIII, Marie Antoinette and one of the mistresses of Charles II all had a Diamond Jim in their lives. US President Andrew Jackson's African Grey had to be removed from the church during his master's funeral service because he kept uttering profanities. At the other end of the social scale were the many pirates who were said to keep African Greys.

It's hardly surprising when you realise that an African Grey can possess an amazing vocabulary, perhaps up to a thousand words. I'm sure he understood what he was saying, rather than simply 'parroting' it. These birds can greet people by name and seem to understand how they relate to their family or social group.

DJ loved the radio and had strong views on several of the BBC announcers. 'Oh, not that bloody fool again!' he'd say whenever a particular radio personality came on air. We don't realise how often we swear until we live with an African Grey Parrot. Often their timing is impeccable, and even if it's not, there's no denying who's responsible. They love to show off, and soak up love, attention and praise. Neither do they confine themselves to replicating human speech: African Greys have been known to reproduce such sounds as running water, the telephone, the front door bell and a dog-owner's whistle, which must have driven the particular dog crazy, not to mention the owners of the telephone and front door bell.

Perhaps their most appealing characteristics are their intense loyalty and loving natures. In the wild they mate for life, and it would seem they are equally devoted to their human companions.

I wish I could tell you that Diamond Jim started to talk or knew the lyrics or at least the names of the jazz and blues numbers I played while we were together at Luswishi River. I avoided playing in front of an audience – jazz and blues didn't rank very highly in the musical tastes of a mining town in the middle of Africa – but I practised regularly, and thought I was doing okay on the harmonica. Sure, it wasn't a piano, but the sixteen-hole chromatic Hohner was nevertheless a beautiful instrument and I wanted to do it justice.

In my imagination I saw DJ as part of an act I was preparing for some imagined future when I would no longer be pursued by the Mafia. DJ would maybe act as a compere, the world's first parrot to introduce a jazz and blues repertoire. No doubt he'd be capable of the odd spontaneous and amusing crack during a performance. But so far I'd had no luck. Apart from dancing, which was impressive and very amusing, DJ hadn't said a single word from a single song. I guess the diamonds he carried in his crop might have been too big a responsibility for one little bird.

I hadn't entirely given up on him, though. He was counting pretty well and learning his colours. I'd laugh and scratch him under the beak because, in truth, all he really had to be was Diamond Jim, whom I had quickly learned to love. My lonely childhood, with no pets and few if any close friends, had not prepared me for the intense feelings I had for this small grey parrot. But I kept working with him, my one ardent hope being that after I finished 'Love Me or Leave Me', he'd learn to say, 'I love you, Bridgett'. Which just shows what a sentimental idiot I was and probably still am.

As I said, after the poker game, things started to improve for me. And then one day, almost two hours before my shift began, I got a message to come on shift half an hour early, to see Mike Tilson, the night manager for number seven shaft. When I got to the shaft head, he briefed me. 'Jack, we've got the risk of a bad flood underground on the eleven hundred level. The diamond drillers on the morning shift were drilling a new ventilation shaft when they tapped into an underground spring.'

'That's pretty unusual, isn't it?'

'Well, it sometimes happens. The surveyors usually pick it up and we pipe the water away. But this time, it came as a surprise. The trouble is the shaft is already about thirty feet deep and filling fast. The pipe fitters can only get two pumps in while they try to fit a pipe to redirect the water into a safe area.'

I wasn't sure I understood. 'You mean, if the shaft fills, then flows over, it will flood . . . ?'

'It will flood the cage shaft and pour down into the fourteen hundred level. We've already evacuated the mine, except for a pipe fitter and his gang, and we've recalled two diamond drillers from the eleven hundred level. The idea is to drill and blast. The blasted rock will partly fill the ventilation shaft, but the main thing is to widen it enough to allow three more pumps to work. We need you to stand by in case there's trouble. I don't have to tell you that what they're doing down there is dangerous work. If the cage shaft floods, it's a long climb to the surface; that is, if you can get to the emergency shaft ladders in time to climb out of the mine.'

'Thanks for nothing, Mr Tilson,' I said with a grin. 'My medic team doesn't come on shift for another twenty-five minutes. Shall I go on ahead?'

'If you would, please, Jack. We'll send them down as soon as they arrive. Shorty Bronkhorst's medic team has to come to the surface as soon as you get down. He's had a bad asthma attack and his team, as you know, can't stay behind without a white medic in charge.'

'Who are the diamond drillers and the pipe fitter?' I asked as I went to get a freshly charged lamp pack and clipped the light to my miner's helmet.

'Piet Wenzel, who you know, I think,' Mike Tilson replied. 'Then a new guy, Klaas Potgieter, I don't think you'd know him, he's only been here two weeks. The pipe fitter is Hungarian, I think: Adorjan Hajdu.'

'Okay. The cage is waiting to take me down; I'll make myself known when I get there.'

The miners' cage was designed to take twenty people up or down at a time but I was the only one in it as it plunged down humming on its cables to the eleven hundred level. When I got clear of the cage, I could hear the blasting hooter going and, shortly after, a muffled explosion. I estimated it was probably about a five-minute walk away.

By the time I got to the blasting site, the air blowers had cleared the smoke from the blast, and I was met by Piet Wenzel, whose opinion of me had improved since that memorable poker game.

'Howzit, Jack?' he said as I approached.

'Fine, Piet; this is an unusual shift for a diamond driller, isn't it? By this time, you guys are usually well pissed,' I joked.

He laughed. 'You can say that again, Jack. I dunno how you do this midnight to dawn stuff. You're a crazy man. It's time you became a diamond driller. We'll train you, man. You've got the size and the brains.'

He then introduced me to the second diamond driller. 'This is Klaas Potgieter; Klaas, this is Jack Reed.' Potgieter nodded but didn't offer his hand. 'Nice to meet you, Mr Potgieter,' I said. Diamond drillers were on the top of the mining heap and a certain formality, while not entirely necessary, was a sign of respect. Piet then turned towards the pipe fitter. 'And this is . . . ah . . .'

I jumped in and extended my hand, smiling. 'You must be Mr Adorjan Hajdu; nice to meet you, I'm Jack Reed.' The pipe fitter seemed pleased to have both his names used and smiled broadly, shaking my hand vigorously.

They and their African gangs were soaked to the skin, and it occurred to me that could be why Klaas Potgieter hadn't shaken hands. But now he turned to Piet Wenzel. 'Hey, is this the guy I heard about, the *kaffir* lover?' He could have said this in Afrikaans and I wouldn't have understood, so obviously it was meant for me to hear. Nice guy.

Piet Wenzel was quick to defend me, also speaking in English. '*Heere*, Klaas, that's old stuff now. Jack is a good guy, n' *regte man* [a real man]'.

But Klaas Potgieter seemed unimpressed and turned away, calling to his black gang to return to his drilling site.

Piet Wenzel turned to me. 'Take no notice, Jack. He's new, from down south. I knew him before, we were together in Randfontein; both of us were on the miners' union committee.' He jerked his head in the direction Klaas Potgieter had taken. 'That one, he's always had a big mouth.' He then explained to me that they had one more drill each to do, two blasts, then they'd lash the walls of the shaft, and the pipe fitter would be able to get two more pumps working; or that was the plan. 'Jack, how come you can remember his name, man? They all the same to me, these foreigners.'

'Blessed with a good memory, I guess.'

'*Ja*, that's why you so good at cards, hey?' He laughed. 'I'll never forget those Congo guys when you spoke to them in French. They shat themselves, I swear it, man, *kaked* their trousers.'

He left to do his final drill and, shortly afterwards, my team arrived, though Samson was off sick with malaria, according to Daniel. I explained the situation in Cikabanga to the remaining three. 'I don't think there will be any problems,' I concluded, to reassure them, then, as an afterthought, I asked, 'Do any of you swim?'

Jackson laughed. 'I born by the river, *Bwana* Jack.'

'Any of you know anything about artificial respiration?'

Daniel put up his hand. 'I have one demonstration long, long time, *Bwana* Jack.'

'Well, they seem to have everything under control and it's probably not something we will need, but I'll give you all a demonstration.'

Artificial respiration was essential knowledge for a medic working on a beach-landing craft. The method taught by the Royal Life Saving Society was known as the Holger Nielsen Method of Artificial Respiration.

Nick Reed, my stepfather, always claimed it was pretty inefficient; in fact, almost ineffectual. If you kept the throat clear, victims of drowning more or less found their own way back to breathing, or died or were probably dead anyhow. 'Right,' I said in Cikabanga, using Jackson as my patient. 'Place the patient on his stomach, with his hands crossed like this, and placed under his forehead. Turn his head to the side, so his mouth and nose aren't covered. Place your hands on his shoulder blades, with the thumbs along his spine, like this.' I demonstrated. 'Then lean forward – one, two – and that presses air out of the lungs, then grab his arms here – three,' I grasped Jackson's upper arms near the elbows, 'and lift – four, five – and his lungs fill with air. And repeat.' I sat back on my heels. 'That's about it.'

I lay down beside Jackson and asked the other two black medics to demonstrate the method on us.

The second blast occurred half an hour or so later, and when the smoke finally cleared, Piet Wenzel's gang started to use crowbars to pry any loose rock from the walls of the shaft – or lash the shaft – to further widen it. Some rocks still clung precariously to the walls and it was important that these were loosened and sent tumbling into the water below.

By lowering a weighted line into the water, we estimated that it was now around ten feet deep. Water was still pouring from the underground spring, but Adorjan Hajdu assured me he could get two more pumps in, and that ought to stop the water rising until he could attach a pipe to the spring's outlet.

Piet's gang, working nearest to us, had just about completed lashing, except for one stubborn slab of rock that clung to the side of the shaft. The men, using a long crowbar, seemed to be having trouble prying it off. Piet pushed two of his gang aside. '*Heere*, man, these *blerrie kaffirs*, you show them how to do it, but they never focking learn,' he said impatiently. He then grabbed a long crowbar from one of the gang and started to work on the slab. Suddenly it came away, knocking him into one of his gang and then straight down some twenty feet into the darkness of the water-filled tunnel. Almost at once, the African he'd struck overbalanced and followed him down. Both disappeared into the black hole and, an instant later, we heard the huge splash as they almost simultaneously hit the water.

'Jesus!' I screamed, then, grabbing the rope we used to measure the depth, I pointed to another rope and yelled for Jackson to grab it. Daniel and Milo, working frantically, wrapped one around Jackson's waist and the other around mine and lowered us into the shaft, feeding out the ropes and shining their headlamps into the shaft so we could see.

My ears strained to detect any sound from the water below, but I could hear nothing. I reached the water first and almost immediately saw the arm of the black guy. Clinging to the rope with one arm I pulled him towards me with the other. As soon as he was close enough, I clamped both arms around his chest and yelled to be pulled up.

I could feel the rock on the sides of the shaft cutting into my back through my heavy woollen miner's vest as they hauled us up, a process that seemed to take an eternity. Hands seemed to come from everywhere to grab at us and then pull us into a clear space. I was gasping and panting, but somehow, with the help of Daniel and Milo, I managed to place the unconscious black miner face down so that I could begin artificial respiration in the manner I'd just demonstrated to my team.

A minute or so later, Jackson emerged with Piet Wenzel, also unconscious. Jackson looked exhausted, so I yelled for Daniel to take over from Jackson and work on Piet, who, I noted, had a serious-looking gash on his forehead. 'Milo, you fix the cut on the *bwana*'s head,' I gasped. The black guy under my hands showed no signs of life, but I kept working on him. If he had any chance of recovering, I daren't stop. *Bloody Samson, where was he when I needed him?* Then, after another minute or so, I felt the black miner's chest heave and he began to cough, expelling a flood of water from his mouth and nose. Still coughing and spluttering, he started to expel more water from his lungs, then painfully drew air into them. It had worked! He was alive. Elated, I yelled over to Jackson, 'Take care of this guy; he's going to be okay, just hold his head clear, watch out he doesn't choke.'

I then leapt to my feet and went over to Daniel, who was working frantically on Piet Wenzel. He looked up at me and his eyes said everything I needed to know. He shook his head silently. I took over and worked on him for a further five minutes, but there was not a sign of life in the white diamond driller. Milo had dressed the cut on Piet's head, taping the dressing down. I ripped it off and examined the wound. It went deep into his crushed skull, and I could see his bloodied brains. Clearly, Piet Wenzel had been dead before he'd even hit the water. 'He's dead, the *bwana* is dead,' I announced to his gang.

'You focking killed him, you *bastard*!' I looked up to see Klaas Potgieter pointing at Piet Wenzel's body with a shaking finger. 'You saved the *kaffir*!' he screamed. 'You saved a focking *kaffir* and let a white man die! I saw it! I saw it with my own focking eyes! You're not going to get away with this, you hear?'

The coroner's inquest held in Ndola reached the conclusion that Piet Wenzel had died from a fractured skull caused by a falling rock, and that he had not drowned. Although the finding was a relief, it didn't alter the fact that a good man had died. Everyone seemed to know that it was the second time I had saved an African's life, but this time *before* attending to the white man. I'd given artificial respiration to an anonymous *kaffir* first, and not to an Afrikaner diamond driller who was supposed to be my friend.

Jannie Coetzee had suspended me, not, I hasten to say, out of malice, but as a precaution. 'Jack, this time they're going to get you. Better you stay away, don't go underground. Shorty Bronkhorst has volunteered to do a double shift. Sorry, man, but I'm going to have to suspend you; the diamond drillers are calling for some blood to be spilled, if you know what I mean.'

The diamond drillers and the miners' union were said to be almost mutinous because I'd been 'allowed to get away with' the African amputation incident, as Jacob's rescue had become officially known. It didn't help that Adorjan Hajdu, the Hungarian pipe fitter, steadfastly maintained that I'd done all I could, that the African was the first to be hauled up, by me, and that Milo had attended to the wound on Piet Wenzel's forehead under my instructions. I was, after all, a 'focking foreigner', so what could you expect?

'Why didn't he leave the *kaffir* and look for Piet Wenzel?' seemed to be the question everyone was asking.

Despite the coroner's finding, I took Jannie Coetzee's advice and remained locked in my rondavel with Diamond Jim. Jannie'd originally posted two black constables outside to protect me if there was any trouble, but after the coroner brought down his verdict, they left. Noel White and the others who'd taken part in the poker game had all come to visit in the lead-up to the coroner's inquest and assure me that they had not joined in the general baying for my blood.

Then, at six on the morning of the day following the coroner's verdict, I woke to the sound of Noel's voice and saw his face at the barred window of my rondavel. 'Quick, Jack, open the door. Lemme in!' he hissed. I jumped up and hastened to open the door, wearing only a pair of pyjama shorts.

'What is it?' I asked, his face telling me enough for me to know that this wasn't a social call.

'Jack, get dressed fast, grab what you can; I've got the van outside, engine running. They're coming for you.'

'Who?'

'Jesus, mate, who fucking knows? A mob of miners, the Krauts, others, what's it matter. We haven't any fucking time. Where's your bag? Ferchrissake, can you stop that fucking bird screeching!'

Five minutes later, with whatever I could grab and with Diamond Jim on my shoulder, we were into the Volkswagen and on the road out of town. Noel had been given just enough warning, it seemed from Jannie Coetzee, and we were away without being seen or followed. I'd locked the door of the rondavel and closed the wooden shutters that covered the barred windows in the rainy season, so nobody would have known I wasn't hiding inside.

On the way to Ndola, Noel said, 'You're not a real fast learner, Jack Reed.' He guffawed, but when I didn't join in, he went on, 'There's a train at eight o'clock that goes south-east, all the way to Beira on the Portuguese East African coast, with the usual coupla hundred stops on the way, of course. You okay for money, mate? I brought some extra cash just in case.'

'Yeah, I'm fine, thanks, Noel. And how will I ever pay you back?'

'You already have, Jack. You're a good mate, and I'll never forget that poker game, and . . . that was a good thing you did, saving those two black guys. I'd like to think I'd do the same, but I doubt it.'

We arrived at the Ndola station with only a few minutes to spare before the train pulled out, but Noel knew the stationmaster, who delayed departure just long enough for him to buy me a first-class ticket and find me a compartment of my own. When I reached for my wallet, he tut-tutted at me. 'Instructions from Jannie Coetzee, mate.' Then he saw me onto the train and into my compartment with Diamond Jim.

Standing on the platform, looking up at DJ and me through the window, he handed me an envelope. 'Jannie says it's what the mine owes you: your copper bonus until the end of the year.'

The guard blew his whistle and the locomotive let out its loud whistle as the train started to move.

'Good luck, buddy!' Noel called. It was the first time I'd heard him say 'buddy'. What a good mate.

We reached the outskirts of the town and five minutes later were travelling through the countryside. I reached into my pocket for my harmonica and began to play 'Love Me or Leave Me' as Diamond Jim kept time on my shoulder with his feet and head. Then, just as I was about to lower the harmonica and sing the lyrics, he began to whistle. He whistled the entire verse without a mistake.

Love me or leave me and let me be lonely
You won't believe me but I love you only
I'd rather be lonely than happy with somebody else . . .

Then, cocking his head on one side, he said in a croaky voice, 'I love you, Bridgett.'

EPILOGUE

Dear Reader,

> *'The time has come,' the Walrus said,*
> *'To talk of many things:*
> *Of shoes – and ships – and sealing-wax –*
> *Of cabbages – and kings –*
> *And why the sea is boiling hot –*
> *And whether pigs have wings.'*

I imagine somewhere in the twenty or so novels I've written, most of the subjects in Lewis Carroll's lovely poem will have been touched upon. But now, alas, my 'use-by' date is almost upon me and there won't be sufficient time to write the sequel to *Jack of Diamonds*.

However, I thought you might like to know what happened to Jack and his offsider, the incorrigible, attention-seeking Diamond Jim.

◄o►

I'd kept in touch with the Ethiopian diplomat Berihun Kidane and his lovely wife, Fenet, whom I'd met on my way to Africa. Once I'd reached Beira on the East Coast I cabled him in Nigeria. Unusually, Fenet replied, insisting in the strongest terms that I travel to Ethiopia, where their family would be able to help me. I cabled Peter Adams, first officer of the *Roybank*, which had brought me to Angola, asking about ships sailing north. He informed me a Bank Line vessel would soon dock in Beira and, while it didn't normally take passengers, he'd make the arrangements. I could then sail further up the coast into the Gulf of Aden and disembark at the port in Djibouti, a small country that was part of French Somaliland and adjoined Ethiopia. From there I could cross the border and travel to Addis Ababa, the capital of Ethiopia, by train.

In Addis I was met by Abrihet, Fenet's younger sister, and at the first sight of her my heart began to pound. Younger than Fenet, and ten years my junior, she'd been a toddler when her family followed the Emperor Haile Selassie into exile, and settled in Bath in England, but, like her sister, she'd received an exclusive public-school education before returning to Ethiopia as a sophisticated Anglophile. Her name means 'she shines', and, I must say, it suited her perfectly. I found myself instantly bewitched.

Diamond Jim and I had been alone for a long time and, although he whistled 'Love Me or Leave Me' each day to remind me of Bridgett, I couldn't convince myself I would ever see her again. Now luck had smiled on me once more, bringing a second gorgeous woman into my life to love, who miraculously seemed to return my feelings. She also grew to adore Diamond Jim, who soon greeted her each morning with the words 'Abrihet, you're beautiful!'

Before long, Abrihet and I were married in Holy Trinity Cathedral in Addis Ababa, with rather more pomp than I would have liked, but Abrihet was from a powerful and devout noble family for whom all the trappings of the Ethiopian orthodox Christian church were necessary. To my dismay Diamond Jim wasn't allowed into the church. At least there was a precedent: President Andrew Jackson's parrot had been ejected from his funeral service because he kept cussing.

Abrihet was a virgin, but quickly proved to be a passionate and generous woman and we were happier than I'd have thought possible.

Within weeks she became pregnant, to the enormous pleasure of her family, for whom fecundity was proof of a successful marriage.

Thanks to her family's connections, I had been put in charge of the Royal Emergency Medical Centre in Addis Ababa. Jack's luck strikes again! It seemed I would never fully free myself from caring women stepping in to help me or even to save my life, but what the heck. I was as happy as I could be away from a jazz club and a card table.

Abrihet's family were close to Emperor Haile Selassie and, knowing of my passion for music, they arranged for me to be one of the musical directors of the emperor's imperial brass band, originally comprising forty Armenian orphans adopted by him and trained as musicians. I didn't like to think of the parallels with my own story – music must have come to the rescue of countless children – but I feel sure that if people played music rather than spoke to each other, this world would be a much better place.

Our daughter was born before our first wedding anniversary, and we named her Ayana Rebekkah – Ayana, meaning beautiful flower, and Rebekkah, meaning to bind. Certainly that little girl bound me to her and her beautiful mother with unbreakable ties, or so I believed.

My mom was desperate to meet her first granddaughter, but Nick and I both thought it was too dangerous. We'd been writing to each other using the private post-office box set up by Nick's contacts in Canadian Intelligence, and my contacts in the Ethiopian diplomatic corps. We were careful never to give away my whereabouts, which made it almost impossible to arrange for my mom to come for a visit. Perhaps I was paranoid, especially after all this time, but I kept remembering how they'd hunted down Johnny Diamond, and now I had at least two precious reasons to live.

One of Mom's letters carried the sad news of Joe's death. That I would never now be able to show him the musician I had become in Las Vegas hit me with renewed strength. I could almost hear him say, 'Jazzboy, you done real good. That phrasing real subtle, my man!' I grieved for the old man who had come closer than anyone to being a father figure to me. With the loss of Joe, Miss Frostbite could no longer continue with her piano routine, and went into retirement. The Jazz Warehouse was purchased by the twins, who now saw themselves as entrepreneurs, with their long, elegant fingers in several pies. Hector was still head chef at the Jazz Warehouse, and his daughter, Sue Stinchcombe, had become a very successful model in Canada.

There is little call for jazz harmonica players or, for that matter, poker players, in Ethiopia, so I had plenty of leisure time to work with Diamond Jim on what started out as a playful jazz routine with a bit of repartee, which we worked out between us. I was constantly amazed by his intelligence and devotion, not to mention his gift for mimicry. I estimated his vocabulary consisted of nearly seven hundred words and numbers, the meaning of most of which he clearly understood.

Almost from the moment she set eyes on him, my little Ayana loved Diamond Jim but, while he tolerated her, he always greeted her with 'Oh boy! Here comes trouble!' Despite sweet-talking Abrihet, Diamond Jim was a one-man bird.

Like most children, Ayana loved music, and would listen happily to anything I played, at first rocking or nodding to the beat, then, as she grew older, singing along in a sweet tuneful voice. Once she tried to sing along with 'Love Me or Leave Me', but only once; Diamond Jim fluffed his feathers furiously and squawked fit to strip the paint from the walls.

I began to teach her music through games and songs, and realised that, with her keen intelligence, she was hungry to learn. So, just for fun, I taught her how to play cards. By the time she was twelve, when Abrihet insisted we move to England for Ayana's secondary education, my daughter was a real whizz at cards. I had weaned myself off poker of necessity, and was determined never to return to it once we were in England. It had brought me too much bad luck. Besides, I wanted to earn a living and keep my family like other men did. I was sick of relying on my wife's family. The blues lends itself wonderfully to the harmonica, and in the UK, with Diamond Jim as part of the act, I hoped that I could resume my life as a performer.

We arrived in London in 1968, the year of the Prague Spring, student riots in Paris and the Beatles' *White Album*. America had launched the first manned Apollo space mission, but was unable to give its citizens equal rights. Black people were demanding to be treated decently; Martin Luther King had died fighting for their rights, and, at the Mexico Olympics, Black American athletes had given a black-power salute, supported by an Australian athlete. Noel White would have been proud of his countryman, and Joe and all my other black friends would have been gratified. It was heady stuff for someone who'd been living quietly at the ends of the earth.

In the UK, the troubles had begun in Northern Ireland, and there were violent demonstrations in the streets of London against the Vietnam War. But, as luck would have it, blues had been rediscovered by a new generation, and I soon found myself in the thick of a jazz and blues scene that was really jumping. It was an era of innovation, the perfect time to introduce my act with Diamond Jim: Jack, Jim & Jazz, or JJ&J. It had a quirky edge, and the music was good. Thanks to Ray Charles, nobody thought twice about a jazz musician performing in dark glasses, and I hoped the disguise and the different name would be sufficient to keep me safe from the Mob. One reviewer said I was the best exponent of this type of music in Europe and, thank God, we quickly became famous. DJ seemed to love performing as much as I did.

When Ayana finished school at seventeen, with first-class results, her mother was delighted that she would be going up to Cambridge. Ayana had grown into a stunningly beautiful young woman. Her Ethiopian elegance combined with her Iroquois and Anglo-Saxon heritage had produced astonishing results. She was just on six feet tall, slender as a reed, and still growing. One night when she was out dancing with friends in a club near Carnaby Street, she was spotted by a Paris fashion identity called Eva Segelov, who ran the Paris School of Modelling. The independent Ayana – or Rebekkah, as she was known to her friends – didn't consult us and, even though she'd been accepted to Cambridge, she left for Paris to train as a model under the name of

Rebekkah Reed, a combination of her second name and my assumed surname.

Eva Segelov was from a Russian Jewish family; feisty, contradictory, ruthless and unpopular within the Paris fashion industry, which spread slanderous rumours about her supposed links with illicit gambling as well as English and French criminal elements. Eva was forthright in her views about the French fashion scene, which, she claimed, was moribund, with petite models who were chosen and trained to be interchangeable, conservative 'clothes hangers'. She wanted to change the fashion business, put some 'guts' into it, and her idea, to the horror of the industry, was to make the model a star. She took one look at Rebekkah and knew she had found the perfect stalking horse, a young woman of such striking beauty that she could never be a mere clotheshorse.

Abrihet was not happy, not happy at all, but assumed modelling would be a passing fad. I extracted a promise from Ayana that she would take up her university studies if she were to prove unsuccessful in Paris and hoped for the best.

Alas, the times were a-changing for me, too, and by the mid-seventies, music was taking a different direction, and one that I was not prepared to follow, even if I'd been able to do so. I'd woken up one day and found that I'd turned fifty in a time when youth meant everything. On top of that I was something of a purist, and either unwilling or unable to adapt to the music of the times. We, DJ and I, would always be able to make a living as performers, but I began to slip from being a top act to being a club act. Diamond Jim and I still performed together as Jack, Jim & Jazz – JJ&J – but we were now regarded as a novelty act, despite my blues harmonica playing being better than ever.

I didn't have time to dwell on my changing fortunes because, in the year Ayana entered the modelling world as Rebekkah Reed, Abrihet was injured when an IRA bomb exploded in Oxford Street. She was rushed to Hammersmith Hospital and I had Ayana come over and stay until her mother was out of danger. Once her condition stabilised, the prognosis wasn't too serious, but then, three weeks after Ayana returned to Paris, my darling Abrihet died from a cerebral haemorrhage.

The months after her death were a blur; I simply couldn't believe I'd lost the second woman I had loved wholly and completely.

But life goes on, and if my act with Diamond Jim had been relegated to small stages in workers' clubs, the occasional nightclub and pub, Ayana, aka Rebekkah Reed, was beginning to make a big name for herself under the tutelage of the redoubtable, outspoken, loud-mouthed Eva Segelov. At a willowy six feet two inches, the stunningly beautiful Rebekkah Reed became an instant sensation. Her popularity soared, magazines begged and queued, and *Harper's Bazaar* dubbed her the most beautiful young woman on earth. The world's first supermodel was born. Of course I was proud, very proud, and wished only that I could have shared her fame and good fortune with her mother.

As Ayana's career began to soar into the stratosphere, mine sank into virtual oblivion. There is a time for everything and my musical career, or rather ours, DJ's and mine, seemed finally to be over. My heart simply wasn't in it. I'd survived the era of the Beatles, Jimi Hendrix and the Rolling Stones, but disco and hard rock finished me. It seemed it didn't matter how good a jazz musician you were, nobody was really interested any more. I earned enough to get by, but not much more.

I'd learned from my mom's weekly letters that Sue Stinchcombe had long ago moved on from modelling, no doubt understanding that she'd need a new career once she could no longer sell her face and body. With her intelligence, guts, organisational flair and people skills, she'd started her own talent agency, dealing with models at first, then branching out into handling musicians and entertainers. The twins had helped finance her business, recognising a savvy woman when they saw one, and even Mac had contributed financially. He'd been right about electric guitars, and his 'McClymont Roadshow' had become famous with the new pop and rock musicians for its tone. I would learn much later that one of the first musicians on Sue's books had been a torch singer whose stage name was Prairie Gold – Juicy Fruit had made it.

Unbeknownst to me, Sue and Ayana had met through the modelling side of the agency when Sue brought her over to Canada for a promotion, (with a multi-thousand-dollar price tag attached) for a leading bank who were savvy enough to see that women *might* just be worth pursuing as customers and investors in their right. It's not hard to guess the name of the bank and its kinky elderly owner, or that the twins would be involved. Sue was completely unaware of Rebekkah Reed's connection to me and had no idea I was in London – no doubt she still thought I was lost somewhere in darkest Africa – and Ayana did not know of my connection with Sue.

I would learn much later that Sue had, of course, kept in touch with Chef Napoleon Nelson, her godfather, who had made his name as a piano player in the GAWP Bar before Bridgett retired from the Firebird when it was sold to Howard Hughes. Bridgett was living somewhere in New York, having financed the education of Jim-Jay Bullnose, who had become a prominent young lawyer. All this came to Sue from Chef Napoleon Nelson, as Bridgett apparently had made no contact with any of the old Las Vegas crowd and had instructed Chef Napoleon Nelson not to breathe a word about the two of us to his goddaughter. Besides, I knew Nick Reed did everything in his power to keep news of me from reaching anyone who'd known me in Las Vegas. It was as if Bridgett and I had never been friends, never loved each other. Perhaps it was for the best, although Diamond Jim always ended his morning serenade with the words 'I love you, Bridgett'.

One of the best things about living in London was the wonderful variety of classical music concerts on offer. I'd never lost my love of classical music, but my life had led me to places where it was rarely played. Now

I was in one of the classical music capitals of the world, and I took full advantage of it. It helped ease my aching heart, and when I listened to beautiful music, I could forget for a moment how much I missed my wife and my lovely daughter.

I went to every concert during the London Proms season at the Royal Albert Hall. Not long after we'd arrived in London, I'd joined the long queue for Prom tickets, with Diamond Jim, as always, on my shoulder. Naturally, he soon became bored, and a bored parrot is a noisy and destructive parrot, who requires a lot of time and attention from his owner to distract him. This is hardly surprising when you understand that these parrots are monogamous, and form lifelong bonds, which can easily last for up to sixty years.

I decided to put on an impromptu performance to distract DJ, playing blues and jazz on harmonica while he did his usual cheeky commentary, whistling along with the songs he knew well. This proved to be a huge success with the crowd and became a feature of the ticket queue each year. Eventually the two of us were caught by TV cameras and appeared on the BBC. Luckily I was wearing dark glasses and a hat at the time, so I was fairly confident I wouldn't be recognised, and surely after all this time and in another country . . . Jack, Jim & Jazz were now known throughout Britain, so I guess we were once again famous in our own small way. Although I had a sneaking suspicion that my parrot was the real star.

Soon we were synonymous with the Proms, a fixture outside the Royal Albert Hall. My sixteen-hole chromatic Hohner super harmonica allowed me to mix my routines with classical and semi-classical music, such as George Gershwin's *Rhapsody in Blue*, and the queuing crowd became an audience in its own right, supplemented by folk who were not in the queue for Prom tickets but were loyal followers of JJ&J.

We worked on several routines. For instance, in one I'd be playing a blues or jazz number and would play a note or two a semitone flat. There'd be a sudden loud whistle from DJ, who would shake his head and shriek, 'No, no, no!' I'd stop playing and he'd say, 'Tin ear! Flat! 'orrible!'

'No, you're wrong, DJ!' I'd protest.

'You're wrong!' he'd insist, then he'd whistle the phrase, pitch perfect. The Prom crowd adored him and he loved all the attention.

My lovely Ayana dealt with the tragic death of her mother by going silent on me. Perhaps because of her personal grief, she became even more consumed with hard work, and when I was fortunate enough to get her on the phone, she was always dashing off somewhere and the conversations were seldom personal. I can't say I didn't mind, because it hurt like hell. She was my everything – my sun, my moon, my firmament.

What I wasn't to know until much later, was that, by thoughtlessly introducing her to card games as a child, I had unwittingly exposed her to the lure of gambling. Her game of choice was blackjack and, while she was still little more than a girl, had become hopelessly addicted. Eva Segelov proved to be her partner in crime; they were both inveterate gamblers addicted to blackjack. Perhaps my daughter was more like me than I cared to admit.

The modelling world isn't easy for young women: there is a lot of money, a lot of pressure, and a lot of parties, alcohol and drugs. Ayana had fallen in with the wrong crowd and, after a very bad run, ended up owing a fortune in gambling debts to one of the most notorious gangs in London.

The first I knew about it was when a Cockney version of Sammy Schischka confronted me after a show for the Prom queue and explained in very colourful language that if I didn't pay his boss a staggering amount of money (I mean, staggering), my daughter's beautiful and now famous face would be permanently disfigured. 'She won't end up with egg on her face,' he said, smiling as if the whole thing were a joke, 'we'll use sulphuric acid, mate.'

Frozen with horror, I was unable to respond as he handed me the number of a private safe-deposit box at a London bank. 'Six weeks, you've got six weeks, matey,' he growled. Then added, 'Or it's your bricks and mortar.' It took me a moment to understand that bricks and mortar was rhyming slang for daughter.

I had a sudden flashback to my gentle stepfather, Nick, talking about trying to patch up a victim of the Mob who'd been attacked with acid. 'Sulphuric acid isn't nice,' he'd said, and I had known then that his understated comment covered unimaginable horrors.

I couldn't possibly raise that kind of money, not if I had months or years. Six weeks was laughable. What made it worse, I couldn't tell anyone about Ayana's problems, for fear it would reach the press and end her career. I spoke to Eva Segelov, who said she too had been a victim of a sting; they hadn't seen it coming and she and her protégée were both up to their eyeballs in debt, potentially ruined. If the tabloids knew about Ayana's gambling habit, or that she had been consorting with gangsters, she'd never be employed again. I could just see the headlines: *The face that launched a thousand chips.*

I had no doubt that the gangsters would follow through on their threat. How could they not? If my daughter defaulted on her debts, her fame would only exacerbate their very public humiliation. Frantic to raise the money any way I could, I contacted Abrihet's family, but I had not reckoned with the conservative and aristocratic Amhara people. Horrified that Ayana would choose to 'flaunt herself' as a model and had, in their view, debased herself, they refused to help. Even Fenet, who I'd thought would be more enlightened, turned her back on us. Perhaps she blamed me for her sister's death; I will never know.

In desperation I began to wonder if there really were diamonds in Diamond Jim's crop. I hated myself for even considering it, but as my finger caressed his breast I'd find myself wondering if they could be gems or merely industrial-grade diamonds. I lay awake at night, tortured by the dilemma I faced: to kill my best and most faithful friend on the basis of a story told to me by simple men in the heart of Africa, or to risk my daughter's face, and possibly her life.

To make matters worse, I was asked to play at the last night of the London Proms, the traditional grand finale of the season. Diamond Jim and I were to perform George Gershwin's *Rhapsody in Blue*, one of our most popular numbers. Heartbroken, I accepted, no longer caring if I were recognised. Time was running out, and I knew that I had to save my daughter, no matter what it cost me. This would be the last time Jack, Jim & Jazz performed together.

When the program finally arrived I gave it a cursory glance. A young American pianist named Steven Rooth would be performing Rachmaninoff. Something stirred my curiosity momentarily, and I read on, noting that he had been toured in Canada by the Sue Stinchcombe Talent Agency. A coincidence, I guessed, and thought no more about it.

I lay awake at night. I couldn't kill Diamond Jim. I told myself that if the diamonds were somehow contained in my own throat, I'd gladly take my life. Oh, god, hadn't I been through enough? I admit I was bitter and sorry for myself and blamed myself for Ayana's gambling addiction: a child's game would destroy everything I loved.

Much later I would learn that, around this time, Sue Stinchcombe had decided to come to London, ostensibly on business, but really for a holiday with her other shareholders, Mac and the twins. While she wasn't responsible for Steven Rooth's appearance at the Royal Albert Hall, she'd contacted him and he'd given her a single ticket to the performance. In return for this favour she invited him to dinner at the Dorchester after the concert, because he'd already met Mac and the twins on his tour of Canada. He accepted and asked if he could bring a guest.

On the final night of the Proms, I prepared myself and Diamond Jim as best I could. Apart from the night of Abrihet's death, it was the worst night of my life, even worse than when Sammy Schischka crushed my left hand. Every loving nuzzle, whistle or squawk, every sign of affection from Diamond Jim, twisted a knife in my heart.

The young American virtuoso appeared before us and I found myself transfixed by his performance. I couldn't help wondering what sort of life I'd have had if only I'd followed the path set out for me by Miss Bates and become a classical pianist. How different might my life have been?

We were on next, and as Diamond Jim and I walked out onto the stage, the audience broke into thunderous applause. They were clearly all regulars, and knew us of old. I felt their warmth and love enfolding us, and I very nearly broke down. But Diamond Jim was a true performer, and kept me focused. The music came to my rescue, and I began to play that long, haunting, sinuous opening to *Rhapsody in Blue*, Diamond Jim prancing and swaying on my shoulder in time to the music.

After the big finale, the crowd went wild, stamping and shouting, then starting up a chant of '*Encore! Encore!*' They damn near lifted the elegant Albert Hall roof. Diamond Jim and I took our bows, but nothing would satisfy the crowd until I raised my harmonica, glanced at my old friend, and began to play Gershwin's 'Summertime'. When that lazy languorous tune finally wound to an end, I waited for the applause to quieten and stepped up to the microphone. 'Thank you, thank you,' I said. 'This is the last performance by Jack, Jim & Jazz . . .' My throat closed up.

Diamond Jim, leaning against the microphone, said, 'That's all, folks. Goodnight and goodbye!'

I could see people in the front row weeping.

Sue was, apparently, close to the front of the stage and couldn't believe her eyes when she saw me walk on. Despite my greying hair and my mangled hand, she instantly recognised Jack Spayd. As soon as I finished speaking, she left and waited outside the stage door, where she finally accosted me as I headed for home with Diamond Jim perched on my shoulder.

My first reaction to seeing someone from Las Vegas after such a public performance was to run, especially after the visit from the Cockney Sammy Schischka but, after a quick look around, I realised that Sue couldn't possibly do me any harm. In moments, we were hugging and Diamond Jim was protesting, and Sue was wiping away tears while I swallowed hard. She invited me and Diamond Jim to the dinner she'd planned, explaining that my old friends from Canada would be there.

'Sue, I can't; you know why.'

'No, Jack, this is different, there's nobody present who can harm you, I promise. The twins, Mac, tonight's soloist, Steven and his mom – a quiet dinner in a private room with old friends, I promise.'

'Diamond Jim will need to come. Will they allow it?'

'You bet.'

I didn't want to tell her this might well be DJ's last supper. We took a taxi to the Dorchester, and Sue filled me in on some of her life since I saw her last. We arrived to an overwhelming welcome from all my old friends and, in my fragile emotional state, I was soon reduced to tears.

Finally, Sue took me by the elbow and said, 'Jack, I'd like you to meet Steven Rooth . . .' I turned as she added, '. . . and his mother.' It was Bridgett, older but as beautiful as ever. For a heartbeat we both gaped at each other, then Bridgett burst into tears. She rushed into my arms and buried her face in my chest.

'Who's this?' Diamond Jim demanded, and Steven Rooth looked as if he wanted to ask the same question. Bridgett and I finally drew apart and gazed at each other.

Her eyes bright with tears, Bridgett said, 'Jack, allow me to introduce you to your son, Steven Jack Rooth.'

It was an unforgettable night, and I felt torn between learning more about my miraculous and extraordinary son I had not known existed, and talking to my lost love. When Bridgett and I were finally alone, I admit, I broke down and told her about the decision I had to face in the next few days – or, rather, the decision I'd already made.

'Jack,' she said, taking my scarred hand in both of hers and kissing it tenderly. 'You gave me my son. I owe you more than I can ever repay. You mustn't harm Diamond Jim.'

I shook my head, unable to speak.

'There's another way,' she went on. 'Will you allow me to talk with the others?'

I nodded. What the hell, I was too distressed and dismayed that just when I had found my love and my astonishing son, I would have to lose my precious Diamond Jim. 'You'll have to leave the room, Jack,' Bridgett said. 'Will you return in half an hour?'

DJ and I went for a walk around the block and returned to the Dorchester roughly half an hour later. When we entered the room, I glanced around at the ring of solemn faces, then suddenly everyone burst into laughter. 'It's done, Jack,' Bridgett said. 'We're all happy to contribute.'

I confess, I fell to my knees and wept again.

'So? What's happening?' Diamond Jim demanded to fresh gales of laughter and not a few tears.

Bridgett kneeled beside me and said in a whisper, 'Jack, you know I still love you. I always have. I've never married – I couldn't – there was only ever you.'

'Oh, Bridgett, I thought I'd lost you forever. I love you, darling, with all my heart,' I managed to stutter.

'Hey! What about me?' Diamond Jim demanded.

'You too, DJ. We can't be parted.' I laughed between my tears.

At some stage during that long night, Bridgett told me that Tony Accardo, the godfather, was dead, and that Manny 'Asshole' de Costa had developed dementia and was in a home for the aged. Sammy had died several years back, in an auto accident, and the Chicago mob had gone completely legit with the sale of the Firebird. Because all the other players were no more, the contract taken out on me had long since been withdrawn, although Bridgett still kept her 'paperwork' in a very safe place.

'Oh, Jack, I've been searching for you for so long. I really began to fear you were dead. Do come back to New York with me and spend some time with us. You need to get to know Steven, your son,' Bridgett said as the sky over London lightened. 'And you must bring Ayana.'

Just then, Diamond Jim let out an ear-piercing shriek, and bobbed up and down. We laughed and Bridgett added, 'And, of course, you'll be accompanied by darling Diamond Jim.'

The End

◄○►

It's been a privilege to write for you and to have you accept me as a storyteller in your lives. Now, as my story draws to an end, may I say only, 'Thank you. You have been simply wonderful.'

With love and admiration,

Bryce Courtenay

ACKNOWLEDGEMENTS

When *The Power of One* was published in 1988 I could never have dreamed that I would be writing the acknowledgements for my twenty-first book twenty-three years later.

As long as I can recall I have always had stories doing gymnastics in my head, and demanding an audience.

Now my wife Christine and my family would be delighted if I chose to take a break as I enter my eightieth year. But I believe it is our stories that define us as a nation and provide an indelible record of where we have come from, and perhaps vital clues about where we may be heading.

Isaac Bashevis Singer, the great Yiddish American writer and Nobel Laureate, once said, 'When a writer tries to explain too much, to psychologise, he's already out of time when he begins.' Someone else once said, when asked if their work contained a message, 'If you want a message, go to Western Union.' Singer believed novelists are entertainers and storytellers and I think he was right. If you enjoy a book, then that is sufficient.

Regardless of the breathtaking developments in technology and medical science, I am often disheartened by the pervading sense of cynicism and disillusionment, not to mention the political rhetoric that takes precedence in the media. But the real stories journalists miss are of the individuals filled with courage, integrity and passion who have tackled the challenges of economic instability, environmental degradation, climate change, and the appalling fact that in our world clean water and food is not shared equally among the growing numbers of people on our tiny planet.

For now, though, I invite you to sit back and enjoy my latest story, be it in paper or on your phone or e-reader (what a wonderful tool the latter is). It is my fervent wish that, when the time comes, I may be remembered by those whom I entertained as a damn good storyteller. I also encourage everyone trying to write a book to take heart – if I can do it, then so can you. So keep on going, kids – much of the effort is simply bum glue. I am constantly astonished and delighted at the breadth of talent I see in my annual writing courses, and in the manuscripts that cross my desk.

Due to some tedious health matters, *Jack of Diamonds* has taken nearly two years to write – an inordinate amount of time for me to complete a book. So it is with a feeling of great relief that I have finally completed it. There hasn't been a lot of time this year to smell the roses, but I saw the first of my spring daffodil shoots break through to announce the end of winter and the coming of summer when you will, I hope, be enjoying *Jack of Diamonds*.

I wish to express my profound gratitude to my readers in Australia and around the world who kindly wait for each of my books. I thank you for your loyalty, your letters, emails and comments on Facebook; these are what continue to encourage me to keep writing. Furthermore, I am constantly amazed by the number of people who approach me in the street and are kind enough to say they enjoy my books. For this generous and personal acknowledgement, I am truly grateful.

Bruce Gee, my long-time researcher, deserves special mention for his agile brain, and lateral approach to problem solving, and for having the honesty and integrity to always speak his mind without fear or favour. I thank you for your invaluable contribution.

Nan McNab, my regular editor, is my tower of strength. It is her opinions I have learned to trust implicitly, even if her comments often result in my having to do many hours of rewriting. Alas, she is seldom wrong and my final draft is always enhanced by following Nan's wise and experienced counsel.

This book was also completed with the help of a wide range of people whose advice and knowledge have been invaluable to me: John Adamson; Patricia Barton; Alida Haskins; Philippe Pee from Guest Apartment Services (Paris); Lorraine Woon; Sam Schischka; Michael Frankel; and, finally, Shanine Mony (South Africa).

Getting old ain't a whole heap of fun, and these past few years I have needed a bit of fine tuning, shall we say, to remain at my computer. I feel enormously privileged to have had the brilliant care of some very special people: Dr Koroush Haghighi, who literally saved my life; Professor Michael Solomon; Dr Peter Grant; Dr Anthony Freeman; Professor Warwick Selby; Dr Irwin Light; and Professor John Rasko and his wife, Associate Professor Simone Strasser; and Associate Professor Eva Segelov. Under their world-class care, 'Lucky' Courtenay continues to make it!

My publisher, Penguin Books, offers me an extraordinary team of dedicated, professional people, whose support I simply could not do without. As you would appreciate, at the present time they are working in the most challenging environment the world of publishing has seen, and while the e-book is here to stay, it has brought drastic changes to the book industry. It is with this in mind that I want to pay tribute to Bob Sessions (Uncle Bob) who is always my first port of call to mull over a problem and who has never once failed me; his dynamic CEO, Gabrielle Coyne; the magical Julie Gibbs; publicity gurus Anyez Lindop and Sally Bateman; Rachel Scully and Anne Rogan in editorial; Carmen de la Rue and Nicole Brown in production; Adam Laszczuk and Alex Ross in design; proofreaders Sarina Rowell and Saskia Adams; and the team of dedicated people who include the army of typesetters, printers, designers, delivery staff, warehouse teams, booksellers and brave shopkeepers.

You are my publishing family, and even in the depths of night as I am struggling to complete a chapter I never feel alone.

Then there are the dear friends and family members who occupy the lining of my soul and whose love, friendship and sense of humour constantly sustain me. My sons and their wives, Brett and Ann Courtenay, and Adam and Gina Courtenay; grandsons Ben, Jake and Marcus; Nima Price and his partner, Kathrine Petersen; Kathleen Brownlie; Margaret Gee and Brent Waters; Shanine Mony and my extended family in South Africa have given me enduring love and support.

My patient and long-term friends who regularly keep in touch even when I don't spend nearly as much time with them as I would like: Robbee Minicola, Irwin and Erica Light, Greg and Lorraine Woon, Peter and Amanda Keeble, Owen Denmeade, Roger and Sandi Rigby, Alex and Brenda Hamill, Anthony and Kerry Freeman, Tony and Cheryl Crosby, Anie Williams, and Alex Van Heeren. I also feel immense gratitude for the love and friendship extended to us by Duncan Thomas, Simon Balderstone AM, David and Carole Baird, Robert Swan OBE (founder of 2041.com), Barney Swan, John Atkin, Karen Thomas, John Adamson and Connie Wang, Marg Hamilton, Patrick Benhamou, Leonard Yong, Megan Grace, Stacey Truscott, Desiree Addinsall, Natalie Bowman, Kamahl, Iain Finlay, Trish Clark, Christine McCabe and Liz Courtenay. Michael Dean and Denis Bertollo also deserve a special note of thanks.

I dare not forget to mention our beloved pets: Tim, always at my feet as I write, and the four cats, Cardamon, Muschka, Ophelia and Pirate, hard at sleep on my desk. Then Leo, the dog next door, barking around 4 p.m. to remind us it's time to take him along with Tim for their afternoon walk and sniff-a-thon.

Finally, but most importantly, I wish to thank my beloved wife, Christine, who is my soulmate and the woman I depend on each and every day, and whose love and support are impossible to put into words. Christine has a distinguished background as a pioneer in the adventure-travel industry, and continues to have a passion for travel that is undiminished, be it in the wilds of the high Arctic, or wandering the streets of Paris, her favourite city.

Christine's imagination, intelligence, capacity for hard work, passion for life and untold kindness to me, our family and friends are an enduring inspiration. I am quite the luckiest man alive to be able to call her my wife.

Christine and I also feel immense gratitude for the fortunate life we continue to lead. We feel it is imperative that we continue to give back to organisations that, with courage and integrity, make a real difference to the lives of others.

Please take a look at their websites and consider joining us in supporting them: The Australian Himalayan Foundation (of which Christine was a founding director); The Thin Green Line Foundation, founded by Sean Willmore; Cure the Future Cell and Gene Trust, founded by Professor John Rasko AO; and Save the Rhino Foundation, begun by Nicholas Duncan. We salute you all and pledge our ongoing support.

Enjoy *Jack of Diamonds*, and my warmest wishes to you all.

Bryce Courtenay
25th of June 2012